Through Their Eyes

A Story of Divided Lands, Shared Dreams, and the Human Spirit That Unites Us

Billy MacLeod MBE

Casover Publishing

Contents

Copyright Notice	VI
Foreword	VII
Introduction	IX
Chapter One	1
Chapter Two	7
Chapter Three	13
Chapter Four	18
Chapter Five	24
Chapter Six	31
Chapter Seven	36
Chapter Eight	43
Chapter Nine	48
Chapter Ten	58
Chapter Eleven	66
Chapter Twelve	74
Chapter Thirteen	82
Chapter Fourteen	88

Chapter Fifteen	94
Chapter Sixteen	102
Chapter Seventeen	114
Chapter Eighteen	120
Chapter Nineteen	130
Chapter Twenty	139
Chapter Twenty One	151
Chapter Twenty Two	158
Chapter Twenty Three	168
Chapter Twenty Four	173
Chapter Twenty Five	191
Chapter Twenty Six	199
Chapter Twenty Seven	209
Chapter Twenty Eight	214
Chapter Twenty Nine	224
Chapter Thirty	231
Chapter Thirty One	240
Chapter Thirty Two	252
Chapter Thirty Three	264
Chapter Thirty Four	272
Chapter Thirty Five	282
Chapter Thirty Six	288
Chapter Thirty Seven	297
Chapter Thirty Eight	304

Chapter Thirty Nine	317
Chapter Forty	328
Chapter Forty One	341
Chapter Forty Two	351
Chapter Forty Three	363
Chapter Forty Four	395
Chapter Forty Five	417
Chapter Forty Six	427
Chapter Forty Seven	440
Chapter Forty Eight	454
Chapter Forty Nine	469
Chapter Fifty	482
Chapter Fifty One	492
Chapter Fifty Two	500
Chapter Fifty Three	516
Chapter Fifty Four	531
Chapter Fifty Five	546
Chapter Fifty Six	551
Billy MacLeod MBE	559

Copyright © 2024

Billy MacLeod MBE

All rights reserved worldwide. No part of this publication may be reproduced, distributed, stored in a retrieval system, or transmitted in any form or by any means—electronic, mechanical, photocopying, recording, or otherwise—without prior written permission of the author or the publisher, except in the case of brief quotations embodied in critical reviews and certain other non-commercial uses permitted by copyright law.

Publisher Information

This book is published by Casover Publishing. The author, **Billy MacLeod MBE**, has asserted their moral right to be identified as the author of this work in accordance with the Copyright, Designs and Patents Act 1988 and international copyright agreements. This work is protected by copyright law in the United Kingdom and internationally under the Berne Convention and other applicable copyright treaties.

Restrictions

Any unauthorised sale, transfer, loan, or reproduction of this book without the publisher's consent is strictly prohibited. This book may not be re-bound or re-covered and then sold without prior consent. Any such actions violate the author's rights and will be pursued by legal action. Please note that the content of this book is protected by international copyright laws and is intended for the buyer's personal use only. If this book is sold, lent, or given away, the new holder is bound by the terms of this copyright notice.

This copyright notice is also intended to serve as a deterrent to copyright infringement, which is subject to legal action and penalties in both the UK and abroad, including the United States.

Contact Information

All inquiries should be addressed to: copyright@casover.com

Publication Details

First Published: 2024

Foreword

The story you are about to read, *Through Their Eyes: A Journey of Two Worlds* by Billy Macleod MBE, offers a rare and poignant glimpse into the lives of two boys caught on opposite sides of a conflict that has defined their existence. Set against the backdrop of one of the world's most enduring struggles, this novel is a powerful testament to the resilience of youth, the complexities of human identity, and the enduring hope for peace.

As publishers, we are proud to bring forward a work that not only informs but deeply moves. Through the alternating voices of Ahmed and Yossi, Billy Macleod brings humanity to the often faceless narrative of the Israel-Palestine conflict. He reveals the laughter, fears, dreams, and doubts that lie behind the walls of separation, showing us that even amidst turmoil, there are moments of beauty, compassion, and connection.

Ahmed and Yossi are not just characters in a book; they are reflections of countless young people across the world who must navigate the harsh realities of conflict while daring to dream of something better. They remind us that in times of division, it is our shared humanity that can offer the most profound hope for a future unmarked by violence.

In this work, we hope you find not just a story of conflict, but also a story of possibility—a narrative that encourages empathy, understanding, and dialogue. It is a call to remember that behind every headline and statistic lies a human life, filled with its own hopes and struggles, much like our own.

BILLY MACLEOD MBE

We are honoured to present *Through Their Eyes: A Journey of Two Worlds*, a story that transcends borders and speaks directly to the heart. May it inspire you as much as it has inspired us.

Casover Publishing

Introduction

Ahmed and Yossi live only 41 miles apart, yet their worlds couldn't be more different.

In the Gaza Strip, Ahmed grows up in Jabalia, surrounded by conflict, loss, and the weight of his father's legacy as a martyr. His childhood is filled with stories of resistance, lessons of sacrifice, and a burning anger that fuels his desire to fight. Trapped in a world of tunnels and whispered plans, Ahmed wrestles with the choices that seem inevitable, questioning whether the path of violence is truly the one he wants to walk.

In Tel Aviv, Yossi's life unfolds in a bustling, vibrant city where the Mediterranean breeze carries the promise of a future filled with possibilities. But beneath the surface of school, football games, and sun-soaked afternoons, there is a lingering fear of conflict - a fear that no child can truly escape. Yossi grapples with the shadow of military service, the weight of his family's expectations, and the hope for peace in a land where violence often seems unavoidable.

Told through alternating perspectives, Through Their Eyes: A Journey of Two Worlds is a powerful story of two boys growing up on opposite sides of a deeply entrenched conflict. As their lives intertwine in unexpected ways, they are forced to confront their beliefs, their identities, and the choices that will shape not just their futures, but the future of their people.

This is a tale of survival, resistance, and humanity, set against the backdrop of one of the world's most enduring conflicts. Through Ahmed and Yossi's eyes, we see two worlds divided by history and politics but united by the shared hope for something more.

Chapter One

AHMED

The cell is dark, the air thick with the stale smell of sweat and rusted iron. Silence presses in from every corner, broken only by the distant hum of a generator and the occasional clang of a metal door echoing down the cold stone corridor, like the ringing of a far-off bell. I lie on the cold concrete floor, the chill creeping into my bones, and I let my mind drift back to Jabalia, to the life I knew before this place, before all the choices that led me here.

I can still see it in my mind: the streets of Jabalia alive with noise and colour, chaotic but familiar. Vendors shout over one another, their voices merging into a chorus that rises and falls like a wave. Children dart between stalls, their laughter bright and carefree, cutting through the din. The smell of falafel frying in hot oil mingles with the sweetness of fresh bread. And always, the sea breeze sweeps through the narrow alleys, carrying the salt and the promise of something beyond the horizon. It was a place where life clung fiercely to every corner, where every breath was a reminder of what it meant to endure.

But I also remember the shadows, the faces that filled our home after my father's death. Our house, like so many in Jabalia, was small but known. My father had died a Shahid - a martyr - fighting the Israelis in the war of 2009. I was nine years old when they came to tell us. I remember the men from Hamas standing in our doorway, their faces solemn, their voices low. My mother, Amal, stood with her head held high, her lips pressed into a tight line, a defiance burning behind her dark eyes. She didn't shed a tear, didn't tremble. There was no room for weakness here. She nodded curtly at the men, muttering a brief, *"Thank you,"* before shutting the door with a firm, finality. But that door closed on more than just the men - it closed on the life we had known. After that day, everything changed.

After the men from Hamas left, my mother knelt in front of me, gripping my face with hands rough from years of hard living. Her touch wasn't gentle, but there was something soft in her gaze - just for me. *"Your father... he was a ,"* she said, her voice steady, but something broke beneath the surface. *"He fought for what was taken from us. You must be strong, Ahmed. You hear me?"* She gripped my shoulders tightly, her eyes burning into mine. *"Like him. Promise me."* Her eyes softened, just for a heartbeat, before the steel returned. *"Promise me."* The words were not a request, they were a command.

And I promised.

But even as I spoke those words, something inside me wavered. I saw the burden of my father's legacy reflected in my mother's eyes, a weight I wasn't sure I could carry. For the briefest moment, I wanted to ask if I could choose a different path, if there was another way. But the question died in my throat. I had to be strong. I had to live up to what was expected of me.

Men began to visit our home - men with rifles slung over their shoulders who spoke in hushed tones and always seemed to be in a hurry. They came to speak with my uncle, Yusuf Al-Masri, who moved in shortly after my father's death. Yusuf was a mountain of a man, broad-shouldered and towering over most, his face a permanent mask of stern resolve. When he visited, he'd give me a firm pat on the head and say in his deep, gravelly voice, *"Ahmed, you are the son of a Shahid. One day, the reasons behind our fight will become clear to you."* His words weren't just for me - they were lessons, warnings. Everyone in the room stood straighter when he spoke, his presence casting a long shadow, commanding the kind of respect that men earned through battle and blood. I looked up to him, both in awe and fear, not wanting to disappoint him.

I remember sitting in the corner of our living room, pretending to do my homework while men gathered around the dim lamp, shadows dancing on the walls. Their conversations were hushed but intense, filled with words like *resistance, sacrifice, freedom*. They spoke of tunnels dug deep beneath the ground, of weapons smuggled through secret routes, of plans to strike back. Occasionally, they would look at me, a small boy with big eyes, and nod approvingly. *"Ahmed, the son of a Shahid,"* they would say. *"One day, you will do great things."*

And I wanted to believe them. From that moment, I felt a ignite within me. I wanted to be more than just the son of a martyr, I wanted to prove myself worthy of my father's name, to earn my place among those men. Every time they spoke of the fight, of the sacrifices yet to come, I felt a surge of pride. I was ready to be part of something bigger, to follow in my father's footsteps.

Yet even then, there were moments of doubt, fleeting thoughts I would quickly suppress. I remember overhearing Yusuf talking to one of the men late at night, their voices barely above a whisper. *"It is not just about the land,"* Yusuf said. *"It is about the message we send. The people must see that we are unyielding, that we will not back down, no matter the cost."* His words were fierce, but there was something in his tone - a hint of something else, perhaps ambition, perhaps desperation. I didn't understand it then, but it stayed with me, a small seed of unease.

My mother took a monthly stipend from Hamas - a payment for my father's sacrifice, she called it. *"This is our right,"* she would tell me. *"Your father gave his life for our people."* The money kept us fed, kept me in school, bought the clothes on my back. But it was more than money, it was a badge of honour in our neighbourhood, a symbol of our family's sacrifice. In Jabalia, we were a family that had given everything for the cause, and that meant something.

Amal was a woman of iron - sharp-eyed, firm-voiced, unbreakable. Mourning had become part of her, the black she wore almost a second skin. People sought her counsel, her guidance. *"The Israelis took your father, our land, our freedom,"* she would say, her voice tight with barely contained anger. *"But they will never take our spirit. One day, Ahmed, you will stand up and fight for what is right."* Her words were not just lessons, they were commands, shaping my very identity.

I was still young when I first sensed it - the tension that clung to the air. I would walk to Al-Amal School every morning, the dust from the streets sticking to my shoes, listening to the chatter of my classmates. We laughed, we joked, but there was always an edge, a seriousness in their eyes that didn't quite match their words. At school, they taught us who our enemies were. *"The Jews,"* they would say, *"the ones who drove our grandparents from their homes, who burned our villages to the ground."* The stories were always about loss, about suffering, about the need to fight back. *"They want to erase us,"* the teachers would whisper, leaning in as if sharing a secret too terrible to speak aloud. *"But we are still here. We will not disappear."*

At first, I didn't fully understand it. All I knew was that the Jews were the reason we lived like this, why my father was gone, why everything seemed broken. I learned to hate them before I ever saw one, before I knew what they looked like, before I even understood what hatred truly meant.

I wanted to be a part of it all, to make my family proud, to carry my father's legacy forward. I didn't see another way, I didn't want to see another way. In my mind, there was no doubt, no hesitation. I was Ahmed Al-Masri, the son of a Shahid. I was meant to fight.

Then there was Fatima, the old woman who lived down the street, always sitting on her stoop, her eyes watching everything. One day, as I walked past, she called me over. *"Ahmed,"* she said softly, *"do not let your heart fill with too much hate. It is easy to hate those we do not know, to see them only as enemies. But remember, they have mothers, fathers, children who laugh. Do not forget that before you pick up a stone."*

Her words felt like a betrayal, a challenge to everything I believed. I wanted to dismiss them, to call them foolish. Instead, I found myself more determined than ever to prove her wrong, to show that my path was righteous, that my father's sacrifice was not in vain. But that night, as I lay in bed staring at the ceiling, her words wouldn't leave me alone. *"They have mothers, fathers, children who laugh."* I told myself she was wrong, that she didn't understand, but her voice echoed in my head, a quiet whisper in the dark.

Now, in this cell, I stare at the ceiling. The walls press in, suffocating, and the air is thick with sweat and metal. I think back to those days, to the sound of my mother's voice, her words of defiance and pride. I think of Yusuf, his voice calm but relentless. *"They will never stop,"* he would say. *"We must resist. We must fight."*

THROUGH THEIR EYES

I remember the faces of the men who visited our home, their eyes hard, their voices filled with a conviction that felt unshakeable. They spoke of glory, of honour, of a cause that was worth any sacrifice. And I believed them. I believed them so much that when my time came, I did not hesitate. I picked up the rifle, I walked the path they had laid out for me. I fought because I believed it was the only thing I could do, the only way to honour my father's name.

But as the days turn into nights in this cell, I wonder - was it worth it? Did I do the right thing? Or was I just another pawn in a game I never fully understood?

I close my eyes, trying to silence the doubts, the questions that gnaw at my conscience. I hear my mother's voice again, as clear as if she were standing beside me. *"You will be strong, Ahmed. You will make us proud."*

I want to hold onto that, to the certainty she had, to the certainty I once had. But it slips through my fingers like sand.

I think about the faces of those I fought. Faces filled with fear, anger, defiance - none of them mattered. They were just enemies, just another threat standing in my way. I never saw them as anything else, never allowed myself to. But then there was him - the soldier. The one who stood with his weapon aimed, his eyes locked onto mine.

For a moment, it was as if time stopped. His gaze seemed to pierce through me, like he was trying to see something I wasn't willing to show. And then... the explosion.

The blast tore through the air, the force ripping everything apart. I felt the heat, the shock, the ground shuddering beneath me. But even in that chaos, I remember his eyes, still fixed on mine, like he was searching for something.

I push the thought away, trying to bury it deep where it can't reach me. I can't let myself dwell on it, can't let that moment make me question. My mother's voice echoes in my mind - *"You will be strong, Ahmed."* But each time I repeat it, the words feel more distant, like they're slipping away from me.

I am here in this cell because I chose this path, because I believed it was the only way. And now, I am left with the memory of his eyes, that moment. I wonder what he saw in mine.

I will not forget. I cannot forget. But I wonder if I have lost something more valuable than I ever knew.

Here in the darkness, I face myself. Here, I find no easy answers - only the echoes of choices that have led me to this point. I am my father's son. But I am also Ahmed, a man searching for something I do not yet understand.

And in this silence, I begin to realise that the hardest battles are the ones fought within.

Chapter Two

YOSSI

The steady rhythm of the machines fills the room, a constant reminder of where I am. The beeping of monitors, the soft whirr of the ventilator - these sounds have become my lifeline, tethering me to this hospital bed. try to block them out, willing myself to drift back to a time before the pain, before all of this. And suddenly, I'm back in Rafah, back in that building by the tunnel entrance.

The air was thick with dust and the acrid smell of smoke, the sound of gunfire echoing through the narrow corridors. We had orders to secure the tunnel, to push forward through the maze of rooms and debris. My heart raced, adrenaline surging through my veins, my weapon ready in my hands. I turned a corner, my boots crunching on broken glass, and there he was - a fighter, his rifle raised, eyes wide with fear and defiance.

I had him in my sights. I could see every detail of his face - the tension in his jaw, the rapid rise and fall of his chest. My finger hovered over the trigger, ready to fire, but I hesitated. For a brief moment, everything slowed. His eyes met mine, and in that instant, I saw more than just an enemy. I saw a man, a young man like me, caught in a situation neither of us had chosen. I saw fear in his eyes, the same fear that gripped me. But there was something else too - something that felt almost like a question.

Why did I hesitate? I still don't know. Maybe I was searching for a sign, some indication that he was more than just a target, more than just another person to eliminate. Maybe I was hoping he'd lower his weapon, that we could somehow find a way out of this without more bloodshed.

But then the explosion came. A deafening blast tore through the air, shaking the very foundations of the building. I felt the shockwave hit me, knocking me off my feet. The force of it sent me crashing against a wall, and everything went black. But even in that chaos, as my vision blurred and the sounds around me faded, I remember his eyes still locked on mine. I could feel the question in his gaze - a question I couldn't answer.

Why didn't I shoot? Why did I stand there staring when I should have pulled the trigger? The moment haunts me. Was it fear? Was it doubt? Or was it something else - a refusal to accept that this was all we were? I don't know. I only know that in those last moments before the darkness took me, I was searching for something in his eyes, something I still haven't found.

I try to push the thought away, to focus on something else. I see the narrow streets of Neve Tzedek, bathed in the soft light of early morning. The sun casts long shadows as I pedal my bike down the cobbled lanes, the warm breeze carrying the scent of fresh bread and coffee from the corner café. Tel Aviv is always buzzing, a symphony of sounds - the chatter of people heading to work, the insistent honking of car horns, the distant hum of the sea mingling with the calls of market vendors setting up their stalls. The city feels like it never sleeps, always moving, always alive. A place where life never pauses.

Our flat is on the third floor of a modest building, once a vibrant blue but now faded. It's small but filled with light and laughter. My mother, Ruth Rosenberg, a doctor, is always in a hurry, juggling a dozen things at once. Yet she never forgets to ask how my day was, always listening with a warm smile that makes everything else seem less important.

One evening, I remember her coming home, looking tired but still smiling. *"Yossi,"* she said as she put down her bag, her voice soft but her hands trembling slightly. *"Tell me, how was football today?"*

I grinned, rushing to her side. *"We won, Mum! Nadav scored twice and Amir saved a goal that was surely going in. You should have seen it!"*

She laughed, her eyes twinkling. *"I'm sure I would have been very proud. Maybe one day you'll both play for Israel."*

But even in her laughter, I saw something deeper - something she never quite said aloud. A flicker of worry that always seemed to linger in the back of her mind. She'd never admit it, but I knew she worried. About me. About all of us.

My father, David Rosenberg, is a lawyer - serious, with big ideas - but his laugh can light up a room, his humour a gentle balm against the world's harshness. I remember him sitting at the kitchen table late one night, papers spread around him. He looked up as I passed by.

"Come here, Yossi," he called softly. *"Look at this."* He pointed to a newspaper headline about peace talks. *"One day you'll understand why these things matter so much. It's not just about politics, it's about people, about you and your friends growing up in a safer world."*

But there was something else in his eyes that night, something that hadn't always been there. A heaviness. I'd hear him at night sometimes, restless in his sleep. My mother told me once, quietly, that he still had nightmares from his time in the army, serving as an infantry soldier. He'd wake up in a sweat, haunted by the past, but he'd always brush it off, telling her it didn't matter. But I knew it did.

"Your father doesn't talk about it much, Yossi," she said one evening, her voice low as we sat on the balcony, the city lights twinkling below. "But those years left their mark. He wants to protect you, but he also knows…" She trailed off, but I understood. He knew it was inevitable.

One evening, as we sat on the balcony, my father turned to me, his face serious. *"Yossi,"* he began, *"there will come a time when you'll have to make choices, difficult ones. And you must always remember to choose what is right, not what is easy."*

I glanced at him, feeling the weight of his words. *"But Dad, what if I'm not ready? What if I don't want to go to the army?"*

He smiled, a comforting smile that made me feel a bit braver. *"Yossi, we all feel that way sometimes. It's normal to be scared. But you're a brave boy, and I know you'll be fine."* His voice was steady, but I could see the shadow of his own memories lingering in his eyes, the unspoken fears he tried to keep at bay. The same fears I was beginning to feel.

And then there's my grandmother, Leah Rosenberg. She lives just a few blocks away in a small flat surrounded by a garden bursting with flowers. Though small, she is indomitable, her eyes always seem to look far beyond the present, as if she sees things the rest of us cannot. A Holocaust survivor, she carries her stories like old scars.

"Never forget, Yossi," she often tells me, her voice soft but firm, a command wrapped in a whisper. *"Always remember where you come from, who you are."* I would sit next to her on the worn sofa, feeling the weight of her hand on mine, trying to understand the things she had seen, the things she had endured. Her words tether me to a past I don't fully understand but know I must honour.

One day, after hearing about another attack on the news, I asked her, *"Grandma, how do you stay so strong after everything you've been through?"*

She smiled a little sadly. *"Because, Yossi, I have to be. For you, for your father, for all of us. Strength isn't about not being afraid, it's about doing what needs to be done, even when you are."*

"But how, Grandma? How do I stay strong?" I asked, feeling small but wanting to understand.

"By remembering who you are, my boy. Always remember," she replied, her voice gentle but firm, her hand squeezing mine a little tighter.

At school, our class was a patchwork of stories. Jews, Muslims, Christians - all from different backgrounds, but none of that mattered to us. We shared desks, played football, and swapped lunches. My best friend, Nadav Levy, lived just a few streets away. We did everything together - football on the dusty pitch, bike rides through the alleyways, swimming in the sea until our skin wrinkled, and the sun set, casting a golden glow over the water.

Unlike me, Nadav couldn't wait to join the army. He talked about it constantly, his eyes lighting up whenever he imagined becoming a paratrooper. For him, it was an adventure, something to look forward to, not something to fear.

"Do you ever think about what it'll be like?" Nadav asked one afternoon as we lay on the grass after a game. *"When we're in the army, jumping out of planes, being paratroopers?"* He grinned, already imagining himself soaring through the air.

I shrugged, trying to match his excitement. *"I don't know... maybe."* But the truth was, I didn't think about it as much as he did. The army felt more like something I had to do, rather than something I looked forward to.

"Come on, Yossi!" Nadav nudged me. *"We'll be in the same unit, jumping together. It'll be amazing!"*

He said it like it was already decided, so full of confidence. I tried to smile, but deep down, I wasn't so sure. Nadav's excitement made me feel my own doubts even more.

It wasn't just the idea of joining the army that scared me. It was everything that came with it. I'd seen the way it changed people. I'd seen the way it changed my dad. What if I ended up like him, waking up in a cold sweat, haunted by things I couldn't control?

"I don't want us to change, Yossi," Nadav muttered. *"I don't want us to stop being who we are."*

I didn't know how to answer him. I didn't want things to change either, but deep down, I knew they would. It felt inevitable.

Samir was the thoughtful one in our group, always deep in his own head but still up for any challenge. A Christian Arab from Jaffa, he saw the world differently from the rest of us. He was adventurous and ready to take on anything, but it wasn't just about thrills for him. There was something else behind his need to push boundaries, something that made him question everything around him.

One day, he stood at the top of an old water tower, looking out over the city, lost in thought. Then, suddenly, his voice broke through the stillness. *"Come on, Yossi! Don't be a chicken!"* His laughter echoed, but I could tell he was daring me for more than just a climb. Samir was always looking for the next big challenge, something that would make us think or see the world differently.

Leila was the calm one, the glue that held us together. She didn't talk much about what she wanted to be when she grew up, but you could always tell she was someone who cared deeply about others. Whenever one of us scraped a knee or had a bad day, she was the first to offer a hand or a comforting word.

One afternoon, after a tough football game where I had taken a hard fall, Leila came over quietly, her expression focused as she knelt beside me. She didn't say anything at first, just handed me a bottle of water and gently checked my leg, making sure I was okay.

"You'll be fine, Yossi," she said softly, her voice steady. And she was right. With Leila around, we always felt like everything would be fine. She had a way of fixing things, of making sure we were all taken care of without ever needing to say it out loud.

As I lie here, I think about my family, my friends, my city. I think about everything that's shaped me, and everything I've been through. I think about the choices I've made and the ones I'll have to make.

But most of all, I think about the eyes of that young man in Rafah, and the question they asked me - one I still can't answer.

Chapter Three

AHMED

The cell is dark, the air suffocating with the smell of sweat and rust. Silence presses in from every corner, broken only by the distant hum of a generator and the sporadic clang of a metal door echoing down the corridor. Each sound jolts me back to life in Gaza - to the heat of the sun on my face, to the sounds of life that filled every corner. I can picture Jabalia clearly: the crowded streets, the tall buildings packed tightly, and the narrow alleys winding between them like a maze. The air was always filled with the cries of vendors, the laughter of children, and the call to prayer from the mosque. But beneath all that, there was something else - an undercurrent, like smoke that never really cleared.

I was still young when I first saw it - not just the tension in the air, but the transformation of boys into something else. It was the summer when my uncle Yusuf took me to a camp hidden in the dunes outside Gaza City. At first, it felt like any other camp - there were boys my age, older boys, all wearing military fatigues, some of them running, others standing in lines as masked men watched over them like hawks. They called it a *"summer camp"*, but it wasn't like the ones I'd heard about from children on television. There were no games, no stories around a campfire.

Here, we learned how to hold a weapon. The rifle was cold and heavy in my hands digging into my shoulder, but it felt strangely natural. *"You will grow into it,"* the instructor said, his voice muffled behind the black cloth covering his face. The other boys looked just as unsure, but we all knew better than to complain. We learned how to fire in the direction of a target, a paper cut-out of an IDF soldier, his face void of expression, his body full of holes by the time we were done. The sound of gunfire echoed in my ears long after the shots stopped.

During training, I tried harder than the others. When the instructors barked commands, I snapped to attention faster. When they demanded push-ups or long sprints in the sand, I forced myself to keep going even as my muscles screamed for rest. I wanted to be noticed. I wanted them to see that I could be strong, like my father, like my uncle. When I closed my eyes at night, I pictured them both looking down at me, nodding in approval.

And when the training was over, they taught us about the mission. We were no longer just boys from Gaza - we were future fighters. *"You will raid their posts,"* they told us, *"Take back what is ours."* We practised storming mock Israeli outposts, imagining ourselves as the conquerors of Jerusalem. Some nights, lying under the canvas of the tents, I would close my eyes and see the city, its golden dome shimmering in the distance, as though I was already there. It was all so vivid, so close, that sometimes I could almost feel the stones of the Old City beneath my feet.

But then came the harder training days - ones where we were blindfolded and led through mock tunnels, told to find our way in the dark. *"Feel the walls,"* the instructors would say, their voices like ghosts in the pitch black. *"This is how you navigate. This is how you survive."* My heart pounded as I stumbled, feeling my way along the rough, cold stone. For a moment, a flash of panic tightened my chest. What if I couldn't find my way out? What if I failed? But then I heard my uncle's voice in my head - *"They will never stop. We must resist. We must fight."* And I pushed on, shoving the fear aside.

At home, my mother Amal spoke of them too, but her voice was always steady, like she was holding back a storm. *"They took your father,"* she would say. *"They will keep taking until there is nothing left of us."* Her words were heavy, filled with something I couldn't quite grasp at the time. But I knew there was pain there and something deeper - an anger that burned just below the surface.

She was a strong woman, my mother. Everyone in Jabalia knew her strength. She carried her pain with dignity, her shoulders always squared, her eyes sharp. Sometimes, though, when she thought I wasn't looking, I would catch her staring out the window, lost in thought. There was something fragile about those moments, something that made me realise that beneath her tough exterior, she feared for me. But she never showed it outright.

"*Ahmed,*" she said one evening as she was preparing dinner, her hands moving deftly over the vegetables. "*You are growing up too fast.*" She looked up briefly, her eyes locking onto mine. "*Soon, you will have to make your own choices. Choices I cannot make for you.*"

"*I know, Mama,*" I replied, though I didn't really understand what she meant. Not yet.

Her expression softened for just a moment, a flicker of the tenderness she reserved only for me. Then her face hardened again, and she turned back to the stove. "*You must be strong, like your father,*" she said, her voice steady. "*But strength is not just about fighting. It's about knowing when to fight and when to endure. Don't rush into this world, Ahmed. It will take everything from you.*"

But I wanted to rush into it. I wanted to be strong like my father, like my uncle.

My uncle Yusuf was different from my mother. He wasn't just angry, he was prepared. He owned a small mechanic's shop filled with old car parts and the smell of oil and rust. To anyone passing by, it looked like a place where cars were fixed and nothing more. But I knew better. I had been around long enough to understand that things weren't always what they seemed.

After school, I would head to Yusuf's shop. I'd help with small tasks - sorting tools, sweeping the floor. But there was always something else going on - something hidden. Men came in and out, their faces serious, their voices hushed. They talked about rockets, about attacks, about plans to fight back. They talked about tunnels - long, winding tunnels under the city, tunnels that could take us anywhere, even into Israel.

One afternoon, Yusuf pulled me aside. "*Ahmed,*" he said, his voice low, "*you're old enough to start understanding what's really happening. This isn't just about fixing cars. This is about fighting back.*"

I felt a strange mix of excitement and fear. *"I want to help,"* I told him, my voice barely above a whisper. *"I want to fight them too."*

He looked at me, his eyes serious but warm. *"You will,"* he promised. *"But first, you need to learn. You need to understand what it means to fight, what it means to resist. It's not just about anger or revenge. It's about being smart, being strong, and knowing when to strike."*

From that day on, I was allowed to listen more, to see more. I saw men bring in bags of fertiliser, pipes, and wires - things that seemed innocent but were not. I watched as they assembled parts that didn't look like much but could do terrible damage. *"We'll make them pay,"* one of the men said once, his voice filled with anger. *"We'll make them bleed for every child they've killed."*

Yusuf would nod, his face calm but resolute. *"They think they are safe,"* he would say. *"They think their walls and guns will protect them. But they are wrong. We will show them they are never safe - not anywhere, not ever."*

He wasn't like my mother. Where she was filled with anger that simmered beneath the surface, Yusuf's anger was cold, controlled. He had a purpose. He believed in what he was doing with an intensity that both inspired and frightened me.

One evening, after a long day at the shop, Yusuf took me to the back and showed me a small hidden entrance. *"This,"* he said, *"is the entrance to one of the tunnels. One day, you will see it for yourself. You will understand why we fight, why we can never stop."*

I stared into the darkness of the tunnel, a cold shiver running down my spine. I wanted to see it, to understand it, to be a part of it. That night, I went home filled with thoughts and plans. My mother looked at me closely, her eyes searching.

"You are growing up, Ahmed," she said softly. *"Soon you will have to choose who you are, what you stand for."*

I knew what my choice would be. I knew who I hated. I knew who I would fight.

Now, lying on this cold, hard floor, I think about those days - about Yusuf's shop, the men who came and went, the tunnels beneath the earth, and the anger that burned inside me. I hold onto that anger because it's mine, a flickering flame that keeps the darkness at bay. Without it, I am hollow - just a man alone in a cell, a shell haunted by doubts that creep in like shadows. And doubts... they are dangerous. They turn resolve into ash. They turn men like me into something breakable.

Chapter Four

YOSSI

The steady beeping of the machines fills the room, a constant reminder of where I am. The soft hum of the ventilator joins the rhythm, and somewhere outside, I can hear the faint shuffle of footsteps. My head feels thick, heavy, like it's wrapped in a fog I can't quite shake. I drift between awareness and something else - something darker, less clear. I'm awake... I think, but it's like I'm caught in the haze of unconsciousness, my mind floating somewhere in between.

I try to focus, to bring everything into sharper view, but it's hard. I can remember flashes - faces, voices, small pieces of the world around me. My parents were here, weren't they? My friends... It all blurs together. I try to push through the fog, but then there's her face. Even through the haze, I remember Yael.

When my eyes first flickered open, she was there, standing by my bedside. She was trying to smile, but I could see it - the strain in her eyes, the way her hand trembled just slightly as she reached out to touch mine. Even though I couldn't fully see her, I could feel her - the scent of jasmine in the air, the sound of her soft, steady breathing. She was there, anchoring me to this moment, to this bed.

"*Yossi,*" she whispered, her voice soft and broken. *"I'm here... I'm right here."*

I wanted to respond, to let her know I could hear her, that I could feel her there beside me. But my body wouldn't obey. My lips barely moved, and my throat was so dry I couldn't make a sound. All I could do was squeeze her hand weakly, hoping she'd understand. Her presence was pulling me out of the haze, out of the confusion, making me feel real again. She leaned closer, her eyes locked on mine, and I felt the warmth of her breath on my skin, stirring something deep within me.

"You've got to fight," she murmured, her voice barely audible. *"Please come back to me, Yossi. We need you."*

I tried to nod, to show her I understood, but the effort was too much. My body refused to cooperate, leaving me trapped in this strange in-between. I closed my eyes again, but I could still feel her hand in mine, her warmth cutting through the sterile coldness of the hospital. She stayed with me, long after I drifted back into the darkness.

I'm alone now, and I let my mind drift. I close my eyes and take myself back, back to a time when life felt simple. I'm twelve years old again, standing in the thick summer heat of Tel Aviv. The sun is beating down, and we're all standing in line at the ice cream stand near the old port. The air smells of salt and sea, and the sound of the waves crashing against the rocks fills the background.

Nadav, as usual, is beside me, nudging me with his elbow.

"You always get chocolate," he teases, grinning.

"Why change what works?" I reply with a smirk, knowing exactly what's coming.

"One day, Yossi, you'll have to try something different." He rolls his eyes dramatically, already knowing I'll ignore his advice.

Amir joins in the teasing, standing next to Leila. *"Maybe he's just scared of new things,"* Amir jokes, laughing as Leila shakes her head at our antics.

"Scared? Me?" I shoot back, laughing with them. *"I just know what I like."*

Ahead of us, Maya and Samir are already arguing about their ice cream choices.

"Mint chocolate is the best," Maya insists, her voice rising in mock outrage.

"You only like it because you have no taste," Samir fires back, grinning at her.

We finally get our ice creams and find a spot to sit along a low wall overlooking the sea, our legs dangling off the edge. The city hums around us - families walking by vendors calling out, and the distant sounds of cars and motorbikes. The warm breeze carries the scent of fresh pomegranates from a nearby stand. As I lick my ice cream, I can't help but think that life couldn't get better than this.

We spent our summers together, riding our bikes down to Jaffa, racing through narrow alleys, and climbing the old stone walls around the clock tower. We played football in the park near my house, our laughter filling the air. We were different - Jews, Muslims, Christians - but we didn't think much about it back then. We were just friends, caught up in our own world.

As I lie here, I think about those differences now, how they were always there, just beneath the surface. But instead of dividing us, they made us stronger, closer.

Nadav leaned back, gazing up at the sky, his mind clearly racing with excitement. *"You ever wonder what it feels like to just fly?"* he asked, out of nowhere, his grin already spreading across his face.

I raised an eyebrow. *"Fly? Like with wings or something?"*

"No, like... jumping out of a plane!" He leaped up from the ground, arms spread wide as if he were already soaring through the air. *"Imagine it, Yossi. The wind in your face, nothing but open sky."* He spun around, laughing.

I couldn't help but laugh with him. *"You'd probably get caught in the trees before you even hit the ground."*

Nadav laughed, shaking his head. *"Nah, I'd land perfectly, like a superhero! You'd be the one stuck up in the branches."*

"You've got it all figured out, huh?" I said, smirking. *"What makes you think I'd even jump?"*

He stopped spinning, looked right at me with that same daring smile. *"Cause you're my best mate, and you'd never let me do it alone."*

I rolled my eyes, but deep down, I knew he was right. *"Fine. But only to make sure you don't do something stupid."*

Amir was different. His family was large and close-knit, and there was always noise and laughter in his house. His father ran a small shop, and his mother was a teacher. They were always welcoming, always making us feel like family. *"You boys are like brothers,"* Amir's mother would say with a smile. And it was true - we were. We'd do anything for each other.

Then there was Maya, from a Druze family. Her parents were doctors, always busy, but never too busy to offer us tea or food whenever we came by. *"Stay, eat,"* her father would insist. *"You're too thin, Yossi!"* He'd tease Nadav too. *"And you, always running like there's a fire behind you!"*

Samir was the jokester of the group, and his father owned a bakery near the Carmel Market. Every morning, Samir would bring us fresh pastries, still warm and dusted with sugar.

"Here," he'd say, handing us each a piece. *"Best way to start the day."*

"Your dad's right," I'd reply, taking a big bite. *"Food really does bring people together."*

"Yeah, but you eat too much of it!" Samir would laugh, making us all join in.

Leila was still the calm one, always there when we needed her. But as we got older, she seemed to take on more of a quiet, watchful role, like she understood things the rest of us didn't. She wasn't just the one patching us up after scrapes and bruises anymore. She had this way of stepping in when things got tense, finding the right words or actions to pull us back from the edge.

I remember one afternoon, after a long day of football and arguments about who fouled who, the tension between Nadav and Samir had started to bubble over. They were both stubborn, and neither of them was backing down. Voices were raised, and it looked like it might escalate.

Leila didn't say much at first, just watched with those calm eyes of hers, letting them shout for a minute. Then, when things were on the verge of boiling over, she walked over and stepped between them. *"Alright, that's enough,"* she said, her voice quiet but firm, like she was the only one in the world who didn't need to raise her voice to be heard.

She put a hand on Samir's shoulder and then turned to Nadav. *"You're both just tired, and you're making this bigger than it needs to be."* They didn't argue with her. She had a way of cutting through the nonsense. In that moment, I realised she was more than just the one who took care of our cuts and bruises - she was the one who kept us together, kept us from falling apart when things got tough.

Later, as we all sat on the grass, cooling down, she looked over at Nadav, who was still fuming a little, and grinned. *"You boys would be lost without me."* Her teasing tone lightened the mood, and we all laughed, tension forgotten.

She didn't have to say it, but I could tell that Leila was already starting to think about the future, about how she could make things better. And even though she didn't talk much about being a medic, we could all see it. She had a natural way of knowing what we needed, even when we didn't.

We didn't talk much about the world outside our games, outside our little bubble. The news, the rockets, the soldiers - they felt distant, like something that happened in another world. But every now and then, the sirens would wail, cutting through our laughter. We'd run for shelter, our hearts pounding, trying to hide our fear from each other.

"It's just a drill," Nadav would mutter, trying to stay calm. But we all knew it wasn't. Leila would move among us, whispering words of comfort, her voice steady as always.

"We're safe here," she'd say, her hand on mine. *"Everything will be fine."*

But things were changing. Even then, I started to notice the soldiers on the streets, the security checks at the mall, the way people glanced over their shoulders. I began to understand that the world was more complicated than I had thought, that we'd all have to face things one day that we weren't ready for.

Sometimes, my grandmother Leah would visit. She'd sit with me and tell me stories of her life before Israel, of friends lost and a world that once existed. She always looked at our group of friends with pride.

"You're lucky, Yossi," she'd say, her voice soft but full of meaning. *"You have friends from everywhere. It's a beautiful thing."*

THROUGH THEIR EYES

I would sit and listen, trying to see the world through her eyes, through the weight of her memories. Once, I asked her if she thought things would ever change.

"I hope so, Yossi," she said, her eyes filled with a deep sadness. *"I pray for it every day. But it takes time. And courage. And understanding."* She paused, smiling at me gently. *"Maybe your generation will find a way."*

Her words stayed with me, made me look at my friends differently, made me wonder what their families were like, what fears they kept hidden, what dreams they held onto.

Now, as I lie in this hospital bed, I think back to those days, to those friends who became my family. I think of my grandmother, her stories and strength, and how she taught me to see the world in a different way. I hold onto those memories because they're real, because they remind me of who I am and where I come from. And I hold onto Yael too, because I know, somehow, that she's waiting for me.

And that's enough for now.

Chapter Five

AHMED

The walls of the cell feel even closer today. The air, thick and stale, clings to my skin. Lying here, I force my mind back to Gaza, to the days when everything was changing so quickly, when I thought I was finally becoming someone - part of something larger than myself.

It all started with small tasks for Yusuf, my uncle. His mechanic's shop was always more than a place for fixing cars. It was where plans were whispered, where resistance took shape. I'd been around for years, cleaning up and fetching tools, but I was always listening, always watching. The men who came to see Yusuf weren't just customers, they were part of the fight. They spoke in low voices, their faces tense as they discussed supply routes, targets, and strategies. I wanted to be involved. I wanted to be part of whatever they were planning.

One afternoon, a man walked into the shop who seemed different from the others. He was tall, with a greying beard and eyes that seemed to pierce through you. The room fell silent as he entered. The men who had been talking stopped and straightened up, their voices dropping to a murmur.

"Yusuf," he called out in a deep, commanding voice. *"We need to speak."*

Yusuf greeted him with a nod of respect, his face serious. *"Of course, Abu Khaled."*

I froze. I had heard the name before - Abu Khaled, a senior figure in Hamas, the one who made decisions about the raids and the tunnels. He was someone to be feared, a man whose name alone made people lower their voices. As he and Yusuf walked into the back room, I tried to stay busy, but my ears strained to catch every word.

They spoke about operations, about moving supplies, about the men who had been taken by the Israelis. My heart raced. This was it - the real thing. These weren't just conversations about small tasks, this was the fight, the one I wanted to be part of.

A while later, Abu Khaled stepped back into the main room. His eyes landed on me, sharp and unblinking. I felt a jolt of both fear and excitement.

"Who is this boy?" he asked, his gaze narrowing as he studied me.

Yusuf's chest swelled with pride as he answered. *"This is Ahmed, the son of a Shahid."*

Abu Khaled's expression didn't soften. He studied me for a moment longer, his eyes hard. *"And what does he do here?"*

"He helps," Yusuf said simply. *"He learns."*

Abu Khaled nodded slowly, his expression thoughtful. *"Good. We need young men like him - those willing to learn and willing to fight."*

A wave of pride surged through me. I wanted to say something, to tell him I was ready, that I could be trusted, but the words stuck in my throat. Instead, I just nodded, my hands clenched at my sides, determination swelling in my chest.

As Abu Khaled turned back to Yusuf, I made a silent vow. This was my chance. I would prove myself. I would show them all that I was worthy of my father's name.

A few days later, Yusuf handed me a folded piece of paper. *"Take this to the man at the market,"* he instructed, his voice low and serious. *"Be quick and careful. Don't let anyone see."*

I ran through the narrow streets, my heart pounding in my chest, eyes darting around as I made my way to the market. The man was there - a fruit seller with a kind face. I handed him the paper, and he nodded, his voice barely above a whisper. *"Good boy. Now, go back to Yusuf. Quickly."*

When I returned, Yusuf was waiting for me. *"Did you deliver it?"*

"Yes, Uncle. I did."

He smiled - a rare, genuine smile. *"Good. Very good."*

From that day on, things began to change. I was given more messages, more tasks. The men at the shop began to see me differently. They'd nod in acknowledgment, patting me on the back as I passed by. I felt like I was becoming someone, like I was part of something much bigger than myself. But it wasn't enough. I needed more than just nods of approval. I needed to show Yusuf - and myself - that I was capable of more.

One afternoon, Yusuf came up to me, wiping his hands on a rag. *"Ahmed, there's something I want you to see,"* he said. His voice was lower than usual, serious. *"Come with me."*

He led me to the small, hidden entrance behind a pile of old tyres at the back of the shop. It was the same entrance he had shown me once before, when he'd talked about the tunnels but never let me inside. But this time, instead of just stopping at the entrance, Yusuf crouched down and gestured for me to follow.

"This is where it begins," he whispered, handing me a small torch. *"You need to see it to understand why we do what we do."*

My heart raced as I followed him into the darkness. The tunnel was narrow, the walls rough, and I could hear the distant sounds of men working - shovels scraping against stone, voices murmuring in the shadows. The deeper we went, the cooler the air became, carrying a damp, earthy scent that clung to my skin. I stumbled a little, catching myself on the uneven walls, but Yusuf's steady steps guided me forward.

"These tunnels are our lifeline," he explained softly, his voice echoing in the small space. *"They let us move freely. Supplies, people, messages - they all flow through here. This is how we survive."*

I nodded, even though he probably couldn't see me. I could barely breathe, my chest tight with a mixture of fear and awe. This was more than just a hidden passage beneath the city. It felt alive, like a breathing entity that connected everything. The flickering light of my torch bounced off the uneven walls, casting long shadows that made the tunnel feel like it was shifting and moving around us.

Yusuf stopped, his hand resting on the wall. *"This is where we fight back,"* he said, his voice low and determined. *"This is where we make them bleed."*

I swallowed hard, the weight of his words sinking in. This was more than just running messages, this was about being part of something much bigger. Something dangerous. But instead of fear, all I felt was a surge of excitement. This was real. This was serious. And I was ready.

Then Yusuf's hand tightened briefly on my shoulder. *"You've come a long way, Ahmed,"* he murmured, his voice softer now. *"But you'll need to go further. This is just the beginning. Don't ever forget what's expected of you."*

His words hit me harder than I'd expected, a rush of pride and pressure washing over me in equal measure. I nodded, a silent promise forming in my mind: *I won't let you down.*

Over the next few weeks, I found myself drawn deeper into this hidden world beneath Gaza, spending more and more time in the tunnels. The air was cool and damp, and the walls seemed to close in around us. It was here that I met Tariq Barghouti, Khaled Mansour, and Bilal Qassem - three boys around my age who quickly became more than just friends. They became my brothers.

We were a tight-knit group, even though we were all so different. We shared our hopes, our fears, our dreams - whispered in the dim light of the tunnels, away from the noise and chaos of the city above. But even as we bonded, I began to notice how different we all were. Each of us carried our own scars, our own motivations for being here.

Tariq was the most intense of the group. He moved with a purpose that seemed too big for his small frame, his eyes always burning with an inner fire that never seemed to die down. There was a rage in him that simmered just below the surface, a constant reminder of the loss he carried with him. His older brother had been killed during a raid two years ago, and Tariq never spoke of him without that unmistakable edge in his voice.

"We can't stop," he'd say, his fists clenched, his voice filled with fury. *"Not until they bleed as much as we have."* His words were like a vow, one he repeated often - always with the same raw intensity.

Khaled was just as quick to anger, his emotions flaring up whenever the fighting was mentioned. He would speak through gritted teeth, his eyes narrowed with determination. *"They think they've won,"* he would mutter, shaking his head. *"But they haven't seen what we're capable of. We'll show them."* Where Tariq's rage burned hot and steady, Khaled's was like a flash of fire, unpredictable and explosive. Sometimes, he'd pace the narrow tunnels, muttering to himself, his hands balled into fists as if he couldn't contain the anger simmering just beneath the surface.

But it was Bilal who caught my attention the most. He was quieter, always thinking, always planning. He wasn't driven by the same raw emotion as Tariq and Khaled, but there was a sharpness to him - a focus. His aggression simmered beneath the surface, emerging only when he was sure of the details. I watched how his eyes would narrow, how his brow would furrow in concentration as he traced lines on a piece of paper, his fingers moving methodically.

"We have to be smart," he'd say calmly, his gaze steady. *"It's not enough to just attack - we have to think ahead. We need to make every move count."*

But it wasn't just his words that made an impact. It was the way he said them. The calm, precise tone, the unflinching logic. Tariq and Khaled would often push back, their anger flaring up at the suggestion of holding back, but Bilal never wavered. He'd just look at them with those sharp, assessing eyes, waiting until their protests died down.

I began to realise that while Tariq's and Khaled's voices were louder, Bilal's carried more weight. He didn't speak often, but when he did, the others listened. Even I found myself holding my breath, waiting for his quiet voice to cut through the tension. There was a patience to him, a determination that made it clear he wasn't just following the fight - he was shaping it, in his own way.

"We need to outthink them, not just outrun them," he'd insist, his voice low but firm. And gradually, I saw the others - Tariq included - start to nod, start to

consider his words. Even though they were quick to dismiss his quiet approach at first, it was hard to ignore the impact Bilal's planning had.

In those moments, I wondered if they ever saw what I did - that Bilal, for all his calmness, was just as dangerous as the rest of us. Maybe even more so, because he didn't act on impulse. He waited, and he watched, and when he moved, it was with precision.

Their different approaches fascinated me, but they also made me question my own motivations. Was I here for revenge like Tariq and Khaled? Or was I searching for a sense of control like Bilal? I didn't know. But one thing was clear: the deeper I got into this world, the more I felt the need to prove myself - to show them that I belonged, that I could be just as strong, just as driven.

Back at home, my mother sensed the change in me. She didn't ask many questions, but I could tell she was watching closely. Her sharp eyes seemed to take in every detail, her expression unreadable as she moved about the house.

"You're spending more time with Yusuf," she said one evening, her voice carefully neutral.

I nodded, unsure of how much to say. *"He's teaching me a lot,"* I replied. *"There's a lot to learn."*

Amal's hands stilled for a moment, and she looked at me, her gaze softening. *"Be careful, Ahmed,"* she said quietly. *"There are many people who will tell you what you should do, but in the end, only you can decide what's right."*

I didn't say anything, but her words stayed with me. I wasn't sure what was right anymore. I wasn't sure if there was a right in all of this. But I knew one thing for sure - I was in too deep to turn back now.

The weeks passed, and I continued working in the tunnels, growing closer to Tariq, Khaled, and Bilal with each passing day. They had become my brothers, and together, we formed a bond that went beyond the work we were doing. We shared our hopes and fears, but we also shared the weight of what we were doing, the knowledge that every step we took could bring us closer to victory - or closer to losing everything.

As we sat in the tunnels one evening, the dim light casting shadows on the walls, Bilal turned to me.

"Do you ever think about what comes next?" he asked quietly, his voice low.

I thought about it for a moment, the question hanging in the air between us. I wasn't sure how to answer. I wasn't sure if I could even imagine a world beyond the fight.

"I don't know," I said finally. *"I guess we'll see."*

He nodded, his gaze thoughtful. *"Yeah. I guess we will."*

And as the days passed, I couldn't shake the feeling that we were all walking a line - one that could lead us to freedom, or one that could consume us all.

Chapter Six

YOSSI

The steady beeping of the machines fades into the background, a dull hum that I barely notice anymore. The pain is there too, constant but distant, as though it's not quite mine. I lie still, eyes half-closed, trapped somewhere between sleep and waking. My body feels heavy, like it's anchored to this bed, but my mind... my mind drifts.

I can almost feel her, like a whisper at the edge of my thoughts. Yael. She's here, I know it. Her presence is so real, so close, it's like I could reach out and touch her if only I could move. I can't see her, but I don't need to. I can smell her perfume - the faint trace of jasmine, warm and familiar. It lingers in the air, wrapping around me like a memory, pulling me out of the haze.

There's a soft rustling, the sound of fabric moving as she shifts in the chair beside me. I can't see it, but I know she's there, always there, waiting for me. Her breathing is slow, steady, like she's been sitting here for hours, watching, waiting for me to wake up. I want to say something, to let her know that I feel her here, that I know she's close. But the words are stuck somewhere deep inside me, trapped behind the fog that clouds everything.

Her hand... I can feel it, just barely, resting on mine. The warmth of her skin seeps into me, and for a moment, the pain fades, the hospital room disappears. It's just us, just this moment. She squeezes my hand gently, and I try to squeeze back, to let her know I'm here, that I'm trying to come back to her. But my body doesn't respond the way I want it to. It never does.

Still, I hold onto that sensation, the feeling of her hand in mine, the sound of her breathing. It's enough to keep me anchored, enough to remind me that there's something waiting for me when I wake up. If I can wake up.

I let my mind slip away, back to a time when everything was easier. We were by the sea, sitting in our usual spot, the air thick with salt and laughter. Nadav was beside me, nudging me like he always did, teasing me about something ridiculous. It was always easy with him, with all of them - Amir, Leila, Maya, Samir. We didn't need to talk about the future back then, didn't need to think about the things that were coming. We just had each other, and that was enough.

We were sitting around a small campfire by the beach, the flames crackling softly as the sun disappeared into the horizon. The warmth from the fire mixed with the cool night air, creating a sense of comfort. Nadav was poking at the fire with a stick, his eyes glowing in the flickering light.

"You know, Yossi," Nadav said, staring into the flames, *"one day we'll look back on this and laugh."*

I raised an eyebrow. *"Laugh at what?"*

He grinned, tossing the stick into the fire. *"At how easy we had it. Sitting here, doing nothing, not a care in the world. You'll see. Things won't always be this simple."*

There was a weight in his words, one I hadn't expected. It wasn't like Nadav to talk about the future like that. Usually, he kept things light, pushing us to enjoy the moment. But this felt different, like he knew something the rest of us hadn't figured out yet.

Leila sat across from us, her fingers idly tracing shapes in the sand. Every now and then, she'd glance up from her doodles and smile. *"We'll probably laugh at how serious you're being right now, Nadav,"* she said, her voice calm, as always.

She continued to draw spirals and patterns in the sand with a stick, her movements slow and thoughtful. It was just like her to be quietly observing, noticing things the rest of us didn't. She always had this way of staying grounded, bringing a sense of calm to whatever was going on around us.

"*You take everything so seriously,*" she teased gently, glancing at Nadav, but her smile was soft, making it clear she wasn't mocking him. She just knew how to lighten the mood, even in moments like this.

Amir chuckled, leaning back on his elbows. "*Yeah, man, you're getting way too deep for a campfire chat. Let's talk about something else. Like, who's the best swimmer? Because we all know it's me.*"

"*In your dreams, Amir,*" Maya shot back, shaking her head as she wrapped a blanket around her shoulders. "*I've seen you in the water. You splash around like a fish out of water.*"

Samir, sitting quietly next to Maya, grinned. "*We could settle this right now, you know. A late-night swim. Winner takes all.*"

Leila sighed, shaking her head. "*Or we could just enjoy the fire and not freeze ourselves to death in the sea.*"

I laughed, the sound carrying through the night. It was moments like these that made me forget about everything else - the army, the future, the things that felt too big to handle. Right now, it was just us and the fire, the quiet lapping of the waves in the background.

Nadav, ever the restless one, stood up and stretched, his face half-hidden in the shadows. "*Fine, no swim. But mark my words, Yossi. One day, we're going to miss this.*"

I didn't answer, just stared into the fire, watching the flames dance and flicker. Part of me knew he was right. We wouldn't always have this - this feeling of freedom, of being untouchable. But for now, I wasn't ready to think about that.

Nadav leaned back, tossing pebbles into the fire, watching the sparks shoot up. "*You know what's gonna be cool?*" he asked, his voice full of excitement.

I glanced over at him. "*What?*"

"*Jumping out of planes!*" He grinned, his eyes wide. "*Can you imagine it, Yossi? We're gonna be like... flying.*"

I laughed, shaking my head. *"You're already flying with those ideas, Nadav."*

"No, seriously!" He sat up, all fired up. *"We'll be paratroopers, jumping out, landing anywhere we want. It's gonna be awesome."*

I rolled my eyes, grinning. *"You'd probably forget your parachute."*

Nadav laughed and nudged me. *"Nah, I'll remember. You'll be right behind me, double-checking everything like always."*

"That's because someone has to stop you from getting into trouble," I teased, grabbing a pebble and tossing it at him.

"Me? Trouble?" Nadav gasped dramatically, then laughed. *"You're just jealous 'cos I'll be jumping first!"*

I shrugged. *"Fine, but I'll be the one who lands without falling on my face."*

Nadav burst out laughing, nearly falling backwards. *"Yeah, right! You? Land smoothly? I'll believe it when I see it!"*

We both cracked up, the firelight dancing in the dark as the sounds of the sea and our friends echoed from the shore.

"We're gonna have the best stories, Yossi," Nadav said, grinning at me.

I couldn't help but smile. *"Yeah, maybe. If you don't break a leg first."*

I think of my parents too, though it feels like a lifetime ago. My mother's voice, always so calm, so reassuring. I can hear her even now, like an echo in my mind.

"You don't have to figure everything out right now, Yossi. One step at a time."

She used to say that all the time, her voice soft and steady as she worked in the kitchen, preparing dinner after a long day at the hospital. I'd sit there, watching her move about the room, her presence making everything seem smaller, more manageable. She had a way of doing that - making the world feel less overwhelming.

My father, on the other hand, was different. He didn't say much, but when he did, it was always simple, always certain.

"You'll be fine, Yossi. You're stronger than you think."

I hear his voice now too, though I wonder if he'd still say those words if he saw me like this - broken, lost in this haze of pain and medication. Would he still believe I'm strong? I'm not sure if I believe it anymore.

But then there's her - Yael. I can feel her, even if I can't see her. The smell of jasmine, the sound of her breathing, the warmth of her hand on mine. She's here, and she's waiting for me. She always has been. I hold onto that thought, onto the promise of her presence, and let it pull me back from the edge. I may not be ready to wake up yet, but I know she's there, and that's enough.

For now, that's enough.

Chapter Seven

AHMED

The air is heavy today, thick with the mingling scents of sweat, dust, and the heat that clings to Jabalia like a shroud. Everything feels intensified beneath the relentless sun - every smell, every sound, every thought. My shirt sticks to my back as I weave through the narrow streets, my mind fixed on the task ahead. I know the boys will be waiting at the corner - Tariq leaning casually against a wall, Khaled pacing with his restless energy, and Bilal standing slightly apart, arms crossed, his eyes scanning the street like a sentinel.

As I approach, they turn towards me, their faces a mix of expectation and tension. There's an unspoken bond between us now, something that wasn't there before. I can feel it in the way they look at me - not just as a friend, but as a leader. Tariq's gaze burns with the same fierce loyalty, Khaled's restlessness quiets, and even Bilal's calculating stare seems to measure my every move. I feel a strange sense of power, a weight that I carry with pride and trepidation. Things have changed. I have changed. And they can sense it too.

Yusuf sees something in me. He calls me *shab* - a term that carries respect, like a young warrior being groomed for battle. Lately, he's taken me aside more often, speaking in low, serious tones about discipline, focus, and our mission.

"You are not just a boy, Ahmed," he tells me, his dark eyes intense. *"You are a leader, like your father before you. And leaders must be strong, unyielding."*

I drink in his words, feeling the swell of pride in my chest. But beneath that pride, something else stirs - something I can't quite name, a flicker of doubt that I push aside. This is the path I've chosen. Or maybe, it's the path that was chosen for me.

My friends - Tariq, Khaled, and Bilal - follow my lead now. When Yusuf speaks, they listen, but their eyes often drift to me, waiting to see how I react. I sense their whispers when they think I'm not listening, calling me *akhuna* - our brother - with an edge of both awe and expectation. I feel the weight of their gaze, the pressure to be the leader they believe I am. We've grown closer, more unified in our purpose, but there's a new intensity between us. We don't laugh as much anymore. Our youth is slipping away, replaced by something harder, something darker.

As we move through the market, Tariq's eyes catch on a group of boys our age lounging against a wall, laughing, playing with a ball. He stops, his frown deepening.

"Look at them," he mutters, disdain dripping from his voice. *"They act like children while we do the work that matters."*

Khaled spits on the ground, his face twisted with contempt. *"They think they're safe because they do nothing, because they hide. They think they're better than us."*

Bilal nods, his eyes narrowing. *"They should be with us, not wasting time."*

A spark of anger flares in me, hot and fierce, but beneath it, something else - something softer that I quickly suppress. I can't afford to question myself, not now. I turn to my friends, my voice cold, steady. *"Let's go talk to them."*

We approach the group with purpose, shoulders squared. The boys stop their game, their faces wary, and I can see the fear in their eyes. They know who we are, what we do. But this time, it's different - they're not just looking at us, they're looking at *me*. I can feel the others watching too - waiting to see what I'll do. I'm no longer just part of the group. I'm leading it.

"You," I say, pointing to the boy in the middle, his dark curls framing a face that suddenly looks much younger. *"Why aren't you with us? Why aren't you doing your part?"*

The boy stammers, looking around at his friends. *"We... we didn't know... we didn't think..."*

I step closer, my face inches from his. *"Didn't think what? That your city needs you? That your people need you? Or are you just a coward?"* The word feels heavy on my tongue, charged with the same anger that had driven me to fight, to prove myself. Out of the corner of my eye, I catch Bilal watching me - his gaze thoughtful, almost questioning, as if he's assessing not just the boy's response, but mine as well.

The boy's face flushes, and I see his hands trembling. There's a rush of power in that moment, a feeling of control that washes over me. But as I stare into his eyes, something twists inside me. *Am I doing this because it's right, or because it's expected of me?* I shove the thought away.

Tariq steps forward, his voice low and menacing. *"Ahmed is right. You should be ashamed."*

Khaled, always quick to act, shoves the boy hard, sending him stumbling against the wall. The others flinch, but they don't move. Bilal's eyes stay fixed on them, daring them to respond.

"We are fighting for something real," I continue, my voice rising with conviction. *"We are doing what is necessary, what is right. And you think you can sit here and play games?"*

One of the boys, braver or more foolish than the others, steps forward. *"We don't want trouble,"* he says, his voice shaky but defiant. *"We just want to live."*

"To live?" I shout, the anger rising in my chest. *"To live while our fathers die, while our brothers fight. Is that all you care about?"*

Before I know it, my fist connects with his face. He cries out, stumbling back, clutching his cheek. The others move to help him, but Tariq and Khaled are already there, pushing them away, their voices harsh, their fists relentless.

For a moment, all I feel is the heat of anger coursing through me. But as the boys fall to the ground, beaten and bruised, that feeling shifts. The power I felt moments ago now feels hollow. *Is this what power is? Is this what it means to lead?*

The fight is quick, a flurry of punches and kicks. We outnumber them, and they are unprepared. When it's over, they lie on the ground, nursing their wounds, their eyes wide with fear.

I stand over them, my chest heaving, my knuckles throbbing. *"Remember this,"* I say, my voice cold. *"Remember where you should stand."*

We walk away, leaving them in the dust. My heart pounds with adrenaline, and I can see the approval in my friends' eyes. Tariq's look is one of triumph, Khaled grins with satisfaction, and even Bilal gives a nod of respect. But inside me, something feels off. The power I thought I wanted, the respect I thought I'd earned - it all feels wrong.

We head to the shop where Yusuf waits for us. He's hunched over the workbench, tinkering with an engine part, the metallic scent of oil mixing with the ever-present dust of the city. As we enter, he looks up, wiping his hands on a rag. There's a pause as he studies us, his eyes sharp, assessing.

"Well?" he asks, his voice calm but laced with expectation.

I recount what happened, keeping my voice steady, trying to sound confident. I feel Tariq and Khaled's eyes on me, their approval boosting my resolve. When I finish, a small smile plays at the corners of Yusuf's mouth.

"Good," he says, his tone calm but firm. *"They need to learn. There is no room for weakness, for hesitation."*

I nod, feeling a flicker of satisfaction. *"Yes, Uncle,"* I reply, but as I speak, a tiny voice in the back of my mind asks if I truly believe this. Was that strength I showed, or something else? Did I lead, or did I just lash out?

Yusuf's eyes linger on me for a moment, studying me in that way he always does, as if weighing my worth. He nods slowly, his expression softening slightly. *"Leadership isn't just about strength, Ahmed,"* he says quietly. *"It's about control.*

Control of others, yes, but more importantly, control of yourself. Doubt is a luxury we cannot afford."

There it is again - that pull, that subtle manipulation, the way he knows exactly what to say to bury my doubts. His words are like a balm, soothing the unease inside me. He doesn't need to force anything, he knows I'll fall into place, just like my father did.

"I understand," I say, though I'm not sure I do.

Yusuf nods, satisfied. *"Good. You're becoming who you were meant to be."*

I stand there, chest tight, his praise mingling with a sense of unease. This is what I wanted, isn't it? To prove myself worthy of my father's name, to be the leader everyone thinks I should be. But then why does it feel so heavy?

"There's more to do, Ahmed," Yusuf adds, his tone sharpening again. *"You've shown them you can lead, but now you need to show them that you can do more. I have something bigger in mind for you and your friends."*

My heart races, excitement and anxiety battling inside me. *"What do you want us to do?"*

He leans in, his gaze never leaving mine. *"We'll talk soon,"* he says softly. *"For now, keep your eyes open, keep your friends close, and be ready."*

I swallow, nodding again. *"Yes, Uncle."*

As we leave the shop, the others look to me, curiosity and anticipation etched on their faces. I offer a tight smile, trying to project the confidence Yusuf wants to see. But inside, questions churn. What will he ask of us? And will I be ready when the time comes?

At home, things feel different. My mother, Amal, greets me with open arms, her voice warm and full of pride. She believes I am fulfilling my father's legacy, that I am becoming the man I was always meant to be. But my sisters - they avoid me now. Layla used to meet my eyes with boldness, but now she barely glances at me. I see the fear in her, in all of them. When I enter a room, their conversations stop, replaced by uneasy silence.

One evening, I overhear them whispering in the kitchen. *"He's changing,"* one of them says, her voice tinged with fear. *"I don't know what to do. He scares me."*

A flash of irritation runs through me, but behind it, something deeper - something I don't want to acknowledge. I tell myself they're too young, too naïve to understand. But their fear, their distance - it gnaws at me, even as I try to push it aside.

Later that night, I confront Layla. She's sitting alone, her back turned, staring at the faint flicker of a candle on the windowsill.

"Why do your friends run when they see me?" I demand.

Layla stiffens but doesn't turn around immediately. When she finally faces me, her eyes are wide, filled with something I hadn't expected - sadness. That sadness pierces through me in a way I wasn't prepared for, stirring something deep inside that I quickly try to bury.

"They're afraid of you, Ahmed. Everyone is." Her voice is soft but steady, as if she's daring me to argue. *"You've changed. You and your friends... you're not the same."*

I glare at her, my jaw tight. *"They should be afraid. If they're not with us, they're against us."*

Her lips tremble, and I see her eyes glisten with unshed tears. She shakes her head, her voice breaking. *"It's not that simple."*

I turn away, dismissing her words. *"You don't know anything,"* I snap, but her words linger, stirring something I try to bury deep inside. There's an ache I can't ignore. Layla's fear, her sadness - it should mean nothing, but it gnaws at the edges of my resolve, threatening to unravel it.

I want to tell her it's for our family, for our father's memory. But would she even understand? Does she see what I'm becoming as honourable, or just... terrifying?

The next morning, I meet with Yusuf again. He's waiting for me at the shop, his expression unreadable as I approach. I square my shoulders, determined not to show any sign of doubt.

"You're doing well, Ahmed," he says, his voice steady. *"You are becoming the leader your father would have been proud of."*

I nod, feeling the weight of his expectations settling on my shoulders. *"What's next?"* I ask, trying to sound eager, strong.

"Patience, shab," Yusuf replies, a hint of a smile on his lips. *"There is always another task, another fight, another battle to be won. But you will know when the time is right."*

The sun beats down on the streets of Jabalia, the heat pressing down like a physical force. There is always another task, another mission, another test. And I will be ready. I *have* to be.

Because this is who I am now. This is who I have chosen to become.

Chapter Eight

YOSSI

The summer sun in Tel Aviv seems never to fade, casting a golden hue over the city, making everything glow with a warmth that feels almost tangible. The days stretch lazily into long, warm evenings, filled with the sounds of traffic, the cries of seagulls, and the distant hum of life. Each morning, I meet my friends by the park, where our bikes rest against the low wall. The familiar sounds of the city waking up around us - traffic buzzing, shop shutters rolling up, and the sea breeze carrying the scents of salt and jasmine - feel like a promise of adventure.

Nadav is always the first to arrive, his wild curls bouncing as he races down the street, always the fastest, always the first to think up some madcap idea.

"Race you to the beach!" he shouts, grinning as he pedals furiously away. I laugh, pushing off after him, with Leila, Amir, Maya, and Samir close behind, our bikes whizzing past the waking city.

The sea sparkles ahead, the air thick with salt and warmth, the scent of fresh coffee drifting from the street stalls. Maya rides with ease, her hair streaming behind her like a flag, a sketchbook always in her backpack, ready to capture the world around her. Samir, steady and quiet, is beside her, his face calm and focused, always calculating the best route, the quickest turn.

Leila's friend, Yael, has started joining us lately. She moved to our neighbourhood a few months ago - a Jewish girl with bright blue eyes and a shy smile. She fits in with us quickly, her laughter blending seamlessly with ours, her curiosity just as boundless. She's quieter than Leila, but there's a spark in her eyes that suggests she's not afraid of a little adventure.

One day, we decide to take her to our favourite spot by the old clock tower in Jaffa. The climb is steep, but the view from the top is worth it - Tel Aviv spreads out below like a patchwork quilt, with the sea stretching endlessly to the horizon. Yael hesitates at first, glancing up at the tower and then back at us as if weighing whether she's ready to be part of this.

The sun was setting low over the rooftops as we all gathered by the old water tower, the place where we'd spent so many long afternoons racing and climbing. Yael stood next to Leila, glancing up at the tower nervously as we all laughed and joked around. Leila had introduced her to the group, and I could tell she was still getting used to us.

"Come on, it's easy," Leila said, nudging Yael's arm. *"I've done it a hundred times. You're just scared 'cos Nadav talks too much about jumping off of things."*

Yael smiled, her fingers fiddling with the strap of her bag. *"It's not that... I'm just... not used to it."*

Leila rolled her eyes, grinning. *"It's fine. If Nadav can do it, anyone can. Trust me."*

Nadav overheard and shot Leila a mock-hurt look. *"Hey! I'm a professional climber, thank you very much."* He threw a playful glance in my direction. *"Unlike Yossi, who's only here to impress someone."* His eyes darted between Yael and me, and I could feel the heat rise to my cheeks.

"Shut up," I muttered, but I couldn't stop the grin from spreading across my face. *"At least I'm not the one constantly falling off and needing Leila to patch me up every five minutes."*

Nadav's laugh echoed through the air, and Leila chimed in. *"He's right, you know. You'd be lost without me."* She nudged Nadav, who made a big show of rubbing his arm like he was injured.

"Fine, fine," Nadav said, throwing his hands up in defeat. *"But when I'm the first to jump out of planes, you'll all be begging me for advice."*

Samir, who had been silently watching us all with a smirk on his face, finally chimed in. *"We'll see about that. You'll probably twist your ankle on the way down."*

Everyone laughed, and even Yael seemed to relax a little. She looked at Leila, a shy smile on her face. *"I don't know how you keep up with them,"* she said, her voice soft but filled with amusement.

Leila shrugged, chuckling. *"You get used to it. Besides, they'd be hopeless without me."* She winked, then turned to the boys. *"Come on, let's show Yael how it's done."*

As Nadav and Samir scrambled to the base of the tower, Leila stayed behind with Yael for a moment. I caught the two of them talking quietly, Leila pointing up at the tower, probably giving Yael some tips on how to climb without getting too scared.

I couldn't help but watch the way Yael smiled, still a bit hesitant but clearly enjoying herself more now that Leila was beside her. It was nice, seeing how easily she fit in with our group, like she'd always been a part of it.

"You coming or what, Yossi?" Nadav called from up ahead, already halfway up the tower.

"Yeah, yeah, I'm coming," I shouted back, stealing one last glance at Yael before following them up.

Yael laughs, and we begin our ascent, gripping the old stones with our hands, our hearts racing with the thrill of it. At the top, we sit on the ledge, legs dangling, watching the city come alive below. The world feels vast and open, and I feel a rush of freedom - a sense that we could do anything, be anyone.

Yael turns to me, her eyes bright. *"Do you ever wonder what's out there? Beyond the sea?"*

I nod, feeling the wind on my face. *"All the time. I want to see it all - every place, every corner of the world."*

"Maybe one day we'll go together," she says softly.

Her words hang in the air, and I feel something shift, something new and exciting. I smile at her, and she smiles back. For a moment, it feels like the world has shrunk to just the two of us sitting on this ledge, dreaming of far-off places. I don't say anything, but I can sense the others watching. Nadav shoots me a sidelong glance, his grin playful, but he doesn't say a word. None of them do. Not yet.

As the days pass, I notice how often Yael's eyes linger on me when we're all together. It's subtle - small, stolen glances when she thinks I'm not looking. I try not to make too much of it, but I feel it - like a current, pulling me towards her in a way I don't quite understand yet.

We spend most of our days by the beach, the sun beating down on us as we race through the sand or dive into the cool, blue water. The city behind us hums with life, but here, it feels like time slows down, like the world is ours and nothing can touch us. Nadav is always the loudest, challenging us to races or inventing some new game that usually ends with us collapsing in laughter.

One afternoon, as we lie in the sand, Nadav leans over to me, smirking. *"You've been quiet lately, Yossi. Something on your mind?"* His voice is teasing, but his eyes are sharp.

I shrug, glancing towards Yael, who's sitting a little apart from the group, drawing shapes in the sand with a stick. I don't know what to say, so I just laugh it off. *"Just enjoying the peace."*

Nadav doesn't push, but I can feel the weight of his unspoken question.

That evening, as we ride back home, I fall behind the group, my thoughts wandering. I can still hear Yael's laughter, see the way her hair catches the last light of the setting sun. There's something about her that's different - something that makes me feel different when I'm around her. I wonder if the others have noticed too. They must have. But no one says anything. Not yet.

As we reach the edge of the park, Yael slows her bike, turning to me with a soft smile. *"Thanks for today, Yossi. It was... nice."*

There's something in the way she says it, something that makes my heart beat a little faster. I nod, unsure of what to say. *"Yeah... it was."*

She lingers for a moment longer, as if waiting for me to say more. But then she turns and pedals away, leaving me standing there, watching her disappear into the dusk.

Later, lying in bed, I replay the day in my mind - her laughter, the feel of the wind on my face, the weight of Nadav's question hanging in the air. I wonder what tomorrow will bring, and if I'll find the courage to say something, anything, that might make sense of these feelings.

But for now, I let myself drift, the sounds of the city outside my window - traffic, voices, the distant crash of the sea - lulling me to sleep. And in that place between waking and dreaming, I can almost feel her presence beside me, soft and warm, like a whisper on the breeze.

Chapter Nine

AHMED

The air feels thick, like it's pressing down on Jabalia, seeping into the darkened tunnels where we gather, heavy with the weight of everything that's coming. It's 2014, and the city seems to hold its breath, waiting for something to break. Following the kidnapping and murder of three Israeli teenagers, the situation exploded. The Israelis blamed Hamas. The whispers of war are louder now, an undercurrent that flows through the streets. Abu Khaled has grown more secretive, his meetings are shorter, his instructions more precise. Yusuf's shop is busier than ever - men come and go at all hours, their faces set in grim lines, their movements sharp and purposeful.

The tunnels - our lifeline beneath the earth - are teeming with activity. Fighters move swiftly, transporting weapons, ammunition, and rockets. My friends and I - Tariq, Khaled and Bilal are no longer just the boys who once played in these streets. We have learned the network of tunnels like the back of our hands. We know every twist and turn, every safe house and storage point. These tunnels are like veins beneath the surface of Gaza, carrying the lifeblood of the resistance.

Our work is crucial, even if it doesn't involve pulling a trigger. We carry messages from one end of the tunnel network to the other, passing information between the fighters. We know which tunnel leads to which exit, which path is safest when the bombing begins. We distribute ammunition. We are the unseen hands that keep everything connected, moving in the shadows where others dare not tread.

"This is our moment," I tell myself, feeling the pulse of adrenaline and purpose in my veins. Abu Khaled's words echo in my mind: *"Every move you make is a strike against the enemy, every step is for our freedom."* I nod to Tariq and Khaled, who look to me for guidance. We are ready. We were born for this.

Abu Khaled has been drilling us on the importance of timing, of choosing the right moment to act. *"They think they can bomb us into silence,"* he growls, his voice low and fierce. *"But they'll learn - Gaza doesn't kneel."*

As Abu Khaled speaks, a surge of pride swells within me. I see the same determination in the eyes of my friends. We know our mission. We know what we stand for. Our fathers and uncles fought before us, and now it is our turn to stand up and resist. There is no room for doubt, only the certainty that we are on the right path.

But as I stand beside my friends in one of the main tunnel chambers, surrounded by crates of ammunition and supplies, I feel a flicker of something else - something I push down quickly. Hani, the bomb maker, is there too, working on his devices, his hands moving deftly over the equipment, checking every fuse and connection. I watch closely, trying to learn every detail, even if I know I'm not ready to handle explosives myself. This is no longer a game. This is real.

"Ahmed," Hani calls, waving me over. *"Take this message to the fighters near the eastern sector. They need to know we're moving the supplies there tonight."*

I take the folded paper from his hands, feeling the weight of the task. I nod and tuck it into my jacket. *"I'll be quick,"* I promise.

He nods, and I move through the tunnel, Bilal at my side. We make our way through the dimly lit passages, careful to keep our steps light and our voices low. The air is cool, thick with moisture, and the walls seem to close in, pressing against our shoulders. The distant hum of Israeli drones overhead reminds us that we are always being watched, always hunted. But we press on, focused and determined.

We reach the eastern sector, finding a group of fighters crouched by a supply cache. I hand over the message, watching as their leader scans the words, his face set with concentration. He nods, folding the paper and tucking it into his pocket.

"Good work," he says, clapping me on the shoulder. "You're doing well. Now head back quickly. It's not safe here for long."

I nod, turning back the way we came, Bilal following closely. As we make our way back through the tunnels, I feel a sense of pride, knowing we are a crucial part of something bigger. Even though our roles might seem small, they are indispensable to the resistance. Every step we take, every message we deliver strengthens our cause. This is the path I have chosen, the path I believe in with every fibre of my being.

But then I catch the flicker in Bilal's eyes, a flash of something I recognise but don't want to name.

"Sometimes, it's like we're playing a role in someone else's game," Bilal murmurs, almost to himself. *"The real decisions are made elsewhere, and we're just moving through shadows."*

I glance at him, surprised by his words. *"But it's what we have,"* I say quietly, though a small knot forms in my stomach. *"It's what we can do."*

He looks at me, searching my face. *"Do you really believe that, Ahmed? Do you believe this is the only way?"*

His question hangs in the air, heavier than the dust around us. *"Of course this is the way,"* I respond firmly, leaving no room for doubt. *"Our fathers and brothers have laid down their lives for this fight. It is our duty to carry it forward. We must be strong. We cannot afford to question the path laid out for us "*

But as we continue walking, Bilal's words echo in my mind. I try to push them away, but they linger like a shadow I can't shake.

When we return to the tunnel's main chamber, Yusuf and a few senior members of Hamas are gathered around a large map, their faces set in concentration. Tariq and Khaled stand off to the side, listening intently, their expressions tense as they absorb every word. Tariq and I exchange glances, then edge closer to get a better view.

One of the older men, his grey beard streaked with sweat, points to a section of the map. *"The northern sector needs these supplies. They're running low on ammunition,"* he says, his voice low but urgent. *"If we wait any longer, they'll be exposed. The Israelis are tightening their patrols."*

Yusuf nods, his eyes moving across the map. *"We'll have to be fast. If we take this route, it'll bring us closer to the main roads. We can't afford to be tracked."*

Bilal leans in, his brow furrowed with concentration. *"It's risky,"* he murmurs, his voice steady but thoughtful. *"The closer we are to the main roads, the more chance there is of running into trouble. We need to ensure there's cover along the way."*

Yusuf glances at Bilal, a flicker of respect in his eyes. *"You're right. We'll need scouts ahead to monitor the roads. If we can't confirm it's clear, we'll have to reroute."*

Beside him, Khaled speaks up, his voice tense. *"Then let's move fast. We've waited long enough. We can't afford to hesitate every time there's a risk."*

"It's not hesitation," Bilal counters, his gaze sharp as he meets Khaled's eyes. *"It's strategy. If we rush, we'll expose ourselves - and if they catch us with the supplies, we lose more than just time."*

Khaled's fists clench at his sides, his jaw tight. *"It feels like we're always holding back. Always waiting."*

Yusuf raises a hand, silencing them. *"Enough. This isn't the time for arguments. We have our orders. This run needs to be smooth. One mistake, and we'll have nothing left for the fighters up north."* His gaze shifts to me, and I straighten instinctively. *"Ahmed, you and the others will be part of the team delivering the supplies. You move when we give the signal. No risks. No mistakes."*

I nod, feeling the weight of his words settle over me. *"We'll be ready."*

The room is quiet, tension simmering beneath the surface. I glance at my friends - Tariq's face set with frustration, Bilal's thoughtful frown, and Khaled's simmering impatience. The pressure is getting to all of us, and it's becoming harder to ignore the cracks forming between us.

"We'll move when the time is right," I say, trying to keep my voice steady. "But we can't afford to make mistakes. We've lost too much already."

Tariq's eyes flash with anger, but before he can respond, a shadow falls across the entrance to the chamber. We all turn as Abu Khaled steps into the room, his presence commanding immediate attention. The tension that had been bubbling between us dissipates, replaced by the familiar weight of his authority.

"What's the status?" Abu Khaled asks, his voice low but resonant.

Yusuf steps forward, giving him a quick rundown of the situation. Abu Khaled listens carefully, his dark eyes flicking from Khaled to Bilal, and then to me. I feel the weight of his gaze, as though he's assessing every thought I haven't yet spoken aloud.

"We'll move on my signal," Abu Khaled says finally, his voice brokering no argument. "No risks, no mistakes. This operation needs to be flawless."

Tariq looks like he's about to protest, but a glance from Abu Khaled silences him. I can see the fire in Tariq's eyes, but for now, he holds his tongue.

"Ahmed," Abu Khaled says, turning his attention to me. "Walk with me."

I follow him out of the chamber, my pulse quickening as we step into the cooler air of the tunnels. Abu Khaled walks with slow, deliberate steps, his hands clasped behind his back. For a moment, neither of us speaks, the silence between us thick with unspoken expectations.

"You've done well," Abu Khaled says at last, his voice low and even. "Your father would be proud."

The mention of my father sends a familiar surge of pride through me, but it's quickly followed by that same flicker of doubt, the one I can't seem to shake. I nod, unsure of how to respond.

"But being a leader isn't just about making decisions," Abu Khaled continues, his tone thoughtful. "It's about managing people. About understanding what drives them, what makes them tick. Tariq is driven by anger, yes, but that anger can be harnessed. Khaled... he's methodical, careful. And Bilal sees things others don't. You must learn to bring them together, to use their strengths."

I swallow hard, the weight of his words pressing down on me. He speaks like he knows every part of me, like he's dissected my thoughts before I've even had them.

"Do you understand?" Abu Khaled asks, his voice softer now, but no less intense.

"Yes," I say, though my voice feels small in the vastness of the tunnel. "I understand."

Abu Khaled nods, satisfied. He places a hand on my shoulder, his grip firm but not unkind. "Good. You'll lead them well. But remember, Ahmed, doubt is a luxury we cannot afford."

His words stay with me as we walk back toward the chamber. I know what he means - he's not just talking about my friends. He's talking about me. About the doubt I try so hard to bury, the doubt that keeps creeping in no matter how much I push it down.

The next day, we prepare for the supply run. Tariq is quiet, his anger simmering beneath the surface, but he follows orders without complaint. Khaled checks the routes under the watchful eye of Yusuf, his eyes scanning the map for any possible threat, while Bilal oversees the packing of the supplies, his mind already thinking two steps ahead.

"Stay focused," Yusuf warns us, his voice low but firm. "If anything happens, keep to the side tunnels until you reach a safe point. You're not there to fight, just to deliver. That's why you don't carry weapons. No one can accuse you of being combatants."

I nod, trying to keep my mind from drifting. The weight of Abu Khaled's words from the day before is still heavy in my chest, and I can't help but wonder if I'm doing enough. If I'm the leader my father was. The leader I'm supposed to be.

We move through the tunnels quickly, the weight of the crates heavy in our hands. The air feels even thicker today, like the walls are closing in, pressing us deeper into the earth. I lead the group, my heart pounding in my chest as we approach the northern sector.

Suddenly, there's a sound - faint, but unmistakable. The low hum of a drone, circling above. We freeze, our breath catching in our throats as we listen.

"They've found us," Tariq whispers, his voice tight with fear and anger.

"No," Bilal says, his voice calm but firm. *"They're searching. We need to move quickly, before they lock on."*

We pick up the pace, our footsteps quick and quiet, the crates shifting in our arms as we weave through the tunnels. My mind races, every step feeling like a countdown to disaster.

As we reach the exit point, I motion for the others to stop. The sound of the drone has faded, but the tension in the air remains. We wait, listening, every muscle in my body coiled with anticipation.

"Now," I whisper, and we move as one, slipping through the exit and into the cover of the trees.

The supplies are delivered, and for a moment, we allow ourselves to breathe. But the weight of the mission hasn't lifted. It's only just begun.

The days blur together, a constant rush of tasks and messages, of slipping through tunnels, keeping our heads down. We hear the reports from above: Israeli soldiers pushing further into Gaza, street by street.

Abu Khaled gathers us again in the tunnels, his face drawn and serious. *"They are coming,"* he warns. *"We must be ready. Every bit of information, every piece of ammunition you deliver, it all matters. Do not lose focus."*

We nod, understanding the gravity of his words. We are not fighters, but we are part of this in our own way. We are part of the web that holds everything together.

The next day, we hear the sounds of gunfire, the rumble of tanks. We run through the tunnels, delivering urgent messages, carrying supplies where they are needed most. We are not on the front lines, but we are in the thick of it, moving through the shadows, keeping things connected.

THROUGH THEIR EYES

The ground shakes violently. A deafening boom above, and then - *crack* - everything comes crashing down. Dust chokes the air, rubble rains from above, and the tunnel fills with smoke. I fall, my ears ringing, my head spinning. When the dust settles, I see Khaled lying next to me, blood trickling down his face.

He groans, struggling to sit up. *"Ahmed... are you okay?"* he asks, his voice faint.

"I'm fine," I reply, grabbing his arm, pulling him up. *"We need to move."*

We stumble through the rubble, Tariq and Bilal close behind. We find an exit, emerging into the chaos above. The city is a warzone, every street a battlefield. We see the IDF soldiers advancing, their guns raised, their eyes sharp.

We duck behind a wall, catching our breath. Tariq looks at me, his face pale. *"What now, Ahmed?"* he asks.

I take a deep breath, my mind racing. *"We keep going,"* I say. *"We keep moving, keep helping however we can."*

He nods, and we move on, the sounds of explosions in our ears, the dust and smoke filling our lungs. We are in the heart of the storm, and there is no turning back.

The days blend together, a haze of delivering messages and supplies. The city is in ruins, buildings crumbling, and the air is thick with smoke. The faces of those around me are strained, their expressions weary. The tunnels, once our refuge, feel suffocating now, like a maze with no clear exit.

We hear of more soldiers coming, of deeper incursions. We carry on with our tasks, doing what we can. There is little sleep and even less time to think.

One night, as we sit in a dimly lit chamber, Bilal turns to me, his voice soft. *"Ahmed... do you ever think about what happens after all this?"*

"After?" I ask, unsure what he means.

"After the fighting, after the war. Do you think we'll even know who we are?" he asks.

I feel a knot form in my stomach. *"I don't know,"* I admit. *"Maybe... maybe we'll be different."*

Bilal nods, his gaze distant. *"I just hope we'll be okay."*

I look around at my friends - Tariq, Khaled, Bilal - and see the same mix of fear and hope in their eyes. For a moment, doubt creeps in again. Are we doing the right thing? Are we helping, or are we just adding to the pain?

I force a smile. *"We will be,"* I say, trying to convince myself as much as him. *"We're strong. We'll find our way."*

But as I speak, a shadow of doubt lingers in my mind. The days ahead are uncertain, and the only thing I am certain of is that we must keep going, keep moving, keep doing what we can. Because this is who I am now. This is who I have chosen to become.

I know the path ahead is not easy, but I am not afraid. I have chosen this fight, this life, and I will see it through. There is strength in knowing your purpose, in understanding your place in the world. This is who I am now, a fighter, a leader. And I will not turn back.

That night, as I lie in my bunk underground, the doubt returns. It clings to me, heavy and suffocating, like the air in the tunnels. I think of Tariq's anger, of Bilal's calculations, of Khaled's steady resolve. And I think of myself, standing at the centre of it all, trying to be the leader they believe I am.

I close my eyes, trying to quiet the noise in my head. But it's no use. The doubt is louder now, impossible to ignore.

"Doubt is a luxury we cannot afford."

Abu Khaled's words echo in the darkness, a reminder of the path I've chosen. Or maybe, the path that was chosen for me.

I think of the days before - before the tunnels, before the missions, before I became someone others looked to. I think of the way we used to run through the streets, carefree, dodging cars, shouting and laughing. We used to be boys with dreams, not soldiers with orders. But now...

"It's different now," I murmur to myself. *"It has to be different."*

But even as I say it, I know the truth. Beneath the mask of determination, the mask I show my friends, there is still a part of me that hesitates, that wonders if we are truly making a difference or if we're just feeding into a cycle that never ends.

I roll over, staring at the rough walls of the bunker, listening to the muffled sounds of movement in the tunnel beyond. I wonder if my father felt this way. Did he lie awake at night, wrestling with the same questions? Did he doubt his place, his choices?

But doubt is weakness. Doubt is something I cannot afford.

I squeeze my eyes shut, willing the thoughts to go away, willing myself to be the leader Abu Khaled and Yusuf believe I am.

Because this is who I am now. This is who I must be.

And as sleep finally takes hold, the last thing I see in my mind's eye is not my father's face, not Abu Khaled's approving nod - it's Bilal's gaze, searching mine, as if waiting for me to tell him it will all make sense someday.

Maybe it will, I think, drifting into uneasy dreams.

Maybe one day, we'll understand.

Chapter Ten

YOSSI

The summer of 2014 is heavy with fear and uncertainty. Tel Aviv, usually vibrant and alive, feels muted, like a city holding its breath. The streets buzz with unease, the sound of daily life undercut by the distant threat of rockets and the relentless news from Gaza. Operation Brother's Keeper, the raids, the arrests - every moment pulls the war closer. Each day, the air grows thicker with tension, the wail of sirens creeping into our routine, replacing the hum of laughter and bikes on the street.

Operation Brother's Keeper dominates the headlines after three Israeli teenagers were kidnapped and killed by Hamas. The military operations that followed, the raids, the arrests - everything spiralled into chaos. Rockets are being fired from Gaza, and the Iron Dome can only do so much. We try to pretend that things are normal, but nothing feels normal anymore. Not really.

The first time the sirens go off, we're at the beach - me, Amir, Leila, Nadav, Maya, and Yael. Nadav is strumming his guitar, a soft melody floating in the sea breeze. Maya is spinning on the sand, her laughter bright above the sound of the waves. Leila and Yael sit close together, their heads bent as they murmur quietly. Leila's arm is slung loosely around Yael's shoulders, her voice soothing as she reassures her friend that things will be fine.

"It's just for a little while," Leila says softly, rubbing Yael's back as if trying to chase away the anxiety she sees building there. *"Tel Aviv is strong. We've been through worse."*

But then the siren cuts through the air, sharp and jarring. The world around us changes in an instant. The beach erupts into chaos, people running in every direction. Yael grabs my arm, her grip tight, her eyes wide with fear.

"Come on, Yossi!" she yells, pulling me toward the nearest shelter. We run together, our feet slipping on the sand, our hearts racing, panic pushing us forward. Leila is right behind us, her hand gripping Nadav's arm, guiding him with a calm that contrasts sharply with the panic in the air.

Inside the shelter, it's cramped and stifling. The murmur of voices, the cries of children - all of it blends into a low hum of anxiety. Leila is beside Yael, her arm wrapped firmly around her shoulders, murmuring softly. I can't hear her words over the noise, but I see the way Yael's shoulders relax just slightly. Leila shifts, catching Nadav's eye. He's gripping his guitar like a lifeline, his face drawn. She nudges him gently, offering a small smile. *"Hey, remember that awful joke about the chicken and the Iron Dome?"* she whispers. Nadav's brow furrows, and then, almost against his will, a small grin tugs at his lips.

"That one's terrible, Leila," he mutters, but he loosens his grip on the guitar, taking a deep breath. Her smile widens, and for a moment, the tension eases.

"It's okay. It'll be okay," I whisper to Yael, though I'm not sure I believe it myself. Leila catches my eye and nods, a small gesture of encouragement, as if to say, *We have to stay strong. For them.*

"I've never been this scared," Yael admits, her voice barely audible. *"It's different when it's here... when it's real."*

I want to tell her that I'm not scared, that I'm strong like my father always says I should be. But I can't. The truth is, I'm terrified. I've never felt fear like this - not even during the drills at school. This is real, and I don't know how to face it. But I have to. For her. For all of us.

"I know," I reply, squeezing her hand. *"But we'll get through this. Together."*

Leila leans in, her voice steady. *"We've got each other, right? That's what matters."* Nadav glances at her, his expression tight, but he nods. The fear in his eyes softens a little, his shoulders relaxing just a fraction under her touch.

The siren stops, and moments later, the ground trembles with a distant explosion. We hold our breath, waiting. Then someone whispers, *"Iron Dome got it."* The tension in the room eases, and slowly, we make our way back outside.

Back on the beach, everything feels different. The sand, the sea, the sky - they've all changed somehow. Nadav tries to lighten the mood with a joke, but it falls flat. We all feel it - the world shifting beneath our feet.

At home, my father is glued to the TV, his face tight with worry. My mother moves around the kitchen, her hands trembling as she chops vegetables.

"It's going to be fine," my father keeps saying, like a mantra. *"We're strong. We'll get through this."* But his eyes betray him, flickering with fear every time the news shifts to new footage of rockets and explosions.

Yael starts spending more time with us after that. She comes over most days after school, bringing pastries from her parents' bakery. We sit on the balcony, talking about everything except the war. With her, I feel a strange calm amid the chaos. It's easier to breathe when she's around. Leila joins us sometimes, always flitting between us and the others, checking on everyone, keeping us together.

One evening, as the sun sets and bathes the city in a warm orange glow, Yael turns to me, her face thoughtful.

"Tell me something real," she says softly. *"Something you've never told anyone."*

I laugh, leaning back. *"That's a big request,"* I say. *"I'm not sure I have any deep secrets."*

She nudges me, smiling. *"Come on, Yossi. I know there's something."*

I pause, then sigh. *"Okay, here's something. Sometimes I feel like I have to be this strong, confident guy like my dad wants... but inside, I'm scared. Really scared."*

Yael's smile softens. *"Me too,"* she whispers. *"I'm scared all the time now. But when I'm with you, it feels a little less terrifying."*

Her words make something inside me unclench, and I reach over, taking her hand. I've never admitted my fears to anyone, not even to Nadav. But with Yael, it feels okay. It feels right.

"I feel the same way," I admit. *"Being with you makes everything feel a bit more... okay."*

Leila watches us from the balcony doorway, a soft smile on her face. *"You two are so obvious,"* she teases lightly. *"But it's sweet."* Her gaze flickers between us, warm and approving, before she disappears back inside.

From then on, something changes between Yael and me. We are closer, more connected. Even when the sirens go off, we run to the shelters together, our hands never letting go. Leila is always right there with us, steady and strong, guiding us through the chaos.

One night, after another rocket alert, we gather at Amir's place. His father has been closing his shop earlier and earlier, worried about the rockets. Amir's older brother, Avi, has been called up, and they haven't heard from him in days. The air is heavy with tension.

We sit in the living room, the TV on but muted. Amir's mother brings us tea, her face tight with anxiety. Yael sits next to me, our knees touching. Leila is beside Nadav, her presence a quiet comfort. She nudges him gently when his shoulders tense, murmuring something that makes his lips twitch into a reluctant smile.

"I just want it to end," Amir says, staring blankly at the muted television. *"I want Avi to come home."* His voice cracks on the last word, and the silence that follows is suffocating.

Nadav, sitting on the edge of the couch, shifts uncomfortably. He's always the first to break the silence, but this time, there's no joke. *"My uncle... he didn't make it,"* he says quietly, his voice hollow. *"A rocket hit his house."* He looks up at us, his eyes stark and empty.

The room goes still. No one breathes, no one moves. I reach out and place a hand on his shoulder. *"I'm so sorry, man."*

Leila is the first to react, wrapping Nadav in a tight hug, whispering softly. He stiffens, and then his shoulders slump, and he leans into her embrace, his face pressed against her shoulder. *"It's okay, Nadav,"* she murmurs. *"We're here."*

Nadav shrugs, his face hard. *"It's just how it is now,"* he mutters, but he leans into Leila's embrace, his shoulders shaking slightly.

Yael turns to me, her eyes filled with worry. *"How do we keep going?"* she whispers. *"How do we just... keep living?"*

I don't have an answer. I feel the same question burning inside me. How do we keep going when everything feels so uncertain, so fragile?

I just squeeze her hand, hoping that is enough.

The days blur into a pattern of sirens and shelter runs. We find cover wherever we can - in shops, in parking garages, in the stairwells of buildings. It becomes a grim game, a routine of survival. But through it all, Leila keeps us steady. She checks in on each of us, her presence like a balm to frayed nerves, always knowing when Nadav needs a distraction, when Amir needs space, when I need a quiet nudge to pull myself out of my thoughts.

One day, as we walk through the market, trying to grasp some sense of normalcy, Yael stops at a stall selling handmade jewellery. She picks up a small silver pendant shaped like a dove, her fingers tracing the delicate lines.

"It's beautiful," she murmurs.

"You should get it," I suggest.

She hesitates. *"I don't know..."*

Before she can finish, I pull out my wallet and pay for it. *"Here,"* I say, handing it to her. *"A gift. For luck."*

She blushes, a smile spreading across her face. *"Thank you, Yossi. I'll wear it always."*

Leila, watching from a few feet away, grins. *"Good choice,"* she whispers as she steps beside Yael, helping her clasp the pendant around her neck. *"A dove for peace."* There's a look in her eyes that's almost wistful, as if she's wishing for a time when that tiny silver bird might truly bring the peace it symbolises.

I feel a warmth spread through me as Yael fingers the pendant around her neck. It's not just a piece of jewellery - it's a reminder that there is still something good in all of this, something worth holding onto.

As time passes, we grow even closer. We talk for hours about our dreams, our fears, the futures we hope for. I find myself thinking about her all the time, wanting to protect her from everything happening around us. Leila watches over us with a fond, amused smile, always the first to pull Yael into a playful hug or whisper something that makes her giggle.

One afternoon, we sit on the beach, watching the waves crash against the shore. It's a rare moment of calm, the sirens have been quiet all day. Yael rests her head on my shoulder, and beside us, Leila sprawls out on the sand, lazily throwing a ball up for Nadav to catch. He keeps missing it on purpose, pretending to stumble, just to make her laugh.

"What do you think will happen?" Yael asks softly.

"I don't know," I admit. *"I hope it ends soon. I hope things can go back to how they were."*

She nods, drawing patterns in the sand with her fingers. *"I hope so too,"* she whispers. *"I don't want to lose this... us."*

I turn to her, feeling my heart race. *"You won't,"* I promise, my voice low but firm. *"I'm here, Yael. Always."*

She studies my face, as if weighing the truth of my words, and then, slowly, she leans forward. Her lips brush against mine - soft, tentative. It's over in a heartbeat, but it leaves me breathless, the world narrowing to just her, just us. For a moment, the sirens, the war, the fear - everything fades.

Leila catches my eye from a few feet away, her expression soft. She murmurs something to Nadav, and he glances our way before making a dramatic show of turning his back, muttering something about *"private moments"* and *"gross romantic stuff."* Leila laughs softly, the sound warm and comforting. She turns back to us, her gaze steady, her presence anchoring us as surely as if she were holding our hands.

But the reality soon returns. The war continues. The sirens blare, reminding us how fragile everything is. Yael and I hold on to each other, stealing moments of peace amid the chaos. We feel older than our years, shaped by a conflict we didn't choose but have to endure. Leila remains the glue that keeps us together, always quick with a joke or a comforting word. She draws us into silly games at the beach, plans surprise picnics in the park - even though we're always glancing over our shoulders for the nearest shelter.

One evening, as we sit on the balcony, Yael looks at me, her eyes steady.

"Whatever happens," she says, *"promise me we'll get through it together."*

I nod, holding her hand tight. *"I promise,"* I whisper. *"No matter what."*

Leila watches us from where she's lounging in the corner, her gaze flickering to Nadav, who's trying to balance a spoon on his nose to make her laugh. *"You're all so dramatic,"* she teases lightly, but there's a soft look in her eyes. *"Of course we'll get through it. All of us."*

Nadav rolls his eyes playfully. *"Well, some of us have to keep the drama alive, Leila. You're too calm - it's unsettling."*

She throws a cushion at him, and for a moment, we're just kids again, laughing as Nadav ducks and the cushion bounces off the wall.

Later that night, as we sit in the quiet of my room, the city outside still humming with distant noises, I find myself asking, *"Do you ever think about leaving?"*

Yael turns to me, surprised. *"Leaving Tel Aviv?"*

I nod. *"Just... going somewhere else. Somewhere far away from all this."*

She sighs, her expression thoughtful. *"Sometimes. But I don't know if running away is the answer. I think... maybe we need to find a way to stay, to make things better here."*

Leila's voice comes softly from the doorway. *"Yael's right."* She steps into the room, sitting beside us. *"Leaving would be easy. But what would we be leaving behind?"*

I look at both of them, feeling a deep admiration swell in my chest. *"You're both right,"* I say softly. *"We can't just leave. This is our home."*

Yael smiles, her gaze shifting between Leila and me. *"We stay,"* she murmurs, and Leila nods firmly, squeezing her shoulder.

The days stretch on, filled with uncertainty. The sirens become part of our routine, a background noise we can't ignore. The fear never quite goes away, but with all my friends beside me, it feels more bearable. We continue to find solace in each other, finding small moments of joy amid the chaos. We laugh, we talk, we dream of a time when things will be better.

But the war does not end. It drags on for seven weeks with over 4,000 rockets fired at Israel from Gaza, pulling us deeper into its grasp. And yet we keep going, holding on to each other, holding on to the hope that someday, somehow, peace will come.

And until then, we stay together, unyielding, facing whatever comes next side by side. Leila's hand on Yael's shoulder, Nadav's jokes cutting through the tension, Amir's quiet strength anchoring us. We are more than just friends now. We are a lifeline, a shield against the storm raging outside. As long as we have each other, we can face whatever the world throws our way.

Chapter Eleven

AHMED

Khaled mutters, his face tight with anger. *"They don't care who they kill. They'll kill anyone."*

I nod, my jaw clenched, but something twists inside me - doubt, perhaps, or something close to it. I glimpse a father cradling a child with a wound on her forehead and wonder if this is what we truly wanted. My stomach churns, the doubt curling like smoke. Are we just fuelling the fire?

Ceasefires come and go, each one shorter than the last. With every resumption of bombing, the intensity grows. Jabalia is hit hard, entire streets are reduced to rubble. The smell of ash and charred wood lingers in the air, a constant reminder of everything we've lost. Footsteps crunch on broken glass, and the streets, once filled with noise and life, now echo with hollow, eerie silence.

One day, Abu Khaled gathers us, his voice low and serious. *"The Israelis are advancing,"* he tells us. *"They're closing in. We can't let them."*

Tariq curses under his breath. Khaled's fists clench. I swallow hard, trying to steady myself, but the fear is always there, like a shadow trailing just behind me. I see Bilal's hollow eyes, dark circles etched beneath them. He has barely slept since his uncle died. Tariq's hands tremble slightly, his breaths shallow. I realise we're all afraid, though we pretend otherwise. We keep moving, keep carrying messages, keep delivering supplies. I remind myself we're fighting for something bigger, something worth every loss.

But the whisper in my mind grows louder: *Are we just prolonging our suffering?* I push it down again, focusing on the tasks ahead.

Then, suddenly, the war ends. The silence that follows is deafening. The guns stop, the bombs cease, but the quiet is heavy, tense. We emerge from the tunnels into a city that no longer feels like home. The buildings stand like broken teeth, the streets choked with debris. The air is thick with dust and smoke, and the people move like shadows, hollow and broken. The smell of burnt metal and stone lingers, and every footstep stirs up more ash, more remnants of what once was.

But the silence is not peace. It's filled with echoes of what we've lost. I walk through streets now reduced to rubble and ash, the ruins of what once were homes and shops, places where I once knew every face, every name. I see children, wide-eyed and hollow-cheeked, picking through debris for anything to eat or wear. I hear a mother's wail as she clutches a photograph - the only thing left of her son who went out one day and never came back. An old man sits by the broken remains of a bakery, his hands trembling as he whispers to himself, rocking back and forth. *Is this what victory looks like?* I wonder.

I think of Bilal, whose uncle died when their shelter collapsed, and of Tariq, who found his brother's body under the remains of their home. I see Khaled's face twisted in pain as he tried to comfort his younger sisters after they lost their father. I see the empty spaces at dinner tables, the missing smiles, and the silence where laughter used to be. Everywhere I turn, I see loss - loss that no speech or slogan can justify.

In the quiet of the night, I lie awake, listening to the wind howling through broken windows. The promises of glory and honour feel hollow now, drowned out by the cries of the bereaved and the sight of so many graves. The men who spoke of resistance, who painted it as something noble and grand, seem so far removed from this reality. I can't help but wonder if any of this was worth it. *Did our struggle really mean anything, or did we simply trade one suffering for another?*

I recall my uncle Yusuf's stern voice: *"There is no price too high for freedom."* But now, looking at the ruins of our lives, I question whether this price is truly ours to pay. I wonder if our sacrifices are just feeding into an endless cycle of vengeance and pain.

At home, my mother's eyes shine with pride. *"You've done well, Ahmed,"* she says, smiling softly. *"Your father would be proud of you."*

But my sisters move like shadows through the house, quiet and watchful. They no longer just avoid me - they look at me as if I am a part of the reason for the misery surrounding us. Layla used to meet my eyes with boldness, but now, when I speak, she glances away, her lips pressed into a thin line. The fear in her gaze is sharper than ever, but this time it's laced with something more. Anger, maybe. Or blame.

"You're back," Amina murmurs one evening, her voice almost a whisper. *"But you're not the same. None of us are."*

She stands by the doorway, hands twisting nervously at the hem of her dress, as if she's trying to wring out the words she's too afraid to say. Layla lingers behind her, arms crossed, her expression guarded.

"You're being ridiculous," I reply, though the words feel heavy, forced. *"I'm still me."*

But Layla shakes her head slowly, her eyes never leaving mine. *"No, Ahmed. You're not. We hardly recognise you anymore. You're so... distant. So angry."*

The words sting more than I want to admit. *"I'm doing what I have to do,"* I say firmly, keeping my tone steady. *"For our people. For our family. You should understand that."*

Layla holds my gaze, then looks away, her shoulders sagging. *"We do,"* she whispers, *"but it feels like we've lost you too."*

Amina, bolder now, steps forward. *"When was the last time you laughed, Ahmed? Really laughed?"* Her voice is soft but piercing. *"You used to joke with us, play with us... now it feels like you're always gone, even when you're here."*

Her words cut deeper than I expect. I remember their laughter, the teasing... but that feels like another lifetime. I'm not that boy anymore. I can't be.

"I'm not a child anymore," I finally say, more defensive than I mean to be. "I have responsibilities. Things that matter."

"*But we matter too,*" Amina murmurs, almost to herself.

There is a weight in her voice that catches me off guard. I see the concern in her eyes, and, for a second, something shifts inside me - a flicker of doubt, an uncomfortable question. *Am I still their brother?* But I push it away.

"*I'm doing this for all of us,*" I insist. "*You may not understand now, but one day you will.*"

Layla sighs, her face softening into a sad resignation. "*I hope so, Ahmed. I really do.*"

Without another word, they turn and walk away. Their absence feels like an accusation, a silent judgment I can't ignore. I try to shake it off, reminding myself of my duty. But their words linger, echoing in the silence of the house, creeping into the corners of my mind.

That night, I sit with Uncle Yusuf. His face is hard, eyes fixed on some distant point. The moonlight filters through the broken shutters, casting long shadows across the room. He watches the world outside like a sentinel, his gaze unblinking, unyielding.

"*You're doing well,*" he says finally, his voice devoid of emotion. "*You've proven your loyalty, Ahmed.*"

I nod, but the words feel hollow. His praise should bring a sense of satisfaction - a feeling of accomplishment - but instead, it twists inside me, a reminder of the growing emptiness I can't seem to shake.

"*Uncle,*" I say slowly, "*do you ever wonder if... if all this is truly making a difference? If the cost is too high?*"

He turns to me sharply, his gaze piercing. For a moment, something flickers in his eyes - something dark and dangerous. "*There is no cost too high for freedom,*" he snaps. "*We do what we must. You must understand that.*"

"*But,*" I persist, my voice wavering slightly, "*the people, our people, are suffering. We've lost so much...*"

Yusuf's jaw tightens, and he leans forward, his eyes burning with intensity. "*And what would you suggest? That we stop. That we let them take everything from us? This is the price we pay, Ahmed. For every victory, there is a sacrifice.*"

I nod again, feeling his words settle heavily on me. *But what if he's wrong?* The question claws at me, refusing to let go. They don't erase the doubt, they don't fill the emptiness inside.

The room falls silent, the tension thick. I glance away, staring out at the shattered city beyond the window. The ruins, the graves, the endless funerals - they blur together in a wash of grey and red, and I wonder if this is all we will ever know. Conflict, loss, and a hunger for a freedom that seems forever out of reach.

"*You're thinking too much,*" Yusuf murmurs, his tone softening just a fraction. "*This is not the time for doubt. Doubt makes you weak. It clouds your purpose.*"

I swallow hard, trying to steady myself. "*I just... I want to know that what we're doing is right. That it's not all for nothing.*"

Yusuf's gaze hardens again, his lips pressing into a thin line. "*Right and wrong don't matter here, Ahmed. Survival does. And if you want to survive - if you want our people to survive - you must put aside these doubts. They will eat you alive.*"

I want to argue, to tell him that it's not just survival I'm worried about. It's the cost - our humanity, our hope. But I bite my tongue, the words dying in my throat. I see the resolve in his eyes, the unwavering conviction that he's doing what must be done. And I wonder if I'm the one who's wrong. Maybe I'm the one who's too weak, too soft to see what needs to be done.

I think about what my sisters said earlier - the fear, the sadness in their voices. *Have I really become so different? So distant?* I used to be the one who made them laugh, who reassured them when the world outside seemed too harsh. Now, I don't even know if I'm capable of comforting anyone.

The silence stretches between us, broken only by the distant sound of the wind howling through the ruins. Finally, Yusuf sighs, his gaze softening just a fraction.

"This is the path we've chosen, Ahmed. There is no turning back. We bear this burden because we must. You must stay strong." His voice drops lower, almost a whisper. *"For them. For everyone who's counting on you."*

His words settle over me like a shroud. *For them.* I think of Layla's eyes, the way she looked at me as if I were a stranger in our own home. I think of Amina's trembling voice, the way she seemed to be searching for something familiar in the shell I've become.

I nod slowly. *"I understand, Uncle."*

But I'm not sure if I do. I'm not sure if I understand any of this anymore. Every step forward feels like stepping deeper into a fog, where right and wrong blur together, where every action leaves a mark I can't erase. But what other choice do I have? This is the path I've chosen, and there's no turning back now.

"Good," Yusuf says firmly, his voice regaining its usual edge. *"There is no place for doubt in this fight. You must keep moving forward."*

Moving forward... But where am I going? I force myself to meet his gaze, trying to mirror his certainty, but all I feel is a growing emptiness, a sense that I'm drifting further away from something I can't even name.

"I will, Uncle," I reply softly. *"I won't let you down."*

Yusuf nods once, sharply, and then turns away, his eyes fixed on the darkness beyond the window.

In the days that follow, I go through the motions - delivering messages, making rounds, offering support to the families who have lost everything. But something is different. The words of my sisters, the questions I can't quite shake, the look in Yusuf's eyes - it all gnaws at me, making every step feel heavier.

One afternoon, as I walk through the ruins of what was once our neighbourhood, I see a group of children huddled together, their faces pale and gaunt. A boy no older than six holds a makeshift toy - a piece of rubble tied with string, dragging it along the ground. His eyes are wide, too old for a face so young. He catches my gaze and stares back, unblinking, unafraid.

"What are you looking at?" I ask quietly, but he says nothing, just keeps staring. I look around, seeing the other children watching me, their eyes dark and hollow.

What do they see when they look at me? A fighter? A hero? Or just another man shaped by anger and war?

I kneel down, my gaze level with his. *"What's your name?"*

The boy hesitates, then whispers, *"Hassan."*

"Hassan," I repeat softly. *"Where's your family?"*

He points to a pile of rubble a few metres away. *"Gone,"* he murmurs, his voice flat, empty.

Something breaks inside me. *"Do you... have somewhere to go?"*

He shrugs, his gaze never wavering. *"I'm waiting."*

"Waiting for what?"

"For the war to end," he replies simply, as if it's the most obvious thing in the world.

I stare at him, my throat tightening. *"It's over,"* I whisper. *"The war is over."*

Hassan shakes his head slowly. *"It's never over,"* he murmurs, his voice heavy with a weight far beyond his years. *"Not for us."*

The words hit me like a punch to the gut. I want to tell him he's wrong, that there's hope, that one day things will be better. But as I look around at the ruins, the shattered homes, the faces etched with loss and pain, I can't find the words.

Because deep down, I know he's right.

I rise slowly, my legs feeling like lead. *"Stay safe, Hassan,"* I say quietly, but he's already looking away, dragging his makeshift toy through the dust.

As I walk away, his words echo in my mind, mingling with the doubts that refuse to leave. *It's never over...* And I wonder if this is what my life will always be - an endless fight, a struggle with no end in sight. If this is what we're destined to become.

Chapter Twelve

YOSSI

The summer of 2014 left its mark on all of us. Nearly three years have passed since the Gaza war, but its shadow stretches long, lingering in every corner of Tel Aviv. The sirens and rockets may have ceased, but the scars are still there - etched into the rhythm of the city, in the way people glance skyward whenever there's a loud noise, in the unspoken understanding between friends who have shared that fear.

Our group has changed too. We're closer now, more solid. The war cemented something between us, a bond that goes deeper than friendship. We've grown up faster than we should have, navigating a world that expects us to be both young and old at the same time. But we're still here, holding on to the fragments of our childhood, even as the reality of our future looms closer.

And there's Yael.

She's been my anchor through all of it - my confidante, my partner. There's no awkward hesitation anymore, no uncertainty. What started with fleeting glances and unspoken words during those chaotic days of war has solidified into something real and steady. We're a couple now, and everyone knows it. There's no need to hide it, no need to explain.

I see it in the way the others look at us - especially Leila. She watches Yael and me with a smile that's both knowing and wistful. Lately, she's been spending more time with Nadav. The two of them seem to drift together naturally, like they share some unspoken understanding. But it's not like what Yael and I have. It's something different - something quieter, more subtle. They're just friends, for now, but I can't help noticing the way Leila's eyes linger on Nadav when she thinks no one's looking.

We're all together one afternoon, lounging on the beach. The sun is high, casting long shadows across the sand. The sea stretches out before us, endless and blue, its waves crashing softly against the shore. It's a rare moment of peace, one of those days where everything feels almost normal.

Yael leans against my shoulder, her fingers tracing idle patterns on my arm. Beside us, Nadav and Leila sit close, talking in low voices. Maya and Amir are a little further away, engaged in some intense debate about which café has the best hummus. Samir is watching them with a bemused smile, shaking his head as they bicker.

"Are they always like this?" Yael murmurs, her eyes on Maya and Amir.

"Always," I reply with a grin. *"It's their version of flirting."*

Yael laughs softly. *"I'm not sure Amir realises that."*

"Probably not," I agree. *"But he'll catch on eventually."*

She shifts, resting her head against my chest. *"What about Leila and Nadav?"* she asks quietly. *"Do you think...?"*

I glance at the two of them. Nadav is gesturing animatedly, and Leila is watching him with that soft smile she reserves just for him, a look that says she's enjoying his company more than she lets on.

"I don't know," I admit. *"Maybe. But I think they're still figuring it out."*

Yael hums thoughtfully, and we lapse into a comfortable silence. I close my eyes, letting the warmth of the sun and the steady rhythm of her breathing ground me. It's strange - how, despite everything we've been through, moments like this still feel precious. Fleeting.

"*Hey!*" Nadav's voice cuts through the air, sharp and teasing. "*You two going to join the conversation, or are you too busy being disgustingly in love?*"

I crack an eye open, smirking. "*Jealous, Nadav?*"

He pulls a face. "*Hardly. But you're making the rest of us look bad.*"

Leila elbows him lightly. "*You're just bitter because Yossi has a girlfriend, and you don't.*"

Nadav gasps dramatically, clutching his chest. "*Leila, you wound me.*"

"*Good,*" she says, grinning. "*Someone has to keep your ego in check.*"

I watch the two of them banter, a strange sense of satisfaction settling in my chest. Leila and Nadav have always been close, but lately, there's something more there - something I can't quite put my finger on. It's not romance, not yet. But it's something that could be, someday.

And then there's Amir and Maya, still arguing, still oblivious to everything except their silly debate. I feel a swell of affection for all of them, these friends who have become more like family. We've all grown up so much, but in some ways, we're still the same kids we were three years ago, still holding on to each other as the world shifts and changes around us.

Yael tilts her head to look up at me, her eyes thoughtful. "*Do you think it'll change us?*"

"*What?*" I ask, brushing a stray curl away from her face.

"*The army. Everything that's coming.*"

I hesitate, then nod slowly. "*Yeah. It will. But we'll get through it. Just like we always do.*"

"*Together?*"

"*Always,*" I promise, leaning down to press a kiss to her forehead.

"Ugh, stop!" Nadav groans loudly, covering his eyes. *"Some of us are still single, you know!"*

We all burst out laughing, the tension breaking. Maya and Amir look over, confused, and Samir just shakes his head, a fond smile on his face.

"Stop torturing Nadav," Leila scolds gently. *"You know he's sensitive."*

Nadav snorts. *"I'm not sensitive, I'm just tired of watching you lot pair off while I'm stuck third-wheeling."*

"You're not a third wheel," Leila says firmly, her gaze softening. *"You're part of this, just like the rest of us."*

He blinks, taken aback by her sincerity. *"Yeah,"* he mutters, glancing away. *"Thanks, Leila."*

They share a look - brief but charged with something unspoken. I wonder if either of them realises it yet, the way they've started orbiting each other more and more. Probably not. But it's there, beneath the surface, waiting.

"We'll always be together," Yael murmurs, snuggling closer. *"All of us."*

"Yeah," I agree, staring out at the horizon. *"Always."*

We sit there, the sound of the waves mingling with our laughter, the sun warm on our skin. For now, we're okay. For now, the future can wait.

But even as we joke and tease, a part of me can't shake the feeling that everything is about to change. The carefree days of our youth are slipping away, replaced by something heavier, something that feels like responsibility. Soon, we'll be stepping into a world that expects more from us - more than we might be ready to give.

But that's for later. For now, I let myself sink into the moment, surrounded by my friends, my girlfriend, and the sound of the sea. Whatever comes next, we'll face it together.

And that's enough.

For now.

As the afternoon turns into evening, we find ourselves on Nadav's rooftop, a familiar place that's become our sanctuary over the years. The city stretches out below us, bathed in the warm glow of the setting sun. It's one of those moments when everything feels suspended in time - like the world is holding its breath, just for us.

But there's an unspoken tension hanging in the air tonight, something we're all feeling but not saying out loud. The conversation drifts between topics - music, movies, random gossip - anything to keep from addressing what's really on our minds. Then, Amir breaks the silence, his voice thoughtful.

"It's crazy to think about, isn't it?" he says, staring out at the horizon. *"In a few months, we'll all be in uniform. It's our turn next."*

Everyone shifts slightly, as if his words have made the rooftop feel smaller. I glance at Yael beside me, and she offers a small, reassuring smile. We're in this together, but the thought of what's coming makes my stomach tighten. There's no running from it.

"Feels like yesterday we were just talking about our plans for the future," Maya murmurs, wrapping her arms around her knees. *"And now it's here. It's not some far-off thing anymore."*

Samir nods slowly, his gaze distant. *"We knew it was coming. But still, it feels... sudden."*

"Tell me about it," Amir sighs. *"Avi's been sending messages from his base, talking about how things are heating up again. He says to be ready. I just hope..."* He trails off, and we all know what he's thinking: *I just hope he comes home safe.*

There's a heavy silence as we let his words sink in. We've all heard similar stories from older siblings, cousins, or friends. But now, it's not just something happening to someone else - it's about to happen to us.

Nadav clears his throat, trying to lighten the mood. *"Well, at least some of us are excited about it,"* he says with a grin, bumping my shoulder. *"I'm gonna be* *a paratrooper, and you"* - he points at me - *"are going to be right there beside me, jumping out of planes."**

I laugh, shaking my head. *"You think I'm crazy enough to jump out of a perfectly good plane?"*

"You won't have a choice, Yossi. I need a buddy up there, and you're it!" Nadav's grin is infectious, and despite myself, I can't help but smile back. It's typical Nadav - always pushing me, always assuming we'll do everything together.

"Just don't get him killed before he even hits the ground," Leila interjects, her tone dry but affectionate. *"Yael would kill you if anything happened to him."*

Everyone laughs softly, the tension easing just a bit. It's these small moments, the teasing and camaraderie, that keep us sane. We cling to them like lifelines, trying to forget the reality pressing in on us from all sides.

"You worry too much," Nadav scoffs, waving a hand dismissively. *"Yossi and I? We'll be landing like pros."*

"Yeah, right," I snort. *"More like you'll land in a tree, and I'll be stuck pulling you down."*

The laughter that follows is genuine, and I catch Leila giving Nadav a look that's part amusement, part concern. They're close - closer than they used to be. I've noticed it more lately, the way her gaze lingers on him, the way he softens when she's around. But it's not something either of them is ready to admit yet.

Yael leans against my side, her fingers lacing through mine. *"You know, Leila's probably right. Someone will have to keep an eye on you two,"* she teases.

"See?" Leila smirks, *"even Yael agrees. She's the sensible one here."*

Nadav rolls his eyes. *"Oh, come on. You're making it sound like I'm a complete liability."*

"You are!" we all chorus at once, the laughter bubbling up again, even stronger this time.

"*Traitors,*" he mutters, but there's a smile tugging at his lips.

After that, the conversation shifts back to safer topics - our favourite memories from the past few summers, stupid things we've done that should've gotten us hurt but somehow didn't. We're talking like nothing is changing, like we're still those carefree teenagers without the weight of the future pressing down on us.

But as the sun dips below the horizon, casting the city in a soft, orange glow, Maya's voice breaks through, soft and uncertain.

"*Do you think we'll change?*" she asks quietly. "*Do you think we'll come back the same?*"

The question hangs in the air, heavy and unanswerable. I squeeze Yael's hand, feeling her fingers tighten around mine.

"*We've already changed,*" Samir murmurs, his gaze distant. "*The war... everything we went through. But maybe... maybe we can choose who we become.*"

Yael nods slowly, her expression thoughtful. "*I believe that*" she says softly. "*We've seen what it's like when you lose yourself in fear and anger. But we can find our way through this. We have to.*"

Amir looks down at his hands, then back up at us, his eyes searching. "*But what if... what if we don't come back at all?*"

Silence falls, heavy and oppressive. It's the question we've all been avoiding, the fear lurking in the back of our minds. But Leila, as always, is the one to break through it.

"*We're coming back,*" she says firmly, her voice steady. "*All of us. And when we do, we'll still be us. Maybe a little different, maybe a little stronger. But we'll still be us.*"

There's something in her voice that makes me believe her, even if just for a moment. I glance at Yael, and she's watching Leila with a small, grateful smile. We're lucky to have her - to have each other.

"*Together,*" I murmur, echoing her words. "*We face it together.*"

The conversation shifts after that, Nadav making an exaggerated comment about how he's definitely going to be the best paratrooper ever. We all groan and roll our eyes, but it's good to hear him talk like that, to hear him joking and confident. It's the way I want to remember us - laughing, teasing, full of dreams and plans.

As the sun disappears completely, the lights of Tel Aviv flicker on, one by one, until the city is a sea of glowing orbs. Yael leans closer, resting her head on my shoulder.

"Thank you," she whispers, her voice almost lost in the breeze.

"For what?" I ask, surprised.

"For believing in us," she says simply. *"For believing we'll get through this."*

I swallow hard, feeling the weight of her words. I want to tell her that I'm not as sure as I sound, that I have doubts too. But instead, I just kiss the top of her head and hold her a little tighter.

"We will," I murmur. *"I promise."*

We sit there, watching the city lights blink softly in the distance, the future stretching out before us, vast and unknowable. Whatever comes next, we'll face it together.

And that's enough.

For now.

Chapter Thirteen

AHMED

The dust of war has settled, but its shadow still lingers over Gaza. The streets are quieter now, yet they hum with a tense energy, like a wound that hasn't quite healed. The ruins - buildings reduced to rubble, homes shattered, entire neighbourhoods hollowed out - are stark reminders of the violence that swept through this place. The smell of smoke and ash still hangs in the air, mingling with the salty breeze from the sea. Life here is fragile, a thin film stretched over the persistent threat of conflict.

Over the years since the war in 2014, my friends and I have become more deeply entangled with Hamas. We've built up a reputation in the community - not to be messed with. Abu Khaled, the local commander, sees us as his most reliable fighters. Every day pulls us deeper into his web, his words like chains around our wrists. *"This is just the beginning,"* he tells us with fierce intensity. *"The world will hear our names, they will know our strength."*

Our training has become relentless. New weapons are brought in - anti-tank missiles, sniper rifles, explosives - and we learn to handle them with increasing skill and confidence. The tunnels beneath Gaza have become more familiar than the streets above. We move through them like shadows, knowing each twist, turn, and hidden route by heart. These underground passages are more than just hiding places, they are lifelines, arteries in a body that refuses to die.

Over time, our bond has grown stronger, but so has the weight of our choices. Tariq and Khaled, my closest friends, have become more volatile, more unpredictable. The war has hardened them in ways I hadn't expected. They handle dissent with a brutality that would have shocked me once. Now, I see them executing men without a flicker of hesitation. Their eyes are cold, their faces blank as they pull the trigger. It's become routine - a chilling transformation that sets them apart from the boys I grew up with. But I am not just a passive observer in this. I lead alongside them, enforcing discipline, carrying out orders. If anything, I've grown harder, more decisive. They follow me because I show no hesitation, no sign of weakness.

Bilal, on the other hand, is quieter. There's a tension in his face, a distance in his eyes, like he's carrying a burden too heavy to share. He does what is required, but I sense his thoughts are elsewhere, hidden behind a wall I can't penetrate. *"We can't afford to be weak,"* he tells me after a particularly brutal confrontation. *"We have to be harder, stronger than them. Otherwise, we lose everything."*

I nod, but a knot of doubt tightens in my stomach. The violence seems to come too easily to Tariq and Khaled now, the hatred too quick to rise. I still believe in our cause, in our fight for freedom, but sometimes I wonder if we're losing something vital in the process.

One evening, Abu Khaled calls me into his office. His eyes are thoughtful, his fingers steepled on the desk before him. *"Ahmed,"* he begins slowly, *"I have been watching you. You have shown great promise, great commitment. But leadership is about more than just strength."*

I nod, unsure where he's going with this. *"I understand, sir,"* I reply, trying to keep my voice steady.

A faint smile touches his lips. *"Good,"* he says. *"I want to introduce you to someone who will help you understand this better."* He gestures toward the door, and a young woman steps in. She is tall, with dark, intense eyes and a quiet confidence that radiates from her. There is something in the way she carries herself - a sense of purpose that commands attention.

"This is my niece, Salma Nasser," Abu Khaled continues. *"She has been involved in our work for some time, in ways you may not yet understand."*

Salma nods at me, her gaze direct. *"I've heard a lot about you, Ahmed,"* she says. *"Abu Khaled speaks highly of your skills and your dedication."*

I feel a mix of pride and curiosity, unsure how to respond. Who is this woman, and why does she make me feel like she's already seen through me?

Abu Khaled leans back in his chair, his gaze shifting between us. *"Salma works in Tel Aviv and gathers information. She crosses into Israel daily to work at a law firm working alongside them. I want you two to work together when she's here."*

Over the next few weeks, Salma and I spend a lot of time together after her work in Israel. We oversee the transport of weapons and supplies - these become our shared tasks.

When she's here, she's sharp, efficient, always a step ahead. I find myself admiring her ability to see beyond what's immediately in front of us.

One evening, she starts talking about her experiences in Israel. *"It's different there,"* she says quietly. *"The streets are clean, the buildings intact. The people... they live without the fear we live with every day."*

I bristle at her words, a surge of annoyance rising within me. *"They are still our enemy, Salma,"* I remind her, my tone sharper than I intended. *"Their comfort comes at our expense."*

She nods, but her eyes hold a conflict that unsettles me. *"I know that. But I've seen their children playing, their schools open and safe. Why can't we have that for our people?"*

Her words hang in the air between us, a challenge I'm not ready to face. *"Because they took it from us,"* I say, my voice firm. *"We have to fight to get it back."*

Salma looks at me, her gaze steady, a hint of doubt flickering in her eyes. *"Maybe,"* she agrees, *"but sometimes I wonder if we're losing ourselves in this fight. Is there another way?"*

I shake my head, unwilling to let her doubt infect me. *"We trust Abu Khaled,"* I say firmly. *"We follow his vision."*

Salma's gaze is unwavering, her expression unreadable. *"I do trust him,"* she says softly, *"but I also trust you, Ahmed. And I think you see things more clearly than you realise."*

Her words stick with me long after. I find myself watching her more closely, trying to understand what she truly believes, feeling a slow, simmering frustration that I can't quite place. Who does she think she is, challenging my beliefs?

At home, my mother's pride in me remains unwavering. *"You are doing what needs to be done, Ahmed,"* she tells me, her eyes filled with fervour. *"You are your father's son."*

But my sisters... they are changing too. Layla and Amina no longer look at me the same way. At first, it was just hesitation, a wariness in their eyes. But now there's something else - an edge, a quiet resolve. They're no longer afraid to confront me.

One afternoon, Layla steps into my room, her face set with determination. *"Ahmed, we need to talk,"* she says, her voice steady.

I look up, surprised by her tone. *"About what?"* I ask.

She takes a deep breath, glancing at Amina, who stands hesitantly in the doorway. *"About you,"* she says. *"About who you're becoming."*

Amina steps forward, her voice soft but clear. *"We're worried, Ahmed,"* she says. *"You're different. Distant. And... angry all the time."*

I feel a flicker of annoyance, but I swallow it down. *"I'm doing what I have to do,"* I reply. *"For our people, for our family."*

Layla shakes her head, a spark of defiance in her eyes. *"But are you doing it for yourself too?"* she asks. *"Or are you just following orders, becoming someone you don't even recognise?"*

Her words hit me harder than I expected. I just stare at her, feeling exposed, seen in a way I don't like.

Amina's eyes soften. *"Show us who you are, not just what you've become."*

I turn away, pretending to busy myself with something on the desk.

Layla's voice is softer now. *"We're still your family, Ahmed,"* she says. *"And we're not giving up on you. Not yet."*

Their words linger long after they've gone, circling my mind like dark birds. I feel a strange mixture of anger and guilt. Salma's questions, my sisters' doubts - they feel like cracks forming in a dam I've tried so hard to keep intact. Something is shifting, and I can't stop it.

One night, I'm sitting on the roof of our house, looking out over the ruined city. The stars are faint, barely visible through the haze of dust and smoke. I hear footsteps behind me, and Salma appears, sitting down beside me in silence. We sit there for a while, neither of us speaking, just listening to the distant sounds of the city.

Finally, she breaks the silence. *"You seem troubled, Ahmed,"* she says softly. *"What's on your mind?"*

I hesitate, then sigh. *"Everything,"* I admit. *"I don't know if this is me anymore."*

She nods, her eyes thoughtful. *"I feel that way too sometimes,"* she confesses. *"But I think it's okay to question things. It's okay to wonder if we're on the right path."*

I glance at her, surprised by her honesty. I feel a flicker of irritation again, not wanting her to see my uncertainty. *"Do you think there's another way?"* I ask, trying to keep my tone indifferent.

She smiles faintly, her expression sincere. *"I don't know, Ahmed. But I think we need to keep searching for it, whatever it might be."*

Her words settle into me like seeds, taking root in the corners of my mind. I realise that the answers aren't as clear as I once thought, that maybe - just maybe - there's room to explore beyond the shadows of the tunnels.

The weeks blur by, the days filled with tasks and missions that occupy my time but do nothing to quell the disquiet within me. Salma's presence, though irregular, is unsettling. She continues to challenge me, to push at the boundaries of what I think I know. I catch myself wondering what she sees when she crosses back into

Israel each day. What does she witness in Tel Aviv that makes her speak with such hesitation about the very fight we're supposed to be committed to?

Abu Khaled's eyes narrow as he studies me over the rim of his cup one evening. The light from a single lamp casts shadows across his face, deepening the lines around his mouth. *"You've been quieter lately, Ahmed,"* he remarks casually, but there's a sharpness in his gaze that makes my skin prickle.

"Just focused," I respond quickly, trying to keep my voice steady.

He nods slowly, his expression unreadable. *"Good. Focus is necessary. But remember this: hesitation is dangerous. In our line of work, a moment's doubt can cost you everything."*

The implication hangs heavy between us. I hold his gaze, forcing myself not to look away, even as my heart pounds in my chest.

"I understand," I say finally, and he gives a small, satisfied nod.

"Good," he repeats softly. *"Because you are meant for something greater, Ahmed. Your uncle saw it, and I see it too. Don't let doubt take that from you."*

He's manipulating me, I realise, to keep me tethered. But even knowing that, I feel the familiar pull of his words, the pressure to live up to expectations I never asked for.

The pressure builds each day and the line between right and wrong feels more blurred than ever. My sisters still watch me with that quiet, wounded gaze, and even Abu Khaled's praise feels hollow now.

I try to drown the doubt in loyalty, in action. But Salma's words keep circling back, poking holes in the certainty I once held so tightly.

What if this isn't the path my father would have wanted for me? What if, instead of becoming the man he hoped I'd be, I'm becoming something else entirely?

The thought haunts me, lingering like a shadow I can't quite escape.

And I wonder if Salma's right - if there's still time to find another way.

Chapter Fourteen

YOSSI

The days are filled with sunshine and laughter, but beneath the surface, there's a tension that hums - an unspoken undercurrent we all feel but none of us acknowledge. Tel Aviv pulses with life: the beaches are crowded with sunbathers, the streets thrum with music and chatter, and the smell of street food mingles with the salty sea breeze. The city is vibrant, pulsating with energy, yet there's a sense we're all pretending, grasping at the last threads of normality we know won't last.

We make the most of these days. My friends and I know our time is running out, that soon we'll be pulled in different directions - into uniforms, into service. But for now, we are here - teenagers trying to grasp the fleeting moments of our youth. We cling to these days as if they might slip through our fingers, savouring every second.

Yael and I spend most of our time together. Her laugh is bright and contagious, and the way her eyes light up when she teases me, or when we find a new spot in the city to explore, is something I've come to rely on. We wander through the narrow alleys of Old Jaffa, climbing to the rooftops to watch the sun dip into the Mediterranean. We invent stories about the people we see, imagining their lives and dreams. We talk about everything - school, the future, what we want to become. There's a lightness when we're together, a sense that maybe, just maybe, everything will be alright.

But there's always the unspoken shadow hanging over us: military service. It's something we've all known was coming, but now it feels closer, more real. We're all waiting for the day when the letters arrive, telling us where to report, where we'll be sent. It's like a storm on the horizon - inevitable and approaching.

One afternoon, as we sit on a bench by the beach, watching the waves roll in, Yael nudges me gently. *"You're still going with Nadav, right?"* she asks, her voice carrying a weight that doesn't match the casualness of the question.

I glance at her, half-smiling. *"You know I am,"* I say quietly.

She nods, her eyes serious. *"Paratroopers."* There's no question in her tone, only a quiet acceptance.

"Paratroopers," I confirm, and I can see the worry flicker in her gaze. Nadav has always wanted to be a paratrooper - jumping out of planes, living the adventure he's always dreamed of. And it's always been understood that I'd join him. But now, with everything becoming real, I wonder if I'm ready for the kind of risk Nadav craves.

"Just... be careful, okay?" she murmurs, squeezing my hand.

I nod. *"I will,"* I promise. *"We'll both be careful."*

Yael smiles, but it's a small, tight thing. *"You're going to be amazing,"* she says softly. *"Both of you."*

Our friends tease us endlessly, especially Leila, who seems to take joy in our relationship. *"So, when's the wedding?"* she jokes one afternoon, making Yael blush and me roll my eyes.

"Not anytime soon," I reply, grinning, *"unless you're planning to be the wedding singer, Leila."*

Everyone laughs, and for a moment, the weight of what's coming lifts. Amir throws his arm around my shoulder. *"Maybe you two will end up stationed together,"* he says, half-joking, half-serious. *"Stranger things have happened."*

"*I'm sure the army will arrange it just for us,*" Yael says, her eyes sparkling with mischief.

But beneath the jokes, there's a shared understanding. We're all thinking about what's to come. Nadav talks endlessly about the paratroopers - the training, the jumps, the camaraderie. He wants us to stick together, to go through this side by side.

Maya, ever the artist, has decided to join something in IT or PR. "*I don't think I could be a soldier in the usual way,*" she admits one evening, "*but I can still serve, still contribute.*"

Amir, the quiet and thoughtful one, has been aiming for the Combat Engineering Corps. "*I've always liked building things,*" he says with a shy smile. "*And maybe this way, I can help protect people, make things safer.*"

Samir, who has always been interested in strategy and puzzles, is set on joining the Intelligence Unit. "*I want to be in a place where I can use my mind,*" he says thoughtfully. "*Where I can see the whole picture, maybe even prevent things before they happen.*"

Leila, with her sharp mind and quick wit, nods in agreement. "*I'm thinking about becoming a Medic,*" she says. "*Someone has to look out for your lot.*"

The days drift by, filled with sun and laughter, but the shadow of what's to come grows longer. Our families try to be supportive but can't hide their anxiety. My father, ever the storyteller, shares tales of his own military service, blending nostalgia with a certain gravity.

"*It's not easy,*" my father tells me one night as we sit on the balcony, the familiar hum of Tel Aviv stretching out below us. The city's lights shimmer in the distance, a web of tiny, glowing orbs against the dark sky. His words are steady, measured, but there's something in his tone that makes me pause. "*But it's important. You'll learn a lot about yourself, about your friends.*"

He's staring out at the skyline, his gaze distant, fingers tapping absently on the arm of his chair. It's a small, almost imperceptible motion, but I know my father too well to miss it. He only does that when something's on his mind, when the words he *wants* to say are caught somewhere deep inside.

"You're worried," I say quietly, more of a statement than a question.

His hand stills, and he turns to look at me, his face shadowed in the soft glow of the balcony light. There's a flicker of something in his eyes - something raw, something that slips past the careful mask he usually wears.

"I'm always worried," he admits slowly, choosing his words with care. *"But it's different this time."*

I don't respond right away, waiting. He's never been one to voice his fears openly, not even during the worst of times. But tonight, there's a tension in his shoulders, a tightness in the way he holds himself.

"Because of the Parachute Brigade?" I ask finally, keeping my voice low.

He nods almost imperceptibly, his gaze drifting back to the city. *"It's a good unit,"* he says, the words coming out flat, devoid of enthusiasm. *"One of the best. But it's not just the training, Yossi. It's... it's the things you see. The things you can't forget."*

He doesn't look at me as he speaks, and that tells me more than anything else ever could. I know my father's stories - his tales of bravery and camaraderie during his service. But I also remember the way he goes silent sometimes, the way his eyes cloud over when the conversation strays too close to certain memories.

"You don't want me to go," I whisper, feeling the weight of his unspoken fears settle around us.

"It's not that," he replies softly, finally turning to face me. *"I'm proud of you, Yossi. So proud. But..."* He hesitates, struggling to put something intangible into words. *"But I know what it's like to come back different. To carry things with you that no one else can see."*

His eyes search mine, and for a moment, I see the vulnerability there - the pain of a father who has been through it himself and doesn't want his son to bear the same burdens.

I swallow hard, unsure of what to say. There's a lump in my throat, a tightness in my chest. *"I'll be okay, Dad,"* I say, but the words feel hollow, uncertain.

"I know you will," he says quietly. *"You're strong. You're brave. But being a soldier is more than just that."* He leans forward slightly, his hand resting on my arm. *"Just... remember who you are, Yossi. And if it ever gets to be too much, if it ever feels like you're losing yourself... don't be afraid to ask for help."*

It's the closest he's come to admitting his own struggles, and it hits me harder than any lecture or warning ever could. I nod, the weight of his words settling in my chest. *"I won't forget,"* I promise, feeling the heaviness of the vow between us.

He gives me a small, tight smile, his hand squeezing my arm briefly before he leans back, the conversation shifting away, the moment slipping back into silence. But the unspoken concern lingers, hanging in the air between us.

My mother, always the worrier, tries to stay positive. *"You'll be fine, Yossi,"* she says with a smile that doesn't quite reach her eyes. I catch the way her gaze flickers over me, the tightness in her expression whenever the topic of the army comes up. *"You're strong. You'll come back safe."*

She says it like a mantra, as if repeating it enough times will somehow make it true. I want to believe her, but the uncertainty is there, lurking just beneath the surface.

Yael's father pulls me aside one day, his expression serious. *"Take care of her,"* he says simply, his voice steady but laced with an edge of vulnerability. *"And take care of yourself."*

I see the worry in his eyes too - the same fear my own father hides behind his calm exterior. It's a look that says more than words ever could, a reminder that the ones left behind carry a different kind of burden.

"I will," I promise, my voice firm. *"We'll look out for each other."*

He nods, his gaze lingering on me for a moment longer, and I know he's not just talking about Yael. There's an unspoken message in the way he looks at me - a plea, almost. *Don't let this war take you away.*

"Good," he murmurs, stepping back. *"That's all I can ask for."*

We all know what's coming, but we try to make the most of the time we have left. We go on trips, spend nights at the beach, have endless barbecues. We talk about everything and nothing, knowing that soon our lives will change in ways we can't yet imagine.

One evening, we gather on the rooftop of Amir's building, looking out over the city. The sun is setting, painting the sky in brilliant hues. Nadav raises a bottle, grinning. *"To us,"* he says. *"To the future."*

We all cheer, clinking our bottles together. Yael leans against me, her head on my shoulder. I wrap my arm around her, feeling a warmth spread through my chest. For a moment, everything feels perfect.

But beneath the surface, I feel the fear growing *"We'll be alright,"* Yael whispers. *"We'll find a way."*

I nod, pulling her closer. *"Yeah,"* I say softly. *"We will."*

Chapter Fifteen

AHMED

It's 2018, and the dust of the past still clings to everything in Gaza. Four years have passed since the last war, but its impact lingers like a shadow that never quite leaves. The city has rebuilt itself in parts, but the scars remain visible - etched into the faces of the people, the crumbling walls, and the stories whispered at night. I feel it every day - a quiet weight that presses down on us all, shaping our thoughts, our decisions, our very existence.

The lessons from my mother echo in my mind like a drumbeat. *"They took everything from us, Ahmed. They will never stop."* She spoke with such certainty, her voice hard, her eyes fierce. Yusuf, too, would speak of hatred like it was the only thing keeping us alive. *"Revenge is our duty,"* he'd say, his voice steady, unyielding. *"We owe it to those who have fallen."*

For me, the war has been a defining force, moulding who I am now, colouring the way I see the world. It's a filter through which I view everything, and I realise I've been changed by it in ways I'm only beginning to understand. I've grown harder, more decisive. My belief in our cause - our fight for freedom - remains firm, but there are moments when Salma's words echo in my mind, making me question whether I truly understand what the end looks like.

"What will we have left, Ahmed, if we destroy everything in the name of freedom?" she had asked me once. I had no answer then, and it troubles me still.

Life has resumed a rhythm of sorts. The days are filled with tasks and training, meetings and missions. Abu Khaled keeps me busy, giving me more responsibility than ever before. I'm no longer just a boy running errands, I'm a leader, someone the younger boys look up to. I teach them how to move silently, how to read a map, how to prepare for whatever might come. They watch me with eager eyes, waiting for guidance, and I do my best to be the leader they need. I've learned to spot fear in their faces, to encourage them with a quiet word, a firm nod, even when I feel the same fear clawing at my insides.

But sometimes, late at night when the city is quiet, my thoughts drift back to Salma's words. *"A future where we don't have to fight anymore."* It sounds like a fantasy - something too far away to even picture. How could we have a future without fighting, without resistance? Everything I know, everything I've been taught, tells me that freedom must be fought for, that there is no other way. But still, her words linger like a splinter I can't quite remove.

Salma is still by my side, and our bond has deepened over these years. She is my confidante, my ally, and sometimes the only one who seems to understand the questions I dare not speak aloud. Her work in Tel Aviv has become a point of tension between us. She crosses the border each day, like thousands of others, to work in a law firm. It's not a mission, not a formal assignment - she's not there to gather intelligence in the traditional sense. But she observes, listens, and tries to piece together the reality on the other side. She talks about it sometimes - the casual conversations she has, the small kindnesses she experiences that make her question everything we've been taught. It's dangerous, what she's doing, but she carries it out with a determination that inspires me, even as it worries me. I find myself admiring her courage, even when it challenges me.

One afternoon, we sit in a quiet corner of a café that's just been rebuilt. The air is filled with the scent of fresh bread and cardamom coffee.

"I heard something today," Salma says, her voice low, almost hesitant. "There's a new plan in motion - something bigger than before. Abu Khaled hasn't shared all the details yet, but I think he will soon."

I nod, taking a sip of my coffee, but my mind is elsewhere. The thought of another plan, another mission, another act of violence... it feels endless.

"Do you ever feel like we're on a loop?" I ask. *"Like we're just repeating the same cycle over and over again?"*

Salma looks at me, her expression thoughtful. *"Sometimes,"* she admits. *"But maybe that's because we haven't found the right way to break it yet."*

Her answer frustrates me. *"What other way is there?"* I reply, a bit more sharply than I intend. *"We fight because we have to. It's the only way we've ever known."*

Salma's hand reaches across the table, lightly resting on mine. *"We have to start somewhere,"* she says, her voice calm but insistent. *"Maybe it begins with asking the right questions, with being willing to see things differently."*

I pull my hand away, feeling a flicker of annoyance. *"I don't know if I'm ready for that,"* I confess, feeling a mix of resistance and curiosity. *"What's the point in asking questions when the answers never change?"*

She smiles a soft, encouraging smile. *"That's a start, Ahmed. At least you're thinking about it. That's more than most people are willing to do."*

Our conversation is interrupted by a call from Abu Khaled. He has summoned me to discuss a new assignment. I stand, feeling the familiar mix of duty and slight irritation at Salma's persistence.

"I have to go," I tell her.

Salma nods. *"Be careful,"* she says quietly. *"And don't forget what we talked about."*

I leave the café and make my way through the crowded streets to the meeting place. As I walk, I think about the boys I trained, their faces eager, excited. I remember the look in their eyes after their first encounter with real danger, the way their hands shook, the way they looked at me, waiting for me to tell them it was okay.

Abu Khaled is waiting for me, his face serious. *"Ahmed,"* he says, *"we have a new mission. This one is important. I need you to take a group of the younger boys and train them for something more advanced. They need to be ready for whatever comes next in the future."*

I nod, my face set in determination. *"Of course, sir. I'll make sure they're prepared."*

But as he speaks, I can't help but feel the weight of his words. Not the words themselves, but what they imply - the willingness to throw more boys into the fire, to sacrifice more lives without hesitation. I think of the youngest, Omar, who always tries to hide his fear with a brave smile, and I wonder if he's ready for what Abu Khaled expects.

He studies me for a moment, then adds, *"Remember, Ahmed, this is not just about fighting. It's about the future we are building, the strength we are showing the world."*

Abu Khaled steps closer, lowering his voice so only I can hear. *"Ahmed,"* he continues, his tone intense, *"this is a test for you as well. You have shown promise, leadership. The boys look up to you. But now you need to prove you can take them to the next level. They need to be ready to fight, to protect, to make sacrifices. Do you understand?"*

His words feel like a knife, sharp and precise. A test. I nod, but my chest tightens, that small whisper in my mind growing louder. *Why does it always have to be a test?*

"Yes, sir. I understand."

He places a hand on my shoulder, his grip firm. *"This is more than just a task. It's a responsibility. I want you to show them what it means to be part of this movement. Make them see what we are fighting for, what we are willing to die for."*

I swallow, trying to suppress the nagging voice that remembers Salma's words. *"I will, Abu Khaled. I won't let you down."*

Abu Khaled nods approvingly. *"Good. Because the future of our struggle depends on boys like you and on how well you prepare those who come after you."*

I leave the meeting, my mind heavy with the weight of his words. I've spent years fighting, training, leading. But what kind of future am I really building? And who am I building it for?

Over the next few days, I throw myself into the training. The boys are eager, their faces bright with the excitement of something new. I show them how to move with purpose, how to stay hidden, how to think quickly under pressure. They look at me with respect, and I feel the weight of their expectations. I see myself in them - the same eagerness, the same need to prove oneself.

"Keep low, stay behind cover until you have a clear shot," I instruct one evening, watching as they try to mimic my movements. *"And remember, no heroics. We are not here to be martyrs. We're here to win."*

They nod, eyes wide, absorbing every word. I can see their belief, their trust. They follow me because I show no doubt, because I project the strength and confidence they crave. But deep inside, the doubts I bury beneath layers of determination feel like stones in my chest. I remember the look in Omar's eyes the first time he held a gun - how his hands trembled until I laid mine over his, steadying his grip.

"It's just a tool," I'd told him softly. *"It's your mind that makes it powerful."*

Now, as I watch him move through the drills, his small frame darting behind cover, I wonder if I've done the right thing. Have I equipped him to survive, or have I merely led him down the same dark path I can't seem to escape?

The boys work hard, pushing themselves to impress me, to earn my praise. And I give it freely, encouraging them, guiding them with the same firm hand Yusuf once used on me. I push the doubts down, burying them under the rhythm of training, the feel of the rifle in my hands, the sound of commands shouted and obeyed.

But at night, when the city settles into uneasy silence, they return, those gnawing doubts, louder and more insistent.

One evening, after a particularly intense session, I see Salma waiting for me outside the training grounds. She's leaning against the wall, her expression guarded but watchful. I feel a flash of irritation - she always seems to know when I'm most conflicted, most unsure of myself.

"What are you doing here?" I ask, my voice sharper than I intend.

She straightens, a small frown creasing her brow. *"I came to see you. Is that a problem?"*

I sigh, rubbing a hand over my face. *"No. It's just... I have a lot on my mind."*

"I can see that," she says softly, her gaze drifting to the boys, now packing up their gear under the watchful eyes of Khaled and Tariq. *"They look up to you, you know."*

"I know," I reply shortly, turning away. *"That's the problem."*

Salma steps closer, lowering her voice. *"It's not a problem, Ahmed. It's an opportunity. You can show them something different, something more than just fighting and killing."*

Her words hit a nerve. *"And what would that be?"* I snap, my frustration spilling over. *"What other choice do we have? Do you think the Israelis will just hand us our freedom if we ask nicely?"*

Salma doesn't flinch, doesn't back down. Instead, she holds my gaze, her eyes steady and calm. *"No, but there's a difference between fighting for freedom and losing yourself in hatred. I see you struggling, Ahmed. I see the doubt in your eyes, even if you won't admit it. You have a choice."*

"You don't understand," I mutter, shaking my head. *"It's not that simple."*

"Maybe not," she agrees quietly. *"But you're not as trapped as you think you are."*

I stare at her, anger and confusion roiling inside me. What does she want from me? What does she expect me to do - turn my back on everything, walk away from all that we've built? I clench my fists, the weight of responsibility pressing down on me like a crushing tide.

"You're asking too much," I whisper, almost to myself.

Salma's expression softens, her eyes filled with something like compassion. *"I'm not asking you to abandon them,"* she murmurs. *"I'm asking you to think - really think - about what kind of future you want to build. For them, and for yourself."*

Before I can respond, a shout from Khaled draws my attention. He's calling the boys over, gesturing for them to line up for inspection. I turn back to Salma, but she's already stepping away, fading into the shadows.

"Just think about it," she says softly, her voice lingering in the air long after she's gone.

I throw myself into the training even harder after that, pushing the boys, pushing myself, trying to drown out the echo of Salma's voice. We train late into the night, until every muscle aches and every thought are blurred with exhaustion. Khaled and Tariq notice, their eyes watchful, but they say nothing. I don't give them the chance.

But the more I try to lose myself in the work, the more her words haunt me. *"What kind of future are you building?"* It's a question that digs deep, a thorn that won't be dislodged.

One day, after a particularly gruelling drill, Omar approaches me hesitantly. His face is flushed, his breathing ragged, but there's a determined set to his jaw.

"What is it, Omar?" I ask, keeping my tone gentle despite the frustration simmering beneath my skin.

"I - I just wanted to say... thank you," he stammers, his voice small but earnest. *"For teaching us. For believing in us."*

The sincerity in his gaze catches me off guard. I feel something twist inside me, something fragile and painful. *"You don't have to thank me,"* I say quietly. *"Just... stay focused. Stay strong."*

Omar nods quickly, his eyes bright with resolve. *"I will, Ahmed. I want to make you proud."*

He scurries off before I can respond, leaving me standing there, feeling hollow. Make me proud. The words linger, a bitter aftertaste I can't shake. What kind of pride can I offer him? What kind of future can I build for boys like Omar, who look up to me with such blind trust?

The doubts are louder now, the cracks in my resolve widening with every passing day. And as I watch the boys train, their faces shining with youthful fervour, I feel a heavy, suffocating weight settle over me.

Because the truth is, I don't know the answer. I don't know what kind of future I'm building anymore. And I don't know if I'm strong enough to find out.

Chapter Sixteen

YOSSI

It is 2018, and the days are moving faster now, drawing Yossi and his friends ever closer to the moment that has always loomed in their future - military service. For years, they've known this time would come, but now it feels tangible, immediate. There's a mixture of pride and apprehension in the air, a sense of stepping into the unknown. While serving feels like an honour and a duty, it's also a step into a world they can't fully predict.

Yossi and his friends cling to the final days of their youth, filling them with moments that feel more precious now. Tel Aviv is alive around them, the city buzzing with the sounds of laughter, traffic, and music. The smell of the sea mixes with the scent of fresh bread from the bakeries, and the warm breeze carries a feeling of late summer - a last lingering embrace of freedom before everything changes.

The atmosphere feels heavier these days. The buzz of the city, once a comforting backdrop, now seems distant. Yossi's senses are heightened - every laugh from a stranger, every rustle of the sea breeze makes him feel as if time is slipping away faster than ever before. There's a dull ache in his chest that comes from knowing that soon everything will be different, and he isn't sure if he'll ever feel this carefree again.

One evening, they gather on the beach, sitting close together as the waves lap gently at the shore. Nadav, his hair tousled by the wind, stares up at the sky.

"It feels like time is slipping away," he says, his voice caught between excitement and anxiety. *"I'm going to miss this... miss all of you."*

Yael, sitting next to Yossi with her fingers intertwined with his, nods. *"Me too,"* she murmurs. *"But we knew this was coming. It's what we have to do. Our duty."*

I listen to Yael's words, feeling a knot tighten in my stomach. I've always known this was coming, but now, on the edge of it, I feel a strange mix of excitement and dread. I've tried to prepare myself, but how do you really get ready for something that might change you forever? My father once told me that no amount of training can truly prepare you for the reality of military life. *"It changes you, Yossi,"* he had said quietly, staring off into the distance. *"And there's no going back."* His words replay in my mind, and I wonder if I'm really ready to face that change.

A few weeks ago, we received our *Tzav Rishon* - the initial call-up for screening and classification. It's the first step into the Israeli Defence Forces (IDF), a sign that our lives are about to change.

"Is everyone ready for the Tzav Rishon tests?" Leila asks, her voice light but her expression serious. *"It's only a few days away."*

Samir nods. *"I've been preparing - going over the psychometric tests, brushing up on my Hebrew and English for the language sections. I'm aiming for intelligence, so I want to do well."*

I push my nerves aside. *"We're about to find out what we're made of,"* I say, trying to sound confident.

Maya, who has been quiet, speaks up. *"I've been thinking about it too. I want to join a unit that focuses on IT and PR."*

I smile at her. *"You'll be perfect for that, Maya. You've always been great at finding stories."*

Maya smiles back, though there's a touch of anxiety in her eyes. *"I just hope they see it that way."*

The following week, we head separately to the military recruitment office for our *Tzav Rishon*. It's a day of tests and interviews to determine our suitability for different roles within the IDF.

I arrive early in the morning. The recruitment centre smells of antiseptic and anxiety, the air heavy with the murmur of low voices and the scrape of chairs against the linoleum floor. I look around at the other faces, wondering if they're feeling the same thing I am - a mix of fear, excitement, and something else I can't quite name. I wonder if they're thinking about the choices we'll have to make, the people we might have to face, the things we might have to do.

The hours drag on as we go through the various tests. I sit through the medical examination, trying to control my breathing, willing my pulse to stay steady as the doctor checks my vitals. The questions he asks feel routine, but every answer feels like a potential mark against me. What if they find something wrong? What if they decide I'm not fit for the Paratroopers? The thought gnaws at the back of my mind.

A doctor checks my vision, hearing, reflexes, and overall physical condition.

"You're in good shape," the doctor comments, scribbling on a form. *"Any injuries or health issues?"*

"No, nothing serious," I reply, feeling a slight sense of relief.

But deep down, I'm still tense. I keep replaying my father's stories in my mind - the long marches, the split-second decisions in combat, the weight of responsibility that never seems to leave. *Am I really ready for that?*

Next comes the psychometric test, a long series of multiple-choice questions assessing logic, language, and mathematical skills. Yossi sits in a room filled with rows of desks, a mixture of anxiety and determination on the faces around him. He takes a deep breath and starts working through the questions, his pencil moving quickly over the paper.

In another room, Samir is also taking the psychometric test. He finds the questions challenging but manageable - his love of puzzles and strategy games has prepared him well for this. He moves through the sections confidently, hoping his scores will be high enough to get him into the intelligence unit he dreams of.

Elsewhere in the centre, Yael undergoes a medical exam, then heads into the psychometric testing room. She's nervous but has been preparing for weeks, practising different types of questions with Yossi and Leila. She aims for a role in the Combat Intelligence Corps, where she will gather real-time information from the field to help guide operations, often working close to combat zones but not on the front lines. She knows her test scores will play a significant role in where she ends up.

Leila, in another section, talks to a career counsellor about her aspirations to become a medic. The counsellor explains the different paths within the Medical Corps, asking about her motivations and why she wants to serve in a medical capacity.

"*I want to help people,*" Leila says earnestly. "*I want to be there in emergencies, to save lives and make a difference.*"

Amir, who has always been good with his hands, is interviewed about his interest in becoming a Combat Engineer. He describes his experience with mechanics and his love for solving practical problems. The interviewer asks about his physical fitness, then hands him a list of tasks to prove he has the endurance and skills required for the role.

"*I'm ready,*" Amir replies with quiet confidence. "*I've been training for this.*"

Maya's turn comes, and she is asked about her interest in Spokesperson's Unit responsible for information policy and external media relations.

Maya's eyes light up. "*I'd love to do that,*" she says. "*It's exactly what I'm passionate about.*"

The officer nods, making notes on his clipboard. "*You'll need to demonstrate both your creative skills and your ability to work under pressure. Are you up for that?*"

"*Absolutely,*" Maya replies, feeling a surge of determination.

After the tests, Nadav and I sit outside the recruitment office, the setting sun casting long shadows over the courtyard. Nadav is quieter than usual, staring at the ground.

"What's going on?" I ask, nudging him lightly with my shoulder.

Nadav hesitates, then sighs. "I've wanted to be a Paratrooper for as long as I can remember," he admits, his voice low. "It's all I've ever dreamed of. But what if I don't make it? What if... what if I'm not good enough?"

His vulnerability catches me off guard. Nadav is always the strong one, the determined one. Seeing him like this is strange, but it makes me realise how much this means to him.

"Hey," I say softly, turning to face him fully. "We'll get each other through this, alright? We're a team. We always have been."

He glances at me, his eyes searching mine. "But what if only one of us makes it? What if I get cut, and you...?"

I shake my head firmly. "Then we keep going. We don't quit, no matter what. And you won't get cut, Nadav. You're one of the toughest people I know. We're going to get through this together."

A small, hesitant smile tugs at his lips. "You really think so?"

"I know so," I reply, my voice steady. "We've been through a lot together. We'll get through this too."

He nods slowly, the tension in his shoulders easing slightly. "Thanks, Yossi," he murmurs. "I needed that."

"Anytime," I say with a grin. "Just remember, when we're out there, it's not just about being strong. It's about having heart. And you've got that, Nadav. In spades."

Nadav's smile grows a bit wider, the worry in his eyes softening. For the first time in days, he looks almost like himself again.

A few weeks later, the results arrive. Each of them receives a letter detailing the next steps: training dates, unit placements, and what they need to do to prepare.

Yossi and Nadav get the news they've been hoping for - they've passed the initial Tzav Rishon assessments and are eligible for the Gibush, the gruelling selection process for the Paratroopers. They immediately message each other, sharing their excitement.

"*We did it, man!*" Nadav writes. "*Now it's time for the Gibush. I've heard it's brutal, but I'm ready if you are.*"

"*Absolutely,*" Yossi replies. "*Let's show them what we've got.*"

As the reality of their next steps sinks in, the friends realise that this is the calm before the storm. They have been accepted into their respective units, but the real challenge lies ahead. The final weeks before they officially begin their military service are filled with preparation, anticipation, and a bittersweet sense of impending change.

Yossi and Nadav intensify their training, running on the Tel Aviv beach every morning, pushing themselves to their physical limits. They do endless sets of push-ups, sit-ups, and pull-ups, knowing that their endurance and strength will soon be put to the ultimate test. Nadav, with his ever-present grin, keeps up the banter, but Yossi can see the tension in his friend's eyes. They are both ready, but they know that the Gibush will be like nothing they have ever faced.

As the days pass, Yossi and his friends focus on preparing themselves mentally and physically for the challenges ahead, knowing they have only passed the initial entrance tests. They spend their time encouraging and supporting one another, sharing their anxieties and excitement about the unknowns they will soon face in their respective units.

They meet regularly, talking about what little they know about the paths they are about to embark on, helping each other stay motivated. Even though none of them have the skills yet for their assigned roles, they share a common determination to prove themselves worthy of the opportunities they've been given. The bond between them grows stronger as they find comfort in their shared uncertainty, knowing they will face whatever comes next together.

The night before Yossi and Nadav leave for the Gibush, they meet their friends one last time at the beach. The mood is a mix of celebration and tension, their usual laughter tinged with the weight of the unknown. They sit in a circle, their feet buried in the cool sand, the waves whispering against the shore.

"*Don't forget to breathe,*" Leila jokes, handing Yossi a small charm she bought at the market earlier that day. "*For luck,*" she says with a grin. "*You'll need it.*"

Yael leans in close to Yossi, her fingers brushing against his arm. "*You've got this,*" she whispers, a soft smile on her lips. "*Just remember why you want this, why it matters to you.*"

Yossi nods, trying to absorb the confidence in her voice, the warmth in her gaze. "*I'll remember,*" he replies, squeezing her hand. "*I promise.*"

They exchange final words of encouragement and jokes, trying to lighten the mood, but the underlying tension is palpable. As they say their goodbyes, the reality of what lies ahead begins to sink in. The next day, Yossi and Nadav will head to the training base, ready to face whatever the Gibush has in store for them.

On the morning of the Gibush, we arrive at the base before dawn. The air is sharp and biting, the sky still a deep indigo as we line up with the other candidates. There's a low buzz of murmurs around us - some nervous, others filled with excitement. I glance at Nadav beside me, his expression calm, but his jaw is clenched just slightly, the only sign of the tension simmering beneath the surface.

The first part is the 2-kilometre run. My heart beats a little faster as I look at the course stretching out ahead of us. I'm not a bad runner by any means, but Nadav's always been faster. The run itself isn't long, but here, it's not just about speed - it's about proving you belong. There's no room for mistakes.

"*Just keep pace with me,*" Nadav murmurs, leaning in slightly. His eyes are steady, encouraging. "*We'll get through this. You're in good shape, just stay focused.*"

We take off at the starting signal, feet pounding against the ground in unison. The cold air fills my lungs, sharp and invigorating. I push myself to match Nadav's stride, settling into a rhythm that feels strong. He glances over his shoulder every few metres, his pace quick and controlled, but not so fast that I can't keep up. It's a small reassurance - that unspoken promise that we're in this together.

As we round the first corner, a few runners begin to surge ahead, their determination palpable. Nadav's eyes narrow slightly, but he doesn't take the bait. He knows the key is consistency, and I follow his lead, breathing hard but steady. Every time I start to feel my pace slip, I focus on Nadav's shoulders just ahead of me, the way he pushes forward, his stride even and sure.

"*Keep it steady, Yossi,*" he calls back over the sound of pounding feet. "*We've got this.*"

We hit the halfway point, and my legs are starting to burn, the muscle fatigue setting in quicker than I'd expected. But I grit my teeth and push through. Nadav is right there, a few paces ahead, his presence pulling me forward. He's holding back, I can tell - adjusting his pace just enough to keep me in sight. Every time I think about slowing down, giving in just a little, he shoots me a quick look, and I force myself to stay with him.

As we approach the final stretch, a few runners falter, their speed dropping off. Nadav glances at me, a quick nod of encouragement.

"*Let's finish strong,*" he says.

I dig deep, ignoring the burning in my lungs, the heaviness in my legs. Together, we push forward, our feet pounding in time. When we cross the finish line, my chest is heaving, but I made it under the time limit - comfortably. I glance at Nadav, and he's grinning, his face flushed with exertion but alight with pride.

"*You did it,*" he says, clapping me on the back, his voice breathless.

"*We did it,*" I correct, managing a grin through my panting breaths.

The run is just the beginning, a warm-up to test our stamina and weed out those who aren't physically prepared. After a short rest, we're thrown into the heart of the *Gibush* - the *Shetach* exercises. The sun is just beginning to creep over the horizon, casting long shadows over the base as we line up, eyes forward, hearts pounding.

"*Ready? Go!*" an instructor shouts, his voice echoing across the field.

We dive into the first drill - sprints up a steep incline, then crawling under a maze of ropes and wires, the earth cold and hard beneath us. I grit my teeth, the sand and grit scraping against my elbows as I drag myself forward. Nadav's just ahead, his movements smooth, controlled. I focus on his form, copying the way he shifts his weight, using his arms and legs to push forward with every ounce of strength he has.

"*Don't slow down!*" the instructor barks. "*Keep moving, or you're out!*"

I feel the pressure mounting, my muscles burning as we push through drill after drill. I lose count of how many times we're ordered to sprint, drop, and crawl again. Sweat trickles down my back, soaking into my uniform, and my breath comes in ragged gasps. But every time I think about easing up, I see Nadav's back, his shoulders tense but steady, his focus unbroken. It keeps me going, pushing through the exhaustion.

"*We're good, Yossi,*" he mutters, glancing back at me as we drag ourselves out of the dirt. "*Just a bit more.*"

The words are simple, but they give me something solid to hold onto. We move on to the sandbag drills - each of us hefting a heavy sack onto our shoulders, the weight almost unbearable after the crawling. My legs tremble under the load, but Nadav is beside me, his jaw set in determination.

"*Stay with me,*" he says quietly. "*One step at a time.*"

We trudge forward, step by agonising step, matching our pace. I feel every muscle in my body straining, screaming for relief, but I push it aside, focusing on Nadav's steady rhythm. We carry the sandbags for what feels like hours, the weight pressing down on us like a physical manifestation of the doubts clawing at my mind. But every time my grip slips, every time my steps falter, Nadav shifts slightly, taking on a little more of the burden, his shoulder brushing against mine in silent reassurance.

When we finally drop the sandbags, my arms are trembling so hard I can barely move. I slump to my knees, my chest heaving, but Nadav crouches beside me, his hand gripping my shoulder.

"You're doing great," he murmurs, his voice low, meant just for me. *"Keep pushing, Yossi. We're almost through this part."*

The instructors don't give us a moment's respite. We're pulled to our feet and shoved into the next drill - stretcher runs across uneven terrain. Four of us hoist the stretcher, Nadav and I taking the front. We grit our teeth as we lift, the weight of the sandbags on the stretcher almost unbearable. But there's no hesitation, no faltering. We move in perfect sync, Nadav matching his steps to mine, our movements fluid and controlled.

"Keep it steady," I call out, my voice strained but firm. *"Don't rush. We've got this."*

The others glance at us, a flicker of relief in their eyes. They trust us to set the pace, to lead them through this. It's a small thing, but it solidifies something between Nadav and me - a silent understanding that we're not just here for ourselves. We're here for each other.

The stretchers grow heavier with every step, the terrain rough and unforgiving. We stumble, our boots sinking into the loose dirt, but we push through, grit and determination driving us forward. By the time we reach the end, I'm barely holding on, my body screaming in protest. But Nadav's still there, his hand steady on the stretcher, his eyes locked on mine.

"Almost there," he mutters. *"Don't quit on me now."*

I give a sharp nod, tightening my grip. *"Never."*

We haul the stretcher the last few metres, our bodies protesting with every step. When we finally set it down, my arms are shaking so badly I can't control the tremors. But we did it. Together.

"Well done," an instructor calls out, his eyes sweeping over us. There's no smile, no warmth, but there's a flicker of respect in his gaze. *"You two - solid teamwork."*

It's a brief acknowledgment, but it sends a rush of pride through me. I glance at Nadav, and he gives me a small, tired smile, the tension in his shoulders easing just a little.

"*Told you we'd make it,*" he murmurs.

"*Yeah,*" I breathe, the exhaustion momentarily forgotten. "*We did.*"

But the relief is short-lived. The next phase is the leadership exercises, and this is where I need to step up. We're split into smaller groups, given complex tasks - building structures out of limited materials, navigating obstacles as a team, making quick decisions under pressure. Nadav stands back, letting me take the lead.

"*Spread the weight evenly,*" I order, my voice clear despite the fatigue. "*We need to stabilise it first. Then we focus on speed.*"

The others hesitate for a moment, but Nadav's quick to jump in, echoing my instructions. "*Do what he says. It's the best way.*"

With Nadav backing me up, the others fall in line. We move methodically, every action deliberate, every movement planned. I feel the eyes of the instructors on us, watching, evaluating. The pressure is immense, but I push it aside, focusing on the task at hand.

When we finish, I catch a brief nod from one of the testers - a silent acknowledgment of our teamwork. It's a small victory, but it's enough to keep me going.

Finally, we're brought in for the interviews. I sit across from a reservist, my body sore but my mind sharp.

"*Why Tzanchanim?*" he asks, his gaze level.

"*Because it's where the best is,*" I reply honestly. "*Because I want to push myself, to be part of a team that makes a difference. And... because I know I can do it.*"

The reservist nods slowly, scribbling something down. "*You showed good teamwork out there. And leadership.*"

I nod, keeping my expression steady. "*Thank you, sir.*"

When it's over, I find Nadav waiting. He looks exhausted, but there's a light in his eyes - determination, relief, pride.

"*Whatever happens,*" he murmurs, clapping me on the shoulder. "*We gave it everything.*"

"*We did,*" I agree quietly.

As we leave the base together, the dawn breaking over the horizon, I feel a strange, quiet certainty settling in my chest. Whatever comes next, we'll face it together.

Chapter Seventeen

AHMED

Ahmed's mission to recruit new members for Hamas began with assembling a team that could execute the task with both precision and subtlety. He understood that this role required careful planning and the ability to connect with potential recruits on a personal level. Not everyone in his circle was suited for this delicate mission, he needed those who could persuade without aggression and navigate this dangerous path without drawing undue attention.

Bilal was an obvious choice. Unlike Tariq and Khaled, who were quick-tempered and prone to violence, Bilal possessed a calm, steady demeanour. He had a way of listening that built trust with just a few words, making him ideal for establishing initial contacts. Ahmed knew Bilal's quiet strength and approachable nature would be crucial in the early stages of recruitment.

Hadi Abu-Salem was another candidate Ahmed considered valuable. Though Hadi was not part of Ahmed's immediate group of friends, he had a quiet intensity that set him apart. Observant and patient, he could make people feel at ease around him, creating deeper connections with those who might be hesitant or unsure. Ahmed believed Hadi's gentle manner would help reach those who felt lost and needed a purpose.

However, Ahmed also knew he needed team members who could enforce discipline and instil urgency once the recruits were brought in. This was where Tariq and Khaled came in. Tariq, known for his ruthlessness and organisational skills, could maintain strict order among the recruits and ensure the training ran smoothly. Khaled, with his fiery spirit and natural authority, would be perfect for pushing the recruits to their limits, preparing them for the harsh realities ahead.

As the sun began to set over Gaza, casting long shadows across the narrow streets, Ahmed stood in a small, dimly lit room at the back of a local community centre. The air was thick with the scent of sweat and dust, the flickering bulb overhead casting long, uneven shadows that seemed to dance with the tension hanging between them.

Ahmed felt a mix of anxiety and determination. This was not the job he had expected, but it was the one he had been given. He glanced at his team, who were still adjusting to their new roles. Beside him were Bilal and Hadi, prepared for the delicate task of initial recruitment. Tariq and Khaled stood a little apart, their eyes sharp, watching Ahmed closely, ready to step in when necessary.

Tariq's gaze flicked to Ahmed, his expression thoughtful yet wary. *"You sure about starting with the schools?"* he asked, his tone measured.

"It's the best way," Ahmed replied, holding his gaze steadily.

Tariq shrugged, his shoulders tense. *"Your call,"* he murmured, a grudging note of deference in his voice. *"But if we waste too much time - "*

"We won't," Ahmed interrupted, his voice calm but firm. *"Trust me."*

Tariq held his gaze for a moment longer before nodding. *"Fine. We'll do it your way."*

Ahmed nodded back, acknowledging Tariq's compliance without letting his own resolve waver. He knew Tariq would follow him, but he also understood that Tariq's patience had its limits.

Abu Khaled broke the silence with a steady, commanding voice. *"Ahmed, this is a critical task. We need young recruits who are ready to learn, to be shaped for the challenges ahead. They must be prepared for any role, and the training must remain secret. We cannot afford mistakes."*

Ahmed nodded, feeling the weight of his responsibility settle like a stone in his chest. *"I understand,"* he replied, his voice steady though his hands felt clammy with sweat. *"But how do we start? Where do we find these recruits?"*

Bilal spoke, his tone serious yet calm. *"We start by looking where young people gather - schools, mosques, the streets. Many of them feel lost, with no clear future. They are frustrated, angry... looking for a purpose. We must offer them that purpose."*

Ahmed thought about the boys he often saw on the streets, aimlessly wandering or sitting in groups, their faces marked by boredom and resentment. He knew these were the ones he needed to reach - the ones who felt they had nothing left to lose.

"We should begin with the schools," Ahmed suggested, his voice firm but with a trace of doubt lurking underneath. *"Speak to the teachers, identify those students who seem restless, who question authority. Then we move to the streets - find those who have already abandoned formal education and need something to believe in."*

Bilal agreed. *"The streets are full of kids with nowhere to go,"* he said. *"They're waiting for someone to give them a reason to fight, a reason to matter."*

Abu Khaled nodded approvingly. *"Good. But remember, discretion is key. No one can know what we are doing, not even their families, until they are ready to commit. The training must be secret. Use safe houses, underground locations, and make sure they understand the importance of silence."*

Ahmed's mind raced with the possibilities and the risks. He caught sight of Abu Khaled's intense gaze, feeling a slight shiver run down his spine. There was something unsettling about the way Abu Khaled's eyes lingered, as if weighing him, testing him.

"Do not let me down, Ahmed," Abu Khaled murmured, stepping closer. His hand landed on Ahmed's shoulder, the grip firm. *"Your father had a vision for you, and I see it too. Remember, hesitation is dangerous. You must lead with conviction."*

The pressure in his chest tightened. *"I won't let you down, sir,"* Ahmed replied, holding Abu Khaled's gaze despite the unease twisting in his gut. He knew this was more than just a task, it was a test of his loyalty, his commitment. Abu Khaled wasn't just watching him - he was moulding him.

In the days that followed, Ahmed, Bilal, and Hadi began their recruitment efforts. They visited schools discreetly, speaking to teachers and identifying students who appeared discontent or rebellious. They approached these students quietly, inviting them to *"special meetings"* in hidden rooms or secluded corners of the school grounds where they could talk more freely.

Bilal and Hadi turned their attention to the streets, engaging groups of boys who loitered around markets or in narrow alleyways. They started with casual conversations about daily life, slowly introducing the idea that there were ways to fight back, ways to make a difference.

One evening, Bilal spotted a young boy standing alone, his shoulders hunched. He struck up a conversation, talking about football and school, watching as the boy's wary expression softened. Eventually, Bilal asked about his family, and the boy's face tightened.

"My brother was killed last year," the boy whispered, staring at the ground. *"He was just trying to help..."*

Bilal placed a hand on the boy's shoulder, his expression gentle. *"That's hard. But it doesn't have to end there. You can make a difference, make sure no one else has to lose their brother."*

The boy looked up, eyes wide with a mix of hope and pain. *"How?"* he asked quietly.

"By standing with us," Bilal replied softly. *"We can help you become strong, so you can protect those who matter."*

The boy nodded slowly, a spark of something fierce in his gaze. Watching from a distance, Ahmed felt a pang of something he couldn't name - a mixture of pride and unease. He turned away, wondering if he was truly giving these boys a chance at strength, or just leading them into more suffering.

In the following weeks, the training began in earnest. Ahmed used the methods he had learned: long runs at dawn, basic combat skills, weapon handling, and silent movement at night. But during one session, a young recruit faltered.

"What are we training for?" the boy asked, his voice trembling slightly. *"Are we... are we going to fight?"*

Ahmed hesitated, his gaze sweeping over the wide-eyed recruits. He glanced at Bilal, who remained silent, waiting.

"We're training for the future," Ahmed replied slowly, choosing his words carefully. *"To be ready for whatever comes."*

The boy nodded, but the uncertainty lingered in his eyes. Ahmed felt a flash of guilt, quickly smothered. He couldn't afford to doubt - not now, not ever.

But as the days wore on, Salma's voice echoed in his mind: *"Sometimes the only thing keeping us human is asking the right questions."*

And Ahmed couldn't shake the feeling that maybe, just maybe, he was starting to forget what it meant to be human.

Despite the progress, Ahmed couldn't shake the sense of unease that seemed to shadow him constantly. At night, Salma's words echoed in his mind, prompting questions he wasn't sure he wanted to answer. He looked at the young recruits, boys with faces that still held traces of childhood, and wondered if he was truly leading them towards a future they would one day want - or simply repeating a cycle of pain and loss.

One day, Tariq cornered him after a training session. *"You're being too soft on them,"* he growled, his eyes flashing with irritation. *"They're not going to learn anything if you keep coddling them."*

Ahmed stiffened but kept his expression neutral. *"They're learning. You can see it in their movements. They're improving."*

Tariq scoffed, crossing his arms. *"Improving? That's not enough. They need to be pushed, Ahmed. They need to be hardened, like we were. You think the enemy's going to go easy on them?"*

"I know what they need," Ahmed replied evenly, meeting Tariq's gaze. *"But there's more to being a fighter than just toughness. They need to believe in why they're doing this."*

For a moment, they stood in tense silence, eyes locked. Then Tariq looked away, shaking his head with a muttered curse. *"You're too cautious,"* he said, his voice low. *"We can't afford cautious."*

"We can't afford recklessness either," Ahmed countered quietly, watching Tariq's jaw tighten. *"They'll be ready. But it has to be done right."*

Tariq didn't respond, just turned on his heel and stalked off. As he watched him go, Ahmed felt a familiar pang of frustration mixed with guilt. Tariq and Khaled trusted him, followed him, but they didn't understand his caution. To them, hesitation was a weakness - one they couldn't afford.

And maybe they were right. But still, the doubts gnawed at him, whispering that there had to be a different way, that pushing these boys too hard, too fast would break something inside them that could never be repaired.

Chapter Eighteen

YOSSI

The days after the acceptance call are filled with a strange mix of excitement and a sense of inevitability. Yossi and Nadav spend their last few moments of civilian life preparing, both mentally and physically, for what lies ahead. There's an unspoken tension between them - a shared understanding that this is the start of something monumental, something that will change them both. The two weeks pass quickly, filled with goodbyes, well-wishes, and quiet moments of reflection.

The evening before Giyus (The Draft), Yossi and Nadav find themselves at their favourite spot by the beach, surrounded by their closest friends. The sunset paints the sky in hues of deep orange and gold, casting long shadows across the sand as the waves roll in gently. They sit in a tight circle, laughter and quiet murmurs mixing with the distant hum of Tel Aviv's nightlife.

"Feels like everything's going to change," Samir murmurs, his gaze distant as he stares out at the horizon. *"I know we've been preparing for this forever, but... now that it's here, it feels different."*

Yossi glances at Samir, understanding exactly what he means. There's a finality to this moment - a sense that the Chapter they're closing tonight will never fully be reopened. They've dreamed of their futures, talked about their goals, but now, the reality of military life looms in a way that's tangible and immediate.

"It is different," Yossi agrees softly, his eyes moving around the circle. He takes in each face, each expression - the people he's grown up with, shared countless memories with. They've always been there, a constant in a world of change, and now they're all about to step into their own separate worlds. *"But it's not the end. We'll find our way back here. We always do."*

Maya looks up from her sketchbook, her smile tinged with sadness. *"A new beginning, maybe. But it's still hard to let go of what we have now."*

Leila nods, her gaze shifting between Nadav and Yossi. *"We've always been together. It's going to be strange not seeing you every day."*

The words hang heavy in the air, laced with the unspoken fears and hopes they all share. Nadav clears his throat, glancing around at his friends.

"We're all going in different directions," he says, his voice steady, though there's a tightness around his eyes that betrays his emotion. *"But we'll stay connected. We'll make time, no matter what. This - "* he gestures around them, at the group huddled close together *" - this doesn't go away."*

There's a murmur of agreement, and Leila's gaze softens as she looks at Nadav, a small smile playing on her lips. *"Yeah. We'll make sure of it."*

Silence falls over the group again, each of them lost in their own thoughts. Yossi turns slightly, feeling Yael's hand slip into his. He meets her eyes, and for a moment, it's just the two of them, the rest of the world falling away.

"Promise me you'll be careful," Yael whispers, her voice low and urgent. *"Promise me you'll come back to me."*

Yossi's throat tightens. He wants to promise her the world, to reassure her that everything will be fine. But he knows better. He knows the risks, the unpredictability of the path they're about to walk. Instead, he squeezes her hand gently.

"I'll do everything I can," he murmurs. *"And you... stay strong. Keep doing what you're doing. We're going to get through this."*

Yael nods, blinking rapidly, a tremulous smile breaking through. *"Okay,"* she whispers, her fingers tightening around his. *"I believe in you."*

Nearby, Nadav and Leila sit a little apart from the rest, the space between them charged with unspoken words. Leila traces patterns in the sand with her finger, not quite looking at Nadav.

"Are you scared?" she asks softly, her voice barely audible over the sound of the waves.

Nadav hesitates, then nods slowly. *"Yeah,"* he admits quietly. *"But... mostly I'm excited. This is what I've always wanted."*

Leila's smile is small and sad. *"I know. You're going to be amazing, Nadav. You always are."*

Nadav opens his mouth as if to say something more, something deeper, but then closes it again, his gaze dropping to the sand. *"We'll see each other again soon,"* he says instead, his voice gruff. *"This isn't goodbye."*

Leila nods, blinking back tears. *"Not goodbye,"* she agrees softly. *"Just... see you later."*

The group lingers like that for a while longer, sharing laughter and quiet moments of reflection. There's a sense of finality to it all, an unspoken understanding that after this night, everything will change. But there's also hope - hope that these bonds, forged over so many years, will hold strong no matter what lies ahead.

As the night deepens, they finally stand, exchanging lingering hugs and promises to stay in touch. Yossi looks around at his friends one last time, committing every face, every expression, to memory.

"Whatever happens," he says, his voice low and steady, *"we don't forget this. We don't forget each other."*

"Never," Samir agrees, his grin returning, fierce and bright.

"Always together," Amir adds, clapping Yossi on the shoulder.

Leila and Maya nod, their eyes bright with emotion.

"Always," Yael whispers, her hand still in Yossi's, her grip tight and warm.

"*Yeah,*" Nadav echoes quietly, his gaze lingering on each of them, as if trying to memorise every detail. "*Always.*"

And then, with one last look, they turn and part ways, each of them heading off into the night, carrying the weight of friendship, love, and hope into whatever the future holds.

The next morning, Yossi stands outside his house, his duffle bag slung over his shoulder, the early morning light casting long shadows across the quiet street. His parents are beside him, their faces a mix of pride and worry.

"*You have everything?*" Ruth fusses, adjusting the strap of his bag even though it's already perfectly in place.

"*I have everything, Mum,*" Yossi reassures her, forcing a smile. He glances at his father, who's watching silently, his expression serious.

"*Remember what I said,*" David murmurs, stepping forward to clasp Yossi's shoulder. "*Stay strong, stay focused. And don't lose sight of who you are.*"

Yossi nods, feeling the weight of his father's words settle over him. "*I won't.*"

Then, with one last hug from his mother and a firm handshake from his father, Yossi turns and heads towards the induction centre, his heart racing. The streets are already filling with other young men and women, all heading in the same direction, all about to take the same leap.

Nadav meets him at the entrance, his grin wide and unrestrained. "*Ready for this?*" he asks, his eyes shining with excitement.

Yossi nods, a surge of adrenaline pushing back the nerves. "*Ready.*"

They step through the gates together, joining the line of new recruits. It's a long, methodical process - filling out forms, getting issued their uniforms, equipment, and finally, their rifles. Yossi holds his rifle carefully, feeling the cold weight of it in his hands. This is real now. He isn't just a candidate anymore. He's a soldier.

"*Look at us,*" Nadav whispers, his voice tinged with awe. "*We're really doing it.*"

Yossi glances at him, a smile tugging at his lips. *"Yeah. We are."*

The days that follow Yossi and Nadav's induction into the Tzanchanim Brigade (The Paratroopers Brigade) blur into a relentless rhythm of sweat, dirt, and exhaustion. Basic training is an unending cycle of physical drills, tactical exercises, and the harsh scrutiny of their instructors. Each morning begins long before dawn, the world around them shrouded in darkness, the air cold and biting as they scramble to fall into formation for the morning run.

Yossi's body aches constantly - the familiar burn in his legs from the endless sprints, the sharp pain in his shoulders from the heavy packs they carry, and the rawness of his hands from gripping ropes and weapons for hours on end. Yet, every time his muscles scream for relief, his thoughts shift to Nadav beside him, his best friend moving with a determination that keeps Yossi's own resolve from faltering.

But it isn't always Nadav setting the pace. Yossi has his own strengths. While Nadav excels at physical endurance, charging through the morning runs and pushing Yossi to keep up, it's in the tactical and leadership drills that Yossi finds his footing. As the days stretch into weeks, Yossi begins to notice how the other recruits subtly look to him when the instructions become complex or when they face new scenarios that require quick thinking.

One gruelling afternoon, after hours of running with weighted packs, the recruits are dropped into the wilderness of the training grounds, tasked with navigating through dense brush and rugged terrain using only a map and compass. The goal is simple: find their way back to base before nightfall. But exhaustion makes the simplest tasks seem insurmountable, and as the shadows lengthen, murmurs of uncertainty spread through the group.

"Yossi," Nadav says quietly, nodding to the map they share. *"What's the call? North ridge or the ravine?"*

Yossi studies the lines on the map, the muscles in his jaw clenching as he makes the decision. *"The ridge. We'll make better time up there, and the visibility is better. It'll be harder, but faster."*

A few of the other recruits glance at each other, hesitant. But Nadav gives a firm nod, his trust in Yossi's judgement clear. *"You heard him,"* Nadav says sharply. *"Let's move."*

They scramble up the rocky slope, sweat pouring down their faces, every breath a struggle. Yossi takes the lead, setting a pace that's gruelling but steady. He doesn't let the pain show on his face, doesn't let the fear of being wrong shake his focus. And when a few of the others begin to lag, Nadav is right there, pushing them forward, taking on some of the weight of their packs without a word.

"Come on," Nadav grunts, helping a struggling recruit over a boulder. *"Stay with us. We've got this."*

As the sun dips below the horizon, casting everything in a dim, dusky light, they crest the ridge. The sight of the training base in the distance is like a jolt of energy through the entire group. They've made it - together.

"Nice call, Yossi," Nadav mutters, clapping him on the shoulder as they trudge the last stretch back to base. Yossi just nods, his chest tight with a quiet pride.

Shooting drills become another battleground for endurance and precision. The hours on the range stretch endlessly, the sun baking down on their backs as they lay prone in the dirt, rifles aimed and steady. Nadav's breathing is always even, his shots hitting the target with an almost casual ease that makes it look effortless. Yossi, though, struggles at first. His muscles twitch, his focus wavers as fatigue sets in.

"Stop thinking about it so much," Nadav whispers once, his voice low and calm. *"You're tense. Just breathe, and let your instincts take over."*

Yossi's hands shake slightly as he takes aim again, the weight of the rifle a familiar pressure against his shoulder. He lets out a long breath, then squeezes the trigger slowly. The shot hits dead centre, the metal clang echoing through the range.

"There you go," Nadav murmurs with a grin. *"I knew you had it."*

From that moment, every time Yossi's mind begins to overthink, he remembers Nadav's advice - just breathe, let go - and his shots grow more confident, his posture steadier.

As the weeks pass, Yossi's knack for quick thinking and his calm under pressure begin to draw the attention of the instructors. During one particularly intense field exercise, the recruits are split into teams and given a single task: set up an ambush and capture the opposing team's leader. With Nadav beside him, Yossi quickly outlines a plan - flanking manoeuvres, strategic positioning, signals for when to move and when to hold.

"We need someone on the high ground," Nadav says, glancing around the rough terrain. *"But we don't have the manpower."*

Yossi shakes his head, already formulating a solution. *"We'll use decoys - two groups, drawing their attention. You and I will go around the side and take out their leader when they're distracted."*

There's no hesitation in Nadav's eyes, just a firm nod. They move silently, coordinating the other recruits with a few quick hand signals. The ambush goes off without a hitch - Yossi and Nadav crash through the underbrush, tackling the opposing leader to the ground before he even knows they're there.

"Well done, Rosenberg," the instructor barks as the whistle blows. *"You used what you had, didn't waste a second. That's the kind of thinking we need."*

Yossi feels Nadav's hand grip his shoulder, a brief squeeze of shared triumph. This is where Yossi shines, where his quick decision-making and understanding of tactics make the difference. And Nadav is always there, backing him up without question, letting Yossi take the lead when it matters.

But the physical training - that's where Nadav pulls Yossi through. Every run, every climb up the ropes, every punishing set of push-ups after a long day in the field, Yossi feels his strength waver. And every time, Nadav is there, setting the pace, his voice low and steady in the dark.

"Keep moving. Don't think. Just one more rep."

They collapse onto their bunks at night, bodies trembling with fatigue, and Yossi shoots Nadav a grateful look. Nadav just grins, his eyes bright despite the exhaustion. *"You carried me today, Yossi. Tomorrow, I'll carry you."*

It's a balance, a constant give-and-take. Where one falters, the other is there to steady them. Where one feels the weight of exhaustion or doubt, the other pushes back with a surge of strength.

On their rare weekends off, they head back to Tel Aviv, their bodies still aching but their spirits lighter. Yossi's heart leaps each time he sees Yael's name flash on his phone, and those brief reunions are a balm to the constant grind of training. They steal a few moments by the beach, holding hands as the waves lap at their feet.

"You look stronger," Yael says quietly, her fingers tracing the calluses on his hands. *"But... tired."*

Yossi just smiles. *"I'm fine. It's worth it, Yael. I'm learning so much."*

They sit together, the weight of unspoken words between them. Yossi notices the way Yael's gaze lingers on his face a moment longer than usual, the way her fingers tighten around his as if trying to hold onto something solid in the midst of change.

"Just promise me you won't push yourself too far," she murmurs.

Yossi's smile softens. *"I'll be careful. And you... stay safe too. We're going to get through this."*

They share a quiet moment, looking out at the darkening sea, the future looming uncertainly ahead. And when the weekend is over, Yossi and Nadav board the bus back to base, feeling the bonds of home and friendship tighten around them like a safety net.

Back at the training grounds, the instructors ramp up the intensity, building up to the final phase of basic training. The days blur together - a relentless grind of physical and mental tests, each one designed to push them past their breaking point.

The toughest of these tests comes one rainy morning. The recruits are woken before dawn, the sky still pitch black, and ordered to assemble on the parade ground. Yossi and Nadav exchange weary looks, their uniforms already soaked through. The rain pelts down in cold sheets, turning the ground into a slick, muddy mess.

"*Today,*" the instructor shouts, his voice cutting through the downpour, "*you'll be completing the endurance course. Each one of you will carry full packs. There's no time limit - just finish.*"

Yossi's shoulders tense as he hoists his pack onto his back, the weight pressing down on him like a boulder. He catches Nadav's eye, seeing the same determination mirrored there. They're ready.

The course is brutal. Mud clings to their boots, slowing every step. They crawl under barbed wire, scramble up steep embankments, and haul themselves over obstacles that seem to loom higher with every lap. Yossi's muscles scream in protest, his breaths coming in harsh, ragged gasps.

But he doesn't stop. He grits his teeth, forcing himself to keep going, even when his vision blurs with exhaustion, even when every fibre of his being begs him to drop to the ground and rest. Ahead, he spots Nadav pushing through, his movements steady and unrelenting.

For a moment, Yossi falters, the pack feeling impossibly heavy. But then he hears Nadav's voice cutting through the roar of the rain.

"*One step at a time, Yossi. You've got this!*"

The encouragement is like a lifeline. Yossi straightens, his resolve hardening. He's stronger than this. He *has* to be.

They trudge through the course together, urging each other on. When Nadav slips in the mud, Yossi is there in an instant, grabbing his arm and hauling him up.

"*Not now, Nadav,*" he grunts, his voice rough with effort. "*You're stronger than this.*"

Nadav lets out a breathless laugh. *"Right back at you."*

By the time they reach the final obstacle - a towering wall of rough-hewn logs - they're both drenched and trembling with exhaustion. Yossi's hands shake as he grips the wet wood, his arms straining as he pulls himself up. For a moment, he thinks he won't make it. His fingers slip, his muscles burn, and his body feels like it's giving out.

But then Nadav is beside him, pushing against his back, steadying him.

"Come on, Yossi," he gasps. *"Almost there."*

With a final burst of strength, Yossi hauls himself over the top, collapsing onto the other side with a grunt. A second later, Nadav lands beside him, both of them panting, their chests heaving.

They lie there for a moment, staring up at the grey sky, the rain falling in relentless sheets around them.

"We did it," Nadav whispers, his voice hoarse but triumphant.

Yossi just nods, too exhausted to speak. But there's a smile tugging at his lips - a smile that lingers even as the instructor's whistle blows, signalling the end of the drill.

They're not just surviving anymore. They're thriving.

And as they stumble back to the barracks, soaked and battered but victorious, Yossi feels something new stirring within him. Confidence. Strength. A sense of purpose that cuts through the exhaustion and pain.

Because this is who he's becoming. A leader. A soldier. A paratrooper.

And whatever comes next, he knows he's ready.

Chapter Nineteen

AHMED

Ahmed's days were filled with more than just recruitment and training, he was slowly realising that his role within the community was evolving into something he hadn't anticipated. As he and his team continued their efforts to draw in new recruits for Hamas, Ahmed began to understand that success required more than secrecy and strategy - it hinged on earning the trust of the local people. The aggressive actions of his past, led by some of his more hot-headed friends, had left a lingering fear that was hard to erase. Ahmed knew he had to change this, and the weight of that responsibility bore down on him every day.

He decided to make himself more visible around the neighbourhood, moving through the crowded markets and narrow streets with a calm, approachable demeanour. He greeted shopkeepers with a smile, helped elderly neighbours carry their groceries, and took time to speak with parents watching over their children. Slowly, he tried to show a different side of himself - the side that cared about the community and wanted to protect it, not intimidate it.

Yet, as he moved through the streets, Ahmed couldn't shake the feeling that his past clung to him like dust. *How do they see me now?* he wondered. *Do they still see the boy whose friends were volent, or can they see that I'm trying to change?* He hoped they would notice his efforts, but he knew it would take time. Trust, once broken, is hard to rebuild. *I have to be patient... I have to show them.*

Ahmed's new approach was met with mixed reactions. Some people remained wary, their memories of his anger and violence too fresh. They would nod at him but kept their distance, their eyes betraying caution. Others, however, seemed cautiously hopeful, curious about the change in his attitude. Ahmed knew it wasn't going to happen overnight. He would have to prove himself again and again, walking a fine line between redemption and rejection.

He began visiting families affected by past violence, expressing his regret and listening to their concerns. *"We need your support,"* he would say earnestly, leaning forward, his voice soft but firm. *"I know there has been fear, but we want to bring change, to build something stronger and safer for our children. The path ahead is difficult, but we want to walk it together."*

But even as Ahmed spoke these words, the fear of failure gnawed at him. *What if they didn't believe him? What if his past was too much to overcome? What if I fail?* He thought it often but never spoke aloud. He couldn't afford to show that doubt.

Gradually, Ahmed began to notice a shift. Some community members started greeting him with nods instead of cold stares. A few even offered words of encouragement, acknowledging his efforts to make amends. It wasn't a complete transformation, but it was a start. Still, the shadow of doubt remained. *Will they ever trust me? Or will I always be seen as the boy who caused pain?*

Bilal and Hadi supported Ahmed's outreach efforts, using their quiet influence to help ease tensions. Bilal, with his calm and friendly manner, spoke with young people who lingered on street corners, making them feel seen and heard. He listened to their frustrations and dreams, patiently explaining how they could channel their energy into something meaningful. Hadi, with his thoughtful approach, would sit down with families, assuring them that their sons would be cared for and would not be forced into anything they didn't understand.

Meanwhile, Tariq and Khaled, known for their more aggressive methods, struggled with Ahmed's new strategy. They had always been the ones to employ force and intimidation, and Ahmed could tell they found his attempts at peace-building frustrating. Though they had agreed to his approach, their aggression was never far from the surface. They were like coiled springs, their tempers held in check but always ready to snap.

One evening, after another exhausting day of outreach, Ahmed sat down with Tariq and Khaled in a quiet alleyway. The tension between them was palpable, and Ahmed knew he had to address it. Tariq crossed his arms, his gaze hard.

"This isn't working, Ahmed," he said bluntly. *"You're wasting time trying to win over people who are more likely to turn on us than stand with us."*

Khaled, standing beside him, nodded in agreement, his fists clenched. *"If you want loyalty, make them fear you,"* he growled. *"That's how it's always been."*

Ahmed took a deep breath, steadying himself. He knew this moment was crucial. If he backed down now, he'd lose their respect - and possibly their support.

"We've tried that already," Ahmed replied calmly, his voice firm. *"And look where it's gotten us. People fear us, yes, but that fear means they'll turn on us the moment they get the chance. We need something stronger than fear - we need trust."*

Tariq's eyes narrowed. *"And what makes you think they'll ever trust us?"*

"Because I'm giving them a reason to," Ahmed said, holding Tariq's gaze steadily. *"By showing them that we're here to protect them, not harm them. That we're building something worth fighting for."*

Khaled scoffed, shaking his head. *"Softness won't win this war."*

"And brutality won't win the people," Ahmed shot back, his tone sharpening. He stepped closer, his eyes blazing with intensity. *"I'm not asking you to abandon our strength, Khaled. I'm asking you to channel it. Use it to show our recruits discipline and determination, not just fear. If you want them to follow us, make them believe in us."*

For a moment, there was silence. Tariq shifted, his jaw clenched tight. Then, almost reluctantly, he nodded.

"Fine," he muttered. *"But if this goes wrong..."*

"It won't," Ahmed interrupted, his voice strong and steady. *"Because I'm not going to let it."*

Khaled stared at him, then let out a low, grudging chuckle. *"You've got guts, Ahmed. I'll give you that."*

Ahmed allowed himself a small, tight smile. *"I need more than guts. I need you both to trust me, like I trust you."*

Tariq's gaze softened just slightly, and he uncrossed his arms. *"We're with you. For now. Just... don't make us regret it."*

"I won't," Ahmed promised, meeting their eyes one by one. *"We're going to win them over - together."*

The moment passed, the tension easing slightly. Tariq and Khaled exchanged a look, then nodded. It wasn't total acceptance, but it was enough for now.

Over the following weeks, Tariq and Khaled began to adjust, albeit slowly. Tariq managed logistics, ensuring the training sessions ran smoothly, but he also started speaking more gently with the new recruits, encouraging them rather than intimidating them. Khaled, with his intense energy, channelled it into motivating the young men during their physical training sessions. He found ways to challenge them without resorting to threats, though Ahmed could tell it was a constant struggle to hold back the fire that burned inside him.

One afternoon, during a meeting with a local elder named Ibrahim, a respected teacher in the neighbourhood, Ahmed was confronted with the mistrust of the past.

"Your friends have caused much pain here," Ibrahim said, his voice heavy with the weight of past wrongs. *"Why should we trust you now?"*

Ahmed met his gaze steadily. *"I know the damage that's been done,"* he replied quietly. *"And I want to fix it. I want to show the young people a better way - a way where they are part of something bigger, something that protects them and their families. I can't change the past, but I want to build a better future."*

Ibrahim studied him, then nodded slowly. *"You have a difficult path ahead of you,"* he said. *"But if you're sincere, you'll have our support."*

Encouraged by this small victory, Ahmed continued to reach out, making connections wherever he could. He knew the path ahead was uncertain, but with his team by his side, he was ready to face whatever came next.

As the days passed, Ahmed's efforts to gain the community's trust slowly began to bear fruit. More families started welcoming him into their homes, and young men who once shied away now approached him with questions about how they could join the cause. Ahmed sensed a shift - subtle, but there. The neighbourhood that had once looked at him with suspicion was beginning to see him as more than just a fighter. They were beginning to see him as a leader.

But this transformation brought new challenges. With each new face that joined their ranks, Ahmed felt the weight of responsibility growing heavier. These boys looked to him for guidance, for reassurance. He knew that one wrong step could send everything crumbling down.

One evening, he sat with Bilal and Hadi in a makeshift office they'd set up in an abandoned building on the edge of the neighbourhood. Maps and charts lined the walls, detailing the locations of training areas, safe houses, and routes for supplies. A single lantern flickered in the corner, casting long shadows across their faces.

"We're getting more recruits than we expected," Bilal observed, his brow furrowed. *"That's a good thing, but... it's a lot to handle. We need to be careful not to grow too fast."*

Ahmed nodded thoughtfully. *"Agreed. But we can't turn anyone away. If they're coming to us, it's because they need somewhere to belong. We just need to make sure we're training them properly."*

Hadi leaned forward, his eyes serious. *"And what about Tariq and Khaled?"* he asked quietly. *"I know they've adjusted, but... I worry they might lose patience. This kind of work isn't what they're used to."*

Ahmed sighed, rubbing a hand over his face. He knew Hadi was right. Tariq and Khaled had been more cooperative lately, but he could sense their frustration simmering beneath the surface. They craved action - something tangible to remind them of why they were doing this. Patience had never been their strong suit.

"I'll talk to them again," Ahmed said firmly. "Make sure they understand the plan."

"And if they don't?" Bilal asked softly, his gaze steady.

"They will," Ahmed replied, his voice resolute. "They're part of this, just like we are. I just need to keep showing them that this approach will work."

Later that night, Ahmed found Tariq and Khaled in the small training yard behind their safe house, working with some of the newer recruits. The boys were lined up in a rough formation, sweating and panting as they completed a series of intense exercises. Khaled barked orders at them, his voice harsh, pushing them to their limits.

Ahmed watched quietly for a moment, taking in the scene. There was discipline here, yes, but there was also fear. The boys looked at Khaled with wide eyes, their bodies trembling with exhaustion. It wasn't the kind of strength Ahmed wanted to cultivate. Fear might drive them now, but it would shatter them later.

"*Enough,*" Ahmed called out, stepping forward.

Khaled turned, his brow furrowed. "*They need to be tougher,*" he growled. "*Weakness gets them killed.*"

"*I'm not saying to go easy on them,*" Ahmed replied, keeping his voice calm but firm. "*But fear isn't the answer. If you want them to fight, make them believe in themselves. Not just in us.*"

Tariq, who had been leaning against the wall, pushed himself upright, his expression guarded. "*And how do you suggest we do that?*" he asked, a hint of challenge in his voice.

Ahmed stepped closer, looking between the two of them. "*By showing them what it means to be strong. Real strength isn't just about how hard you can hit. It's about control. Restraint. Knowing when to push and when to hold back. If they only follow orders out of fear, they'll never truly be loyal. They'll break the moment things get tough.*"

Khaled crossed his arms, his eyes narrowed. *"And you think talking to them gently will make them better fighters?"*

"No," Ahmed said quietly. *"But making them feel valued will. Make them understand why we're doing this, and they'll push themselves harder than we ever could. You both know what it's like to be driven by something bigger than yourself. That's what we need to give them."*

For a long moment, there was silence. Tariq and Khaled exchanged a look, then turned back to Ahmed.

"You're asking a lot," Tariq murmured. *"To change everything we've done... just like that."*

"I'm not asking you to change who you are," Ahmed said steadily. *"Just the way you show it. You're both strong - stronger than any of us. Let them see that strength in a way that inspires them, not just scares them."*

Khaled exhaled sharply, shaking his head. *"You really think this will work?"*

"I do," Ahmed replied, his gaze unwavering. *"But I need you both to believe in it too."*

There was another long pause, then, slowly, Tariq nodded.

"Alright," he said grudgingly. *"We'll try it your way."*

Khaled grunted, his expression still sceptical. *"For now,"* he muttered. *"But if they start slacking off..."*

"They won't," Ahmed interrupted, his voice firm. *"Because you won't let them. Use your strength to push them, Khaled. Just don't crush them in the process."*

Khaled stared at him for a moment longer, then finally nodded. *"Fine,"* he said, his tone resigned. *"But you'd better be right about this."*

Ahmed allowed himself a small smile. *"Trust me,"* he said softly. *"This will work. We're building something more than just soldiers here. We're building a future."*

As the days turned into weeks, Ahmed's new approach began to take root. Tariq and Khaled, true to their word, adjusted their methods - though with visible reluctance. Tariq focused on teaching the recruits strategy and tactics, encouraging them to think before they acted, to plan and consider the consequences of their decisions. Khaled, while still intense, shifted his focus to building resilience, pushing the boys to dig deeper, to find strength in places they didn't know existed.

The change wasn't immediate, and there were moments of friction - times when Khaled's temper flared or when Tariq's patience wore thin. But slowly, Ahmed could see the results. The boys began to respond differently, not just obeying commands but asking questions, seeking to understand the purpose behind their training.

One evening, after a long day, Ahmed found himself sitting on the roof of their safe house, gazing out over the quiet streets of Gaza. The stars were faint, barely visible through the haze of the city. He heard footsteps behind him and turned to see Salma approaching.

"I heard what you did with Tariq and Khaled," she said softly, sitting down beside him.

"It's not much," Ahmed replied, his voice low. *"But it's a start."*

Salma smiled, a gentle, approving smile that made something inside him relax. *"You're changing things, Ahmed. For the better. You're showing them there's more to this fight than just force."*

He glanced at her, studying her expression. *"Do you really think that?"* he asked quietly. *"Sometimes I wonder if I'm just delaying the inevitable."*

"No," she said firmly, placing a hand on his arm. *"You're giving them hope. And that's something we need more than anything."*

Ahmed looked out over the city again, his heart heavy but his resolve strong. *"I hope you're right,"* he murmured. *"Because we're going to need every bit of it for what's to come."*

The road ahead was still fraught with uncertainty, but Ahmed knew one thing for sure - he was willing to fight for this, for the trust he was building and the future he was shaping. One day at a time, he would continue on this path, leading his team and his people towards something greater. Something they could all believe in.

Chapter Twenty

YOSSI

The air is thick with anticipation as the recruits assemble in the pre-dawn darkness, the chill biting through their fatigues. Yossi stands in formation beside Nadav, feeling the weight of his gear pressing down on his shoulders. His combat backpack is heavy, stuffed with nearly 25 kilograms of equipment - extra clothing, rations, water, and survival gear. The rifle slung across his chest adds another burden, its cold metal a stark reminder of the gravity of what lies ahead.

This is it - the final march of basic training, Yossi thinks, tightening the straps on his backpack. Around him, murmurs of nervous energy ripple through the ranks. They all know this will be the longest, hardest march they've faced yet - thirty kilometres through the rough, unforgiving terrain of the Samaria hills. The culmination of every gruelling hour they've spent pushing themselves beyond what they thought possible.

An instructor's voice cuts through the low hum.

"*Recruits! Today you prove yourselves. This is not about speed, but about endurance. Stick together, support each other, and finish as a team.*"

Yossi glances over at Nadav, who nods back, his expression set and determined. For weeks, they've pushed through every challenge together - tactical drills, endless sprints, and heavy lifts. Nadav has always been the stronger of the two when it comes to pure physical stamina, charging ahead even when others began to falter.

But tonight, it's not just about strength. It's about who can dig deeper when it matters most.

The order to begin comes sharply.

"*Move out!*"

They start at a brisk pace, the rhythmic crunch of boots on gravel and dirt forming an unbroken cadence. The night is silent except for the sounds of their breathing and the clinking of equipment. Each soldier is burdened with over thirty kilograms of weight, the packs seemingly growing heavier with every step. Yossi can feel the pressure in his lower back, the tightness in his calves as they navigate the uneven ground.

As they climb the first steep hill, Yossi's mind flashes back to the months of training that led them here - the runs before dawn, the punishing obstacle courses, and the constant pressure to prove themselves worthy. His legs are screaming, but he grits his teeth, refusing to show any sign of weakness. He looks around at his fellow recruits, seeing their tired faces, their laboured breathing, and knows they're all suffering. They've been pushed to their limits again and again, and now they're about to be pushed further.

Nadav's voice comes through the darkness, low and steady.

"*One step at a time, Yossi. Just keep moving.*"

Yossi nods, feeling a rush of gratitude. That's what Nadav does - keeps moving, keeps pushing, no matter the pain. But this march isn't just about making it to the end. It's about how they finish.

As they crest another hill, a sharp cry comes from somewhere behind them. Yossi's head snaps around, spotting a figure slumped on the ground. His heart sinks as he recognises Amit Cohen, a determined but quiet boy who's struggled with endurance since the start. His ankle is twisted awkwardly as he struggles to get up.

No, Yossi thinks, gritting his teeth. *Not now, Amit. Don't quit.*

"*Cover me,*" Yossi mutters to Nadav, and without waiting for a response, he drops back, kneeling beside the fallen recruit.

"*Amit, can you stand?*" he asks urgently, eyes scanning Amit's pale, pain-drawn face. They've shared quiet words of encouragement during training, but this moment feels different - more urgent, more real.

Amit looks up, his face twisted in pain, but nods weakly. "*I - I think so. But my pack... it's too much. I can't -*"

"*Don't worry,*" Yossi interrupts, bending down to shift some of the weight from Amit's pack onto his own shoulders. It's brutal, the added load digging into his already strained muscles, but he grits his teeth and pulls Amit up. "*Lean on me,*" he murmurs, his voice firm but encouraging. "*We're going to do this together, alright? Don't think about the distance, just stay with me.*"

Amit nods, his eyes wide with a mixture of pain and gratitude as he limps along beside Yossi. Yossi can feel his own strength waning, the straps of the packs cutting into his shoulders, but he forces himself to keep going. He catches Nadav's eye up ahead, and his friend slows slightly, giving Yossi a quick nod of approval before moving to help another recruit struggling under the weight of his own gear.

"*Push through,*" Nadav urges, his deep voice cutting through the murmur of exhaustion. "*Don't think about it - just keep moving. One step at a time.*"

That's Nadav's strength - his ability to keep others moving forward, no matter how broken or beaten down they feel. Yossi watches as Nadav loops an arm around one of the heavier-built recruits, practically dragging him up a steep incline, refusing to let him falter.

"*Stay with us!*" Nadav shouts, his voice filled with that stubborn energy that never seems to fade, even when his own legs are quivering under the strain. "*We don't leave anyone behind!*"

They march on through the night, the terrain growing more treacherous as the path narrows and winds through rocky outcroppings. The darkness is disorienting, the only light coming from their flashlights and the faint glimmer of stars above. Sweat mixes with the dust caking their skin, the air thick with the scent of wet earth and exhaustion.

Yossi's muscles scream for relief, every step a test of willpower. But he keeps pushing, pulling the limping Amit beside him. It's a torturous pace, every metre feeling like a mile, but slowly, they make progress. As the hours pass, he starts calling out softly to the other recruits around him.

"Just a little further... We're almost there... Stay together..."

His voice is calm, even when he's trembling with effort. He knows that if he falters, the others will too. They look to him now, the way they do in drills, and he can't let them see his own doubts, his own pain.

But it's Nadav who keeps their spirits high. As they stumble over rough patches, Nadav starts cracking jokes, his voice light and teasing despite the strain etched into his face.

"This is nothing," he calls out, grinning through the sweat streaming down his cheeks. *"Wait till we're doing this carrying each other!"*

A few tired chuckles ripple through the group, and for a moment, the exhaustion fades, replaced by a fierce determination to keep going, to finish this together. That's the difference between them - Yossi guides, steady and thoughtful, while Nadav drives them forward, fierce and unrelenting.

As dawn breaks, the first rays of sunlight spilling over the hills, they finally see it - the silhouette of the training base in the distance. A murmur of relief sweeps through the recruits, but the march isn't over yet. The last stretch is uphill, a brutal incline that tests every ounce of strength they have left.

Yossi's legs are shaking, and Amit is almost collapsing beside him. He catches Nadav's gaze one last time. They nod to each other, wordlessly agreeing - *this is where we make our stand.*

With a guttural cry, Yossi pulls the struggling recruit forward, matching Nadav's relentless pace step for step. The other recruits fall into line behind them, shoulders straightening, backs stiffening. The officers watching from ahead begin to murmur, noticing the sudden shift in energy.

Together, they crest the final hill and stumble onto the training ground, a ragged but united line of soldiers. Their packs slump to the ground, breaths heaving, faces streaked with dirt and sweat. For a moment, there's nothing but silence - then a quiet cheer rises, growing louder as the realisation sets in.

They did it.

Yossi turns to look at Nadav, who's grinning fiercely, his face lit with a pride that mirrors Yossi's own.

"*Well done, Rosenberg*," Nadav says, his voice rough but full of warmth. "*You led us through that one.*"

Yossi shakes his head, smiling despite the pain. "*We did it together.*"

After the march, the recruits are ordered into formation, their breaths coming in ragged gasps. Yossi can barely feel his legs - every muscle is trembling, his entire body numb from exhaustion. But he stands tall, shoulders squared, his gaze steady.

An officer steps forward, his eyes sweeping over the formation. There's a pause - a moment of silence as he looks at each of them in turn, his expression unreadable.

"*You've done well*," he says finally, his voice carrying across the stillness. "*You've pushed yourselves past your limits. You've proven that you have what it takes to continue forward in the Tzanchanim Brigade. Today, you're not just recruits. You're soldiers.*"

Yossi feels a rush of pride swell in his chest, the words cutting through the exhaustion. He glances at Nadav beside him, seeing the same pride mirrored in his friend's eyes.

"*This is only the beginning*," the officer continues, his gaze hardening. "*The real challenges lie ahead in Advanced Training. But today... today, you can be proud of what you've accomplished.*"

There's a moment of stillness, then, one by one, the recruits are called forward. Each recruit steps up to the officer, who places a unit pin into their trembling hands - a small symbol, a badge that marks them as soldiers of the Tzanchanim

Brigade, representing the blood, sweat, and pain they've poured into these past weeks.

When Yossi's name is called, he steps forward, his heart pounding. The unit insignia feels almost surreal in his hands - light and yet so heavy with meaning. He looks up at the officer, who nods once, a faint smile touching his lips.

"Well done, Rosenberg."

Yossi swallows hard, nodding in return. "*Thank you, sir.*"

He steps back into formation, the pin clutched tightly in his hand. Around him, the other recruits are doing the same - standing a little taller, a little straighter. And when the ceremony ends, the officer takes a step back, letting his gaze linger on the line of new soldiers.

"*Starting today, you are officially soldiers of the Tzanchanim Brigade,*" he announces, his voice firm. "*You've earned your place here. But don't get too comfortable. This was only the beginning.*"

A murmur ripples through the line - half pride, half trepidation.

"*You will now go on a week's leave to rest and recover,*" the officer continues, raising his voice over the shifting of bodies. "*Take the time to regroup, to spend it with your families. Because when you return, we'll begin Advanced Training.*"

Yossi feels his heart lift at the thought of seeing his family and friends again - a much-needed break after everything they've endured. Beside him, Nadav lets out a long breath, his shoulders visibly relaxing.

"*Use this time well,*" the officer warns, his tone turning stern. "*Because when you come back, it's only going to get tougher. Much tougher. You've proven that you have the potential to be paratroopers. Now, you will prove that you can become true soldiers of the Tzanchanim Brigade.*"

There's a moment of silence as the weight of his words sinks in. Then the officer steps back, his gaze sweeping over them one last time.

"*Rest well. And be ready.*"

With a final salute, he dismisses them. The recruits stand frozen for a second, the reality of what they've just achieved mingling with the looming shadow of what's still to come.

Yossi turns slowly, looking down at the insignia in his hand. Around him, the others are doing the same - some staring at it in disbelief, others clutching it to their chests as if it's the most precious thing in the world.

"*We did it,*" Nadav murmurs beside him, his voice filled with quiet wonder. "*We're really soldiers now.*"

Yossi looks up, meeting his friend's gaze. He nods slowly, a smile breaking across his face. "*Yeah. We did.*"

They're soldiers of the Tzanchanim Brigade now.

But this is just the beginning.

The week's leave comes as a welcome relief after the brutal march, but the reality of it sets in the moment Yossi steps off the bus in Tel Aviv. His entire body protests every movement, his legs stiff and uncooperative, his shoulders raw and aching. Each step sends a jolt of pain shooting up from his blistered feet, and the small of his back burns where the straps of his pack have rubbed his skin raw.

"*Feels like I'm walking on knives,*" he mutters to Nadav as they hobble down the street, their packs long discarded but the weight of exhaustion still pressing heavily on them.

Nadav lets out a low groan, his expression twisted in a wry grin. "*I think I left half my skin back on that hill. Never thought I'd be grateful for a proper bed again.*"

Yossi laughs softly, though even that small action makes his ribs ache. "*You and me both. Just try to keep up, old man.*"

They move slowly, each step a reminder of the gruelling ordeal they've just endured. By the time they reach their homes, Yossi's feet are swollen and tender, his shoulders rubbed so raw that every movement sends a sharp sting radiating through his back. He winces as he turns the key in the lock, the simple action feeling like a monumental effort.

The door swings open, and the familiar warmth of home washes over him. His mother, Ruth, rushes forward, her face tight with worry.

"*Yossi!*" she exclaims, her hands fluttering around him as if she doesn't know whether to hug him or scold him for pushing himself so hard. "Look at you - what have they done to you?"

"*I'm fine, Mum,*" Yossi says gently, though he can't hide the wince as she brushes against a sore spot on his shoulder. "*Just... a little worse for wear.*"

Ruth's eyes narrow, and she shakes her head, muttering under her breath as she ushers him inside. "*A little worse for wear, he says... You need rest, proper food, and those wounds cleaned up.*"

Yossi allows himself to be fussed over, letting his mother tend to his blisters and bruises. The familiar smells of home - fresh bread, the hint of rosemary and thyme from the kitchen - wrap around him like a balm. For the first time in weeks, he feels truly at ease.

"*You need to let those heal,*" Ruth frets as she smooths a bandage over the angry red patch on his shoulder. "*You can't go back like this. Tell them you need more time.*"

Yossi shakes his head gently. "*I'll be fine, Mum. I've got a week. I'll heal.*"

His father, David, stands quietly in the doorway, watching with a thoughtful expression. He doesn't speak much, just offers a nod of approval now and then. Yossi knows his father understands - he's been through this himself, years ago. There's a silent respect between them, a bond forged not just by blood but by shared experience.

"*I'm proud of you,*" David murmurs quietly as Yossi sits back, the worst of the stinging now soothed by the salve Ruth applied. "*You showed strength out there - real strength.*"

Yossi nods, the words sinking deep. "*Thanks, Dad.*"

The first few days blur by in a haze of rest and recovery. Yossi spends hours lying on the sofa, his body too sore to move much. He receives a constant stream of messages from Nadav, each one a mix of complaints and humour, as if they're both trying to convince themselves that they're not as broken as they feel.

"*Still alive?*" Nadav texts one morning, followed by a series of exaggerated 'dying' emojis.

"*Barely,*" Yossi replies, a smile tugging at his lips. "*But hey, we've got a week, right?*"

But it's when Yossi finally meets up with Yael that he feels a true sense of relief. The moment he sees her waiting at their favourite café, her face lighting up as he limps toward her, all the pain and exhaustion seem to melt away.

"*You look terrible,*" she murmurs, her fingers brushing gently over his arm as they sit down. "*How are you feeling?*"

"*Like I've been run over by a truck,*" Yossi admits, but his smile is genuine. "*But seeing you makes it better.*"

They spend the afternoon together, walking slowly along the beach, stealing quiet moments and whispered words. Yael's presence is a soothing balm, her laughter a welcome distraction from the dull ache that has settled into his bones. Nadav and Leila join them later, their reunion filled with laughter and the kind of teasing that only long-time friends can share.

"*Look at us,*" Leila jokes, glancing between Yossi and Nadav as they sit in the sand, still visibly stiff and sore. "*The mighty paratroopers, barely able to move.*"

"*We'll be back in shape soon,*" Nadav grumbles, though his eyes sparkle with amusement. "*Just give us a few days.*"

But even as they laugh and share stories, Yossi can feel the change in the air. They aren't just the carefree friends they were before, there's a new weight to their interactions, a sense of distance that has crept in, shaped by the trials of their training and the paths they're now walking.

The days pass quickly, a blur of shared meals, long talks, and quiet moments of reflection. But as the week draws to a close, Yossi feels the pull of the future tightening around him, the sense that something is shifting, something is waiting to be said.

One evening, Yossi and Yael sit together on the beach, the cool breeze ruffling their hair. Yossi hesitates before speaking, his voice tentative.

"Yael, I've been thinking a lot... about us, about what comes next."

Yael looks at him, her expression gentle.

"What are you thinking?" she asks softly.

Yossi takes a deep breath, his heart pounding.

"I love you, Yael. I feel like we have something real, something worth holding onto. I... I want to ask you to marry me."

For a moment, there is only the sound of the waves crashing against the shore. Yael's eyes widen in surprise, then soften with emotion.

"Yes, Yossi," she whispers, tears glistening in her eyes. *"Yes, I will marry you."*

Yossi's heart swells with joy.

"Really?" he asks, a smile spreading across his face.

"Really," she laughs, nodding. *"I want to spend my life with you."*

They sit there in the darkness, the stars beginning to twinkle above, holding each other as if the world has suddenly shrunk down to just the two of them. It feels like a promise, a vow shared under the vastness of the night sky.

Encouraged by their shared decision, Yossi speaks with his parents, Ruth and David, about his intentions the next day.

"I think I want to ask Yael to marry me," he confesses, excitement and a hint of nervousness in his voice.

Ruth smiles warmly.

"Yael is a wonderful girl, Yossi. We would be very happy to see you two together. But maybe it's best to wait until your military service is complete before getting married."

David nods thoughtfully.

"Focus on your service first, but if you are certain about your feelings, you should speak to her parents. It's respectful to ask for their approval before you propose."

Feeling supported, Yossi decides to meet with Yael's parents. To his relief, they are delighted, seeing the happiness in their daughter's eyes whenever she speaks of him. With their blessing, Yossi feels a sense of completeness - a sense that everything is falling into place.

Yossi and Yael made a quick stop at David's office. As Yossi stepped inside to speak with his father, Yael lingered in the small reception area, glancing around curiously. Her eyes settled on a young woman sitting at a desk in the corner, her dark hair pulled back neatly, a focused expression on her face as she sorted through a stack of files.

Feeling a little out of place, Yael approached her with a friendly smile. *"Hi,"* she said softly. *"I'm Yael. You must be new here?"*

The woman looked up, startled for a moment, then offered a polite smile. *"Yes, I am. I'm Salma,"* she replied. Her voice was soft, accented slightly, and there was a cautiousness in her gaze that caught Yael's attention.

"It's nice to meet you, Salma," Yael said warmly, extending her hand. Salma hesitated briefly, then shook it gently. *"Do you like working here?"* Yael asked, genuinely curious.

Salma nodded slowly. *"Yes, I do. Your… Mr Rosenberg is a good boss,"* she said, choosing her words carefully. *"Very fair."*

Yael's smile widened. *"That sounds like him,"* she agreed. *"I hope we see each other more. Maybe we could have coffee sometime?"*

Salma's eyebrows lifted in surprise. *"Coffee?"* she echoed, her gaze searching Yael's face as if trying to gauge her sincerity.

"Yes, coffee," Yael repeated with a laugh. *"I'd love to get to know you better."*

Salma hesitated, then nodded slowly, a small, genuine smile forming on her lips. *"I'd like that,"* she said softly.

Just then, Yossi stepped out of David's office, glancing between the two women. "*Everything okay?*" he asked, curious.

"*Just making a new friend,*" Yael replied lightly, glancing back at Salma. "*See you soon, Salma.*"

Salma nodded, watching them go, a thoughtful expression on her face as Yossi and Yael exited the building. Something about Yael's warmth lingered in the air, making Salma wonder if perhaps, for the first time, she had found a genuine connection in a place where she had always felt like an outsider.

As the week drew to a close, Yossi and Nadav packed their bags again, the soreness lingering but their spirits lifted. Yossi kept Yael's words and the promise they had made close to his heart, a light that guided him through the anticipation and the uncertainty of what lay ahead.

"*Ready to get back to it?*" Nadav asked, his grin bright despite the shadows under his eyes.

"*More than ready,*" Yossi replied, his gaze steady. "*Let's do this.*"

With a final glance at Tel Aviv's skyline, they boarded the bus back to the base, knowing that whatever challenges awaited them, they had something real to fight for.

Chapter Twenty One

AHMED

A strange calm had settled over Gaza, a deceptive stillness that made the streets feel like the surface of water - placid, yet ready to ripple with the slightest disturbance. Occasionally, missile strikes from Gaza into Israel triggered retaliatory bombings, shaking buildings and unsettling nerves. Yet, for now, there was a pause in the violence - a temporary respite that everyone knew could end at any time.

Ahmed walked through the quiet streets, feeling the eerie stillness wrap around him like a shroud. Every step felt heavier, his breaths shallow, as if the very air carried the weight of unspoken fears. He glanced around, noticing how people moved - hurried, heads down, wary of the peace that could break like a wave against rocks. It was a fragile calm, a silence that hummed with the tension of what lay beneath. Ahmed knew better than to trust it. *A pause,* he thought, *nothing more than a breath between battles.*

Under the watchful eye of Abu Khaled, he had become more deeply involved in the plans of Hamas. The older leader had taken a particular interest in Ahmed, impressed by how he had built connections with the local community, gaining their trust while fulfilling his duties as a recruiter. Ahmed's ability to balance his responsibilities with genuine engagement had not gone unnoticed. Abu Khaled saw in him the potential for a role beyond that of a mere recruiter.

Yet, despite the praise, Ahmed felt the growing weight of expectation on his shoulders. Sometimes he wondered what his father would say if he saw him now.

Pride, perhaps? Or disappointment? Would he understand the sacrifices Ahmed made, the lives he traded for this role? The thought of his father, the long talks they used to have, flickered briefly in his mind, only to be pushed away by the urgency of the present.

Meanwhile, Salma wrestled with her own conflicts. Her brief conversation with Yael lingered longer than she expected. The ease in Yael's smile, the way she spoke without fear or anger - those small details felt like a glimpse into a world Salma thought she'd never know. Yael had been kind, curious, and sincere in her empathy, treating Salma not as an outsider but as a person worthy of understanding. This had stirred something unfamiliar in Salma - a confusion that gnawed at her. She found herself thinking about that moment often, about how easily they had connected, even though, under different circumstances, they might have been seen as enemies.

Back in Gaza, Salma continued her daily routine: working at the law firm in Tel Aviv during the day and returning home before nightfall. Each time she crossed back into Gaza, the stark contrast between the lives on either side of the border became more apparent. She noticed the crumbling buildings, the scarcity of essential services, and the constant undercurrent of fear and uncertainty that enveloped her city. Every time she saw another tunnel being dug or heard whispers of a new plan for a large-scale operation, a sense of frustration and futility grew inside her.

The memory of an afternoon in Tel Aviv, just a few weeks prior, stayed with her. She had walked past a café, the air thick with the aroma of fresh bread and coffee. A mother had been laughing with her child, both oblivious to the world around them, their smiles full of light. Salma had stood there for a moment too long, her gaze lingering on the scene, an unfamiliar tightness growing in her chest. The world felt so close, yet so impossibly far.

One evening, after a long day, she sat with Ahmed in the small courtyard of his home. The sun was setting, casting a warm orange glow over the rooftops. She watched the fading light, her thoughts heavy.

"It's strange," she murmured, almost to herself, *"how they live over there. They talk about next week like it's a promise. They make plans as if the world isn't on the edge of breaking."*

Ahmed listened, sensing the conflict in her words. He fidgeted with the edge of his sleeve, avoiding her gaze. *"Their lives are easy,"* Ahmed said, his voice flat. *"They don't have to worry about tomorrow like we do."*

Salma sighed, her voice tinged with frustration. *"But what if we could have that too, Ahmed?"* she pressed, leaning forward. *"What if we could make plans without holding our breath?"* 'Sometimes I wonder... if all the money spent on tunnels and weapons was instead used to rebuild our streets, create jobs, open new schools... maybe things could be different. Maybe we wouldn't have to fight so hard just to survive.'

Ahmed felt a flicker of doubt, a brief hesitation, but he pushed it aside. He glanced away, his jaw tightening. *"If we don't defend ourselves, Salma, there won't be a future. Tunnels, rockets - they're the only things keeping us alive. You know that."*

Salma fell silent, her expression troubled. She looked down at her hands, tracing invisible patterns on the table. *"Maybe,"* she said softly, not breaking eye contact. *"But what if we're building a cage for ourselves, Ahmed? Maybe there's another way - one where we're not always waiting for the next blow to fall."*

Ahmed's face hardened, his eyes narrowing as he tried to push back the doubt creeping in. *"You're talking about dreams,"* Ahmed shot back, shaking his head. *"Dreams don't keep us alive."* His voice was tight, almost pleading. *"This is survival, Salma. We don't have the luxury to think that way - not now."*

Salma nodded, though her gaze remained distant. 'I know,' she whispered, 'but I still think... maybe it's worth considering.'

Ahmed, now more deeply embedded in the organisation, sensed that something significant was coming. Abu Khaled had hinted at a large-scale operation, something designed to take the fight to the enemy. The details remained vague, but the urgency was clear: preparations needed to begin immediately. The focus was on expanding the tunnel network, strengthening their defences, and intensifying the training of recruits.

Ahmed threw himself into the work with renewed determination. He saw it as a challenge, an opportunity to prove his value to the movement. His friends - Khaled, Hadi, Tariq, and Bilal - were equally committed, each playing a vital role. Tariq, with his sharp mind, managed logistics, ensuring supplies and resources were in place. Khaled, with his intense energy, pushed the recruits harder than ever, drilling them in endurance, discipline, and combat skills. Meanwhile, Hadi and Bilal focused on engaging with the community, building support for Hamas and recruiting new members.

Hadi, with his calm and thoughtful manner, spoke with parents and elders, listening to their concerns and explaining the importance of the movement's objectives. He assured them that their sons would be cared for, not coerced, and that their contributions would be meaningful and safe.

Bilal, equally charismatic but with a more fiery spirit, connected with the youth on the streets. He engaged them in conversations about their frustrations and dreams, presenting Hamas as a path to finding purpose and dignity in a world that often seemed devoid of both.

Amid the preparations, Ahmed could not ignore the growing murmurs among the people. Many were questioning why so much money and effort were devoted to tunnels and preparations for war when the needs of daily life - clean water, healthcare, decent housing - remained unmet.

He had heard their voices - the mothers who worried about feeding their children, the fathers who wondered why they couldn't fix the broken pipes or repair the crumbling homes. He understood their frustration, their need for something more immediate than tunnels and weapons. Ahmed felt the weight of these concerns but knew he could not let them distract him. *If we don't protect ourselves,* he thought, *what good will all the rest be?* And yet, even as he justified the need for preparation, he couldn't completely silence the questions creeping into his mind.

One night, after supervising another long day of tunnel construction, Abu Khaled pulled Ahmed aside. *'You are doing well, Ahmed,'* he said, his voice low and measured. *'But remember, what we build here is not just for today. It's for tomorrow, for the next battle and the one after that. We must always be ready.'*

As Abu Khaled spoke, Ahmed felt a flicker of uncertainty. He understood the necessity of preparation, the need to be ready for whatever came next. But Salma's words echoed in his mind, her vision of a future without tunnels and rockets, a future where the streets were filled with laughter instead of fear. He pushed the thought aside, focusing on Abu Khaled's steady gaze. *This is my path,* he reminded himself. *I chose this.* But still, the doubts lingered, whispering to him in the quiet moments when no one was watching.

'I know, Abu Khaled. I'm committed to this. But I also see the frustration among our people. They wonder why we aren't using our resources to build a better life now.'

Abu Khaled's face hardened, his tone sharp. *'And what good is a better life if we are not safe to enjoy it? What good are schools if they are bombed? What good are hospitals if they are destroyed? We must make sacrifices now for a greater future.'*

Ahmed nodded, trying to silence the echo of Salma's voice in his mind. He walked through the streets later that night, Abu Khaled's words still heavy on his shoulders. *We must always be ready.* He repeated the phrase silently, almost like a prayer, but felt a gnawing unease growing inside him. He paused for a moment, looking at the faces around him - the children playing in the dust, the men gathered in small groups, their voices low. *What if Salma is right?* he thought suddenly. *What if we're spending everything on tomorrow and forgetting about today?* He shook his head, pushing the thought away. *No, I can't afford to think like that. Not now.*

Salma continued her work at the law firm in Tel Aviv, her internal conflict deepening with each passing day. She watched the normality of life in Israel - the bustling streets, the cafés filled with people, the children playing in parks - and felt a quiet envy. She wondered what it might be like to live without the constant fear that defined life in Gaza.

But she also knew her place was at home, with her family, her people, and the struggle that shaped their existence. Her conversations with Ahmed grew more charged. She shared her observations and frustrations, and though Ahmed listened, she could see the conflict in his eyes. He was torn between his loyalty to the cause and the reality of life in Gaza.

One evening, she spoke frankly to him, her voice thick with emotion. *'Ahmed, I see so much suffering here. I see children with no shoes, families without enough food. And I think... what if all this effort, all this money, was used to build us up instead of tearing others down?'*

Ahmed looked at her, feeling the full weight of her words. He opened his mouth to respond but hesitated, running a hand through his hair. *'I understand, Salma,'* he replied softly. *'But this is the path we've chosen. It's not easy, and it's not perfect, but it's the only one we have right now.'*

Salma sighed, wrestling with her conflicting thoughts. She respected Ahmed's commitment, admired his leadership, but she couldn't help but wish for a different future - one that didn't revolve around tunnels, rockets, and an endless cycle of conflict.

As the days passed, preparations intensified. The tunnels grew deeper, the training more rigorous. Ahmed's status in the community continued to rise, and he found himself increasingly viewed as a leader, a bridge between Hamas and the people of Gaza. But with this respect came a sharper awareness of how precarious their situation was. The large operation Abu Khaled had hinted at loomed ahead, a shadow on the horizon, and though no one knew exactly when it would come, everyone knew it was inevitable.

That night, as they rested after another long day, Tariq turned to Ahmed. *'You've been quiet,'* he remarked. *'What's on your mind?'*

Ahmed hesitated. *'I'm just thinking about the people... about what they want from us.'*

Tariq nodded, his expression thoughtful. *'They want everything, Ahmed. And sometimes we can't give it to them. We can't give them peace, only the chance to fight for it.'*

Ahmed sighed. "I know. But sometimes... I feel like we could give them more." He glanced down at his hands, fingers flexing unconsciously, as if trying to grasp the shape of that elusive 'more'."

Tariq stared at him for a moment before replying, *'Maybe. But first we have to survive.'*

Ahmed kept his focus on his tasks - his recruits, his friends, and his responsibilities. He had chosen this path and was bound to see it through. But as he looked at the faces around him - the hopeful, the weary, the fearful - he couldn't help but wonder if he was leading them toward something better... or into ruin.

He looked around at the faces of his friends, his recruits, and the people who depended on him. They saw him as a leader, a bridge between the fighters and the community. But he also saw their doubt, their fear of what lay ahead. *Can I really be what they need?* he wondered. *Can I lead them through this... and into something better?* The questions gnawed at him, and he realised that the path he had chosen was far more complicated than he had ever imagined.

For now, all he could do was prepare, build, and wait.

Chapter Twenty Two

YOSSI

Yossi and Nadav arrived at the IDF's Parachuting School, Bahad 8, for the first phase of their Advanced Training: the Parachuting Course (Kurs Tsanchanim). This three-week course was the first obstacle and challenge before earning the coveted red berets - the symbol of the Paratroopers Brigade at the end of the four-month training course. It was going to be intense, demanding, and unlike anything they had faced before.

The mood at the training base shifted the moment the recruits learned what was next. There was a buzz of energy and anticipation, something sharp and electric in the air. This was the moment they had been waiting for - the start of their parachute training. It was the phase that defined the Tzanchanim Brigade, the experience that set them apart. But for Nadav, it was more than that. It was a dream coming true.

"Can you believe it, Yossi?" Nadav asked, his grin wide and unrestrained as they stood in line outside the parachute school on their first day. *"This is it. This is what I've always wanted."*

Yossi couldn't help but smile at his excitement. The enthusiasm radiated off Nadav like a beacon, lighting up the faces of those around him. For weeks, they'd pushed through punishing drills, endured sleepless nights and bone-weary days, but this was what Nadav had always talked about. Yossi remembered the countless conversations they'd had growing up, where Nadav had waxed lyrical about the thrill of leaping from a plane and the rush of air as you floated through the sky. Now, they were here, about to make that leap - literally.

"You'll finally get to put all those hours of daydreaming to use," Yossi teased, nudging him lightly. *"Let's see if it's as good as you've imagined."*

Nadav chuckled, his eyes gleaming. *"Better. I just know it."*

The training began with classroom instruction. Yossi and Nadav sat among a room full of eager recruits, listening intently as the instructors explained the fundamentals of parachuting. They covered everything from the mechanics of a parachute and the correct way to pack it, to the aerodynamics of a safe jump and the proper body position during descent. The atmosphere was serious, focused, every recruit knew that mastering this knowledge could mean the difference between life and death.

The gravity of the situation weighed heavily on Yossi. Every detail mattered. The room, usually full of camaraderie and banter, now felt hushed. Even Nadav was uncharacteristically silent, scribbling down notes as if his life depended on it. *"This is real,"* Yossi thought. The idea of jumping from an aircraft at such heights sent shivers down his spine, but there was no room for hesitation.

After the classroom sessions, the physical training intensified. The recruits ran drills designed to build the specific muscles needed for parachuting - sprints, strength training, and exercises that tested their endurance to its limits. Yossi and Nadav pushed themselves hard, knowing their bodies had to be ready for the challenges ahead.

"You've got this, Yossi," Nadav would say, clapping him on the back. *"Just think about that red beret."*

Yossi nodded, determination in his eyes. *"I'll earn it,"* he replied. *"We both will."* Yet, as determined as Yossi was, the fatigue was starting to set in. His muscles burned after each training session, but there was a greater fire inside him - the drive to succeed.

But as much as Nadav had anticipated this, it was Yossi who adapted to the training with surprising ease. The instructors quickly separated the recruits into groups for the initial ground phase, teaching them how to assemble and pack their parachutes, explaining the mechanisms and the importance of precision. The training was meticulous, every movement and detail scrutinised. For many, the instructions seemed overwhelming - a tangle of straps, cords, and procedures to memorise. But for Yossi, it just... clicked.

On the second day, they were given their first practice static-line chute pack to prepare. Nadav's hands fumbled a few times, normally calm and collected, suddenly struggling to manage the fine details. He cursed under his breath as one of the cords snagged.

"Need a hand?" Yossi asked, already stepping closer. He took Nadav's chute and ran through the procedure slowly, showing him the best way to fold the nylon, how to avoid twists in the lines.

"I thought I'd be a natural at this," Nadav muttered, shaking his head. *"I don't get it."*

Yossi's expression softened. *"Hey, we're just getting started. You'll get the hang of it. I know you will."*

Nadav grinned, his confidence returning. *"Thanks, mate. You're pretty good at this, though. Maybe you've got a secret talent for not dying horribly from great heights."*

"Maybe," Yossi replied with a grin. *"Or maybe I just really don't want to mess this up. After all, it's a long way down."*

Once their chutes were packed, they moved to the static line jump platforms. The instructors drilled them repeatedly - learning how to exit the aircraft in a precise, controlled manner.

"Jump, count 1,000, 2,000, 3,000, 4,000, check canopy!" the instructor's voice barked, drilling the rhythm into their heads.

The first practice jumps were from a tower - leaping off a high platform attached to a long wire that simulated the exit from a plane. It was meant to teach them the proper body positioning and timing. They practised over and over, Yossi adjusting quickly to the motion, landing with ease. But Nadav struggled, his muscular build making it harder to maintain the streamlined form required for a smooth descent.

"You're overthinking it," Yossi said after Nadav's third rough landing. *"Just relax. Trust the line to do the work."*

Nadav snorted. *"Easy for you to say."* But the next time he jumped, he focused on keeping his posture loose and steady. It wasn't perfect, but it was better.

The real test came when they were led out to the airstrip. The sight of the C-130 Hercules, massive and imposing against the blue sky, sent a shiver down Yossi's spine. This was no simulation. This was the real deal.

"Alright, listen up!" the jump instructor shouted over the drone of the engines. *"Today, you're going to learn what it means to be a paratrooper. This isn't about bravery - it's about skill. Follow the procedure and remember there's no room for hesitation."*

"Yes, sir!" they chorused, voices strained with anticipation.

As the plane taxied down the runway, Yossi felt a surge of nerves. Nadav was beside him, his hands gripping the shoulder straps of his harness tightly.

"You ready?" Yossi asked, his voice barely audible over the roar of the engines.

Nadav swallowed hard, then nodded. *"Born ready."*

As they stood at the jump door, wind roaring past, it was Yossi who felt the rush of clarity, the sense of everything falling into place. He watched the red-light blink to green, the instructor's hand tapping his shoulder.

"Go!"

Yossi stepped forward, the motion automatic, drilled into him by countless practice jumps. One second, he was inside the plane, and the next, he was falling - hurtling through the air, the roar of the wind filling his ears. He counted steadily in his head:

"1,000... 2,000... 3,000... 4,000 - check canopy!"

The static line pulled taut, jerking him sharply. His parachute billowed out with a loud snap, filling with air and slowing his descent. Yossi looked up, his heart racing, and saw the canopy spread perfectly above him, the green and brown fabric a stark contrast against the vast expanse of blue sky. Relief flooded through him, followed by a rush of exhilaration.

I did it.

For a moment, Yossi hung there, suspended in mid-air, marvelling at the stillness after the chaos of the exit. The world below seemed small and quiet, the drop zone a patchwork of green fields and dusty terrain. He glanced around, spotting the other recruits drifting nearby, their chutes blossoming like flowers. Some wobbled awkwardly, adjusting their positions, but Yossi felt steady, his hands guiding the toggles with ease as he drifted towards the drop zone.

Below, the ground rushed up to meet him, and Yossi shifted his body, preparing for the landing. Knees bent, feet together - he touched down with a controlled roll, the impact jarring but manageable. Quickly, he gathered up his chute, adrenaline still coursing through his veins. He glanced up just in time to see Nadav descending, his chute swaying erratically.

Yossi's heart clenched as Nadav hit the ground hard, tumbling sideways in a flurry of dust. He rushed over, his pulse pounding in his ears.

"You okay?" he called, skidding to a halt beside his friend.

Nadav grunted, wincing as he pushed himself up, his face flushed. *"Yeah,"* he muttered, brushing dirt off his gear. *"Just - just a little bumpy."*

"It's all right. Next time, keep your elbows tucked in tighter when you exit. It'll stop the spin."

"Right. Tighter. Got it." Nadav shot him a crooked smile. *"Guess I'm just not as graceful as you, mate."*

"It's not about grace, it's about control," Yossi replied, his tone light but firm. *"You'll get it."*

Their second jump was smoother. This time, Nadav focused on keeping his body rigid as he stepped out of the plane, and his chute deployed without a hitch. He landed a bit roughly but managed to stay on his feet. Each time they went up, Nadav improved, his confidence growing with every descent. By the third jump, he was grinning when he hit the ground, shaking off the dirt with a whoop of triumph.

"See? Told you you'd get it," Yossi called, laughing as Nadav jogged over.

"Yeah, yeah," Nadav panted, but there was a spark of pride in his eyes. *"Just wait till I'm the one showing you up next time."*

But it was the fourth jump that tested them both. As the plane gained altitude, a gusty wind picked up, rattling through the fuselage. Yossi could feel the change in the air, the way the plane seemed to lurch slightly as it fought the turbulence.

The jumpmaster's voice was tense. *"Wind's picking up! Stay focused, stick to your training. Remember your count and watch your descent!"*

Yossi swallowed, his gaze flicking to Nadav. His friend looked pale, his knuckles white where they gripped his harness.

"Nadav," Yossi murmured, leaning close. *"Stay calm. You know what to do."*

Nadav nodded stiffly, his jaw clenched. *"Yeah. Just... got to get it right."*

The green light blinked on, and Yossi watched as the first few recruits jumped, their figures buffeted by the wind as they tumbled out. When it was his turn, he hesitated for a split second - then jumped.

1,000... 2,000... 3,000... 4,000 - check canopy!

The wind caught him immediately, jerking him sideways. Yossi fought to stabilise, adjusting the toggles until his descent smoothed out. But as he looked around, his heart leapt into his throat.

Nadav's chute was tangled, the canopy twisted and flapping wildly. He was spinning, arms flailing as he struggled to regain control.

"Nadav!" Yossi shouted, though he knew his friend couldn't hear him over the roar of the wind. He watched, helpless, as Nadav pulled desperately on the risers, his body jerking violently in the harness.

Then, with a wrenching twist, the canopy snapped open, the lines straightening. Nadav stopped spinning, his descent stabilising just in time for a hard, jarring landing. Yossi let out a breath he hadn't realised he'd been holding, relief washing over him.

By the time Yossi touched down and sprinted over, Nadav was already on his feet, breathing hard but grinning fiercely.

"That was close," Nadav gasped, his eyes wide with adrenaline.

Yossi grabbed his shoulders, his heart still racing. *"You all right?"*

"Yeah," Nadav breathed, his grin still in place. *"Better than all right. I didn't panic."*

Yossi shook his head, a smile tugging at his lips. *"You're a madman, you know that?"*

"Takes one to know one," Nadav shot back, clapping Yossi on the back.

By the fifth and final jump, they were moving like seasoned paratroopers. Each recruit stepped out with confidence, their motions fluid and controlled. Yossi's descent was smooth, his landing almost perfect. Nadav followed close behind, touching down with a solid roll.

As they gathered on the drop zone, the jump instructor approached.

"Rosenberg," he barked, eyes narrowing on Yossi. *"Excellent form out there. You're a natural."*

Yossi blinked in surprise, then nodded. *"Thank you, sir."*

The instructor turned to Nadav. *"And you, Levy - keep working on those exits. You've got potential."*

"Yes, sir," Nadav said, a new determination in his voice.

Packing up their chutes, Yossi grinned at his friend. *"See? I told you you'd get it."*

"Yeah, yeah," Nadav replied, but his smile was wide. *"Just wait till I'm the one showing you up next time."*

They were ready for whatever came next. Together.

As Yossi and Nadav walked back to the barracks after completing their final parachute jump, the exhaustion mingled with the sense of accomplishment in every step. The thrill of the jumps still buzzed in their veins, but a new challenge loomed on the horizon.

"*Well, we've done it,*" Nadav said, his voice carrying a mix of pride and lingering adrenaline. "*We're officially paratroopers.*" He glanced at Yossi with a grin, wiping sweat and dirt from his forehead. "*Now comes the fun part, right?*"

Yossi chuckled, though his eyes were thoughtful. "*If by fun, you mean hauling even heavier packs, running even longer distances, and being pushed to the edge again and again... yeah, definitely fun.*"

Nadav shook his head, but his smile never wavered. "*Bring it on. I want to see what we're made of.*" He adjusted his pack as if testing his shoulders, already bracing himself for the physical strain to come.

"*You know it's not going to be easy,*" Yossi murmured, glancing around at the other recruits, who were murmuring quietly amongst themselves, some still flushed with the thrill of parachuting, others clearly anxious about the next phase. "*They're going to ramp everything up from here - combat fitness, endurance training... we're talking forty-kilometre mascot with over thirty-five kilos on our backs.*"

Nadav's grin only widened. "*Sounds perfect. That's what we signed up for, right?*"

"*Maslul Krav too,*" Yossi reminded him, a flicker of excitement in his voice. "*They'll have us on that combat track with full gear - walls, ropes, planks, the whole thing. And then there's the night courses.*" He shook his head, unable to hide his admiration for what they were about to face. "*Moving under pressure, low visibility... it's going to test everything we've got.*"

Nadav nodded slowly, the playful light in his eyes replaced by a steadier, more determined gleam. *"Yeah, it's going to be hell,"* he said quietly. *"But I can't wait to see what we're capable of, Yossi. This is where we really prove ourselves."*

Yossi met his gaze, and for a moment, there was no teasing, no bravado - just an unspoken agreement. They were in this together, ready for whatever lay ahead.

"Let's show them what we can do," Yossi said softly.

"Together," Nadav echoed, the word carrying a weight of commitment.

They turned towards the barracks, already steeling themselves for the next phase of training - the phase that would push them beyond anything they'd ever experienced. But they were ready. They had to be.

Because the real test of becoming a paratrooper wasn't just jumping out of planes.

It was surviving everything that came after.

That evening, after the adrenaline of the final jump had settled and the recruits were given a few precious hours to rest, Yossi found a quiet corner of the base and pulled out his phone. He dialled Yael's number, his fingers trembling slightly with the mix of fatigue and excitement still coursing through him.

The phone rang twice before she answered.

"Yossi!" Yael's voice was bright, filled with warmth that seemed to reach across the miles between them. *"How did it go?"*

Yossi leaned back against the wall, letting the sound of her voice wash over him like a balm. *"I did it, Yael. I completed the parachute course. I'm officially a paratrooper now."*

There was a beat of silence, and he could almost picture her face, her eyes widening with joy.

"You did it?" she breathed, and then there was a burst of laughter - light and pure. *"I knew you would! I'm so proud of you, Yossi!"*

His lips curved into a tired but genuine smile. *"I think I surprised myself a bit. It was tougher than I expected, but... I made it through. We both did - Nadav too."*

"You're amazing," she murmured softly, and the sincerity in her voice made something tighten in Yossi's chest. *"I wish I could have been there to see you."*

"You were, in a way," Yossi said quietly, his voice steady. *"I thought of you every time I felt like I couldn't push any further. And when I jumped... it was like you were with me."*

There was a pause, then a gentle sigh on the other end. *"I miss you, Yossi. I can't wait for the day when we're not saying goodbye every time we talk."*

"Soon," he promised softly, his gaze drifting up to the darkening sky, imagining her there, looking at the same stars. *"I'll get through this, and then we'll have all the time in the world."*

"One step at a time, right?" she teased lightly, and he could hear the smile in her voice.

Yossi nodded, even though she couldn't see it. *"Yeah... one step at a time."*

They talked a little longer, sharing small moments and thoughts, holding onto the connection they had built, even across the distance. And when they finally hung up, Yossi felt something warm settle in his chest - a sense of calm, of purpose.

He slipped the phone back into his pocket, took a deep breath, and turned towards the barracks.

Because the next Chapter of his training was about to begin.

And he was ready.

Chapter Twenty Three

AHMED

Gaza was caught in a strange, uneasy calm - like a bowstring pulled taut, vibrating with the tension of what lay ahead. It wasn't peace, just the heavy, expectant silence before the storm. Ahmed had risen in prominence within Hamas, increasingly seen as a key figure in their efforts to build and prepare. Under the watchful eye of Abu Khaled, Ahmed had proven himself as a leader who could connect with the community, recruit effectively, and inspire trust. But now, there was an unspoken urgency in every meeting, a feeling that all their work was converging on something monumental. It thrilled him - yet sent a cold shiver down his spine. Was this what he'd been preparing for, or something far darker?

One afternoon, Abu Khaled approached Ahmed with a serious expression. *'Ahmed,'* he began, his voice low, *'we need to make a trip to Rafah. There's someone there who wants to meet you, someone whose decisions can change everything.'*

Ahmed felt a knot tighten in his stomach. He had heard about these secret meetings, whispered conversations with high-ranking officials, but he had never been invited to one himself. Rafah, with its network of tunnels and proximity to the Egyptian border, was a place of critical importance. This wasn't just another routine visit, it was something significant.

As they drove through the crowded streets of Gaza, the dust from the last bombings still hung in the air, and with each bump in the road, Ahmed's thoughts churned. *'Why me? Why now?'* The knot in his stomach tightened. The weight of it settled on his shoulders, heavier with each mile they covered.

The following morning, Ahmed and Abu Khaled set off for Rafah. The journey was tense, the air thick with dust and the lingering smell of smoke. As they approached the city, Ahmed's senses sharpened. The scent of burning wood mixed with the acrid tang of dust, and plainclothes men loitered near doorways, their eyes tracking every movement. Armed guards stood at discreet intervals, their fingers grazing the triggers of their rifles - a silent reminder of the ever-present danger. Ahmed's pulse quickened. *'They're expecting something,'* he thought, *'something big.'*

Their destination was unexpected: a compound used by an international aid agency, tucked away in a quiet part of the city. The compound, with its high walls and guarded gates, seemed an unlikely setting for a clandestine meeting. As they passed through the gates, Ahmed couldn't shake the feeling that they were entering a place where secrets lived, where decisions were made that could change everything.

Inside, the atmosphere shifted. Aid workers moved about, seemingly absorbed in their duties, yet the tension beneath the surface was palpable. Abu Khaled led Ahmed through a side door, past several rooms bustling with activity. More guards stood watch at every corner, their expressions unreadable. Finally, they reached a nondescript door at the back of the compound. Two men with rifles slung over their shoulders nodded to Abu Khaled and stepped aside.

The room they entered was sparse, furnished only with a table and a few chairs. At the far end of the room sat a man whose presence commanded immediate attention. He was dressed simply, his face partially obscured by a keffiyeh, but his posture radiated authority.

'Ahmed Al-Masri,' the man began, his voice calm yet firm, *'I am Abu Yasser. I lead the Al-Qassam Brigades.'*

Ahmed felt a surge of nerves, a mix of fear and pride. *'This is the man I've heard so much about,'* he thought, feeling the weight of Abu Yasser's reputation press upon him. *'The man who plans in the shadows and strikes with precision.'* His voice was calm, his words deliberate. Ahmed sat up straighter, trying to mirror the authority in Abu Yasser's gaze. *'Stay calm,'* he told himself. *'Show him you're ready.'* But beneath his composed exterior, his thoughts whirled with the enormity of what was being asked of him. *'A coordinated effort... all of Gaza... what will it mean for us?'*

Abu Yasser leaned back, his fingers tapping rhythmically on the wooden table. *'I've heard about you, Ahmed. Abu Khaled says you have a gift for making people trust you. We need that... now more than ever.'* His eyes, sharp and calculating, seemed to pierce through Ahmed's calm façade.

Abu Yasser motioned for Ahmed to sit. *'Your work in Gaza City has been effective, and you've managed to build trust and respect among the people. But we need more than that now.'*

Ahmed nodded, his mouth dry. "*I'm here to do whatever is needed*," Ahmed said, keeping his voice firm. He straightened his shoulders, hoping it disguised the tremor of unease he felt under Abu Yasser's gaze.

Abu Yasser leaned forward, his gaze intense. *'We are preparing for something much larger, a coordinated effort that will involve all of Gaza. It will be unlike anything we've done before - an operation that will take the fight directly to the enemy.'*

Ahmed listened carefully, pride and anxiety swirling in his chest. *'What do you need from me?'* he asked, though he wasn't sure he was ready for the answer.

'There are others like you,' Abu Yasser explained. *'Leaders in Gaza City, Khan Yunis, Beit Hanoun, and other areas. You are all being prepared for this. Your role is to continue what you're doing: recruit, train, and build. But also ensure that your men are ready for anything. When the time comes, all of you will be brought together, unified for a single purpose.'*

Ahmed nodded, trying to process the enormity of what was being asked of him. *'And when will this happen?'* he asked, though he wasn't sure he wanted to know.

Abu Yasser's expression remained inscrutable. *'When the time is right. For now, focus on your work. Keep everything discreet, maintain your cover, and make sure your men are prepared. Remember, our strength lies in our readiness and our secrecy.'*

Ahmed nodded again, his mind racing. *'I understand,'* he said quietly, though a part of him screamed, *'Do I really?'*

'Good,' Abu Yasser said, his voice lowering to a quiet intensity. *'I have faith in you, Ahmed. Don't let us down.'*

As Abu Yasser's words hung in the air, Ahmed felt his hands clench involuntarily. His pulse quickened, a sharp pang of fear rippling through him. *'Don't let us down.'* The weight of that expectation pressed on him like a heavy stone. He knew the consequences if he failed - they all did.

The drive back to Gaza City was silent, Ahmed's mind churning with the implications of the meeting. *'They've chosen me,'* he thought. *'But for what?'* The weight of Abu Yasser's words pressed on him like a vice, squeezing his chest until he could barely breathe. *'When the time is right,'* he had said. But when would that be? And what would it mean for the people he cared about, for the future they all imagined but rarely spoke of?

That evening, Salma was waiting for him at home. She could see the tension etched across his face as soon as he walked in.

'Ahmed, what happened?' she asked gently, her eyes filled with concern.

Ahmed's expression remained stoic, his voice measured. *'More planning, more preparation,'* he said simply, not wanting to reveal too much. *'We're getting ready for something larger. I don't know when or how, but it's coming.'*

Salma looked at him closely, sensing his internal conflict. "*And how do you really feel about that, Ahmed*?" she pressed, her gaze searching his face.

Ahmed hesitated, his voice low and controlled. "It's not about feelings,' he snapped, then softened his tone. 'It's about what must be done. This is duty - our duty.'

She nodded, though she felt a pang in her chest. *'But Ahmed, at what cost? I see the strain in your eyes, the way it wears on you.'*

As he looked at her, the guilt gnawed at him. He had shared so little of what truly weighed on his mind, and yet, how could he? He could never tell her the full extent of what they were planning, of what it might cost. His jaw tightened, a flicker of frustration crossing his face. *'Salma, I can't afford to let emotions in. Not now.'* His voice trembled slightly, betraying the certainty he was trying to project.

Salma sighed, sensing his distance. *'I just want you to stay true to yourself, Ahmed... to the person you were before all this.'*

He looked away, his expression hardening. *'Maybe that person doesn't exist anymore,'* he muttered more to himself than to her.

Later that night, Ahmed found himself on the rooftop again, staring at the city below. The lights flickered like distant stars, but to him, they felt more like fading embers. He thought of the mothers holding their children close, the fathers trying to shield their families from fear. *'Are we the protectors,'* he thought bitterly, *'or are we just giving them more to fear?'*

His thoughts drifted to Salma and her vision of a different future. A small voice inside him whispered, *'Could that be possible?'* But he silenced it quickly. *'No, I can't think like that. Not now. I have a duty... a purpose.'*

He thought of the mothers holding their children close, of Salma's quiet hope for a different future. What would happen if he failed them? Could he live with the consequences? His duty, his purpose, had always been clear. But now, standing on the precipice, he couldn't help but wonder if the path he had chosen would lead them all into darkness.

Ahmed continued his role with renewed focus, but a part of him began to feel more isolated. He buried his doubts deeper, hiding them behind a facade of determination. But he couldn't help but wonder if he was truly on the path he was meant to walk, or if he was merely following the shadows of those who had come before him.

For now, Ahmed remained trapped - between the weight of expectations and the growing shadow of doubt that whispered, louder each day, that the path he was on might lead them all into ruin.

Chapter Twenty Four

YOSSI

Yossi and Nadav stood at attention with the rest of the recruits, listening as the instructor outlined the next stage of their training. The days of parachuting through the sky were behind them - now they were back on solid ground, preparing for the gruelling weeks ahead.

"From this point on, you're going to be pushed harder than ever," the instructor's voice boomed. *"The next few months will define you as soldiers. Physical conditioning, endurance, combat drills, urban warfare, and live-fire exercises. If you want to earn that red beret, you'll have to prove yourselves every single day."*

The recruits were silent, their eyes hard with determination. They knew what lay ahead. This was where the real test began - where they'd be shaped into the kind of soldiers who could fight under any conditions, in any terrain, against any threat.

The physical conditioning phase ramped up the intensity of everything they'd faced in basic training. Each morning started with punishing runs, sometimes stretching up to 15 kilometres, with the recruits carrying over 35 kilograms of gear. The goal was simple: push them to the brink, then push them further.

Yossi's body ached with every step, his muscles burning as they slogged up hills and pounded through muddy trails. But no matter how brutal the pace, no matter how heavy the pack on his back, he kept his focus locked on the path ahead.

Beside him, Nadav moved with relentless energy, his face set in fierce concentration. *"Come on, Yossi,"* he would grunt, teeth gritted against the strain. *"Just keep moving. One more hill, one more step."*

The endurance marches became a constant feature of their days, the distance increasing steadily until they were covering up to 40 kilometres in a single stretch. The recruits stumbled through the dark, their boots heavy with mud, their packs cutting into their shoulders.

One night, after hours of marching, Yossi's legs felt like lead, his back screaming in protest. He glanced at Nadav, seeing the same exhaustion etched into his friend's face.

"You still with me?" Yossi murmured, his voice rough.

Nadav shot him a weary smile. *"Always, mate."*

The obstacle courses added to the physical grind - the infamous *Maslul Krav* (Combat Track) testing every ounce of their strength and agility. They hauled themselves over walls, crawled under barbed wire, and balanced across narrow beams, all while wearing their full combat gear. Nighttime courses were particularly brutal, the darkness transforming the obstacles into looming threats.

Yossi felt his hands shake as he gripped a high wall, the weight of his gear dragging him down. But he set his jaw, pulling himself up inch by inch, refusing to let go. Below him, Nadav was already moving, his muscles bunching as he swung over the wall with a grunt of effort.

"Get up here, Yossi!" Nadav barked, his voice sharp. *"We don't have all night!"*

With a final burst of strength, Yossi hauled himself over, landing heavily beside Nadav.

"Nice of you to join me," Nadav teased, a grin flashing in the dark.

"Shut up and move," Yossi muttered, but there was no heat in his words - only the shared determination that kept them pushing through.

The physical conditioning was just the beginning. The next phase shifted their focus to tactical training, throwing them into high-pressure combat scenarios that tested not just their bodies, but their minds and instincts.

The mock towns of the urban warfare training grounds were like a maze of concrete and steel - multi-storey buildings, narrow alleys, hidden snipers, and booby traps at every corner. Yossi led his squad through the twisting streets, his heart pounding as they cleared room after room, the echo of simulated gunfire ringing in his ears.

"Move, move!" he shouted, his rifle up as they sprinted across an open courtyard.

Nadav was right behind him, his face set in a grim mask of concentration. *"Left side clear!"*

They swept through the buildings in a blur of motion, the air thick with tension. Every decision mattered. A wrong move could mean losing their entire team in a real battle.

Yossi ducked around a corner, signalling for Nadav to take point. *"Check that alley. I'll cover."*

Nadav nodded sharply, slipping forward with his rifle raised. The alley was empty, but the training was teaching them never to trust appearances. Every shadow could hide an enemy, every open door a potential death trap.

As the days passed, their movements grew sharper, more coordinated. Yossi's commands came quicker, Nadav's responses instinctive. They moved like a single unit, each step calculated, each position covered.

The real test came during a live-fire exercise, the mock town filled with the deafening cracks of real ammunition. Yossi's pulse thundered in his ears as he led his squad through the maze of buildings, the air thick with smoke.

"Upstairs, now!" he shouted, pointing to a narrow staircase.

Nadav was already moving, his boots thundering up the steps. A moment later, the crack of his rifle echoed through the building, followed by a shout of *"Target down!"*

Yossi grinned, adrenaline surging through him. They were becoming something more - more than recruits, more than trainees. They were becoming soldiers.

The urban warfare training gave way to long days in the wilderness, where they learned to survive and fight in the harshest conditions. The rugged terrain around the base became their classroom - thick forests, rocky hills, and steep ravines testing their every step.

They practised camouflage and concealment, moving silently through the underbrush, their bodies blending into the landscape. Yossi's face was smeared with mud, his uniform streaked with dirt as he crept through the undergrowth, his eyes scanning for movement.

"Stay low," he whispered to Nadav, his voice barely a breath. They had to cross a clearing without being detected, the instructors watching from hidden positions.

"We've got this," Nadav murmured back, his body coiled with tension.

They moved like shadows, slipping through the grass without a sound. Yossi's heart pounded, but his mind was calm, focused. This was where he felt alive - where every sense was sharp, every instinct honed.

The final phase of their training combined everything they'd learned, pushing them through a series of live-fire exercises that tested their ability to function under extreme pressure. The recruits were split into squads, each led by rotating commanders, and thrown into combat scenarios that simulated the chaos of real battle.

Yossi found himself leading his team again, the weight of responsibility heavy on his shoulders. They moved through the course in a staggered line, rifles up, eyes sharp.

"Contact, left!" Nadav shouted, dropping to one knee as he fired.

Yossi reacted instantly, his commands clear and precise. *"Flank left! Suppressive fire on my mark!"*

They moved like a machine, each recruit falling into position. The air was filled with the roar of gunfire, the sharp crack of rounds zipping past. But Yossi's voice never wavered, his orders cutting through the chaos.

When the exercise ended, Yossi's squad stood panting in the aftermath, their faces smeared with dirt and sweat. The instructors stepped forward, nodding approvingly.

"Good work, Rosenberg," one of them said gruffly. *"You held your team together under pressure. Keep it up."*

Yossi nodded, his chest tight with pride. They were getting closer. The final test - the Masa Kumta - was just over the horizon.

"We're almost there," he murmured to Nadav as they gathered their gear.

Nadav grinned, his eyes fierce. *"One step at a time, right? We've got this."*

Yossi looked out at the horizon, his heart steady.

"Yeah," he said softly. *"We've got this."*

The final phase awaited, and they would face it together. One step at a time.

Yossi stood in the darkness, adjusting the straps of his pack as he stared at the long line of recruits assembling in the predawn chill. They were about to embark on the Masa Kumta - the Beret March - arguably the toughest challenge they had faced so far. This wasn't just a test of physical endurance, it was a rite of passage, the defining moment that would transform them from trainees into fully-fledged soldiers of the Parachute Brigade. Everything they'd done, every gruelling march, every sleepless night, had led them to this point.

The distance loomed large in everyone's minds - 90 kilometres of relentless terrain, carrying nearly 40 kilograms of gear: full combat packs, ammunition, water, and weapons. It was more than just a march. It was a marathon of pain and perseverance that would push them beyond their breaking points.

Beside him, Nadav shifted his weight, his face grim but determined. "*This is it,*" he murmured quietly. There was no grin this time, no light-hearted banter. Just the steady resolve of someone who knew that failure wasn't an option.

Yossi nodded, his own nerves a tight coil in his stomach. "*Yeah. This is where we earn it.*"

As the commander called them to attention, the recruits fell silent, their breath visible in the cold morning air. The tension was palpable - a mix of fear, anticipation, and fierce determination. The order rang out sharply, cutting through the stillness.

"*Move out!*"

The march began slowly, boots crunching over gravel in unison. The first few hours were deceptively easy, the rhythm of their steps almost hypnotic. But Yossi knew better than to let his guard down. They'd learned the hard way during Basic Training that the true challenge of these marches lay not in the beginning, but in the grinding hours that came after - the moments when exhaustion set in, and the mind started to waver.

The terrain shifted rapidly as they made their way out of the training grounds and into the rugged hills surrounding the base. They trudged up steep inclines that made their legs scream, the loose rocks sliding underfoot, threatening to send them tumbling. The straps of Yossi's pack cut into his shoulders, the weight pressing down like a boulder on his back. His feet were already aching, the blisters from earlier marches rubbing raw with each step.

Around them, the air was filled with the sounds of laboured breathing and the occasional stumble as recruits struggled to keep up. Yossi glanced over at Nadav, watching his friend's face tighten with concentration. Nadav was strong - one of the strongest in their unit - but even he couldn't ignore the strain.

"*Stay steady,*" Yossi murmured, his voice low but firm. "*We've got a long way to go.*"

Nadav grunted in response, shifting the weight of his pack. "*Yeah, tell me that when we're halfway.*"

Hours passed in a blur of sweat and pain. The sun crept higher, beating down on them with an unforgiving heat. By midday, Yossi could feel his legs trembling under the strain, his shoulders numb from the constant pressure of the pack. The trail narrowed as they made their way along a rocky ridge, the ground dropping away sharply on one side. A recruit a few paces ahead of them stumbled, nearly losing his footing.

"*Careful*!" Yossi barked, stepping forward to grab the recruit's arm, steadying him before he could fall. The recruit looked back, face pale and eyes wide with exhaustion.

"*Thanks*," he muttered, barely able to catch his breath.

Yossi gave a tight nod, his own chest heaving. "*Just focus. One step at a time.*"

The recruit nodded weakly, his gaze fixed on Yossi. It was in that moment, as Yossi held the line steady, that he realised they were all looking to him - to keep them together, to keep them moving. The thought sent a surge of determination through him. They couldn't afford to falter. Not now.

"*Keep your heads up*!" he called, his voice carrying over the line. "*Eyes forward. We finish this together.*"

Nadav fell into step beside him, his jaw clenched against the strain. "*Nice speech, Rosenberg,*" he muttered, his voice a low rasp.

Yossi smirked, glancing at his friend. "*You just focus on keeping those legs moving. Don't think I haven't noticed you limping.*"

"*Just a little twist,*" Nadav replied nonchalantly, but Yossi saw the flash of pain in his eyes. Still, Nadav didn't complain. He just gritted his teeth and pushed on, the same unyielding strength that had carried him through every challenge.

The hours blended into one long, unending march. Day turned into night, and still, they kept moving. The cold crept back in as the sun disappeared, the darkness swallowing them whole. Yossi's vision blurred, his limbs numb and uncooperative. But he forced himself to keep going, one step after another, driven by the knowledge that this was the final hurdle.

"*Just a little more,*" he murmured to himself, his voice almost lost in the wind. "*We're almost there.*"

When the sky began to lighten again, the first pale streaks of dawn painting the horizon, they crested the final hill. Below them, the outline of the training base was just visible - a tiny speck of civilisation after what felt like an eternity of wilderness.

"*We made it,*" Yossi breathed, his chest tight with emotion. He glanced at Nadav, seeing the exhaustion etched into every line of his face, but also the spark of triumph in his eyes.

"*Yeah,*" Nadav whispered, a smile breaking through the grime and sweat. "*We did.*"

With a final push, they marched into the training grounds, a ragged line of soldiers. Packs thudded to the ground as they dropped to their knees, gasping for breath, their bodies trembling with fatigue.

"*You've completed the Masa Kumta!*" the commander's voice rang out, clear and strong. "*Well done, soldiers.*"

Yossi barely registered the words. His mind was hazy, his body screaming for rest. But as he glanced around, seeing the weary but proud faces of his fellow recruits, a sense of satisfaction settled over him. They had done it. They had earned this.

After the Red Beret March was complete, the recruits sat scattered around the final checkpoint, exhausted but triumphant. Medics moved among them, checking for any injuries or signs of dehydration. Yossi and Nadav sat together, catching their breath and sharing relieved smiles. The weight of their packs was finally off their shoulders, but the emotional weight of the accomplishment lingered.

Amidst the crowd, they spotted Leila, who assigned to oversee the recovery, making her way toward them with a bright grin.

'*Leila!*' Nadav called out, his face lighting up. He stood, despite the pain in his ankle, and opened his arms wide as Leila approached.

Leila rushed over, and they hugged tightly, laughter and excitement filling the air. *'I can't believe you made it!'* she exclaimed, her eyes shining with joy. *'You look exhausted, but in one piece!'*

Yossi joined in, pulling Leila into a quick, playful embrace. *'It's so good to see you, Leila,'* he said warmly. *'We've missed you.'*

Leila nodded, still smiling broadly. *'I've missed you both too. It feels like forever since we've all been together like this.'* She then looked down at Nadav's ankle and noticed him wincing slightly.

'Nadav, what's going on with that ankle?'

Nadav shrugged, trying to appear nonchalant. *'Just a little twist during the march. Nothing serious.'*

Leila rolled her eyes affectionately. *'You're always trying to downplay things,'* she said, moving to kneel beside him. *'Let me take a look.'*

Yossi grinned as Leila began tending to Nadav's injury. As she worked, he leaned back, staring up at the sky letting Leila take care of him, as always. They'd made it. They were paratroopers now.

And soon, they'd be stepping into the next Chapter of their journey.

The day of the Beret Ceremony - *Tekes Kumta* - arrived with the setting sun casting a golden hue over the training grounds of Bahad 8. Yossi and Nadav stood shoulder to shoulder with their fellow recruits, their uniforms crisp despite the exhaustion still evident on their faces. This was what they had been working towards, what every drop of sweat, every sleepless night, and every moment of doubt had led to.

Yossi scanned the crowd, his heart racing as he searched for familiar faces. He saw his parents standing off to the side, their faces glowing with happiness and pride. His mother, Ruth, waved excitedly when she caught his eye, tears shimmering in her eyes. His father stood beside her, his expression serious yet unmistakably proud. And then, there was Yael. Her smile lit up her entire face, and her eyes sparkled with so much emotion that Yossi felt his breath catch. She looked at him like he was the only person in the world.

Just next to them, Nadav's family stood clustered together, their faces equally radiant. Nadav's mother, a short but strong woman with a warmth that shone through her smile, beamed with pride, clapping loudly as she caught sight of Nadav in formation. His father, a tall, broad-shouldered man who rarely showed emotion, wore a smile that softened his usually stern features. And beside them was Leila, standing close to Nadav's parents, her gaze fixed on him. Her expression was soft, her eyes brimming with admiration and relief. She looked proud - prouder than Yossi had ever seen her.

Nadav caught sight of them too, and for a moment, his gaze lingered on Leila. She smiled at him, her eyes holding his for just a second longer than necessary, and Nadav's face lit up with a smile that was different from his usual grin. It was gentler, quieter - a smile meant just for her. But then the moment passed, and Nadav turned back to face forward, his posture straightening as the ceremony began.

'Can you believe we made it?' Nadav whispered beside him, his voice a mix of disbelief and pride.

Yossi nodded, swallowing against the lump in his throat. *'Barely,'* he replied with a chuckle. *'But we're here.'* His stomach churned with anticipation. This was the moment they had worked so hard for. It felt surreal to think they had survived everything - from the intense physical training to the fear of their first jump - and now, they stood ready to be recognised as full members of the Parachute Brigade.

Their commanding officer, a seasoned veteran with a presence that commanded respect, stepped forward to address them. His voice was calm yet filled with the weight of authority as he began to speak.

'Today, you stand before us not as recruits, but as soldiers of the Parachute Brigade,' he said, his gaze sweeping over them. *'You have faced the challenges, endured the hardships, and proven yourselves worthy of wearing the red beret. This beret represents not only the honour of our brigade but also the trust that is placed in you to protect our nation and each other.'*

The words sank deep into Yossi's heart. He had heard speeches like this before, but this time, it felt personal. The weight of the red beret was not just about achievement - it was about responsibility. He glanced briefly towards Yael again, his thoughts drifting to the future they had talked about, and he wondered if the responsibilities of a soldier would pull him further from the dreams they had shared.

'One by one, step forward as your name is called and receive your red beret,' the officer commanded.

Each recruit stepped forward, heads held high as they received the symbol of everything they had fought for. Yossi's name was called, and he moved forward, every muscle tense, every nerve on edge. His commanding officer handed him the red beret with a solemn nod.

'Well done, soldier,' the officer said quietly, his voice carrying a note of respect. *'You've earned this.'*

Yossi took the beret, feeling its weight in his hands. Slowly, almost reverently, he placed it on his head, his chest tightening with a surge of emotion. He turned, scanning the crowd for his family, and saw them cheering, their faces beaming with pride. Yael's smile never faltered, her eyes brimming with tears of joy. Their connection, even from a distance, felt electric, and for a moment, Yossi felt invincible.

Nadav stepped forward next, receiving his beret with the same mix of nervousness and pride. As he turned to Yossi, their eyes met in a silent acknowledgment of all they had endured together. They didn't need words to express what they felt. They knew this was a moment they would never forget.

The rest of the ceremony passed in a blur of cheers, applause, and salutes. And then, it was over. The recruits - no, the soldiers - stood together, red berets on their heads, eyes alight with a pride that nothing could diminish.

After the ceremony, there was a celebration. Friends and family flooded the training grounds, embracing the new paratroopers and sharing in their joy. Yossi found Yael in the crowd and pulled her into a tight hug, lifting her off the ground as he spun her around. Her laughter rang out, pure and joyful, and he held her close, never wanting to let go.

'I'm so proud of you,' Yael whispered, tears in her eyes. *'You've done it, Yossi. You're really a paratrooper now.'*

He smiled, his voice low and filled with emotion. *'I couldn't have done it without you,'* he said softly. *'You kept me going through all of it.'*

Yael pulled back slightly, just enough to look into his eyes. *'I'm always here, Yossi. I always will be.'* Her words were a promise, one that they both needed.

Nadav, meanwhile, was swept up by his family, his parents and siblings all talking at once, their excitement palpable. But his gaze kept drifting back to Leila. She stood a little apart, smiling softly as she watched the family celebrate. When their eyes met, Nadav's smile softened, and for a moment, it seemed like he might say something - something important. But then his mother called out to him, breaking the moment, and he turned away, his smile fading slightly.

Yossi caught the exchange and raised an eyebrow as Nadav turned back. *'Everything okay?'* he asked quietly.

Nadav shrugged, glancing over his shoulder at Leila. *'Yeah. Just...'* He trailed off, his expression unreadable. *'It's good to see everyone here.'*

Yossi didn't press. He knew better than to push Nadav when he was like this - thoughtful and uncertain. But he couldn't help glancing between his friend and Leila, wondering if they would ever take that step they'd been dancing around for so long.

As the night wore on and the celebration wound down, Yossi and Nadav found a quiet corner, away from the noise and bustle. The weight of the red berets on their heads felt both strange and reassuring.

'It feels surreal, doesn't it?' Yossi said, adjusting his beret.

Nadav nodded, his grin wide. *'Yeah, but we earned it. Every bit of it.'* He looked out over the grounds, the training base now dim under the fading light. *'You ready for what's next?'* There was an underlying tension in his question. Both of them knew that the hardest challenges were yet to come.

Yossi smiled, though a part of him felt the weight of what was to come. *'As ready as I'll ever be.'* He thought of Yael, of the life he wanted to build, and of the unknown future that stretched out before them. He knew that while this moment was a victory, the path ahead was still full of uncertainty.

But for now, they had made it. They had earned their place in the Parachute Brigade, and nothing could take that away.

With their training complete, Yossi and Nadav returned to Tel Aviv for a week. The transition from the intensity of the Paratroopers' training back to the relative calm of civilian life was jarring. Yossi felt an odd sense of detachment as he stepped off the bus, his red beret tucked neatly under his arm. The bustling streets of Tel Aviv felt distant, almost unfamiliar after weeks of constant training. The scent of falafel and the hum of traffic surrounded him, but his mind was still back at Bahad 8, reliving the relentless challenges he had endured.

Yael met Yossi at the station. The moment she saw him, her face lit up, and she ran into his arms. They embraced tightly, neither wanting to let go. It felt like a lifetime since they had last held each other, and for Yossi, this moment grounded him in a way that no amount of training could. The familiar scent of Yael's hair brought a wave of comfort he hadn't felt in weeks, a reminder that this, too, was part of his life.

'I've missed you,' Yossi whispered into her hair, his arms still wrapped around her.

'I've missed you too,' Yael replied, tears forming in her eyes as she pulled back slightly to look at him. *'We have a whole week together. Let's make every second count.'*

Yossi smiled, though a part of him still carried the weight of his recent experiences. He wanted to be fully present, to cherish this time with Yael, but the demands of his role, the reality of his new responsibilities as a paratrooper, gnawed at the edges of his thoughts. His muscles ached from the Beret March, and even though he was back in the comfort of Tel Aviv, the weight of the red beret reminded him that this respite was temporary.

They spent the week rediscovering each other, wandering the familiar streets of Tel Aviv, talking about their hopes, their fears, and their dreams for the future. Every moment felt precious, as if time had become more fragile, a reminder of how much they had missed each other. Yossi couldn't help but notice the small things he had taken for granted before - the sound of Yael's laughter, the feel of her hand in his, the simplicity of walking together through the city. But even as they shared these moments, there was a tension in the air. Yossi knew that their time was limited.

One evening, as they sat on a bench overlooking the beach, the sun setting over the Mediterranean in a wash of orange and gold, Yael turned to Yossi with a serious expression.

'Do you ever think about what it will be like when all this is over?' she asked softly, her voice filled with a mix of hope and concern.

Yossi paused, looking out at the horizon. The rhythmic sound of the waves lapping against the shore filled the silence between them. *'Every day,'* he replied after a moment. *'I think about it all the time. I imagine a life where we can just... be. No more separations, no more wondering when we'll see each other again. Just us, together.'*

Yael smiled, though her eyes glistened with unshed tears. *'That's what keeps me going, Yossi. Knowing that there's a future for us, waiting on the other side of all this.'* Her words hung in the air, heavy with the weight of unspoken fears - the fear that maybe that future wouldn't come as easily as they hoped.

Yossi reached over, gently taking her hand in his. *'We'll get there,'* he whispered, his voice filled with determination. *'I promise.'* But even as he said the words, a part of him wondered how many promises he could truly keep. The demands of the military were growing, and with each passing day, the reality of war and service felt more inescapable. He wanted to believe in a future with Yael, but the uncertainty of what lay ahead loomed over him like a dark cloud.

Before Yossi's time in Tel Aviv ended, he visited his father, David, at home. It had become a tradition for them to have long conversations after Yossi returned from the field, and this time was no different. They sat on the roof of their apartment block, the late afternoon sun casting long shadows across the ground, the warm scent of citrus trees filling the air. Yossi felt a sense of peace being here, but he couldn't shake the feeling that he had changed, that he no longer fit as easily into this life.

David listened intently as Yossi recounted his experiences in the Parachute Course, the Beret March, and the ceremony. There was pride in David's eyes, but also a quiet concern that only a father could feel. He had seen Yossi grow into a man, but he also knew the cost of the life Yossi had chosen.

"You've grown, Yossi," David said, his voice thoughtful. "*I can hear it in the way you talk. You've seen things now that change a man.*"

Yossi nodded slowly. "*Yeah... it's hard to explain, but it feels like a part of me shifted. I feel stronger, but at the same time, I know there's a lot more to come. I don't think I've even scratched the surface of what this life really means.*"

David leaned forward, his expression serious. "*You've always been strong, Yossi. And I'm glad you have Yael by your side. She's a strong, wonderful young woman.*" He paused, letting the words settle before continuing. "*But you need to pace yourself. Take things one step at a time. You have a lot ahead of you, but you'll get there. Don't let it weigh you down all at once.*"

Yossi appreciated his father's wisdom, but it was easier said than done. Every step forward seemed to bring new challenges, new responsibilities, and he wasn't sure how long he could keep shouldering the load. But for now, he nodded, taking comfort in the fact that his father understood.

David's gaze softened, but there was a note of gravity in his voice. "*Listen, son... I know you're going to see things - things that will change you. I've been there myself, and I know how easy it is to try and push it all down. But don't bottle it up inside. Talk about it - whether it's with me, with Nadav, or with Yael. Just make sure you let it out.*"

Yossi looked down, his father's words hitting closer to home than he expected. "*What if I can't?*" he murmured quietly. "*What if it's too much?*"

David reached over, placing a firm hand on Yossi's shoulder. *"That's when you have to lean on the people around you. You don't have to carry it alone. Trust me - if you try to shoulder it all, it'll eat away at you. Don't let it. Share it. Even if it's hard, even if you don't know where to start... just don't keep it locked up."*

Yossi swallowed hard, a knot forming in his chest. He had always been the one others leaned on - whether it was Nadav during training, or his friends back in Tel Aviv. But now, with his father's steady gaze holding his, he realised just how much those words meant. His father knew. He understood.

"I'll try," Yossi said softly, meeting his father's eyes. *"I promise, I'll try."*

David gave a small, approving nod, a smile tugging at the corners of his mouth. *"That's all I ask, Yossi. Just try. And remember - you're not alone in this."*

"Thanks, Dad," Yossi murmured, his voice thick with emotion. He looked out at the sun setting over the porch, casting everything in a warm, golden light. There was still so much ahead of him - so many unknowns and unseen challenges. But in that moment, with his father's hand still resting on his shoulder, he felt a little more prepared to face them.

For now, that was enough.

Yael stopped by David's office again, carrying a small bag filled with freshly made sandwiches. She spotted Salma at her desk, deeply engrossed in her work.

"Hey, Salma," Yael called softly, catching her attention.

Salma looked up, surprise flickering across her face before it melted into a smile. *"Yael! What brings you here?"*

"Thought you might like a break," Yael replied, lifting the bag. *"I brought us some lunch. Would you like to join me?"*

Salma hesitated for just a moment, then nodded, setting her work aside. *"That sounds nice. Thank you."*

They moved to a small corner of the office, sitting side by side as Yael unpacked the sandwiches. The scent of roasted vegetables and freshly baked bread filled the space, and Salma's expression brightened.

"You didn't have to go through all this trouble," Salma murmured, taking a bite.

"It's no trouble at all," Yael insisted with a smile. *"It's nice to share a meal, isn't it?"*

They ate in comfortable silence for a few moments before Yael glanced at her thoughtfully. *"I was wondering... how difficult is it, travelling back and forth from Gaza every day?"*

Salma paused, choosing her words carefully. *"It's... not easy,"* she admitted, her voice quiet but steady. *"The journey is long, and the checkpoints can be unpredictable. But it's worth it. I want to do something meaningful, and this job gives me that chance."*

Yael nodded, admiration softening her gaze. *"It takes a lot of strength to do what you do, Salma. I can't even imagine how hard it must be."*

"We all have our challenges," Salma replied gently. *"But... it means a lot to hear that from you."*

They exchanged a small, genuine smile - a quiet understanding passing between them. It was just a shared lunch, a brief conversation, but it felt like something more. Another step toward a bridge they were both cautiously, but willingly, building.

As the week drew to a close, Yossi and Yael faced their coming separation with a mixture of sadness and resolve. The seven days had passed too quickly, and the prospect of being apart again weighed heavily on them. Yossi held Yael close, feeling the warmth of her body against his, the bittersweet moment of knowing he had to leave once again.

'I'll be back soon,' Yossi whispered, holding Yael close, his breath warm against her hair. *'We'll get through this, Yael. We always do.'*

Yael nodded, her arms tightening around him. Her eyes were bright with unshed tears, but she managed to smile through them. *'I know, Yossi. Just promise me you'll come back to me.'*

Yossi gently cupped her face in his hands, forcing her to meet his gaze. *'I promise. Always.'* His voice was steady, but inside, he felt the weight of that promise more deeply than ever before. He knew the dangers that lay ahead, and the uncertainty of the future loomed over them like a shadow, but he meant every word.

They shared a lingering kiss, the kind that felt both like a farewell and a promise for the future. When Yossi finally pulled away, it was only to embrace his parents, thanking them for their endless support.

Nadav was waiting for Yossi as they prepared to leave, his usual grin lighting up his face. *'Ready?'* he asked, already shouldering his pack.

Yossi glanced back at Yael one last time before nodding. *'Yeah, I'm ready.'*

As they boarded the transport to join their new unit on the Lebanese border, Yossi stared out of the window, his mind filled with thoughts of Yael, his family, and the journey ahead. The familiar weight of responsibility settled over him again, but this time, it didn't feel so overwhelming. With Nadav by his side, and with the strength of the friendships and love that carried him forward, Yossi felt ready for whatever came next. He knew the challenges were far from over, but for the first time, he truly believed that he could face them.

Chapter Twenty Five

AHMED

The year 2020 brought intensified focus on Gaza's militant factions, and Ahmed found himself at the centre of it all. Under a veil of secrecy, he and his team worked relentlessly to expand the network of tunnels beneath the city. Recruits from the local population were tasked with digging and fortifying access points hidden in schools, hospitals, and private homes. These concealed entrances would allow fighters to emerge at will, moving through the underground passages like ghosts. Hidden rooms were also constructed - small, fortified spaces meant to hold hostages, well away from potential rescuers.

But more was at stake than just tunnel work. An urgency filled the air - a sense that something bigger was building with each passing day. Whispers circulated among the higher ranks about a new phase of operations - an offensive campaign that would take the fight directly to Israel's doorstep. Ahmed had been involved in many drills before, but this felt different. The factions were coming together in a way that suggested they were gearing up for something much larger.

One afternoon, Abu Khaled summoned Ahmed to a private meeting. The older man's eyes were hard, his voice low and measured.

"'We're preparing for something beyond anything we've done before,' Abu Khaled began, his tone laced with urgency. 'The operation, codenamed Strong Pillar, will bring together not just our forces, but every faction. No hesitation. No weakness. You'll have command of your unit - total control. Can I count on you to lead this?'"

Ahmed felt a tightening in his chest, a quickening of his pulse. *Why now? Why me?* he wondered, even as he kept his face impassive.

"'*What's the real objective?*" Ahmed asked, forcing his voice to stay steady. His mind raced. There had to be more to this than just a drill. Why the urgency? Why him?"

Abu Khaled leaned closer, his gaze intense. '*We will train near the Erez Checkpoint in the north of Gaza, close enough to simulate an actual breach of the border defences. The objective is to practise breaking through barriers, storming buildings, infiltrating Kibbutzim, and taking hostages. This training must be as realistic as possible. Every detail counts.*'

Over the next several weeks, fighters from Hamas, Islamic Jihad, and smaller factions gathered at the designated training area near the Erez Checkpoint. The terrain, with its mix of open fields and clusters of abandoned buildings, provided the perfect setting to simulate an attack on Israeli border communities. The air was thick with tension as militants prepared for the extensive training exercise.

The first phase focused on breaching border defences. Teams practised cutting through barbed wire, scaling walls, and using makeshift explosives to breach fences. Ahmed oversaw the operations, coordinating his team through radio communication. Fighters moved swiftly, their movements choreographed by his commands.

'*Team One, advance!*' Ahmed called into his radio, watching as a group of fighters sprinted towards a simulated barrier. '*Team Two, cover their flank and prepare for the breach!*'

Explosions sounded in the distance, echoing across the training grounds. The trainees drilled relentlessly, repeating the same manoeuvres until they could execute them flawlessly.

Next came training for infiltrating secured areas. Old buildings had been repurposed to mimic the layout of a typical Kibbutz - high gates, narrow entrances, and a network of small houses and community buildings. Under Ahmed's direction, the fighters practised scaling gates, climbing over walls, and storming buildings.

They rehearsed how to move silently, eliminate security personnel, and capture hostages without raising an alarm.

'Speed is key,' Ahmed instructed during one of the sessions. *'The element of surprise is our greatest advantage. Hit fast, hit hard, and then vanish.'*

He directed the fighters through complex scenarios involving multiple stages of assault. Some teams practised using vehicles and motorbikes to quickly traverse the terrain, while others were tasked with breaching doors and windows. The fighters trained in small units, manoeuvring through rooms, shouting commands, and covering each other's backs.

The drills were intense and repetitive. Combatants practised storming rooms filled with mock hostages, learning to quickly subdue their targets and move them to hidden locations. The emphasis was on efficiency - rapidly identifying threats, neutralising them, and securing strategic points.

During breaks, Ahmed huddled with his commanders, refining strategy and adjusting tactics based on their observations. He communicated constantly with the different units, ensuring that everyone knew their roles. The fighters were taught to adapt on the fly, responding to changing conditions and making quick decisions under pressure.

Over the next few days, the training intensified further. The drills moved into night operations, with the fighters practising under the cover of darkness. Ahmed coordinated movements using vehicles and motorbikes, navigating rough terrain to simulate the quick strikes needed in real combat. He remained in constant communication with the teams, directing them as they practised evading drones, hiding from surveillance, and using tunnels to reposition quickly.

Ahmed's performance in command and control did not go unnoticed. He remained calm under pressure, coordinated multiple units effectively, and made quick decisions. One afternoon, as the sun began to set over the training area, two senior commanders approached him.

'Ahmed, come with us,' one of them said, his tone serious. Ahmed felt a surge of nerves but concealed it with a nod, handing over his headset to another fighter before following them.

They drove him to a secluded building at the edge of the camp. Inside, a group of senior Hamas members sat around a table, their faces stern and focused. Ahmed recognised a few from previous meetings, but most were new to him.

One of the men, a grizzled veteran with a hard gaze, spoke first.

'Ahmed Al-Masri, you have shown yourself to be a capable leader. Your coordination during the exercises has been exemplary. Because of this, we have selected you for an important role in what is to come.'

Ahmed swallowed, keeping his voice steady. *'I'm ready to serve however I can.'*

The veteran nodded.

'We are planning a significant operation - a coordinated attack targeting key locations inside Israel. The goal is to breach their defences, storm strategic positions, and take hostages. It will involve multiple factions, and you will have a critical role in leading part of this effort.'

Ahmed's mind raced as he absorbed the gravity of the words. *When is this operation supposed to take place?*

'When the time is right,' the man replied. *'Until then, your job is to continue preparing your men. They must be ready, disciplined, and capable of executing commands without hesitation.'*

Another commander spoke, his voice measured.

'Understand, Ahmed Al-Masri, the Israeli response will be severe. Our strength must come from our readiness. We strike hard, and then we wait. We know the retaliation will be intense, and our hope is that it ignites a larger conflict, drawing other nations into the fight.'

Ahmed nodded slowly, processing their words.

'And what about the international community?' he asked cautiously.

The veteran commander replied,

'We have others working on that front. Supporters outside of Gaza, those in other nations, and certain media channels. They will shape the narrative, present us as the oppressed, and highlight our struggle. Your focus is here, on the ground. Leave the rest to those who handle that side of the battle.'

Ahmed felt a cold shiver run down his spine. He understood his role clearly: he was to prepare for war, to lead the fighters into what would likely be a bloody and prolonged conflict, while others dealt with the political and media dimensions.

'I understand,' he said firmly.

The commanders exchanged approving glances.

'Good,' the senior member said. *'We believe in you, Ahmed Al-Masri. Do not let us down.'*

For the next few days, Ahmed stayed at the training grounds, overseeing his team's exercises with renewed intensity. He felt the weight of the secret he carried, the responsibility of his role in the upcoming operation. Every manoeuvre, every drill took on new meaning, and he pushed his men harder, knowing they needed to be flawless when the time came.

When the exercise finally concluded, Ahmed felt a deep exhaustion settle over him. He had not slept properly in days, his mind consumed by the enormity of what lay ahead. He longed to return home, to find some comfort in familiar surroundings.

When he finally made it back, it was late in the evening. Salma was waiting for him, her face lined with worry. She could see the weariness in his eyes, the tension in his posture.

'Ahmed,' she began softly, *'where have you been? You haven't come home in days. What's going on?'*

Ahmed hesitated, feeling the strain of holding everything inside.

'It's just... the training,' he said quietly, trying to keep his tone steady. *'There's a lot happening, a lot to prepare for.'*

Salma frowned, sensing there was more to it.

'But why this intensity? What are you really training for?'

Ahmed's frustration flared.

'Salma, I've told you, it's just preparation!' he snapped, immediately regretting his harsh tone. He saw the hurt in her eyes, and guilt washed over him.

'I'm sorry,' he muttered, softer this time. *'I'm just... tired.'*

Salma took a step closer, her voice gentle but firm.

'Ahmed, I've seen what's happening - the digging of tunnels, the new entrances in schools, hospitals, and even people's homes. It's not just training anymore. It feels like we're preparing for something big. And I'm scared, Ahmed. I'm scared that a war is coming, right here, to where we live.'

Ahmed felt a surge of guilt and frustration. He had hoped she wouldn't notice the full scale of their preparations, but Salma was sharp - she always had been. He looked away, his jaw tightening.

'Salma, you know we must be ready for anything. We can't afford to be caught off guard.'

Salma shook her head, her eyes filled with a mix of fear and concern.

'But why here, Ahmed? Why are we making our homes into battlegrounds? Our schools, our hospitals... our streets? You're putting all of us in danger.'

Ahmed's face hardened.

'You think I want this? You think I enjoy turning our city into a fortress? This is the reality, Salma. We don't have a choice. If we don't prepare, we'll be overrun.'

Salma's voice trembled.

'I understand that we need to defend ourselves, but this feels different. This isn't just about defence anymore. It's like... we're inviting the fight here. And I'm worried about what that means for our families, for our friends. What will happen to us?'

Ahmed's heart pounded. He wanted to reassure her, to tell her everything would be okay, but he knew he couldn't make such promises.

'I know you're scared,' he said softly, *'but we're doing this to protect our people, to give ourselves a fighting chance. I can't just sit by and wait for them to come to us. We must be ready to strike back.'*

Salma took a deep breath, trying to steady herself.

'But at what cost, Ahmed? What if this leads to more suffering, more loss? I don't want to lose you, or anyone else. I don't want our home to become a war zone.'

Ahmed felt a lump in his throat, torn between his duty and the fear he saw in her eyes.

'I don't want that either, Salma,' he whispered, his voice thick with emotion. *'But this is the path we're on. I must follow it, even if I don't have all the answers.'*

Salma's eyes glistened with unshed tears.

'Just... be careful,' she pleaded. *'And remember that there's more at stake than just the battle. Our lives, our future - they matter too.'*

Ahmed nodded slowly, feeling the weight of her words settle over him like a heavy shroud.

'I'll remember,' he promised quietly, though he wasn't sure how he could balance the demands of his role with the growing uncertainty in his heart.

He squeezed her hand, trying to offer some comfort even as he felt the turmoil within himself grow.

'I'm doing what I think is right, Salma. I hope... I hope you can understand that.'

Salma nodded, but her expression remained troubled.

'I just don't want to see you get lost in this, Ahmed. I don't want to lose you to a fight that never seems to end.'

Ahmed felt the sting of her words, knowing she was right in many ways. He pulled her closer, holding her tightly, as if trying to shield her from the reality that loomed over them.

'I promise,' he whispered again, though the uncertainty in his own heart made it feel like a fragile vow.

As they stood there in the dimly lit room, both of them knew that their world was shifting beneath their feet, and that the choices they made in the coming days would shape everything that followed.

Chapter Twenty Six

YOSSI

Yossi and Nadav arrived at their new assignment - a small, rugged field base along the Israeli-Lebanese border. The base sprawled over a rocky hillside, a stark contrast to the orderly barracks they had left behind. Sandbags were piled high around the perimeter, and barbed wire twisted along the edges, forming a crude but effective barrier. Dirt pathways snaked between makeshift tents and rough-built shacks, blending almost seamlessly into the landscape. It felt as if the camp had grown from the earth itself, a part of the rugged terrain.

The air buzzed with the hum of generators, punctuated by the distant crackle of radio transmissions. This was a place built for function, not comfort - a frontline outpost where every soldier knew that an alert could come at any moment. Tension hung in the air, a constant reminder that they were only a heartbeat away from action. But beneath that tension, there was also a sense of purpose. Everyone here understood what was at stake.

As they stepped off the transport vehicle, a lean, weathered soldier with sharp eyes and a no-nonsense demeanour approached.

'Welcome to the border,' he said, extending a hand. *'I'm Samar (Staff Sergeant) Aviad Halevi. You're the new guys, right?'*

Yossi nodded, shaking his hand. *'Yes, Samar, Rosenberg and Levy.'*

Samar Halevi offered a brief smile. *'Glad to have you both. Listen up: this isn't like the base you're used to. Here, things work differently. We've got routines, but they're built around constant readiness. You learn discipline from knowing what could happen, not from someone yelling orders.'*

He gestured around the camp. *'Everyone here has a job, and every job matters. Get settled quickly - we don't have the luxury of easing you in.'*

Yossi and Nadav quickly adjusted to the rhythms of life at the field base. The living conditions were rough: small tents or shacks served as sleeping quarters, and communal areas, like the makeshift mess tent and the communications station carved into a hollowed-out section of the hillside, were minimal. Dust seemed to settle on everything, and the ground was uneven underfoot, a constant reminder of the rugged terrain they were living in.

Yossi was assigned to a reconnaissance team responsible for monitoring the border for any unusual activity. The work was intense, requiring constant vigilance - scanning hills and valleys with binoculars and infrared cameras, always alert for signs of trouble. Each sweep of the terrain was accompanied by a quiet tension, as if the landscape itself might shift to reveal a threat.

Nadav, meanwhile, was placed with a quick response team, always on standby to react to any incident along the border. They practised rapid deployments, moving out of the base and into the field within minutes of receiving an alert. The team maintained a state of near-constant readiness, their gear packed and ready to go at all times.

From the outset, Yossi and Nadav noticed how different this was from their training. There were no drill sergeants barking orders, no strict formations. Instead, discipline was quieter, more ingrained - a matter of survival. The soldiers moved with an easy confidence, but always with an undercurrent of readiness, as though a single wrong move could trigger a cascade of consequences.

Yossi adapted quickly to the new dynamics. His role demanded a keen eye for detail and the ability to spot even the smallest changes in the landscape that might signal a threat. He communicated constantly with his team through short radio bursts, calling out coordinates and marking suspicious movements on maps. The pressure to avoid missing anything important weighed heavily on him, making each day feel like a delicate balancing act between focus and fatigue.

Nadav focused on building camaraderie with his quick response team. His role required not just physical endurance but also the ability to think quickly and act decisively. He soon gained a reputation for his calm under pressure and his skill with heavy gear and weapons. His humour and willingness to help made him a trusted member of the team.

Life at the field base was demanding, but it fostered a strong sense of camaraderie. The soldiers relied on one another not just for their safety but for the safety of the entire unit. Yossi and Nadav were welcomed into this tight-knit group, where bonds were forged over long nights on watch, shared meals, and countless moments of tension and relief.

'Out here, you learn to read people fast,' Eitan, a veteran soldier, told them one day. *'You've got to know who's got your back when things go sideways.'*

Yossi nodded. *'I get it. Trust matters out here.'*

Nadav quickly established himself as a reliable presence in the unit. He volunteered for the toughest tasks, whether it was carrying heavy supplies up steep hills or taking the hardest shifts on watch. His easy-going nature and ability to laugh in the face of adversity made him popular among his comrades.

Yossi, too, earned respect with his sharp instincts and calm demeanour. He quickly learned the intricacies of reconnaissance work, developing a knack for interpreting the subtle signs that might indicate a threat. His team began to look to him for guidance, trusting his judgement in situations where split-second decisions could make all the difference.

One evening, during a rare break, Yossi found himself thinking of Yael. He pulled out his phone and saw a new message from her.

'I hope you're okay. I miss you. The border feels so far away.'

Yossi smiled, feeling a warmth spread through his chest. He quickly typed back:

'I'm good. Just tired, but I'm doing what I have to do. I miss you too, more than you know. We'll see each other soon, I promise.'

Yael replied almost immediately:

'I'll hold you to that. Stay safe, Yossi.'

Yossi stared at the message for a long moment, feeling the strength in her words. He pocketed his phone, a renewed sense of determination coursing through him.

'Message from Yael?' Nadav asked, raising an eyebrow.

Yossi nodded. *'Yeah, she says she misses me.'*

Nadav grinned. *'Of course she does. And I'm sure she's counting the days till you're back.'*

Yossi laughed, but there was a seriousness in his voice. *'Me too. But I know we're where we need to be. This is our time.'*

In quieter moments, when they were off-duty, Yossi and Nadav would talk about their future, their dreams, and the people waiting for them back home.

One evening, as they sat on a hillside watching the sun dip below the horizon, Nadav broke the silence.

'You think about Yael a lot, don't you?' he asked, his tone thoughtful.

'Every day,' Yossi admitted. *'She keeps me grounded, reminds me why we're doing this. She's my anchor.'*

Nadav nodded, understanding. *'That's good. We all need someone or something to hold on to out here. It makes all this... bearable.'*

Yossi glanced at Nadav. *'And for you? What's your anchor?'*

Nadav paused, thoughtful. *'I think it's you, mate. Knowing we've got each other's backs... that gets me through.'*

Yossi smiled, touched by his friend's words. *'Same here, Nadav.'*

As the days passed, the bonds between the soldiers deepened. Yossi found himself more attuned to the subtle dynamics of the group, noticing who needed encouragement, who needed space, and who just needed someone to listen.

One evening, he saw a young soldier, Ari, sitting alone, looking out over the darkened landscape. Yossi approached him.

'Hey, Ari,' Yossi said gently. *'You doing alright?'*

Ari looked up, surprised but grateful for the interruption.

'Yeah, just... missing home, I guess. It's hard sometimes, you know?'

Yossi nodded. *'I get it. We all do. But we're here for each other. If you ever need to talk, I'm around.'*

Ari smiled, his expression softening. *'Thanks, Yossi. That means a lot.'*

Back in the base, Nadav continued to excel in his role with the response team. One afternoon, after a particularly intense drill, he sat down next to Yossi.

'You know,' Nadav began, *'I never thought I'd be able to handle this kind of pressure. But being here, with you and the team... it makes it feel possible.'*

Yossi nodded. *'We're all stronger than we think. And when you've got people you trust... that makes all the difference.'*

Despite the constant tension, they felt a growing sense of purpose. They knew why they were there and what was at stake. Their roles were not just about maintaining a presence, they were about protecting their country, their families, and their future.

In the evenings, as the sun dipped below the horizon, Yossi and Nadav often sat together, sharing a quiet moment before another long night. They talked about their families, friends, and the lives they had left behind. They spoke of Yael and their dreams for the future - dreams that seemed both near and impossibly far.

'We're learning a lot out here,' Yossi said one night, looking over the darkened hills. *'But I think we're also learning who we really are.'*

Nadav nodded. *'We're becoming the soldiers we trained to be,'* he replied. *'And whatever comes next, we're ready for it.'*

Yossi smiled, feeling a sense of calm. They had made it this far, and they would continue to face whatever challenges came their way - together.

In a dimly lit room filled with computer screens and satellite feeds, Yael, sat at her station in the Combat Intelligence Unit, her eyes fixed on the live footage streaming from surveillance drones near the Erez Crossing. The video feed revealed a large group of armed men moving in a coordinated manner across a dusty field just north of the crossing. The area was scattered with makeshift barriers, vehicles, and clusters of men - clearly indicating a large-scale training exercise.

Yael zoomed in on the scene, her fingers deftly manipulating the controls to enhance the resolution of the feed. *"We've got multiple squads engaging in what looks like breaching exercises,"* she muttered to Samir, who was also watching intently, leaning over her shoulder.

Samir, deep into his work in Intelligence, nodded, his eyes narrowing as he studied the footage. *"They're simulating an attack scenario,"* he remarked. *"See how they're moving in formation, practicing cutting through barbed wire, and setting small charges to breach barriers? They're preparing for an offensive, likely targeting a settlement or a Kibbutz across the border."*

Yael adjusted the feed, switching to an overhead thermal view. *"And look at the vehicles,"* she pointed out. *"They've got pickups and motorbikes positioned on the outskirts, ready for rapid insertion and extraction. This isn't defensive training - they're gearing up for something bigger, probably a cross-border raid."*

Samir switched to a different drone angle, capturing the scene from another direction. *"Over there,"* he indicated, *"A group is conducting close quarters combat drills, moving through what looks like a mock-up of residential buildings. This is definitely preparation for urban combat, house-to-house engagements, maybe even hostage-taking scenarios."*

Yael frowned, leaning closer to the screen. *"I count three different factions here - Hamas, Islamic Jihad, and smaller groups, all training together. They're using the area near the Erez Crossing as a rehearsal space for a coordinated assault."*

"*That's concerning*," Samir agreed. "*It's a strong message that they're unifying their efforts, which suggests they're planning a large-scale, coordinated offensive. We need to escalate this intel immediately.*"

Yael nodded and quickly grabbed her radio. "*This is Unit 47*," she reported. "*We have confirmed visual on Hamas and allied factions conducting joint military exercises near the Erez Crossing. Activities indicate preparation for an offensive operation involving breaching border defences, infiltration tactics, and urban warfare. Recommend heightened alert status. Over.*"

As she finished the transmission, Yael's thoughts briefly flickered to Yossi on the ground near the Lebanese border, aware that the exercise unfolding before her could be the precursor to something far more significant. She bit her lip, pushing her concern aside as she refocused on the task at hand. "*Let's keep tracking their movements*," she said, glancing at Samir. "*We need to be ready for any escalation.*"

"*Agreed*," Samir replied, his voice tense. "*We need to make sure everyone on the ground is prepared.*"

Yael nodded, silently hoping that Yossi and his unit were ready for whatever lay ahead.

Samir sat in a small, secure briefing room deep within the intelligence headquarters. Around him, a group of senior officers, including his direct superior, Lieutenant Colonel Arik, waited for his report. The room was quiet, save for the faint hum of the projector, which displayed images and video clips captured near the Erez Crossing on a large screen at the front.

Samir took a deep breath, steadied himself, and began. "*Over the past several days, we've monitored increased activity near the Erez Crossing. Multiple factions, including Hamas, Islamic Jihad, and smaller militant groups, have been conducting joint exercises in a secured area close to the border.*"

He clicked a button, and a series of drone images flashed on the screen: groups of armed men moving in coordinated formations, practicing breaching manoeuvres against makeshift barriers, setting small charges, and conducting house-to-house combat drills in mock-up buildings.

"*As you can see,*" Samir continued, "*These drills are far more extensive than routine training. They've been simulating offensive scenarios, including breaching border fences, storming buildings, and conducting urban combat and hostage-taking operations. They're also using motorbikes and vehicles to practice rapid insertion and extraction, which suggests preparation for a coordinated cross-border assault.*"

The officers around the table exchanged glances, some frowning, others nodding slightly. Lieutenant Colonel Arik leaned forward, resting his chin on his hand. "Samir," he began, his tone measured, "*What's your assessment of the threat level here? Is this something we should be worried about?*"

Samir hesitated for a moment, choosing his words carefully. "*Sir, given the scale and intensity of the training, it's clear they're preparing for something more than just defensive operations. The cooperation between factions suggests a unified effort, which we know has been rare in the past. I recommend raising the alert level and conducting further reconnaissance to understand their objectives.*"

Lieutenant Colonel Arik tapped his pen against the table thoughtfully, then sighed. "*Samir, I appreciate your thoroughness,*" he said, his voice calm but firm. "*But exercises like these are not uncommon in Gaza. Hamas and the other factions often use these shows of force to demonstrate unity or to prepare for potential escalations. This isn't the first time they've conducted large-scale training near the Erez Crossing, and it likely won't be the last.*"

Samir nodded, but he couldn't shake the feeling of unease. "*Sir, I understand,*" he replied cautiously, "*but the specific nature of the drills - breaching, urban combat, and hostage scenarios - suggests a shift towards offensive capabilities. I believe it warrants closer monitoring.*"

Arik leaned back in his chair, considering this. "*We'll keep an eye on it, of course,*" he said finally, "*But at this point, there's no indication of an imminent threat to our border positions or settlements. We have to be careful not to overreact to every move they make. Their goal is often to provoke a response from us, to make us jump at shadows.*"

Another officer chimed in, *"And if we start treating every exercise as a sign of an impending attack, we risk exhausting our resources and spreading our forces too thin."*

Samir continued his presentation, clicking to advance the slideshow to a new series of images. The photographs displayed on the screen were grainy but clear enough to capture the tension in the room. The officers leaned forward, their focus sharpening as they took in the faces.

"In these recent images," Samir began, pointing to the screen, *"We have observed a number of key figures at the training grounds near the Erez Crossing. Several senior Hamas members - known for orchestrating past operations - have been seen entering a small building at the edge of the compound. This structure, based on our intelligence, is likely being used for high-level meetings and briefings."*

He paused, letting the weight of his words sink in. *"What stands out here,"* Samir continued, *"Is the presence of these known leaders, but also someone who is new to us."*

Samir clicked to the next slide, revealing a photograph of fighter. The image showed the fighter in the midst of training exercises, directing a group with a handheld radio, his expression focused and determined. *"This individual,"* Samir pointed out, *"Has been observed multiple times during the exercises. He appears to be in a leadership position, orchestrating movements, and issuing commands to various combatant groups."*

Lieutenant Colonel Arik, seated at the head of the table, leaned forward. *"Do we have an identification on him?"*

Samir shook his head slightly. *"Not yet, sir. He's new to us. From what we've seen, he's not someone we've encountered in our previous intelligence assessments. But he's clearly playing a significant role in the ongoing training."*

Samir clicked again, showing a second image of the fighter - this time, captured entering the same small building used by the senior Hamas members. The timestamp indicated it was shortly after one of the more intensive training sessions. *"Here,"* Samir continued, *"We see him entering the building where the senior *members were meeting. It suggests that he may have direct access to higher command or is being brought into their circle."*

The room went quiet for a moment as the officers absorbed the new information. Lieutenant Colonel Arik spoke up, "*If he's someone new but already in a leadership position and being brought into these meetings, he could be important. We need to know more about him.*"

Samir nodded. "*Yes, sir. We're currently working to identify him, and we'll increase our monitoring efforts to learn more about his background, his role, and his potential significance in these exercises.*"

Lieutenant Colonel Arik tapped his fingers thoughtfully on the table. "*Good. Keep this individual in your sights. Find out who he is, where he came from, and what his connections are to the senior leadership. If he's becoming a key player, we need to understand his purpose.*"

Samir agreed, knowing the task ahead would require careful observation and analysis. As he got up to leave the briefing room, he made a mental note to prioritise gathering more intelligence on this unknown figure who had suddenly appeared on their radar. The fighter was an enigma, and they needed to uncover his story before it became a threat.

"*Understood, sir,*" he said. "*We'll continue to monitor the situation closely and update you with any new developments.*"

Lieutenant Colonel Arik nodded. "*Good. Keep your team on it, but don't escalate without further evidence. For now, maintain standard alert levels. Dismissed.*"

Amir nodded, saluting briefly before gathering his notes. As he left the room, he felt a mixture of resignation and determination. He knew his instincts were telling him that something more significant was brewing.

Chapter Twenty Seven

AHMED

Ahmed stood on the rooftop, the cold wind biting through his jacket like a blade. Below, Gaza sprawled in a shroud of darkness, the city holding its breath, as if waiting for something inevitable. The distant rev of a car engine, the murmur of voices, the sharp slam of a door - each sound echoed in the silence, like ghostly reminders of a life he barely recognised anymore. His mind drifted back to Salma and their last conversation. He could still see the worry etched across her face, hear the tremble in her voice as she questioned their path.

Is this really how we protect our people? she had asked, and Ahmed hadn't had an answer then. He still didn't. He stared out over the city, feeling the weight of the question pressing down on him like the very air itself.

His phone rang, shattering the stillness. It was Tariq. His voice was tight, clipped.

"Ahmed, we need you at the safe house. Now."

The urgency surged through him like a jolt of electricity. He left immediately, moving quickly through the narrow streets, his thoughts whirling. The weight of his responsibilities pressed down like a heavy stone on his shoulders. When he reached the safe house, Tariq and Khaled were already there, their faces tense, shadows dancing in the dim light. Bilal and Hadi stood nearby, speaking quietly with a small group of new recruits, their voices calm and measured as they laid out the vision to the eager young men.

Ahmed nodded to Bilal and Hadi before turning to Tariq. *"What's going on?"*

Tariq's expression was grim. *"A patrol near the Erez crossing spotted one of our tunnel exits. It's only a matter of time before they investigate further."*

Khaled, jaw clenched, cut in sharply. *"If they find that tunnel, we lose months of work. It'll set back our preparations for the operation."*

Ahmed's mind raced. The tunnel was crucial to their plans and losing it would be a significant blow. But acting too hastily could draw even more attention. He paused, the pressure mounting like a vice.

"Alright," he said, forcing his voice to remain steady. *"We need to seal it, but we have to leave no trace."* He turned to Bilal and Hadi. *"Create a distraction - organise something near the area that draws attention away from the tunnel. Make it look natural."*

Bilal nodded, his expression calm, almost serene. *"We can handle that. We've built connections, people trust us. We'll make it look like a community gathering - nothing suspicious."*

Hadi's voice was softer but equally firm. *"And we'll use it to strengthen recruitment, bring in more young men. The community needs to feel our presence, not our absence."*

Tariq's impatience flared, his eyes hard. *"What about sealing the tunnel? We need to act now."*

Ahmed turned to Tariq and Khaled. *"You two handle the tunnel. Get our best men and make sure it's done quickly and quietly. No mistakes."*

Khaled's gaze darkened. *"If they get too close, we deal with them. No hesitation."*

Ahmed hesitated, feeling a flicker of doubt pass through him. *"No unnecessary violence, Khaled. We handle this smart, not reckless."*

Khaled's eyes narrowed, his jaw set in defiance, but he nodded slowly. *"Fine, but if it comes to it, we act."*

The tension in the room crackled like electricity. Ahmed could feel the weight of their expectations - each decision a potential flashpoint for bloodshed. He took a deep breath, pushing aside the gnawing fear that every choice he made was leading them further down a path from which there was no return.

As the meeting broke up, Ahmed found himself standing alone, watching his friends. Tariq and Khaled, always ready for a fight, willing to take risks without hesitation, Bilal and Hadi, who moved in quieter ways, speaking softly, building trust with every word. And here he was, caught between them - torn between his loyalty to his people and his growing doubts - doubts planted by Salma's words and watered by the reality he faced each day.

Can we really protect our people by turning Gaza into a fortress? he wondered, the thought slipping through his mind like a poison. *Can we ever hope to win by sacrificing everything we hold dear?*

On the walk home, Ahmed's thoughts grew heavier. He remembered a time when he was younger, sitting on his mother's lap, listening to his father speak with fierce intensity about the injustices they had suffered. *"Never forget what they did to us,"* he had growled, his eyes blazing with a hatred that seemed endless. *"We will take our revenge, Ahmed. We will make them pay - every single one of them."* His mother's hands had tightened around his shoulders, as if trying to keep the fury from swallowing him whole.

Yusuf's anger, his unwavering belief in revenge, and Abu Khaled's cold detachment were all part of the same narrative. He recalled a recent conversation with Abu Khaled, who had dismissed concerns about civilian casualties with a wave of his hand.

"They are collateral," he had said coldly. *"Necessary sacrifices for a greater cause."*

Ahmed knew he was being pulled deeper into this war, every day more entangled in the plans of those above him. He also knew they didn't care about Gaza or its people. They cared only about starting a war they believed would bring a new reality. And he was part of that now, whether he wanted to be or not.

When he reached home, Salma was waiting for him. Her eyes met his, searching for some sign of the young man she had known before he was dragged in so deep.

"Ahmed," she began softly, stepping forward. *"I know you feel trapped, that you think there is no other way. But every time I see another tunnel, another preparation for war, I wonder... is this really what we want? Is this really how we protect our people?"*

Ahmed sighed, her words settling over him like a heavy blanket.

"Salma, I'm... lost," he whispered, his voice cracking. *"I used to know what was right, but now... I only keep moving because it's all I know. Somehow, I have to believe it will protect us, but I don't even trust that anymore."*

Salma stepped closer, her hand reaching out to touch his arm.

"Every time I hear another rumour about a new tunnel, or an attack being planned, I feel sick, Ahmed. Is this really the life we want for our children? To live in fear, preparing only for war?"

Ahmed's face remained stoic, his emotions buried deep.

"I understand what you're saying, Salma, but we have no choice. This is the path we are on, and I have to see it through."

Her eyes searched his, a mix of frustration and fear.

"Just remember, Ahmed," she whispered, *"that the fight isn't the only thing that defines us. There's more to who we are, more to what we could be."*

Ahmed nodded, feeling the conflict within him deepen.

"I'll try to remember," he said quietly, though he wasn't sure if he could find a way to see beyond the fight, beyond the hatred that had been so deeply ingrained in him.

As they stood together in the dimly lit room, Ahmed felt a moment of clarity, a fleeting sense that perhaps there was another way. But it was gone as quickly as it came, lost in the shadows of their world - a world that demanded choices he wasn't sure he was ready to make.

Later that night, Ahmed returned to the rooftop. The wind had grown colder, the city's lights flickering like fading stars. He stared out into the darkness, his thoughts a tangled web of doubt and determination. He knew the path he was on, but he could no longer see where it would lead.

There's no turning back now, he thought, feeling the chill of fear creep through him. *I've gone too deep. Any sign of hesitation, and they'll see me as a threat. And I know what happens to threats.*

He closed his eyes, feeling the wind whip against his face.

If I want to survive, I have to be strong. Unyielding.

Opening his eyes, he looked out over the city, listening to the faint sounds of life around him. He knew he was trapped, not just in a war with those outside, but in a battle within himself - a battle with no clear end in sight.

Chapter Twenty Eight

YOSSI

Yossi and Nadav had fully integrated into their unit along the tense border with Lebanon. Each day stretched into long hours filled with patrols, observation posts, and unrelenting vigilance. Both had proven themselves reliable soldiers, earning respect for their dedication, sharp instincts, and camaraderie with their comrades. Their consistent performance had not gone unnoticed by their commanding officers.

Within the IDF, the promotion system for enlisted men is structured, and both Yossi and Nadav were quickly moving up the ranks. Due to their exemplary conduct, they were promoted from Rav Turai (Corporal) to Samal (Sergeant). The rank of Samal marked a step up in leadership and responsibility.

The promotion ceremony was simple but meaningful, held at their field base near the border. Standing before their platoon, they received their new rank insignia from their Commanding Officer, Lt. Colonel Arad - a chevron with a small star. Yossi felt a swell of pride. He and Nadav had come a long way from their initial days of basic training, now recognised as leaders within their unit.

Yet, as the insignia was pinned to his uniform, Yossi felt a conflicting mix of pride and apprehension. With this new rank came a deeper involvement in the complexities of their mission. He was no longer just a soldier, he was a leader, responsible for making hard calls. But what did that mean when the lines between right and wrong blurred with every skirmish, every order to advance? Was he becoming a better soldier, or was he losing a part of himself?

Yossi glanced at Nadav during the ceremony. His friend wore a proud expression, but Yossi knew Nadav's thoughts must mirror his own - was this promotion a step forward, or the beginning of a path that would take them somewhere else?

Shortly after their promotion, there was a noticeable increase in activity along the border. Hezbollah had grown more aggressive, their movements frequent and visible. The presence of Hezbollah fighters became larger, more organised, and confident. It was clear they were testing the resolve of the IDF, probing defences and seeking vulnerabilities.

Yossi and his unit were on more frequent patrols, ordered to remain vigilant. One afternoon, Yossi and Nadav's sections were conducting a routine patrol near a narrow valley close to their base when their radio crackled with an urgent message from the forward observation post.

"*Hezbollah fighters spotted moving toward your location,*" came the tense voice. "*Prepare for engagement.*"

Yossi's heart kicked into high gear. He glanced at Nadav, who was positioned with his own team further down the valley, separated by about a hundred metres of uneven terrain. They exchanged a look - a silent understanding that they would have to fight this one as separate leaders, not as battle partners standing shoulder to shoulder.

"*Stay sharp, everyone,*" Yossi called to his squad. "*Nadav's unit is on our left flank, we'll cover the right. Keep your sectors clear, and eyes on the target.*"

He pressed his Pressel switch, adjusting the frequency to reach Nadav's comms. "*Nadav, how's your position?*"

"*Good to go, Yossi. We're setting up cover here. If they push right, we'll be ready to pin them down,*" Nadav's voice crackled back, tense but focused.

The valley was thick with scrub and rocky outcrops, providing ample cover for an enemy force. The sun had begun to set, casting long shadows that could hide movement. The air was heavy with anticipation, the scent of earth and dust mingling with the sharp tang of metal from their weapons. Yossi's unit quickly took positions, crouching behind boulders and low bushes. They waited, weapons ready, ears straining to hear beyond the rustling of the wind.

Minutes later, they heard the soft crunch of footsteps and whispered Arabic. Yossi raised his hand, signalling his men to stay down. Through the trees, he made out shapes - Hezbollah fighters creeping towards them, clearly preparing for an ambush.

"*Engage on my command... wait... wait...*" Yossi whispered into his radio, his pulse pounding.

A twig snapped underfoot, the sound unnaturally loud in the stillness.

"*Fire!*" Yossi shouted.

The air erupted with gunfire. Yossi's section opened fire, their rifles spitting rounds into the advancing enemy. The Hezbollah fighters, caught by surprise, hesitated before returning fire. Bullets zipped past Yossi's head, thudding into the dirt around him. Each shot felt like a hammer striking the air, the sound reverberating off the valley walls.

Yossi's men fought with precision, taking cover and firing controlled bursts. He focused on keeping their formation tight, ensuring no gaps for the enemy to exploit. But as more Hezbollah fighters poured in, he knew they were getting pressed.

"*Nadav, we're getting pinned down here!*" Yossi shouted into his radio. "*I need suppressive fire on my right!*"

"*Roger that. Hold your position, we'll lay it down for you,*" Nadav replied.

Yossi's radio crackled as Nadav's section unleashed a barrage of fire. Yossi took advantage of the distraction, directing his squad to adjust their formation and push up slightly. Just then, a Hezbollah fighter emerged from behind a boulder, aiming a rocket-propelled grenade (RPG) launcher.

"*RPG on the right!*" Yossi called out.

Nadav's voice came through sharply. "*I see him. We've got him covered!*"

One of Nadav's men, fired a precise burst.

Rounds hit the Hezbollah fighter as the RPG fired, with the projectile whistling high into the air and exploding against a rock off target, sending shrapnel flying. The smell of burning rock and metal filled the air, sharp and acrid.

"*RPG neutralised!*" Nadav confirmed, his voice calm despite the chaos.

More Hezbollah fighters advanced under the cover of fire. Yossi's men fought back, their rifles blazing. The ground shook with grenades, and the relentless exchange of gunfire thickened the air with smoke and cordite that stung their eyes and throats. The taste of smoke and adrenaline lingered on Yossi's tongue, the line between survival and loss so thin it almost felt like it would snap.

Hezbollah reinforcements poured in, and Yossi saw their numbers swell.

"*We need to hold this line!*" Yossi shouted to his men. "*Don't let them flank us!*"

Over the radio, Nadav's voice was tense. "*We're taking fire on the left! I'll try to push through and take out their command!*"

Yossi nodded, knowing Nadav couldn't see him but feeling the solidarity in their shared goal. "*Do it. We'll hold here.*"

Yossi pressed the Pressel and coordinated a renewed defence. His squad laid down a deadly pattern of fire, holding the line as Nadav's team swung wide, targeting a cluster of fighters directing the attack.

Nadav's voice cut through the radio again. "*Command is down. Keep the pressure on!*"

Yossi's men responded instantly, pushing back the enemy with everything they had. Finally, the Hezbollah fighters began to fall back, dragging their wounded. Yossi's unit held their fire, maintaining their positions.

"*Ceasefire!*" Yossi ordered. "*Stay alert, they could be regrouping.*"

A tense silence fell over the valley, broken only by distant shouts and the groans of the injured. The sound of wind rustling through the scrub suddenly felt loud, as if the earth itself was holding its breath.

"*Count off!*" Yossi called, needing to know if his men were all accounted for.

One by one, his comrades called out, but one voice was missing.

"*Where's Eli?*" Yossi shouted, scanning the area.

"*He's hit!*" Itai yelled, pointing to a prone figure. Yossi crawled over and saw Eli clutching his shoulder, blood seeping through his uniform. The sight of the blood seemed to freeze the world for a moment before instinct kicked in.

"*Stay with me, Eli,*" Yossi said urgently, gripping Eli's hand. "*We're getting you out of here.*"

"*Nadav, we've got a man down!*" Yossi shouted into his radio.

"*I'm on my way!*" Nadav's reply was immediate.

When Nadav arrived, they lifted Eli together, keeping low as they moved him to safer ground. Yossi's mind was racing - he was a leader now, but how many more times would he have to drag a friend out of the line of fire?

"*We need to get him to a field hospital now!*" Nadav shouted over the wind, the urgency in his voice cutting through the haze.

Yossi nodded. "*Everyone fall back in formation. We're moving out!*"

They carefully made their way back to the base, Eli's life in their hands. The silence that followed the retreat felt almost deafening, the adrenaline leaving Yossi's veins and making his limbs feel heavy. As soon as they reached the perimeter, a medic team took over, and Yossi watched, anxiety gripping his chest, as they prepared Eli for transport.

Yossi felt as though he was being pulled in two directions - his duty to command his men, and his desire to stay with Eli, his friend. But the urgency in Nadav's gaze settled his internal conflict.

"We need to make sure he's alright, Yossi. Come with me."

Yossi and Nadav volunteered to accompany Eli to the field hospital. The drive was tense, each bump in the road eliciting a moan from Eli. Yossi found himself praying silently for his friend's survival. He couldn't lose him - not like this.

When they finally arrived at the field hospital, Yossi immediately spotted Leila, busy with another patient. She wore the same focused, professional expression that he had seen so many times, but when she noticed them, her face lit up with a mix of surprise and relief.

"Yossi! Nadav!" she called out, rushing over with a bright smile. *"I didn't expect to see you two again so soon."*

Yossi grinned despite the tension. *"Leila! Is it just coincidence, or are you following us around?"*

Nadav laughed. *"Yeah, you seem to turn up everywhere we go."*

Leila chuckled, her eyes twinkling with that familiar spark of mischief. *"Well, someone has to keep an eye on you two troublemakers. Besides,"* she added, her tone becoming more serious, *"I volunteered to be attached to the Parachute Brigade as a medic. Thought it'd be good to be close to my friends... you know, just in case."*

Yossi and Nadav exchanged a quick, grateful look. It was a relief to know she was close by, even if the circumstances were less than ideal.

"Smart move," Yossi said warmly. *"And we're glad you're here. Eli took a hit - needs your expertise."*

Leila nodded, her expression turning immediately professional as she turned to assess Eli's wound. *"Alright, let's get him stabilised first,"* she said, her hands moving with practised ease as she cleaned and dressed his injury. *"He's lost a lot of blood, but we can handle it."*

Yossi and Nadav stood back, watching as Leila worked quickly and methodically, her presence somehow soothing the frantic energy coursing through both of them.

Once Eli was stable, Leila turned back to them, a soft smile breaking through her serious expression.

"*He's going to be okay,*" she assured them. "*We'll get him the care he needs.*"

Yossi let out a breath he hadn't realised he'd been holding. "*Thanks, Leila. You're a lifesaver.*"

Leila shrugged modestly. "*Just doing my job, Yossi. But it's good to see you both, even like this.*"

Nadav, still riding the wave of relief, grinned, a bit more relaxed now. "*It's good to see you too, Leila. Maybe next time, we'll run into you without bullets flying.*"

Leila laughed softly, the sound a welcome break in the tension. "*That would be nice, Nadav. But you two seem to attract trouble.*"

As they continued to talk, Nadav's gaze lingered on Leila. He could see the dedication in her eyes, the way she moved with purpose. He remembered their carefree days growing up, but now he felt something deeper - a connection formed through shared experience. Her calm in the midst of chaos reminded him that there was still softness in the world, even here.

"*Leila,*" Nadav began hesitantly, "*it's been a long time since we've really talked. I've missed that.*"

Leila looked at him, her eyes softening. "*I've missed it too, Nadav. You know, I think about those days often... when things were simpler, and we didn't have to worry about all this.*" She gestured around them, indicating the harsh realities of their current lives.

Nadav nodded slowly. "*Yeah, those were good days. But I think... I think this has made us stronger in ways we never imagined.*"

Leila reached out and squeezed his hand briefly. "*It ha*s," she agreed quietly. "*But don't forget, strength doesn't mean hardening yourself completely. There's still room for softness, for caring... even here.*"

Nadav felt a warmth spread through him at her words. He knew she was right - there had to be more to this life than just surviving. "*I won't forget,*" he promised softly. "*And maybe when all this is over... we can find that simplicity again.*"

Leila's eyes searched his face, and for a moment, the war, the uniforms, and the distance between them faded away. "*I'd like that, Nadav. I'd like that a lot.*"

As they prepared to leave, Leila hesitated, then spoke earnestly.

"*Nadav, keep in touch, okay? Don't let this be the last time we see each other until another crisis.*"

Nadav nodded, his smile genuine. "*I promise, Leila. I'll keep in touch.*"

They shared a brief, meaningful look before Yossi and Nadav turned to leave. Their conversation was interrupted by a call from their commanding officer, requesting a debrief on the skirmish.

"*I have to go,*" Yossi said, his tone resigned but respectful. "*Duty calls.*"

Leila nodded, her gaze lingering on both of them. "*Take care of yourself, Yossi. And you too, Nadav.*"

Nadav nodded. "*You know we will. And you stay safe, Leila.*"

Yossi and Nadav returned to their field base, where they debriefed their commanding officer. Their patrol had successfully repelled the enemy and avoided serious casualties. The CO Lt. Colonel Arad commended them for their leadership.

"*Good work,*" he said. "*Hezbollah is getting bolder. Stay sharp.*"

Yossi nodded, his expression serious. "*Yes, sir. We're ready for whatever comes.*"

The tension along the border continued to grow. Hezbollah fighters were more visible, and another confrontation seemed imminent. As they settled into their quarters for the night, Yossi looked over at Nadav, catching his friend's gaze.

"*We're going to have to stay one step ahead of them,*" Yossi murmured.

Nadav nodded, his face set. *"We will. But whatever comes, we'll face it together."*

They shared a silent moment of understanding. Each knew that the challenges ahead would be harder, the stakes higher. But for now, they were ready - each leading their squads, each standing firm against the gathering storm

Yael was hard at work in the intelligence unit, the focus shifting to the unknown target from Hamas. His movements were a top priority. Samir and his team were tasked with tracking him, trying to understand his role in the organisation. They placed undercover operatives in Gaza, working to get closer to him and uncover his significance.

The challenge was significant. The target moved with a confidence that suggested he knew he was being watched. His group was intimidating, keeping people at a distance. The intelligence team observed him attending meetings, training sessions, and interacting with other leaders. They documented his routines and contacts.

From the safety of the intelligence unit, Yael worked tirelessly, analysing surveillance images. The unknown fighter appeared more often than others, always at the centre of activity, always purposeful.

Then one day, as Yael flipped through images, her heart skipped a beat. In one, she saw the fighter walking in Jabalia with a familiar figure beside him - Salma.

Yael's breath caught in her throat. There was no mistaking it, Salma was there beside him, walking calmly.

Confusion and concern surged within her. *What was Salma doing with him? Was she in danger, or was she involved?*

Yael needed to find out more. She reached out to Samir.

"Samir, I need to flag something," she said, forcing her voice to remain calm. *"There's someone connected to our target. I think I know her."*

Samir turned to her, his gaze sharp. *"Who is she?"*

Yael hesitated. "*Her name is Salma Nasser. I met her at David's office in Tel Aviv. I need to understand what she's doing with him. Can we get more resources on this?*"

Samir's eyes narrowed thoughtfully before he nodded. "*We'll look into it. Let's find out everything we can.*"

Yael felt a knot of worry tighten in her stomach. She hoped Salma was safe, but deep down, she knew this was just the beginning of something more complicated.

Chapter Twenty Nine

AHMED

As 2021 unfolded, the relentless pace of training weighed heavily on Ahmed and his men. Every day became a gruelling test of endurance, packed with drills, exercises, and constant preparation. For months, rumours of a mission had swirled, leaving everyone restless and uneasy. Finally, word came through: a large-scale assault deep into Israeli territory was being planned for the following year. This operation would be no routine mission, it was intended to make a powerful statement and shift global opinion in their favour.

But as the year dragged on, it became clear that the timeline was more fluid than anyone had expected. Whispers among the senior leadership hinted at the need for more preparation. Tunnels required reinforcement, and more weapons and ammunition were being smuggled through the networks from Egypt. The operation was pushed back repeatedly, allowing for more thorough preparations, but each delay increased the tension among Ahmed's men, who were growing anxious for action. Every postponement stretched the days longer, making each one feel more unbearable. Ahmed could see the exhaustion in their eyes, even when they tried to hide it.

The training ground in southern Gaza buzzed with a tense, almost frantic energy. Fighters from all over the Strip had gathered - members of Hamas, Islamic Jihad, and smaller allied groups. New equipment - paragliders for aerial assaults, stockpiles of weapons, and advanced ammunition - had arrived through secret tunnels, signalling a new phase of readiness. Everyone knew the clock was ticking, but no one knew the exact deadline. Ahmed wondered whether they were truly ready for what was coming. He tried to push the thought away, but it lingered in the back of his mind, like an itch he couldn't scratch.

Ahmed's responsibilities had expanded significantly. He now coordinated multiple teams, ensuring seamless communication across various groups. Hadi and Bilal managed the motorbike assault team, training fighters to infiltrate deep behind enemy lines using motorbikes. Tariq and Khaled led the ground assault units, conducting practice raids on a mock kibbutz and drilling their men in close-quarters combat. Each unit trained with relentless intensity, rehearsing their parts in a complex, multi-faceted plan.

Tariq and Khaled would lead their units in pickups, each truck carrying four to five fighters in the back, armed and ready to respond at a moment's notice. The pickups were stripped down for speed and manoeuvrability, their backs reinforced to carry men and equipment without compromising agility. The trucks were meant to punch through enemy lines quickly, drop fighters deep into the target area, and provide rapid-fire support. Behind them, Hadi and Bilal's motorbike teams would follow - each bike carrying two fighters, one to drive and one to provide suppressive fire with automatic rifles. The motorbikes would zigzag through rough terrain, using their speed and small profile to evade detection and reposition quickly.

Ahmed's own command was a tactical unit, equipped with three pickups, each armed with heavy machine guns mounted on the back. His fighters moved with precision, responding instantly to his sharp, clipped commands. From his position in the lead pickup, Ahmed's voice crackled over the radio:

"Pickup One, ease back - too exposed on the left. Motorbike Unit, shift right and cover their flank."

His eyes darted between the pickups and motorbikes, noting every movement, every potential weakness. He adjusted their positions like pieces on a chessboard, guiding each element of the assault with practised precision.

"No mistakes. Every second counts," he muttered under his breath, his voice drowned out by the roar of engines and the crackle of gunfire.

The teams practised coordinating their assaults over and over, drilling each manoeuvre until it became second nature. Engines roared, dust swirling in the air as the trucks accelerated, tyres churning up the ground. The fighters in the back leaned out, rifles braced against the truck's sides as they aimed and fired, the heavy thud of automatic fire blending with the sharp cracks of the rifles. The motorbikes shot forward, weaving between the pickups, their riders crouched low to minimise their profile. Ahmed kept his focus sharp, watching for any mistakes, ready to call out corrections.

The training sessions were relentless - under a scorching sun, in pouring rain, and through the cold of night. The constant roar of engines, the crack of live ammunition, and the roar of fighters shouting commands kept everyone on edge. Ahmed moved between the teams, using the radios to guide their attacks and push them harder, knowing they needed to perfect their coordination. He could see the strain on his fighters' faces - their nerves fraying as they practised the same drills endlessly, their muscles taut with anticipation and fatigue.

However, the delays in launching the attack were taking a toll. The men grew impatient, their morale fragile. Small arguments flared over trivial matters, fuelled by deeper frustration. Ahmed could feel it - his men were like coiled springs, wound too tight and ready to snap. He knew he had to act before things broke down completely.

The tension erupted a few days later. During a live-fire exercise, two fighters in Tariq's unit got into a heated argument over a misfired shot. Within seconds, fists were swinging. The fight spread, other men jumping in, shouting and swinging wildly. Tariq stormed in, shoving the fighters apart with brute force. But the men were beyond reasoning - pent-up frustration turning into violence. Ahmed leapt from his truck, fury etched on his face.

"*Enough!*" he roared, grabbing one of the fighters by the collar and slamming him against the side of a pickup. "*You want to fight? Fight the real enemy!*"

But the fighter struggled, shouting back: "*We're tired of this! Tired of training like dogs while they sit back and wait!*"

Without thinking, Ahmed struck him across the face. The sound of the slap echoed across the yard. The men froze.

"I said, enough!" Ahmed's voice dropped low, dangerous. *"You think I'm not tired too? You think I don't want to move forward? But we do this right, or we all die!"*

Tariq stepped in, his face flushed with anger. *"You can't keep holding us back, Ahmed. The men are falling apart!"*

Ahmed's eyes narrowed dangerously. *"Enough of this!"* he growled, stepping forward until Tariq was forced to back up a step. He turned to the rest of the fighters, his expression hard.

Later that evening, the tension carried over to the safe house. Ahmed gathered his closest leaders - Tariq, Khaled, Bilal, and Hadi - in the dimly lit room, their faces shadowed by the flickering overhead bulb. Tariq and Khaled still wore the simmering resentment from earlier, their expressions hard and unyielding. Ahmed could feel the undercurrent of defiance crackling between them.

He stood at the centre of the room, his posture rigid, arms crossed. For a moment, he let the silence stretch, his gaze fixed on each of them in turn.

"I called you here because this has to end now," Ahmed began, his voice low but charged with intensity. *"Today was a disaster. If this keeps up, we won't even make it to the real battle. The men look up to you, and right now, you're failing them."*

Tariq leaned forward, his jaw clenched. *"Failing them?"* he echoed, disbelief and anger colouring his tone. *"You think we're failing them? We're the ones holding them together while you keep us in this endless cycle of drills and delays."*

Khaled stepped in beside Tariq, his fists clenched at his sides. *"You keep saying 'we're not ready.' Well, the men don't want to hear it anymore. They're ready, Ahmed. They're more than ready. But you - are you?"* His eyes narrowed, challenging.

Ahmed felt his own anger rising, but he forced himself to remain still, his expression cold. *"This isn't about what you or I want, Khaled. We're under orders."* His voice dropped lower, each word sharp. *"And if you think defying them will get us anywhere, then I'll take you in front of Abu Khaled myself."*

The threat hung in the air, heavy and dangerous. Tariq's face flushed with fury. He took a step forward, his shoulders tense. *"You'd do that, wouldn't you? Just hand us over?"*

The room felt like it was on the verge of exploding. For a heartbeat, Ahmed thought Tariq would swing at him. But he stood his ground, his gaze unwavering. *"I will if I have to,"* Ahmed said softly, dangerously. *"You want to question my leadership? Fine. Go ahead. But if you think for a second that I'll let you undermine me, you're mistaken."*

Hadi and Bilal exchanged uneasy glances. Bilal shifted, clearing his throat softly. *"Ahmed, none of us want that. We're all just... frustrated."* His voice was calmer, less confrontational. *"But these delays - how long can we keep this up? The men are at their breaking point."*

"We're all at our breaking point," Ahmed replied, his voice tight. *"But losing control now? Turning on each other? That's exactly what the enemy wants. Do you think they're sitting back, unprepared? No."* He took a step forward, looking each of them in the eye. *"There's going to be a huge battle in the future - something like nothing we've ever seen before. But right now, I am in charge. I'm making the decisions, and I need you to back me up. Or I'll find someone else who will."*

Tariq and Khaled stared at him, their expressions defiant. For a long moment, no one moved.

Then Ahmed's face softened, just slightly. *"We've been through too much together,"* he said quietly. *"You're more than just soldiers to me. You're friends. But I can't have you undermining me like this. I need you to trust me. We have to hold the line until the time is right. If we fail now, everything we've done will mean nothing."*

Tariq's fists loosened, the anger in his eyes dimming just a fraction. Khaled's shoulders relaxed, though his expression remained tight. Slowly, grudgingly, they nodded.

"*Fine,*" Tariq muttered, his voice rough. "*We'll wait. But this can't go on forever, Ahmed. You know that.*"

"*I know,*" Ahmed murmured, letting out a slow breath. "*And when the time comes, we'll move. But not a second before.*"

The tension in the room eased, though it didn't disappear entirely. They were still on edge, still wary. But for now, they would follow him. He could feel it.

As they turned to leave, Ahmed caught Tariq's arm, holding him back for a moment. "*Tariq,*" he said softly, his voice low enough that only Tariq could hear. "*I don't want to stand against you. But if it comes to it, I will. Don't force my hand.*"

Tariq's eyes widened slightly. Then he nodded, his gaze unreadable. "*I won't.*"

Ahmed released him, stepping back. "*Good.*"

As they filed out, Bilal offered Ahmed a small, tight smile. "*You did the right thing,*" he murmured. "*They needed to hear it.*"

"*Maybe,*" Ahmed replied, rubbing the back of his neck. "*But I need them with me, not just following orders because I threatened them.*"

Bilal paused in the doorway, his gaze thoughtful. "*Then make sure this ends on your terms, Ahmed. Show them you have a plan. Because right now, all they see is delay.*"

Ahmed watched him go, a strange sense of foreboding settling over him. He had won a small victory tonight, but it felt hollow. If he couldn't control his own men, how could he expect to control what came next?

Later that night, Ahmed stood alone on the rooftop of the safe house, the cold wind biting at his skin. He stared out at the darkened city, his thoughts churning.

The memory hit him like a punch to the gut - 2014. The streets of Jabalia, reduced to rubble, smoke still curling from the ruins. He could still smell the stench of burning flesh and charred wood, could still hear the screams - endless, piercing screams that tore through the chaos. He had walked through the aftermath, stepping over bodies twisted in unnatural shapes, a child's lifeless hand reaching out from beneath a collapsed wall.

"Where were you when my family died?" a woman had screamed at him, her eyes wild with grief, clutching the limp form of her son. He had stared at her, numb. What could he say? What comfort could he offer?

He shook his head, his chest tight. *We're trying to protect them. To give them a future.* But even as the thought formed, it rang hollow. How many more would suffer because of his choices? Because of what he was planning?

The leaders don't care, he thought bitterly. *They speak of liberation, but they live far from the line of fire.* He felt trapped. *But now I know too much. If I waver, they'll see me as a threat - a threat they'll eliminate.*

The weight of his position pressed down on him, heavier than ever. There was no way out - not without consequences.

I can't think like this, he told himself fiercely. *I have to stay strong - for the men. For our people.* But as he stood there, staring into the darkness, the doubts gnawed at him.

Could he truly protect them? Or were they marching toward another disaster?

As 2021 ended and the operation continued to be delayed, Ahmed prepared himself and his men for the challenges ahead, knowing that soon everything they had trained for would be put to the ultimate test. He could feel the tension building like a storm on the horizon, and he prayed he was making the right decisions - for his men, for his people, and for himself.

Chapter Thirty

YOSSI

After eighteen months stationed at a forward operating base on the Lebanese border, Yossi and Nadav had become accustomed to the relentless rhythm of patrols and skirmishes. The tension of the front line had become a constant backdrop to their lives, forging a camaraderie that grew stronger with each passing day. Together, they faced danger, shared moments of quiet reflection, and formed a bond that felt unbreakable.

One scorching afternoon, they sat on the edge of a makeshift bunker, savouring a rare moment of calm. The sun beat down mercilessly, the air thick with dust and sweat.

"Do you ever wonder what home's going to feel like?" Nadav asked quietly, his gaze lingering on the shimmering heat of the hills. *"You know... to be somewhere that doesn't have this constant edge?"*

"All the time," Yossi said, a faint smile tugging at his lips. *"But I don't think we'll ever really leave this behind... we've become something else out here."*

"Yeah, tougher, maybe," Nadav nodded slowly. *"But... it's not just that. We've had to make calls - ones that change people's lives forever. I never imagined it'd feel like this."*

Yossi offered a small, reflective smile. *"We've still got time left,"* he said quietly. *"Plenty of it, by the looks of things. But I wonder... will we even recognise the people we used to be when we get back?"*

Nadav shrugged, his expression thoughtful. *"I hope so, Yossi. I think we've become better in some ways - more resilient, more aware of what really matters. But maybe we've lost something too... the part of us that was innocent."*

Yossi fell silent, the weight of Nadav's words settling over him. He had often wondered the same - whether their shared experiences had taken something from them, something they might never get back. They had become hardened, but at what cost? He was about to respond when the crackle of the radio cut through the quiet.

The radio buzzed sharply, interrupting the uneasy silence that had settled between them. *"Contact, contact, contact!"* The voice over the radio was strained, electric with tension. *"Enemy movement - north ridge!"*

Yossi and Nadav leapt to their feet, adrenaline flooding their veins. Within moments, they were assembling their sections and moving into position.

Yossi led his men to the edge of a densely forested area. As he peered through the undergrowth, he spotted a Hezbollah sniper team setting up an ambush just ahead.

"Stay down," Yossi murmured, eyes fixed on the movement ahead. *"Nadav, sweep left. We'll box them in from the right. Make every shot count."*

Yossi felt the weight of leadership settle on his shoulders like a heavy pack. Every decision he made could mean the difference between life and death, not just for himself but for the men who looked to him for guidance. He had to be strong, had to be decisive, but he also felt the constant, gnawing fear of getting it wrong. *Is this what leadership really is?* Yossi wondered. *Making calls that could take or save lives?* In the quiet moments before the storm, he questioned whether he was truly prepared to bear this burden.

Nadav nodded, his expression tense but focused. He signalled to his team, and they began to manoeuvre into position while Yossi crept forward, inching through the thick brush. The air was hot and heavy, every sound amplified in the stillness. Yossi's breath came in shallow bursts, his mind racing through the possibilities. He could feel the tension in his muscles, the pressure of command weighing heavily on his chest. Was he making the right choice? Would this decision cost lives or save them?

Suddenly, a shot rang out, and Yossi saw one of his men, Avner, crumple to the ground, wounded.

"Cover fire!" Yossi shouted, his voice cutting through the air like a whip. *"Keep them pinned down!"*

Ignoring the hail of bullets, Yossi crawled forward under heavy fire to reach Avner. Nadav shouted, *"Yossi, no!"* but Yossi kept moving, driven by instinct. When he finally reached Avner, he grabbed him by the shoulders and dragged him to safety behind a small ridge, his heart pounding in his chest.

"Stay with me, Avner," Yossi murmured, pressing a bandage to the wound. *"You're going to be okay."* But as he said it, a familiar doubt crept in. *What if I can't keep them safe? What if this decision gets someone killed?*

He signalled to Nadav, and together they launched a flanking manoeuvre. Nadav's team fired accurately, pinning down the enemy while Yossi's section moved in from the side. The Hezbollah fighters, caught by surprise, were quickly overpowered.

As the dust settled and the cries of the wounded filled the air, Yossi felt a strange mix of relief and emptiness. They had survived another day, another battle - but to what end? The faces of the men he had just fought alongside, their expressions hardened by fear and adrenaline, seemed to blur into the faces of those they fought against. Who were they, really, in this endless cycle of violence? Could there be another way? A path that did not involve death at every turn.

The firefight was brief but intense. As the radio crackled again with the all-clear, Nadav rushed over to Yossi, a grin of relief spreading across his face. *"One of these days, your luck's going to run out, you know that?"* Nadav muttered, shaking his head but unable to hide the relieved smile tugging at his lips.

"Had to be done," Yossi replied, still catching his breath. *"Couldn't leave him out there."*

Nadav's grin faded slightly, his tone becoming more serious. *"I get it. But... don't make a habit of being a hero. We need you here."*

Yossi nodded, understanding the concern behind Nadav's words. *"I hear you. But sometimes, you just have to do what feels right."*

That night, as he lay in his bunk, Nadav's words looped through his mind: *We need you here.* It wasn't the first time he'd been told that. Running out into the open like that... Was it courage, or just plain stupidity? How many more times could he tempt fate before the cost was more than he was willing to pay?

A few days later, Yossi and Nadav were summoned to the Commanding Officer's tent once again. This time, the CO's expression was serious, but there was a glimmer of pride in his eyes.

"Sit down," he said, gesturing to the chairs in front of his desk. Yossi and Nadav exchanged a curious glance as they took their seats.

The CO continued, *"I wanted to bring you both in to inform you that I've recommended you for commendations based on your actions during the last engagement. "Samal Rosenberg, I've put you in for the Medal of Distinguished Service. You saved your man's life under fire - that's the kind of bravery we honour. And Samal Levy, the Chief of Staff Medal of Appreciation for the way you kept your head and coordinated the attack. Exceptional leadership, both of you."*

Yossi felt a rush of pride and humility at the same time. A medal? It felt surreal, especially after everything he had been through. Nadav grinned, then quickly composed himself, his own pride evident.

"And" the CO added, *"your recommendations have already been approved. There will be a ceremony back in Tel Aviv where the medals will be presented. I'm sending you both home for a few weeks of leave. You've earned it."*

Yossi's heart swelled at the thought of seeing his family, especially Yael, after so long. Nadav nodded, the relief of being able to go home clear in his smile.

"But there's more," the CO continued, his tone shifting to a more serious note. *"I also want to recommend both of you for Officer Training. You've demonstrated*

qualities we need in our leaders. Think it over during your leave. The IDF needs men like you."

Yossi and Nadav nodded, still absorbing the weight of the moment. Officer Training? Yossi's mind whirled. It was an honour, but it also meant more responsibility. *Am I ready for that?* he wondered. Leadership had already tested him in ways he never imagined.

"Thank you, sir," Yossi said finally. *"We'll think about it."*

The CO stood, extending his hand. *"Enjoy your time at home and think hard. You both have a lot to offer."*

As they left the tent, Nadav looked at Yossi, his expression thoughtful. *"What do you think?"*

Yossi smiled, feeling a mix of excitement and uncertainty. *"I don't know, Nadav. I'm glad we're going home. But staying on... it's something we need to think about carefully."*

Nadav nodded. *"Let's see what our families have to say."*

They walked back to their quarters, knowing the next few weeks would be filled with decisions that would shape their futures.

Yael's heart pounded as she waited for Samir to respond. She had recognised Salma in the surveillance photographs - Salma, now seen alongside the man who was under intense scrutiny for his militant activities. Involving Samir would escalate the situation, but Yael needed answers.

Samir leaned over to study the photograph. *"You're sure it's her?"* he asked.

"Positive," Yael replied. *"Salma works at David's law office in Tel Aviv. I've met her several times."*

Samir's expression hardened. *"Alright, I'll escalate this. We need to find out why she's there and what ties she has to the target."*

Yael nodded, feeling a mix of relief and apprehension. *"Thanks, Samir. I just... I hope she's not involved in anything dangerous."*

"Let's hope," Samir said grimly. *"But we have to assume the worst until we know more."*

Within an hour, they were called into a meeting with senior officers. Yael felt a jolt of nerves as she entered the room, where several stern faces turned toward her. The commanding officer, a middle-aged man with a grizzled beard, spoke first.

"Rav Turai Cohen, you've flagged someone you recognise in these surveillance images. What we need now is every detail you can provide," the officer said, his gaze sharp and unyielding.

Yael took a deep breath. *"Her name's Salma Nasser. She's at a law firm in Tel Aviv - same office as my fiancé's father, David. She always seemed to want to bridge the divide, to understand people on both sides. But seeing her here... with him... I'm not sure what to believe anymore*

The officer nodded. *"We need to know if she's involved willingly or if there's more to this. We'll be looking closely at her movements. For now, continue to monitor the situation. We may need you to be part of further inquiries."*

Yael nodded, her mind racing. She left the room, her thoughts swirling with possibilities. She couldn't shake the feeling that Salma was more than just a random civilian caught in this web. Her connection to the target had to mean something, and Yael was determined to find out what.

After her tense day in the operations room, Yael stepped outside, her head still buzzing with the weight of everything she'd seen. Her phone rang, and her heart skipped a beat when she saw Yossi's name on the screen.

"Yossi..." she answered, trying to keep her voice steady, but she could feel a lump forming in her throat.

"Yael," Yossi's voice came through, warm but edged with an intensity she hadn't heard in a while. *"I have news. Nadav and I... we've been in the middle of something*

intense, and... we're coming home for a few weeks. I'm being awarded a medal. It's... it's something big."

A wave of relief and joy surged through Yael, her breath catching. "*Yossi, that's... incredible. I've been so worried about you,*" she breathed, her voice trembling slightly.

"*I know,*" Yossi replied gently. "*I know you have. But we're okay. I'm okay. And I need you to get some time off if you can. I want us to have these weeks together. Just you and me, away from everything.*"

Yael closed her eyes, feeling tears spill over, warm against her cheeks. "*I'll make it work, Yossi, I swear. I'll talk to anyone I have to... I'll make it happen. We need this time. I've missed you... so, so much.*"

Yossi's voice softened, filled with a mixture of yearning and hope. "*I've missed you too, more than I can say. I want to hear everything, Yael. Everything you've been through, every thought that's crossed your mind. I want us to feel close again... not just through these calls, but truly together.*"

"*I want that too,*" Yael whispered, her voice breaking slightly. "*I've felt so lost without you. Like I'm just... waiting for my life to start again.*"

Yossi sighed, his own emotions catching in his throat. "*I know the feeling. But we're coming back, and we're going to figure this out. Together. No more waiting. I promise.*"

Yael's tears flowed freely now. "*I'll make sure everyone is there for you, Yossi. We're all so proud. But more than anything, I just want to see you. I want to hold you and feel like... like everything's okay, even if just for a moment.*"

Yossi smiled, a warmth spreading through his chest. "*I promise, Yael. We'll have our time. We'll talk about everything - our dreams, our fears, and what comes next.*"

When they finally hung up, Yael sat still for a moment, her heart pounding in her chest. She felt a mix of anticipation and worry, but above all, a powerful yearning to be with him, to hold him close and never let go again. She quickly dialled another number.

"Hello, Mum?" she began, her voice trembling but full of hope. "Yossi's coming home, and he's getting a medal. We need to plan... we all need to be there."

Across the base, Yossi called his parents. "Mum, Dad, it's me," he began, unable to hide the smile in his voice. "I'm coming home for a few weeks... and there's going to be a ceremony."

He heard his mother gasp on the other end. "Yossi, are you alright? What happened?"

"I'm fine, Mum, really," he said softly. "It's for a medal... something that happened up here. It's... it's hard to explain over the phone, but I want you both there. I need you all with me."

His father's voice broke in, filled with pride. "Not for anything, Yossi. Just say when and where, and we'll be there."

Yossi felt a wave of emotion rush over him, his throat tightening. "Thank you," he whispered. "I just... I can't wait to see you all."

As he hung up, Yossi closed his eyes for a moment, letting himself feel the full weight of everything. The fear, the relief, the love - it all mixed together, making him feel more alive than he had in months. He knew these few weeks would be precious, a chance to reconnect, to remember why they fought so hard, and what they were fighting for.

Back in their quarters, Yossi and Nadav packed their bags, readying themselves for the journey home. The thought of seeing their families and friends filled them with a sense of anticipation they hadn't felt in months. But they also knew that the time ahead would bring new challenges, new decisions.

"Think we'll stick around, after all this?" Nadav asked quietly, his hands pausing over the folds of his uniform.

Yossi paused, considering. "I'm not sure, Nadav. I want to go home, be with everyone, feel what normal is again. But... being here, it's done something to me. I just don't know what it means yet."

Nadav nodded. *"I guess we'll see,"* he said with a smile. "Whatever happens, I'm glad we've got each other in this."

Yossi grinned, feeling a sense of peace settle over him. *"Yeah,"* he agreed. *"Together."*

And with that, they shouldered their bags and stepped out into the bright, hot sun, ready to make the journey back to the people and places they loved, even as the world around them remained uncertain and full of shadows.

Chapter Thirty One

AHMED

Ahmed sat in the dimly lit room, feeling the tension thick in the air. The leaders were gathered around, their faces shadowed, their expressions serious. They spoke in confident tones, outlining the full scope of the upcoming attack on Israel - a massive, coordinated assault that aimed to strike deep into Israeli territory. It was unlike anything they had attempted before, a bold move meant to shift the balance of power.

As Ahmed listened, his stomach tightened. The operation sounded grand and ambitious, but as the leaders continued, he sensed a troubling vagueness in their words. They spoke about making a powerful statement, about changing the dynamics of the conflict, but they were light on specifics. There were no clear directives on targets, no precise timing, and no concrete steps his teams would need to follow.

Ahmed's role was described as pivotal. He would command multiple teams, coordinating assaults on high-value targets. Yet, the lack of clarity gnawed at him. He knew Israel's response would be swift and brutal, and without detailed planning, their chances of success seemed thin. The leaders' enthusiasm did little to ease his unease. He could feel the knot of dread tighten in his chest as he thought of the lives - on both sides - that would be lost in this gamble.

As the meeting ended, Ahmed lingered behind, his mind buzzing with questions. The room emptied, but Ahmed stood rooted to the spot, haunted by doubts he could not express aloud. His head pounded as he replayed the conversation over and over, trying to find some concrete detail, some assurance that they were on the right path. But nothing came. Only more uncertainty.

As the last of the leaders left, he found himself alone with Abu Khaled. The older man's eyes narrowed slightly, watching Ahmed with a calculating gaze.

"Speak your mind, Ahmed," Abu Khaled said quietly. *"I can see something is troubling you."*

Ahmed took a deep breath, steadying himself. Now was not the time to mince words. He stepped forward, his posture tense but determined. *"With respect, Abu Khaled, I'm starting to lose my men."* He paused, choosing his words carefully. *"They've been training and waiting for years, and they're tired of hearing about 'plans' with no action. Last week I had to confront them - and I nearly lost control."*

Abu Khaled's expression remained inscrutable, but his gaze sharpened. *"Lost control?"*

Ahmed nodded, his eyes hardening. *"Tariq and Khaled were on the verge of challenging my authority in front of everyone. If we don't act soon, we'll lose more than just patience - we'll lose discipline, and then we'll lose everything. I need something to tell them. Anything that will stop the doubt from spreading further."*

For a long moment, Abu Khaled was silent, his gaze never leaving Ahmed's face. Then he leaned back slightly, his lips pursed in thought. *"I understand your concerns,"* he murmured slowly. *"But you must remember, timing is everything. One wrong move, one premature strike, and we risk losing the entire operation."*

Ahmed swallowed his frustration. *"And if we wait too long? If they lose faith in the mission? They're not just soldiers, Abu Khaled - they're our friends, our brothers. I'm trying to hold them together, but I need something concrete."*

Abu Khaled's eyes narrowed. *"What are you asking for?"*

"A timeline. An assurance that we are moving forward. Something I can show them - give them hope that this isn't just talk. They need to know we're not just wasting time, risking our lives in endless drills."

Abu Khaled sighed deeply, his gaze softening just a fraction. *"There are things at play that you do not see, Ahmed. But I'll speak to the others. I'll see what can be done to give you some clarity."*

Ahmed nodded slowly, recognising the small victory. *"Thank you. That's all I'm asking for. I'll keep the men in line until then, but I need something more than words."*

With that, he turned and left, his heart still heavy but with a glimmer of hope. He had taken a risk confronting Abu Khaled, but it was a risk he had to take. Now, he just had to make sure he could bring his men back from the edge.

That evening, Ahmed returned to the safe house. Tariq, Khaled, Bilal, and Hadi were already there, their expressions guarded as he entered the small, dimly lit room. He could feel the tension simmering beneath the surface, could see the wariness in their eyes as they waited for him to speak.

He stood at the centre of the room, his gaze sweeping over them. *"I spoke to Abu Khaled,"* he began quietly, his voice firm but calm. *"I told him everything - the frustration, the doubts. I told him that if something doesn't change soon, we risk losing the fighters. He listened."*

Tariq scoffed softly, crossing his arms. *"And what did he say? More empty promises?"*

Ahmed shook his head. *"No. He's going to push for a clearer timeline. He understands the risk."* He took a deep breath, meeting each of their gazes in turn. *"I know you're angry, and I know you don't trust me right now. But I'm telling you - things are going to move. We just have to hold on a little longer."*

Khaled's eyes narrowed, his jaw clenched. *"And if they don't? If they just keep dragging it out?"*

Ahmed stepped closer, his voice dropping to a low, intense murmur. *"Then we go to them together. If I have to drag Abu Khaled out of his seat and make him look these men in the eye, I'll do it. But I need you with me."*

The room was silent. For a long moment, no one spoke. Then, slowly, Tariq nodded, the hardness in his gaze softening just a little. *"Alright,"* he muttered. *"But we're trusting you, Ahmed. Don't make us regret it."*

"I won't," Ahmed replied quietly, holding his gaze. *"I promise."*

The tension in the room eased, if only slightly. Bilal leaned back, exhaling softly. *"So, what's the plan until then?"*

Ahmed looked around, his expression steady. *"We keep training. But no more drills for the sake of it. We focus on readiness, making sure every man knows his role inside out. And we wait for word from Abu Khaled."*

Hadi nodded thoughtfully. *"Alright. But you'll keep us informed, won't you?"*

"Always," Ahmed assured him. *"From now on, I'm not hiding anything. We're in this together."*

Slowly, grudgingly, they nodded. It wasn't perfect - it wasn't complete trust - but it was a start.

As the meeting broke up and the others filed out, Tariq lingered behind. He hesitated, then stepped closer. *"Ahmed... I'm sorry,"* he murmured, his voice rough. *"I shouldn't have challenged you like that. I just... I didn't see where we were going."*

Ahmed clapped him on the shoulder, a faint smile tugging at his lips. *"You were right to question me, Tariq. I need you to keep pushing me, even when I don't want to hear it. But next time - "* his voice lowered, turning serious, *"- don't do it in front of the men. You and I... we've been through too much for that."*

Tariq's gaze softened. *"I know. I won't let it happen again."*

Ahmed nodded, feeling a weight lift from his chest. *"Good. Because we're going to need each other for what's coming. Whatever it is."*

As Tariq left, Ahmed stood alone for a moment, the tension finally easing from his shoulders. He had made progress tonight - small, tentative steps, but progress, nonetheless. Now, he just had to keep them moving forward.

With a final, deep breath, he turned and walked out into the night, his mind already racing with the next steps. He would hold the line. He would keep them together, no matter what.

Because if he didn't, everything they had built would crumble. And that was a risk he could not afford to take.

The next morning, Ahmed called his leaders together once more. This time, there was a new energy in the air - a shift from the simmering frustration of the previous days. Tariq, Khaled, Bilal, and Hadi gathered around a large, roughly drawn map of their tunnel system, spread out on a table in the dimly lit safe house. The tunnel network stretched like a web beneath Gaza, with branches extending in every direction, crisscrossing under schools, mosques, and homes. They had spent months creating these passageways - paths for movement, escape routes, storage spaces. But Ahmed had a new purpose for them now.

As the men leaned in, Ahmed tapped the centre of the map, where their command post was marked. *"We've been training for attack after attack, drilling for infiltrations, surprise assaults, and breaches. But now, we switch focus. The reality is, no matter what we do, Israel will respond - hard. They'll strike back with everything they have. And when they do, our men need to be ready to defend every inch of these tunnels."*

The group exchanged wary glances. Tariq was the first to speak, his brow furrowed. *"You want us to focus on defence? But isn't that a sign we're preparing to lose?"*

Ahmed shook his head firmly. *"No. We're preparing to hold the ground we take. Every second we hold out, every moment we delay them, is a victory in itself. We make them bleed for every metre, make it so costly that they can't press forward. If we defend these tunnels correctly, we can keep striking back from the shadows - hit and fade."*

Bilal nodded slowly, his expression thoughtful. *"And with the tunnels, we can move our units without being seen. We control the space underground, not them."*

"Exactly," Ahmed said, leaning forward. *"We're not abandoning the plan. We're adding to it. So, each of you will be responsible for a section of the tunnel system.*

Bilal, you take the northern sector, where most of the escape routes are. Khaled, you'll have the southern routes that connect to the deeper tunnels leading towards the Egyptian border. Tariq, I want you on the east, focusing on the approach towards the Israeli settlements. And Hadi, you take the west, near the coast, to secure any possible breaches from a naval strike."

As he assigned each leader their section, he watched their reactions carefully. The shift in strategy wasn't just about defence, it was about re-engaging their focus, giving them new purpose. He saw it in the way their shoulders straightened, the way their eyes sparked with determination. This was something different - a challenge that they could sink their teeth into.

"I'll be overseeing all of it," Ahmed continued, his gaze sweeping over them. *"I'll coordinate movements between each sector from our central command post. You'll each have your own command points within your sectors. The focus is on defence, but we'll keep small units ready to launch counterattacks if they try to push in too deep. We're not just holding them back - we're making them pay for every step."*

A murmur of agreement rippled through the group. The change in dynamic had already sparked a shift in their attitudes. Where there had been doubt and restlessness, now there was anticipation - a sense of purpose.

"We'll also rotate our units through each of the sectors," Ahmed added. *"I want every fighter to know the layout of every tunnel - every hidden chamber, every choke point. No matter where they're deployed, they need to know how to move like they belong there."* He glanced at Hadi, whose specialty had always been guerrilla tactics. *"Hadi, you'll be in charge of setting up false exits and traps. We need to create confusion if they breach us - give them false leads, draw them into kill zones."*

Hadi nodded sharply, his lips curving into a grim smile. *"I'll make it a maze for them. They won't know which way is up."*

"Khaled," Ahmed turned to the fiery leader. *"You'll work on creating fortified positions - strongholds where we can mount heavy resistance if they push too far. Use whatever you need - concrete, sandbags, armoured plating. I want each of your positions to be a fortress."*

"Done," Khaled agreed, his jaw set with determination.

"*Tariq,*" Ahmed continued, "*focus on mobility. I want your units to be able to move quickly through the eastern tunnels. We'll need to be able to shift men and equipment fast if they come at us with full force. And we need to be able to hit their rear units if they try to sweep us out.*"

Tariq's eyes lit up at the prospect. "*Fast strikes, quick exits. I'll get them moving like ghosts.*"

"*And Bilal,*" Ahmed finished, "*you keep your men in the north on constant alert. We need those escape routes open, but also monitored. I don't want any surprises. If they find a way in from there, we need to know immediately.*"

Bilal's expression was calm, thoughtful. "*I'll make sure we have eyes on every exit. They won't slip through.*"

As the meeting concluded, Ahmed felt a weight lift from his shoulders. For the first time in weeks, there was a sense of cohesion - a feeling that they were working towards something tangible, something they could control. As his leaders dispersed, moving to brief their own teams, Ahmed turned his attention to the overall coordination.

He watched the new training unfold from his command pickup, positioned just outside the main entrance to the tunnels. Radios buzzed as his leaders called out positions, guiding their men through the new defensive drills. The fighters moved differently now - no longer just running assault patterns, but setting up ambushes, preparing fallback positions, and creating defensive lines.

The northern sector, under Bilal's command, practised rapid evacuation drills - slipping in and out of hidden exits, sealing doors behind them, and laying traps to slow any potential pursuers. The fighters moved with precision, retreating down side tunnels and reappearing in unexpected places. Bilal's calm voice crackled over the radio, directing their movements with unerring accuracy.

In the south, Khaled's men were fortifying their strongpoints. Heavy barriers went up, machine-gun positions were established, and caches of ammunition were hidden behind layers of concrete and sand. The sound of drilling and hammering echoed through the underground, punctuated by Khaled's sharp commands.

To the east, Tariq ran his men through rapid-response drills, shifting them from one end of the tunnel to the other with practised efficiency. His voice was a constant presence over the radio, barking orders, pushing them to move faster, to anticipate every scenario.

Hadi's group to the west was a flurry of activity, setting up false exits, creating dead ends, and rigging sections of the tunnel with booby traps. He was meticulous, placing tripwires and remote-detonated explosives with a surgeon's precision, his tone calm and focused as he guided his men through the maze he was constructing.

Ahmed coordinated it all, his voice cutting through the airwaves as he moved between sectors. *"Tariq, pull back your men - let Khaled's group hold the line. Hadi, seal off the western tunnel and prepare for a controlled detonation. Bilal, deploy a secondary unit to the northern sector, we need to secure that escape route."* He shifted between channels, adjusting, refining, shaping the defence until every fighter knew exactly where they needed to be.

It was a different kind of fight - one that required patience, precision, and discipline. But he could see the change in his men. The frustration was easing, replaced by a focused intensity. They were no longer just waiting - they were preparing. And that made all the difference.

For now, Ahmed had restored some semblance of control. But he knew this was only the beginning. The real test would come when the enemy finally arrived - when every decision he made could mean the difference between life and death for the men who had put their trust in him.

And when that time came, he prayed that all their training, all their preparation, would be enough. Because if it wasn't, everything they had built would be buried beneath the rubble.

As the days wore on, clarity seemed further away. On the streets of Jabalia, the tension was palpable. People moved quickly, eyes darting nervously. Ahmed could feel the fear in the air every time he walked through the market with Salma, every time he caught the wary glances of those who sensed something was coming but didn't know what.

One afternoon, an elderly man approached Ahmed, his voice trembling. *"Ahmed, what's happening? Are we safe?"*

Ahmed forced a smile, trying to reassure him. *"We're doing everything to protect you,"* he said, though the words felt hollow even to his own ears.

The man's eyes were filled with fear. *"But at what cost? We don't want another war. We just want to live."*

Ahmed nodded, feeling the frustration around him. He looked into the old man's eyes and saw the reflection of his own doubts. *Am I protecting them or leading them to their doom?* he wondered. *"I understand,"* he said quietly, *"but we have to stand up for ourselves, to defend our homes."* Yet even as he spoke, the weight of those words pressed on him.

As they continued walking, Salma turned to him, her face serious. *"They're scared, Ahmed. They see the fighters, the weapons... they know what's coming."*

"I know," Ahmed replied, his voice tight with frustration. *"But without orders, we're all in the dark. And if we don't fight, we lose everything."*

Salma shook her head, her eyes filled with concern. *"I just hope we don't end up losing everything in trying to protect it."*

Her words stayed with Ahmed long after their walk had ended. As they returned to the base, his mind replayed the conversation over and over. Was he leading his men to victory, or were they all hurtling toward something far more destructive? His stomach twisted with anxiety, and he felt a fresh wave of fatigue wash over him.

As the weeks of continuous training and drills dragged on, Ahmed felt his nerves fraying. He was aware of the growing danger he faced, not just from the Israelis but from within his own ranks. The lack of clarity, the constant waiting - it was like standing on the edge of a cliff, knowing the ground could give way at any moment.

At night, when the camp was quiet, Ahmed found himself staring at the ceiling, Salma's words echoing in his mind. *Was he leading his people to freedom, or to their doom?* He had pledged to protect them, but now he wasn't sure what that even meant anymore.

He thought of the people of Jabalia, their anxious faces, their whispered fears. Could he really protect them? Or was he just leading them deeper into an abyss? The weight of their hopes and fears pressed on his chest, suffocating him in the dark. He rolled onto his side, staring into the shadows of the room.

There must be another way, he thought, though the idea felt like a fleeting whisper, quickly drowned by the reality of his situation. He was too far in to turn back now.

Over the next few months, Ahmed watched the training evolve, the defensive strategy taking shape in the dimly lit, labyrinthine tunnels that snaked beneath Gaza. Each day, his fighters grew more accustomed to the underground warfare they would face - learning to navigate the twisting passageways, setting traps, fortifying positions, and moving silently through the shadows. His men were no longer just assault troops - they were defenders now, guardians of a hidden world beneath the surface, prepared to make every metre a battlefield if the enemy dared to enter.

Ahmed's command pickups moved constantly between sectors, monitoring the progress, offering corrections, and, when needed, pushing his leaders to refine their tactics. The radio crackled almost nonstop with updates and questions - requests for supplies, confirmation of movements, reports of completed fortifications. He kept a tight grip on it all, coordinating their efforts like a conductor guiding a complex symphony, each note precise, every movement calculated.

And as he moved through the darkened passages, watching the fighters lay down mines, conceal firing positions, and rehearse their tactics over and over again, he couldn't help but reflect on just how close he had come to losing it all. The memory of that argument with Tariq and Khaled, the simmering frustration of his friends, and the rising tension that had threatened to tear them apart - all of it felt like a shadow that still lingered at the edges of his mind.

He remembered the rage in Tariq's eyes, the bitterness in Khaled's voice, and how, in that split second, everything had been on the brink. It could have gone either way. For the first time, he had felt real fear - not of the Israelis, but of his own men turning against him, of everything he had built fracturing and falling apart. And when he had confronted Abu Khaled, demanding clarity and a path forward, he had known he was risking his position, perhaps even his life. Yet, he had done it, because he had to. Because if he hadn't, he would have lost them forever.

But now... now they were working together again. He could see it in the way they moved, the way his friends called out orders, the way the men followed without hesitation. The change from attack to defence had been exactly what they needed - a new challenge, a new focus. Each of his leaders had embraced their roles, transforming their sections of the tunnel network into veritable strongholds. The fighters, too, had found a renewed sense of purpose. They were no longer idle, no longer waiting. They were building, preparing, readying themselves for whatever came next.

Ahmed leaned against the rough stone wall of the central command post, his eyes tracing the lines on the map in front of him. He had been at the edge, teetering, and now... he felt them pulling back, unifying once more. It had been touch and go - one wrong move, one moment of weakness, and they would have slipped away from him. But somehow, he had brought them back.

He glanced up as Tariq's voice crackled over the radio, sharp and confident. *"North Sector secured. Defensive lines reinforced. Requesting permission to rotate the squads."* Ahmed smiled faintly as he keyed the mic.

"Permission granted, Tariq. Good work. Keep pushing."

Switching frequencies, he heard Khaled coordinating the construction of another strongpoint, his voice strong and sure, guiding his men through the latest set of orders. *"Stack the sandbags higher - cover every angle. This position needs to hold, no matter what."*

In the distance, Bilal's soft, calm tones drifted through the static, advising his men on how to conceal traps and false exits, his usual patience and quiet authority filling the airwaves.

And then Hadi's voice cut in, giving quick, precise instructions to his own unit as they set up more barriers and false walls, his mind always one step ahead, anticipating where the enemy might try to push through.

Ahmed took a deep breath, feeling a sense of pride swell in his chest. It was as if, for the first time in months, the pieces were falling back into place. He had his friends back beside him, their respect and trust renewed. And more importantly, the fighters believed in him again. They weren't just following orders - they were committed, focused, ready.

He knew they still stood on a precipice, teetering between victory and disaster. One wrong move could still unravel everything. But for now, they were holding together, and that was something. A fragile stability, a tentative unity - but it was enough to build on.

The tunnel lights flickered slightly as a rumble reverberated through the earth above. Somewhere, far off, another strike - another reminder of the storm that was always waiting just beyond the surface. But Ahmed didn't flinch. They were as prepared as they could be, and now, when the time came, they would be ready.

"We'll show them," he murmured softly, almost to himself, his voice lost in the hum of the radios and the distant murmur of his men's voices. *"We'll make them pay for every step."*

And for the first time in what felt like an eternity, Ahmed believed it. They were no longer on the brink - they were in control. He had brought his fighters back, steadied the course, and now... they would face whatever came next, together.

Chapter Thirty Two

YOSSI

Yossi and Nadav returned home for their two weeks of leave, feeling a mix of relief and excitement. The long-awaited medal ceremony, set to honour their bravery, was scheduled at a military base near Tel Aviv - the very place where they had first undergone basic training. As they approached the base, memories of those intense months flooded back, creating a deep sense of anticipation and reflection.

On the day of the ceremony, the sky was a brilliant blue, and Israeli flags fluttered in a soft breeze. Yossi and Nadav stood tall in their crisp IDF dress uniforms, each wearing the red beret of the Parachute Brigade, a powerful symbol of their unit's elite status. Their uniforms were immaculate, their expressions serious yet filled with pride.

Friends and family filled the stands, a sea of familiar faces radiating quiet pride and joy. Comrades from different units stood among them, some wearing the same red berets, others in their own distinctive colours. The air was thick with unity and purpose, this day belonged not just to Yossi and Nadav but to everyone who had been part of their journey.

When the commanding officer called Yossi and Nadav forward, their names echoed across the parade ground, and the applause surged around them like a wave. Yossi scanned the crowd and spotted his parents and Yael in the front row, their faces glowing with pride. Nearby, Nadav's family stood smiling, their eyes filled with emotion.

A senior officer stepped forward to present the medals, his voice clear as he praised their courage and leadership. Yossi received the Medal of Distinguished Service for his bravery under fire, while Nadav was awarded the Chief of Staff's Citation for his exceptional leadership and support during the operation. As the medal was pinned on Yossi's chest, he caught a glimpse of his mother wiping away a tear, her hand pressed to her lips. His father stood beside her, his face set in pride, his shoulders squared as if carrying Yossi's honour himself.

Yossi glanced down at the medal, feeling its weight both literally and metaphorically. His mind flickered briefly to the chaos of that firefight - Avner on the ground, bullets whizzing past. His heart pounded in the present, but he stayed composed as the applause surged once more. He caught Yael's gaze in the crowd, and the noise of the applause seemed to fade. Her smile was bright, but he noticed a flicker of concern in her eyes - a question hanging in the air between them. He knew this was a proud moment, but it was also a crossroads, a turning point for the life they wanted together.

After receiving his medal, Nadav looked out at the sea of faces and found Leila's gaze. She stood just behind his family, her eyes fixed on him, filled with unspoken admiration. He offered her a small smile, and she nodded, her expression saying more than words ever could.

After the ceremony, there was a rush of embraces, handshakes, and congratulations. Yossi was overwhelmed by the love and support of those around him. As he moved through the crowd, he caught Yael's eye, and they shared a knowing smile. They both understood that this moment was about more than just their courage, it was about the quiet strength of their loved ones, who had stood by them through every challenge.

"You did it, Yossi!" his mother whispered, her arms wrapped tightly around him. Yossi's father smiled, his eyes gleaming with pride.

"I always knew you were destined for something great, son," David said softly. "Today, you've proved it."

Nadav's mother clasped his hand, her grip firm. "*We're so proud of you, Nadav,*" she said, her voice thick. His father merely nodded, the approval in his gaze speaking volumes.

With two weeks of leave ahead, Yossi felt a freedom he hadn't experienced in months. It was a rare chance to reconnect with his family, friends, and, most importantly, to spend time with Yael. Decisions about his future in the military could wait - this was a time to savour the present, to embrace the warmth of those who mattered most.

That evening, Yossi and Nadav's families and friends gathered for a celebration at a local venue, festively decorated with fairy lights, music, and the scent of fresh food in the air. Laughter filled the room - a rare sound after months of tension and separation. The celebration was lively, with toasts raised in their honour and stories shared. Yossi looked around, deeply grateful for the people in his life. His parents embraced him warmly, and Yael stood by his side, her hand in his, her eyes shining with pride and relief.

Yossi smiled and nodded his way through congratulatory handshakes and embraces, but his thoughts were elsewhere. The weight of his decision was still pressing down on him. The moments of celebration felt bittersweet, as if the joy of the evening was tainted by the uncertainty he couldn't shake. He knew he couldn't ignore it any longer, especially with Yael right there by his side. He needed to talk to her - to share the doubts gnawing at him.

He caught her eye from across the room. She seemed to sense his urgency, excusing herself from a conversation with her parents, and made her way over to him.

"*Hey,*" she said softly, noticing the seriousness in his expression. "*Want to go for a walk?*"

He nodded, grateful. "*Yeah, let's get some air.*"

They slipped away from the crowd, stepping out into the cool night. The sounds of the celebration faded as they walked down a quiet path, lit by soft streetlights. For a while, they strolled in silence, their footsteps echoing softly against the pavement, until Yossi finally stopped and turned to face her.

"There's something I need to talk to you about," he began, his voice low, almost hesitant.

Yael's expression grew serious, her eyes searching his. *"I figured,"* she replied gently. *"Is it about the officer training, Nadav mentioned it?"*

Yossi nodded, swallowing hard. *"Yeah... They've offered me a place. The Brigade Commander wants me to go through with it, to become an officer."*

Yael's eyes softened, but she stayed quiet, waiting for him to continue.

He took a deep breath, the words spilling out before he could stop them. *"I'm not sure I want to do it, Yael. And it's not because of Nadav, or the guys, or even the thought of leaving them behind. It's... it's because of us."*

Yael blinked, caught off guard. *"Us?"* she echoed softly. *"What do you mean, Yossi?"*

He ran a hand through his hair, searching for the right words. *"Becoming an officer... it means more time away, more responsibilities, more... everything. I'd have to commit to years more in the army, years that I thought we'd have together, building our future, planning our life. I'm worried that if I take this path, I'll lose sight of what's really important - of what we've been dreaming of, what we've been building."*

Yael's face softened, a tender expression crossing her features. *"Yossi,"* she whispered, *"I understand where you're coming from, I do. But is that really what's holding you back? Are you worried about our future, or about choosing a path that might change it?"*

Yossi's thoughts raced. He wanted to tell her more, to explain the heavy sense of dread he had about taking on more responsibility - about leading men into battle, about carrying their lives in his hands. But the words stuck in his throat. He nodded, feeling a rush of emotion welling up inside him. *"I don't want to lose what we have,"* he said, his voice breaking slightly. *"I don't want to wake up one day and realise I've put my career ahead of us, that I've sacrificed the life we've talked about - the home, the family, everything."*

Yael reached for his hand, holding it tightly. *"Yossi,"* she said, her voice steady but filled with warmth, *"our future isn't just about a plan or a timeline. It's about us, who we are together. Yes, becoming an officer might mean more time away, more challenges... but it could also mean a better future for us, one where you're doing what you're meant to do, what makes you happy."*

He shook his head, a conflicted look on his face. *"But what if it doesn't make me happy?"* Yossi murmured. *"What if it takes me away from you, from everything I love?"*

Yael took a step closer, her gaze unwavering. *"Yossi, we can't build our future on 'what ifs.' We have to trust that whatever happens, we'll face it together. I want you to be happy, to find your purpose. And if that means becoming an officer, then I'm here for it. But if you feel it's not right for you, then we'll find another way. We always do."*

Yossi's shoulders sagged slightly, the tension easing a little at her words. *"I just... I'm scared, Yael. Scared of making the wrong choice, scared of losing you... scared of losing us."*

"It's hard for me too, Yossi," she admitted softly. *"Every time you leave, every time you're gone... I worry. But I can't hold you back from doing what you're meant to do, just because I'm afraid."*

Yael reached up, brushing a tear from his cheek with her thumb. *"You won't lose me, Yossi,"* she whispered fiercely. *"Not to any decision, not to any job. I love you, and that's not going to change. But I need you to believe that we're stronger than this, that our future isn't as fragile as you think."*

He swallowed, his throat tight with emotion. *"I love you too,"* he murmured. *"More than anything. And I want to build a life with you, a real life, where we're not always waiting for the next leave, the next break. I want to be there for you, every day, not just in between missions or deployments."*

Yael smiled, a tear glistening in her eye. *"I want that too,"* she said softly. *"But I also want you to be true to yourself, to who you are. And I know that part of you wants this, wants to lead, to make a difference. Don't turn away from that just because you're afraid of what it might mean for us. We're strong, Yossi. We can handle it."*

Yossi nodded slowly, feeling the weight of his responsibility both as a soldier and as her partner. *"I guess... I just needed to hear that,"* he admitted. *"Needed to know that you're okay with it, that you're with me, no matter what."*

Yael squeezed his hand, her smile warm and reassuring. *"Always,"* she promised. *"Whatever path you choose, I'm here. And we'll find our way together, like we always have."*

Yossi took a deep breath, feeling a sense of calm washing over him. The doubts were still there, but they felt smaller now, less insurmountable. He knew the decision wasn't going to be easy, but with Yael by his side, he felt stronger, more certain.

"Thank you," he whispered, pulling her into a tight embrace. *"Thank you for believing in me... in us."*

Yael hugged him back, her voice a soft murmur against his ear. *"Always, Yossi,"* she repeated. *"Always."*

They stood there for a moment, holding each other under the stars, the world around them fading away. Yossi knew there were challenges ahead, but he also knew that with Yael, he could face whatever came next.

Nadav found himself drawn to Leila. They hadn't seen each other since their last encounter at the field hospital, and he felt a surge of excitement mixed with nervousness.

"Hey, Leila," Nadav greeted, his voice carrying a warmth that surprised even him.

Leila turned, her face lighting up with a smile. *"Nadav! I was hoping we'd get a chance to talk. It feels like ages."*

Nadav nodded, his grin widening. *"Yeah, it does. How've you been?"*

Leila chuckled softly. *"Busy, as usual. But it's good to be here, with everyone, celebrating something positive for a change."*

Nadav felt a rush of affection. *"Yeah, it's nice to feel... normal, you know? Even if it's just for a little while."*

They moved to a quieter corner of the venue, away from the bustling crowd. Leila glanced at Nadav, a playful look in her eyes. *"So, are you following me around, Nadav?"*

Nadav laughed. *"Maybe I'm the one who should be asking you that. What are you doing attached to the Parachute Brigade?"*

Leila shrugged, smiling. *"I volunteered. Wanted to be close to my friends - close to you and Yossi. I figured someone had to patch you up when you inevitably get yourselves into trouble."*

Nadav's expression softened. *"I'm glad you did. It's good to know we've got you looking out for us."*

Leila's smile grew more tender. *"And I'm glad to be here, Nadav. It means a lot to me."*

There was a brief silence between them, comfortable yet charged with something unspoken. Leila took a small step closer, her gaze warm. *"Maybe, during these two weeks, we could... spend some time together? Just us?"*

Nadav swallowed, feeling his heart quicken. *"I'd like that. A lot,"* he said, his voice a little huskier than he intended.

Leila's smile widened, and for a moment, the bustling room faded away, leaving just the two of them in a quiet, unspoken understanding.

As Yossi, Yael, Nadav, and Leila settled around a quieter table, Yossi felt the weight of his decision pressing down on him. The celebration continued in the background, filled with music and laughter, but he knew it was time to talk to Nadav about what came next.

He glanced at Yael, who gave him a small, encouraging smile. He took a deep breath and turned to Nadav, clearing his throat to get his attention.

"Nadav," Yossi began, his voice steady but carrying a hint of seriousness. *"I've been thinking a lot about what comes next... about the officer training."*

Nadav nodded, his expression tightening slightly, as if he'd been expecting this. *"Yeah, I've been thinking about it too,"* he admitted. *"They made it pretty clear they want both of us to go."*

Yossi nodded. *"They did. And... I've decided I'm going to do it. I'm going to go for officer training."*

There was a pause, a slight flicker of something in Nadav's eyes - maybe a mix of pride and something else, something heavier. He took a breath, his shoulders straightening a little. *"I'm not surprised, Yossi,"* Nadav said, his voice calm but tinged with a bit of tension. *"I always figured you'd go for it. You've got what it takes to be an officer - the leadership, the way you think things through. You'll be great at it."*

Yossi appreciated the support in Nadav's words, but he could sense the underlying unease. *"Thanks, Nadav,"* he replied sincerely. *"But I was hoping... that maybe you'd join me. I mean, we've been through everything together up until now. I can't imagine going through this without you."*

Nadav looked down at the table, fiddling with the edge of his glass. *"I know,"* he said quietly. *"But... I've been thinking about it too. And I don't think it's the right path for me."*

Yossi felt a pang of disappointment, but he nodded slowly. *"Why not?"* he asked, trying to keep his tone gentle. *"I thought... I thought we could do this together, like always."*

Nadav sighed, looking up to meet Yossi's gaze. *"I know. And it's not that I don't want to be by your side - I do. But becoming an officer... it's a whole different world, Yossi. It's a different kind of responsibility. I don't know if that's where I belong."*

Yossi's brow furrowed. *"You're one of the best leaders I've ever known, Nadav. The guys look up to you, they trust you. Why wouldn't you take that further?"*

Nadav shrugged, a conflicted look on his face. *"Because I like where I am,"* he said slowly. *"I like being in the field, right there with the team. I like knowing that when things get tough, I'm right there beside them, not a step removed, not behind a desk or a map, planning from a distance. I want to stay with the unit as a career soldier, an NCO. I want to be the one they can count on, up close, where it matters most."*

Yossi listened, feeling a mixture of understanding and frustration. *"So, you're saying... you'd rather stay an NCO? Stay where you are?"*

Nadav nodded. *"Yeah,"* he replied. *"I think that's where I belong. And it doesn't mean we're not together, Yossi. We'll still be in the same brigade, the same unit. Only difference is... now you get to tell me what to do,"* he added with a small, teasing grin.

Yossi's expression softened, a grin spreading across his face. *"Oh, is that right? You think I'm looking forward to giving you orders?"*

Nadav chuckled, some of the tension easing. *"Let's be honest, you've been doing that unofficially for years. This just makes it official."*

Leila, who had been quietly observing, laughed. *"I think you both know this doesn't change anything. You're still Yossi and Nadav - just with a few more stripes and responsibilities."*

Yael smiled, nodding. *"Exactly. And besides, Nadav, you'll have plenty of chances to give Yossi a hard time when he's stressed over some officer paperwork."*

Nadav laughed, the tension fully dissipating. *"Oh, you better believe it,"* he said, his grin widening. *"I'll be right there to remind him not to take himself too seriously."*

Yossi relaxed, feeling a wave of relief. *"I guess I can count on you for that,"* he said, clapping Nadav on the shoulder. *"Just promise you'll still have my back, even if I'm the one in charge."*

Nadav's expression softened into something more genuine. *"Always, Yossi,"* he said earnestly. *"Just like always."*

Yossi nodded, feeling a warmth spread through him. *"Alright then,"* he said, raising his glass. *"To new roles, new challenges, and the same old friendship."*

Nadav clinked his glass with Yossi's. *"To that,"* he agreed. *"And maybe to giving you a few more grey hairs along the way."*

They all laughed, the mood lifting as the conversation flowed back to the easy banter they were used to. The decision had been tough, but it felt right. No matter their different paths, their bond remained unbreakable.

As the evening progressed, the group of friends - Yossi, Nadav, Yael, Amir, Maya, Samir, and a few others - slipped away from the noise of the party to their favourite spot on the beach, a quiet cove they had claimed as their own years ago. The moon hung low in the sky, casting a soft, silver glow over the sea. They sat in a circle on the cool sand, their voices mingling with the sound of the waves gently lapping against the shore.

Nadav spoke first, his voice filled with nostalgia. *"Remember how we used to come here after school, talking about our dreams and plans?"*

Amir grinned. *"Yeah, those were simpler times. Back when we thought getting into the right unit was the hardest thing we'd ever face."*

Maya laughed softly, her eyes shining with fond memories. *"And now look at us - different paths, different dreams, but somehow... still the same in a way."*

Yossi gazed out at the waves, his thoughts drifting. *"I've been thinking a lot about what comes next,"* he admitted. *"After everything we've been through, I just want to find peace - whatever that means for each of us."*

Yael squeezed his hand gently, her voice warm. *"I think we all do, Yossi. But maybe finding peace starts with moments like this - with people who know you, who understand where you've been and where you want to go."*

Samir nodded. *"No matter what happens, we have to stick together. Who else would put up with our nonsense?"*

They fell silent, listening to the gentle rhythm of the sea, each lost in their own thoughts. Yet in that moment, they felt a renewed connection, a rekindling of the friendship that had carried them through so much. They spoke of hopes, fears, and dreams, talking late into the night under the stars, holding on to the promise of staying close, no matter what the future held.

Yossi looked around at his friends, emotion swelling within him. *"No matter what comes next, I'm grateful for all of you. We've got each other, and that's what matters."*

They nodded, smiles on their faces, as the waves continued to break gently on the shore. It was a moment of quiet unity, a reminder of the strength they found in one another - a strength that would guide them through whatever lay ahead.

Yael had received her orders from the intelligence services just before her leave, but she kept them to herself, knowing she needed to use her time wisely. Yossi remained blissfully unaware of her mission as they made plans for their two weeks together. The days passed in a blur of family gatherings, long walks, and quiet moments of reconnection. But beneath the surface, Yael's mind was constantly turning, trying to balance the joy of being with Yossi with the weight of her responsibilities.

Yossi decided to spend some time with his father, David, catching up and sharing his hopes and concerns about his future in the IDF. Meanwhile, Yael took the opportunity to speak with Salma, arranging to meet her at David's office. Salma greeted her warmly, and they settled into a quiet corner, their conversation beginning light and easy.

"I was hoping we could catch up," Yael began, smiling warmly. *"I've always admired your strength, managing the work here and everything back in Gaza. It must be so challenging."*

Salma's smile faltered slightly, and she nodded. *"It is,"* she admitted. *"Every day feels like I'm caught between two worlds. Here, it's calmer, more stable... but as soon as I cross back into Gaza, it's like stepping into another reality. The contrast is jarring."*

Yael nodded sympathetically. *"I can imagine,"* she said softly. *"Do you ever think about staying here longer if it was possible, maybe working and living in Tel Aviv full-time? It might make things a bit easier."*

Salma hesitated, her eyes flickering with uncertainty. *"I think about it sometimes,"* she replied. *"There are moments when I see what life could be like here... without the constant fear, the tension. But it's not so simple. My family is everything to me. They are in Gaza, and I can't imagine leaving them behind."*

"I get that," Yael said gently. *"It's hard to balance what you want with the reality of your responsibilities. But you have a lot of potential, Salma. You could make a real difference, wherever you choose to be."*

Yael leaned forward slightly, her voice soft. *"Salma, I hope you know... if you ever need anything, you can reach out to me. I mean that."* She forced a smile, willing her own doubts to remain hidden behind the warmth of her words.

Salma's face softened. *"That means a lot, Yael. Thank you."* she murmured. *"I just wish things were clearer. Some days, I feel like I'm living in a shadow, always waiting for the next crisis. It's exhausting."*

Yael offered a sympathetic smile. Yael's smile wavered slightly, guilt twinging in her chest. *"Anytime,"* she murmured, wishing she could mean it more sincerely.

Salma smiled, a hint of gratitude in her eyes. *"That means a lot, Yael. Thank you."*

Yael returned the smile, though her heart was heavy with the knowledge she couldn't share. She saw the conflict in Salma's eyes, the struggle to balance her ties to Gaza with the pull of a different life in Tel Aviv. Yael felt an urge to reach out more, to help bridge the chasm between two worlds. But she knew that trust was fragile, and this was a delicate dance - one wrong step could shatter everything.

Later, when Yael reunited with Yossi, he could see something was on her mind. *"Everything okay?"* he asked gently, his eyes searching hers.

Yael nodded, masking her concerns with a soft smile. *"Yeah, just... thinking about a few things,"* she replied, taking his hand. She felt a wave of gratitude for this brief moment of calm, knowing that the days ahead would likely bring more challenges, both for herself and for those she loved.

As they walked together along the familiar streets, the future - uncertain as it was - seemed a little less daunting with him by her side.

Chapter Thirty Three

AHMED

Ahmed sat among the senior leaders, the atmosphere thick with tension. The dimly lit room buzzed softly with the low hum of voices and the rustle of papers, adding to the weight of anticipation. He sat straight-backed, his eyes alert, as Abu Khaled leaned forward, his face a mask of seriousness.

"This is it, Ahmed," Abu Khaled began, his voice low but steady. *"You and your men are to start preparing the ground. We need you to conduct reconnaissance along your sector of the border, observe Israeli positions, and monitor troop movements. You'll be coordinating with other units, but your zone is critical. We need to know exactly where they're weak and where they're strong."*

Ahmed nodded, absorbing the information. *"Understood. But is there a timeline?"*

The older man shook his head slowly. *"Not yet. But things are building up. We need detailed intelligence to plan the attack. Your secondary task - equally important - is to identify and establish missile positions."*

"Missile positions?" Ahmed repeated, feeling a ripple of unease. The implications were clear.

"Yes," Abu Khaled confirmed, leaning forward. *"We are preparing a massive missile strike to overwhelm the Iron Dome. Thousands of missiles will be launched simultaneously to flood their defences. Each one has to be concealed so well that no drone or satellite can spot them. Once they are fired, the enemy will retaliate*

brutally. We need these missiles positioned in a way that ensures their maximum use and reduces exposure."

"Over a thousand?" Ahmed echoed softly, masking the flicker of unease that crossed his face. He kept his voice steady, but inside, a cold dread settled. *We're not just preparing for a fight,* he thought. *We're planning for devastation.*

"Yes, over a thousand," Abu Khaled said evenly. *"Just in your sector alone. We'll be spreading them across Gaza, but each zone will carry a significant share. Your men need to find safe spots - places that are hidden yet accessible. Once they're positioned, we'll also need storage facilities at each site. This is going to be a long-term operation, spread over a year or more. You have to be meticulous. No mistakes."*

"And the observation posts?" Ahmed asked.

"They need to be along the border," Abu Khaled said, *"from the north, near Erez Crossing, all the way down to the south, near the army camp at Re'im, covering every key area in between. Your men will watch the Israelis from hidden positions, using tunnels to enter and exit without being seen. If the enemy notices even a hint of activity, everything could be compromised."*

"I understand," Ahmed murmured, his mind racing. *"And my leaders - should they rotate through these posts?"*

"No," Abu Khaled replied firmly. *"Your leaders will organise the shifts, but the observation will be done by trusted men under their command. This is too critical for them to be caught out in the open."*

Ahmed nodded again, his eyes narrowing slightly as he considered the logistics. *"And what about the missile positions?"*

"Those will be spread throughout your sector," Abu Khaled said. *"They must be positioned far enough from the border that they aren't easily detectable. Use the tunnel network. Build special pits and shelters, and make sure they're camouflaged from above. Every position must be reviewed and approved before any missile is moved."*

He paused, his gaze drilling into Ahmed's. *"Once the locations are identified, we'll need to move quickly. The missiles have to be positioned without being seen. This means coordinating teams, watching for drones, and ensuring there's no sign of activity visible from above. It's risky, but it's what's been ordered."*

Ahmed took a deep breath, his mind buzzing. *"I'll get started,"* he said quietly.

"Good," Abu Khaled said, sitting back. *"Remember, Ahmed - this isn't just about gathering information. It's about creating a network that can sustain a war. One misstep, and the entire plan could fall apart."*

With that, the meeting ended. Ahmed left the room, his mind swirling with the gravity of the new orders. His role had expanded again - now, he wasn't just preparing men for an assault. He was building a web of defences, hiding an arsenal that could set the region ablaze.

Back at the safe house, Ahmed gathered his four leaders. They sat around a small, wooden table, the dim light casting shadows across their faces. He could see the curiosity and the tension in their eyes as he laid out the orders.

"We've got a new task," Ahmed began, keeping his voice calm and steady. *"We need to set up observation posts along the border, from Erez Crossing in the north to Re'im in the south. Each OP must be completely hidden, with tunnel access so movements can't be seen from the Israeli side. Once the positions are established, they need to be manned in shifts - trusted men only."*

He paused, looking each of his men in the eye. *"I'm putting each of you in charge of a sector. Tariq, you'll cover the north. Khaled, take the south. Bilal and Hadi will set up post in between these two locations, this will be our area of operations. I want detailed reports on every viable location. No mistakes, no loose ends. If you're not sure about a spot, discard it. We can't afford any slip-ups."*

The men nodded, their faces serious.

"There's more," Ahmed continued, his voice lowering. *"This is a long-term operation. Over the next year, we'll be hiding over a thousand missiles in our sector alone. They'll be positioned away from the border - around Gaza City. We're talking about built up areas near hospitals, schools and populated areas, the places they won't*

strike... any place that won't be visible from above. Each site will also need to have storage for the missiles."

"This isn't a rush job," Ahmed said slowly. "We've got time, but we need to be precise. Every site has to be perfect, every movement unseen. We'll train separate teams for this - people who can move discreetly, who can dig and build without drawing attention."

He leaned forward slightly, his gaze hard. "I don't need to tell you how risky this is. The Israelis will be watching. One mistake, and they'll know something's up. So, take your time. Do it right."

Tariq shifted in his seat. "What if they get suspicious? What if we start losing men?"

"Then we adapt," Ahmed replied firmly. "If they notice us, we pull back, change tactics. But we keep going. This is what's been ordered, and we'll see it through."

For a moment, the room was silent. Then Khaled nodded slowly. "We'll get it done."

"Good," Ahmed said quietly. "Once the observation posts are up and running, I want a list of every potential missile site by the end of the month. After that, we'll start training the new teams."

The men nodded again, their expressions set. As Ahmed watched them, he felt a strange mix of emotions - determination, worry, and a flicker of pride. They had been on the brink before, but now they were back on track, focused and united.

"Stay sharp," he warned as they rose to leave. "We're going to be under the microscope from here on out. Every move counts."

They nodded, filing out silently, leaving Ahmed alone with his thoughts. As he stared at the empty chairs, he felt the familiar weight of responsibility settle over him once more. The stakes had never been higher, but at least now, his men were with him again.

It had been touch and go, but they were back on his side. For now.

Weeks turned into months as Ahmed and his men meticulously set up the observation posts and began the laborious task of identifying and securing missile sites across their designated sectors. The hidden network they were building expanded deep into Gaza City and its surroundings. Each site was carefully chosen, concealed beneath homes, hospitals, and schools - any place where it would be least expected and hardest to detect.

The atmosphere in Gaza began to shift as word of unusual activities spread through the community. The streets buzzed with hushed whispers, and wary glances followed Ahmed's fighters wherever they went. Families were being relocated, neighbourhoods subtly reshaped to accommodate hidden bunkers and shelters, and civilians began to notice that something ominous was in the air.

Even Ahmed could feel the difference. People were on edge, watching with fear and suspicion as trucks rolled through their neighbourhoods at odd hours, always accompanied by armed fighters. His men moved under the cover of darkness, but there was no hiding the tension that rippled through the city like a current. And it wasn't just the civilians who felt it - Ahmed's fighters, despite their training and discipline, were growing more restless each day.

One evening, as Ahmed returned to the safe house from another long day at the command centre, he found Salma waiting for him in the living room, her arms crossed, and her face set in a worried frown. The moment he stepped inside, he sensed the tension radiating from her.

"Ahmed," she began, her voice low and firm, *"we need to talk."*

He paused, studying her expression. *"What's wrong?"* he asked cautiously, though he already had a sinking feeling he knew what this was about.

"What's wrong?" Salma repeated, her voice rising slightly. *"People are scared, Ahmed! They're saying the fighters are moving into the neighbourhoods, that strange things are happening at the schools and hospitals. Families are being told to move without explanation. They don't know what's going on, but they know it's bad."*

Ahmed sighed heavily, running a hand over his face. *"Salma, you know I can't talk about this."*

"But you can see what's happening, can't you?" she pressed, stepping closer. *"People are nervous. They're afraid. And when people are afraid, they start making assumptions. They're starting to whisper that something big is coming - something that's going to put us all in danger. The tension is thick enough to cut through. You must feel it."*

"I do," Ahmed admitted, his shoulders sagging slightly. *"But this is how it has to be. I'm doing what I can to keep everyone safe."*

"Safe?" Salma's eyes widened, disbelief flickering across her face. *"By putting them in the middle of a battlefield? Is that safety, Ahmed?"*

"Lower your voice," Ahmed warned, glancing toward the windows. *"You know people are listening."*

"Then maybe they should hear!" she shot back, her voice dropping to a fierce whisper. *"Because what's happening right now is wrong. People are being used. They're being turned into human shields, and for what? What are you fighting for, Ahmed?"*

He clenched his fists, feeling anger flare up in his chest. *"I'm fighting for us, for our future, for our freedom!"* he hissed. *"You know that!"*

"Freedom?" Salma's voice softened, turning sad. *"What kind of freedom are we building if it's built on fear and bloodshed? What's the point if there's nothing left of us when it's over?"*

Ahmed turned away, his jaw clenched. He couldn't answer her - not truthfully. The orders he'd been given were clear, and deviating from them wasn't an option. But the doubt Salma's words stirred in him was like a knife twisting in his gut. He'd spent so long convincing himself that he was doing the right thing, that this was all necessary, but now... it was getting harder to believe.

"Salma, this is bigger than you or me," he murmured, staring down at the ground. *"If we don't prepare now, if we don't build up our defences, we'll be crushed the moment the fighting starts."*

"And what about the people?" Salma demanded softly. *"The mothers, the children - do they know they're part of your defences now? Do they get a say in any of this?"*

Her words struck him like a blow. Ahmed squeezed his eyes shut, willing himself to keep control. *"You know I don't have a choice,"* he whispered, his voice tight. *"If I stop now, everything falls apart. The leaders -"*

"The leaders don't care about us," Salma interrupted sharply. *"They don't care about the people you're trying to protect. They care about making a statement, about using us to score points on a global stage. And you know that, Ahmed. I see it in your eyes every time you come home."*

For a moment, the room was silent, the weight of her words hanging heavy between them. Ahmed swallowed hard, opening his eyes to meet her gaze.

"I have to see this through," he said quietly. *"If I don't, it won't just be me who pays the price. They'll kill me, Salma. They'll kill you, our families, everyone. We're in this, whether we want to be or not."*

Salma's shoulders slumped, the fire draining out of her. *"I know,"* she whispered, her voice small and broken. *"But I can't watch you turn into someone I don't recognise. Please, Ahmed... remember why you're doing this. Don't let them turn you into another one of their pawns."*

Ahmed felt a pang of guilt twist in his chest. He stepped forward, reaching out to cup her face gently. *"I'm still me,"* he murmured, his voice softer now. *"I'm still fighting for us. I'm just... doing what I have to do."*

Salma's eyes searched his, pain and worry swirling in their depths. She didn't say anything, but she didn't pull away either. Instead, she leaned into his touch, her eyes closing briefly.

"Just... be careful," she whispered. *"Don't let them take everything from us."*

"I won't," Ahmed promised, though even as he said it, he wasn't sure if he believed it himself.

In the weeks that followed, the placement of missiles continued, slowly and methodically. Ahmed and his leaders coordinated the movements like clockwork, using the tunnels to transport the weapons and teams to the designated sites. The observation posts along the border remained active, men rotating through shifts under Tariq's and Khaled's watchful eyes, reporting every Israeli patrol, every hint of movement. Meanwhile, the concealed pits were dug deeper into Gaza City, each one hidden with meticulous care.

Ahmed remained vigilant, overseeing every detail, ensuring no mistakes were made. The tension in the city grew with each passing day, but he kept his men focused, kept them working. This was their reality now - moving in shadows, balancing on a knife's edge. There was no room for error, no room for doubt.

But every night, when the city fell quiet and he lay beside Salma, Ahmed felt the weight of his choices pressing down on him, heavier than ever. He was pulling his men together, rallying them around a cause that seemed to grow murkier with each new order. He was following orders, carrying out the mission, but each step brought him closer to a line he wasn't sure he could cross.

The storm was building, and he was in too deep to turn back. But as he looked at Salma's sleeping form, he couldn't shake the feeling that no matter what happened next, he'd already lost something precious. Something he might never get back.

Chapter Thirty Four

YOSSI

Yossi and Nadav returned to the forward operating base after their two weeks of leave, their minds still processing the whirlwind of events that had unfolded. The time away had been filled with celebration, reflection, and decisions that would shape their futures. As soon as they arrived back at the base, a runner met them with orders to report immediately to the commanding officer's tent.

The two friends exchanged a glance, both aware this was the moment they had anticipated. They walked through the familiar landscape of the base, weaving through the maze of sandbagged positions and makeshift shelters. The sounds of radio chatter and shouted commands filled the air. As they neared the tent, Nadav smirked.

"Think he already knows what we're going to say?" he asked.

Yossi gave a slight nod, a smile playing at the corners of his mouth. *"Probably, but it's time we said it out loud."*

They pulled back the flap and stepped inside. The commanding voice of Lieutenant Colonel Arad greeted them from behind a table cluttered with maps and reports.

"Come in!"

They snapped to attention, and Arad looked up, his sharp eyes scanning them both. *"At ease, Samals,"* he said, his tone calm but firm. *"I trust you had a good leave?"*

"Yes, sir," they replied in unison, their voices steady.

Arad leaned back slightly in his chair. *"Good. I'm sure you've had time to consider the recommendation for officer training. Let's hear your decisions."*

Yossi spoke first, his voice clear. *"Sir, I've given it a lot of thought, and I'm ready to accept the recommendation for officer training. I understand what's at stake, and I'm prepared to take on the responsibilities and challenges ahead."* He'd been mulling it over during his leave, thinking of his time in the field and the kind of leader he wanted to become. The decision hadn't been easy, but it was right.

Arad nodded, just slightly, as if this was what he had expected. *"Good to hear, Samal Rosenberg. You've shown potential, but remember, becoming an officer is more than just a title. You'll need to prove yourself, starting with the Gibush at Bahad 1."*

"I understand, sir. I'm prepared," Yossi replied, determination steady in his voice.

Arad's gaze shifted to Nadav. *"And you, Samal Levy?"*

Nadav squared his shoulders, standing a little taller. *"Sir, I've made my decision to stay with the unit as an NCO. Leading from the front, being right there with my men - that's where I belong. It's where I can do the most good."* His voice was resolute, but there was a brief flicker of emotion in his eyes. Nadav had thought long and hard about this, realising his strength lay in leading from the front, with his men, not in an officer's role. It hadn't been easy turning down the opportunity, but he knew it was the right choice for him.

Arad's expression softened slightly. *"I respect that decision, Samal Levy. The unit needs experienced NCOs, and you've always been strong in that role. Are you ready for what it means to stay on as a career soldier?"*

"Yes, sir," Nadav replied. *"That's where I can make the most difference."*

Arad nodded again. *"Very well. Samal Rosenberg, you'll report to Bahad 1 next week for the Gibush. If you pass, you'll proceed to officer training. Samal Levy, you'll continue with your duties here."*

He stood up, signalling the end of the conversation. *"I'm proud of both of you. You've made thoughtful decisions. The unit is better for it. Dismissed."*

Yossi and Nadav saluted and left the tent. As soon as they were outside, Nadav chuckled, breaking the tension.

"Well, it's official. You're going to Bahad 1."

Yossi grinned. *"Yes, but first, I have to get through the Gibush."*

Nadav had his own paperwork to complete. He made his way to the Company Office Tent, filling out forms to officially become a career soldier. In his statements, he emphasised his commitment to the unit and his belief that he could make the most difference as an NCO. There was a sense of satisfaction as he signed the documents - this was where he belonged. A brief interview followed, and within a week, he received his approval. The men in his unit welcomed the news with enthusiasm. Nadav felt a sense of pride and contentment, knowing he was exactly where he wanted to be.

A week later, as Yossi prepared to leave for Bahad 1, Nadav was there to see him off, offering a firm handshake.

"You know you're going to crush it, Yossi. Just remember - you're already the leader they need. Bahad 1 is just about showing them what I already see."

Yossi nodded, smiling. *"I'll do my best. But hey, don't go slacking off without me here to keep you in check."*

They shared a final smile, both knowing that while their paths were going in different directions, their bond would remain unbroken. But as Yossi walked away, Nadav felt a twinge of something else - wondering how different things might be once Yossi returned as an officer. He shook the thought away. Whatever happened, they'd make it work.

A week later, Yossi found himself standing on the training grounds at Bahad 1, the IDF's Officer Training School. The selection process, known as the Gibush Kavatzim, was underway. Yossi had already proven his physical fitness in the Parachute Brigade, but here, it wasn't just about endurance or strength. It was about leadership, quick thinking, and decision-making under pressure.

During the leadership exercises, Yossi was tasked with leading a small team through simulated missions, navigating rough terrain and managing unexpected challenges. The evaluators watched closely, scrutinising how he communicated, motivated his team, and made tactical decisions in real time. He drew on his experience from the field, issuing clear instructions and maintaining his composure, even when things went wrong. He knew this was his chance to prove he could lead, not just follow.

Later, Yossi faced a series of interviews and psychological evaluations. He sat across from a panel of officers and psychologists, answering questions about his motivations, experience, and understanding of leadership.

"Why do you want to become an officer?" one of the officers asked, leaning forward.

Yossi spoke plainly. *"I've seen what good leadership can do. It changes outcomes, builds trust, and keeps men safe. I want to be that leader."* He paused, wondering if they'd understand how much this meant to him, how deeply he felt the responsibility of leadership. The panel nodded, their faces betraying nothing. They were assessing not just his words, but his character and resolve.

A few days later, the results were posted. Yossi's heart pounded as he searched the list. When he saw his name, a rush of relief and pride filled him. He had passed. Officer training at Bahad 1 was next.

He couldn't wait to tell Nadav and the others. As he walked away from the board, he felt a renewed sense of purpose. The next Chapter was beginning, but he also knew the stakes had just gotten higher.

After receiving the news that he had passed the selection process, Yossi was granted a few days of leave. He decided to spend this time with Yael in Tel Aviv. The city was alive with energy, a stark contrast to the regimented environment of the base. He relished the freedom of these brief days, knowing they were a rare respite before the next Chapter began.

He arrived at Yael's apartment, a smile spreading across his face as she opened the door.

"*Hey,*" he said, pulling her into a warm embrace.

"*Hey yourself,*" Yael replied, grinning. "*How does it feel to have a few days of freedom before becoming an officer?*"

"*Feels pretty good,*" Yossi admitted. "*But I'm even happier to spend them with you.*"

They spent the afternoon wandering through the streets of Tel Aviv, sharing stories and laughter. As the sun dipped below the horizon, they found a quiet bench in a nearby park. Yossi sensed there was something on Yael's mind.

"*What's up?*" he asked gently.

Yael took a deep breath, her gaze drifting to the skyline. "*I've been thinking a lot about what comes next,*" she began. "*And I've decided not to stay in the military after my service ends in six months.*"

Yossi nodded, squeezing her hand. He had suspected as much. "*I had a feeling that might be your decision,*" he said softly. "*What do you want to do instead?*"

Yael smiled thoughtfully. "*I've been talking to a security consultancy firm in Tel Aviv. It seems like a good fit. I'd still be using my skills, just in a different way. And... it might give us more stability, a chance to really build something together.*"

Yossi felt a surge of warmth in his chest. This was the direction he had hoped for, and now, with her decision made, he saw a clearer path for them both. "*I think that sounds perfect,*" he said. "*And speaking of building something together... I've been thinking too.*"

He took a deep breath, turning to face her. "*Yael, I know we've talked about the future - about building something together. Well, I don't want to wait anymore. When I finish officer training... will you marry me?*"

Yael's eyes widened, then broke into a wide smile. *"Are you serious?"* she asked, though her voice was filled with joy.

Yossi grinned. *"Completely serious. I want us to start our lives together, properly, no more waiting. What do you say?"*

"Yes," Yael said, laughing. *"Yes, of course, I'll marry you!"*

They embraced, and Yossi felt a deep sense of peace and happiness. The future was still uncertain, but this was a certainty he wanted more than anything.

The next day, Yossi and Yael decided to share their news with their parents. They gathered both sets of parents at a small café, where Yossi's and Yael's parents met them with curiosity and anticipation.

"Okay, you two," Yael's father said with a smile. *"What's this all about?"*

Yossi took Yael's hand, and they both looked at their parents. *"We have some news,"* Yossi began. *"We've decided to get married... after I finish officer training."*

There was a moment of stunned silence, and then their mothers' faces lit up with joy.

"Oh, that's wonderful!" Yossi's mother exclaimed, tears of happiness already glistening in her eyes. Yael's mother reached over to squeeze her hand, smiling broadly.

"This is great news," Yael's father said, nodding. *"We're so happy for both of you."*

Yossi's father clapped him on the back, beaming. *"We'll start planning right away,"* he declared. *"We'll handle the wedding arrangements, send out the invites to all your friends - you two just focus on getting through this training and finishing your service."*

Yael laughed. *"That's a lot of work for you all. Are you sure?"*

Yossi's mother waved her hand dismissively. *"Of course, we're sure. We've been waiting for this day for a long time. And besides, it gives us something to do while you two are busy with your careers."*

Yael's mother nodded in agreement. *"Leave everything to us. Just promise to come back in one piece, both of you."*

Yossi and Yael exchanged a glance, their hands still intertwined.

"We promise," Yossi said softly, squeezing Yael's hand.

Back at Bahad 1, Yossi's officer training was in full swing. The days were intense, filled with tough physical drills, leadership exercises, and tactical simulations designed to test every aspect of his abilities. He faced each challenge with determination, driven by the goal of becoming the kind of officer his men could trust and respect.

He thought of his friends often - Leila, beginning her nursing journey, Nadav, steadfast in his role as a career soldier, Amir, always ready as an EOD specialist, Samir, vigilant in intelligence, and Maya, thriving in the tech world. Their paths were moving in different directions, but the strength of their friendship remained a constant.

As Yossi completed another day of training, he felt a deep sense of gratitude for the people in his life and the journey they were all on. They were each moving forward with courage and conviction, ready to face whatever came next.

Leila had recently left the IDF to pursue her dream of becoming a nurse. With some time to herself before her studies began, she enjoyed a bit of freedom and reflection. Nadav, on a short break from his unit near the border, suggested they meet for coffee. They hadn't had much time to talk lately, and Nadav was eager to catch up.

They met at a small café near the park, where the warm scent of fresh pastries and the soft hum of conversation created a relaxed atmosphere. Leila arrived first, settling at a table outside under a shade umbrella. Nadav appeared a few minutes later, a smile on his face despite the tension of his recent duties.

"Hey, sorry I'm late," he said, taking a seat. *"Had some last-minute stuff to sort out before leaving the unit."*

Leila smiled warmly. *"No worries, Nadav. It's good to see you. How are things at the border?"*

Nadav shrugged, his smile turning slightly wry. *"Busy, as always. It's been pretty tense lately, but I'm getting used to the idea of staying on as a career soldier. It's where I need to be, I think."*

Leila nodded, sipping her coffee. *"I think it's great. You've always been solid out there. The unit is lucky to have you staying on."*

Nadav chuckled. *"Thanks. And you? How does it feel, leaving the IDF?"*

Leila thought for a moment, then smiled. *"It feels right,"* she admitted. *"I loved my time as a medic, but I'm ready for a new challenge. Becoming a nurse feels like the next step for me. I'll miss the military, but I'm excited about what comes next."*

Nadav nodded thoughtfully. *"You're going to be great at it,"* he said sincerely. *"You've always been the one who knew how to take care of everyone... even when you were patching me up in the field."*

Leila laughed, a light blush spreading across her cheeks. *"Well, someone had to keep you out of trouble,"* she teased.

Their conversation flowed easily, from shared memories of their service to their hopes and dreams for the future. Nadav found himself more relaxed than he'd felt in weeks, enjoying Leila's company in a way he hadn't expected.

As they finished their coffees, Nadav hesitated before speaking. *"You know,"* he said softly, *"I've really enjoyed today. We should do this again... maybe dinner next time?"*

Leila's eyes brightened, and she felt a flutter of excitement in her chest. *"I'd like that,"* she replied, smiling. *"I'd like that a lot."*

Nadav grinned. *"Great. It's a date, then."*

They stood up, a new energy between them as they said their goodbyes. As Leila walked away, she felt a lightness she hadn't felt in a while. This new Chapter wasn't just about her career - it might be about something more.

Amir remained in the IDF as an EOD (Explosive Ordnance Disposal) specialist, focusing on detecting and neutralising IEDs (Improvised Explosive Devices) and booby traps. His unit stayed close to the border of Gaza, where tensions always simmered. Amir's days were filled with training exercises and preparation, ensuring his team was ready for any potential threat. It was serious work, but Amir understood its importance - being prepared could mean the difference between life and death.

During a break, Amir received a call from Yossi, who was in the middle of his officer training.

"Hey, Yossi! How's officer school treating you?" Amir asked.

"Tough, but good," Yossi replied with a laugh. *"How about you? Any excitement on your end?"*

"Not much," Amir said. *"Just keeping busy and staying ready. You know how it is."*

"Yeah, I do. Stay sharp, Amir. We need you at the wedding, not stuck defusing something."

Amir chuckled. *"Don't worry, I'll be there. And you better pass that training!"*

They ended the call with a sense of camaraderie, each knowing they were where they needed to be.

Yael and Samir continued their work in military intelligence, analysing data and monitoring activities. The long hours and constant vigilance were exhausting, but both understood the value of their work.

One evening, while reviewing some reports, Samir glanced over at Yael.

"So, you're really leaving in six months?" he asked casually.

Yael nodded. *"Yes, it's time. I've been in this world long enough, and I think I'm ready for something new. Plus, with the wedding coming up, it feels like the right time for a change."*

Samir smiled. *"I'm happy for you both. You deserve it. But I'm going to miss having you around here."*

Yael chuckled. *"I'll miss working with you too, Samir. But we've got six months left to make a difference. Let's make them count."*

"Absolutely," Samir agreed. *"Let's make sure we do."*

They shared a moment of understanding before returning to their work, knowing that change was on the horizon but that their commitment to their duties remained steadfast.

Maya had transitioned out of the IDF to enter the tech industry, joining a promising start-up in Tel Aviv. Her strategic thinking and analytical skills were already proving invaluable in the fast-paced world of tech. Her days were filled with meetings, coding sessions, and the constant challenge of innovation. It was a big shift from her military service, but Maya was thriving.

She sent a quick text to Yossi: *Hey, just letting you know - I'm officially a techie now. Start-up life is wild, but I'm loving it!*

Yossi replied with a smiley face: *That's brilliant, Maya! I knew you'd do great. Don't forget us little people when you make it big.*

Maya laughed, feeling a sense of fulfilment in her new role. She was ready to embrace whatever came next, knowing her friends would always be there to support her.

Chapter Thirty Five

AHMED

For months, Ahmed's fighters had been meticulously gathering intelligence along the border. They mapped Israeli movements, observed patrol patterns, and identified potential vulnerabilities. The information was painstakingly compiled, every detail passed up the chain to the senior command. Now, as the late summer of 2022 began to wane, Ahmed received new orders that promised to test everything they had learned.

One humid morning, a summons came from the Hamas High Command. The meeting took place in a dimly lit room deep within the labyrinthine tunnels beneath Gaza City. Ahmed moved swiftly through the narrow passageways, the walls damp and the coolness of the underground air clinging to his skin. When he entered, he found several senior commanders seated around a table, their expressions grave and intent.

Abu Yusuf was the first to speak, his voice echoing in the confined space, carrying authority and a sense of urgency.

"We are approaching a critical phase of our operation," he announced, his gaze sweeping the room. "The intelligence you've gathered has been invaluable, and we're ready to move forward. Your new task is to conduct detailed reconnaissance during the Jewish holiday of Simchat Torah on the 16th of October. This is a period of vulnerability, and we need to know everything - movements, weaknesses, changes in routine."

Ahmed listened intently, understanding the significance of the mission. They intended to strike when the Israelis' guard might be down, using the holiday as a cover for their operations. But the risks were immense. One mistake, and the entire operation could unravel with devastating consequences.

Abu Khaled, sitting silently to the side, leaned forward, his gaze fixed on Ahmed. *"This is a highly sensitive operation. Use any means necessary to gather the intelligence, but you must not raise suspicion. Keep your men hidden. We need you to prepare a report, and you will present it directly to us."*

As the briefing concluded, another commander, Abu Fadel, caught Ahmed's arm. His grip was firm, his voice low and edged with a warning. *"Ahmed Al-Masri, this mission is crucial. We are counting on you. Do not let us down."* He paused, his gaze piercing. *"How is Salma, and your family?"*

Ahmed's chest tightened. A subtle but clear reminder that his family's safety depended on his success. *"They're well,"* he answered evenly, refusing to show any fear.

Abu Fadel nodded, his smile thin. *"Good. Keep it that way."*

Suppressing the unease that rippled through him, Ahmed left the meeting with a new understanding of just how high the stakes had become. One wrong move, and it wouldn't just be him paying the price.

Back at their safe house, Ahmed gathered his four leaders - Tariq, Khaled, Bilal, and Hadi. They sat around the small wooden table, the dim light casting sharp shadows on their faces. He could see the curiosity and tension in their eyes as he relayed the new orders.

"The intelligence we've gathered has been valuable," Ahmed began, his voice calm but laced with urgency. *"Now we have a new mission based on that information. We need to focus on the period around the Jewish holiday of Simchat Torah. During this time, the Israelis will likely be distracted, their guard lowered. We need to know everything about their security during the holiday - movements, routine changes, any gaps we can exploit."*

He glanced around the room, meeting each man's gaze. *"This is not just about watching. It's about understanding their patterns, finding weaknesses we can use when the time comes. Our reports have to be perfect. No mistakes."*

Tariq frowned slightly. *"And what if we get caught? What if they notice us?"*

"Then we pull back," Ahmed replied firmly. *"We adapt. We change tactics. But we do not stop. This mission is critical."*

He paused, allowing the weight of his words to sink in. *"The Israelis will be celebrating the holiday of Simchat Torah soon. During that time, their focus may shift. We need to know if there are any changes in their routine - patrol movements, shift rotations, any gaps in their defences."* His gaze moved from one man to the next. *"This is not just about observing. It's about understanding. The information we collect will be used to plan the next steps. If we miss something, if we misread them, the consequences will be severe."*

Tariq frowned slightly. *"What exactly are we looking for? They're always on alert."*

"Anything out of the ordinary," Ahmed clarified. *"More troops, fewer troops, shifts in the guards' patterns. Anything that could indicate a change in their focus. Remember, even a small detail could make the difference."*

Bilal leaned forward. *"What's the real goal here, Ahmed? Are they planning something big?"*

Ahmed hesitated, choosing his words carefully. *"They haven't told me everything, but I believe they're waiting for the right moment to strike. And when they do, it'll be massive."*

The men exchanged uneasy glances, understanding the gravity of the situation.

"We'll keep observing," Khaled said quietly. *"But we need to know - what happens after this?"*

Ahmed shook his head. *"For now, we stick to the plan. This mission is just the beginning. Once we have the information, I'll present it to the commanders, and they'll decide what comes next. Until then, we need to keep a low profile and avoid detection."*

"And the missile sites?" Khaled asked, his tone cautious.

"The missile sites remain the priority," Ahmed said firmly. *"This new mission doesn't change that. We need to stay on track - identify locations, prepare the sites, and keep everything hidden. But we cannot afford to lose sight of what's happening along the border."*

The room fell silent as they absorbed the orders. Then Tariq nodded slowly. *"We'll get it done."*

"Good," Ahmed said quietly. *"But remember - this isn't just about gathering information. It's about laying the groundwork for something bigger. Stay focused, stay alert, and above all, stay safe. One mistake, and we're finished."*

With that, they rose and left the room, moving silently into the shadows of the night. As Ahmed watched them go, a sense of unease tightened in his chest. They were stepping into dangerous territory, and the risks were higher than ever.

Later that evening, Ahmed returned home, the weight of the day pressing down on him. As he stepped inside, he saw Salma waiting, her face calm, though her eyes brimmed with concern. She stood as he entered, her gaze searching his.

"You're back," she said softly, a mixture of relief and apprehension in her voice.

"Yes, it's been a long day," he replied, trying to sound neutral, though he knew she'd see through it.

Salma stepped closer, her eyes never leaving his. *"Ahmed, I don't need to know every detail,"* she began quietly, *"but I can see something is weighing on you. You've been more tense than usual."*

Ahmed sighed, feeling the familiar tug of frustration and guilt. *"We're being asked to gather intelligence for something significant. It's... delicate."*

Salma's expression softened, but there was an edge to her voice. *"Ahmed, I know you feel the weight of this. But sometimes I wonder if we're just repeating the same patterns, going in circles."*

Ahmed's jaw tightened. *"You always say that Salma. But what else can we do? If we don't act, we risk everything."*

Salma touched his arm gently. *"I'm not saying we do nothing, Ahmed. But think about the cost. Every move we make, every escalation... it has consequences. For us, for the people here. I see the fear in their eyes every day."*

He turned away, trying to suppress the doubt gnawing at him. *"What do you want me to do, Salma? Just stand back and watch?"*

"No," she replied softly, her voice firm. *"I want you to think about why we're doing this. What are we really fighting for? Are we trying to win, or just trying to survive?"*

Her words hit deeper than he wanted to admit. *"I don't know,"* he whispered. *"But it's all I've known."*

Salma squeezed his hand. *"Just remember, Ahmed, there might be another way. Maybe it starts with us, with people like you, daring to see things differently."*

Ahmed nodded slowly, feeling a lump in his throat. *"I promise, I'll think about it,"* he said, though he wasn't sure how he could keep that promise.

In the days leading up to the holiday, Ahmed's men began to gather intelligence, quietly, carefully. Workers returning from Israeli towns reported back with what they had overheard - small details, whispers, rumours.

"*We've heard them talking,*" one worker reported. "*Some of the soldiers are looking forward to spending time with their families. They're hoping for an easier day.*"

Another added, "*I noticed fewer guards at the checkpoints today. Some of them seemed less alert, distracted.*"

Ahmed felt the pressure building. "*Keep listening, keep observing. Do not miss anything. We must know exactly how things stand before the holiday begins.*"

Ziad, a worker, glanced nervously at Ahmed. "*We're doing what we can... but it's dangerous. The Israelis are on edge too. What if they catch us?*"

Ahmed's expression hardened. *"Then make sure they don't catch you. Your families are relying on you. We all are."*

The workers left, their fear palpable. Ahmed hated pushing them so hard, but he saw no choice. *They need to understand,* he thought, *the cost of failure is too great.*

Before sunrise on the day of Simchat Torah, Ahmed's men were in position, hidden in carefully chosen spots along the border. The air was cool, the silence only broken by distant sounds of nature. The orders were simple but demanding, remain invisible, observe everything, and report back.

As the sun climbed, the holiday began. Ahmed's men lay low, binoculars trained on roads, checkpoints, and Kibbutzim. They watched the soldiers' movements, noting subtle changes - reduced patrols, relaxed demeanour, fewer vehicles. Ahmed felt a flicker of hope. *This is what we were waiting for.*

By nightfall, the team began their careful withdrawal, waiting for darkness to cover their tracks. Ahmed watched as his men returned, nodding at them, feeling a mix of relief and pride in their discipline.

The next day, he gathered the team to compile their observations. Each fighter reported what they had seen - reduced presence, distracted soldiers, quieter posts. Ahmed pieced together the information into a comprehensive report. *A pattern is forming,* he thought. *Now, to confirm it.*

Later that afternoon, Ahmed met the workers again. They provided additional details about troop numbers and atmosphere. One mentioned overhearing that security was lighter because some soldiers had been granted leave.

Ahmed nodded. *"This is good. We have what we need. Make sure no one knows you spoke to us. Keep your heads down."*

As they left, he felt a gnawing doubt. *Is this enough? Will it ever be enough?*

Salma, watching from a distance, saw the strain etched into his face. *He's playing a dangerous game,* she thought, *and we're all just pieces on his board.*

Chapter Thirty Six

YOSSI

Yossi tightened the straps of his gear, his eyes scanning the rugged training grounds of Bahad 1, the IDF's Officer Training School. The familiar weight of his equipment settled on his shoulders, but this time felt different. Although he had served with distinction in the Parachute Brigade, this was a new level of challenge. The instructors knew his experience, so they had designed a condensed yet intense programme focusing on leadership, strategy, and decision-making rather than basic training.

The early days were filled with advanced exercises that tested Yossi's ability to lead under pressure. One morning, he found himself guiding a small team through a simulated mission designed to push them to their limits. The terrain was rugged, and the obstacles relentless. It wasn't just about physical endurance - Yossi had to think on his feet, adapting to new challenges and making quick, effective decisions.

During a tactical simulation, Yossi had to lead his team through an ambush. They were pinned down, and he had to decide whether to push forward or pull back. He chose to retreat, recognising that the risk was too great. Afterward, an evaluator approached him.

"Why didn't you push forward when you had the chance?" the officer questioned, raising an eyebrow.

Yossi met his gaze steadily. "*My priority is my men's lives. Winning at any cost isn't worth it if it means losing them needlessly. That's not leadership - that's gambling.*"

The officer nodded, jotting down notes. "*A sound decision. But remember, sometimes the risk is necessary.*"

Yossi knew he was being watched, every decision weighed and measured. As he continued through the training, he received frequent text messages from Nadav:

"*Word's out that the platoon's betting on you. I put my money where my mouth is, so don't make me regret it!*"

Yossi laughed to himself, appreciating the support and banter from his friend. These messages kept his spirits high and reminded him that, no matter where his path led, he had a strong network of comrades behind him.

Meanwhile, in Tel Aviv, Yael was navigating her final six months in the IDF with a growing sense of urgency. She continued working closely with Samir in military intelligence, monitoring increased activity in Gaza. Their team had recently identified a new key figure: Ahmed Al-Masri. His name had surfaced through undercover operatives, along with the names of his associates Tariq Barghouti, Khaled Mansour, Bilal Qassem, and Hadi Abu-Salem.

They were slowly piecing together the network.

During a meeting with her senior officers, the atmosphere was tense.

"*We've confirmed Ahmed Al-Masri's name, along with several of his close associates,*" one of the officers began, pointing to the names on the screen. "*He's a high priority, and it's clear he's planning something significant.*"

Yael nodded, her expression serious. "*And we already know about Salma. She is either Al-Masri's partner or wife. She's been appearing frequently in surveillance footage. Given her proximity to him, she could provide vital insights into his plans.*"

The officer acknowledged her point. "*Yes, we're aware of Salma Nasser's connection to Al-Masri. Your earlier identification was critical.* "*We need to use that connection carefully. Keep things casual - maybe meet her while you're at David Rosenberg's office discussing wedding plans. Think you can manage that?*"

Yael agreed. *"I can. Our interactions have been casual so far, and I think I've managed to build some trust. I'll continue to meet her when opportunities arise, but we'll need to be careful - any sudden increase in contact might make her wary."*

The officer leaned forward. *"Good. Gather whatever you can - details about Al-Masri's movements, his communications, any hint of an upcoming operation. But remember, Salma mustn't sense she's under any suspicion. We can't afford to lose this connection."*

Over the next few weeks, Yael continued her routine visits to David's office, ostensibly to discuss wedding arrangements. She often ran into Salma by chance, seizing these opportunities to build rapport. Each time, she kept the conversation light, sharing snippets about her life, the upcoming wedding, and her hopes for the future.

One day, as they chatted, Yael casually remarked, *"Sometimes, I wish things weren't this way. I imagine how different life could be... Maybe, in another world, we could actually be friends. Does that ever cross your mind?"*

Salma seemed taken aback but smiled slightly. *"I think about that too,"* she admitted, her guard lowering just a fraction. *"It would be nice, wouldn't it?"*

Yael nodded, sensing a small breakthrough. Over the following weeks, she continued these interactions, gradually building a foundation of trust. Salma grew more comfortable around her, and Yael noticed small slips of information - mentions of places and names - that she carefully noted without pressing further.

In her work with Samir, Yael noticed a worrying trend. Al-Masri's activities were intensifying, there were more movements, more meetings, and encrypted communications suggesting something significant was being planned.

One evening, she and Samir compiled their findings into a report for their senior officers.

"We're seeing clear signs of preparation for a large-scale operation," Yael explained. *"Al-Masri is central to this, and the involvement of his associates indicates a coordinated effort. We have reason to believe an attack is imminent."*

Samir nodded in agreement. *"We need to act on this intelligence. Waiting could be dangerous."*

The response from their superiors was less urgent than they had hoped.

"We'll continue to monitor the situation," one officer replied, seemingly dismissing their concerns. *"But without more concrete evidence, we can't escalate our response."*

As Yael left the room, a heavy weight settled in her chest. She was playing a dangerous game, trying to balance her duties with the growing bond she felt with Salma. A part of her wondered if she could keep deceiving someone who had done nothing to deserve suspicion - yet the stakes were too high to let her emotions cloud her judgement.

"They're not taking this seriously enough," she muttered to Samir. *"If we're right and they don't act, people could get hurt."*

Samir sighed. *"I know. But we'll keep pushing. We can't let this slip through the cracks."*

On the border, Nadav was engaged in regular operations. The situation with Hezbollah had intensified, with several small-scale clashes erupting. He kept in touch with Leila, though their meetings were less frequent due to his duties.

During one of their calls, Nadav's tone was apologetic. *"I'm sorry I can't see you more often. Things have been hectic here. But as soon as I get a break, I promise we'll meet up."*

Leila understood the situation. *"I know, Nadav. Just stay safe. We'll meet when we can."*

Nadav smiled, his voice warm. *"I'll make it happen, don't worry. I'm looking forward to it."* Though a part of him feared how much longer they could keep their relationship alive with the constant dangers of the front line.

Leila felt a sense of anticipation building. Their connection had grown deeper, and she knew they were both committed to making it work despite the challenges.

Back at Bahad 1, Yossi's officer training was reaching its most demanding stage. Each day brought new challenges, pushing him further physically, mentally, and emotionally. The instructors had raised the bar, testing every aspect of the candidates' leadership potential.

Yossi was assigned more complex tasks, often having to lead a diverse group of soldiers through a series of simulated combat scenarios. These exercises required not just strategic thinking but also a keen ability to inspire and maintain the morale of his team in the face of adversity.

During one such exercise, Yossi found himself in charge of a platoon navigating a mock urban environment under heavy fire. The simulation was designed to mimic the chaos and unpredictability of real combat. Smoke filled the air, and the sounds of explosions and gunfire echoed around them. Dust clung to their clothes, and the sharp smell of cordite burned in the air. Yossi could feel the tension in his men, sensing their anxiety as they moved through narrow alleys and cleared buildings.

He paused, taking a deep breath before issuing his orders. "Bravo, secure the left flank and lock down that building. Charlie, cover their advance from the ridge. Delta, stay with me - we're moving in. Quick, quiet, and stay connected. We move as one - let's make it count."

His voice was calm, steady, and authoritative. Even in the midst of simulated chaos, Yossi maintained his composure, reading the situation and adapting his tactics on the fly. His team responded to his leadership with confidence, executing his plan with precision.

By the end of the exercise, Yossi's platoon had achieved all their objectives with minimal "casualties." The evaluators nodded in approval, taking notes as Yossi regrouped his men for a debrief.

"*Good work out there,*" he said, his voice carrying a mix of praise and constructive feedback. "*We stayed tight, kept our heads, and adapted when needed. Remember, it's not just about following orders but understanding the bigger picture.*"

The final weeks brought a series of endurance challenges and tactical drills designed to push each candidate to their limits. Yossi knew that every moment counted, and he refused to let fatigue or self-doubt creep in. His experience in the Parachute Brigade had taught him resilience, but this training demanded something deeper - a relentless drive to excel, to prove himself worthy of the officer's rank.

During a particularly gruelling multi-day exercise, Yossi and his unit were tasked with a long-distance march through difficult terrain while carrying heavy packs. The route was deliberately challenging, with steep climbs and rough paths that tested the endurance and spirit of the candidates.

Yossi could feel the strain in his muscles and the fatigue setting in, but he kept pushing forward, encouraging his team along the way. *"Stay focused, keep the pace,"* he called out. *"We're almost there. Don't think about the pain, think about why we're doing this."*

His words resonated with the men, and they pushed through, reaching the checkpoint ahead of schedule. When they arrived, an instructor looked at Yossi with approval. *"Well done, Samal Rosenberg. You've set a high standard for the others."*

The final evaluation was a comprehensive field exercise that combined all aspects of the training. It was designed to test not only tactical knowledge and physical endurance but also leadership under extreme pressure.

Yossi's team was assigned a mission to capture a heavily fortified objective. He was given minimal information and had to make quick decisions with limited resources. The evaluators watched closely, looking for any sign of hesitation or poor judgement.

Yossi assessed the terrain and enemy positions swiftly. He gathered his team and outlined his plan with clarity and precision. *"We'll create a diversion to draw their fire while our main force moves in from the south. Keep radio communication tight and stay alert for any changes. This is about speed and surprise."*

The operation unfolded as planned. Yossi led from the front, maintaining control and adapting as the situation changed. When an unexpected obstacle emerged, he quickly adjusted the plan, directing his team with confidence and calm under fire. His ability to remain composed and decisive impressed the evaluators.

The final evaluation was over, and the day had come for the formal Beret and Sword Ceremony, the IDF's equivalent to a commissioning parade. The newly commissioned officers stood in perfect formation on the parade ground at Bahad 1, the same place where they had begun their gruelling training months before. Family, friends, and senior officers gathered to witness the culmination of their journey.

Yossi stood among his fellow graduates, his heart pounding in rhythm with the steady drumbeat that accompanied the march. The sun beat down on them, glinting off the polished swords each new officer held at their side, a symbol of the authority and responsibility they now carried. The red beret of the Parachute Brigade rested proudly on Yossi's head, marking him out among officers from other units.

The commanding officer, a seasoned and respected figure, approached the centre of the parade ground. His voice was firm and clear as he addressed the assembled officers. *"Today marks the completion of one of the most demanding courses in the IDF. You have proven yourselves worthy of the rank and responsibility you now bear. Each of you will return to your units to lead with integrity, with courage, and with honour."*

The officer paused and turned toward Yossi's cohort, scanning the line of new officers before his gaze rested on Yossi. *"There's one officer who has stood out - not just for his tactical skills, but for his resilience and leadership. It's my honour to recognise Segen Mishne Yossi Rosenberg as the top graduate of his cohort."*

A murmur of quiet approval rippled through the ranks as Yossi was called forward. He stepped forward with precise military formality, his heart swelling with pride as he saluted the commanding officer. The officer extended his hand in recognition, and as Yossi shook it, he felt the weight of the achievement.

Segen Mishne Rosenberg, the officer continued, his tone both formal and warm, *"you have embodied the qualities we expect from our finest leaders. Congratulations. You now carry the responsibility of guiding others with the same excellence you have shown here."*

Yossi, keeping his emotions in check, responded firmly. *"Thank you, sir. I'll do my best to live up to it."*

The officer smiled briefly, lowering his voice slightly. *"You have your choice of postings, Segen Rosenberg. Think carefully about where you want to go. The Parachute Brigade will welcome you back, but wherever you serve, you have a bright future ahead of you."*

Yossi saluted once more and returned to his place in the formation, feeling the immense pride of the moment wash over him. As the ceremony concluded and the officers marched off the parade ground, Yossi felt the weight of the sword at his side and the symbolism of the beret on his head. His journey as an officer had just begun, but he knew he had earned his place.

As Yossi finished his training, Yael was wrapping up her final days in the military. She had secured her new job at the security consultancy firm in Tel Aviv, and her senior officers had called her in for a final meeting.

"We're sorry to see you go, Rav Turai Cohen," one of the officers began. *"But we understand your decision. "Before you go, we need you to stay in touch with Salma - informally, of course. We've already run it by your new firm, and they're fine with it. Your insights could still be invaluable."*

Yael nodded, understanding the gravity of their request. *"I'll do what I can, sir."*

As she left the meeting, she felt a mixture of relief and anticipation. Her new life was about to begin, and she was ready to face whatever challenges lay ahead.

Back in Tel Aviv, wedding preparations were in full swing. Yael and Yossi's mothers had finalised the arrangements, and everything was falling into place. Yael had given them input where she could, balancing her excitement with her responsibilities.

Yossi, now at the end of his training, could finally look forward to the future. He had proven himself, and now, with his officer's rank and his choice of assignments, he was ready to take on new challenges. But more than anything, he was ready to start his new life with Yael.

As he packed up his belongings and prepared to leave Bahad 1, Yossi felt a deep sense of fulfilment. The road had been long and demanding, but he had come through stronger and more determined than ever. He knew the next Chapter of his life was just beginning, and he was ready to embrace it with open arms. Though as he done the straps up in his bergan, a flicker of concern passed through his mind - he couldn't help but think about how fragile peace was in this region, and how quickly life could change.

With his training behind him and his future wide open, Yossi set his sights on the next great adventure - his wedding and the life he would build with Yael. The path ahead was filled with promise, and he was eager to take his first steps.

Chapter Thirty Seven

AHMED

Several weeks after the surveillance operation during the Simchat Torah holiday, Ahmed was summoned to hand in his report to Hamas High Command. The meeting was set to take place in Khan Younis, in a discreet location well-suited for avoiding prying eyes and Israeli drones. The small, nondescript building was tucked away in one of the city's more congested quarters, where the tight web of alleys and overhanging buildings provided cover and shadows.

The streets were alive with the last murmurs of the day, the sharp calls of vendors mingling with the smell of grilled meat and diesel fumes from the narrow alleys. Ahmed arrived in the early evening, the streets bustling with vendors packing up their stalls for the day. The air was thick with dust, and the aroma of fresh falafel and grilled meats mingled with the scent of street food. He moved quickly, avoiding eye contact, his face set in a neutral mask. Every step felt calculated, each movement controlled. He knew his every move was being watched, nothing could be left to chance.

Inside the building, a few guards nodded at him, their expressions unreadable. Ahmed stepped into a narrow hallway that led to a room with a heavy, metal door. He knocked twice, the sound dull against the thick metal. After a pause, the door creaked open, and one of the commanders beckoned him inside. The air inside felt stale, thick with the scent of cigarette smoke, and the low hum of a ceiling fan did little to ease the tension in the room.

The room was dimly lit, the only light coming from a single overhead bulb that cast long shadows across the walls. Abu Yusuf sat at the head of a large wooden table, flanked by Abu Khaled and several other senior figures. Abu Fadel stood near the door, his arms crossed, his face set in a stony expression. Ahmed felt a tightening in his chest as he took his seat at the opposite end of the table.

Abu Yusuf wasted no time. *"Ahmed Al-Masri, we need to hear your report in full detail,"* he began, his voice firm. *"What did you and your men observe during the Simchat Torah surveillance?"*

Ahmed cleared his throat, aware that every word counted. *"Our men observed a significant reduction in Israeli patrols and a noticeable drop in alertness among their forces during the holiday period. There were fewer guards at key checkpoints, and their general demeanour was more relaxed. They seemed less vigilant, likely due to the festive nature of the holiday."*

He could feel his heart beating a little faster. *Do they believe me? Is this enough?* He quickly brushed aside the doubts. Now wasn't the time for weakness.

Abu Yusuf nodded, a slight frown on his face. *"And what of the intelligence from the workers?"*

Ahmed continued, *"The workers reported similar observations. Some overheard conversations indicating that security rotations were adjusted to allow more soldiers to take leave. They mentioned that security was lighter and that some of the personnel appeared less attentive than usual."*

Abu Fadel, who had remained silent, finally spoke, his voice carrying an edge of scepticism. *"And do you trust this information, Ahmed Al-Masri? Do you trust the workers?"*

Ahmed met his gaze, holding it steady. *I have to show confidence.* "Yes, I do. They understand the consequences of giving us false information. They have provided consistent details that align with what our own men observed." As he spoke, Ahmed wondered if he sounded as assured as he hoped. The room's silence, the unblinking stares - it was all designed to make him doubt.

Abu Fadel nodded slowly, but his expression did not soften. *"Very well,"* he said, *"but know this, Ahmed Al-Masri: we are relying on you and your men. This operation is critical. We cannot afford any mistakes. Understand?"*

Ahmed nodded, feeling a chill run down his spine. *"I understand."*

As the meeting concluded, Abu Fadel approached Ahmed with a seemingly friendly smile, though his eyes were sharp, probing. He placed a hand on Ahmed's shoulder, guiding him away from the others, towards a quieter corner of the room.

"Ahmed Al-Masri," he began, his voice light, almost conversational, *"this operation is more critical than ever. We're all counting on you to deliver precisely what we need."* There was a moment of silence, and then, with deliberate slowness, he pulled out a small, grainy photograph from his pocket and handed it to Ahmed.

Ahmed felt a chill run through him as he looked down at the image. It was a candid shot of his mother, sisters, and Salma, seemingly taken from a distance. They were going about their day, unaware they were being watched. His mother's headscarf fluttered slightly in the wind, Salma appeared to be talking to his youngest sister, a faint smile on her lips. His heart raced. They looked so vulnerable, so innocent in that moment, and yet, they were pawns in a game they never chose to play.

"They look well, don't they?" Abu Fadel commented casually, his tone calm but his eyes never leaving Ahmed's face. *"It's good to see that they are safe and... happy."*

Why show me this now? Ahmed's mouth went dry, his hand tightening around the photograph. He forced a neutral expression, even as his heart pounded in his chest. *"Yes,"* he managed to say, his voice steady despite the tension building inside him. *"They look well."*

Abu Fadel nodded slowly, still smiling. *"I thought you'd appreciate the gesture,"* he said softly. *"You see, we are all invested in keeping them that way. But that relies heavily on you, Ahmed, on how well you perform your duties."*

There was a pause, the air between them thick with unspoken meaning. *"Make sure you don't disappoint us,"* Abu Fadel added, his voice dropping to a near whisper, his gaze intense.

I have to keep calm, Ahmed told himself, though the fear gnawed at him. He met Abu Fadel's eyes, the unspoken threat as clear as day. *"I understand,"* he replied, each word weighed with control. *"I won't fail."*

Abu Fadel's smile widened just a fraction, his expression almost mocking. *"Good,"* he murmured, giving Ahmed's shoulder a firm squeeze before releasing it. *"It would be a shame if anything were to disrupt their peace."* The pressure from Abu Fadel's hand felt like an iron grip, his fingers digging in just enough to remind Ahmed that nothing was ever truly safe.

Ahmed felt the sting of the veiled threat and the surge of anger and fear that came with it. He knew then, more clearly than ever, that every step he took was being watched, every decision scrutinised. And the stakes, already impossibly high, had just become even higher.

This is my life now - forever on edge, forever wondering.

Returning to the safe house in Gaza City, Ahmed felt a simmering frustration. He found Tariq, Khaled, Bilal, and Hadi already gathered, their faces tense and expectant. The room was stifling, the small fan in the corner doing little to ease the oppressive heat.

Before Ahmed could speak, Tariq was already on his feet. *"What now, Ahmed?"* he demanded, his tone sharp. *"Are we going to sit around again and wait for another signal? When are we going to take real action?"*

Khaled, sitting with his arms crossed, added, *"The men are restless. They want to fight. They've been training, they're ready. Why are we just playing spy games?"*

Ahmed felt his temper flare. *Why do they always question me?* The strain of the day, the pressure from his superiors, and now the frustration from his own men were pushing him to the brink. *"Do you think this is easy for me?"* he snapped, his voice rising. *"Do you think I don't want to fight? I am following orders! This isn't just about what we want - it's about what's necessary."*

Tariq's face reddened with anger. *"But when? When will it be necessary? We are soldiers, not spies!"*

Ahmed slammed his hand down on the table, the sound echoing through the room. *"We wait until the right moment! You think we can just charge in whenever we feel like it? You think I enjoy sitting here, waiting for the next move, wondering if this will be the time we are finally allowed to strike?"* Do they think I'm weak? That I'm losing control?

Khaled's frustration boiled over. *"Maybe you've forgotten what it means to be a fighter, Ahmed! Maybe you're getting too comfortable, giving reports and playing it safe!"*

Ahmed's expression darkened, his hands trembling with suppressed rage. *"You think I'm comfortable?"* he shouted. *"Do you know what it's like to sit in front of those men, to be told that if we fail, our families are at risk? Do you think I don't carry that weight every day?"*

The room fell into a heavy silence, the intensity of Ahmed's outburst leaving the others momentarily stunned. Tariq and Khaled exchanged a glance, their anger not entirely quelled but understanding the depth of Ahmed's strain. I need them to see... to understand the pressure I am under.

Ahmed took a deep breath, trying to steady himself. *"We all want to fight,"* he said, his voice quieter but no less forceful. *"But we fight when it's time. Until then, we prepare. We gather every piece of information, every advantage we can. That is our job. If you can't handle that, then maybe you should reconsider your place here."*

Tariq finally nodded, though he still looked unconvinced. Khaled muttered something under his breath but said no more. Ahmed knew he had to keep them in line, there was too much at stake.

They must understand. If they break, we all break.

After Ahmed returned home, Salma immediately noticed the tension radiating from him. His usual stoic demeanour seemed more strained, and there was a heaviness in his step as he moved around their small living space. His face was drawn, his eyes clouded with a mix of frustration and fear.

Salma watched him closely, her concern deepening. He looked like a man carrying an invisible weight, one that threatened to crush him at any moment. She could sense something had happened, something more serious than the usual pressures of his role.

"*Ahmed,*" she began softly, her voice cutting through the heavy silence. "*What is it? What did they say?*"

Ahmed hesitated, his back still turned to her as he stared out of the window. For a moment, he seemed lost in his thoughts, caught between what he could share and what he needed to protect. *How much should I tell her?* Finally, he turned to face her, his expression a mix of anger and resignation.

"*They made it clear what's at stake,*" he muttered, his voice barely more than a whisper. "*They reminded me of the cost of failure... in their own way.*"

Salma's heart quickened. "*What do you mean? What did they say?*"

Ahmed clenched his jaw, his hands balling into fists at his sides. "*Abu Fadel... he asked how you were. How my family was.*" His voice faltered for a moment, a flicker of pain crossing his face. "*He talked about how well they looked, how healthy they seemed.*"

Salma felt a chill run down her spine. The words hung in the air like a threat. "*So, they're watching us... all of us,*" she whispered, her voice tinged with fear.

Ahmed nodded, his face hardening. "*Yes. And they're making sure I know that. If I fail, if I step out of line... they'll come after you, after them.*"

Salma's expression shifted from fear to anger. "*Ahmed, this is too much. They're not just using you, they're holding your family hostage to ensure your compliance. You can't keep letting them manipulate you like this.*"

Ahmed's shoulders sagged, a look of helplessness crossing his features. "*What can I do, Salma? If I resist, if I push back... they will take it out on you, on Layla and Amina. I can't risk that.*"

Salma moved closer, gripping his arm tightly. *"But you're losing yourself in the process, Ahmed. They're turning you into someone I barely recognise, and I can see the toll it's taking on you."*

Ahmed's eyes met hers, filled with a mixture of regret and determination. *"I know,"* he admitted softly. *"But I have no choice. Not if I want to keep you safe, to keep them safe."*

Salma shook her head, her eyes brimming with tears. *"There's always a choice, Ahmed. Even if it's a hard one. You can't keep sacrificing yourself, and us, to their cause."*

Ahmed swallowed hard, his face a mask of inner turmoil. *"I don't know how, Salma. I don't know how to break free without risking everything."*

Salma held his gaze, her voice firm but filled with emotion. *"You can't let them control you through fear. Don't let them win."*

Ahmed nodded slowly, but his heart was heavy. *I know she's right, but what can I do?* He knew she was right, but the path forward seemed more uncertain than ever. He feared that no matter what he chose, they were already caught in a game where every move came with a cost.

But for now, I have no choice. I must keep moving.

Later that night, Ahmed felt the weight of the day bearing down on him. The frustration from Tariq and Khaled, the tension in his meetings, the pressure from Abu Fadel - all of it was grinding him down.

He looked around the dimly lit space, his thoughts on his family and Salma. *What if I fail?* he thought, a cold sweat forming on his brow. *What if it's not enough?*

He closed his eyes, forcing the doubts away. There was no room for weakness, no room for second-guessing. He had to stay strong. He had to see this through, for his men, for his family... for himself.

Chapter Thirty Eight

YOSSI

Yossi tightened the straps of his bergan, feeling the tension of the past months begin to ease. He was now officially *Segen Mishne Rosenberg*, a newly commissioned officer. With his commanding officer's blessing, he had been granted a month of leave to marry the woman he loved. The extended leave was a rare privilege but well-earned after his time serving on the border and six months of gruelling officer training. His new posting as Platoon Commander on the Lebanese border wouldn't start until later in the year, giving him precious time to begin this new Chapter of his life.

As Yossi stepped out of the camp gates for the last time, a mixture of exhilaration and uncertainty surged through him. The drive back to Tel Aviv allowed him to reflect on the journey that had brought him here - relentless training at Bahad 1, late nights studying tactical manuals, and the constant pressure to prove himself. His determination had carried him through, but now, for the first time in months, he allowed himself to focus on something else - Yael, their life together, and the future they were about to embrace as a married couple.

He wondered if he was truly prepared for this new phase of life. Would he be able to balance the demands of his military career with the responsibilities of being a husband? Would Yael understand the times he would be away, the dangers he might face? These questions circled in his mind, but as Tel Aviv's skyline came into view, his doubts softened. He knew, above all, that he loved her deeply, and that had to be enough.

Upon arriving in Tel Aviv, he headed straight for Yael's apartment, practically sprinting up the stairs two at a time. He paused at her door, catching his breath, his heart racing - not from the climb, but from the anticipation of seeing her. For a brief moment, he hesitated, feeling the weight of all the changes about to unfold. Then, he knocked.

The door swung open, and there she was. Yael's face lit up with a wide smile, her eyes bright with joy at the sight of him.

"Yossi!" she exclaimed, throwing her arms around him.

He held her close, inhaling the familiar scent of her hair, feeling all the distance and tension between them dissolve in an instant. *"I missed you more than I can put into words,"* he murmured, his voice barely steady.

"I've missed you too," she replied, pulling back slightly to look into his eyes, her expression a blend of joy and relief. *"I can't believe we're finally here."*

He smiled, brushing a strand of hair from her face. *"It's real,"* he said softly, *"and it's everything I've been dreaming of."*

They stood there for what felt like an eternity, wrapped in each other's arms, as if time itself had stopped. The world outside seemed distant and irrelevant, all that mattered was this moment of connection. Yossi felt his heart steady against hers, a quiet reminder that, despite everything, they had made it here.

The days before the wedding were a whirlwind of activity. Family and friends arrived from across the country, filling their home with warmth and anticipation. Nadav had come down from the border, taking leave to stand by Yossi's side as his best man. Leila was with him, their blossoming relationship adding another layer of joy to the gathering.

Yossi noticed how Nadav and Leila moved around each other, laughing and exchanging glances that spoke of a new connection. Nadav leaned in to whisper something in Leila's ear, and she threw her head back in laughter, her eyes sparkling with delight. Yossi's heart swelled with happiness, and with a mischievous grin, he decided to have a bit of fun.

"Well, look who's gone soft on us," Yossi teased, giving Nadav a playful nudge. *"Weren't you the one always saying I was 'whipped' when it came to Yael? What happened to that no-nonsense soldier?"*

Nadav laughed, pretending to take offence. *"Easy target, mate. You practically wore your heart on your sleeve! Besides,"* Nadav shot a wink at Leila, *"no one ever told me how good it feels to let someone in."*

Leila blushed slightly but quickly shot back, *"And here I thought you were a serious soldier, Nadav. Turns out you're just as soppy as Yossi!"*

Yossi chuckled, remembering how Nadav had teased him when he first realised he was in love with Yael. *"Ah, so the tables do turn, don't they? Just remember, I've got years of payback stored up, and a wedding is the perfect place to start."*

Nadav raised his hands in mock surrender, though there was genuine happiness in his eyes. *"Alright, alright, I concede. You've got me."*

Yossi felt a wave of nostalgia. It reminded him of the first time he realised he loved Yael - the quiet certainty, the joy of finding someone who truly understood him. He couldn't help but smile.

Amir, who had remained in the IDF as an EOD specialist, came from his base, his usual intensity softened by the excitement of seeing his friends. Maya had taken a break from her hectic life in Tel Aviv's tech scene, and Samir was there too, his normally analytical expression softened by a rare smile. Yossi felt a deep sense of gratitude as he saw all these faces around him - people who had shared his highs and lows, his victories and doubts.

The preparations were filled with warmth and camaraderie. Yossi and Yael's friends helped with everything: stringing fairy lights, arranging flowers, and practising dances for the celebration. There was laughter and teasing, stories shared from their years in service, and the kind of deep, unspoken bond that only long-standing friendships create.

The night before the wedding, they all gathered at Yossi's parents' home for a final dinner. As they passed around dishes of homemade food, Yossi found himself recalling memories - training exercises, late-night talks, the shared fear before missions. Someone pulled out a camera, and they huddled together, capturing a moment that felt timeless - a snapshot of friendship, love, and shared history that would stay with them forever.

That night, Yossi lay in bed, staring at the ceiling, his mind racing. Despite the day's joy, a knot of nervousness had formed in his stomach. He thought about all that lay ahead - the commitments, the changes, the unknowns. He picked up his phone and sent a quick message to Nadav, who was staying at a nearby hotel.

"Be honest - am I really cut out for this, Nadav?" Yossi typed, his thumb hovering over the screen before hitting send.

A few moments later, his phone buzzed with a reply. Nadav's response was swift and direct. *"Yossi, you've stared down enemy fire without blinking. If you can handle that, standing by Yael's side is a walk in the park. You've got this."*

Yossi chuckled, feeling some of the tension ease. *"Yeah, maybe you're right,"* he muttered, setting the phone down on the bedside table. But in his heart, he knew that this, too, was a kind of battle - a different one, but a battle, nonetheless.

The following day dawned with the sun dipping low over Tel Aviv, painting the sky in hues of gold and pink as guests gathered for Yossi and Yael's wedding. The venue, a charming garden near the city's coastline, was set with delicate floral arrangements, and the scent of fresh blooms filled the air. A warm, soft breeze carried the sounds of laughter and chatter as friends and family arrived, their faces bright with anticipation and joy.

Yossi stood under the chuppah, the traditional wedding canopy, his maroon beret neatly positioned on his head, and his polished medals catching the setting sun's rays. As he waited for Yael, he felt his palms sweat, his heart racing in a way that had nothing to do with fear and everything to do with love. He glanced over at Nadav, who gave him a reassuring nod.

On the other side of the chuppah, Yael stood in her flowing white gown, her hair adorned with small white flowers. Her eyes sparkled as she looked around at the gathered friends and family. Beside her was Leila, her *Shoshvinah*, dressed in a light blue gown that matched the calmness in her eyes. Leila had recently started her nursing training, but today she was fully present as Yael's closest confidante, holding her bouquet and whispering words of reassurance and love.

As Yael approached, Yossi felt his breath catch in his throat. She looked radiant, like a vision from his dreams. He thought of all the moments that had brought them here - the challenges, the separations, the small, precious times they had stolen together. He realised how much she meant to him, how much he needed her by his side, not just today but every day forward.

When it was time for the vows, the atmosphere grew quiet and expectant. Yossi and Yael faced each other, holding hands, their gazes locked. Yossi took a deep breath, his voice steady but his heart pounding.

"Yael," he began, his voice filled with emotion, *"I vow to stand by you, to hold you up when the world feels too heavy, and to love you fiercely, with everything I am. You're not just my partner, Yael - you're my heart, my anchor."* I know there will be tough days, and there will be times when my duty takes me away from you. But I vow to always come back, to always fight for what we have, because you are my reason, my home."

Yael's eyes shone with unshed tears. *"Yossi,"* she replied, her voice gentle but unwavering, *"I promise to be your strength when you feel weak, your laughter when times are dark, and to love you with every beat of my heart, for the rest of my days."* Together, we will build a life filled with love and laughter, no matter where it takes us."

With their vows exchanged, the rings were slipped onto their fingers, and the rabbi recited the blessings. Yossi then broke the glass under his foot, the symbolic shattering echoed by a chorus of joyful *"Mazal Tov!"* from the guests, their voices rising in a jubilant cheer.

The celebration that followed was filled with joy. Nadav took the microphone, his grin mischievous.

"Ladies and gentlemen, I have the privilege of being Yossi's Shoshvin, which means I get to tell you all the embarrassing stories," he joked, prompting laughter from the crowd. "And believe me, there are plenty. But here's the thing - now that Yossi

is my Platoon Commander, I have to start calling him 'Sir' or 'Segen Rosenberg'! Can you imagine?"

He paused, letting the laughter grow. *"In reality, though, I've been taking orders from Yossi all my life! Whether it was following him into some wild adventure when we were kids or doing whatever he said during training, he's always had me following his lead."*

Nadav turned to Yossi with a mock salute. *"So, here's to you, Segen Mishne Rosenberg... I guess I'd better get used to calling you 'Sir' from now on!"*

The crowd erupted in laughter, and Yossi shook his head, grinning. Nadav's tone softened as he continued, *"But seriously, I've known Yossi my whole life, and I've never seen him happier than he is today with Yael. They're perfect for each other, and I'm honoured to stand here with them."*

Leila stepped forward next, a soft smile on her lips. *"Yael has always been the kind of friend who is there no matter what,"* she began, glancing fondly at Yael. *"But I've known Yossi even longer - since we were children, in fact. We grew up together, and he's been my friend for as long as I can remember. When I first introduced Yael to our group, I knew she would fit right in, but what I didn't expect was how quickly she and Yossi would connect. And, of course, it took a bit of a gentle push from me to get Yossi to finally ask her out,"* she added with a playful grin, drawing laughs from the crowd.

Leila continued, her voice warm. *"Watching them now - my oldest friend and the dearest person I've ever known - it's like seeing two halves finally make a whole. They've found something real, something rare, and I couldn't be happier for them."*

As the laughter from Nadav's and Leila's speeches began to die down, Yossi took the microphone, a smile spreading across his face. He glanced around at the gathered crowd, his friends, and family, feeling a wave of emotion. He cleared his throat, playfully shaking his head at his friends.

"Well, after those speeches, I'm not quite sure how I can follow up," he began, drawing a chuckle from the crowd. *"Thank you, Nadav, for reminding everyone just how much you've suffered following my lead all these years,"* he said with a wink.

"And Leila, thank you for sharing our secret - that it took a little nudge from you to get me to ask Yael out. I guess I owe you more than I thought!"

He turned to Yael, his expression softening. *"But in all seriousness, I've been blessed in more ways than I can count. To have grown up surrounded by friends like you, who have been with me through every battle, both in the field and in life, is something I'll never take for granted. And now, to be standing here with you, Yael, my best friend and my love, is more than I could have ever dreamed of."*

He paused, his voice steady but full of emotion. *"Yael, you have this way of making the impossible seem possible, of turning every challenge into a shared adventure. You've shown me a kind of love that is fearless, a love that's full of hope and laughter. I promise to spend the rest of my life trying to be worthy of that love, to be the husband you deserve."*

Yossi looked out at the guests, his eyes shining with gratitude. *"Thank you all for being here with us today, for being a part of our journey. Here's to friends who are like family, to love that lasts a lifetime, and to all the adventures still to come."*

He raised his glass, and the room erupted in applause and cheers, with Yossi and Yael standing arm in arm, surrounded by those who loved them most.

The evening continued with more speeches, toasts, and endless dancing. The photographer moved around, capturing every moment - the laughter, the shared glances, the embraces. One photo, in particular, stood out: Yossi and Yael standing arm in arm, surrounded by their friends who had been there through every twist and turn of their journey. They were all there, together, despite their different paths - some still in service, others building new lives outside the military. The photograph captured not just the moment but the spirit of enduring friendship that bound them all.

A few days later, Yossi and Yael arrived in Eilat, their honeymoon destination on the shores of the Red Sea. The city, with its sun-soaked beaches and crystal-clear waters, was a perfect escape. They stayed at a quiet resort tucked away from the main tourist areas, where the only sounds were the gentle lapping of waves and the distant calls of seabirds.

Their days were filled with adventure and relaxation. They snorkelled in the vibrant coral reefs, marvelling at the colourful marine life. One morning, they took a boat trip to swim with dolphins, laughing like children as the friendly creatures swam around them. They hiked through the nearby Red Canyon, the sun casting dramatic shadows on the rock formations as they navigated the winding paths.

In the evenings, they dined under the stars, enjoying fresh seafood and local delicacies, their conversations flowing easily from shared dreams to light-hearted jokes. On their final night, they enjoyed a candlelit dinner on the beach, the waves providing a soothing background. The soft light illuminated their faces, highlighting the joy in their eyes.

They spent their last day in Eilat exploring the desert, taking a jeep tour through the rugged landscape. They stopped at a high vantage point, overlooking the vast expanse of sand and rock. The setting sun painted the sky in shades of orange and purple.

Yael turned to Yossi, her eyes glinting with affection and amusement. *"I love you, Segen Rosenberg,"* she said with a playful grin.

Yossi laughed, pulling her close. *"And I love you too, Mrs. Rosenberg."*

They stood there, wrapped in each other's arms, letting the moment linger. It was just them, the desert, and the endless sky above, a perfect ending to their honeymoon - a moment of peace before returning to the world that awaited them.

Back in Tel Aviv, Yossi settled into the rhythm of his extended leave, enjoying the extra time he had been given. But even with a month away from his duties, he knew he couldn't let himself grow complacent. The demands of his role as a Platoon Commander were never far from his mind, and he needed to stay sharp, both physically and mentally.

Every morning, Yossi laced up his running shoes and set out for a long run along the waterfront, the vibrant heart of Tel Aviv stretching out before him. The cityscape was a blend of modern high-rise buildings, their glass facades reflecting the sun's golden glow, and older, charming structures that whispered stories of the city's past. The salty sea breeze filled his lungs as he ran along the promenade, the sound of waves crashing softly against the shore.

To his left, the golden sands of Tel Aviv's beaches were dotted with early morning sunbathers and joggers, some stretching, others deep in conversation. A few surfers braved the gentle waves, their boards cutting through the water with smooth, practiced ease. Further out, sailboats and yachts bobbed gently in the harbour, their white sails standing tall against the clear blue sky. The waterfront was alive with activity - a fusion of relaxation and energy that captured the spirit of the city he loved.

These runs helped Yossi clear his mind and prepare for the challenges ahead. He felt the tension leave his body as he pushed himself, his muscles warming to the familiar rhythm. With each stride, he focused on the discipline that had guided him through his military career, knowing that soon he would need to channel it once more. The tranquillity of these moments by the sea contrasted sharply with the intensity of his duties, but they provided a necessary balance, grounding him for what was to come.

While Yossi focused on staying in peak condition, Yael used the extra time to continue her work. She visited David's office, finding reasons to meet with Salma again, carefully maintaining the trust she had begun to build. Each conversation was light, seemingly casual, but Yael was always listening, always watching for any clues, any pieces of information that might help. She knew there was something significant happening in Salma's world, something that made her feel uneasy.

One afternoon, as they sat in David's office sharing coffee, Yael noticed a change in Salma. Her friend seemed more anxious than usual, her eyes flickered around the room as if searching for unseen threats, and her hands trembled slightly as she held her cup. Salma seemed to shift her posture frequently, crossing and uncrossing her legs, her movements almost restless. Her smile was thin, a mask trying to hide something deeper.

Yael decided to lighten the mood and break the tension. *"I don't think I've told you much about the wedding,"* she began with a smile. *"It was beautiful, Salma. We had it in a garden near the coast, with the sunset over the sea, and all our friends and family around us. It was everything I'd dreamed of."* She paused, hoping to see Salma relax. *"And the honeymoon... well, Yossi and I spent a few wonderful days in Eilat, by the Red Sea. Just us, the sun, and the sea - it was like stepping out of time."*

Salma managed a faint smile. *"It sounds lovely,"* she replied, but her eyes seemed far away, as if her thoughts were elsewhere. Her fingers tapped lightly on the table, betraying her nervousness.

Yael continued gently, hoping to draw her back. *"It really was. But, you know, as wonderful as it was, there was a part of me that couldn't fully relax... knowing how things are at the moment, the uncertainty... everything feels so fragile."*

At this, Salma's face tightened slightly, and Yael saw a tear slip down her cheek. She quickly brushed it away, but Yael had already noticed. *"Salma,"* she said softly, leaning forward, *"is everything alright? You seem... worried."*

Salma hesitated, her gaze dropping to her hands. Her shoulders hunched slightly, as if she were trying to make herself smaller. *"I'm fine, really,"* she murmured, but her voice wavered. *"It's just... things have been difficult lately."*

Yael reached out, touching her hand gently. "*Is there someone you trust? Anyone you can lean on?*" Yael asked gently. "*You shouldn't have to carry this alone.*"

Salma hesitated again, her eyes clouded with uncertainty. *"No... not really,"* she admitted, her voice barely audible. *"There's no one... not like that."*

Yael squeezed her hand, feeling the tension in Salma's trembling fingers. She sensed that Salma was holding back something important, something she was afraid to say. *"I'm here for you,"* she reassured her. *"If there's anything you need to share, anything you need help with... you don't have to face it alone."*

Salma nodded, a tearful smile crossing her face for a brief moment. *"Thank you, Yael,"* she whispered. *"That means more than you know."*

As they parted, Yael couldn't shake the feeling that something was very wrong. Salma's fear seemed almost palpable, like a shadow hovering between them. Yael wondered if Salma was in some kind of trouble, something that she was too afraid to speak about.

A sense of unease settled over her as she left the office, a nagging feeling that this was just the beginning of something much larger. She knew she needed to keep her guard up and stay close to Salma - there were things left unsaid, and secrets that needed to be uncovered.

As the days moved forward, both Yossi and Yael felt the weight of their responsibilities growing. Each of them knew they were playing their parts in something much larger than themselves, something that could shift in a moment. And as they prepared for what lay ahead, the city around them continued its rhythm - bright, bustling, and unaware of the silent storms brewing just beneath the surface.

As the end of Yossi's leave drew near, a sense of heaviness settled over their home. The day before his return to the unit, the reality of the separation loomed over them like a dark cloud, casting a shadow on their final hours together.

That morning, they lingered over breakfast, their conversation quiet and filled with unspoken thoughts. Yael watched Yossi's face as he spoke, trying to memorise every detail - the way his eyes crinkled when he smiled, the faint scar on his cheek from a childhood fall. She fought back the tears that threatened to spill, unwilling to let him see how much this goodbye was tearing her apart.

Yossi sensed her struggle, his own heart aching with the knowledge that soon he would have to leave her again. He reached across the table, taking her hand in his, holding it tightly, as if trying to hold on to this moment just a little longer.

As the day slipped away, they went through the motions of packing his bergan, their hands moving mechanically, neither willing to acknowledge the inevitable. When everything was finally ready, Yossi stood at the door, his bergan slung over his shoulder. He turned to face Yael, his eyes filled with a mixture of love and sorrow.

"Yael," he began, his voice catching slightly. *"I hate that I have to leave you again... It never gets easier. But I promise, every day I'm gone, I'll be thinking of you. No matter where I am, or what I'm doing, you're always with me."*

Yael felt a lump form in her throat, her voice breaking as she replied. *"I know, Yossi. But... it's so hard to let you go again, especially now, after everything."* She took a deep breath, tears spilling down her cheeks. *"I try to be strong, but... if something happened to you..."*

Yossi pulled her into a tight embrace, holding her as if he could somehow protect her from all the fears and uncertainties that lay ahead. *"I'm coming back, Yael. No matter where I go, I'll always find my way back to you. You're my home, my heartbeat... the reason I'll keep fighting."*

They clung to each other, neither wanting to be the first to let go. Yael buried her face in his chest, inhaling his scent, trying to etch it into her memory for the days and nights ahead when he would be far away. She felt his heartbeat against her cheek, steady and strong, and she closed her eyes, willing herself to remember the rhythm.

Finally, Yossi pulled back slightly, lifting her chin with his fingers. *"Look at me,"* he said softly, his eyes searching hers. *"We've faced so much already. We'll get through this, too. We have to hold on to that."*

Yael nodded, though her tears continued to flow. *"I love you, Yossi,"* she whispered, her voice trembling. *"So much it hurts."*

"I love you too, more than anything," he replied, his own eyes brimming with tears. *"And I promise, I'll be back before you know it."*

They kissed deeply, a desperate, lingering kiss that spoke of all the words they couldn't find, all the fears and hopes tangled between them. When they finally pulled away, Yael pressed her forehead against his, her breath shallow and ragged.

"Stay safe," she murmured, her fingers gripping his jacket. *"Please, stay safe."*

Yossi nodded, his voice a whisper. *"I will."*

With one last look, he turned and walked out the door, his steps slow, each one feeling like a weight pressing down on his heart. Yael stood in the doorway, watching him until he disappeared from view, her hand raised in a silent wave, her tears falling freely now that he was gone.

As the door closed, the emptiness of the house seemed to press in around her. She knew she had to be strong, to hold on to the promise of his return. But in that moment, all she could feel was the ache of his absence and the uncertainty of the days ahead.

She closed her eyes, whispering a silent prayer for his safety, and for the strength to endure the waiting once more.

Chapter Thirty Nine

AHMED

The atmosphere in the safe house was thick with tension, a tension that had been building for weeks. Ahmed sat at the head of the table, his eyes moving across the faces of his men - Tariq, Khaled, Bilal, and Hadi. These were his closest allies, men he had fought alongside for years. But now, their camaraderie felt strained, stretched thin by the endless waiting and growing uncertainty.

Tariq was the first to speak, his frustration clear in his tight voice. *"Ahmed, we can't keep this up. The men are starting to talk. They think we're just being strung along with empty promises. They're beginning to doubt."*

Khaled, always blunt, jumped in before Ahmed could respond. *"They're not wrong, Ahmed. We were promised a chance to fight, to actually do something. But instead, we're sitting here, doing nothing. This isn't what any of us signed up for."*

Ahmed felt the familiar heat of irritation rising but forced himself to take a deep breath. He knew he couldn't meet their anger with more anger. He needed to bring them back on his side. *"I get it,"* he began, keeping his voice steady but firm. *"I feel it too. But listen, we're not being strung along, we're getting ready for something much bigger than any of us."*

Tariq's eyes narrowed. *"Bigger? What do you mean?"*

Ahmed leaned forward, lowering his voice, making sure each word carried weight. *"I can't give you all the details yet... but trust me, I'll know more soon. I've been summoned. I'm getting briefed on the full plan, and after that, we'll know exactly when and where we're going to strike."*

Khaled scoffed, crossing his arms tightly. *"And we're just supposed to take your word for it?"*

Ahmed met his gaze, unwavering. *"Yes, Khaled, you are. You know me. We've been through this together. You know I'm no coward, and I've never lied to you. If I say something big is coming, then you've got to trust me on this."*

Bilal, who had been silent until now, nodded slowly. *"Ahmed's right,"* he murmured. *"He's never led us wrong before. If he says there's a plan, then there's a plan."*

Ahmed gave Bilal a brief nod of gratitude, then turned back to the others. *"Think about it,"* he pressed on. *"Why would the leadership have us waiting if it wasn't for something big? This isn't just some minor skirmish. It's something that could change everything. That's why it's taken so long."*

Tariq seemed to hesitate, his expression softening a bit. *"So... what do you want us to do, Ahmed?"*

Ahmed's tone sharpened. *"I need you to calm the men down. Talk to them. Let them know our time will come, but we need discipline and patience. If we lose focus now, we risk everything. Can you do that?"*

Khaled sighed, some of the tension easing from his shoulders. *"Alright, Ahmed. We'll talk to the men. But you'd better be right about this. We can't hold them back much longer."*

Ahmed nodded, his voice firm. *"I know. Just a little longer. I promise."*

The room fell silent, the weight of his words hanging in the air. Tariq finally nodded, a reluctant smile tugging at his lips. *"We're with you, Ahmed. Just... don't keep us waiting too long."*

Ahmed allowed himself a brief smile in return. *"I won't."*

As his men began to disperse, the tension in the room slowly ebbed away. Ahmed felt a small sense of relief. He had managed to buy some time, to keep his team focused. But he knew the clock was ticking. He had to deliver on his promise. And soon.

Later, as he sat alone, Ahmed felt a knot of anxiety tighten in his stomach. He had given them hope, but he still didn't know the full extent of what was coming. His mind wandered to Salma and the promises he'd made to her. He had to make sure he didn't fail - not just for his men, but for her. What if this was the moment he lost everything? He could only hope that when he was summoned, he would finally have the answers they all needed.

Just a little longer, he told himself. *Just a little longer, and then we will know.*

He closed his eyes, pushing the doubt away. For now, he had to keep his men steady, keep them believing. But if they lost faith, if they broke, everything would fall apart. Failure wasn't just a personal fear anymore - it was a threat to everything he'd fought for, including his family. Failure was not an option. Not now, not ever.

A few weeks had passed since Ahmed's tense meeting in Khan Younis, and now he had finally been summoned again. The message came through familiar channels, terse and direct, instructing him to report to a meeting in Rafah. Ahmed knew the location - a large, inconspicuous warehouse, hidden behind a web of tunnels that connected it to various points throughout the city. The complexity of the network made it difficult for the IDF to monitor or locate their gatherings. Ahmed had been there before, but this time felt different, this time, it felt final.

He moved through the tunnels, his steps quick but cautious, his footsteps echoing through the narrow, dim passageways. The air was cooler underground, but it clung to his skin like a reminder of the world above - a world closing in around them. A bead of sweat ran down his back despite the chill. His mind raced. *This is it. This is the moment we've been waiting for.*

As he emerged from the tunnel into the warehouse, Ahmed saw dozens of men gathered - leaders from various factions, each representing a different part of their resistance. He felt the weight of their presence, the gravity of what was to come reflected in their hardened faces. He quickly noted that none had brought their men with them, only the senior commanders and key decision-makers were present. These were the people who would each lead a part of the broader plan. Ahmed recognised some from past operations, their faces familiar, hardened by years of conflict.

The room was charged with anticipation. Ahmed moved to his place among the Hamas delegation, nodding to a few he recognised. As he settled, he felt the weight of the moment pressing down on him. They were all here for one reason - to be briefed on a plan that was more ambitious than any before.

At the front, Abu Yusuf and Abu Fadel stood side by side, their faces serious. Beside them were leaders from nine other factions, including Islamic Jihad, the Popular Resistance Committees, and smaller groups with unique capabilities and agendas. It was rare to see these often-divided leaders in one place, united by a common cause.

A senior commander from Hamas, known for his strategic brilliance, stepped forward to address the group. The room fell silent.

"Brothers," he began, his voice steady and resonant, *"you have been brought here because you are the most trusted leaders within your organisations. Today, we stand on the brink of an operation that will redefine our struggle and our resistance."*

He paused, letting the words sink in. *"What we are about to embark upon is the most ambitious plan we have ever conceived. The goal is clear: to deliver a blow so significant, so unexpected, that it forces our enemy to reconsider its actions and its presence on our land."*

His gaze moved slowly across the room, meeting the eyes of each leader in turn. *"You have all been chosen for your capabilities, your experience, and your commitment. Today, you will receive an overview of the plan, but only what is necessary for you to know. No one will know the entirety of the operation except a select few. This is for our security and the success of our mission."*

Ahmed felt a chill run through him. The secrecy, the careful compartmentalisation of information - this was more than just another attack. It was clear they were planning for every possibility, including the worst-case scenarios.

"The date is set," the commander continued, his tone unwavering. *"October 7th, 2023, the day of the Simchat Torah holiday. We believe it is when our enemy will be most vulnerable, their defences at their weakest. We will strike simultaneously across multiple points. Each of you will lead a team that is critical to this operation's success."*

Ahmed glanced around the room, seeing the seriousness etched on the faces of those around him. This was real. This was happening.

The commander continued, *"After this initial briefing, you will be separated into smaller groups. Each of you will be given specific instructions and details about your roles and targets. You are not to share this information with anyone outside your group. The success of this mission depends on absolute secrecy and precise coordination."*

Ahmed nodded slightly, understanding the importance of what was being asked. He knew these men, he had trained with some, fought alongside others. But today, they were all bound by a shared purpose, leaving no room for personal agendas or misunderstandings.

Another senior figure, a leader from Islamic Jihad, took the floor, outlining logistics - coordinated efforts, the timing of each strike, the need for flawless execution. It felt like every word carried the weight of the months of planning that had led to this point. Every detail seemed meticulously planned, with no margin for error.

After the general briefing, Ahmed was led to a corner where Abu Fadel waited. They moved into a more private area. Abu Fadel handed Ahmed a small folder. *"Inside,"* he said, *"you will find the specifics of your role - your target, your objectives, the resources at your disposal. Memorise it, then destroy it. This information is for you alone."*

Ahmed took the folder, his hands steady despite the adrenaline coursing through him. The weight of responsibility pressed down on him with each page he scanned - maps, coordinates, a list of equipment, names of operatives. Each word felt like a nail driving home the finality of the mission ahead.

Back at the safe house, Ahmed gathered his core commanders - Tariq, Khaled, Bilal, and Hadi.

"*Alright, listen closely,*" Ahmed began, his voice steady and commanding. "*What I'm about to tell you is classified. You are all sworn to secrecy. This does not leave this room. Understood?*"

The men nodded, their faces serious. They understood the gravity of his words.

Ahmed took a deep breath, then continued. "*Our target is a Kibbutz located just 4 kilometres from the Gaza border. Our mission is to attack this Kibbutz and take control of Route 232, the main road that runs alongside it. This road is critical - it's the primary route for any IDF reinforcements heading toward the border. Our job is to block it, disrupt their response, and prevent them from stopping the larger operation.*"

He paused, letting his words settle in. "*If we fail to take and hold Route 232, the entire operation could be jeopardised. The road is our lifeline. If we control it, we control their movement. That's why we've been given this role. We're not just one of seventy different attacks along the Gaza border, we are key to stopping the IDF from mobilising quickly to counter the other assaults.*"

Tariq and Khaled exchanged a quick glance, realising the significance of their role. Bilal and Hadi leaned in, absorbing every detail.

"*We need to train specifically for breaching the border fence,*" Ahmed continued. "*This will require machinery and explosives. The fence is fortified, but not impenetrable. We must be swift and precise. Once we breach it, our combatants will move through in pickup trucks and on motorbikes, heading directly for our targets.*"

He pointed to a map spread across the table, highlighting their approach route and the positions of the IDF patrols. "*I'll be in overall control,*" he said, "*coordinating all groups from Route 232. Bilal and Hadi, you two will lead what we're calling the mobile unit using motorbikes. Your task is to secure the road and keep it under our control. Use all necessary force to stop any IDF convoys or reinforcements that try to pass. This is our most critical line of defence.*"

Bilal and Hadi nodded, their faces serious. They understood the magnitude of their assignment.

Tariq, Khaled, Ahmed continued, turning to the other two commanders, *"you will lead the direct assault on the Kibbutz. Your objective is maximum destruction and to take as many hostages as possible. The hostages will be brought back to Gaza, dispersed across different locations. This needs to be chaotic, the enemy should have no idea where their people are or how many we have. It will give us leverage."*

Khaled, usually the more impulsive of the group, shifted in his seat. *"How many combatants do we have for this?"* he asked.

Ahmed met his gaze. *"Enough for the job,"* he replied firmly. *"You'll have two teams of fighters in pickups, trained for urban combat and hostage-taking. You need to move fast, be decisive. Once the breach is made, go in and don't stop until it's done."*

Tariq nodded, but there was a question in his eyes. *"And the timeline?"*

Ahmed straightened. *"October 7th, the Simchat Torah holiday. The enemy will be distracted, their defences lowered. Now you know we weren't stringing anyone along, there was a purpose to our surveillance. We hit them hard, fast, and without mercy."*

"The attack will start with a huge missile attack, that's what you have been working for over the last months, our teams will be the first across the border in our sector, but others will follow to support us."

A moment of silence fell over the room. The men absorbed the enormity of the task. Ahmed felt their tension but also their resolve. They had waited for this. They had trained for this.

"There will be seventy different attacks along the length of Gaza," Ahmed continued. *"We're part of a much larger strategy. Remember, we're not alone. Each group has its own target, its own mission. But for us, the key is Route 232. Hold that road, and we hold the upper hand."*

He paused, then added, *"And this attack, it's only the beginning. The first part of the plan."* He leaned forward, his tone growing more intense. *"The second part is dealing with the Israeli retaliation, which is why we've been building these tunnels and stockpiling ammunition for months. Their response will be like nothing we've seen before, and we have to be ready."*

His words hung in the air, heavy with the reality of what was to come.

"The aim is to bring in other Arab nations, to ignite a response that could wipe out Israel, and to get world opinion on our side. This will take sacrifice. A lot of it."

His commanders exchanged glances, shock and resolve mingling on their faces.

Khaled spoke first, his voice low but steady. *"You're serious... you think this could really draw in the whole region?"*

Ahmed nodded. *"That's the plan. But it won't be easy. It will be the hardest fight we've ever faced. And it starts with us."*

Bilal's eyes narrowed. *"So, this is why we've been preparing, why we've been waiting... not just for the attack, but for what comes after."*

"Exactly," Ahmed affirmed. *"We need to be ready for the next phase, for the retaliation. This is bigger than us, bigger than Gaza. But if we succeed, the impact will be felt across the world."*

Tariq leaned back, considering Ahmed's words. *"It sounds like a suicide mission... but it also sounds like our only chance."*

Ahmed nodded slowly. *"That's exactly what it is. Our only chance."*

The room fell silent again, each man contemplating his role in the operation. Ahmed felt a renewed sense of purpose, he saw it reflected in the eyes of his commanders. They understood now, this was not just another attack - it was the opening move in a much larger game.

"Get your teams ready," Ahmed concluded. *"We don't have much time. Train hard, stay sharp, and remember what we're fighting for."*

The men nodded, understanding the gravity of the situation. They dispersed to begin preparations, their movements purposeful and determined. As they left, Ahmed felt a mixture of anxiety and resolve. The clock was ticking, and the time for action was fast approaching.

For the first time in a long while, Ahmed felt that perhaps they had a chance. But with every plan in place, there came the risk that something would go wrong. The fear of that outcome gnawed at him. Perhaps this time, they could make a mark so significant, so undeniable, that it would change everything.

After the intense briefing with his leaders, Ahmed returned to his small, dimly lit apartment in Gaza City. The weight of the mission still pressed on his shoulders, but there was a renewed clarity in his mind, a focus that had been missing for weeks. Each step back to his apartment felt heavier, the reality of what he was about to do hitting him with more force. He had secured the loyalty of his commanders and prepared them for the scale of what was coming. Now, all he could do was wait for the final call to action.

As he stepped through the door, he found Salma sitting on the edge of their worn-out sofa, her eyes immediately searching his face. She could see the tension he carried and feel the burden of what he wasn't saying. She had been waiting for him, as always, but tonight there was a different tension in the air. She could sense the change in him, the way his body carried a new strain, a fresh burden.

"You're late," she said softly, her voice filled with concern.

Ahmed nodded, setting his bag down with a weary sigh. *"There was a lot to discuss,"* he replied, keeping his tone measured. He could see the worry etched into her features, the way her hands fidgeted slightly on her lap.

Salma hesitated, then stood and moved closer to him. *"Ahmed, you look... different. What happened today? Was it another meeting with the commanders?"*

Ahmed met her gaze, struggling with how much to tell her. Could he really protect her by shielding the full truth? He didn't know anymore. He felt the familiar tug-of-war between protecting her from the full reality and knowing she could see through his silence. Finally, he decided to give her something, just enough to calm her fears.

"Yes," he admitted, his voice low. *"There was a meeting. A significant one. Plans are moving forward, and everything is becoming clearer now."*

Salma's eyes narrowed slightly. *"And? What does that mean for you... for us?"*

Ahmed took a deep breath, choosing his words carefully. *"It means we have a role to play, a critical one. The operation is bigger than we thought. It's going to involve many people, from different groups, all working together. But our part is vital. We have to be ready."*

He saw anxiety flicker in her eyes, the way her brows knitted together. *"And you?"* she pressed gently. *"Are you ready for this?"*

Ahmed swallowed, feeling the weight of her question. Was he ready? It wasn't just his life on the line anymore. *"I have to be,"* he answered quietly. *"There is no other choice."*

Salma stepped closer, her hand reaching for his. *"Ahmed, I know you're doing what you think is right, but I see what it's doing to you. Every day, you come back with more weight on your shoulders. This... this is changing you."*

He squeezed her hand, feeling the warmth of her touch against his skin. *"I know,"* he whispered, his voice filled with a mix of regret and determination. *"But I need you to trust me. I'm doing this for us... for all of us."*

Salma's eyes softened, and she nodded slowly. *"I do trust you, Ahmed. I always have. But I'm scared... for you, for our family. I just want to know that when this is over, we'll still have each other."*

Ahmed felt a tightness in his chest, a knot of fear and love tangled together. He had to believe in the future they were fighting for, even as it felt like the ground beneath them was crumbling. *"We will,"* he promised, though the uncertainty of his own words stung. *"We have to believe that Salma."*

She held his gaze for a long moment, then finally nodded. *"Just... come back to me,"* she said softly, her voice breaking a little. *"No matter what happens, just come back."*

Ahmed pulled her into a tight embrace, feeling her heartbeat against his chest. *"I will,"* he whispered, more to himself than to her. *"I promise."*

They stayed like that for a while, holding on to each other in the quiet of their small home, the world outside still moving with its chaotic rhythm. For a brief moment, they found solace in their closeness, in the simple act of being together.

But as Ahmed held her, he knew time was running out. There wasn't enough time for them, for their love. There never had been. The operation was drawing nearer, and soon he would have to step into the unknown, to face whatever lay ahead. He had made his choices, committed to his path, but the fear of what it might cost them, of what he might lose, lingered at the edge of his thoughts.

For now, though, he held on to Salma a little longer, knowing that moments like these were fleeting, precious… and perhaps soon, too rare to count on.

Chapter Forty

YOSSI

Yossi stood outside the tent that served as the CO's office at the Forward Operating Base. The rugged terrain of the Lebanese border stretched out behind him, a stark reminder of the challenging environment he would soon face again. The mountains loomed in the distance, their rocky slopes bathed in the early morning light. Unlike much of Israel, this landscape was dominated by steep ridges, dense thickets, and hidden valleys, where every movement required caution, and each step could prove treacherous.

He took a deep breath, letting the cool mountain air fill his lungs as he prepared to meet his CO, Lieutenant Colonel Arad. His new rank, *Segen Mishne* (Second Lieutenant), still felt unfamiliar on his shoulders, the weight of his responsibilities beginning to settle. Yossi was eager yet conscious of the challenge ahead - leading a platoon in such difficult terrain would be a true test of his skills and resolve.

Yossi parted the tent flap and stepped inside. The interior was sparse but functional, with a large map of the border pinned to one wall and a sand table in the centre displaying the contours and strategic points of their area of operation. Lt. Col. Arad stood behind a makeshift desk covered with papers, his eyes scanning over a report. As Yossi approached, the CO looked up, his expression softening into a brief smile.

"Segen Mishne Rosenberg," Arad greeted, using the formal address for a Second Lieutenant. "Congratulations on coming first in your Officer Training course. I've heard nothing but good things from Bahad 1."

"Thank you, sir," Yossi replied, standing at attention, his back straight and his chin held high.

Arad nodded, gesturing for Yossi to stand at ease. "You've done well, Yossi. Coming top of your course is no small feat, especially at Bahad 1 - Israel's prestigious officer training school. You've proven your capability, but now it's time to demonstrate it in the field."

"Yes, sir," Yossi affirmed, his voice steady. He knew that no amount of training could fully prepare him for what lay ahead, but he was ready to rise to the challenge.

Arad's expression grew more serious. "I'm assigning you to command the second platoon - Samal Levy's platoon. I know you two are close friends, and that could either work in our favour or become a complication. I need to know if you're ready to lead without letting personal relationships interfere."

Yossi met his gaze directly, his voice unwavering. "I'm ready, sir. I understand the importance of my role and the need to maintain a professional distance when it comes to command decisions. I won't let our friendship cloud my judgement."

The CO studied him for a moment, then nodded. "Good. Because this is a critical time, and your platoon will play a vital role in our operations. The situation here on the border is unpredictable, and we need to be prepared for anything. I trust you can handle this."

"I won't let you down, sir," Yossi replied.

Arad's expression softened slightly. "I believe you, *Segen*. But remember, this terrain is unforgiving. You've seen it before, but now you'll need to navigate it as a leader. Stay sharp and keep your men ready. Dismissed."

Yossi saluted, then turned and left the tent, the weight of his new responsibilities sinking in. He had been given command of Nadav's platoon, and he knew that leading men he counted as friends would be one of his greatest challenges. But he also felt a deep sense of pride and determination. He had earned this position, and he would prove himself worthy of it.

Yossi stepped out of the CO's tent, squinting slightly against the midday sun. The harshness of the environment hit him again - the rugged terrain beneath his boots grounding him to the moment, reminding him of the ever-present dangers. He moved toward the group of soldiers gathered in a loose semicircle, noticing a mix of familiar and new faces. Some of the men broke into grins as they spotted him, while others looked on with cautious curiosity.

Yossi stopped in front of them, hands on his hips, and let a grin spread across his face. "Alright, listen up!" he called out, raising his voice to be heard over the noise of the camp. "I know some of you might've had a few bets going while I was off at Officer Training. I heard rumours that half of you thought I'd come back to another platoon." He raised an eyebrow playfully. "And the other half thought I'd get lost somewhere in the mountains of Bahad 1!"

A ripple of laughter went through the group, a few of the veterans nodding in agreement. Yossi chuckled, enjoying the light-heartedness. "Well, it looks like I'm back and ready to take over this platoon. And to those of you who bet on me ending up here with you lot - congratulations, you've won yourselves some shekels."

There were cheers and good-natured shouts, and Yossi could feel the tension ease. He continued, still smiling but with a firmer tone. "But all joking aside, I'm glad to be back. I know what this unit is capable of, and I'm looking forward to seeing what we can accomplish together. The terrain here, as you know, is tough, and the situation can change in a heartbeat, but I've no doubt that we'll rise to the challenge, as always."

He glanced over at Nadav standing near the centre of the group. "Nadav, looks like we're back at it again, my friend. I hope you're ready to keep me out of trouble."

Nadav grinned and replied, "I've been doing that for years, Yossi. I mean, *Segen*. But don't worry, I'm ready."

The men laughed again, the atmosphere relaxed but attentive. Yossi nodded, appreciating the camaraderie forming. "Alright, enough messing around. We've got work to do. We'll be running drills and getting everyone up to speed, especially those of you who haven't worked with me before. We need to be ready for anything, and that means moving fast, thinking smart, and keeping each other safe out there."

A few of the soldiers nodded, and Yossi could see some of the newer faces starting to soften, the initial caution beginning to fade.

"Now," Yossi continued, his tone more serious but still warm, "I know we've got a lot of talent in this platoon, and I trust each and every one of you to do your part. We're going to keep training, keep honing our skills, and we'll do it together, as a team. So, let's get to it. Samal Levy, take half the men and start prepping the vehicles. I'll take the rest, and we'll run through some drills on movement and cover. Meet back here in an hour."

Nadav gave a quick nod, grinning. "Got it, *Segen*. Let's see if these guys can keep up."

Yossi laughed. "Let's show them what this platoon is made of!"

As Yossi turned to start his own preparations, he felt a surge of energy. The light-hearted banter had done its job, setting a positive tone, and he could already sense the beginnings of trust forming among the men. It was a small start, but it was a good one.

The days settled into a steady rhythm - a mix of intense training, patrols along the rugged terrain, and moments of camaraderie that knit the platoon together. As Yossi adjusted to his new role as Platoon Commander, he focused on building trust and unity among his men. He made it a point to observe each soldier, identifying their strengths and weaknesses, encouraging them when needed, and maintaining firm but fair discipline.

The terrain here was unforgiving, with its steep hills and narrow passes, but it offered an ideal setting for the kind of rigorous drills that Yossi knew would prepare his men for whatever lay ahead. Every day, he led them through exercises that honed their skills in navigation, stealth, and rapid response. They practised moving silently through dense brush, communicating without words, and setting up ambushes in the rocky outcrops that dotted the landscape. Yossi pushed them hard, knowing that only by testing their limits now could they be ready for the unpredictable realities of the border.

One evening, after a particularly gruelling day of drills and a long patrol along the border, Yossi found himself drawn to a rocky outcrop overlooking the camp. He needed a moment to himself, a chance to reflect. The sun was dipping low, casting a warm, amber glow across the rugged terrain. From this vantage point, he could see the whole camp, the tents nestled against the backdrop of rolling hills, with the boundary of Lebanon in the distance. The harshness of the land felt almost like a mirror to his inner state - both unyielding and demanding.

He sat down on a flat rock, feeling the coolness of the stone seep through his fatigues. For a few minutes, he just breathed in the evening air, allowing the tension of the day to leave his body. His thoughts drifted to Yael, to the feel of her hand in his during their wedding ceremony, the way her eyes had shone with love and determination as they exchanged their vows. He could almost hear her voice, soft and steady, reminding him to keep faith, to stay strong.

A wave of longing swept over him, a deep ache settling in his chest. He missed her with an intensity that caught him by surprise, a stark reminder of the life he had left behind to return to this place. But with the ache came a surge of determination. He had chosen this path, knowing full well the sacrifices it would demand. He had made a promise to her - to be the best man he could be, both for her and for his country.

Yossi looked out over the landscape, the sun now a sliver on the horizon. The rugged terrain, with its shadows growing longer, seemed almost to reflect his own resolve. He had a platoon to lead, men who depended on him to make the right decisions, to guide them through the uncertainties of their mission. He also had a promise to keep to Yael, a promise to return to her, whole and unbroken, despite the risks that lay ahead.

He stood up, feeling the cool breeze against his face, a breeze that seemed to carry with it a whisper of encouragement. He had no illusions about the challenges that were coming, the difficult days and tough decisions that awaited him. But he also knew he had the strength and the will to face them.

With a renewed sense of purpose, Yossi turned back towards the camp. He could hear the distant sounds of his men, their voices carrying through the still evening air. He smiled, a quiet confidence settling over him. There was work to be done, and he was ready to lead them, ready to face whatever came next.

He began the descent back towards the camp, his steps firm and steady. Yossi knew this journey had only just begun, but he was prepared to see it through - every step, every challenge, every day. And with that thought, he moved forward, his resolve unwavering, his mind clear.

He had a mission to complete, and he would do it with everything he had.

Yael had settled into her new routine at the consultancy firm, but her instincts from her service were far from dormant. She continued to cultivate her relationship with Salma, carefully balancing friendliness with subtle observation. Today, she decided to bring coffee for them both, using it as an opportunity to engage Salma in casual conversation.

Arriving at the office with two cups of coffee, Yael approached Salma's desk ."Morning, Salma! Thought you might need a little caffeine boost," she said, placing one of the cups on Salma's desk.

Salma looked up, surprised, her eyes brightening momentarily."Oh, thank you, Yael. You read my mind!" She took a sip, smiling, though there was a slight tension in her posture, as if her thoughts were elsewhere.

"Long night?" Yael asked casually, pulling up a chair beside her.

Salma nodded, her gaze dropping momentarily to her cup."Yeah, you could say that. Things have been a bit hectic..." She trailed off, catching herself, as if realising she had said too much.

Yael leaned back, keeping her tone light."Anything interesting?" she asked, feigning casual interest.

Salma hesitated, then seemed to shake off whatever had been on her mind ."Oh, nothing really," she replied quickly. "Just the usual family stuff." She took another sip of her coffee, her eyes momentarily distant.

Yael continued to chat about mundane matters, hoping to keep the conversation relaxed. As they spoke, Salma seemed to relax a little, her guard dropping. Yael noted the subtle change, recognising the opportunity to gather more insight.

"It's been a strange few weeks," Salma muttered absent-mindedly, almost to herself, before she realised her mistake. Her expression shifted, and she quickly added,"I mean, you know, just with work and everything."

Yael caught the slip but pretended not to notice."Yeah, I get it. Things can get overwhelming sometimes," she said, offering a sympathetic smile.

Salma nodded, a hint of unease still in her eyes."Exactly... Anyway, thank you for the coffee, Yael. I really needed this." She flashed a tight smile, clearly eager to move on.

"Anytime," Yael replied, returning the smile. She kept her tone light, letting Salma feel in control of the conversation once more.

As Yael left the office, she made a mental note of Salma's mistake. It was a small crack in her composure, a fleeting moment that had passed quickly. But in her line of work, such moments were where the truth often slipped through.

She sent a discreet message to her old unit command, mentioning the brief but telling lapse in Salma's words. It wasn't much, but it was a start. The unease that Salma had shown indicated something deeper beneath the surface, and Yael knew it was only a matter of time before more slipped through.

Yael knew she had to keep the conversation going, building on the foundation of trust she had established. Salma had let something slip today, and Yael would be ready to catch more next time.

Yossi stood among the other platoon commanders in the tent that served as their briefing room, the fabric walls rustling slightly in the wind. The base was always bustling with activity, but today there was a different tension in the air, a sense of something looming just beyond the horizon.

Lt. Col. Arad stood at the front, his face set in a serious expression. The dim light from the overhead lamp cast shadows across his features, adding to the gravity of the moment. As he waited for the murmuring to die down, Yossi glanced around at the other platoon commanders. Everyone seemed to be on edge, their expressions tight with concentration.

Arad began speaking, his voice steady and commanding."We've received new intelligence from our drone surveillance," he started, his tone making it clear that this was no routine update. "There's been a noticeable increase in movement by Hezbollah forces along the border. A lot more than we've seen in recent months."

He paused, letting the words sink in before continuing."Our intelligence sources have confirmed that a significant number of Hezbollah combatants have recently returned from Syria, where they've been engaged in heavy fighting. These are battle-hardened troops, well-equipped, and they pose a clear and present threat to our position here."

A murmur went through the room. Yossi felt a knot tighten in his stomach. He knew what this meant. Those who had fought in Syria would not be easily deterred, they were experienced and likely looking for new engagements.

Arad continued, his voice cutting through the low whispers."We need to increase our vigilance. Starting immediately, there will be more patrols, including at night. We must monitor any movement carefully and be prepared for any potential threats. Our orders are clear: observe but do not engage. We need to know what they're planning without giving away our own position."

He turned slightly, looking directly at Yossi."Segen, your platoon has been assigned a night patrol," he said. "You're to head out after sunset and move along Sector Charlie. Your mission is to observe any activity across the border, identify possible infiltration points, and report back. No engagement unless absolutely necessary. Understood?"

Yossi nodded."Understood, sir."

Arad's gaze swept across the rest of the commanders."The same goes for all of you. Stay alert, stay hidden, and report anything unusual. We can't afford to lose the element of surprise. Dismissed."

The commanders began to disperse, talking quietly amongst themselves. Yossi lingered for a moment, considering the gravity of the orders.

As Yossi stepped out of the CO's tent, he caught sight of Nadav, who was already waiting for him near the tent entrance, a serious expression on his face. The dimming light of the late afternoon cast long shadows across the rugged terrain of the base, but Yossi could see the alertness in his friend's eyes, always ready for whatever came next.

He nodded at Nadav, signalling him over. "Nadav, there's a night patrol tonight," Yossi said without preamble. "Get the men to sort their kit out. I want everyone ready for a briefing at 1700."

Nadav nodded sharply, his expression focused. "Got it, Yossi," he replied, already moving to relay the orders.

Several hours later, as the clock ticked closer to 1700, the platoon gathered in a loose semicircle around Yossi. The atmosphere was tense but controlled, the men understood the importance of this mission. Yossi could see they were prepared, their gear neatly laid out, and their faces calm with the quiet confidence of soldiers who had been here before.

Yossi waited for a moment, ensuring he had everyone's attention. "Samal Levy has already informed you that we will be on a night patrol this evening, and you should all have your gear ready," he began, his voice steady and clear. "Our task is to observe Hezbollah movements along the border. We are not to engage unless there is no other choice. Our objective is to remain unseen, gather intelligence, and return without detection."

He turned to Nadav. "Samal Levy, you will be with Team Bravo in the centre," Yossi continued. "This will allow you to coordinate between the teams and manage movements on the ground. Make sure all sections know their roles and are properly prepared."

Nadav gave a firm nod, already making mental notes.

Yossi then looked out over the men. "Team Alpha will cover the northern approach along the wadi. Team Bravo, led by Samal Levy, will take the central route, which is more exposed but gives a good line of sight for observation. Team Charlie will handle the southern flank, using the cover of trees and rocks."

He turned to the team leaders."Rav Turai (Corporal) Goldstein, take Alpha along the northern route. Rav Turai Ben-Ami, you're with Bravo in the centre. Rav Turai Malka, you take Charlie to the south."

Yossi continued,"The support team will be with Bravo. The Negev gunners will cover any open ground where we might be spotted. Keep yourselves concealed behind natural cover - rocks, low brush, anything that keeps you out of sight but ready to provide suppressive fire if needed."

He glanced over at the sniper."Rav Turai Ben-Shimon, you're with Team Alpha. Use the higher ground to provide overwatch. Pick your spots carefully, you're our eyes in the dark."

Yossi then addressed Amit, the radio operator."Amit, you'll handle all the radio traffic. Stick close to me and keep the communications minimal. We're sticking to pre-arranged signals only. We can't afford any mistakes."

He turned back to the medic."Rav Turai Gavriel, you'll be positioned with Bravo in the centre. This will allow you to get to any team quickly if needed."

Yossi took a step back, scanning the faces of his men."Remember, our mission is observation. Do not engage unless absolutely necessary. Stay silent, stay sharp. We've trained for this, and we know what to do."

A unified response came back from the men:"Understood, sir!"

Satisfied, Yossi nodded."Alright then, gear up get some food and be ready. We move at 2000 hours."

Yossi watched as Nadav and the men made their final preparations, confident in their readiness. The operation ahead would test them all, but he knew they were capable. As Yossi turned to start his own preparations, a quiet determination settled over him, guiding his every step.

As the final preparations were completed, Yossi gave the signal, and the platoon began to move out. The men slipped into the darkening landscape, each step deliberate and quiet. The only sounds were the faint crunch of gravel under boots and the whisper of fabric brushing against gear. They moved in single file, taking care to avoid any unnecessary noise that could give away their position. Night had fully descended, the sky a canopy of stars providing just enough light to outline the rugged terrain ahead.

Yossi kept his eyes forward, his senses sharp as he led from the rear, allowing the teams to fan out to their designated positions. Nadav, in the centre with Bravo, signalled for his team to spread out along their assigned route, using the natural cover of rocks and sparse vegetation. Ahead, Alpha team, with Rav Turai Goldstein, moved to the northern approach, taking up positions along the wadi where the ground sloped gently upward, providing a good vantage point. To the south, Charlie team, led by Rav Turai Malka, moved into a more densely wooded area, using the trees and low shrubs to remain concealed.

The night stretched on, the silence around them punctuated only by the occasional rustle of leaves or the distant call of a night bird. The soldiers adjusted their night vision goggles, scanning their sectors, watching for any signs of movement across the border. Each man knew his role, and the tension, while ever-present, was underpinned by a sense of quiet confidence.

The platoon had been in position for several hours, the stillness of the night stretching into the early hours of the morning. The men were settled, their eyes constantly scanning the darkness, each soldier's breath slow and measured to maintain their cover. Yossi remained in his position with Amit, listening to the quiet murmurs of the night and the occasional rustle of leaves in the cool breeze.

Then, just after midnight, the first signs of movement were reported from Alpha team. A single, deliberate click on the radio from the sniper alerted the rest of the platoon. Yossi felt a surge of anticipation as he focused his NVGs on the northern approach, where the signal had come from. The men waited, their senses heightened, scanning the terrain for any hint of activity.

Nadav, with a double click, passed the signal along over the radio. The entire platoon held their breath, NVGs trained on the area, waiting for the shapes to emerge from the shadows. Moments later, the outlines of figures began to take form - a large group moving in a loose formation across the rugged landscape.

Through the NVGs, the figures became clearer - dozens of Hezbollah fighters moving with disciplined caution. Yossi noted their professionalism, a stark contrast to what they had observed before. These were likely the hardened fighters recently returned from Syria, carrying heavy loads and what looked like rockets and other equipment. The men were heavily laden, each bearing cylindrical shapes resembling rocket tubes and larger packs that suggested ammunition or additional gear.

Yossi's eyes narrowed as he observed the group moving deliberately, cautious to stay unnoticed, yet pressing forward with clear intent. He tapped Nadav on the shoulder, a silent signal to continue monitoring and relay the observation back to the other teams. Nadav responded with another series of quiet clicks, ensuring the platoon remained coordinated and aware of the situation.

The platoon maintained their positions, silent and unseen, gathering as much intelligence as possible. Each section passed updates in series of pre-arranged clicks, keeping communications to a minimum. The professionalism of the enemy fighters confirmed their suspicions - these were indeed the newly arrived Hezbollah combatants from Syria.

For the next couple of hours, the platoon observed the movement, noting the direction and size of the group, the type of equipment they carried, and their formation tactics. Yossi knew this was vital information for the CO and the Ops Room.

As the first light of dawn began to creep over the horizon, Yossi signalled the platoon to pull back. The order was passed through a series of radio clicks, each team moving with practised stealth, ensuring they remained undetected. The men moved quickly but cautiously, maintaining their cover until they reached a safe distance from the border.

Back at the base, Yossi wasted no time. As soon as the platoon was through the gates, he gathered the men in a loose semicircle near the main tent. The early morning light was just beginning to filter through the camp, casting long shadows over the weary soldiers. They stood with a mix of exhaustion and alertness, still running on the adrenaline from the patrol.

Yossi took a step forward, his face serious but satisfied. "Alright, listen up," he began, his voice steady. "You all executed the plan well tonight. We did what we came to do, and most importantly, we did it without being seen. Good work."

He paused, allowing a moment for his words to sink in, then continued. "Section commanders, I want to hear from each of you about what you observed. We need to compile everything for the CO, so he gets the full picture."

One by one, the section commanders stepped forward, each giving a quick but detailed report. They spoke of the size of the Hezbollah group, the equipment they were carrying, and the direction they were moving. They described the professionalism of the fighters, the disciplined way they handled their movements, and their likely status as hardened troops recently returned from Syria. Yossi listened carefully, taking mental notes, occasionally asking for clarification or additional details.

Once the last of the reports was given, Yossi nodded in approval. "Good, that's exactly what we needed. I'll take this to the CO and provide him with a full briefing. You've done your part well."

He turned to Nadav standing at his side. "Nadav, make sure the platoon squares away their gear properly. Everything needs to be checked, cleaned, and stowed correctly. After that, get them to the mess for breakfast. Make sure they eat something decent, and then they can get some sleep."

Nadav gave a quick nod. "Understood, Yossi. I'll take care of it," he replied, already moving to address the men.

Yossi watched as Nadav moved through the ranks, giving instructions in his usual calm, efficient manner. The men dispersed, some heading for the equipment shed, others towards the mess hall, their movements still carrying the quiet discipline that had marked the night's mission.

Satisfied that everything was in good hands, Yossi turned towards the CO's tent, ready to deliver his report.

Chapter Forty One

AHMED

The weeks leading up to October 7th blurred into a relentless cycle of training, secrecy, and preparation. Each day felt like a new test, a fresh challenge to overcome. Ahmed could feel the tension tightening in his chest with every passing moment - a mix of anticipation and anxiety that never seemed to leave him. Every whisper in the tunnels beneath Gaza carried the same urgency, every glance exchanged between his men was filled with unspoken fears and hopes.

By late December 2022, Ahmed had been summoned again to the training site, a place now etched into his mind - a grim reminder of their mission. The site lay just 1.6 kilometres from the Erez crossing, next to an international aid distribution centre. Its location had been chosen with deliberate intent, positioned under the watchful eyes of Israeli observation posts and mere kilometres from the border. The message was clear: they were being watched, but they would not flinch.

Ahmed had learned to sense the constant surveillance, the gaze of the Israeli observation towers and elevated boxes less than a mile away. He imagined the soldiers peering through their binoculars, watching as smoke rose from their explosions, observing as they prepared. The training ground had been dug several metres below ground level, partially hidden from view, but Ahmed knew the Israelis could see the smoke, the movement, the shadow of something larger taking shape.

He often wondered what those soldiers thought, staring across the border, seeing them train so openly. *Did they feel a flicker of fear? Or were they, like him, hardened by years of conflict, simply doing their duty, eyes fixed on the enemy?* But Ahmed knew they hadn't seen everything. They hadn't seen the full scope of what was being planned, the depth of their determination. The plans had been whispered, the orders given, and now his men moved with a new intensity - their steps heavier, their breaths sharper. They were no longer just preparing, *they weren't just preparing for another fight, this time, it was for something that truly mattered.*

Ahmed scanned the training ground and felt a surge of pride mixed with fear. His men were practising storming mock Israeli military bases, seizing hostages, and destroying security barriers with a fierce determination he hadn't seen before. The drills were relentless, designed to simulate the *liberation* of settlements near Gaza. That's how the leadership spoke of it - liberation, as if they were freeing something that had been taken from them.

They trained repeatedly, honing their skills in urban combat, using the terrain to their advantage, moving like shadows through narrow alleyways, scaling walls, and clearing rooms in rapid succession. Each day brought new scenarios, new threats to consider, and new ways to strike.

The mock buildings were filled with dummy targets, plaster walls splintered by bullet holes, smoke rising from small, controlled detonations. In the distance, he could hear the low rumble of mock tanks being overrun, the sound of engines revving and tyres skidding over dirt and gravel. It was a cacophony of preparation, a symphony of war that filled his senses and steeled his resolve.

Let them watch. We're watching too, he thought, the weight of his rifle grounding him against the cold wind. He could feel the dust on his face, the sweat that clung to his skin despite the chill. He knew the enemy was observing closely, analysing every move, every tactic. But that was part of the plan, wasn't it? To let them see just enough, to let them think they knew, while the real plan unfolded in the shadows, unseen.

His commanders had told him this was the moment to prove themselves. This was what they had been waiting for. His men felt it too - the fear, the anticipation, the determination. They moved with a new urgency, their faces set with grim focus. There was no room for hesitation now, no room for doubt.

Ahmed's gaze drifted over his men, noting their concentration. He wondered if they, like him, felt the weight of unseen eyes. *The Israelis might think they understand, but they only see what's meant to be seen.* Ahmed was sure of that. He knew that the time for waiting was over, soon, it would be time to act.

As the sun dipped below the horizon, casting long shadows over the training ground, Ahmed took a deep breath and let it out slowly. He turned back towards his men.

'Keep moving,' he called out, his voice cutting through the evening chill. *'We have to be better, faster. The enemy is watching, but we are ready.'*

He watched as his men continued their drills, their movements precise, their faces focused. They had a plan now, a real plan, and every man there knew it. The leadership had made sure of that. Every training session, every whispered order in the tunnels, every night spent studying maps and rehearsing tactics - it all led to this moment.

Ahmed felt the weight of it all settle on his shoulders. The responsibility, the fear, the hope. *We are ready, but so is the enemy. And soon, the world would know just how ready they were.*

Ahmed returned home each night with the weight of the day still clinging to him - the scent of dust and cordite lingering on his clothes, the echo of drills still ringing in his ears. The contrast between the intense, disciplined world of the training ground and the fragile peace of his small apartment grew starker with each passing day. He walked through the door, his eyes immediately finding Salma, who sat on the edge of their worn-out sofa, her face a mask of quiet worry.

Salma had always been good at hiding her fear, but Ahmed could see the subtle changes in her - her fingers gripping the edge of a cushion, her eyes flicking to the window every time a distant sound broke the silence. Her movements were more careful, as if each step was measured, calculated. When she spoke, her voice held a tightness that hadn't been there before.

'You're late,' she said softly, trying to keep her tone light, but Ahmed could hear the edge beneath the words. He nodded, setting his bag down, feeling the weight of it all pressing into his shoulders.

'Training ran over,' he replied, his voice gruff, tired. He didn't offer more. He knew she understood, but he also knew that understanding didn't bring her peace.

Salma watched him closely, her eyes searching his face. *'Is it... getting worse?'* she asked, her voice barely above a whisper, as if speaking too loudly might shatter the fragile calm between them.

Ahmed hesitated. He wanted to reassure her, but after years of living through airstrikes and violence, he knew there were no guarantees, no promises that would hold true.

'It's getting... closer,' he finally admitted, choosing his words carefully. *'But we're not alone this time. Others will come to help us - other Arab states, maybe even the world. They'll see what's happening and they'll put pressure on Israel. This time, things will be different.'*

Salma nodded, but he could see her shoulders tense, the flicker of fear in her eyes that she tried to hide behind a brave smile. *'Different,'* she repeated, the word sounding hollow in the small space between them. *'And what about when they retaliate? Because they will, Ahmed. You know they will, and it won't just be like last time. It will be worse... much worse.'*

Ahmed felt a tightening in his chest. He had seen the fear in her before, but this was different - deeper, more visceral. *'We have no choice, Salma,'* he said, trying to keep his voice steady. *'This is our fight... our duty. If we don't stand now, then when?'*

Salma's eyes filled with tears she refused to let fall. *'And what about the people, Ahmed? What about us, the ones who have to live with the consequences? I've seen what they do. I've heard the bombs. I've felt the ground shake under our feet... I've watched mothers bury their children.'*

Her words cut deeper than he expected. Ahmed turned away, blinking hard to push down the doubts that crept up in moments like this. *'I know,'* he whispered, his voice tight. *'But we have to believe it will be different this time. We have to believe that we can make a difference, that this is worth it.'*

Salma shook her head, her voice trembling. *'I just want to live, Ahmed,'* she said, her tone raw. *'I want to live with you, to be normal, like the people I see in Israel. Why can't we have that? Why do we always have to fight?'*

Ahmed felt a surge of anger rise in his chest. *'You think I don't want that?'* he snapped, his voice sharper than he intended. *'You think I don't dream of something better? This isn't about what we want, Salma. This is about what we have to do.'*

Salma flinched at his tone, and immediately, Ahmed regretted it. He saw the hurt in her eyes, the fear that his anger was hiding something deeper. He reached out, his hand trembling slightly, and touched her arm gently. *'I'm sorry,'* he murmured, his voice softening. *'I didn't mean... I just... I don't know any other way.'*

Salma stepped closer, her hand finding his, squeezing tightly. *'I know, Ahmed,'* she whispered. *'But I'm scared. I'm scared of losing you... of losing everything.'*

Ahmed felt the ground shudder beneath his feet. He glanced up instinctively, recognising the sound all too well - the distant rumble of an airstrike. The strike was a clear message: their activities had not gone unnoticed. A thick plume of smoke rose in the distance. *They know,* Ahmed thought. *They've been watching closely, and now they're striking back.*

He could see the tension in his men's faces as they regrouped. Some were wide-eyed, others stone-faced, but all of them knew this was no ordinary exercise.

Ahmed's thoughts flicked back to Salma, back at home, her face filled with fear. *She will have heard by now.*

He quickly grabbed his radio, steadying his voice despite the turmoil inside. "Stay alert," he called out, his tone calm but commanding. "They know we're here. This is a test of our resolve. Keep moving, stay hidden, and follow the orders." The men nodded, their expressions taut with tension but ready.

In the command centre, the atmosphere was heavy with tension. The leadership of Hamas had gathered around the table, the news of the Israeli airstrike still fresh, hanging in the air like smoke. Abu Khaled, his face grim, leaned forward, slamming his fist onto the table.

"They think they can intimidate us by bombing one of our sites?" he snarled, his voice low but fierce. *"We knew this was a possibility, and yet, we continue to prepare. This only proves they are afraid. They see our strength, our determination, and they know they cannot stop us."*

Another leader, calmer but equally resolute, nodded in agreement. *"We must adapt, use this to our advantage. Change the training locations again, keep them guessing. They cannot bomb what they cannot see."*

Abu Khaled turned to Ahmed, who had just entered, his face still flushed from the heat and dust outside. *"Ahmed, you've been on the ground. What's the morale of the men?"*

Ahmed took a moment to compose himself, weighing his words carefully. *"The men are shaken, but they are ready. They understand that this is part of the struggle. They know what's at stake, and they're prepared."*

Abu Khaled nodded, a small smile of satisfaction crossing his face. *"Good. Then let's make sure the Israelis see just how ready we are."*

At home, Salma stood by the window, her hands gripping the edge of the windowsill so tightly her knuckles had turned white. She had heard the strikes - felt them, even from here. The air was thick with dust, a haze that seemed to settle over everything.

Her heart raced as she paced the small room, trying to keep herself calm. Every time Ahmed left, she felt this same gnawing fear, but today was different. The airstrikes were closer, more direct, and she knew they were aimed at disrupting whatever Ahmed and his men were planning.

"Why now?" she whispered to herself, her voice trembling. *"What do they know? What will they do next?"*

The thought of retaliation gripped her, memories of past escalations flashing through her mind. She had seen what happened when the Israelis decided to strike back - heard the bombs, felt the ground tremble, and seen the smoke rising from shattered buildings.

"They're trying to stop him... to stop all of them," she thought, a wave of dread washing over her. Her hands shook as she reached for her phone, desperate to hear Ahmed's voice, to know he was safe. But there was nothing - no call, no message. Just the sound of sirens in the distance and the murmurs of concerned neighbours gathering outside.

Back at the training site, Ahmed's mind raced. The Israeli response in April had been faster and more precise than they'd anticipated. The reality of their exposure was stark - they could no longer afford to train openly, not with the enemy's eyes constantly watching.

We have to be smarter, he thought, feeling a tightening in his chest. *If they know what we're doing, they know where we're vulnerable.*

He gathered his men around him, their faces drawn tight with tension. *"We can't afford to stay in one place for too long,"* he began, his voice firm but quiet. *"We move quickly, change locations, keep them guessing. This is a new phase of our fight. We've trained for this. Now we adapt."*

The men nodded, their resolve hardening. They had not been broken by the strike - if anything, it had steeled their determination. The Israeli airstrikes had been a blow, but they would not deter them.

The leadership reconvened, the discussions more urgent now. They had to change tactics - train in smaller groups, move locations constantly, and use every piece of cover available. The enemy was watching, and they had to become invisible.

Abu Khaled leaned forward, his voice a low growl. *"We train at night. We use the tunnels more effectively. Every step we take, they will wonder if it's real or a distraction. We will be a shadow they cannot catch."*

The others nodded in agreement, the plan already forming in their minds. They would continue despite the risks. Every bomb, every strike only confirmed that their preparations were working, that their plans were moving forward.

When Ahmed finally returned home that evening, Salma was waiting for him, her eyes filled with fear and anger. *"I heard the bombs,"* she said, her voice breaking. *"How close were you?"*

Ahmed hesitated, then closed the door behind him. *"Close enough,"* he answered, trying to keep his voice steady. *"But I'm here. I'm fine."*

Salma shook her head, tears brimming in her eyes. *"And next time? What about next time, Ahmed?"*

Ahmed walked over, placing his hands gently on her shoulders. *"We have to keep going, Salma. We have to believe that what we're doing is right."*

"But what if it's not?" she whispered, her voice trembling. *"What if all this does is bring more pain?"*

Ahmed pulled her into an embrace, feeling the weight of her fear pressing against his chest. He had no answers, no reassurances to give, but he held her close, hoping it would be enough, at least for now.

In the aftermath of the April airstrike on their training site, Hamas made a decisive shift. The bombing near Erez Crossing had been a stark warning, and now, every member understood what was coming. The next phase of their preparation moved underground - deep into the network of tunnels beneath Gaza. The fight would come to them, and they had to be ready.

Throughout the spring and summer months, the leadership of Hamas met repeatedly in the command centre, their tension growing with each meeting. The recent Israeli airstrikes had forced them to adapt quickly. The Israelis had shown they were vigilant, striking whenever they sensed a threat. Abu Khaled and the other leaders knew they had to turn the tables, using their intimate knowledge of the terrain to their advantage.

"We draw them in," Abu Khaled declared during a late April meeting, his voice edged with determination. *"The Israelis will come, believing they can flush us out. But we'll guide them into a trap, then vanish. When they think they've got us, we retreat into the tunnels, only to reappear behind them and strike."*

He scanned the room, meeting the eyes of each commander in turn. Every fighter, every leader, had to commit to this strategy without hesitation. The directive was clear: expand their network of tunnels and create access points in unexpected places - inside schools, family homes, even beneath children's beds. These exits would allow them to engage the enemy swiftly, disappear, and then launch surprise attacks from elsewhere.

"The tunnels are our greatest advantage," Abu Khaled continued, his tone hard. *"We must use them as escape routes and ambush points. They will never know where we'll surface next."*

As the months passed, Ahmed found himself spending more time in the tunnels, the familiar pathways now taking on a renewed sense of purpose. The dim lights flickered overhead, barely piercing the thick darkness. The tunnels were noisy and cramped, filled with the constant sound of drills, commands bouncing off the concrete walls. The men rehearsed how to navigate the labyrinthine network swiftly, memorising routes and practising their retreats.

"We draw them in above ground, retreat quickly, then strike from behind. Keep practising your routes!" Ahmed shouted over the clatter, his voice sharp, slicing through the chaos.

His men moved with determination. They drilled tirelessly, learning every path by heart, knowing that every exit could offer them an advantage. The stakes were high, and every man felt the urgency.

The final days were a blur of activity - last-minute drills, final checks, briefings, and whispered conversations in dimly lit rooms. Every man knew his role, every man understood the stakes. The air was thick with fear and determination, the tension palpable.

On the night before the attack, Ahmed returned home to find Salma waiting for him. Her face was pale, her eyes searching his as he entered. She sensed that this time was different - that this time, he might not come back.

He moved towards her, his steps heavy. *"Salma,"* he began softly, reaching for her hands. *"I have to go."*

Her eyes filled with tears, but she didn't look away. *"I know,"* she whispered, her voice cracking. *"I knew this day would come."*

Ahmed pulled her into his arms, holding her tightly, feeling her heartbeat against his chest. *"I love you,"* he murmured, his voice thick with emotion. *"Whatever happens, remember that. Always."*

Salma clung to him, her tears falling freely. *"Come back to me,"* she pleaded, her voice barely audible. *"Please... come back."*

He held her close, wanting to say more, to promise her everything, but the words caught in his throat. Finally, he pulled back, brushing his hand against her cheek. *"I'll try,"* he whispered.

And then, without another word, he turned and left, the door closing softly behind him. Salma stood there, listening to his footsteps fade away, her heart heavy with dread. She knew he was walking towards something that could change everything - something that could take him from her forever.

And as she stared at the closed door, she felt a deep, aching emptiness settle within her, knowing that whatever happened next, nothing would ever be the same again.

Chapter Forty Two

YOSSI

The work on the border continued with relentless intensity, mirroring the urgency that had marked their missions in recent months. Patrols were more frequent now, their purpose clear: to observe the increasing movement of Hezbollah fighters across the rugged, unpredictable terrain. The intelligence reports Yossi had reviewed in the past few days had confirmed their worst fears - missiles were being moved into hidden bunkers in the mountainous regions, a new and troubling development. The atmosphere at the field base was charged, every soldier could feel the weight of heightened tension, aware that something was shifting on the other side of the border.

Yossi and Nadav, now well-established in their roles as trusted leaders, were at the forefront of every mission. Their platoon had become one of the most dependable units, frequently tasked with the toughest operations. Over time, the bond between Yossi and Nadav had strengthened, translating into seamless communication on the battlefield. They operated almost instinctively, reading each other's movements and anticipating decisions, a dynamic forged in countless patrols and skirmishes.

But the strain was beginning to show. The constant vigilance, long nights, and ever-present threat had taken their toll. Yossi could see the fatigue in his men's faces, in the way they moved - slower than before - and in the silence that settled over them during moments of rest. He felt it himself - an exhaustion that settled deep in his bones, far beyond the usual weariness of hard duty. There were days when he thought of their last patrol, the ambush they narrowly avoided, the injuries they patched up in the field - constant reminders of how close they always were to the edge.

One afternoon, after another gruelling patrol, Yossi and Nadav were called to the CO's tent. They exchanged a glance, sensing the urgency but also something different in the air. As they entered, the CO looked up, his expression softer than usual.

"Sit down, both of you," Arad began, his tone direct but less stern than they were accustomed to. *"I've been watching you two, and I see the toll this is taking. You're both due for some leave."*

Yossi and Nadav exchanged a surprised look. Leave was a rare privilege these days, a luxury almost forgotten in the endless cycle of missions and patrols.

"Second week in April," Arad continued. *"You're both heading home to Tel Aviv. Take some time, recalibrate, and come back ready. We need you at your best."*

Yossi felt a mixture of relief and hesitation. The thought of seeing Yael, of spending time away from the tension of the border, filled him with anticipation. Yet, he knew how hard it would be to leave the platoon, even for a short time. The faces of his men flashed in his mind - tired, determined, always ready, but now showing signs of wear.

"Thank you, sir," Yossi replied. But before he could stop himself, he added, *"Sir, if I may... the men are slowing down too. The constant patrols, the stress - it's wearing on them. I'd like to request a rotation for the platoon to go on leave as well, even if it's just for a week at a time."*

The CO paused, considering Yossi's words carefully. He gave a slight nod, a sign of respect for Yossi's thoughtfulness. *"You care about your men, Segen Rosenberg. That's good. I've noticed it too. We can arrange a rotation. A few at a time for a week's leave, starting as soon as possible."*

Yossi felt a surge of relief. *"Thank you, sir. I'll draw up a rota for who should go first. It will mean a lot to them."*

Arad nodded again. *"Do that. And make sure it includes you and Samir Levy in April as agreed. You've both earned it."*

As they stepped out of the CO's tent, Nadav clapped Yossi on the shoulder. *"You've got a knack for this leadership thing."*

Yossi smirked, trying to mask his own sense of relief. *"I just hope they see it that way. Let's get that rota sorted before they think I'm bluffing."*

Nadav grinned. *"Looks like we're all getting a bit of a break then. Tel Aviv, here we come."*

They walked back towards their quarters, the prospect of leave giving them a renewed sense of energy, a lightness that had been missing for too long. For a brief moment, they allowed themselves to imagine normalcy - a life beyond the constant threat of conflict, even if it was only for a few weeks. Yossi knew it wasn't much, but it was something. And sometimes, in moments like these, something was enough.

The morning after his meeting with the CO, Yossi called his platoon together. They gathered in the small clearing outside their tents, a familiar spot where they'd often received their orders. The early light filtered through the trees, casting long, dappled shadows on the ground, and a light breeze carried the scent of earth and pine. The men stood in a loose formation, curiosity mixed with fatigue on their faces. Yossi could see the toll of the continuous operations, the strain etched into their expressions.

Yossi took a deep breath and looked at his men - each one of them tired but still standing tall, still ready. He knew they needed this, probably more than they realised. He began with a steady, confident voice, *"Alright, listen up. I spoke with the CO yesterday, and I've managed to secure some leave for all of you."*

A ripple of surprised murmurs ran through the platoon. A few men exchanged glances, a hint of disbelief in their eyes. Yossi saw shoulders straighten, a few brows lift in cautious hope.

"I know it's been a long stretch," Yossi continued, *"and you've all been pushing hard. We've been given the go-ahead to start rotating home leave. Everyone will get a week,*

starting tomorrow. We'll do it in shifts to keep the platoon operational, but each one of you will get time to go home."

He watched as the news settled in, the reality of it slowly dawning on them. For a moment, there was silence, and then a low buzz of conversation spread through the group. Relief began to break across the faces of the soldiers - some smiled, others nodded appreciatively, and a few clapped their comrades on the back.

"Finally, some good news!" Rav Turai Ben-Yamin, one of the squad leaders, said, his face breaking into a wide grin. *"A chance to see our families, sleep in a real bed... it's like a dream."*

Yossi allowed himself a small smile. *"Check the rota I've posted outside the briefing tent. We'll be starting with three of you tomorrow, and then we'll rotate every week. Make sure you're ready when your turn comes."*

The men's reactions varied - some looked up at the sky as if giving thanks, while others were already discussing their plans. Yossi could hear snippets of conversation: *"I can't wait to see my kids," "My mum's cooking...," "I've got a bed with my name on it."*

Nadav, standing next to Yossi, leaned in with a knowing grin. *"About time someone thought of this."*

Yossi nodded. *"Yeah, we've been running on fumes. They need a break... and so do we."*

Rav Turai Yair, another section leader, stepped forward with a grateful expression. *"Thanks, Sir. This is... it's exactly what we needed."*

Yossi nodded, meeting Yair's eyes. *"Just make sure that when you're home, you get proper rest. Come back ready to pick up where we left off. We're still in the middle of it, and we need everyone sharp."*

"Yes, Sir!" came the unified reply from the men, their voices carrying a renewed energy, a spark that had been dimming over the past few weeks.

Yossi watched them break into smaller groups, heading to check the rota and discuss their upcoming leave. It was a small respite, but it was something - a glimpse of normalcy in a world that had been anything but.

As the men dispersed, Nadav turned to Yossi. *"You're right - they've been needing this more than they know."*

Yossi glanced over at the men, his expression softening as he saw their faces light up with a bit of hope. *"We all do, Nadav. Even a few days away can make a world of difference."*

Nadav chuckled. *"And in six weeks, it'll be our turn. Tel Aviv, here we come."*

Yossi smiled, a fleeting image of home flashing through his mind, but he quickly pushed it away. There was still work to be done, still missions to lead. But for a brief moment, he allowed himself to enjoy the small victory - a little light breaking through the constant haze of duty and tension.

He looked back at Nadav. *"Make sure they're squared away. They need this, and we need them to come back in one piece, ready for whatever comes next."*

Nadav nodded. *"You got it, Yossi. They'll be ready."*

Yossi and Nadav packed their bags and climbed into their 'David' armoured jeep, the sturdy vehicle rumbling to life as they prepared for the journey back to Tel Aviv. The sun was high, casting long shadows over the rocky terrain as they drove through the familiar landscapes, they had come to know so well - the dust-covered plains, the sharp, jagged rocks, and the sparse vegetation that clung desperately to life in this harsh environment.

Inside the jeep, the air was thick with the mix of diesel and sweat, but there was a noticeable lightness between the two men. They had driven this route many times, yet today felt different - filled with the promise of something more than just another mission.

Nadav leaned back in his seat, his fingers drumming lightly on the dashboard. *"You know,"* he said with a grin, *"I almost forgot what it feels like to drive without a destination that involves an ambush, or an intel drop."*

Yossi chuckled, keeping his eyes on the road ahead. *"Yeah, it's been a while since we've had a mission to 'relax and recharge.' I almost don't remember how to do that."*

Nadav laughed. *"Well, I think it starts with something cold and refreshing by the beach. Maybe a few hours of not looking over our shoulders."*

Yossi nodded, his smile softening as he thought of Yael. *"And seeing the people who make it all worthwhile."*

Nadav's grin widened. *"Leila's going to be so surprised. I told her it might be another month. Didn't want to get her hopes up."*

Yossi glanced at his friend. *"Yeah, same with Yael. I didn't want to promise anything until I knew for sure. But it'll be good to see them, to be around people who remind us why we're doing all this."*

The road stretched ahead of them, winding through the hills, as they moved from the barren landscape of the border towards the outskirts of Tel Aviv. The scenery gradually shifted - more trees, a hint of green here and there, and the distant shapes of buildings coming into view.

Nadav sighed contentedly, looking out the window. *"You know, Yossi, sometimes I think we're crazy for doing this. But then I remember these moments... the chance to just be ourselves, even if it's just for a few days."*

Yossi nodded. *"Yeah, I get it. It's like we're living two different lives. One minute we're soldiers, the next... just two guys heading home."*

As they neared the camp in Tel Aviv, both men grew quiet, lost in their thoughts. The city's skyline appeared on the horizon, and the sense of anticipation grew stronger with each passing mile. The air seemed fresher, lighter, as if Tel Aviv itself was welcoming them back.

Finally, they reached the camp's entrance. The familiar sight of soldiers moving about, the sounds of drills in the background - it felt almost surreal to be back here for something other than a briefing or debriefing.

As they pulled up, Yossi spotted Yael and Leila waiting near the gate, their faces lighting up with excitement as the jeep approached. Yossi could feel his heart quicken, a rush of warmth spreading through him as he saw Yael wave enthusiastically.

"Look at that," Nadav chuckled, *"our welcoming committee."*

They parked the jeep and climbed out, hardly able to contain their smiles. Yael was the first to reach Yossi, wrapping her arms around him in a tight hug.

"Welcome home," she whispered, her voice filled with emotion.

Yossi held her close, feeling the tension of the past months begin to melt away. *"It's good to be back,"* he murmured.

Leila embraced Nadav with equal enthusiasm. *"I can't believe you're really here!"* she exclaimed, her eyes bright with joy.

Nadav grinned, lifting her off the ground slightly. *"Surprise! We finally made it."*

The four of them stood there for a moment, soaking in the reunion, the relief of being together again. The weight of their duties seemed to lift, replaced by the simple joy of being with those they cared about most.

"Alright," Nadav said, slinging an arm around Leila's shoulders, *"who's ready for a drink at the beach?"*

Yael laughed, the sound light and carefree. *"I thought you'd never ask. Let's go find a spot by the water."*

They made their way down to one of the many beachside bars that lined the Tel Aviv coastline. The sun was beginning to set, casting a warm glow over the sand and the Mediterranean Sea, painting the sky in shades of pink and orange. The air was fresh and salty, a welcome change from the dusty tension of the border.

They found a table on the terrace of a lively bar, shaded by a thatched roof, with a perfect view of the water. The soft murmur of conversations and the clink of glasses mingled with the sound of waves crashing gently on the shore. It was a place filled with life and peace, far from the demands of their military duties.

Nadav grinned as he dropped into a chair beside Leila. *"This is exactly what I needed,"* he said, stretching his arms wide. *"Feels good to be back."*

Yossi nodded, his arm still around Yael. *"More than good,"* he replied. *"Feels like we've stepped into a different world."*

They ordered a round of beers, the cold bottles arriving quickly, droplets of condensation forming on the glass in the warm evening air. Yossi took a long sip, relishing the cool liquid that seemed to wash away some of the dust he had carried with him from the frontlines.

"So, how's everything been with you two?" Yossi asked, looking between Yael and Leila.

Leila laughed, leaning back in her chair. *"Non-stop! It feels like Tel Aviv never takes a break, and neither do we."*

Yael nodded. *"I've been thrown into the deep end at the new job,"* she admitted with a small smile. *"The work at the security company is intense, but it keeps me sharp."*

Yossi's eyes softened. *"I knew you'd handle it. You always do."*

Yael squeezed his hand, her smile growing wider. *"Thanks,"* she said, turning to Leila. *"And what about you? How's the nursing going?"*

Leila's face lit up. *"Oh, it's been a whirlwind!"* she said. *"I'm learning so much, and every day is different. It's exhausting, but in a good way. It feels... important."*

Nadav nudged her playfully. *"Look at you, saving lives every day,"* he teased.

Leila laughed, her eyes sparkling. *"Well, someone has to balance out what you two do,"* she joked.

The group laughed, the tension from the border fading with each shared smile and light-hearted comment. They moved on from work to lighter topics, reminiscing about old times, sharing funny stories, and planning the days ahead.

Yossi felt the stress of the past months melting away. He hadn't laughed like this in weeks, and the sight of Yael's carefree smile anchored him in a way that nothing else could. Here, with his closest friends, he could almost forget the weight he had been carrying.

"Alright, enough about work," Nadav interjected, leaning back in his chair. *"We've got two whole weeks off. What's the plan?"*

Yael raised her beer bottle, a gleam of mischief in her eye. *"How about we start with a beach day tomorrow?"* she suggested. *"Let's make the most of this time, right from the start."*

Leila nodded eagerly. *"Yes! A day with nothing but sun, sea, and just relaxing sounds perfect."*

Yossi chuckled. *"Count me in,"* he agreed. *"We've earned it."*

Nadav lifted his bottle. *"To two weeks of freedom,"* he toasted. *"No patrols, no orders, just us and whatever we want to do."*

They all clinked their bottles together, their spirits high, a moment of unity that reminded them why they fought, why they endured.

As the night deepened, they remained at the bar, watching the stars gradually emerge over the water, the city lights twinkling along the shoreline. For now, they were just four friends enjoying the simple pleasures of life - cold beers, a warm breeze, and the soothing sound of the sea.

And for that moment, it was enough.

The days of leave passed in a blur of family gatherings, familiar comforts, and the rare luxury of uninterrupted rest. Yossi and Nadav spent much of their time visiting their families and catching up with old friends. For Yossi, being home with Yael felt like a soothing balm, every moment was cherished, a brief reprieve from the constant tension of the border.

One afternoon, Yossi and Yael decided to meet David for lunch. They arrived at his office, a bustling hub in the centre of Tel Aviv, and waited in the reception area. Yael's gaze drifted over to Salma, who was sitting at her desk, looking more withdrawn than usual. Salma's eyes were fixed on her computer screen, but it was clear she was lost in thought, her expression tense and distant.

Yael approached her with a friendly smile. *"Salma, hi,"* she said softly, trying not to startle her.

Salma blinked, as if pulled from a deep thought, and quickly mustered a smile, though it didn't quite reach her eyes. *"Oh, Yael, hello,"* she replied, her voice wavering slightly.

Yael could sense something was wrong. *"You okay? You look a bit... distracted,"* she offered, keeping her tone light.

Salma hesitated, her fingers nervously playing with a pen. *"It's... it's just been a tough few days,"* she admitted quietly.

Yael nodded, drawing closer, her voice gentle. *"I heard about the air strike near the Erez Crossing. I can't imagine how difficult that must have been."*

Salma's eyes filled with tears, and she quickly looked down, her voice barely more than a whisper. *"Some people I knew were there,"* she confessed. *"It's... it's just so close now."*

Yael's heart ached for her. She could see the fear etched on Salma's face, the way her shoulders seemed to curl inwards as if trying to shield herself from some unseen danger. *"I'm so sorry, Salma,"* she said softly, placing a comforting hand on her arm. *"If there's anything I can do..."*

Salma shook her head slightly, wiping away a tear with the back of her hand. *"I just worry... for all of you,"* she said quietly, her voice wavering with emotion. *"Things feel different now. Please, take care."*

Yael felt a knot form in her throat as she nodded. *"We will, Salma. I promise."* She reached out, giving Salma's arm a gentle squeeze, trying to convey reassurance in the face of her obvious fear.

Salma nodded, but Yael could see that the fear lingered in her eyes. As they turned to leave, Yael glanced back, noticing the way Salma's shoulders seemed to hunch with the weight of her worry. It stayed with Yael, that quiet fear, like a whisper she couldn't quite ignore.

After a few moments, Yossi joined them, and they made their way out for lunch with David. But Salma's quiet desperation lingered in the back of Yael's mind, a gnawing concern that was hard to shake.

Towards the end of their leave, Yossi, Nadav, Yael, and Leila gathered once more at a beachside restaurant. The sun dipped low over the sea, casting a warm, golden glow over the water. The sound of waves gently lapping against the shore provided a soothing backdrop to their conversation.

They ordered their meals and settled into easy chatter about their plans and the small joys of being home. But soon, the conversation shifted back to the news.

"I heard there was another air strike in Gaza," Leila remarked, her tone thoughtful as she glanced at Yael. *"Near the Erez Crossing, right?"*

Yael nodded, her expression serious. *"Yes, Salma mentioned it the other day... she seemed really scared. It's like she knows something is about to happen,"* she said, a hint of worry in her voice.

Yossi exchanged a look with Nadav. *"Things have been tense,"* he admitted, carefully choosing his words. *"There's been more Hezbollah activity on the border. We've seen them moving weapons, setting up new positions. It could be connected, or it could be nothing... hard to say for sure."*

Leila leaned in, concern evident on her face. *"Do you think it's building up to something bigger?"* she asked quietly.

Nadav shrugged, his face calm but serious. *"We've been on edge for months,"* he replied. *"Always prepared, always watching. But you never really know until it happens."*

Yael squeezed Yossi's hand, her brow furrowed. *"Just... promise me you'll be careful, okay?"* she said softly, her eyes searching his.

Yossi smiled, trying to keep things light. *"Always,"* he said with a wink. *"We've got a good team, and we know what we're doing."*

Nadav raised his beer. *"To knowing what we're doing, and to staying safe,"* he toasted with a grin, trying to lift the mood.

They all clinked their glasses, and for a moment, the tension seemed to fade, replaced by the warmth of friendship and the comfort of familiar faces. They stayed at the restaurant long after their plates had been cleared, sharing stories and laughter, savouring these rare moments of peace.

But beneath the surface, the worry remained, a silent undercurrent that ran through every conversation, every glance exchanged. They all knew their time together was fleeting. Soon, they would return to their posts, back to the uncertainty and the danger that awaited them.

For now, though, they held onto these moments, cherishing the time they had, knowing that in their world, nothing was ever guaranteed.

Chapter Forty Three

AHMED

Ahmed stood before his men in the pre-dawn darkness of 7th October, his voice unwavering as he delivered the final briefing. The room was cloaked in shadow, a single bulb flickering above, casting jagged shapes across tense, expectant faces. The faint hum of distant machinery filtered through the walls, and the air smelled of sweat and gun oil - a sharp, metallic scent that mingled with the faint trace of incense clinging to the commanders' clothes. Determination and dread coiled in Ahmed's chest, tightening with every breath. Today would not just change everything - it would redefine everything.

"Listen closely," he began, his voice cutting through murmured prayers and whispered breaths. His gaze locked onto each of his commanders - Tariq, Khaled, Bilal, and Hadi. Tariq's sharp, calculating eyes, Khaled's stony determination, Bilal's restless energy, and Hadi's cool composure met his own. Each man a blade, honed and tempered, ready to strike.

"Today, we move. The plan is simple, but the execution must be flawless. One mistake, and it all falls apart." He paused, letting the gravity of his words settle like a weight in the room.

The men shifted subtly, jaws tightening, shoulders stiffening. A few glanced at each other, brief flickers of nerves in eyes that quickly hardened. Ahmed could see them anchoring themselves, readying for the bloodshed to come.

"We have several teams assigned to breach different points along the security fence. The breach teams will blast through with explosives and mechanical diggers, ripping the barrier apart. Once the fence is down, Tariq and Khaled, you will lead your teams straight across the border. Your target is Kibbutz Be'eri. You'll breach, secure Route 232, and move directly to the junction leading to Kibbutz Be'eri." He jabbed his finger against the map spread out on the table, its edges curling from use.

"A fleet of white pickup trucks and motorbikes will take you there. Speed and surprise are our weapons. Get in fast, hit them hard, and leave nothing to chance."

His voice carried a steady confidence, but Ahmed knew his men understood the stakes. Failure here wasn't just defeat - it was dishonour. He turned his attention to Bilal and Hadi, their eyes locked on him with fierce intensity.

"You two will lead the Mobile Squadron on motorbikes as we've planned and practised. Your task is to secure the southern end of Route 232 - control it with an iron grip." He let the words hang in the air before continuing, his tone lower, sharper. *"After securing the road, you'll attack the festival at Re'im. Latest reports indicate there are still many people there. Be cautious of the military base nearby, but if you can, strike it - kill everyone you find."*

He straightened, his presence dominating the small, cramped space. *"I will be travelling with the Command-and-Control Team. Once we reach Route 232, we'll secure the road to protect you from incoming IDF and to destroy anyone escaping along the road from the festival."*

Ahmed's gaze swept over the men, seeing their jaws clench, the flicker of adrenaline sparking in their eyes. They were ready. *"We start with a barrage of rockets fired into Israel from all over Gaza. The aim is to create confusion - disorientation - keep them guessing, looking the wrong way. The moment the rockets launch, you breach the fence. Show no mercy, but if you see anyone of value - someone we can use - take them alive."*

His voice lowered, turning hard as steel. *"If you capture anyone, report it to me on Route 232. I will decide what happens next."*

He paused again, scanning their faces - the flicker of nerves, the clenched jaws. He could sense the tension thickening in the air, an almost tangible force pressing in from all sides. His heart hammered steadily in his chest, a rhythm in time with the barely audible clicks and shifts as his men adjusted their rifles, the creak of leather holsters punctuating his words. He took a deep breath, the room's weighty silence settling over his shoulders like a mantle.

"This is it, brothers. This is what we've bled for, the day we carve our mark into their land. The day they will know our strength. Stay focused, stay disciplined, and trust in our plan. Allah is with us."

For a moment, the room was still. The flickering bulb cast distorted shadows that seemed to pulse in rhythm with the men's steady, deliberate breathing. Then came the soft shuffling of feet, the tightening of hands around rifles, and the whispered murmur of prayers, filling the air like a final plea to the heavens.

Ahmed took a deep breath, sensing the fear mingling with resolve. His voice softened, lowering to a near-whisper that demanded their full attention. *"May our actions today bring honour to our cause and fear to our enemies. Go now and make them remember us."*

The men moved with hushed urgency, their steps purposeful. The scrape of boots against concrete, the muted clinking of ammunition - each sound seemed amplified in the stillness. Ahmed watched them leave, feeling the familiar weight settle over his shoulders - a mix of responsibility, fear, and something darker he couldn't quite name. He needed to stay calm, to hold firm as the storm broke.

He turned back to the map, his gaze tracing the borderlines, the junctions marked in sharp, red lines. This land - this small strip of contested soil - had cost them dearly. He closed his eyes briefly, forcing his thoughts to clear, muscles taut with the need to act. Today would change everything. One way or another.

Behind him, the room emptied out, the silence that followed heavy and thick. He took a final, steadying breath, then picked up his radio.

"Command, this is Ahmed. Finalise preparations. We move at 0630."

Bilal's gaze swept over the small, makeshift courtyard, lingering on each man's face as if silently committing them to memory. The early morning air was thick with tension, a suffocating weight that pressed down on the fighters, coiling tighter with every second that passed. Shadows clung to the corners, and the muted pre-dawn light painted their figures in shades of grey, making them appear as ghosts - silent, watchful, waiting for the order that would hurt them into a maelstrom of violence.

The men shifted with nervous energy, hands twitching over weapons, shoulders tense with suppressed anticipation. Muscles coiled like springs, ready to snap at the slightest signal. The muffled scrape of boots against gravel and the soft rustle of tactical vests were the only sounds in the oppressive silence. The acrid scent of sweat, mingled with oil and dust, hung heavy in the still air. Bilal could almost taste it on his tongue, the bitterness of it matching the anticipation that gnawed at his gut.

Just a few metres away, Hadi stood flipping through a set of notes with deliberate calmness, his face a mask of unyielding focus. His movements were methodical, precise - each turn of the page slow and deliberate, as if he were absorbing every line, every instruction, even though Bilal knew Hadi had memorised them all long ago. His gestures were measured, controlled - a stark contrast to the tension simmering around him. To the untrained eye, he might have seemed dispassionate, detached, but Bilal could see the minute signs of readiness in the subtle flex of his fingers, the way his gaze flicked up to scan the courtyard between each page turn.

A faint glow pulsed from the rear of one of the motorbikes lined up along the courtyard's edge, casting red shadows on the dusty ground, each flash punctuating the silence like the slow beat of a drum. The lights cut through the darkness, a reminder of the chaos coiled just beneath the surface - a signal, a warning of the fury about to be unleashed.

This was the final, agonising calm before the storm - the silence that seemed to hold its breath, knowing that with the next command, the world would explode into fire and fury. Every heartbeat stretched long and thin, the men's eyes darting, muscles twitching with the need to act. To fight. To kill.

Bilal took a slow, deliberate breath, letting the anticipation settle into a sharp edge of focus. This was the moment they'd prepared for, every plan, every drill leading to this point. And yet, for all their readiness, he could see the flicker of fear in a few of their eyes - the fear that came when you stood at the precipice, staring into the unknown.

"Steady," he murmured, his voice low, almost inaudible, but it carried through the still air, grounding them. He saw shoulders relax minutely, the tension bleeding out just enough to sharpen rather than weaken. They needed the fear - it would keep them alert, quick, ruthless.

Hadi glanced up, meeting Bilal's gaze, and gave a single, sharp nod. Everything was in place. Every man was ready.

The two shared a brief, wordless exchange, an unspoken understanding passing between them. Hadi's fingers stilled on the page, and slowly, deliberately, he folded the notes and tucked them into his pocket. There was no need to speak. The time for words had passed.

Bilal turned back to his men, his eyes hard, his stance steady. The courtyard felt like a coiled spring, wound so tightly that a single breath might shatter the fragile silence. *"We go when the rockets launch,"* he murmured, eyes scanning the faces before him. He saw resolve, determination, and the spark of something darker - something that mirrored the fire burning in his own chest.

The minutes crept slowly towards 0630, and the air seemed to thrum with anticipation. Ahmed stood beside Tariq and Khaled, his gaze fixed on the distant horizon where the border lay hidden in the morning haze. All around them, men crouched low, rifles clutched tightly in their hands, their eyes scanning the skyline. The stillness was suffocating, broken only by the occasional murmur or the faint shuffle of a boot against gravel. The Command-and-Control team was poised, every man on edge, waiting for the strike that would signal the start of something far greater than any battle they had fought before.

Then, just as the second hand swept past 0630, the silence shattered.

The first missiles streaked into the sky with a deafening roar, leaving fiery trails that crisscrossed the air above Gaza. One after another, rockets shot upwards, filling the dawn with the thunderous noise of engines igniting and metal piercing through the stillness. The ground seemed to vibrate beneath Ahmed's feet as more and more rockets launched, lighting up the sky with a chaotic dance of fiery tails. The sheer force of the barrage reverberated through the air, a pulse of raw power that throbbed through the men, sharpening their resolve.

Ahmed could see it now - missiles arcing high into the sky, disappearing briefly before reappearing as distant flashes towards the Israeli side. Each launch sent a shiver of excitement and dread rippling through the ranks. It was as if the world itself held its breath, the booming echoes carrying a single message: *The time has come.*

Ahmed grabbed his radio, his voice cutting through the explosions. *"Breach, breach, breach!"* he commanded.

The order echoed across the radios, reaching Khaled and Tariq just ahead of him at the northern breach and Bilal and Hadi to the south. As soon as the command was given, the breach teams surged forward - shadowed figures racing towards the fences against the backdrop of chaos. Explosives detonated simultaneously, erupting in a series of thunderous cracks as the metal barriers shuddered, sending plumes of dust and debris high into the air. The thick steel crumpled and collapsed, twisted wire and shattered posts falling in jagged heaps. The sound of tearing metal mixed with the steady roar of rockets overhead, each launch echoing like a relentless war drum.

In both locations, as the dust settled, the mechanical diggers rumbled forward, their engines roaring to life. One machine lurched ahead, its massive shovel scraping against the remains of the fence, shoving twisted iron aside with a shriek of protesting metal. Smoke poured from its exhaust as it cleared a path, the grinding and clanking reverberating through the ground.

With the fences breached, Tariq and Khaled's men were the first to push through at the northern point, a convoy of white pickup trucks packed with fighters surging forward. The vehicles tore through the gap, each bristling with men wielding machine guns and RPGs, eyes fixed ahead with fierce determination. Flanking the pickups, a squad of motorbikes roared alongside - riders hunched low over the handlebars, with another fighter seated behind, rifles slung across their backs. Dust and smoke swirled around them as they shot forward, tyres skidding over the uneven ground, engines growling as they cleared the border and sped onto Route 232.

"Go, go!" Khaled shouted, leaning out of the lead pickup, his voice barely audible over the deep-throated roar of rockets streaking overhead. The fighters in the trucks braced themselves, weapons at the ready, scanning the horizon as they sped towards Route 232 and onwards to Kibbutz Be'eri.

Simultaneously, on the southern end, Bilal and Hadi's squads stormed through their own breach in a mirror image of the northern assault. White pickups filled with armed men surged through the opening, followed closely by motorbikes weaving around the vehicles with practised precision. The engines roared as they pushed forward, the convoy snaking through the breach and heading towards the southern sector of Route 232.

Ahmed's Command-and-Control Team moved in next at the northern breach, slipping through the gap with practised efficiency. A line of white pickups fitted with heavy machine guns thundered behind Khaled and Tariq's teams, the mounted weapons swivelling slowly as they cleared the border. Each truck was packed with men, their faces set in hard lines, rifles clutched tightly as they took their positions.

The path was clear - the road ahead lay open. With engines roaring and weapons bristling, the assault teams surged forward, dust rising in their wake.

The attack had begun.

Bilal and Hadi led the charge down the southern stretch of Route 232, a convoy of over a hundred motorbikes roaring through the deserted roadways. Each bike carried two fighters - one at the handlebars, eyes locked ahead, the other seated behind, rifle balanced across his lap, ready to engage. The riders moved in a tight formation, engines growling like a swarm of angry wasps. The man at the rear of each bike sat poised, his gaze sweeping the surroundings, finger resting lightly on the trigger. It was a column of mobile firepower, each pair primed to strike at a moment's notice.

The wind whipped past as they sped forward, dust trailing in their wake. The first light of dawn cast long shadows across the asphalt, the pale sun filtering through the trees lining the road.

"*Slowly... let's not lose the others,*" Hadi called out, his voice steady over the roar of engines. The fighters weaved in and out, staying tight, every movement controlled and disciplined. It was a scene of organised chaos, the armed men blending seamlessly with the growl of the machines.

Suddenly, a flash of movement ahead - a cluster of cars appeared, headlights piercing through the morning light, racing towards them from the festival site at Re'im. Bilal's gaze narrowed as he raised his hand, signalling the men to spread out across the road. The bikes fanned out like a net, blocking the entire stretch of Route 232. The lead car skidded, tyres squealing, the driver's face a mask of panic.

"*Fire!*" Bilal's command rang out, and in an instant, the rear riders lifted their rifles and opened up. Gunfire erupted, deafening against the roar of engines. Bullets punched through windscreens and doors, shredding metal and glass. The vehicles swerved wildly, one car spinning out of control as the driver slumped forward, lifeless. Another car lurched to a stop, riddled with holes, the figures inside slumped over in a twisted tableau of death.

The convoy moved on, the fighters firing with deadly precision, their faces set in grim determination. The air was thick with the acrid stench of gunpowder and burnt rubber. As the last of the cars ground to a halt, smoke curling from shattered windows, Bilal signalled his men to close ranks again. The bikes swarmed back together, engines snarling, rifles still trained on the smoking wrecks.

The brief encounter was over, the road littered with the twisted remains of those who had tried to flee. Without a word, Bilal and Hadi pushed their men forward, engines roaring as they continued their relentless advance up the southern route. The attack was underway, and there would be no mercy.

The last of the cars lay still, smoke curling up from shattered windows and twisted metal. The fighters circled around, eyes sweeping for any movement, but there was none. Bodies slumped over steering wheels, faces contorted in terror and blood. Bilal and Hadi exchanged a look - grim satisfaction mingled with cold resolve.

The road was theirs.

"*Secure the area!*" Hadi barked, his voice cutting through the fading echo of gunfire. He pointed to a group of fighters. "*You, stay here. No one gets past this point.*" The men nodded sharply, peeling off from the convoy and positioning their bikes along the wreckage, weapons still trained on the ruined vehicles.

Bilal turned to the rest, raising his rifle. "*The rest of you, with us! We move on the festival entrance. No delays.*"

Engines roared to life again as the remaining motorbikes formed up behind their leaders. With a final glance at the men securing the road, Bilal and Hadi twisted their throttles, tyres kicking up dirt as they accelerated forward, leading the main force down Route 232. The roar of over a hundred bikes surged together, the fighters hunched low over their handlebars, weapons at the ready.

Ahead, the entrance to the festival loomed in the distance - an expanse of tents and makeshift structures, still teeming with people unaware of the death racing towards them. Bilal and Hadi's eyes were fixed on the target. They would show no hesitation.

There was only the mission, and the path ahead lay clear. Without slowing, they pushed forward, leaving the men behind to hold the road, while the rest charged towards the festival like a wave of steel and fire.

At the same moment Bilal and Hadi were securing the southern stretch of Route 232, Tariq and Khaled's convoys pushed through the breach at full speed, engines roaring as they tore through the dust-choked road. Behind them, Ahmed's Command-and-Control Team followed closely, the heavy machine guns mounted on their white pickups swivelling slowly as the fighters scanned for any signs of movement.

The sun had fully crested the horizon now, casting a harsh, unforgiving light over the landscape. The barren stretch of Route 232 unfolded before them, a narrow line cutting through the scrubland and fields. Tariq and Khaled's pickups were packed with men, rifles bristling from every side, and RPGs resting on shoulders, the fighters' eyes sharp and focused. Flanking the vehicles, motorbikes buzzed alongside, riders weaving in and out, the men at the rear gripping their weapons tightly, ready to fire at a moment's notice.

The convoy moved like a serpent of steel and fire, a column of armed power sweeping south. The kilometres ticked by rapidly, tyres eating up the distance as they sped along the deserted road. The men remained silent, tension crackling through the ranks as they pushed closer to their objective. With every passing minute, the sense of urgency grew, the roar of engines blending with the distant rumble of rockets still streaking overhead - a constant reminder of the chaos they were about to unleash.

The convoy rumbled to a halt as they reached the junction leading into Kibbutz Be'eri, the heavy tyres grinding against the asphalt. Dust billowed around them, mingling with the acrid stench of exhaust fumes. Tariq and Khaled's teams veered off the main road, engines roaring as they swung into position, forming a loose perimeter around the entrance. Behind them, Ahmed's Command-and-Control Team spread out across the junction, blocking off the route and fortifying their hold on the area.

Ahmed's vehicles, fitted with heavy machine guns, lined up along the road, weapons trained in both directions. Men jumped down from the trucks, fanning out across the intersection. The fighters moved quickly, setting up firing positions and preparing for the inevitable response from the IDF. Ahmed's eyes flickered over the scene, taking it all in - the angles, the approach, and the best vantage points. His men had their orders: hold the junction at all costs.

The junction was now a choke point - any Israeli forces trying to reach Kibbutz Be'eri would have to come through them, and any fleeing vehicles from the festival would be caught in the crossfire. It was the perfect spot to both command and control the operation, a node from which they could direct the assault and respond to any unforeseen developments.

He lifted his radio, taking a deep breath to steady himself. The time had come.

"All units, prepare for the attack." His voice was calm, deliberate, cutting through the static.

The fighters moved in like a pack of wolves, dismounting from their motorbikes and spilling out of the white pickups, spreading through the grounds like a tide of death. Engines still roared, rifles were raised, and the first shots rang out - sharp and explosive - tearing through the early morning stillness. It was a coordinated strike - swift, brutal, and without mercy. They moved with lethal precision, fanning out to block every exit, guns trained on the mass of people still trying to comprehend what was happening.

"All units, move to the target. Block every exit - stop the cars leaving," Ahmed's voice crackled over the radio, cold and commanding.

Bilal pressed his radio to his lips. *"Copy, Commander. We're moving in. It's chaos - hundreds of vehicles trying to leave. We'll stop them, but some are heading your way."* He glanced at Hadi, who gave a sharp nod, and the men began to fan out, weapons ready, engines rumbling as they spread through the festival grounds.

Panic erupted instantly. People abandoned their cars, scrambling out of vehicles and sprinting in every direction, screams piercing the air. A young woman in a black top and white shorts, her red shawl flaring behind her like a banner, tore across the field, her eyes wide with terror. Behind her, others stumbled through the dust, faces twisted in fear, some glancing over their shoulders as gunfire cracked and spat around them.

The initial strike was pure chaos. The fighters opened fire into the packed line of cars, bullets shattering windscreens and ripping through metal and flesh. People dropped where they stood, bodies crumpling against the cars they had moments ago hoped would take them to safety. The gunmen moved among the vehicles, shooting indiscriminately. The sharp *crack, crack, crack* of rifles punctuated the panicked screams. Glass exploded, tyres burst, and engines sputtered out as the fighters laughed and shouted to one another, eyes alight with the thrill of the hunt.

"Allahu Akbar!" one of the men bellowed, raising his rifle triumphantly after putting a burst of bullets into a fleeing man's back. Another fighter responded with a savage cheer, a grin splitting his face as he pivoted, emptying his magazine into the windscreen of a nearby car. The driver's head snapped back, blood splattering across the inside of the glass. Others took up the cry, voices lifting in fierce, jubilant praise.

"Allahu Akbar!" they shouted, repeating it like a mantra. They called out to each other, congratulating every kill with shouts and gestures, as if it were some kind of twisted game.

The woman in the red shawl stumbled, nearly falling as she sprinted through the open field. She darted between the bodies, eyes darting wildly, gasping as she glanced back. One of the fighters spotted her, his smile widening as he raised his rifle, the barrel tracking her erratic movements. But before he could pull the trigger, another gunman shouted, *"Leave her! We'll get her later - focus on the others!"*

The laughter that followed was cruel, echoing over the screams and the relentless rattle of gunfire.

"Keep shooting! Don't let them escape!" Hadi roared, his voice carrying above the din.

Gunfire rattled and cracked as the fighters unleashed a storm of bullets into the panicking masses. The woman ran, adrenaline driving her forward as men and women fell around her, screams filling the air. A group huddled behind a row of vehicles - an older man and two women, crouching low, eyes wide with horror. One of the gunmen turned, grinned, and squeezed the trigger. Blood sprayed, and the three figures collapsed, their bodies twitching as the fighters moved on without a second glance.

"Allahu Akbar!" another shouted, firing into a cluster of people trying to shield themselves behind a car. The fighters cheered as the bullets struck home, more voices picking up the chant, praising God with every life taken.

Bilal moved through the carnage, his rifle barking out in steady bursts. He didn't flinch, didn't hesitate. His men were doing exactly what they'd been ordered to - creating chaos, spreading terror. He saw a group of festival-goers trying to flee across the open ground, abandoning their cars and sprinting towards the fields. His eyes narrowed.

"Cut them off! Don't let them reach the trees!"

The woman in the red shawl kept running, legs pumping furiously as if sheer will alone could carry her to safety. She didn't look back, didn't see the people collapsing behind her, their desperate cries swallowed up by the cacophony of violence. She glanced to her left and saw another woman stumble and fall, crying out as she tried to crawl through the dirt. Without hesitation, a gunman fired a short burst, and the crawling woman slumped, blood pooling beneath her.

But somehow, through pure luck or determination, the girl in the red shawl managed to break away, sprinting further and further from the carnage. Her heart hammered, chest burning, as she pushed through the chaos, the red shawl whipping around her like a flag of defiance.

Behind her, Bilal's and Hadi's men continued their rampage, sweeping through the festival grounds with calculated ruthlessness. More people tried to make a run for it, some darting between the cars, others sprinting across the open fields. But the gunmen were everywhere, rifles barking, the air thick with dust and smoke, the stench of blood and burnt rubber hanging heavy.

At the same time as Bilal and Hadi started the attack on the festival, Khaled's team moved swiftly towards the yellow electric gate, the early morning light casting long, eerie shadows across its steel frame. The gate loomed tall and fortified, a daunting barrier, but it was not one they hadn't planned for. The scent of dew clung to the cool air, mingling with the faint tang of metal and oil. Ahead, the guard at the small gatehouse stood motionless, his posture relaxed, blissfully unaware of the approaching threat.

"Attack teams in position," Khaled murmured into his radio, eyes locked on the guardhouse. He glanced back at his men, their expressions hard and determined. *"All units, prepare to breach."*

Ahmed's voice crackled through. *"You have the green light. Move in."*

Khaled gestured sharply, and one of his men, his face set with grim determination, raised his rifle, taking careful aim. The crack of the gunshot shattered the morning stillness, the echo reverberating off the surrounding buildings. The guard crumpled to the ground, his body folding in on itself in a lifeless heap. There was no time to linger, no room for doubt.

"Get over that gate!" Khaled barked, his voice cutting through the tension like a whip.

A wiry young fighter with a scar running down his cheek scrambled up the side of the gate, his fingers gripping the cold steel bars. The metal felt icy beneath his hands, sending a shiver down his spine. He swung himself over the top, narrowly avoiding the coils of barbed wire, feeling the sting of adrenaline coursing through his veins. Landing with a thud on the other side, he sprinted towards the gate control panel, his breath coming in sharp, ragged bursts.

With a flick of his wrist, he found the emergency override switch. For a moment, his fingers hovered, searching for the right button among the worn, greasy controls. Then, with a swift, decisive movement, he flipped the switch.

The gate began to hum, the metal groaning and creaking as it slowly slid open. Khaled's team didn't wait for it to fully retract. With engines revving, the fighters surged forward through the widening gap, each one eager to unleash the violence they had long prepared for.

"Move! Move!" Khaled shouted, his voice cutting through the growl of engines, leading his team through. The pickups and motorbikes sped past him, tyres skidding over gravel and dirt, kicking up clouds of dust as they spread out to establish a perimeter. Fighters dismounted swiftly, rifles shouldered as they advanced on foot, covering each other in tight, coordinated movements as they pushed down the narrow paths winding between homes.

The vehicles drove into the heart of the kibbutz, the acrid smell of exhaust fumes mingling with the sharp tang of dust and burnt fuel. Inside the kibbutz, the first residents appeared, blinking in confusion as they stumbled from their homes, faces painted with a mix of shock and dawning fear. Khaled's men moved with intent, rifles raised, eyes darting left and right, scanning for any sign of resistance.

The realisation spread like wildfire among the inhabitants, and then came the first screams - high-pitched, piercing the air in frantic bursts. Shots rang out, echoing off the stone walls and quiet lanes, and those who tried to flee were cut down without hesitation, bodies crumpling where they stood. Blood splattered the walls, staining the quaint cottages of the kibbutz with sudden violence.

"Clear every house!" Khaled commanded, his tone icy and resolute. *"No survivors if they resist!"*

The team moved with ruthless efficiency, pushing deeper into the kibbutz, house by house. They smashed through doors, kicking them in or firing into locks, spilling into living rooms and kitchens with weapons raised. The familiar, metallic scent of cordite hung heavy in the air, mingling incongruously with the fragrance of freshly cut grass and the sweet aroma of blooming flowers from the small gardens - an unsettling contrast to the chaos unfolding.

Curtains flapped in the wind from shattered windows, while distant cries of startled birds taking flight mingled with the panicked screams of those trapped within the onslaught. The fighters advanced with practised, unfeeling precision, their movements almost mechanical. The assault was swift and brutal, every second punctuated by the sharp crack of gunfire, the hollow thud of bodies hitting the ground, and the desperate wails of those caught in the path of destruction.

Khaled and his men coordinated their movements with military precision, weaving through the narrow streets, forcing their way into every home, systematically hunting down anyone who might pose a threat - or anyone who simply crossed their path.

On the opposite side of the Kibbutz, Tariq's team zeroed in on the kindergarten, the focal point of their assault. Intelligence from those who had worked there had pinpointed it as the largest safe room in the kibbutz, situated on a narrow road directly across from the medical centre. Tariq understood the urgency - capturing it swiftly was critical to their plan.

He crouched behind the rusted shell of an abandoned car, the cold metal biting into his back, his eyes locked on the narrow road ahead. The kindergarten was close - just beyond the bend - but the way was blocked. A small kibbutz security team had taken up defensive positions at both junctions of the road, determined to protect those who had managed to reach the safe room. They were few in number, but they fought with everything they had, every shot a testament to their desperation.

They think they can hold us back, Tariq thought with a sneer, his lips curling into a tight, disdainful smile. His breath fogged slightly in the crisp morning air, the scent of damp earth mingling with the acrid odour of cordite. He had already lost several of his men to the defenders' stubborn resistance. Each time they tried to advance, the defenders pushed them back, refusing to yield an inch. The sharp cracks of rifles and the deafening booms of grenades filled the air, punctuating the silence with bursts of chaos. Bullets ricocheted off walls, windows shattered, and smoke hung thick in the air, mingling with the sharp tang of burning wood and charred metal.

Tariq's patience wore thin. The battle was dragging on too long, the defenders were holding their ground longer than he had anticipated. He watched as another of his fighters crumpled to the ground, a bullet tearing through his chest, blood spraying onto the dusty road in a vivid crimson arc. Tariq cursed under his breath, tasting the bitterness of dust and frustration on his tongue. This was supposed to be quick, a swift strike to seize the kindergarten. Instead, they were caught in a bloody stalemate.

We need to break them, Tariq decided, his expression darkening with cold resolve. He raised his hand, signalling sharply for his men to split up and assault both ends of the narrow road simultaneously.

The fighters surged forward, moving like shadows between the cover of low walls and hedges, ducking behind children's bicycles and overturned garden furniture as they advanced, while the defenders continued to pour fire down on them from their entrenched positions. Tariq gritted his teeth as another one of his men went down, his body convulsing in the dirt, fingers clawing at the earth in a desperate, futile attempt to cling to life.

He felt a flicker of anger, quickly smothered by the cold, ruthless clarity that had served him so well. *They will pay for this,* he thought grimly, eyes narrowing as he tracked the muzzle flashes from the defenders' rifles.

There would be no more delays. It was time to crush them.

Khaled moved through the kibbutz with calculated coldness, his senses attuned to the task at hand. His nostrils flared as he inhaled the acrid smoke rising from burning wood and fabric. His boots crunched over broken glass and soft grass, and he could feel the fine grit of dirt settling on his skin, the weight of his weapon familiar in his hands. Ahmed's instructions echoed in his mind: *create maximum chaos and fear, take hostages if they have value, discard the rest.*

"Valuable ones," he reminded himself, his gaze sweeping across the frightened faces of the residents. *The rest are expendable.*

His men dragged families from their homes, the desperate cries and sobs filling the air. Khaled quickly assessed each one, his eyes cold and calculating. He saw the terror in their eyes, heard the frantic pleas for mercy, but his heart remained unmoved, his focus unbroken. He pointed at a man and his wife, ordering his fighters to separate them from their two young children. The children screamed, reaching out for their parents, but Khaled's men yanked them away, indifferent to their cries.

Ahmed's voice crackled over the radio, sharp and direct. *"Khaled, remember, we need valuable hostages. Look for foreign nationals, anyone who could be of use. But keep it moving."*

Khaled nodded to himself, already scanning the crowd for suitable targets. He turned to one of his men. *"Take the woman. Kill the man,"* he ordered, his voice devoid of any emotion.

The woman struggled, her voice rising into a desperate wail as she was dragged towards the line of pickups. Khaled raised his weapon and shot the man in the chest, watching dispassionately as his body crumpled to the ground, his children's screams piercing the air.

"Take them too," he commanded, his tone as flat as if he were discussing cargo, not lives.

The moment was cold, calculated - designed to break the will of those around. Moving down the line, Khaled made quick, ruthless decisions.

"Take that one," he said, pointing to a middle-aged woman clutching a young boy. *"She could be valuable, looks like a foreigner. Take the boy too."*

Another crackle from Ahmed came through the radio, this time tinged with urgency. *"Khaled, don't waste time. If they resist, shoot them. Only keep those who have real value."*

Khaled's gaze swept over the trembling figures before him, pausing on a group of elderly residents forced to their knees, their hands tied behind their backs. He hesitated only for a moment before shaking his head dismissively.

"No value," he muttered. *"Kill them."*

Without a flicker of hesitation, his fighters raised their rifles and opened fire. The bodies slumped forward, lifeless, the sound of gunfire echoing across the kibbutz, mingling with the distant cries of dogs barking frantically, their howls filled with fear.

Meanwhile, his men continued to separate families, forcing some into the pickups while others were dragged aside and executed on the spot. A young woman, clutching an infant to her chest, was shoved roughly into the dirt. Khaled stepped forward, grabbing the infant from her arms. He stared at her, his eyes cold, weighing his options.

He spoke into his radio. *"Ahmed, we've got a woman and a child here. What's the order?"*

Ahmed's voice returned, cold and pragmatic. *"Take them both if you think they could be useful. If not, kill them."*

Khaled's expression hardened. *"We take both,"* he decided, pushing the woman and the child towards one of the trucks.

He turned to another group, pulling a man from the crowd who was pleading in broken Arabic. Khaled paused, then nodded to his men. *"Take him,"* he ordered. *"He might be worth something."*

The process continued, brutal and methodical. Khaled's men moved quickly, barking orders, shooting anyone who resisted or who they deemed of no value. A man tried to run, and without a second thought, Khaled shot him in the back, watching impassively as he crumpled to the ground, his face twisted in pain and fear.

His heart pounded with a mixture of adrenaline and cold, detached focus. He lifted his radio again. *"Ahmed, we've got a mix - some foreigners, some women and children. Should we send more back?"*

Ahmed replied swiftly. *"Yes, but keep it quick. And remember, we're here to make a statement. Let them know what fear is."*

Khaled acknowledged the command and turned back to his men. *"Load them up!"* he shouted. The fighters began roughly herding the captives into the backs of the trucks, ignoring their cries and pleas. The terrified sobs of those being taken mingled with the distant echoes of sporadic gunfire, the thick smell of smoke hanging in the air.

The trucks positioned themselves at the end of the road, engines idling, ready for a swift exit back to Gaza.

As the trucks filled, Khaled took a moment to survey the scene. Bodies lay scattered across the kibbutz, pools of blood staining the earth, mingling with the vibrant colours of flowers in small, tidy gardens now trampled underfoot. The sound of distant weeping carried on the wind, a haunting melody against the backdrop of the destruction.

He nodded to his men, satisfied that the mission was proceeding as planned. With a final check, he confirmed over the radio. *"Command, we're sending the hostages back. The rest... they're not coming back."*

Ahmed's voice responded, devoid of emotion. *"Understood, Khaled. Get them out. We have what we came for."*

Khaled turned away, his gaze sweeping over the devastation they had wrought. There was no remorse, no hesitation - only the cold certainty of a mission completed.

On the other side of the kibbutz, the battle raged on for hours. Both sides exchanged fire in a fierce, bitter fight, the air thick with the acrid stench of gunpowder and the sharp crack of rifle shots. Tariq pushed his men hard, driving them forward with shouts and threats, but the kibbutz security team held firm, fighting back with everything they had. The green grass around the houses was littered with spent shell casings, trampled underfoot, stained with dirt and blood. The resistance of the kibbutz security team, their stubborn refusal to give in, only made Tariq more determined to crush them.

He could hear the defenders shouting to one another, issuing brief, hurried commands in Hebrew. He glimpsed them darting between trees and bushes, using the thick foliage for cover. Tariq watched them through narrowed eyes, seeing the defiance in their movements, the flashes of their rifles firing back. His men were pinned down behind walls, crouching low to the ground, the sharp, metallic tang of gunpowder filling their nostrils, sweat dripping down their brows, mingling with the dust and dirt kicked up by the chaos.

The resistance was fierce, almost desperate. The defenders were clearly running low on ammunition, but they fought with every last ounce of strength they had. Tariq could see some of his men grinning manically as they fired at anything that moved, revelling in the chaos, the sheer thrill of the fight. They tore through small gardens, kicking over potted plants, crushing flower beds underfoot, and smashing through windows as if it were a game. A few fighters rummaged through the homes they passed, tearing open fridges and grabbing food and drinks, casually snacking while bullets flew past.

Tariq ignored their behaviour, his focus locked on the enemy and the plan at hand. The rage simmered in his chest, building with every passing second, like a kettle slowly reaching its boiling point. He wanted this over. He wanted the defenders crushed beneath their feet, broken and defeated.

After several gruelling hours, he sensed a shift. The defenders' fire slackened, their shots becoming more sporadic. Tariq watched closely as they began to pull back, inching towards the small medical centre, their last place of refuge. Their movements were desperate and ragged, their bodies hunched low, trying to avoid the relentless barrage raining down on them.

Now we've got them, Tariq thought, his lips curling into a thin smile. Seizing the moment, he turned to his second-in-command, his voice low and flat. *"Prepare the grenades,"* he ordered, his gaze never leaving the retreating defenders.

His men moved swiftly, pulling the pins from their grenades, fingers gripping tightly around the smooth metal spheres. Tariq's eyes were cold, calculating. He could see the desperation in the defenders' movements as they scrambled for safety, their retreat a pitiful, stumbling effort. They were cornered, trapped like rats. There would be no escape.

"On my mark," Tariq shouted, his voice slicing through the chaos. He watched his men, their muscles coiled like springs, grenades ready to be hurled. The defenders were almost at the door, clustered together in a tight knot, a last-ditch attempt to hold their ground.

"Now!" he roared.

The grenades arced through the air, dark shapes silhouetted against the smoke-filled sky. They landed among the defenders, exploding in bursts of deafening thunder. The force of the blasts shook the ground, sending plumes of dust and debris skyward. Screams of pain and terror erupted as bodies were flung in all directions. Blood and dust mingled in the air, a gruesome mist hanging over the scene as the smoke cleared.

Tariq's eyes narrowed, scanning the wreckage. The defenders lay crumpled on the ground, some motionless, others writhing in agony, clutching at shattered limbs and torn flesh. He watched dispassionately, feeling no pity, no remorse. This was war. This was what it meant to defy them.

"Push forward!" he barked, signalling his men to advance. The fighters surged ahead, weapons raised, faces set in grim determination. There would be no mercy. No reprieve. They moved like a tidal wave of destruction, sweeping over the remnants of the defenders.

The medical centre loomed ahead, a squat, unassuming building now marked for ruin. Tariq's gaze fixed on it, his jaw clenched. *This ends here.*

With a final, brutal push, they would finish it.

Near the edge of the festival grounds, Bilal noticed an ambulance, its red lights still flashing weakly against the chaos. A small group of people had taken refuge inside, their faces pressed against the windows, wide-eyed and pale with terror. Without a moment's hesitation, Bilal signalled to his men.

"Fire on the ambulance!" he commanded sharply.

The fighters raised their rifles in unison, unleashing a torrent of bullets into the vehicle. The deafening staccato of gunfire filled the air. Glass shattered, metal crumpled under the relentless assault, and within moments, the ambulance erupted in flames. The screams of those trapped inside were swallowed by the roar of the explosion, the once-life-saving vehicle now a burning pyre of death.

To the right, a group of terrified revellers had huddled together inside a makeshift bar, desperately seeking shelter behind flimsy fridges and upturned barrels. Hadi's gaze locked onto them. He pointed sharply, his face a mask of cold resolve.

"In the bar - finish them!" he ordered, his voice cutting through the pandemonium.

The gunmen turned, rifles snapping into position as they unleashed a deadly volley into the tent. Bullets tore through the thin fabric, puncturing fridges, ricocheting off barrels, and finding flesh with brutal efficiency. One by one, the bodies fell, collapsing over each other in a tangled heap. Their hiding place offered no protection against the merciless onslaught. The air was thick with the smell of blood and cordite, the ground littered with the broken forms of those who had sought refuge.

Bilal felt the weight of the command settle heavily on his shoulders as he advanced through the carnage, his finger tight on the trigger. He saw another group attempting to flee, their panicked movements betraying them. Without a second thought, he fired into the crowd. Bodies crumpled under the relentless hail of bullets, collapsing like rag dolls amidst the chaos.

He glanced at Hadi, who nodded grimly, eyes steeled with resolve. They were doing what they had come to do. No hesitation. No mercy.

Smoke coiled upwards in thick, acrid tendrils, a mix of burning fuel and human flesh. The stench clawed at Bilal's throat, but he ignored it, his gaze sweeping over the scene. The ground was soaked in blood, bodies sprawled haphazardly across the earth like discarded dolls. He took it all in - the destruction, the ruin, the finality of it. They had done what they were sent to do, executed their orders to perfection.

Raising his radio to his lips, Bilal's voice was calm, almost detached. *"Area is secure, Commander. We have many hostages, but most are dead or hiding."*

Ahmed's voice crackled back through the static, cold and emotionless. *"We regroup on Route 232."*

Bilal gave one final glance over the festival grounds, the bodies strewn across the earth like broken toys. No remorse. No regret. Just the cold reality of war.

"Let's finish this," he muttered to Hadi. *"We're done here."*

Bilal called over a group of fighters who had corralled the remaining hostages, their captives crying or screaming, confusion and terror etched on their faces. Hadi, ever efficient, had already begun organising the transport - the motorbikes and pickups that would ferry their captives back into Gaza.

With brutal precision, a grim convoy formed, a line of vehicles that promised more horror to come. The fighters, their faces smeared with dirt and streaked with blood, loaded the last of their captives, the screams of the terrified hostages blending into the roars of the engines. The convoy started to pull away, leaving behind only death and despair. For those still breathing, the nightmare was far from over.

Bilal and Hadi gathered the rest of the transport, their fighters re-mounting their motorbikes and revving engines. With a grim satisfaction, they turned their bikes and pickups onto the road, engines roaring as they headed back towards Ahmed and the Command Team. Shouts of victory echoed among them, a twisted jubilation that hung heavy in the air as they sped away.

They left behind a trail of destruction - the sounds of weeping and the sight of broken bodies etched into the dirt. The festival grounds were nothing more than a graveyard of shattered dreams and ruined lives.

Six hours had passed, six hours of death and destruction. The assault was over, but the war had just begun.

On Route 232, Ahmed's team was strategically positioned along the road, weapons primed, eyes scanning the horizon. The distant cracks of gunfire and the deep rumble of explosions from the Nova Festival at Re'im filled the air, a grim soundtrack to the unfolding assault. A steady stream of vehicles appeared, headlights blazing in the dawn light, as festival-goers - terror-stricken and desperate - sped away from the chaos they thought they'd escaped. But they had driven straight into another ambush.

The first cars came into view, tyres screeching against the asphalt as drivers frantically tried to maintain control. Ahmed's team sprang into action. A burst of machine-gun fire shattered windscreens, tore through metal, and struck flesh. An RPG hissed as it flew, slamming into a car in the middle of the convoy. A deafening explosion followed, sending debris and flames skyward, the searing heat washing over the fighters like a wave.

Panic rippled through the convoy. Drivers swerved and braked, trying desperately to avoid the burning wreckage blocking their path. Some attempted to turn around, their tyres squealing as they reversed wildly, but there was no way out. Ahmed's men continued their merciless assault, their faces set like stone.

"Push forward!" Ahmed barked into the radio, his voice cold and unyielding. *"Clear the road. No survivors."*

His men advanced with deadly precision, leaving a trail of wreckage and bodies in their wake. Cars flipped, colliding into each other, turning into blazing infernos. The stench of burning fuel and scorched metal filled their lungs, mingling with the acrid smell of gunpowder and smoke. The desperate cries of the dying were drowned out by the relentless roar of the flames.

Suddenly, a group of festival-goers veered off the road, abandoning their car, and sprinted towards a small concrete bomb shelter situated by a bus stop. Ahmed's sharp eyes tracked them as they scrambled inside.

"Take the shelter!" Ahmed ordered, his gaze fixed on the small structure. *"Do not let them get away."*

His men approached cautiously, weapons raised. One of them lobbed a hand grenade through the entrance. Then, to their disbelief, the grenade was hurled back out, landing just a few feet away. They barely had time to duck as it detonated, spraying shrapnel and dust into the air.

"Again!" Ahmed snarled.

Seven times they repeated the exchange - seven grenades thrown, seven times they were hurled back. Each detonation sent shockwaves through the fighters, the stubborn resistance enraging them further. Ahmed clenched his teeth, fury simmering just beneath the surface. Finally, on the eighth attempt, one of his men managed to angle the grenade just right. A few seconds later, there was a dull thud, followed by smoke and cries of pain..

"Get them out!" Ahmed commanded.

His fighters approached warily. Inside, they found a horrific scene. The bodies of those who had been hiding were sprawled across the floor, some motionless, others groaning in pain. Blood smeared the concrete walls, pooling on the ground beneath the wounded.

One young man, cradling a bloodied stump where his hand used to be, looked up at Ahmed's men with wide, terrified eyes. He tried to speak, but no sound came out - only a strangled gasp as he was hauled roughly to his feet.

"Take them as hostages," Ahmed ordered, his voice devoid of emotion. *"The injured too. They'll make good bargaining chips."*

The fighters moved quickly, dragging the survivors out of the shelter, roughly pushing them towards the waiting pickups. Some stumbled, struggling to keep up as blood dripped from their wounds. Others were thrown into the vehicles like sacks of grain, their eyes glazed over in shock.

The man with the missing hand was shoved into the back of a truck. He slumped against the side, breathing hard, his face twisted in pain. One of Ahmed's men leaned in close, his voice low and mocking.

"Should have stayed in there, eh?" he sneered, prodding the wound with the barrel of his rifle.

The man flinched but said nothing, his gaze unfocused, barely conscious.

"Allahu Akbar!" one of the fighters shouted, raising his weapon in triumph.

The others echoed the cry, their voices ringing out across the road as they loaded the captives. Some of the men slapped each other on the back, grinning as if they had just completed a great feat. Their laughter, a cruel and twisted celebration, filled the air.

Ahmed stood to the side, watching with cold detachment. His gaze shifted to the burning wrecks scattered along the road, the bodies of the dead and dying littering the asphalt. He took a deep breath, the acrid scent of smoke and death filling his lungs.

This is what we came for, he thought grimly. *This is what they will remember.*

"Secure the rest of the road," he ordered into the radio, turning away. *"And keep moving. We've got more to do."*

The fighters nodded, engines roaring to life as they set off again, leaving the shattered remains of the ambush behind. The trucks carrying the hostages sped ahead. The cries of the wounded faded into the distance, swallowed by the rumble of tyres on asphalt and the steady thrum of gunfire still echoing from the festival.

For Ahmed, it was just another victory in a day of bloodshed.

On the other end of the road, Bilal and Hadi's teams moved into position, blocking any escape.

At a leisurely pace, Khaled and his team continued clearing the houses, moving with the unhurried calm of predators certain of their dominance. People had locked themselves into safe rooms, desperately trying to cling to some semblance of security. But the order went out without hesitation: burn the houses. The scent of smoke grew stronger, mingling with the acrid tang of fear and sweat, the odour of charred wood and burning fabric filling the air, thick and suffocating. Flames began to lick greedily up the sides of the buildings, and soon the crackling of fire drowned out the distant cries and muffled sobs coming from within the sealed rooms.

Khaled watched the smoke billowing upwards, dark and acrid, blending with the early morning haze as it spread ominously across the kibbutz. His men moved with grim determination, kicking open doors, checking rooms, and dragging out anyone they found hiding inside. Occasionally, they paused to rummage through kitchens, tearing open cabinets, biting into fruits left on counters, or gulping water from half-empty bottles found in fridges. Some even laughed - carefree in their cruelty - as they helped themselves to snacks or drinks, wiping their mouths with the back of their hands before moving on to their next target. The taste of the stolen food mixed with the metallic tang of blood and the acrid scent of cordite lingering in the air.

Inside one house, a fighter casually picked up a child's toy - a small, stuffed bear left abandoned on the floor. He stared at it for a moment, as if contemplating its innocence, then tossed it into the fire, watching it smoulder and blacken, a slow smile spreading across his face. Another fighter, his boots crunching over broken glass, nudged a small bike with his foot, its tiny wheels spinning uselessly. With a sneer, he kicked it aside, sending it skidding across the lawn, its bell ringing out a hollow, haunting chime that echoed eerily in the chaos.

In the garden of one home, a cat darted out, eyes wide with terror, its sleek fur a blur of panic. But it was caught in the crosshairs of one of Khaled's men. The shot rang out, a sharp crack that cut through the air, and the cat dropped silently to the ground. The men laughed, their voices harsh and mocking - a jarring contrast to the gentle rustling of the trees swaying in the wind. Nearby, a dog whined and scratched frantically at a door, desperately seeking safety, but a fighter shot it without a second thought, the animal's yelp cut short, leaving only silence in its wake. The scent of cordite mingled with the sweet, earthy smell of freshly cut grass, an almost surreal mix of brutality and normality.

Khaled's eyes roved over the small gardens, noting the neatly planted flowers, the little potted herbs, the children's drawings stuck to windows. To him, they were just signs of the enemy's life - lives now uprooted, torn apart, their belongings discarded and trampled underfoot. There was no sympathy, no regret, only a cold satisfaction as he surveyed the chaos they were creating. Every broken toy, every shattered window was a testament to their power, a message carved in violence.

He continued down the street, stepping over a discarded bicycle, its wheels still spinning as if desperately trying to maintain some semblance of motion in a world gone mad. His boots crunched on gravel and broken flowerpots, the shattered remnants of peaceful lives laid waste by the violence he had unleashed. The delicate scent of jasmine from a nearby bush mingled incongruously with the thick smoke, a fleeting reminder of what the kibbutz had been before it was transformed into a smouldering battlefield.

A volley of grenades was hurled into the medical centre, shattering windows and blowing the doors off their hinges in a cacophony of destruction. The explosions rocked the building, sending plumes of smoke and shards of debris flying in all directions. Tariq's men surged forward, weapons raised, their figures silhouetted against the swirling smoke as they fired relentlessly into the interior. The few remaining defenders who still clung to life were quickly overwhelmed, their desperate cries drowned out by the deafening roar of automatic gunfire.

As the smoke cleared, Tariq and his men moved through the devastated building, stepping over twisted bodies, feeling the slickness of blood under their boots. The acrid smell of smoke and burnt wood permeated the air, mingling unpleasantly with the faint, sterile scent of antiseptic from the shattered medical supplies. Broken syringes and torn bandages lay scattered amidst the wreckage, pitiful remnants of a place meant to heal, now reduced to a slaughterhouse.

The floor was treacherous, slick with blood and strewn with debris. Tariq advanced with a single-minded purpose, his expression cold and focused, checking every corner, every room, making sure nothing and no one was left alive. His heart pounded in his chest, adrenaline still coursing through his veins. The destruction they had wrought filled him with grim satisfaction - a brutal sense of accomplishment.

His voice was flat, devoid of any emotion as he keyed his radio. *"Building cleared. No survivors,"* he reported to Ahmed, his tone reflecting the ruthless efficiency of the assault. There was no hesitation, no remorse - just the cold, hard reality of war.

Suddenly, Ahmed's voice burst through the radio, sharp with urgency. *"Incoming IDF units!"*

Khaled's head snapped up, his eyes narrowing as adrenaline surged through him. He grabbed his radio and called out to his men. *"Hold your positions!"* he barked, his voice cutting through the noise like a whip. He could see the dust rising in the distance, the faint glint of sunlight reflecting off the metal surfaces of the approaching vehicles.

The rumble of engines grew louder, and the rapid bursts of gunfire signalled the start of the battle. Tariq's team, having just cleared the medical centre, moved swiftly to join Khaled. They sprinted across the open ground, ducking behind garden walls, vehicles, and any available cover as bullets whistled past, shattering windows and chipping away at brickwork in deadly bursts.

"To Khaled's line! We hold them here!" Tariq shouted over the cacophony of battle, waving his men forward to take defensive positions alongside Khaled's team. The two groups converged, quickly setting up along the narrow street, rifles raised and eyes sharp. Tariq glanced at Khaled, his face streaked with dirt and sweat, a silent understanding passing between them - a wordless pact sealed in the midst of chaos.

"Focus fire!" Khaled ordered, his voice strong and steady. *"Don't let them get close!"*

His men unleashed a barrage of gunfire, filling the air with the sharp cracks of rifles and the high-pitched whine of bullets slicing through the air. The acrid smell of cordite thickened, and smoke began to drift lazily down the street, casting a hazy veil over the carnage.

Tariq crouched low behind a stone wall, his rifle steady as he fired in short, controlled bursts. He could see the IDF soldiers advancing with grim determination, moving from cover to cover, their movements precise and disciplined. *"Short bursts! Conserve your ammo!"* he shouted to his men, urging them to stay focused amidst the pandemonium.

The IDF forces, despite being outnumbered, pressed forward with calculated efficiency, using the natural cover of the kibbutz - the trees, hedges, and garden walls - to inch closer. Each movement was covered by suppressive fire, but Khaled's fighters, entrenched behind solid cover, held their ground, their weapons trained on the narrow approach.

A soldier fell, struck by a burst from one of Khaled's men, his body crumpling onto the grassy verge. Another IDF trooper darted behind a low wall, a bullet whizzing past his head and splintering into the nearby tree trunk. The air was thick with the sounds of battle - gunfire, shouted orders, and the distant wail of alarms blending into a maddening symphony of chaos.

"Tariq, cover the left!" Khaled shouted over the din. *"I'll hold the centre!"*

Tariq nodded, signalling his men to shift their fire. The tension was palpable - sweat dripping down their faces, dust clinging to their clothes. Each fighter fired carefully, aiming with deadly precision, conserving ammunition, knowing that every shot had to count.

The battle intensified. The IDF soldiers, undeterred by the relentless fire, continued their methodical advance, closing the gap and forcing Khaled's fighters to adjust their positions. Tariq saw one of his men take a direct hit, the fighter collapsing to the ground with a strangled cry. He gritted his teeth and fired back, the shots sharp and deliberate, covering the man's desperate crawl to safety.

Khaled, firing steadily from his position, watched grimly as another of his fighters went down, blood spraying across the dirt. His voice cut through the chaos once more. *"Hold the line! Do not let them get closer!"*

The radio crackled with Ahmed's voice, urgency now seeping through every word. *"Khaled, Tariq, prepare for withdrawal! You've bought enough time. Get everyone out now - fall back to Gaza immediately!"*

Khaled didn't hesitate. *"You heard him!"* he roared. *"Begin the retreat! Move in pairs - cover each other!"* He turned sharply to Tariq, his eyes hard. *"We pull back in phases, you take the left, I'll cover the right."*

Tariq relayed the orders, his voice sharp and unyielding. *"Fall back by groups! Keep firing! Keep moving!"*

The fighters began to pull back methodically, their movements disciplined, firing in short bursts to cover each other's retreat. The IDF sensed the withdrawal and pressed harder, but Khaled's men held their ground, using the buildings and overturned vehicles for cover. Tariq fired, watching as another IDF soldier darted behind a tree, the bullet missing him by inches and splintering the bark into jagged fragments.

The fighters reached the waiting vehicles, piling inside with hurried efficiency. Khaled grabbed the radio again, his tone firm and commanding. *"Last units, board the pickups!"*

The fighters scrambled into the vehicles, engines roaring to life as the convoy started to pull away. Tariq and Khaled climbed into the last pickup, still firing as they withdrew, the sound of gunfire mingling with the deafening roar of engines. Dust and debris billowed behind them as the convoy sped off, tyres kicking up a storm of grit.

The sharp staccato of gunfire faded into the distance, replaced by the steady thrum of engines and the pounding of their hearts. The kibbutz, now a smouldering battlefield marked by the ruins of shattered homes and charred bodies, grew smaller in the rear-view mirror - a bleak reminder of the devastation they had wrought.

Ahmed's voice crackled through the radio once more, steady but tense. *"Well done, both of you. Get back here quickly."*

Khaled nodded at Tariq, a brief nod of acknowledgement passing between them. They had held the line just long enough, but both knew it was a temporary victory. The real fight was far from over.

As the convoy sped towards Gaza, dust hung thick in the air, mingling with the fading echoes of the battle, a grim harbinger of the violence that still loomed ahead.

The missions had converged, each unit completing their brutal tasks with ruthless efficiency. Radios buzzed incessantly with reports and orders, a chaotic symphony of victory and destruction. Ahmed listened to the final transmissions, his voice calm but unwaveringly resolute. *"Regroup on Route 232. We hold here until further orders. Today, we have made our mark. Prepare for what comes next."*

The fighters, bloodied but triumphant, began their retreat, knowing they had struck fear deep into the heart of their enemies. Eyes hardened and faces smeared with dirt and sweat, they moved with the grim satisfaction of a mission completed. The battlefield bore the scars of their assault - smouldering wreckage, shattered homes, and the cries of the broken.

As the sun climbed higher, casting long shadows over the devastation, the smoke from the kibbutz and the festival site merged, swirling together in a thick, dark plume. It rose ominously into the sky like a signal fire of war - a stark reminder of the terror they had unleashed and the chaos that still smouldered in their wake.

Chapter Forty Four

YOSSI

Yossi and Nadav pulled into Tel Aviv as the late afternoon sun dipped toward the horizon, casting a warm, golden hue over the city. Their *David* jeep rolled up to the entrance of the military base, where they parked with a final lurch. As the engine cut out, both exhaled deeply, feeling a fleeting sense of relief as the tensions of the day began to melt away.

They stepped out of the jeep, stretching their weary limbs, taking a moment to breathe in the salty air of the coastline. Yossi looked around, catching sight of Yael and Leila approaching, their faces lighting up as they drew nearer. Yael waved excitedly, her smile wide, while Leila followed with a look of quiet joy.

Yossi and Nadav grinned, their exhaustion momentarily forgotten. They embraced the two women, feeling the comfort of being together again, even if only for a short time.

"At last, a break!" Yael exclaimed, a playful sparkle in her eyes. *"I thought they'd never let you go."*

Leila laughed softly, her arm wrapped around Nadav. *"We've got plans,"* she said. *"A whole week to relax and enjoy ourselves."*

With a shared glance, they all piled into Yael's car, leaving the *David* jeep behind at the base. As they drove away, the familiar sights of Tel Aviv, bathed in the warm glow of the setting sun, seemed to promise a brief escape from the realities they had faced.

The group arrived at a beachfront restaurant they frequented, a cosy spot where the waves lapped gently against the shore just a few metres away. The atmosphere was light and welcoming, a stark contrast to the intensity of their duties on the Lebanese border. They settled at a table with a perfect view of the sea, the rhythmic sound of the water offering a soothing backdrop. Over plates of freshly grilled fish and glasses of wine, they talked about everything and nothing - future trips, favourite beach spots, and the joy of simply being together.

For now, it felt as if the world outside their bubble didn't exist. No duties, no threats - just the quiet companionship of those they cared for.

Later, back at their apartment, Yossi and Yael continued to talk late into the night. They made plans for the holiday - trips to the countryside, lazy mornings by the sea, catching up on lost time. The world outside seemed distant and almost unreal, they felt alive and free, savouring each other's company. The week stretched ahead of them like a promise - a rare chance to unwind, to breathe deeply, to forget, even if only for a moment, the weight of their responsibilities.

The following morning, just as the first light of dawn began to filter through the curtains, the shrill wail of air raid sirens shattered the stillness. Yossi jolted awake, adrenaline immediately surging through his body. He leapt out of bed and rushed to the window. His eyes widened as he saw multiple rocket trails arcing across the sky, followed by the distant booms of explosions somewhere in the city.

"Yael!" he called urgently. *"Get up! We're under attack!"*

Within moments, he had his phone in hand, dialling Nadav. *"Nadav, did you hear that? Meet me at the base. We need to find out what's going on."*

"On my way," came Nadav's tense but steady reply.

Yael was already pulling on her clothes. *"I'll drive you,"* she said. *"Let's get moving."*

They hurried out of the apartment and were soon joined by Leila and Nadav, who arrived moments later. There was fear in their eyes, but also determination. Yael drove Yossi to the military base, her hands gripping the steering wheel tightly. Leila did the same with Nadav in the car behind them.

When they reached the base, the scene was chaotic. Soldiers were running, vehicles revving, and the sound of distant explosions filled the air. Yossi and Nadav leapt out of the cars, quickly scanning for anyone who could provide some information.

"What's happening?" Yossi demanded of the first officer he encountered.

The reply was hurried and vague. *"Reports are still coming in... The Erez Crossing is under attack, but that's all we know at the moment. Communications are a mess."*

Yossi's expression tightened. *"We need ammunition and gear,"* he said, turning to Nadav. *"Let's see what we can do."*

They quickly geared up, strapping on vests, grabbing their rifles, and checking for ammunition. They knew they might be walking into a dangerous situation, but standing by was not an option. As they prepared, they turned to Yael and Leila, who were standing just outside the armoury, watching them with worried eyes.

Yossi stepped over to Yael, his face softening for a moment. He pulled her into a tight embrace. *"Stay safe,"* he whispered. *"We'll be back soon, I promise."*

Yael nodded, her voice choked with emotion. *"Just... come back to me."*

Nearby, Nadav hugged Leila tightly. *"Look after each other. We'll sort this out and be back soon."*

With a final glance at the women they loved, Yossi and Nadav turned back to their jeep. The time was 07:30. The sun was already climbing higher in the sky, and they knew they had no time to waste.

As Yossi and Nadav drove toward the Erez Crossing in their *David* jeep, the scene around them became increasingly chaotic. Cars and trucks sped past in the opposite direction, headlights flashing, horns blaring - a frenzied exodus of civilians desperate to escape whatever horror lay ahead. Yossi tightened his grip on the steering wheel, his jaw clenched as he navigated through the growing tide of vehicles.

Nadav, sitting beside him, had his phone pressed to his ear, speaking urgently. *"Yael, what else can you find out?"* he asked, his voice strained with worry. He listened intently, nodding at her response, then glanced at Yossi. *"She's putting us through to Samir at the Intelligence unit. He might have more information."*

Moments later, a new voice crackled through the line - Samir's voice, tense and hurried. *"Nadav, Yossi, listen carefully. The Erez Crossing has been breached. We're looking at a full-scale assault. There are reports of numerous casualties... it's a mess."*

Yossi exchanged a glance with Nadav, the weight of the news sinking in. *"How many?"* he asked, his voice firm but low.

"We don't have exact numbers yet," Samir replied, his tone grim. *"But it's bad... very bad. And it's not just the crossing. We're getting reports of heavy fighting near Sderot. It seems like they're pushing further in."*

Yossi nodded, his decision immediate. *"We're heading there now."*

Samir's voice came back sharply. *"Be careful. We're still piecing things together, but it's chaos out there. Watch your backs."*

"Understood," Nadav replied before ending the call. He turned to Yossi, who was already accelerating, weaving around the vehicles still streaming away from the border. *"Did you hear that?"* Nadav asked, his voice steady despite the urgency. *"Sderot's under attack too."*

Yossi nodded. *"I heard. We'll check it out. If they've breached the crossing, they'll be trying to move deeper. We need to find out what's happening."*

As they neared the outskirts of Sderot, the sound of intense fighting reached their ears - distant gunfire, the sharp crack of rifle shots, and the deeper thud of explosions. Smoke billowed on the horizon, and the air was thick with tension and the acrid smell of burning.

Nadav scanned the area ahead. *"It sounds like a war zone,"* he muttered, his eyes narrowing as he spotted plumes of smoke rising above the rooftops.

Yossi nodded, his focus unwavering. *"It is a war zone. Stay alert. We're going in."*

They continued to push forward, the sounds of battle growing louder with each passing second, the stakes becoming clearer with every turn of the wheel.

Yossi and Nadav brought their *David* jeep to a sudden halt, the engine purring softly as they took in the scene ahead. The narrow road leading to the cluster of houses was strewn with debris, and the acrid stench of smoke filled their nostrils. They exchanged a quick glance, fully aware that this vehicle might be their only way out.

"Let's leave it here," Yossi murmured, his voice steady. *"We might need it later."*

Nadav nodded in agreement. *"Weapons ready,"* he said, double-checking his rifle and ensuring he had enough ammunition. Yossi did the same, and they quickly disembarked from the jeep, moving swiftly but cautiously toward the sounds of gunfire and shouting that filled the air.

The sharp crack of automatic gunfire echoed off the walls of the houses, mingling with the shouts of the attackers and the cries of terrified civilians. They could see the flickering flames through the smoke, houses already ablaze, sending plumes of thick black smoke into the clear sky.

They came upon the body of a civilian sprawled lifelessly on the ground, clothes soaked with dark red stains - a stark reminder of the chaos unfolding. Yossi's jaw tightened, and he exchanged another look with Nadav. No words were needed - they both knew what had to be done.

Ahead, they spotted a group of Hamas fighters, clearly identifiable by their distinctive gear. One of them was perched atop a white pickup truck, his camouflage uniform caked in dirt and sweat. His eyes were fixed intently on the houses he was firing into. A green headband bearing Arabic script was tied around his forehead, marking his allegiance to the Izz ad-Din al-Qassam Brigades. The fighter manned a PKM machine gun mounted on a tripod, sending a relentless stream of bullets into the buildings, showing no mercy.

"That's our target," Yossi whispered, his voice barely audible over the din.

The pickup was flanked by more fighters, each similarly dressed in camouflage and balaclavas, their green headbands stark against the smoke and ash. Yossi and Nadav quickly took cover behind a low wall, assessing the situation.

"We need to take out the truck first," Yossi said quietly. *"On my count... ready?"*

Nadav gave a brief nod. *"Ready."*

"Three... two... one... Now!" Yossi commanded.

They sprang into action, rifles raised. Yossi took aim at the fighter on the truck, his finger squeezing the trigger with practised precision. The shot rang out, and the fighter staggered back, struck squarely in the chest. He fell, his grip on the PKM loosening as he crumpled to the ground. Nadav followed up with quick, precise shots, taking down two more fighters who were caught off guard by the sudden attack.

With the machine gun silenced, Yossi and Nadav pressed their advantage. They moved from cover to cover, keeping low and using the terrain to their benefit, firing methodically and pushing the militants back.

"Keep moving!" Yossi urged. *"Don't let them regroup."*

The remaining fighters, realising the attack had turned against them, began to retreat, firing sporadically as they pulled back. Yossi and Nadav advanced, hearts pounding but focus unwavering, driving the attackers further away from the civilian homes.

As the militants vanished into the distance, Yossi and Nadav paused briefly, taking in the scene around them. They knew they had only moments to catch their breath - the fight was far from over.

They moved swiftly, the acrid smell of burning wood and plastic filling their nostrils as they navigated through the chaos. The crackle of flames consumed the air, accompanied by the occasional distant pop of small-arms fire. The taste of smoke coated Yossi's mouth, and he could feel the grit of ash settling on his tongue, mixing with the sweat dripping down his face. His heart was pounding in his chest, a rhythm matched by the adrenaline coursing through his veins.

Yossi glanced over at Nadav, his eyes narrowed in concentration. *"Nadav, find a high point. We need overwatch,"* he said, his voice steady but urgent. *"Keep an eye out in case those bastards come back."*

Nadav nodded, scanning the nearby structures. *"Got it,"* he replied, spotting a house with a flat roof that would give him a decent view of the area. *"I'll get up there."*

Yossi watched as Nadav clambered up the side of the house, using the window ledges and a drainpipe to pull himself up. He kept his rifle slung over his shoulder until he reached the roof, then immediately dropped to a prone position, eyes scanning the terrain. From his vantage point, he could see the flicker of movement further down the road, shadows flitting between the trees.

"Keep your eyes open," Yossi muttered to himself as he approached the first house. The door was slightly open, swaying gently in the smoky breeze. He pushed it open slowly, the creak of the hinges echoing in the stillness. Inside, the air was thick with dust and the scent of burnt wood. He could feel his skin prickling with sweat, the coolness of the house a sharp contrast to the heat outside.

His boots crunched on broken glass as he made his way through the living room, eyes darting from corner to corner, his senses on high alert. The house was eerily silent, but he could sense that people were hiding somewhere within. Moving cautiously, Yossi followed a hallway to a reinforced door, the kind used for safe rooms. He could hear muffled whispers behind it, the sound of frightened breathing.

He raised his voice just enough to be heard. *"IDF! It's safe to come out!"* he called, his tone firm but reassuring.

For a moment, there was no response. Then, slowly, the door cracked open, and a man's face appeared, eyes wide with fear. He glanced quickly at Yossi, scanning his uniform, the realisation dawning.

"We need to go, now," Yossi instructed. *"Are there any weapons in there?"*

The man nodded, his voice shaky. *"Yes, I'm former IDF... we've got a couple of handguns, some ammo."*

"Good," Yossi said, giving a curt nod. *"Get them and get your family out. We need to move quickly."*

The man disappeared back behind the door for a moment before returning with a rucksack, his wife and three children nervously stepping out behind him. The children's eyes were wide, and the woman clutched them close, her face pale with terror.

Yossi led them toward the door, glancing back outside and shouting up to Nadav. *"All clear?"*

Nadav, lying flat on the roof, his rifle trained down the road, called back, *"For now, but I see movement about a kilometre away. Looks like they're regrouping."*

Yossi turned to the man. *"Start clearing out the other houses. Get everyone out of their safe rooms and bring them here. Keep them behind cover,"* he ordered, his voice taut with urgency.

The man nodded, a look of determination replacing his fear. *"Understood,"* he replied, rushing towards the next house, his family following closely behind.

Yossi could feel his pulse racing, the tension in the air thick enough to taste. He glanced up at Nadav again, his mind racing. Every second counted, and he knew they had to get as many civilians out as they could before those fighters returned.

Nadav, he called out, *stay sharp. This isn't over yet.*

Nadav's response came back quickly, *"I'm on it, Yossi. I'll let you know the moment they get closer."*

Yossi nodded, his senses heightened, every sound, every movement becoming more acute. The calm before the storm was over, now, they had to act swiftly if they wanted to save lives.

Yossi moved over to the white pickup where they had taken out the gunner and carefully inspected the weapon mounted on the back. It was a PKM machine gun, belt-fed with linked ammunition, perfect for sustained fire. He found several belts of ammo still in the vehicle, each one loaded with over a hundred rounds. He quickly unhooked the weapon from its mount, bundled up the belts of linked ammo, and slung them over his shoulder. Nearby, he checked the fallen fighter's backpack and discovered even more ammunition, along with a few grenades. Grabbing the backpack, he hurried back to where Nadav was keeping watch.

He called up to Nadav, shouting, *"Present for you!"* as he tossed the PKM and the belts of ammo up to him.

Nadav caught the weapon with a grin. *"Now you're talking!"* he replied, a new edge of confidence in his voice. The weight of the machine gun felt reassuring in his hands, and he quickly set it up on his vantage point, the linked ammo belt ready to feed through the weapon. *"Let them try now,"* he muttered to himself, scanning the area for any movement.

Yossi watched as Nadav settled back into position on the roof, the PKM now at the ready. His friend looked steadier, more prepared for what was to come.

By this time, the former IDF soldier Yossi had sent to clear out the other houses returned, leading a small group of about fifteen civilians. They huddled together, their faces a mix of fear and hope.

Yossi quickly assessed the group, his eyes falling on a few who seemed to be carrying something. *"Anyone have any spare 5.56mm ammo for my M4?"* he asked. Two men nodded, and he gestured for them to hand it over. Yossi had a gut feeling that this day would be far from over, and he needed as many magazines as possible, both for himself and for Nadav.

As the men passed over the additional magazines, Yossi turned to the first man he had met, the former IDF soldier. *"Get these people into cars, and take them out of here,"* he instructed, quickly explaining the safest route out of the area.

The man nodded, understanding the urgency. But before they could move, the sharp crack of gunfire filled the air. Bullets whizzed past them, hitting the walls and the ground around them. Nadav immediately returned fire, the PKM roaring to life in short, controlled bursts, the belt-fed rounds spitting out with a heavy, metallic rhythm. Each burst sent casings clattering to the ground, and the distinctive smell of gunpowder filled the air.

"Go, now!" Yossi shouted at the group, motioning for them to get moving. Nadav's bursts kept the attackers' heads down, buying the civilians precious seconds to get to their vehicles.

Nadav, his eyes fixed on the distance, muttered under his breath, *"Come on, show yourselves."* He kept sweeping the area with the PKM, ready to unleash another volley the moment he spotted any movement.

Yossi felt the tension in the air, every sense heightened - the acrid taste of dust and cordite on his tongue, the echoing crack of each shot, the sweat beading on his forehead despite the morning chill. He could hear his own heartbeat thundering in his chest, could feel the weight of every decision pressing on him. But he pushed the thoughts aside. They had to get these people to safety, and they had to survive.

As the cars began to move, he shouted up to Nadav, *"Keep them covered until they're clear!"*

Nadav nodded, still scanning the horizon. *"I've got them,"* he replied, his voice steady. He squeezed the trigger again, sending another burst of linked rounds downrange, each shot a reminder that they were still in the fight.

As the vehicles carrying the civilians roared away, the sound of their engines gradually fading, Yossi and Nadav remained vigilant, their eyes scanning the immediate area. Yossi crouched low behind a crumbling wall, his senses alive with the tension of the moment. He could hear the faint rustle of movement ahead - footsteps crunching on gravel, the faint murmur of voices in Arabic. The enemy was regrouping, and he knew they wouldn't stay hidden for long.

A sharp whistle cut through the air. Nadav, from his elevated position, called down, *"Yossi! Left side, they're moving up!"*

Yossi glanced left, just in time to see a group of fighters attempting to flank them, creeping along the edges of a dilapidated house. The fighters were using the sparse cover of trees and debris to advance. He could see the flashes of green headbands and the dark shapes of weapons in their hands. His heart pounded in his chest, the weight of the moment pressing down on him. But his training kicked in.

"I see them!" Yossi shouted back, quickly raising his M4 Carbine and taking aim. He squeezed off several precise single shots, the weapon's recoil sending vibrations through his shoulder. Each shot rang out with a sharp crack, echoing off the surrounding walls. One of the fighters dropped instantly, then another. The others hesitated, ducking back into cover.

Nadav laid down a burst of suppressing fire from the PKM, the rapid clatter of the belt-fed rounds hammering through the air like a drumbeat. The smell of burnt powder filled Yossi's nostrils, acrid and thick. *"I'm keeping them pinned!"* Nadav yelled, his voice hoarse from shouting.

Yossi nodded, even though Nadav couldn't see him. *"Good! Keep it up!"* he replied, glancing quickly to his right. He spotted another group trying to move through the narrow alleyways, sneaking up to their flank. He pivoted, adjusting his aim. He steadied his breathing, his finger resting lightly on the trigger. The taste of dust was on his lips, the air heavy with tension and the distant scent of burning.

"Three more on the right!" Nadav called out from above, his voice urgent but controlled.

"Copy that!" Yossi responded, switching targets with fluid precision. He aimed carefully, sighting down the barrel, and squeezed the trigger. Another fighter fell, and then another. *"Two down!"* he shouted.

Nadav's gun barked again, the sound almost deafening in the close quarters. Brass casings flew from the PKM, clinking against the concrete roof tiles, a steady rhythm in the chaos. *"We've got this,"* Nadav muttered to himself, his focus unwavering. *"Just hold them."*

The firefight dragged on, the air thick with smoke and the acrid smell of gunpowder. Yossi felt the sweat running down his back, trickling uncomfortably beneath his body armour. His mouth was dry, his muscles tense, but he stayed focused, his eyes darting from one potential threat to another.

"Yossi, they're falling back!" Nadav shouted suddenly, his tone a mixture of surprise and relief.

Yossi risked a quick glance over the wall and saw it too - the fighters were pulling back, retreating toward the deeper part of Sderot. White pickups began to appear, screeching to a halt, and the fighters clambered in, their shouts of frustration and anger barely audible over the roar of the engines.

"They're moving out!" Yossi yelled, his voice strained but firm.

"Yeah, I see it," Nadav called back. *"Let's keep an eye on them. Don't let them regroup!"*

Yossi nodded, watching as the pickups sped away, dust kicking up in their wake. His hands trembled slightly from the adrenaline, the weight of the M4 now feeling heavier in his grip. He took a deep breath, trying to steady himself, the taste of fear still lingering in his mouth. *"Stay sharp,"* he murmured, half to himself, half to Nadav.

Nadav nodded from his rooftop position, his eyes still scanning the horizon. *"They might come back,"* he warned, his voice a low growl. *"But they know we're here now. That might make them think twice."*

Yossi gave a short nod, wiping the sweat from his brow with the back of his hand. *"Yeah... or they might just come back harder,"* he replied grimly.

The air was still thick with tension, but for the moment, the street was quiet again. The battle wasn't over, but they had won this round.

The sounds of gunfire echoed through the streets, a chaotic mix of sharp cracks and deeper, booming reports. Yossi and Nadav exchanged a glance, their faces set with determination. Nadav's ears perked up at a distinct sound among the barrage - familiar, almost comforting in its familiarity. *"That's 5.56,"* he muttered, recognising the calibre of IDF weapons. *"Could be some of ours nearby."*

Yossi nodded, tightening his grip on his M4. *"We need to move,"* he called out to Nadav. *"Get back in the vehicle, we'll head toward the sound."*

With swift, precise movements, they climbed back into the David jeep, the vehicle's engine rumbling to life beneath them. They moved cautiously, navigating through the narrow streets, the distant sound of gunfire growing louder with each passing second. As they approached the area where the shooting was most intense, Yossi brought the jeep to a halt. *"This is close enough,"* he said, turning to Nadav. *"We go on foot from here."*

They exited the vehicle and began to advance, keeping to cover, moving through the shadowed alleyways. The smell of gunpowder hung heavily in the air, mingling with the scent of smoke and the acrid stench of burning rubber. Yossi's heart pounded in his chest, but he focused on the mission, on the sounds guiding them closer to the fight.

As they approached, they spotted a group of Hamas fighters. Yossi signalled to Nadav, and they moved into position, Nadav setting up with the PKM, while Yossi found cover with a better view of the fighters. *"On my count,"* Yossi whispered, and Nadav nodded, his eyes never leaving his sights.

"Now!" Yossi shouted, and they sprang into action. Nadav laid down a burst of suppressive fire, the PKM chattering loudly, short, controlled bursts to avoid wasting precious ammo. Yossi took aim, picking off the fighters one by one with well-placed shots. He could see the panic set in among the enemy, their movements becoming frantic and uncoordinated.

"Yossi! One on the truck!" Nadav shouted as a gunner mounted on a pickup truck began firing in Yossi's direction. Yossi ducked down, feeling the impact of rounds hitting the wall behind him, plaster and dust filling the air. *"Cover me!"* Yossi yelled, shifting to a new position.

Nadav adjusted his aim and squeezed the trigger, his bullets striking the gunner squarely in the chest. The gunner slumped over, and one of Nadav's rounds pierced the fuel tank. A moment later, the truck erupted in flames, sending a plume of black smoke into the sky. The remaining fighters, seeing their support vehicle ablaze, began retreating once more.

Yossi took the chance to call out. *"IDF! IDF! Hold your fire!"* he shouted in Hebrew, his voice carrying over the crackling flames.

From behind a barricade, a voice responded, shaky but relieved. *"IDF here!"* Yossi moved towards the voice, keeping his weapon raised, signalling Nadav to follow.

They moved cautiously toward the group and found six IDF reservists, their faces pale, eyes wide with fear and exhaustion.

Yossi immediately took charge, his tone firm but reassuring. *"You're under our orders now. You follow what we say, and we'll get through this. Understood?"*

The reservists nodded, clearly relieved to see them. Yossi began checking their weapons, noting their anxious expressions. *"Count your ammo!"* he ordered. *"Do you have any more stashed nearby?"*

"About 300 rounds between us," one of the reservists replied, his voice shaky.

Yossi nodded, quickly doing his own check. He and Nadav still had enough to hold their own for now. *"Nadav, what's your status?"* Yossi asked, turning to his friend.

Nadav glanced up from his position, still watching the surroundings carefully. *"Used about 25 rounds from my M4 so far. Full belt on the PKM and eight grenades left."*

Yossi nodded, feeling the weight of the situation but remaining composed. *"We've got enough for now,"* he said, looking back at the reservists. *"Stay close, keep your heads down, and follow my lead. We need to move, find better cover, and get an idea of what we're facing."*

The reservists nodded, determination slowly replacing their fear. Yossi felt a spark of hope - small, but enough to keep him moving forward.

They moved cautiously, keeping to the shadows, eyes darting around for any signs of movement. Every sound seemed louder, every shadow more ominous, but they pressed on. They had people to save, and they weren't going to stop until every last civilian was out of harm's way.

Yossi quickly began issuing orders to the reservists. *"Alright, listen up,"* he said firmly, *"I want you to split into pairs. Start going through these houses and check for survivors. Make sure you check the safe rooms in each one. Announce yourselves as IDF, we don't want anyone mistaking you for the enemy. Bring anyone you find back here and stay low. Use cover and be quick. Nadav and I will provide overwatch."*

The reservists nodded, their fear replaced by determination, and immediately set off in pairs, moving from house to house, cautiously keeping to the shadows and using walls and debris as cover. Yossi took a moment to catch his breath and decided it was time to call Samir at the Intelligence unit. His fingers fumbled slightly as he dialled, the weight of the situation pressing heavily on his shoulders.

The phone rang twice before Samir's voice came through, tense and hurried. *"Yossi? What's your status?"*

"We've managed to get a few civilians out," Yossi reported. *"Hamas fighters are all over Sderot, and we're trying to clear a path for any more we find. What's the situation like on your end? And do you need us anywhere specific?"*

Samir's voice was grim. *"It's bad, Yossi. A massive attack all along the border. Many Kibbutzim have been overrun, and we're receiving reports of high casualties. Proceed with extreme caution, we don't know the full extent of their plan yet."*

Yossi felt a cold chill despite the heat. *"Understood. We'll keep moving civilians out as we can. Keep me updated if there's anything specific we need to know."*

Yossi took a deep breath. *"Understood. But, Samir, I need you to do something for me."*

"What is it?" Samir asked, urgency in his tone.

"Get a message to Yael and Leila. Tell them Nadav and I are fine, that we're helping out where we can. Tell them not to worry," Yossi said, his voice softer now, a brief moment of vulnerability slipping through.

There was a moment of silence before Samir responded, *"I'll get the message to them. Stay safe out there, Yossi."*

"Thanks, Samir," Yossi replied, feeling a slight weight lift from his chest. *"And keep me posted if you get any new intel."*

He ended the call and turned to Nadav, who had kept his eyes trained on the streets. *"Samir says it's huge - Hamas has hit multiple locations along the border. High casualties, Kibbutzim overrun. We're in the middle of something big, Nadav."*

Nadav swore under his breath, his grip tightening on the PKM. *"We're not letting them take anyone else. We'll get these people out, and then we'll see where we're needed."*

While Nadav continued his watch, Yossi ducked into one of the nearby houses, moving quickly through the kitchen. He found a fridge and pulled out several bottles of water and some cold meats and snacks, enough to sustain them for a while. He returned to Nadav, tossing him a bottle. They drank thirstily, the cool water providing a momentary relief from the intense heat.

Moments later, the reservists returned, leading a group of about twenty civilians. Some were elderly, others were children, their faces pale and filled with fear. Yossi wasted no time. *"Get the children into the David,"* he ordered, *"squeeze them all in."*

Once the children were packed in, he turned to two of the reservists. *"Drive them back to the first safe location we secured earlier. One of you stays with the kids. The other, come back with the vehicle for more."*

The reservists nodded and sped off in the jeep, dust kicking up from its wheels. The rest of the group remained vigilant, eyes scanning for any sign of enemy movement.

Bit by bit, they repeated the process, extracting the remaining civilians in groups, moving them from cover to cover. The tension was palpable, every sound seemed louder, every shadow seemed to move. Yossi's heart pounded in his chest, and he could feel the weight of each step, the urgency in every move they made. Sweat dripped down his back despite the cooling breeze that occasionally swept through the streets of Sderot. Nadav, ever vigilant, kept his gaze fixed on the horizon, his finger resting lightly on the trigger of the PKM, ready to fire at any sign of trouble.

Finally, as the last group was loaded into the David jeep, Yossi and Nadav spotted an IDF convoy positioned along the road in the distance. Relief washed over them, but they knew their job wasn't done yet. *"Let's get moving,"* Yossi said, nodding towards the vehicles. *"We need to get these people to safety."*

They continued the extraction, guiding the civilians carefully through the chaotic streets of Sderot, past burning buildings and wrecked cars. The air was thick with the acrid smell of smoke and cordite, and the sounds of distant gunfire still echoed through the neighbourhood. Yossi felt every muscle in his body tense, his senses heightened to a razor's edge, his mind focused on getting them out alive.

Nadav covered their rear, his eyes constantly scanning for any movement, any sign of a new threat. He could feel the strain in his arms from holding the PKM at the ready, the heaviness of his breath as he tried to control his anxiety. Every now and then, he glanced over at Yossi, who was leading the group, his face set with determination.

Slowly but steadily, they made their way out of the heart of Sderot, weaving through alleyways and side streets, always keeping to cover. They moved quickly but carefully, aware that any wrong turn could expose them to more Hamas fighters. The civilians moved in frightened silence, their eyes wide with fear, their footsteps hurried and uncertain. Yossi and Nadav stayed close, whispering words of reassurance, urging them forward.

As they moved, Yossi noticed shadows flitting in the periphery of his vision. He halted, scanning the area. *"Nadav, they're tracking us,"* he muttered under his breath.

Nadav nodded, his gaze shifting to where Yossi had pointed. *"I see them,"* he replied quietly. *"Keep moving. I've got this."*

Nadav swung his weapon around, aiming in the direction of the shadows, and fired a quick burst. The rounds cracked through the air, echoing off the nearby buildings. He saw movement - a few fighters ducking down, keeping low, trying to avoid his line of fire. He fired again, short, controlled bursts, keeping the pressure on them. The Hamas fighters kept their heads down, staying out of sight, reluctant to advance under his steady fire.

"Yossi, go!" Nadav shouted, his voice strained but determined. *"I'll hold them off."*

Yossi nodded and pushed the group forward, moving them faster, hearing the staccato bursts from Nadav's PKM behind him. He knew they had to keep going, to reach safety. The sound of gunfire grew louder, more intense, as Nadav kept up his suppressing fire, preventing the fighters from advancing on them.

After what felt like an eternity, they finally cleared the outskirts of Sderot. The sounds of battle grew fainter, replaced by the quieter, more distant sounds of the countryside. Yossi and Nadav could see the nervous relief on the faces of the civilians, some of whom began to whisper prayers of thanks.

They pushed on a little further until they came across a place of relative safety - a cluster of buildings that had remained untouched, and beyond them, an IDF unit positioned in a defensive line. The soldiers there were setting up checkpoints, their weapons drawn, eyes scanning for any further threats.

Yossi waved to the soldiers, who quickly recognised them and began moving forward to assist. He turned back to Nadav, a weary but relieved grin spreading across his face. *"We made it,"* he said, his voice edged with exhaustion but also triumph.

Nadav nodded, wiping the sweat from his brow, still keeping his weapon at the ready. *"Let's get these people over to the unit,"* he replied. *"Then we can see what they need us to do next."*

They led the civilians towards the IDF soldiers, who immediately took them in, offering water and medical attention. Yossi could feel the tension in his body begin to ease, but he knew this was just one part of a much larger battle. For now, they had done what they could.

But he also knew that whatever lay ahead, they would face it together, just as they always had.

Yossi took a deep breath, feeling the weight of the day settle on his shoulders, and prepared himself for whatever would come next.

As Yossi and Nadav sat to one side, gulping down water and catching their breath, the adrenaline of the morning's firefight still coursing through their veins, a woman approached them. Her face bore the marks of exhaustion and fear, but her eyes held a glimmer of gratitude. She paused for a moment, reading the nametags on their fatigues.

Segen Rosenberg, Samal Levy, she said, her voice steady despite the tremor of relief that undercut it. *"We can't thank you both enough for saving our families. This... this will not be forgotten."*

Yossi glanced at Nadav, feeling a sudden flush of embarrassment. The unexpected recognition caught them both off guard. The weight of her words felt heavy, almost too much to bear after everything they had just been through. They had been trained to act, to save lives, to fight when necessary - but not to receive praise like this.

Nadav gave a sheepish smile, his hand instinctively reaching up to rub the back of his neck. *"It's, uh, it's what we're here for,"* he managed to reply, his voice awkwardly humble.

Yossi nodded in agreement, though he could feel a tightness in his chest. *"We're just glad we could help,"* he added quietly.

Before either of them could say more, the woman reached out and pulled them both into a tight, grateful hug. For a moment, neither Yossi nor Nadav knew what to do. They stood there, somewhat stiffly, feeling the warmth of her embrace, feeling the raw emotion she poured into that simple gesture.

After a moment, she stepped back, tears glistening in her eyes. *"Thank you,"* she whispered again, her voice breaking slightly.

Yossi and Nadav exchanged a glance - both feeling a mix of pride and discomfort. They hadn't done it for the thanks, and yet, standing here, with a stranger's arms wrapped around them in gratitude, they felt the weight of what they had achieved settle in a different way.

"It's okay," Yossi finally said, finding his voice. "You're safe now. That's what matters."

The woman nodded, giving them one last grateful look before she turned away, rejoining the other civilians who were now receiving help from the IDF unit.

Yossi and Nadav watched her go, still feeling the unexpected warmth of her appreciation.

For a moment, they were silent, both lost in their own thoughts. Then Nadav chuckled softly. *"Guess we made quite the impression, huh?"*

Yossi smirked, shaking his head. *"Yeah, I suppose we did,"* he replied. *"Let's just hope we can keep making them."*

Nadav raised his water bottle in a mock toast. *"To making impressions,"* he said with a grin.

Yossi clinked his own bottle against Nadav's, a small smile spreading across his face. *"To making it through today,"* he corrected, and they both took another long drink, the taste of dust and adrenaline slowly being washed away.

After replenishing their ammunition from the IDF unit, Yossi and Nadav wasted no time. It was still early afternoon, and they were determined to keep pushing forward. The air was hot and heavy, thick with the acrid smell of smoke and the distant sounds of sporadic gunfire. The reality of what lay ahead sharpened their focus as they prepared to engage with the enemy again.

With a few additional IDF soldiers for support and a truck ready to evacuate any civilians they found, they set off once more, navigating through the war-torn streets of Sderot. The truck followed closely, its engine growling low as they pressed deeper into the town. As they moved, they remained alert, scanning the ruins and debris for any signs of life or movement.

The first engagement came quickly. They spotted a group of Hamas fighters trying to regroup, likely searching for more targets. Nadav laid down suppressive fire with the PKM machine gun, forcing the fighters to duck for cover. Yossi flanked to the left, moving between the burnt-out shells of cars and rubble, picking off the fighters with precise, controlled shots.

Their training and coordination shone through, they communicated with short, sharp phrases, their movements fluid and practised. *"On your left, Nadav!"* Yossi shouted as a fighter emerged from behind a wall. Nadav turned and fired a short burst, the rounds hitting their mark.

The firefight lasted only minutes, but it felt like hours. Eventually, the remaining fighters retreated, leaving behind a trail of chaos. Yossi and Nadav wasted no time and quickly began searching the nearby houses. They found several civilians, huddled in fear, and led them to the waiting truck.

They continued this pattern throughout the afternoon - engaging with enemy fighters when necessary, moving quickly from house to house, calling out to survivors, and guiding them to safety. Each time they rescued a group of civilians, Yossi felt a mix of relief and urgency. Every life saved was a victory, but he knew there were still many more who needed help.

As they reached the outskirts of another cluster of houses, the smell of smoke was thicker, more pungent. The cries of frightened civilians echoed around them, mixed with the crackle of gunfire. Yossi led the group cautiously, hand raised to signal quiet. *"Stay close,"* he whispered to Nadav, who nodded, eyes scanning the surroundings.

They moved swiftly, Nadav providing overwatch while Yossi and the IDF soldiers cleared houses. They found another group of civilians, terrified and huddled together in a small room. Yossi spoke calmly, *"We're IDF. We're getting you out."* Slowly, they coaxed them out of hiding, reassuring them as they moved them toward the truck.

As the day wore on and the shadows grew longer, they made several more trips, repeating the process, encountering pockets of resistance along the way. Each time, they engaged with the enemy fighters, using the element of surprise and their knowledge of the terrain to their advantage.

By the time the sun dipped low on the horizon, they had rescued over 150 civilians. The town of Sderot was quieter now, but the tension in the air remained thick. The Hamas fighters had been pushed back, but Yossi and Nadav knew they weren't gone.

With the last group of civilians safely loaded into the truck, Yossi and Nadav finally paused to catch their breath. They could hear the distant sounds of IDF units engaging along Route 232. They exchanged a glance, knowing they had done all they could for now.

Suddenly, an IDF officer appeared, ordering them to stand down. *"You've done enough today,"* he said, his tone both stern and grateful. *"We've heard about what you two have done. Thank you."*

Yossi nodded, fatigue starting to set in. He glanced at Nadav, who looked equally exhausted but still alert. *"Let's get back to Tel Aviv,"* Yossi said.

As Nadav drove, Yossi called Yael, who was with Leila. *"We're safe,"* he said, relief evident in his voice. *"We're on our way back... see you soon."*

Chapter Forty Five

AHMED

As the first rockets launched from Gaza at 6:30 AM, Salma awoke to the sharp, ear-splitting whoosh of outgoing missiles tearing through the dawn sky. The sound was different this time - louder, more deliberate, like the city itself was roaring into the air. The concussive blasts that followed echoed across the buildings, rattling the windows of her small flat and jolting her upright in bed. Her heart pounded against her ribs as she realised that this was not the usual sporadic fire she had grown accustomed to - this was something different, something much bigger.

The whoosh of rockets leaving their launchers continued, rhythmic and relentless, shaking her to her core. Panic bubbled up in her chest. She had known this moment was coming, had sensed it in Ahmed's quiet intensity, in the tension that had seeped into their recent meetings. Yet now that it had begun, fear clenched her insides with a cold grip.

Salma rushed to the window, her breath quickening. Outside, the streets were already filled with people - neighbours stepping out of their homes, their faces a mix of confusion and dread. In the distance, she could hear the faint, rhythmic thud of more rockets launching, each one like a heartbeat pounding in her ears. She wrapped her arms around herself, feeling the prickle of sweat on her skin despite the early morning chill. Her eyes darted across the horizon, searching for any sign of what was to come next. The sky was streaked with smoke, dark and curling, as if the city itself was exhaling in fear.

Salma hesitated for a moment, torn between staying inside, hidden and safe, or stepping out into the unknown. She could feel the cold tiles beneath her feet, grounding her, pulling her in two directions. She knew she needed to see for herself, to understand. *What has Ahmed done? What is happening?* Her thoughts swirled like a storm, each one colliding with the next.

Steeling herself, she rushed out into the early morning light, the streets of Jabalia already alive with frenetic energy. The air was thick with the acrid smell of burning, a metallic tang that stung her nostrils and clung to her throat. The sky above was streaked with smoke from the rockets that had launched just moments ago, leaving a faint metallic taste on her tongue. Salma's heart pounded in her chest as she tried to make sense of the chaos unfolding around her.

People spilled out of their homes, gathering in small groups, their faces painted with a mixture of excitement and fear. Salma could hear snatches of conversations - hushed voices buzzing with speculation, trying to piece together what was happening. A young boy ran past her, clutching his mother's hand, his eyes wide with a mixture of awe and terror. An older woman, her face lined with years of hardship, muttered prayers under her breath, her hands trembling.

Salma moved through the crowd, trying to remain inconspicuous, to blend in as she made her way towards the marketplace. Her senses were overwhelmed - the cacophony of voices, the smell of sweat and smoke, the taste of dust in her mouth. She felt a knot of anxiety tighten in her stomach. She didn't know what she was looking for, only that she needed to understand, to see what was happening with her own eyes.

The sound of engines revving filled the air, and she turned to see a group of young men mounting motorbikes, their expressions set with grim determination. They wore makeshift uniforms - some in fatigues, others in civilian clothes with scarves wrapped around their faces. She heard one of them shout, *"For Gaza!"* before they sped off down the narrow streets, leaving a cloud of dust in their wake. Salma felt a shiver run down her spine as she watched them go, a part of her knowing they were heading towards the border, towards the fighting.

Around her, more men began to move with purpose. Some were loading themselves into battered pickup trucks, others clutching rifles, shouting to one another in a hurried frenzy. Salma caught fragments of their words - *"the breach," "the Israelis," "our chance."* There was an electricity in the air, a fervour that seemed to grip everyone around her. She realised with a sinking heart that many of these men, civilians only moments ago, were now heading to join the assault.

The hours stretched on, a haze of tension and waiting. The sun climbed higher in the sky, the heat intensifying, causing sweat to bead on Salma's brow. She wandered through the streets, feeling like a ghost amidst the hysteria building around her. She watched as women gathered in tight clusters, whispering nervously, some speaking in excited tones, sharing snippets of news that filtered back from the border. A rumour spread that the fighters had broken through, that they were bringing back hostages. Salma's heart sank, a wave of nausea washing over her.

She saw a few men, faces flushed with excitement, returning to the city on motorbikes, shouting to anyone who would listen, *"They've captured them! They're bringing them back!"* The crowd erupted in cheers, and Salma felt a surge of dread. She knew what this meant - there would be no peace, no safety. This was only the beginning.

As the sun began its slow descent, shadows lengthening on the dusty streets, the rumble of engines returned, louder this time, more vehicles than before. Salma's breath caught in her throat as she watched the first of the pickups appear, rolling into Jabalia like a wave. The crowd around her erupted into wild cheers, men and women shouting, waving flags, their faces alight with triumph. Jubilation spread like wildfire, transforming the streets into a chaotic celebration.

Faces glowed with exultation, hands raised in victory as the fighters paraded through. They hoisted their rifles high, some firing celebratory shots into the air. Salma saw young boys, barely more than children, grinning as they pumped their fists, their eyes wide with excitement. The crowd surged forward, reaching out as if to touch the victors, to absorb a piece of their triumph.

But then Salma's gaze shifted to the hostages.

Packed into the back of the pickups, their bodies hunched and trembling, were men, women, and children. They were tied, their hands bound behind their backs, eyes wide and hollow with fear. Blood streaked some of their faces, others had bruises blossoming across their skin. One woman, her hair matted and face streaked with dirt, sat crumpled against the side of a pickup, her shoulders shaking as she sobbed quietly, her mouth moving silently in what seemed to be a desperate prayer.

Another man, his face smeared with blood, clutched the stump of his arm, his eyes glazed with shock and pain. He sat slumped against the metal siding, his head lolling as if too heavy for his neck to support. A fighter leaned over him, grinning, his voice carrying mockingly over the roar of engines.

The man didn't respond, didn't even seem to register the words - only stared blankly into the crowd, his gaze unfocused, lost. Salma felt her stomach twist violently. The hostages' expressions of abject terror and resignation stood in stark contrast to the jubilant cheers surrounding them. It was a cruel contrast - their suffering feeding the crowd's sense of triumph, every sob and whimper drowned out by the roar of approval.

Then, amidst the chaos, she saw him.

Ahmed's pickup appeared, its engine growling as it rolled through the streets. In the back, armed fighters sat rigidly, rifles in hand, their faces set with grim determination. But it wasn't the fighters that drew Salma's attention. It was Ahmed himself, standing in the front, his gaze sweeping over the crowd.

For a moment, their eyes met.

Salma's heart clenched painfully as she looked into his face. For the briefest instant, a flicker of something - shame, perhaps - crossed his features. His eyes darkened, and he quickly looked away, the mask of detachment slipping back into place. She could see it - the weight of what he had done, the burden of his choices. But it was gone in an instant, buried beneath layers of resolve.

A wave of nausea surged through Salma as she took in the sight of him, standing tall in the vehicle, directing his men with an almost practised ease. The man she had known, the one she had thought she understood, was gone - replaced by this cold, calculating figure who seemed almost to revel in the chaos he had unleashed.

She watched as Ahmed turned sharply, speaking into the radio clipped to his vest, his voice carrying clearly over the din. *"Take them to the holding area. Separate the wounded - we need to evaluate their condition before the next stage."* He spoke with a calm authority that made Salma's blood run cold. These people - these hostages - were no longer human in his eyes. They were pieces on a board, assets to be used and discarded.

The fighters jumped down from the trucks, dragging the captives roughly out, ignoring their cries of pain and protest. The woman Salma had noticed earlier was pulled to her feet, her head bowed in defeat as she stumbled forward. Another hostage, a young girl with dark hair matted against her face, was yanked from the vehicle, her eyes wide with terror as she was shoved towards the group of fighters waiting nearby.

The crowd cheered wildly, surging forward as the hostages were paraded through the streets. Salma's heart pounded as she watched Ahmed turn his gaze back towards her. This time, there was no shame - only cold determination. He lifted his chin slightly, a silent command in his stance.

Do not intervene. Do not ask questions.

Salma felt a wave of revulsion so strong it almost made her stagger. Her vision swam for a moment, the bile rising in her throat as she struggled to breathe. This - *this* - was the man she had defended, the man she had believed in? The one she had argued for, time and time again, when others had whispered doubts about his methods. She had seen the idealist in him, the one who spoke of freedom and dignity for their people. But this? This was a stranger. A monster.

Ahmed's eyes lingered on her for a fraction of a second longer, and for a moment, she thought she saw something break in his gaze. But then he turned away, barking orders to his men, his expression hardening. The mask was back in place, the ruthless commander fully in control.

Salma watched, numb, as the hostages were herded away, their cries swallowed by the roar of the crowd. She wanted to scream, to shout at them to stop, to demand that they see what she saw. But the words caught in her throat, choked by the horror and helplessness that gripped her.

As the vehicles rolled forward, Salma stumbled back, her legs trembling. She felt hollow, empty, as if something inside her had shattered irreparably. The world around her seemed to blur, the triumphant shouts of the crowd and the low growl of engines fading into a distant roar. She had thought she understood what this war meant. She had thought she knew the cost.

But she hadn't. Not really.

Not until now.

The pickup carrying Ahmed began to pull away, the fighters still standing guard, their weapons held high. The crowd pressed closer, waving and cheering, their faces alight with fervour. Salma could only stand there, rooted to the spot, watching as the man she had once thought she knew disappeared into the dust and chaos.

She realised, with a sickening certainty, that whatever part of him had once been redeemable, whatever glimmer of the man she had known, was gone. Buried beneath layers of bloodshed and vengeance.

Salma turned away, bile rising in her throat. She stumbled through the crowd, her breath coming in shallow gasps, her vision blurred. She felt as if the ground were shifting beneath her feet, the world tilting on its axis. *What have we become?* she thought, a wave of despair crashing over her. *What have we done?*

She didn't know where she was going, didn't care. She just needed to get away, to put distance between herself and the horror unfolding around her. But no matter how far she ran, she knew she would never escape this feeling - this sickening, soul-crushing certainty that everything she had fought for, everything they had sacrificed, had been twisted into something unrecognisable.

And somewhere, deep in the chaos, Ahmed felt it too.

He stood in the back of the pickup, staring out over the sea of cheering faces, his heart a hard, unyielding knot in his chest. He had made his choices. He had walked this path willingly. But the look on Salma's face, the revulsion in her eyes... It cut deeper than any blade ever could.

He felt something tighten around his heart, a hollow ache that he had thought long since buried. For a moment, just a moment, he wondered if he could ever turn back. If there was any way to reclaim what he had lost. But then the thought was gone, swept away by the tide of reality and resolve.

This is war, he told himself, his jaw clenching. *There is no room for weakness. No room for doubt.*

Ahmed moved with purpose through the streets of Jabalia, his mind racing with a mix of victory and urgency. The operation had gone better than expected, they had struck deep into Israeli territory, captured hostages, and spread chaos just as planned. But he knew they could not linger. His team had to get the hostages to safety, to the tunnels, before the inevitable retaliation came.

The city was buzzing with frenetic energy. The locals were out in force, cheering as his convoy of mud-streaked pickups returned, waving flags and shouting slogans. But amidst the jubilation, Ahmed felt a knot of unease tightening in his stomach. His instincts, honed by years of conflict, told him something wasn't right.

Without warning, the roar of jets overhead. The familiar, terrifying sound of Israeli aircraft cutting through the air. Ahmed's breath caught in his throat as he looked up, squinting against the brightness of the sky. His heart pounded as he calculated their position, the possible targets.

Moments later, the first explosion shook the ground beneath his feet. He staggered slightly, eyes widening as a plume of smoke rose from the direction of the safe house. The very place they were heading, the place where they had always regrouped, where he had held countless meetings. The shockwave of the blast sent a wave of dust and debris rolling down the street, hitting him like a physical force.

"Get down!" he shouted instinctively, dropping low, signalling to his men to do the same. Another blast followed, this one even closer. The ground trembled, and Ahmed could feel the vibrations deep in his bones. For a moment, everything seemed to freeze. He could hear the ringing in his ears, the shouts of his men, the cries of the civilians around him.

And then it hit him. They had been watched. The Israelis had known of the safe house, had known the locations that had been kept secret for so long. They had marked this place, waited for the right moment, and struck with precision.

His mind raced, thoughts tumbling over one another. *How long have they known? How did they know? And if they knew about the safe house, what else do they know?*

Ahmed's eyes flicked towards his men, who were now scrambling for cover, some looking back towards him, waiting for orders. He needed to think fast. He felt the anger rise within him, a searing, burning frustration that they had been outmanoeuvred, that they had been watched. He clenched his fists, feeling the sweat on his palms, the taste of dust on his lips.

"*Move! Now!*" he barked into his radio, his voice sharp, cutting through the chaos. "*Fall back to the secondary location!*" He knew they had to get out of there immediately. The airstrike had not only taken out the safe house but had sent a clear message. They were vulnerable, exposed.

Ahmed's team began to move quickly, darting through the narrow alleyways, using the buildings for cover. The crowd was in disarray, the initial celebration turning to panic. He could see the fear in their eyes, the same fear that gripped him, that spurred him on.

Ahmed's gaze flicked towards the horizon where the smoke continued to rise. His stomach churned with a mix of fear and fury. *The Israelis have seen us, they've watched us, and now they're responding with force.* He knew this was just the beginning. The retaliation would come hard and fast, and they needed to be ready.

As he pushed forward, his radio crackled again. "*Commander,*" a voice came through, breathless, "*the safe house's gone... completely levelled.*"

Ahmed's jaw tightened. *That could have been us.* That had been the plan. He had been moments away from leading his men into that very building.

"*They were watching us,*" he muttered under his breath, his voice low, a dark edge to his tone. "*They knew exactly where to strike.*"

He glanced over his shoulder, scanning the faces of his men. They were alert, waiting for his next move. He had to keep them focused, had to keep them moving. "*In to the tunnels,*" he ordered, "*and keep low. We're not out of this yet.*"

As they moved, his thoughts kept returning to the airstrike, the precision, the timing. The implications were clear: they had been watched, closely monitored, perhaps for months. *There are eyes on us, eyes that know our every move.*

Ahmed felt a cold chill run down his spine. The stakes had just been raised. *We've sent our message, but the response is already coming, and it will be relentless.*

He glanced back one more time, towards the smoke-filled sky, towards the place where their refuge had once stood. His jaw clenched, his fists tightening around his rifle. He felt the weight of what was coming, the weight of every decision he had made, and every decision he would have to make.

"*Keep moving,*" he called out again, louder this time, rallying his men. "*We need to stay ahead of them. We have to be ready.*"

As they pushed further into the city, Ahmed's mind was already turning to the next steps, to the new plans they would need to make, the new risks they would need to take. They had started a fire, and now, they would have to survive the flames.

As the dust settled and the roar of jets faded into the distance, Ahmed pushed forward through the narrow, winding streets of Jabalia. His mind was still reeling from the airstrike. The precision of it, the timing - *we were too exposed*. The safe house is gone, reduced to rubble in moments. He felt the weight of what he had set in motion pressing down harder with each step.

His radio crackled again, Tariq's voice coming through with a sense of urgency. "*Commander, we've regrouped near the secondary point. Awaiting further orders.*"

Ahmed took a breath, trying to steady his racing thoughts. "*Hold your position,*" he replied sharply. "*I'll be there soon. We need to get everyone underground.*"

He cut the transmission, eyes darting around the chaos. The streets were a mess of shouting and movement, civilians ran in every direction, panic setting in as they realised what was coming. The air was thick with dust and smoke, and the acrid smell of burning was already beginning to fill his nostrils.

Then, in the midst of the chaos, he spotted Salma.

She was standing a short distance away, her face pale, her eyes wide with fear. For a moment, their gazes locked, and time seemed to stop. Ahmed felt a jolt of something deep in his chest - was it guilt? Regret? He couldn't tell. Her expression was a mixture of shock and a knowing sadness, a kind of resigned understanding that seemed to cut through him more sharply than any of the noise around them.

He took a step towards her, almost on instinct, as if drawn by some invisible force. "*Salma,*" he called, his voice hoarse, barely audible above the din. She didn't move at first, then with a last look with what looked like disgust, she turned and walked away leaving him staring after her.

Chapter Forty Six

YOSSI

Yossi and Nadav arrived back at the military camp in Tel Aviv, their faces lined with exhaustion and dust from the long drive. The base, with its orderly rows of buildings and the Israeli flag fluttering in the evening breeze, offered a strange sense of comfort amidst the chaos of the day. The low hum of activity was punctuated by distant shouts, the grinding of vehicle engines, and the metallic clink of equipment being loaded and unloaded.

As they pulled up in their David jeep, Yael and Leila rushed toward them, their expressions a mixture of relief and worry. Yossi barely had time to turn off the engine before Yael threw her arms around him, her grip tight, her face buried against his shoulder. He could feel the tension in her body, the tremor in her fingers, the fear that had gripped her all day. There was a fleeting sense of peace in the embrace, but it was fragile, teetering on the edge of the tension that still lingered.

Leila wasn't far behind, embracing Nadav with equal fervour. The moment was thick with emotion - joy at seeing them alive, anxiety over what they had just endured. The faint smell of sweat and dust mingled with the cool evening air.

"I was so worried," Yael whispered, her voice trembling. *"We heard about everything happening near the border, but we didn't know if you were safe."* Her fingers dug into Yossi's back, as if afraid he might vanish again.

Yossi stroked her hair gently, feeling the grit on his palms, whispering back, *"I'm here, Yael. We're both here. It was... a long day, but we're okay."* His words were soft, almost a plea to reassure her, but underneath them lay the weight of everything unsaid - the danger, the close calls.

Leila glanced at Nadav, her eyes searching his face. *"What happened out there? It sounded... terrible."*

Nadav gave a tired nod. *"It was,"* he admitted, his voice heavy. *"But we did what we could. We got people out, saved as many as we could."* He ran a hand through his hair, the gesture doing little to soothe the tension that still clung to him.

Before they could say more, the CO of the camp approached, flanked by several senior officers. His expression was serious, but there was a glint of respect in his eyes. *"Rosenberg, Levy,"* he greeted, his voice firm and authoritative. *"We need to debrief you both right away. Your actions today... well, we need to hear everything."*

Yossi exchanged a quick look with Nadav and then back at Yael and Leila, giving them a small nod. *"We'll be right back,"* he murmured. *"Stay here, okay?"*

Yael and Leila nodded, watching as Yossi and Nadav followed the CO and the officers towards a nearby building. The weight of the day's events hung heavy over them, and as they walked away, Yossi felt the adrenaline beginning to ebb, replaced by a bone-deep exhaustion that made every step feel like wading through mud.

Inside the briefing room, the atmosphere was tense. The air felt thick, heavy with anticipation. The CO gestured for them to sit down, and they took their seats across from a panel of senior officers who seemed eager, almost impatient, to hear their account.

"Let's start from the beginning," the CO said, leaning forward, his eyes focused intently on Yossi and Nadav. *"What did you see out there, and how did you decide to act?"*

Yossi took a deep breath, the acrid taste of dust still lingering in his mouth, gathering his thoughts. *"We were on leave in Tel Aviv when the sirens went off,"* he began, recounting the events of the morning. *"We headed for the base, but it was *clear there wasn't much information coming in. When we heard about the breach at Erez Crossing and the situation in Sderot, we decided to go out and see what was happening."* His words were measured, careful, but underneath them was a current of urgency, as if he was still racing against time.

Nadav nodded, adding, *"We took the David jeep and made our way towards the crossing. As we got closer, we could see civilians fleeing in panic, cars coming towards us. That's when we heard the sounds of intense fighting near Sderot."*

The officers listened intently, their pens scratching against notepads, the sound cutting through the silence like a knife. Yossi continued, *"We found ourselves in the middle of it - Hamas fighters everywhere, shooting indiscriminately. We took cover, returned fire, and managed to rescue some civilians hiding in the houses. It was chaos... pure chaos."*

"And how many hostages did you rescue?" one of the senior officers asked, his pen poised, ready to capture every word.

"At least twenty in the first group," Yossi replied, his voice steady but weary. *"Then we regrouped with some IDF reservists and continued, bringing out more civilians throughout the afternoon and into the night. We must have saved around 150 by the end of it."*

The CO nodded, clearly impressed. *"You both showed exceptional bravery out there,"* he said, his tone softer now, almost admiring. *"Your actions saved lives, and the IDF will not forget that."*

Yossi and Nadav exchanged a brief glance. They both knew they had done what they could, but there was no time to dwell on it. The CO's voice brought them back to the present. *"Rest for now,"* he said, *"but be prepared. We'll need every soldier ready for what comes next."*

Yossi nodded, feeling the weight of the day's events pressing down on him like a physical burden. He turned to Nadav as they stood up, a silent understanding passing between them. *"We'll get through this,"* he murmured, the words more a promise to himself than anyone else.

Nadav gave a tired smile, a flicker of determination in his eyes. *"Together,"* he replied.

As they exited the building, Yael and Leila were waiting for them, their faces a mix of relief and lingering worry. Yossi walked up to Yael, pulling her close, his heart finally settling into a steadier rhythm.

"Let's go home," he whispered, his voice thick with emotion. *"For tonight, let's just go home."*

They nodded, and together, they made their way back to the jeep, ready for a moment of peace amidst the storm.

Yossi woke up with a start, his body tensed as if expecting a sudden noise or movement. The faint early morning light was creeping through the curtains, casting long shadows across the room. He lay still for a moment, listening to the familiar sounds of Tel Aviv outside - the distant hum of traffic, a dog barking somewhere. But beneath the normalcy, he felt a strange, heavy weight in his chest. The events of the previous day came rushing back to him, and he knew that their brief respite was over.

He turned his head to see Yael lying beside him, her face calm in sleep, but even in rest, he could see the faint lines of worry etched on her brow. He reached over and gently touched her shoulder, feeling the warmth of her skin.

"Yael," he whispered softly, his voice barely a breath. *"Wake up."*

Her eyes fluttered open, and she blinked a few times, disoriented before her gaze focused on him. *"Yossi?"* she murmured, still half-asleep.

"We need to go," he said quietly. *"We have to report to the mobilisation unit."*

Yael nodded, the fog of sleep quickly clearing from her eyes. She sat up, rubbing her face. *"I had a feeling,"* she replied. *"Let me get dressed."*

Yossi picked up his phone and quickly dialled Nadav's number. After a few rings, he heard his friend's groggy voice on the other end. *"Nadav, it's time. We need to get to the mobilisation unit."*

Nadav's tone sharpened instantly. *"Understood. I'll meet you there with Leila."*

"See you soon," Yossi replied, ending the call. He turned back to Yael, who was already pulling on her clothes. *"Ready?"*

"Ready," she nodded, a flicker of determination in her eyes.

Within minutes, they were in their car, heading towards the mobilisation centre. The streets of Tel Aviv were quieter than usual, the tension in the air almost palpable. As they drove, Yossi stole a glance at Yael, who was staring straight ahead, her face tense, her fingers gripping the seat.

"What's on your mind?" Yossi asked, keeping his tone light, though he already sensed the answer.

Yael hesitated for a moment before speaking. *"There's something you should know,"* she began, her voice low, almost hesitant. *"I've been watching this build-up for months... and I tried to warn my senior officers. I told them what I was seeing, what I thought might happen, but they didn't take it seriously."*

Yossi felt a cold weight settle in his stomach. *"What do you mean? What were you seeing?"*

"Salma," Yael replied, her voice almost a whisper. *"She's been... close to someone in Hamas. I spotted her with one of their leaders. I don't know what she knows, but she's been more worried than usual, and I've been reporting everything I could back to my unit."*

Yossi frowned, processing the information. *"You think she knew something?"*

"I don't know," Yael said, frustration clear in her tone. *"But I kept trying to get the message across that something was coming, that something didn't feel right."*

Yossi's hands tightened on the steering wheel. *"And they didn't listen?"*

Yael shook her head, a mixture of anger and resignation in her eyes. *"Not enough."*

Yossi nodded, understanding the weight of what she was saying. *"Well, we're all listening now,"* he said grimly. *"And we're going to need every bit of information we can get."*

They continued the drive in a tense silence, each lost in their thoughts, until they arrived at the mobilisation camp.

The atmosphere inside was crackling with tension. Soldiers and reservists were moving quickly, filling out forms, receiving orders, and preparing for deployment. The air was thick with a mix of urgency and anticipation, and Yossi could feel the adrenaline coursing through him as they walked towards the registration desk.

Nadav and Leila were already there, waiting in line. Yossi caught Nadav's eye and nodded. *"Let's get in line and find out where they want us,"* he muttered to Yael, who gave a brisk nod in agreement.

As they approached the desk, a harried-looking officer glanced up. *"Name, rank, unit?"* he asked in a clipped tone.

"Segen Yossi Rosenberg, IDF Paratroopers, currently assigned on the Lebanese border," Yossi responded crisply.

The officer nodded and made a quick note. *"And you?"* he asked, turning to Nadav.

"Samal Nadav Levy, also IDF Paratroopers, same unit," Nadav replied, his tone steady.

The officer glanced at Yael and Leila. *"And you two?"*

"Yael Rosenberg," Yael answered. *"Former Combat Intelligence Corps, now with a private security firm, but I'm ready to return to my old unit."*

Leila stepped forward. *"Leila Cohen, a trainee nurse and former medic, currently working in Tel Aviv."*

The officer scribbled their details down, then looked up at them, his face serious. *"Right, wait here for a moment. We'll see where you're needed."*

They stood in tense silence for a few minutes until the officer returned. *"Okay, listen up. Yael Rosenberg, you're to report to your old unit in Intelligence. They need your experience. Leila Cohen, you're to head back to your hospital, they're calling up all medical personnel right now."*

Yael and Leila nodded, already prepared for this.

The officer turned to Yossi and Nadav. *"As for you two, you're to contact your CO on the Lebanese border. It sounds like they want you back there as soon as possible."*

Yossi nodded. *"Understood."*

He stepped aside, pulling out his phone to call their CO. The line rang only once before it was answered. *"Segen Rosenberg, reporting in,"* Yossi said briskly. *"We're at the mobilisation centre. What are your orders, sir?"*

His CO's voice was calm but firm. *"Yossi, it's good to hear from you. We need you back here, on the border. Things are tense, and with what's happening down south, we can't afford to take any chances. Hezbollah might see this as an opportunity to strike."*

"Understood, sir," Yossi replied. *"We'll leave immediately."*

He ended the call and turned back to Nadav. *"We're heading back to the border. Grab whatever gear you need, we're leaving in ten."*

Nadav nodded, already moving towards their David Jeep to prepare. Yael pulled Yossi aside, her face a mix of worry and determination.

"I told you, she whispered. *"I warned them about Salma and what I saw... I just hope they're taking it seriously now."*

Yossi squeezed her hand. *"They are, Yael. And you did everything you could. Now we just have to do our part."*

They shared a brief, tight embrace before parting ways. Yossi watched as Yael and Leila headed off to their respective assignments. He and Nadav climbed into their vehicle, feeling the weight of the moment.

As they pulled away from the camp, Yossi glanced at Nadav. *"Back to the border,"* he said quietly.

Nadav nodded. *"Back to the border,"* he echoed.

They drove on, ready for whatever lay ahead, knowing that their roles were about to become even more critical in the days to come.

Yossi and Nadav drove in silence for a while, the road stretching out before them, winding through the landscape as they made their way back to the Lebanese border. The David Jeep rumbled beneath them, a steady, comforting sound amidst all the uncertainty.

After a while, Nadav glanced over at Yossi, breaking the silence. *"Crazy day yesterday,"* he said, a hint of disbelief in his voice.

Yossi nodded, keeping his eyes on the road. *"Yeah,"* he replied quietly. *"Felt like it all happened in a blur. One minute we were driving through Sderot, the next... well, we were right in the middle of it."*

Nadav chuckled softly, but there was no humour in it. *"I've got to admit, when you suggested heading to the firefight, I thought you'd lost your mind."*

Yossi shrugged. *"Didn't feel like we had much of a choice. People needed help."*

"True," Nadav agreed. *"But you know, the way those reservists looked at us... like we were some kind of madmen."*

Yossi shook his head. *"We did what we had to do. What anyone would have done in our place."*

Nadav gave a small smile. *"Not everyone would have taken on dozens of armed fighters with the rounds we had. But you're right, we were just doing our job."*

The modesty in Yossi's tone was genuine. To him, and to Nadav, their actions were nothing extraordinary. It was just another day in the life of a soldier - one where you made split-second decisions and hoped they were the right ones. They didn't dwell on the chaos or the danger, they just did what was necessary to protect their people.

After a moment, Yossi's expression grew more serious. *"Yael told me something this morning,"* he began, glancing over at Nadav.

Nadav raised an eyebrow. *"What's that?"*

"She said she'd been talking to Salma. She'd seen her with one of the Hamas leaders," Yossi explained. *"Apparently, she'd reported it to her senior officers, but they didn't take it seriously."*

Nadav's brow furrowed. *"Salma? The woman from the office?"*

"Yeah," Yossi nodded. *"Yael was trying to get more information from her, but Salma didn't say much. Still, it makes sense now, doesn't it? All the build-up, the training right under our noses... And no one acted."*

Nadav let out a long breath. *"That's tough. Sounds like Yael did everything she could. But it's frustrating to think that maybe... just maybe... someone could have pieced it all together if they'd listened."*

Yossi nodded in agreement, gripping the steering wheel a little tighter. *"It's hard not to think about what might have been... if someone had paid more attention."*

"Or if we'd known more ourselves," Nadav added. *"But we can't change what's happened. Just got to deal with what's in front of us now."*

Yossi sighed. *"Yeah, you're right."*

They drove on, the tension from the camp slowly creeping back into the vehicle. The landscape around them grew more rugged, the familiar terrain of the border drawing closer with every mile.

For a while, neither of them spoke, both lost in their own thoughts. The immensity of the past 24 hours weighed heavily on them. The audacity of the attack, the lives lost, the chaos that had unfolded - it was all still sinking in. The call-up of reservists, the deployment of troops... It felt like they were on the brink of something much bigger, a storm that had only just begun.

As they approached their base, Yossi could see the heightened activity - vehicles moving, soldiers rushing to and fro, the tension almost palpable in the air. He glanced at Nadav, who looked equally focused.

"Looks like they're expecting something," Nadav murmured, his eyes scanning the scene.

Yossi nodded, pulling the Jeep to a stop. *"Yeah... everyone's on edge."*

They got out of the vehicle, the weight of the situation settling on their shoulders like a heavy cloak. Whatever lay ahead, they knew it would demand everything they had. As they walked towards their unit, Yossi couldn't shake the feeling that their actions, no matter how small or ordinary they felt to them, were part of something far more significant - a turning point in a conflict that was only just beginning to unfold.

Yael arrived at her old unit, the gates of the intelligence compound opening before her. The familiar sounds and sights of the place filled her senses - a mix of tension and controlled chaos. Soldiers were hurrying about, phones ringing off the hook, and screens filled with real-time footage from the border zones. Her heart raced, a mixture of anxiety and determination coursing through her veins.

As she walked inside, she was met by several familiar faces. Samir was the first to spot her, his face breaking into a relieved smile. *"Yael! Good to see you back,"* he said, moving quickly towards her.

"Good to be back, Samir," she replied, managing a tight smile of her own. *"Although I wish it were under different circumstances."*

He nodded, his expression sobering. *"Yeah, no kidding. We could really use your eyes on this. A lot has happened."*

He motioned her to follow, leading her through the labyrinth of the intelligence centre. The walls were covered with maps, images, and reports tacked up in a rush. The place buzzed with activity, the air thick with urgency.

"Right," Samir began as they reached a small workstation set aside for her, *"we've got a lot of feeds coming in, and we need to start piecing together what's happening*

on the ground. You're going to help us sort through this. I know you've been watching this build-up closely... now's the time to put that knowledge to use."

Yael nodded, slipping into the seat and adjusting the headset over her ears. *"I'm ready,"* she said, her voice steady. *"Tell me what you need."*

He handed her a stack of satellite images and pointed to a live feed on a screen in front of her. *"We're getting multiple reports of Hamas movements, and we're trying to map their positions and objectives. Focus on this quadrant first,"* he indicated a section of the map. *"We need to know where they are most concentrated, where they're falling back, and where the next likely strike will be."*

Yael scanned the images quickly, her sharp eyes darting over the details. She knew this terrain well - too well. She began to mark potential routes, identifying patterns and areas that looked like staging points or fallback positions.

As she worked, Samir kept her updated on incoming intel. *"We're hearing reports of more movements in Jabalia. We need to confirm if they're regrouping or preparing for another strike."*

Yael nodded, zooming in on a set of recent images. *"I'll focus on the area,"* she replied, her concentration intense. She knew the stakes were high, every detail mattered.

Across the city, Leila had returned to the hospital, stepping back into the familiar rush of the emergency room. It was a controlled chaos, nurses and doctors moving swiftly between beds, voices urgent and tense. The smell of antiseptic hung heavy in the air, mingling with the scent of sweat and fear.

Leila's heart tightened at the sight of the wounded. The wards were full, many beds occupied by civilians caught in the crossfire of the attacks. She quickly found her supervisor, a tall, thin woman named Rivka, who greeted her with a weary smile.

"Leila, I'm so glad you're here," Rivka said, placing a hand on her shoulder. *"We're stretched thin, and there are so many injured coming in from all over. We need everyone we've got."*

Leila nodded, already rolling up her sleeves. *"Just tell me where you need me,"* she replied, her voice resolute.

Rivka handed her a list of patients. *"Start with the triage, assess who needs immediate attention, and move them through as fast as you can. We're running out of space, and we need to prioritise."*

Leila took a deep breath, trying to steady herself. She moved quickly between the beds, checking pulses, speaking softly to the injured, and relaying information back to the doctors. The scenes of pain and fear were overwhelming, but she focused on her training, letting it guide her hands and keep her mind steady.

Each time she heard the wail of an ambulance arriving, her heart clenched. She knew there would be more - a never-ending stream of casualties, each one a story of suffering and survival.

As the day wore on, both women found themselves fully immersed in their duties. Yael's fingers moved deftly over the keyboard, eyes locked on the screens, analysing every detail. She felt a deep sense of purpose, a determination to do whatever she could to help prevent further attacks. Every movement of the enemy, every strategic position identified, felt like a small victory in a war that had only just begun.

Leila moved between patients with a similar resolve. She treated burns, staunched bleeding, comforted the frightened. Her training took over, and she found herself working with an almost mechanical efficiency, her emotions kept at bay by the urgency of the work.

Yet, in the quiet moments between tasks, both women felt the weight of the situation bearing down on them. They were doing what they could, but they knew that the situation was far from over. The stakes were high, the dangers real, and the impact would be felt by everyone they loved.

Back at the intelligence unit, Yael shared a brief look with Samir. *"We're doing everything we can,"* he said quietly, sensing the weight on her shoulders.

She nodded. *"I know,"* she replied. *"But it's not enough just to know. We have to act, to prevent more of this."*

And across the city, Leila, wiping sweat from her brow, looked at the lines of stretchers and whispered to herself, *"Just keep going. One life at a time."*

Both women, in their own way, were ready to face whatever came next.

Chapter Forty Seven

AHMED

In the first days, the Israeli bombardment came in relentless waves, each strike more precise and devastating than the last. Missiles roared through the sky, screaming down with an eerie, mechanical precision that left little room for error. They targeted not just buildings, but the very heart of Hamas's operations - the places they believed were hidden deep underground, far beyond the reach of Israeli eyes. Apartment blocks were reduced to hollow, charred shells, their façades blown apart as if gutted from the inside. Shops, cafés, and homes - once filled with life - collapsed into mounds of debris, choking the narrow streets with twisted rebar and shattered glass.

What had been the lively, bustling cityscape of Jabalia was now a scarred battlefield. Craters pockmarked every street corner, deep gouges in the earth that belched black smoke into the already suffocating air. Each explosion seemed to tear another piece out of the city's soul, leaving behind only ash, ruin, and the cries of the wounded. The sky above was thick with plumes of acrid smoke, dark and menacing, rising from the centre of the city as if the very ground was burning from within.

But it wasn't the devastation on the surface that unnerved Ahmed. It was the strikes on the tunnels - their lifeline, their sanctuary. For years, they had laboured in secret, digging deep into Gaza's sandy soil, constructing a labyrinthine network of tunnels that spanned miles beneath the surface. These underground passageways were more than just escape routes, they were conduits for weapons, supplies, and the very command structure that kept the fighters coordinated. They were meant to be safe havens, undetectable and indestructible. And yet, within days, they were crumbling under the precision of Israeli bombs.

The first hit came without warning. A deafening roar echoed through the tunnel systems, followed by a series of shuddering booms that reverberated through the narrow passages. Dust and rock rained down, filling the air with a choking cloud of debris. Fighters scrambled for cover, their shouts lost in the chaos. Lights flickered and then died, plunging sections of the tunnels into suffocating darkness. Men stumbled blindly, their voices rising in panicked cries as they groped their way through the choking haze. Those who were closest to the explosions were trapped instantly, the passageways collapsing around them in a lethal avalanche of concrete and sand.

Panic spread like wildfire. Communications, already tenuous, were severed as the primary control nodes were obliterated in quick succession. The radios crackled with urgent, disjointed voices - Ahmed's leaders desperately calling for reinforcements, medics pleading for help as they tried to reach the injured. But the tunnels, once bustling with the hum of activity and command, were now death traps. Fighters who had once moved confidently through the passageways now found themselves cornered, unable to retreat as more sections caved in, sealing them off from escape.

"Section three, we've lost contact!" a voice had shouted over the radio in the first hours of the bombardment, the panic clear in his tone. *"Commander, they've hit the munitions storage - direct strike! It's gone... it's all gone..."*

Gone. Ahmed had listened in stunned disbelief as report after report came in. Underground caches they had spent months, even years, painstakingly concealing were being hit with pinpoint accuracy. Missile launch sites buried deep beneath layers of reinforced concrete were obliterated as if they were nothing more than cardboard cut-outs. Each strike was a message, clear and chilling: *We know where you are. We see everything.*

How? How did they know? Ahmed's mind churned with the implications. For nearly a year, they had concealed these locations - moving equipment in the dead of night, hiding entrances under ordinary-looking houses, using false signals and decoys to mislead any prying eyes. And yet, the Israelis were hitting them with terrifying precision. It was as if someone had drawn a map for them, marked out every critical node, every vulnerable spot. Their secrets, guarded so jealously, were laid bare.

As he moved through the battered remains of the tunnels, stepping over the bodies of the dead and wounded, Ahmed felt a cold sweat trickle down his spine. This wasn't just a military setback - they had been watching their every move. Their entire network was compromised. The thought sent a shiver of dread through him. If they could pinpoint the tunnels, what else did they know?

Around him, fighters worked frantically to shore up the remaining passageways, their faces drawn and pale under the weak glow of emergency lanterns. The tunnels echoed with the harsh clanging of metal and the muffled groans of the injured. Medics moved swiftly, their movements urgent and practised as they tried to stabilise those caught in the initial blasts. But there was only so much they could do. The air was thick with the smell of blood, sweat, and fear.

"Commander," a young fighter called out, his face smeared with dirt and blood, eyes wide with panic. *"The tunnels... they're collapsing. We need to get out - we can't hold - "*

Ahmed rounded on him, his expression hard. *"We can't leave. We hold our positions,"* he snapped, the weight of the situation pressing down on him like a physical force. If they abandoned the tunnels now, the Israeli ground forces would sweep in unopposed. But even as he spoke, he knew the truth. *We're losing.*

He turned sharply, motioning for the remaining officers to gather. *"We need to regroup,"* he said, keeping his voice low but firm. *"Set up fallback positions. Move the wounded to the secondary tunnels. And for God's sake, keep the entrances clear. We can't afford to lose any more men in a bottleneck."*

But the reality was inescapable. Every time they regrouped, there were fewer men, more haunted eyes staring back at him, their hope eroding with every strike. The tunnels, once their greatest asset, were now traps. And above them, the Israeli forces waited, patient and calculating, ready to pounce as soon as the last defences crumbled.

Ahmed felt his chest tighten with a mixture of fury and dread. They had to survive until the ground forces arrived. It was the only chance they had to even the playing field, to force the Israelis into close combat where the tunnels would still give them some advantage. But as each explosion rocked the fragile ground, sending fresh cascades of rubble tumbling through the tunnels, he knew time was running out.

The air was thick with dust, and every breath felt like it scraped his lungs raw. Fighters stumbled through the narrow passageways, their faces smudged with soot and desperation. Some were injured, limping or clutching hastily bandaged wounds. Others were barely more than boys, their wide eyes reflecting the horror of what they were witnessing.

"Stay strong," Ahmed muttered under his breath, though he wasn't sure if he was speaking to his men or to himself. *"Hold on. Just a little longer."*

But even as he said it, he couldn't shake the gnawing sense of dread that had taken root in his gut. This was no ordinary battle. The Israelis weren't just breaking their defences - they were dismantling them piece by piece, systematically tearing apart everything they had built.

And deep down, in the part of his mind he tried to keep buried, Ahmed knew: *They were waiting for the kill.*

By the second week, the IDF began to push into the city itself. The ground shook with the tread of tanks and the rattle of gunfire. The Israeli forces advanced methodically, backed by drones and air support, clearing one block at a time, street by street. Jabalia had become a labyrinth of rubble, the streets narrowed by debris, and the buildings crumbling around them. The civilians who remained had retreated into the shadows, hiding in the remnants of their homes, caught between Hamas fighters and Israeli forces.

Hamas fighters tried to hold their ground, but the losses were staggering. The Israeli forces were relentless, and for every ambush that succeeded, three more of Ahmed's men fell. Tariq, his most trusted lieutenant, had been among the first to die. His death, in a violent skirmish at a key intersection, left a void that no one could fill. Now, more than two-thirds of the fighters that had once moved under

Ahmed's command were gone, cut down by airstrikes, artillery, or the precision gunfire of Israeli soldiers.

The city was unrecognisable. Streets where children once played football and vendors sold their goods were now battlefields. Burnt-out cars littered the roads, and shattered glass sparkled in the sunlight like deadly confetti. Buildings that still stood were pockmarked with bullet holes and the scars of explosives. Bodies, both of fighters and civilians, lay strewn across the ruins, some buried beneath the rubble, others left where they had fallen. The air reeked of smoke, decay, and blood.

Despite the overwhelming Israeli firepower, Hamas fighters, including Ahmed, had no choice but to keep fighting. Every retreat felt like a slow death, every fallback another defeat. But the men followed him, their eyes filled with fear but also with the determination that came from knowing there was no escape. They were fighting not just for their lives, but for something far more intangible - an idea, a belief that refused to die, even in the face of overwhelming destruction.

By the third week, Jabalia was a shell of its former self. Buildings no longer stood, entire blocks had been levelled, and the streets were so filled with debris that movement became difficult, almost impossible. The sound of distant artillery had faded, replaced by the steady crack of rifles and the heavier thump of machine-gun fire. Israeli forces were now deeply entrenched within the city, moving with precision, clearing out any remaining resistance.

Ahmed and what remained of his unit had retreated to a basement beneath a half-destroyed building. It was damp and dark, lit only by the faint glow of a flickering lantern. His men, exhausted and battered, sat in silence. The radio beside him crackled occasionally, but the news was always the same: more losses, more ground taken by the enemy.

He stared at the maps spread out before him - maps that had once been marked with positions of strength but were now covered in red, each circle representing another area lost to the IDF. The reality was sinking in. Jabalia was lost. The city was theirs only in name now, and even that was slipping away.

Ahmed clenched his fists, feeling the weight of every decision, every life lost under his command. The IDF was closing in, and the fight was nearing its end. But even now, with so few men and almost no hope of victory, he could not let go.

Promises of support had been made. Ahmed had sat in meetings with leaders, officials who assured him that help was coming, that the tide of war would shift. But here, in the heart of the destruction, it felt like they had been abandoned. Qatar, Lebanon, Jordan - none had sent the aid they spoke of. Their words, once hopeful, now felt hollow, a distant echo as the city crumbled around him.

Where are they? he thought bitterly. *They promised us aid, fighters... yet we're left to die here alone.*

Ahmed had seen men fall, their hopes pinned on the idea that their Arab brothers would come. But as the weeks dragged on, the only ones left standing were those willing to fight and die in the ruins of Gaza. *The world watches,* he thought, *but no one moves to help.*

Ahmed moved swiftly through the shattered remnants of Jabalia, his steps sure, but his heart heavy with the weight of what he was witnessing. Around him, the city lay in ruins, every street and alleyway transformed into a surreal nightmare of twisted steel, shattered concrete, and burning debris. The streets that had once echoed with the laughter of children and the bustle of markets were now empty corridors of destruction, filled only with the low moan of the wind and the distant crackle of burning rubble.

Buildings that had stood proudly just weeks before were now hollowed-out husks, their façades ripped away to reveal the broken remains of lives interrupted - beds overturned, tables splintered, a child's toy half-buried in the dust. Everywhere he looked, the scars of war were etched deeply into the very bones of the city. Craters, some wide enough to swallow a car, gaped like open wounds in the streets, while the few remaining structures leaned precariously, their walls sagging under the strain of relentless bombardment.

Ahmed's men moved in tight formation, their expressions grim, their weapons held close. Each fighter held a length of rope tied to a hostage, the thin lines taut with tension. The hostages stumbled along, their faces pale and drawn, eyes darting nervously as they took in the devastation around them. Ahmed could see the fear in their expressions, the exhaustion. A woman, her wrists raw from the ropes, limped heavily, struggling to keep up. The fighter tethered to her gave the rope a harsh tug, and she staggered forward with a whimper, her gaze fixed on the ground.

What have we done? The thought struck Ahmed with unexpected force as he looked out at the ruins of the city he had sworn to defend. Salma's voice, soft but insistent, echoed in his mind. She had warned him for years that this would happen, had pleaded with him to find another way, to see beyond the cycle of violence. *This will only bring destruction,* she had said, again and again. *They will destroy everything, Ahmed. They will destroy us.*

He hadn't listened. He had been so sure then, so confident that they were doing what needed to be done, that the sacrifices were necessary. But now, seeing the charred remains of Jabalia, the broken bodies of his men and the terrified faces of the hostages tethered to his fighters, doubt gnawed at him like a living thing.

They slipped through the ruined streets, keeping low, eyes scanning constantly for any sign of movement. The Israeli drones buzzed overhead like angry insects, their presence a constant, oppressive reminder that they were never truly safe. Every time one of the fighters glanced upwards, Ahmed could see the fear in their eyes - the fear of being caught in the open, of being turned to ash in an instant by a missile strike. The very thought of it made his skin prickle with a cold sweat.

A few blocks away, a column of smoke rose lazily into the sky, marking the spot where an apartment block had collapsed. He could hear the faint, desperate cries of people trapped beneath the rubble, their voices growing fainter by the minute. There would be no rescue. Not here. Not now.

The horror of it all settled over him like a shroud. What had once been a proud city was now a wasteland, its people reduced to refugees, scavengers picking through the debris of their lives. His men marched forward, grim and silent, their faces drawn with fatigue and fear. And in their midst, the hostages - their eyes hollow, their shoulders slumped - moved with the same mechanical obedience, driven on by the knowledge that any sign of resistance would mean death.

"Don't even think about it," growled Khaled, as the man tied to his rope hesitated, looking back over his shoulder at the burning city. *"Keep your head down and keep moving, or I'll put a bullet in your back."*

The man, his face pale and streaked with dirt, nodded quickly, his shoulders hunched in defeat. Khaled's expression was hard, unyielding, but as he turned away, Ahmed caught a glimpse of something in his eyes - weariness, and perhaps a flicker of something darker, something close to shame.

Ahmed pressed on, pushing the thoughts aside. They had to survive, no matter the cost. He looked over at Bilal, who marched beside a woman clutching the hand of a small child. The boy couldn't have been more than six or seven, his cheeks smudged with ash, his wide eyes staring blankly ahead. Bilal kept his gaze forward, but Ahmed noticed the way his grip on his rifle tightened every time the child stumbled.

"Hadi," Ahmed murmured softly, who was bringing up the rear with the last of their group. *"Keep an eye on the perimeter. We need to move quickly, before the drones pick up on our movement."*

Hadi nodded, his face tense with concentration as he scanned the rooftops, the rubble-strewn streets. The tunnels had been their world, their sanctuary. But out here, exposed and vulnerable, they were little more than prey. And the predators were circling.

They rounded a corner, the wreckage of a collapsed building looming above them like the twisted skeleton of some long-dead beast. As they emerged into the open street beyond, Ahmed's breath caught in his throat.

Before them, a tide of humanity surged southward, a desperate river of civilians fleeing the devastation. Families huddled together, clutching what few belongings they could carry. Mothers and fathers, their faces lined with exhaustion and fear, guided their children through the ruins, eyes fixed on the horizon. Old men and women, bent and frail, shuffled along at the edges of the crowd, their faces masks of pain and determination.

Ahmed's fighters blended in, slipping into the flow of people as if they had always been part of it. The hostages were scattered among the crowd, each one tethered to a different fighter, their terrified eyes darting from side to side as they moved. To anyone watching from a distance, they looked like just another group of refugees, just another fragment of the human tide pouring out of Jabalia. But Ahmed knew better. He could see the tension in the way his men moved, the cold, watchful glances they cast around them.

"Stay close," he muttered to Bilal, keeping his voice low. *"Don't let them break off. If they try anything..."*

"I know," Bilal murmured back, his expression hardening. *"They won't get far."*

They trudged forward, the weight of the war pressing down on them like a physical force. The civilians around them had no idea of the danger hidden in their midst. The IDF watched from a distance, armoured vehicles positioned on high ground, the barrels of their tanks and machine guns trained on the road below. Every so often, Ahmed caught a glint of sunlight reflecting off a scope or a gun barrel, a silent reminder that the slightest misstep could mean death.

As they moved deeper into the crowd, Ahmed felt the tension building. The hostages were silent, their expressions blank, but he could see the desperation in their eyes - the desperate hope for a chance, any chance, to escape. He could feel it too, the fear gnawing at the edges of his own resolve. *Is this what it has come to? Using people like shields, hiding among them like rats?*

The thought twisted like a knife in his gut, but he pushed it down, burying it beneath layers of resolve. They had no other choice. They had to survive, to regroup, to fight another day. Whatever the cost.

"Keep moving," he whispered, his voice lost in the roar of the crowd. *"Don't look back."*

And they didn't. Step by step, they moved south, into the unknown, with nothing but the hope that they might still find a way to survive the flames consuming everything behind them.

Salma crouched low in the shadows of a crumbling wall, her breath coming in shallow, uneven gasps. The early morning light barely filtered through the thick smoke hanging over Jabalia, mingling with the acrid stench of burning rubber, concrete, and scorched flesh. Explosions thundered in the distance - steady, relentless - echoing through the narrow alleyways that had once been filled with the sound of children playing and the hum of daily life. The once-celebratory cheers that had greeted the return of the fighters were gone, replaced by screams of panic and the guttural cries of the wounded piercing the air.

She had known this would come, had felt it in her bones as soon as she saw the pickups return with the hostages. She had known that the war would come to their doorsteps. But knowing was one thing, witnessing it now, feeling the ground shudder with each blast, was another. The devastation was total. The air itself seemed to vibrate with pain and fear, the smoke and dust so thick it stung her eyes and coated her throat, making every breath an effort.

Salma pressed her back against the cold, rough brick, her hands trembling uncontrollably. She had spent hours since dawn moving cautiously through the labyrinth of broken streets, sticking to the shadows, avoiding the main roads where Israeli drones hovered like silent predators, always watching, always waiting. She had seen too many bodies already - men, women, children and many fighters, their rifles still clutched in lifeless hands. Some lay where they had fallen, faces frozen in expressions of shock and terror. Others were buried beneath the rubble, just a glimpse of an arm or a leg visible among the jagged concrete slabs.

The evacuation had begun - everyone knew that. The exodus had started almost as soon as the first bombs fell, a tide of people desperate to escape the rain of death that tore through buildings as if they were paper. But not everyone could leave. Hamas had set up roadblocks, stopping cars, turning back families with cold, hard eyes and even colder words. She had seen it with her own eyes - mothers clutching children, their faces streaked with fear and dust, turned back at gunpoint. *Stay,* the men had barked, their fingers twitching on the triggers of their rifles. *We need you here.*

Salma's heart clenched with anger at the memory. *This is their home too, their lives - not just pieces on a chessboard.* The injustice of it boiled inside her, but she forced it down. There was no time for anger now, no time for anything but survival.

She kept moving, her family close beside her. Her mother and younger brother stayed close, each gripping the other's hand as they made their way through the throngs of people. The crowd surged and shifted like a living entity, a mass of frightened souls all pressing southward, seeking some elusive safety. The sounds of the exodus surrounded them - the low murmur of worried voices, the occasional sharp cry of a child, the muttered prayers of old women clutching their rosaries as if the beads could somehow shield them from the destruction raining down around them. Nearby, a woman sobbed quietly, her face hidden in her hands, shoulders shaking with the force of her grief.

The crowd thickened as they neared the so-called safe corridor set up by the IDF. But it didn't feel safe. Unlike other checkpoints, there were no soldiers standing guard along the path, no one directly managing the flow of people. The IDF watched from a distance, their armoured vehicles and tanks positioned on ridges and high ground, just visible through the haze of smoke. The soldiers were unseen, but Salma knew they were there - always observing, always ready. The distant sight of the armoured columns, poised and waiting, cast a heavy shadow over the civilians as they moved through the open road.

The safe corridor itself stretched endlessly - a wide, cracked road packed with a sea of people, all moving in one direction, southward, towards what they hoped was safety. From the crumbling outskirts of Jabalia, thousands of men, women, and children poured through, moving as one - a human tide desperate to escape the devastation behind them. The road was flanked by the remnants of buildings, many still smouldering from the bombardments. Overhead, power lines sagged, and the sky was streaked with the smoke of the distant city, now fading into ruin.

The atmosphere was thick with a mixture of desperation and grim determination. The people around Salma shuffled forward, their faces drawn and weary, their clothes stained with dust and sweat, eyes glazed with exhaustion.

A woman nearby stumbled, clutching a toddler to her chest, her face pale and streaked with dirt. Salma's mother reached out instinctively, steadying her, and the woman nodded gratefully, tears streaming down her face.

"Thank you... thank you," she whispered, her voice choked with emotion, and Salma's mother only nodded, her own face a mask of quiet pain.

Salma kept her head down, her senses on high alert, listening for any sound that might signal danger. The distant rumble of artillery continued, a menacing reminder of the destruction they were fleeing. The air was thick with dust, acrid smoke, and the metallic scent of blood. She could feel the desperation of the people around her, could hear it in their voices - a low, collective hum of fear and uncertainty, punctuated by the occasional gasp or sob.

A few metres ahead, she saw an elderly man stumble, his legs giving way beneath him. A young boy, perhaps his grandson, struggled to keep him upright, his thin arms trembling with the effort. Salma's brother moved to help, slipping under the man's other arm, and together they managed to keep him moving, step by step.

"*Thank you, thank you,*" the boy whispered, his voice breaking with gratitude. The old man's eyes were dull, his gaze fixed on some distant point beyond the horizon, as if he had already left his broken body behind.

Salma glanced back over her shoulder, scanning the crowd for any familiar faces, any sign of hope or reassurance. But there was nothing - just a sea of weary, frightened people, all of them heading south, away from the destruction. She knew they were being watched, tracked by both sides, caught in a conflict that had spiralled far beyond their control. And she felt so small, so powerless.

Keep going, she told herself, pushing back the tide of guilt and doubt that threatened to drown her. *Just keep going.*

The sound of the explosions grew fainter as they moved further south, but she knew it wasn't over. Not yet. There would be no quick resolution to this. And as they walked, the thought gnawed at her - how many more would die before this nightmare finally ended?

But there was no time for that. Not now. She had to stay focused, to keep moving. There would be time for thinking, for grieving, later. For now, all that mattered was getting her family to safety. One step at a time, she told herself, one breath after another. And she kept walking, determined not to look back.

Her mother moved beside her, silent and resolute, gripping her brother's hand tightly. Salma could see the exhaustion etched into every line of her face, the pain she carried in her eyes. But there was also a stubborn determination there - a refusal to give in, to let go.

We have to survive, Salma thought fiercely. *We have to, no matter what.*

The crowd swelled and shifted around them, pressing in from all sides. Children cried, their voices thin and reedy amidst the murmur of thousands of desperate souls. Old women whispered prayers under their breath, their fingers moving rhythmically over the beads of their rosaries. Young men, their faces hard and set, kept their heads down, their eyes scanning warily for any sign of trouble.

As they moved through the corridor, Salma felt the weight of the war pressing down on her like a physical force. The fear, the desperation, the anguish of those around her - it was suffocating. She could feel it in every step, hear it in every voice, see it in every hollow, haunted gaze.

They were all searching for something - safety, peace, a place where they could rest without the constant fear of death hanging over their heads. But where could such a place exist now? Gaza had become a labyrinth of destruction, every city and village scarred by the unrelenting violence. The south, they said, was safer, but for how long? How long before the war followed them there too?

Salma shook her head, trying to banish the dark thoughts. She had to focus on the present, on the path ahead. One step at a time. One breath. One heartbeat.

And then, as they crested a small rise, she caught sight of the sea of people stretching out before her - a vast, shifting mass of humanity, all moving in the same direction, all driven by the same desperate need to escape.

How many of us are left? she wondered, staring out over the crowd. *How many will survive?*

But there was no answer, no way of knowing. All she could do was keep moving, keep pushing forward, step by step, breath by breath.

The corridor stretched on, an endless road of suffering and fear, the sky above a bleak, smoke-filled expanse. Salma's feet ached, her body screamed with exhaustion, but she didn't dare stop. Not when every second could be the difference between life and death.

And so, she kept walking, her mother beside her, her brother's hand in hers. They walked together, a small, fragile line of hope amidst the chaos.

The sound of artillery rumbled in the distance, a grim reminder of the world they were leaving behind. The world they might never see again.

But for now, they were still moving. Still alive. And that was all that mattered.

One step at a time.

One breath.

One heartbeat.

And they kept going, into the uncertainty of the south, with nothing but the hope that somewhere, somehow, they might still find a place where they could be safe again.

Where the war couldn't reach them.

Where they could finally rest.

Chapter Forty Eight

YOSSI

Yossi and Nadav arrived back at their Forward Operating Base on the Israeli-Lebanese border just as the first reports of missile fire came through. The camp was a flurry of activity, soldiers moved quickly, their expressions tense, and the sound of shouted commands filled the air. The distant rumble of explosions echoed from the hills, signalling the beginning of something they had all feared.

Yossi felt his chest tighten as they made their way toward the CO's tent. *"Looks like we've walked straight back into it,"* he muttered to Nadav.

Nadav nodded, his face grim. *"Doesn't look like it's going to get easier any time soon."*

As they entered the tent, Lieutenant Colonel Arad was hunched over a map spread across a table, his expression taut with concentration. He looked up as they approached, nodding in acknowledgment.

Segen Rosenberg, Samir Levy, good to have you back, Arad began, a faint smile tugging at his lips despite the tension in his eyes. *"I hear you two were quite busy yesterday on the Gaza border. Word travels fast."*

Yossi exchanged a glance with Nadav, both of them looking slightly embarrassed. *"We did what we had to, sir,"* Yossi replied modestly.

Arad nodded, his tone shifting to urgency. *"Well, it seems you've come back just in time. Hezbollah fired their first missiles into Israel earlier today. Our intelligence suggests this is only the beginning. We're on high alert."*

Yossi glanced at Nadav, who gave a slight nod. *"What are our orders, sir?"*

Arad pointed to the map. *"For now, we need to strengthen our defences. I want patrols increased along the border, especially in areas where the terrain could offer cover for their fighters. Begin fortifying the perimeter with additional sandbags and barriers. Keep everyone alert - this could escalate at any moment."*

Yossi and Nadav listened intently, absorbing the information. The CO continued, *"No one knows for sure how far Hezbollah is willing to go, but we have to be ready. Expect more missiles. Expect more attacks. Make sure your men are prepared."*

"We'll get on it right away," Yossi replied, his voice steady.

Outside the tent, a sense of urgency propelled Yossi and Nadav forward. They headed to the assembly area where their platoon waited, a mix of seasoned soldiers and a few fresh faces who had joined in the last rotation. The air was thick with tension, but also a faint hum of anticipation. Everyone sensed the gravity of the situation.

"Alright, listen up!" Yossi called out, his voice cutting through the murmur of conversation. The platoon gathered around, eyes sharp, sensing that something significant was unfolding.

Nadav stepped forward, his face serious. *"We've got a situation. Hezbollah fired the first missiles into Israel earlier today, and we're expecting more. This is just the beginning."*

Yossi continued, *"The CO wants us to increase patrols along the border, particularly in areas where the terrain gives them cover to set up launch sites. We're also going to keep an eye on the known spots where they've been firing missiles. If we see any activity, we'll be calling in strikes from fast air to neutralise the threat."*

A murmur of understanding ran through the group. The stakes were clear to everyone.

"When you're not on patrol," Nadav added, *"you'll be working in shifts to reinforce our positions - adding sandbags, digging trenches, whatever it takes to prepare for a potential escalation. We don't know how far this could go, so we have to be ready for anything."*

Before Yossi could continue, one of the more seasoned soldiers, Eli, raised his hand with a grin. *"Did you have a nice holiday break, then, Sir? I hear you've been quite the busy boys down south."*

The entire platoon erupted in laughter, and Yossi felt his cheeks flush with embarrassment. Nadav chuckled beside him, shaking his head. *"News travels fast, it seems,"* Yossi replied, attempting to hide his smile.

"Yeah, well, you save a bunch of civilians and take on a few dozen fighters, people tend to talk," Eli quipped, still grinning.

Yossi waved his hand to regain control of the group. *"Alright, alright, enough of that. Back to business. We're here now, and this is where we focus. Keep your heads in the game. We've got a job to do, and we need to stay sharp."*

Nadav nodded, his voice firm. *"Remember, we're all in this together. Watch each other's backs out there. Stay alert, stay safe. Let's show them what we're made of."*

The platoon quieted down, but a few smirks remained on their faces. Yossi and Nadav couldn't help but feel a sense of pride mixed with the embarrassment. Their men were ready - focused but still able to find a moment of levity amidst the tension. They'd need that spirit in the days to come.

"Alright, you've got your orders," Yossi said more seriously now. *"We'll head out on patrol in ten. Let's get moving."*

The platoon dispersed, energy heightened, each soldier preparing for the next task. Yossi turned to Nadav with a grin. *"I guess we're not the only ones who've been busy."*

Nadav laughed. *"No, but it looks like they're ready. Let's hope that's enough."*

They moved off to join their men, knowing the days ahead would be challenging, but confident in their team and their preparation.

At the Intelligence Centre, Yael worked tirelessly, her gaze fixed on the monitors displaying live feeds from drones over Gaza and the northern borders. The screens were filled with moving images of chaos - the relentless churn of military activity, the frantic movement of civilians, trails of smoke rising from freshly struck targets. Her fingers moved deftly across the keyboard, pulling up data, cross-referencing known operatives, and passing information up the chain.

The ground was being pounded by artillery and airstrikes, buildings collapsing into plumes of dust and debris. Through the drone feeds, she saw patterns emerging - Hamas fighters popping up in different locations, almost as if they were ghosts.

The tunnels, she realised, her mind racing. Quickly, she began analysing the footage, identifying entry and exit points the fighters were using to disappear and reappear. She clicked on her headset. *"Samir, I'm seeing movement patterns that suggest they're using a network of tunnels. Fighters are popping up in multiple locations within minutes."*

Samir's voice crackled through the earpiece. *"Roger that, Yael. I'll forward this to ground command. Can you mark the likely tunnel entrances?"*

"I'm on it," Yael replied, her fingers moving swiftly across the keyboard. She highlighted areas on the digital map, marking potential tunnel entrances and exit points.

Moments later, Samir's voice came again. *"Good work, Yael. We'll relay this to the units on the ground. Hopefully, they can narrow down the locations and target the tunnels effectively."*

Yael nodded, her eyes still scanning the screens. The drone feeds showed the entry of IDF ground troops into the heart of Jabalia. She watched as soldiers advanced cautiously, moving through the narrow alleys, their progress punctuated by sudden bursts of gunfire and flashes of explosions. Buildings collapsed, the ground shook from detonations - every step forward seemed met with fierce resistance.

Her stomach twisted at the sight. It was different watching it all unfold from the sterile distance of a screen, knowing that real people, real lives, were caught in the crossfire. She took a deep breath, pushing back the emotion. There was no place for hesitation here. Lives depended on the speed and accuracy of her information.

During a brief lull, Yael leaned back in her chair, eyes closing for a moment. Her thoughts drifted to Yossi. *Where is he now?* she wondered. *Is he safe?* She had heard from him earlier, but it had been brief - a short message to let her know he had reached the border safely. She found herself longing for more, a word, a sign that he was alright.

"Yael," Samir's voice broke through her thoughts, softer this time. She turned her head to see him standing beside her, a concerned look on his face. *"You alright?"*

She managed a small smile. *"Yeah, just... wondering about Yossi."*

Samir nodded, pulling a chair closer. *"Tough position up there with Hezbollah firing missiles. But if anyone can handle it, it's him."*

Yael looked down, her fingers tracing the edge of the keyboard. *"I know. It's just... seeing all this,"* she gestured to the screens, *"it makes you realise how close everything is... how fragile."*

Samir placed a hand on her shoulder, a gesture of comfort. *"He's tough, and he's got Nadav with him. They'll be alright. You just keep doing what you're doing. It makes a difference, you know."*

She nodded, feeling a little lighter, and returned her focus to the screens. *"Yeah, I know. I just wish I could do more."*

Samir gave her a reassuring smile. *"You're doing more than most. Keep at it. We'll get through this."*

Yael watched as another explosion lit up the screen, a building in Gaza City reduced to rubble. Her heart ached for the lives caught in this relentless conflict. She blinked hard, pushing the emotion back down, and refocused on the task at hand. There was still so much to do.

"*Alright,*" she murmured to herself, eyes narrowing in concentration, "*let's find them.*"

Her focus shifted to the exodus in Jabalia and Gaza City. Civilians were streaming south, heeding evacuation orders. Her task was critical: to identify any Hamas operatives who might be trying to blend in with the fleeing crowds. Leaning closer to the screen, Yael scanned every face, every shadow. The heat signature overlays showed clusters of people, but the resolution wasn't always perfect.

"*Come on... show yourselves,*" she murmured, running a new round of facial recognition scans.

Her screen pinged, a name flashing across the system. Her breath caught in her throat: *Salma Nasser*. The system confirmed her identity among a group moving south. Yael felt a surge of mixed emotions - relief and doubt. *At least she's alive*, she thought. But then, doubt crept in. Was Salma just an innocent woman caught in the turmoil, or was there something more? Had their past conversations been more than they seemed?

She shook her head, pushing the thoughts aside. There wasn't time to dwell on personal concerns now. She returned her attention to the screens, watching the unfolding destruction in Jabalia and Gaza City.

Leila moved swiftly through the crowded corridors of the hospital, her hands steady but her heart pounding. The air was thick with the scent of antiseptic and the sharp, metallic tang of blood. Casualties were coming in waves - soldiers, civilians, all marked by the chaos of the front lines. The injured groaned softly, some screaming in pain, while the medical staff worked with focused intensity.

She glanced at the stretchers being wheeled past, unable to stop the flicker of fear that crossed her mind. Each face could have been Nadav's or Yossi's, and the thought tightened her chest. She tried to push it away, to focus on the task at hand, but the fear lingered, a shadow she couldn't escape.

As she bandaged wounds and checked vitals, she found herself scanning each new arrival, dreading the moment she might recognise a familiar face. Her hands moved with practised skill, but her thoughts were miles away, imagining the border, the sound of missiles, and the faces of the people she cared about most.

During a brief lull, Leila leaned against a wall, trying to catch her breath. Her mind wandered to Nadav and Yossi. *Are they safe?* she wondered. *How long before one of them ends up here?* The fear gnawed at her, but she forced herself to push it aside. There was no time to dwell on her worries - only time to keep going, to keep helping, and to hope that her friends stayed out of harm's way.

After months of relentless patrols along the Israeli-Lebanese border, Yossi and Nadav felt the weight of exhaustion settling into their bones. Day after day, they moved through the rugged terrain, scanning the horizon, watching for any sign of Hezbollah rocket sites. The tension never eased, it lived in every breath, every step. Each time they ventured out, they called in air strikes on any targets they identified, their voices steady over the radio despite the weariness tugging at them.

The situation had worsened in recent weeks. Hezbollah had shifted their focus, targeting local Israeli villages with rocket fire, hoping to strike fear into the hearts of the civilians and disrupt daily life. These attacks had become a relentless threat, forcing the IDF to take swift action to protect their people. The Parachute Brigade had been deployed to evacuate over 80,000 civilians from the area, an effort that required meticulous coordination and bravery under fire. Soldiers moved through the affected towns, ushering families into buses and armoured vehicles, guiding them south to safer ground. It was a massive, dangerous undertaking, but they knew they had no choice - the civilians had to be saved.

The camp had taken several direct hits over the past weeks. Missiles from Hezbollah had struck with terrifying accuracy, ripping through the air and leaving craters in their wake. Yossi could still hear the haunting sound of explosions ringing in his ears, even during rare moments of quiet. The threat was constant, pressing in from all sides, fraying their nerves and stretching their endurance to its limits.

Reinforcements had begun to arrive - a mixture of seasoned reservists and fresh faces needing guidance. Armour rumbled in, combat engineers followed, and the camp swelled with new life and fresh challenges. The Parachute Brigade's efforts to evacuate civilians meant that their base was now a hub of activity, not only a forward military post but also a staging ground for humanitarian operations. It fell to Yossi and Nadav to bring these new arrivals up to speed. The two men found themselves running endless drills, giving hurried lessons in border patrols, and pushing the tired men through exercises to ensure everyone could face the dangers ahead.

One morning, just before dawn, Yossi and Nadav stood in the briefing tent, rubbing sleep from their eyes as they reviewed their orders for yet another patrol. This one, however, had a twist. They were to provide protection for a team of combat engineers clearing IEDs along a suspected route. Hezbollah fighters had been seen laying these traps, hoping to cripple their movements and delay their response.

As they studied the map, marking the danger points and possible ambush sites, a familiar voice called out from the back of the tent. Yossi looked up, a tired smile breaking across his face.

"Amir!" he exclaimed, seeing his old friend from their childhood. Amir was with the EOD team, his face smudged with dirt, his eyes bright despite the weariness that touched them all.

"Yossi, Nadav," Amir greeted them with a quick, warm handshake. *"Didn't think I'd be seeing you two in a place like this. Or maybe I should have guessed."*

Nadav chuckled, *"It seems trouble always finds us, doesn't it?"*

They shared a brief moment, exchanging updates and jokes, recalling the easier times before this conflict had consumed them all. But the moment didn't last long. The clock was ticking, and the mission called them back to focus. Amir's expression turned serious as he handed Yossi a more detailed map.

"We've identified at least three locations where they've placed IEDs," Amir explained. *"We'll need to clear those before you can safely patrol the area. I'll need your team to cover us. Keep your eyes peeled, they like to strike when we're distracted."*

Yossi nodded. *"We've got your back, Amir. Stay sharp, and let's get this done quickly."*

The briefing ended, and they moved out, each soldier knowing their place and role. As they walked towards their vehicles, Nadav nudged Yossi.

"Feels like we're always starting over, doesn't it?" Nadav said with a half-smile. *"Same war, different day."*

Yossi sighed, glancing over at Amir, who was already checking his equipment and talking to his men. *"Yeah, but at least we're still here to do it,"* he replied quietly. *"Let's just hope it stays that way."*

They climbed into their jeep, weapons ready, eyes scanning the horizon. The weight of the past months settled heavily on their shoulders, but they knew they had to keep moving. They had a job to do.

Yossi and Nadav gathered their platoon for the patrol briefing, the mood tense but focused. The fatigue of the past months was etched on their faces - lines of exhaustion under their eyes, shoulders weighed down by the constant strain. Yet, there was a flicker of anticipation among them, they knew today's mission was crucial.

As they entered the briefing room, Yossi's eyes landed on Amir, their old friend, stood by the map, surrounded by his Explosive Ordnance Disposal (EOD) team. He looked up, and a grin spread across his face. *"Yossi! Nadav! Glad to have you watching our backs."*

"Amir," Yossi responded with a tired smile. *"Just like old times."*

Amir nodded, the camaraderie evident despite the gravity of the situation. *"Yeah, we've got our work cut out for us today. Hezbollah's been busy planting IEDs along the routes. We're here to clear them so you boys can keep doing what you do best."*

Nadav chuckled. *"And we're here to make sure you get to do your job without any interruptions."*

They exchanged a few more words, but there wasn't much time for pleasantries. The CO's voice cut through the room. *"Alright, listen up! The Engineers will be clearing obstacles on Route 43, where Hezbollah has been observed setting up IEDs. Segen Rosenberg, your platoon will provide protection for Samal Shalev's team. We've got reports of enemy activity in the area, so be prepared for contact. Move out in ten!"*

The group nodded, and Yossi gave Amir a pat on the shoulder. *"Let's get this done, and we'll catch up properly later."*

The patrol moved cautiously along the dusty road, the heat of the day pressing down on them like a heavy blanket. Yossi's eyes were constantly scanning the surroundings, looking for any signs of movement. The sound of their boots crunching on the gravel seemed louder than usual, the silence around them thick with tension.

Ahead, Amir's team was already at work, methodically searching for and dismantling the IEDs. They worked with quiet efficiency, every move calculated, every step deliberate. Yossi admired their focus, their calm in the face of danger. He knew what it was like to do a job that required that level of concentration. One mistake, one lapse in attention, could be fatal.

Suddenly, a burst of gunfire erupted from the hills to their left. Yossi's instincts kicked in immediately. *"Contact left! Take cover!"* he shouted, dropping to a knee and raising his weapon. His platoon scattered, taking positions behind rocks and debris, returning fire to suppress the enemy.

Amir's team froze for a moment, but Yossi's voice cut through the chaos. *"Amir, keep working! We've got you covered!"*

Nadav, beside Yossi, was already calling in their position, requesting air support while directing his men's fire. The air was filled with the sharp cracks of rifles and the heavier thumps of machine guns. Yossi could see the Hezbollah fighters moving in the distance, trying to get a better angle on Amir's team.

"Rafi! Take your squad and flank left!" Yossi ordered. *"Keep them pinned down!"*

Rafi nodded and signalled to his squad, moving quickly through the underbrush to outmanoeuvre the enemy.

Amir's voice came through on the radio, tense but focused. *"We're almost done here, Yossi. Just a few more minutes."*

"Take your time but hurry up!" Yossi replied with a grin that masked his own nerves.

The firefight continued, but Yossi's platoon held their ground, their disciplined fire keeping the Hezbollah fighters from advancing. Minutes felt like hours, but finally, Amir's voice crackled over the radio again. *"We're done! All clear!"*

"Good! Fall back to our position!" Yossi shouted.

Amir's team began to pull back, moving quickly but carefully. Yossi's men provided covering fire, their bullets slicing through the air, keeping the enemy pinned down long enough for Amir's team to reach safety.

"Move, move, move!" Yossi shouted, directing his men as they began their own withdrawal, maintaining a controlled, defensive retreat.

As they fell back to the vehicles, Yossi felt a rush of relief. They had done it. Amir and his team were safe, the obstacles cleared. They piled into their vehicles and sped back to the Forward Operating Base, the adrenaline still coursing through their veins.

Back at the base, they dismounted and immediately headed for the debriefing room. The CO was waiting, his expression one of calm focus.

"Well done, everyone," he began. *"Samal Shalev, your team cleared the route, and Segen Rosenberg, your platoon handled the contact perfectly. But this is far from over. Samal, you've got another location to clear, and Segen Rosenberg, your platoon will be on standby for the next patrol."*

Yossi nodded. *"Understood, sir."*

As the debrief ended, Amir approached Yossi and Nadav once more. *"No rest for the wicked, huh?"*

Yossi smiled. *"Seems like it. Stay safe out there, Amir."*

"You too, both of you," Amir replied, giving them a final nod before heading off with his team.

Yossi watched as Amir disappeared into the crowd, then turned back to Nadav. *"Another day, another mission."*

Nadav sighed. *"And no end in sight."*

Yossi nodded. *"But we keep going. We have to."*

And with that, they prepared for whatever would come next, knowing that each day could be their last, but determined to face it head-on.

Yossi and Nadav stood in the CO's tent, their boots still coated in dust from the day's patrol. Lieutenant Colonel Arad looked up from his desk, his expression unreadable.

"Gentlemen," Arad began, his tone serious but calm, *"we've received new orders. The entire unit is being redeployed to the urban training base near Gaza. We're going to start preparations for a potential operation inside Gaza itself."*

Yossi and Nadav exchanged a glance, understanding the gravity of the news. *"When do we leave, sir?"* Yossi asked.

"You have a month," Arad replied. *"During that time, you'll be handing over to a new unit arriving in the next few days. Your task is to take them out on patrols, show them the lay of the land, familiarise them with the area, and make sure they're up to speed on the threats we're facing here."*

Nadav nodded. *"Understood, sir. We'll make sure they're ready."*

Arad continued, *"One more thing - congratulations are in order. Segen Rosenberg, you're being promoted to Segen Rishon (Lieutenant). And Samal Levy, you're promoted from Samal to Samar (Staff Sergeant). You've both earned it."*

A flicker of pride crossed their faces. *"Thank you, sir,"* Yossi replied. *"It's an honour."*

Arad nodded but then leaned in slightly, his voice dropping to a more serious tone. *"However, there's something else you need to be aware of. There's an investigation underway into your actions on October 7th. Statements are being taken from everyone you interacted with that day."*

Yossi and Nadav felt a jolt of surprise. *"An investigation, sir?"* Nadav asked cautiously.

Arad nodded. *"Yes, it's something big. I can't go into details just yet, but know that this is a good thing. You both did something extraordinary, and I am extremely proud of you. Just keep your heads down, do your jobs, and let the process take its course. You'll be informed as things develop."*

Yossi and Nadav exchanged another look, a mix of concern and curiosity in their eyes. *"Understood, sir,"* Yossi said finally.

Arad gave a firm nod. *"Good. Now get back out there and do what you do best. Make sure that new unit is ready - they'll need to be."*

They saluted and left the tent, feeling the weight of new responsibilities and the mystery of the investigation hanging over them. Yossi turned to Nadav as they walked back toward their men.

"Promotion, new orders, and an investigation... quite a day," Yossi remarked with a faint smile.

Nadav chuckled. *"Never a dull moment, eh? Let's focus on getting this new unit up to speed. We've got a month to make sure they're ready for anything."*

Yossi nodded. *"And then we head south to Gaza. One step at a time."*

As they moved through the camp, they felt a renewed sense of purpose. The days ahead would be challenging, but they were ready to face them head-on, together.

The month passed quickly, filled with long days and even longer nights. Yossi and Nadav, along with their men, took the new unit out on daily patrols, sharing every detail they had learned over nearly two years on the Lebanese border. They navigated the rugged terrain, pointed out hidden threats, and ran through drills that had become second nature to them. Each day was a test, ensuring that the new arrivals were ready to take over.

By the end of the month, the handover was complete. The new unit had proven themselves capable, and Yossi and Nadav felt a sense of satisfaction in knowing they had done their part. Still, a hint of anxiety remained, they were moving on to something even more uncertain, something they had only begun to prepare for.

On the morning of their departure, the Parachute Brigade assembled by their vehicles, the sun just beginning to rise over the hills. The air was filled with a mix of anticipation and relief. Yossi looked around at the familiar faces, his men, his friends. He could see the exhaustion in their eyes, but also a spark of determination.

Nadav came up beside him, giving him a light punch on the shoulder. *"Ready for a new Chapter?"* he asked, a grin spreading across his face.

Yossi nodded, smiling. *"Ready as I'll ever be,"* he replied. *"It's strange to leave this place, but I'm glad to be moving forward."*

They both turned as Lieutenant Colonel Arad approached, his expression a mix of sternness and respect. *"You've done well here, all of you,"* he said, his voice carrying over the assembled soldiers. *"You've faced down every challenge thrown your way. Now, we've got a new task ahead of us. It won't be easy - urban warfare never is - but I know you're up to it."*

The men nodded, absorbing his words. There was no need for a long speech, they all understood what lay ahead. The training would be intense, the stakes high. But they were the Parachute Brigade. They knew their purpose, and they trusted in one another.

"Mount up!" Yossi called out, and the men moved to their vehicles with purpose. Engines roared to life, and the convoy began to roll out. Yossi climbed into his jeep, Nadav beside him, both looking back one last time at the landscape they had called home for so long.

As they drove away from the border, Yossi felt a wave of emotions - relief at leaving this place of constant tension, pride in what they had accomplished, and a steely resolve for what was to come. The road ahead was uncertain, filled with new dangers and new challenges, but they would face it together.

They moved south, toward the Baladia Urban Warfare Training Centre, located at the Tze'elim base in the Negev Desert. Here, they would train for the intense, close-quarters combat scenarios they might face in Gaza. Leaving behind the hills of the Lebanese border, they knew this was the end of one Chapter and the beginning of another. As they drove, Yossi looked at his men in the convoy, saw the determination in their eyes, and knew they were ready for whatever came next.

And so, the Parachute Brigade set off toward the unknown, engines rumbling, dust rising behind them. Ahead lay new battles, new tests of courage and skill. They were heading to Baladia to prepare for Gaza, where the stakes would be higher than ever. But they were ready. They had to be.

Together, they would face whatever came next.

Chapter Forty Nine

AHMED

Salma gripped her brother's hand as they moved south through the IDF Safe Corridor. Her mother followed closely, clutching a small bag of essentials. The heat was stifling and sweat trickled down Salma's back. There was no time to think of comfort, only safety.

The road was crowded with families, the elderly, and children - all walking with fear etched into their faces. Every step felt heavy, but the hope for safety kept them moving. The distant rumble of explosions made them duck instinctively. Salma's heart raced, but she forced herself to stay calm. Her family needed her to be strong.

After hours of walking under the scorching sun, they reached the outskirts of Khan Yunis. The city overflowed with people - those fleeing from the north, desperate for shelter. The narrow streets were packed. The sounds of crying children and desperate shouts filled the air.

They made their way to a temporary shelter in a local school. The building was already crammed with families, every room and hallway filled to capacity. Barely enough space to sit, but at least they had a roof. Salma found a small corner near a window where she spread a blanket for her mother and brother.

The night was restless. Tension hung in the air, and every sound seemed louder in the crowded school. Salma's mother held her brother close as he whimpered in his sleep. Salma couldn't rest. Her mind kept racing back to Ahmed. *Where was he? Was he safe?*

Ahmed and his men moved quickly through the crowded streets of Khan Yunis. Though far from the fiercest fighting, the city now bristled with tension as civilians and militants sought refuge. The air felt thick, as though it was holding its breath. The influx of people from Jabalia and Gaza City hadn't gone unnoticed. Fear and determination intermingled among the crowd.

His men followed silently, leading the hostages they had taken from the north. Some looked dazed, others defiant, but all remained quiet. They knew the consequence of attempting to escape - death.

Ahmed approached a small, hidden building down a narrow alley. Hamas guards in civilian clothes nodded as he passed. Inside, a local Hamas leader, a middle-aged man with a thick beard, awaited him. He greeted Ahmed with a firm handshake.

"*Ahmed Al-Masri,*" the leader said, his voice low and controlled, "*you made it. The situation is fluid, but we still hold control. What do you bring?*"

Ahmed gestured to the hostages. "*Prisoners from the north. They're ready for the safe houses or tunnels. They've been silent.*"

The leader's expression remained impassive. "*Good. Some will go to the safe houses. Others, underground.*"

Ahmed watched as operatives led the prisoners away into the shadows, before turning back to the leader. "*We need to regroup, resupply. My men are exhausted, but ready. Where do you need us?*"

The leader's eyes sharpened. "*Rafah,*" he said curtly. "*The tunnels between here and Rafah are our lifeline. They connect our arms and ammunition. The IDF is intensifying their attacks. We need fighters there to protect them.*"

Ahmed nodded. "*We'll be ready. Give us the tunnel route, and we'll hold whatever position you need.*"

The leader smiled slightly. "*Come, I'll show you.*"

He led Ahmed and a few men down a narrow corridor, descending into the tunnels. The air cooled as damp earth filled their nostrils. Dim lights flickered, and the sound of distant drilling echoed faintly.

"*The IDF is using everything they have,*" the leader whispered. "*Bunker-busters, drones, special forces. We've rebuilt many tunnels, but some are still vulnerable. We must keep the routes open, especially between Khan Yunis and Rafah. We've already lost several.*"

Ahmed listened, the gravity of the situation sinking in. "*And Rafah?*" he asked.

"*Still under our control, but fragile,*" the leader replied. "*It's our supply hub, but also a target. The tunnels to Egypt are critical for weapons and supplies. You'll defend them.*"

They reached a chamber where a crude map of the tunnel network was spread across a table. The leader pointed to the lines connecting Khan Yunis to Rafah. "*These are the primary routes. Use them to get to Rafah. Once there, coordinate with the commanders. Protect the tunnels and supply lines at all costs.*"

Ahmed nodded. "*Understood. We'll leave immediately.*"

The leader gave a sharp nod. "*Go quickly. The longer you stay above ground, the greater the risk. And Ahmed...*" He paused, meeting Ahmed's gaze. "*Failure is not an option. Our fight depends on these tunnels.*"

Ahmed felt a cold shiver pass through him, but he pushed it aside. "*We won't fail,*" he said firmly. "*We know what's at stake.*"

Ahmed gathered his men, and they began descending deeper into the tunnels, heading south toward Rafah. The air grew colder, the lights dimmer, but the path ahead was clear. They moved with purpose, their steps echoing off the narrow walls. This was their lifeline, their last stand. They had to make it count.

As they moved, Ahmed's mind raced. He knew the risks and the dangers ahead. But there was no turning back. Not now. Not ever.

The next morning, Salma learned from a relief worker that it might be safer to continue south to Rafah, where more organised shelters were available. After a quick discussion with her mother, they decided to press on. The walk to Rafah was shorter but just as exhausting. Salma's brother complained of sore feet, and her mother grew weaker with every step. But they had no choice. The threat of violence pushed them forward.

When they reached Rafah, the streets were just as congested as Khan Yunis. Military activity was closer now, and warnings of airstrikes echoed over loudspeakers. They found refuge in a school run by an aid agency - a large, fading blue building. The walls were chipped, the windows broken, but it was a shelter. Salma led her family through the courtyard and found a small space to settle.

Her mother sank to the ground, exhausted. Salma spread a blanket, watching as other families did the same. Children played in the courtyard, some laughing, others crying. Adults exchanged hushed conversations. The school, once a place of learning, had become a temporary refuge for people who had lost everything.

But Salma found no peace. A storm of emotions churned inside her. Everything was spiralling out of control. And it all came back to Ahmed. There was a time when she had believed in their fight. She had been complicit, gathering information for him and her uncle, Abu Khaled. She had believed in the righteousness of their cause.

But now, as she looked around at the suffering, she questioned everything. The destruction was too much. The faces of the displaced haunted her. *Had she contributed to this?*

Ahmed, the man she loved, had been manipulated. At first, he had been so sure, so determined to fight for something larger. But as time dragged on, she saw him for what he truly was - a pawn. Her uncle and the leaders of Hamas twisted his convictions, using fear to control him. There was no turning back for Ahmed now. He was trapped, and it tore Salma apart.

She had once believed in the fight, even when she had gathered information in Tel Aviv. Her conversations with Yael had opened her eyes to another way. Yael had been an enemy but had shown her the possibility of peace. Coexistence wasn't a dream - it was possible. Salma had tried to tell Ahmed, sensing deep down that he wanted peace too. But Hamas had him in their grip. Every time he wavered, they pulled him back.

Salma couldn't help but wonder: *Could I have stopped this?* If she had been braver, if she had spoken to Yael. But her loyalty to Ahmed had kept her silent. Now, that silence weighed heavily. She had chosen loyalty over peace, and it seemed too late.

As she sat in the dusty courtyard, watching her brother sleep, jets roared overhead. The violence had no end. Her heart ached with the weight of choices not made. Could she ever forgive herself? Could she ever find a way out of the dark tunnel she had been pulled into?

She wasn't sure. Her only focus now was to protect her family, even if that meant turning her back on the path she and Ahmed had once walked.

Several weeks after arriving in Rafah, Ahmed and his men were summoned to a meeting deep within the tunnels. The air was colder here, thick with the scent of damp earth. It pressed down on them like the weight they had carried for far too long. Khaled and Hadi had just returned from their assignments and joined Ahmed as they moved toward the chamber.

The tunnels felt tighter here, the claustrophobic walls closing in. But it wasn't just the tunnels that made Ahmed feel trapped. His men were silent, their faces hollow with exhaustion. Dirt clung to their skin, sweat caking in layers. Their clothes were stiff from days of wear. Their eyes told the real story - haunted by the losses they had seen and the friends they had buried. Ahmed could feel their unspoken desperation. They had been fighting for too long. The war hung heavy on their shoulders, but there was no rest, no respite. It was either fight or die.

As they neared the meeting room, Ahmed caught the scent of freshly cooked food. His stomach twisted. How long had it been since any of them had eaten a proper meal? They had been surviving on scraps, scavenging what little they could. But as he stepped into the chamber, he saw Abu Khaled and Abu Fadel standing over a map. The two commanders were clean - immaculate even. Their clothes were pressed, not a single thread out of place. Their faces were calm, their bodies well-fed.

The contrast struck Ahmed hard. His own men, battle-worn and grim, stood just inside the room like ghosts of themselves, while these men, who claimed to lead, looked untouched by the suffering outside. It made Ahmed's stomach churn with disgust. *How could they look so fresh, so pristine, while his men carried the dirt and blood of the battlefield on their backs?*

Abu Khaled looked up. His eyes flicked briefly to Ahmed before returning to the map. He showed no sign of noticing the state of Ahmed's men. *Of course not,* Ahmed thought bitterly. *He hasn't seen the frontline in weeks.*

"*The IDF is closing in,*" Abu Khaled began, his voice measured, almost detached. "*They're preparing for a ground assault, moving closer to Rafah and Khan Yunis.*"

Ahmed kept his expression neutral, though the tension gnawed at him. "*We've reinforced the key positions along the tunnels,*" he replied. "*Khaled and Hadi have been overseeing the defences. We're ready if they advance.*"

Abu Fadel nodded, but his jaw tightened. "*Our supply lines are critical. If they cut us off, we lose everything. We can't let that happen.*"

Khaled, always sharp, stepped forward. "*We've set traps along the main routes. Secondary passages are reinforced, and we're rotating the guards. We'll keep them guessing.*"

Hadi added, his voice steady but laced with fatigue, "*The men are on edge, but they're prepared. If the IDF pushes, we'll push back harder.*"

Abu Khaled nodded, his gaze still on the map. "*Good. But stay flexible. The IDF has drones, satellites, spies. They're adapting. We need to stay ahead.*"

Ahmed felt the tension coil in his gut. He looked at Abu Khaled, standing there so calm, so certain. Something inside Ahmed snapped. He thought of the promises - the ones Abu Khaled had made months ago. That reinforcements were coming, that the other Arab nations would step in, that their allies would crush the IDF from the north while they held the south. He glanced at his men, at their hollow faces, and realised he couldn't hold it in any longer.

He took a step forward, his voice tight. "*Where are they?*"

The room stilled. Abu Khaled's eyes narrowed slightly, as if he hadn't understood the question. "*Where are who?*"

Ahmed's heart pounded, but he kept his voice controlled. "*The other Arab nations. The ones you promised. You said they would step in. That they would stop the Israelis before they reached us. But here we are.*" He gestured sharply at the map, his frustration breaking through. "*The IDF is closing in. Where are they, Abu Khaled? Where are the allies you spoke of?*"

Khaled and Hadi exchanged a glance. This wasn't how things were done. Questioning the leaders was dangerous. *But we're dying out there,* Ahmed thought bitterly. *We have the right to ask.*

Abu Khaled's face remained impassive, but a muscle in his jaw twitched. He slowly straightened, his eyes cold as they fixed on Ahmed. "*You dare to question me, Ahmed? I told you - everything is under control. We are winning this war.*"

Winning? Ahmed's mind reeled at the word. It was delusional. The tunnels were crumbling, the IDF was closing in from all sides, and they were bleeding fighters faster than they could replace them. The men at his side - his brothers - were starving, exhausted, barely holding on. And yet here stood Abu Khaled, looking as though he hadn't missed a meal in months, telling him they were winning?

Ahmed clenched his fists, forcing himself to stay calm. "*My men are dying,*" he said quietly, his voice like a knife in the silence. "*We are holding on by a thread. Every day we lose more ground. More lives. And you stand here and tell me we're winning?*"

Abu Khaled's eyes flashed with anger. "*Careful, Ahmed,*" he warned, his voice low and dangerous. "*You may have fought well, but don't forget your place. I make the decisions here. You're a soldier. You follow orders. I've told you - we have a strategy. And we are not losing.*"

Ahmed swallowed the bile rising in his throat. His men, standing behind him, shifted uncomfortably. He could feel their tension, their disbelief. They had seen the reality of the war. They had seen the blood, the bodies, the ruin. And yet they were being asked to believe this lie - that everything was under control. That they were winning.

Abu Khaled leaned in closer, his voice dropping lower. "*I suggest you focus on your task, Ahmed. Keep your men in line. Hold the tunnels. The rest is none of your concern.*"

Ahmed stared at the commander, feeling the weight of every lie that had been told. He had followed, he had believed. But now, standing here, filthy and worn, while these men feasted on lies and luxury, he knew the truth. *We've been abandoned,* he thought. *And we're being led to our deaths.*

With a curt nod, Ahmed stepped back. There was nothing more to say. The tension in the room was suffocating, but he wouldn't fight this battle here. Not now. His men were waiting. They were the only truth he had left.

Salma and her family stayed in the crowded shelter in Rafah for weeks. The days blurred together as they struggled to survive. The schoolyard, once filled with children's laughter, had become a sea of desperate people, all waiting for food, water, anything. Each day, aid trucks arrived but hope quickly turned to frustration. The trucks were full, but the people's hands remained empty.

Hamas controlled everything.

Salma watched in horror as fighters took control of the food and water supplies. Aid meant for civilians was intercepted, distributed only to those loyal to Hamas or to the fighters themselves. For the rest, there was nothing. She saw long lines of people waiting for hours, only to be turned away. Some were beaten for daring to ask.

One afternoon, Salma saw a man trying to take food for his children. His cheeks were hollow, his eyes wild with desperation. He was caught by one of the guards. There was shouting, then a gunshot. The man fell, lifeless, the small bag of bread still clutched in his hand.

A cold shiver ran down Salma's spine as she turned away, gripping her brother's hand tightly. The message was clear: Hamas wouldn't hesitate to kill their own to maintain control. Fear ruled the streets, and survival had become a daily battle.

Despite the aid trucks arriving regularly, little reached the starving masses. The food, the water, the essentials - everything was siphoned off by Hamas to sustain their fighters or sold on the black market. Rumours spread that some leaders were hoarding supplies, profiting while their people starved. Salma's stomach churned with anger and disgust. This wasn't the future they had fought for. It wasn't the justice she had believed in. Everything had twisted into something unrecognisable.

Her family had no choice but to scavenge. On good days, they found scraps of food from sympathetic neighbours or shared rations with other families. Water was rare, often coming from broken pipes or makeshift containers. Every drop was precious.

Hunger gnawed at them constantly. Her mother, frail to begin with, had grown weaker. Her brother's energy had drained away, replaced by a quiet lethargy that broke Salma's heart. But what hurt most was knowing that this suffering, this endless cycle of violence and deprivation, had its roots in the choices made by people like Ahmed - people she had once trusted.

The longer they stayed, the more Salma realised there was no escaping Hamas's grip. The violence, the hunger, the fear - it all felt inescapable. Yet, through it all, she couldn't shake the thought: *Could things have been different?* If she had made different choices, if she had spoken out earlier, maybe, just maybe, they wouldn't be here now.

As Ahmed led his men through the narrow tunnels, his thoughts wandered back to a time before the war, before he had become entangled in this life. The sound of their footsteps echoed off the cold walls, but Ahmed's mind wasn't in the present. He was thinking about the men who had shaped his path, who had led him here - most of all, Abu Khaled.

Abu Khaled had been a part of his life since he was a boy, a constant presence, guiding him deeper into Hamas. He remembered how Abu Khaled had spoken to him, his voice filled with conviction, his words crafted to instil loyalty, pride, and a sense of duty. Back then, it had all made sense. Back then, Ahmed had been desperate to belong to something bigger than himself.

Abu Khaled had known that, of course. He had seen the hunger in Ahmed's young eyes, the need for purpose, and had used it to pull him closer, deeper into the cause. At first, it had seemed noble - the fight for freedom, for their people - it had felt righteous. But over time, Ahmed began to see how he had been shaped, manipulated. He wasn't just another fighter in the cause, he was Abu Khaled's tool, moulded from boyhood to serve a purpose that wasn't his own.

The realisation made his stomach churn as he moved through the dark tunnel. *How long have I been blind? How long has Abu Khaled been pulling the strings, making sure I'd never leave?* Ahmed had trusted him, admired him even, but now he saw that it had never been about loyalty or justice. It had always been about control.

Khaled and Hadi flanked Ahmed, their movements precise, their breaths shallow, but Ahmed's thoughts were heavy. Khaled's sharp eyes scanned the dark space ahead, while Hadi, normally the more light-hearted of the two, had grown quieter. The loss of Tariq still weighed on them all.

But more than the death of his comrade, it was the weight of the truth that pressed on Ahmed's chest. He couldn't shake the feeling that all of this - the tunnels, the endless fighting - was the result of a lifetime of manipulation. Abu Khaled had known exactly what he was doing, using Ahmed's need for belonging, twisting it into something unrecognisable.

And then there was Abu Fadel. If Abu Khaled had moulded him, it was Abu Fadel who had made sure he would never escape. When Abu Fadel had sensed any doubts, it was he who had stepped in with threats. He had looked Ahmed in the eye and made it clear: *failure wasn't an option.*

"*Your family, Ahmed. Think of them. Think of Salma.*"

The threats had been so effective. How could Ahmed even consider walking away when he knew his family, the woman he loved, were under threat? Abu Fadel had played on his greatest fear - losing them. Ahmed hated him for it. Hated the way he had used his love for Salma as a weapon to keep him in line.

Salma... Her face flashed in his mind. She had tried, again and again, to make him see. She had told him there was another way, that the fight wasn't the only path. She had begged him to see the truth, but every time she spoke, Abu Khaled's teachings and Abu Fadel's threats drowned out her voice. Every time Ahmed had thought about leaving, he had been reminded of what was at stake.

His mind swirled with guilt. He had failed her. He had failed himself.

"*I miss Tariq,*" Khaled muttered suddenly, breaking the silence. "*He'd know how to handle this.*"

Ahmed's jaw clenched. Tariq had been more than a comrade. He had been a friend - someone who had believed in the fight as much as Ahmed had once believed. But now Tariq was gone, and all that was left were the ghosts of those promises.

"*We can't mourn now,*" Ahmed said, his voice steady but empty. "*Tariq would want us to finish this.*"

But what did finishing even mean? Ahmed had followed orders, led men into battle, buried friends in the dirt of this endless war, but where was the victory? Where was the freedom they had been promised? The leaders still talked of it, still fed the men their lines about a coming triumph, but Ahmed knew better now. They were clinging to a lie.

Hadi nodded, his voice hushed with grief. "*I keep thinking about him too. About what he'd say now. He'd tell us to keep our guard up. Not to give the enemy an inch.*"

Tariq would have said that, yes. But Tariq hadn't seen the things Ahmed had seen. He hadn't lived long enough to realise that the leaders - men like Abu Khaled and Abu Fadel - weren't fighting for the same reasons they were. They were playing a game of power, using men like Ahmed as pieces on the board. And they had no intention of losing, even if it meant sacrificing everyone.

As they neared a key tunnel intersection, Khaled turned to Ahmed, his voice businesslike. "*We've reinforced the entrances like you asked, but the northern access points are exposed. We need more men up there.*"

Ahmed stopped, weighing the situation. His mind was focused on the task, but he couldn't shake the heaviness inside him. "*Good thinking. Take a team and set up additional checkpoints. Make sure everyone knows - we can't lose those positions.*"

Khaled nodded, already planning his next move. "*Understood. We won't let them through.*"

"*I'll go with him,*" Hadi added. "*We'll cover more ground together.*"

Ahmed nodded, hearing the weariness in their voices but knowing there was no time for rest. Not now. He looked at both men, feeling a strange sense of pride, mixed with guilt. These men followed him, trusted him, even as the world around them crumbled. "*Stay sharp,*" he said. "*The enemy will be looking for any weakness. Don't give them one.*"

Khaled and Hadi disappeared down the dimly lit tunnel, leaving Ahmed alone with his thoughts. The memory of Abu Khaled's promises and Abu Fadel's threats weighed heavily on him. *How did I let them do this? How did I let them use me like this?*

He had believed in the cause once, believed in the fight for freedom. But now he saw it for what it was - control, manipulation, lies. Abu Khaled had taken him from a boy and moulded him into a fighter, a leader, and when doubt crept in, Abu Fadel had used his family, his love for Salma, to make sure he never left. Now, there was no way out. Not for him. Not for his men.

He turned back to the logistics, pushing the weight of his thoughts aside. There was still work to be done. The flow of weapons and ammunition from Rafah to Khan Yunis was critical. The IDF was trying to close the tunnels from Egypt by targeting the Philadelphia Corridor, trying to choke them off. If they lost the tunnels, they lost everything.

Ahmed called for Bilal, who was overseeing the supply lines. "*What's the status of the next shipment?*"

Bilal, holding a clipboard, glanced at his notes. "*More ammo and supplies from Egypt hopefully within the hour. I've instructed that the supplies come by the longer route to avoid detection, but we need more guards along the southern junction. It's exposed.*"

Ahmed nodded, the weight of responsibility pressing down on him. "*I'll send men to reinforce that position at once.*"

Bilal nodded, his face tight with worry. "*Good call. The fighters in Khan Yunis are counting on these supplies.*"

"*We won't let them down,*" Ahmed said firmly. But even as he spoke, he couldn't shake the doubt gnawing at him. *How long can we keep this up?*

Ahmed turned away, his thoughts heavy. They had to keep the supply lines open - for now, for survival. But deep down, Ahmed knew the truth. They weren't just running out of time. They were running out of lies to keep them going.

Chapter Fifty

YOSSI

Yossi's David jeep crawled slowly into the training area, its engine rumbling softly over the sand-blown ground of the Tze'elim base. The first thing he noticed was the sight of soldiers huddled beneath makeshift tarpaulins stretched between vehicles. The sun beat down relentlessly from a cloudless sky, casting sharp, unforgiving shadows on the desert floor. The tarps, tied to tank turrets and vehicle frames, created small pockets of shade where the soldiers sought relief from the punishing heat.

He scanned the scene. Underneath the tarps, tank crews sat on folding stools or directly on the dusty ground, their faces streaked with sweat and grime, uniforms stained dark from dirt and sand. Some soldiers leaned over tactical maps, their voices low as they plotted manoeuvres and attack routes. Others methodically cleaned their weapons, each movement slow and deliberate - a ritual to keep their hands steady and minds focused.

Nearby, a few men leaned back against the massive tracks of their Merkava IV tanks, eyes closed, snatching whatever precious moments of sleep they could before the next drill. Yossi could see the exhaustion etched into their faces, bodies slack but still poised, hands never far from their rifles.

Under another cluster of tarps, the IFV and APC crews moved with quiet urgency, reloading ammunition and performing last-minute checks on their weapon systems. Commanders crouched over maps, tracing routes and positions with their fingers, rehearsing every step, memorising every move. The air was filled with a low hum of anticipation - a collective breath held in the moments before the storm.

Nearby, the combat engineers sat in small groups, their tools and explosives laid out neatly beside them. They sipped water from canteens, wiped sweat from their brows, and exchanged quiet words. Their faces betrayed a mix of focus and apprehension. Yossi watched as they glanced at their hulking D9 Caterpillar bulldozers - armoured giants with reinforced blades and steel jaws, ready to breach walls or clear mines when the order came. The engineers would be among the first to move, and the knowledge showed in their expressions, a blend of determination and dread.

Further on, the artillery crews and spotters gathered around, their attention fixed on range calculations and firing coordinates. Yossi knew their role would be crucial - providing the precise, immediate fire support needed for the infantry to advance into Rafah. Some loaded shells into transport vehicles, while others peered through binoculars, practising their roles as forward observers, their faces set with concentration.

Yossi turned his gaze back to the broader scene, feeling a weight settle deep in his chest. The scale of the preparation, the sheer number of soldiers, vehicles, and equipment - it was overwhelming. This was no small operation, it was a full-scale assault, an all-out effort to break through the defences of Rafah and dismantle the stronghold, piece by piece.

He felt a knot tighten in his stomach. *'This is bigger than anything we've done before,'* he murmured to Nadav, his voice barely audible over the noise of engines and machinery.

Nadav, gripping the steering wheel, nodded, his expression serious. *'Bigger, yes,'* he replied. *'But we're ready, Yossi. We've trained for this. We know what to do.'*

Yossi tried to muster a smile, but the weight of the moment pressed on him like a heavy burden. *'Yeah,'* he agreed. *'We're ready. But this... this is different. Look at them - everyone's on edge. You can feel it in the air.'*

Nadav glanced at him briefly, then back to the road. *'We've been in tough spots before,'* he said, his voice calm but firm. *'This is just another mission. We go in, do our job, and we come out. Together.'*

Yossi nodded, feeling a mixture of anxiety and resolve. *'Together,'* he repeated softly, as their jeep continued through the preparation area. He knew that soon, all this would be put to the test. For now, he would focus, stay sharp, and ready himself for what lay ahead.

The Baladia Urban Warfare Training Centre was a maze of crumbling buildings, narrow alleys, and mock battle zones. Three weeks of intensive training stretched before them like a daunting mountain to climb. As a newly appointed Segen (Lieutenant), Yossi felt the weight of leadership on his shoulders more than ever.

At the start of the first week, Yossi stood with his men in the makeshift briefing room, the heat pressing down like a heavy blanket. Around him, his platoon was sweating, their faces serious but eager. He glanced at Nadav, now Samar (Staff Sergeant) and closest confidant, who caught his eye and nodded. Nadav was always ready, always calm under pressure - Yossi knew he could rely on him to keep the men steady.

'In this first week,' the instructor barked, *'you'll engage in various urban combat scenarios. This isn't just about shooting. This is about room-clearing, CQB (Close Quarters Battle), ambushes, and counter-ambush tactics. Every building, every alley could be a trap. We need you to think fast, move faster, and trust each other completely.'* You will be using the MAGAV system (Multiple Integrated Laser Engagement System) throughout the training and all results will be checked. So, if you hear a beep you are down.

Yossi took a deep breath, feeling the tension in the room coil like a spring. His men were looking to him for direction. *'Alright, you heard him,'* he said, his voice steady but commanding. *'We start now. Eyes open, heads down, and stick to your training.'*

The days that followed were relentless. Yossi led his platoon through room-clearing exercises, moving quickly through narrow hallways and tight spaces. His voice was calm and clear as he issued commands. *'Move, move! Cover left, check your corners!'* He knew that every step could be their last if they weren't careful.

They practised ambush tactics, learning to anticipate enemy movements, set traps, and react within seconds. Yossi felt the weight of every decision, every order. The men looked to him for confidence, and he gave it to them. Nadav was right there, coordinating team movements, ensuring every soldier knew their role.

One afternoon, they faced a sniper scenario. Yossi and his men had to move through an open area while simulated enemy snipers took shots from hidden positions. *'Stay low! Use cover!'* Yossi shouted, feeling adrenaline spike while Nadav flanked to the right, motioning his men to keep moving. Yossi trusted Nadav with his life, and it showed in the way they worked together - seamlessly, like parts of a well-oiled machine.

The second week brought a new challenge - subterranean warfare training. Yossi had heard about the tunnels beneath Rafah, the intricate web that Hamas had carved deep into the ground. Now, he would learn to navigate and fight in those dark, claustrophobic spaces.

The entrance to the training tunnels loomed ahead, a dark, gaping maw in the earth. Yossi felt a shiver run down his spine. *'Okay, listen up,'* he said to his men, his voice low and serious. *'This is going to be different. In these tunnels, it's not just about combat - it's about survival. Stick close, follow orders, and keep your heads clear.'*

They moved into the tunnels, and the world above seemed to vanish. It was dark, damp, and the walls seemed to close in around them. Yossi led the way, feeling the weight of the earth pressing down from above. Every step was a calculated risk. *'Nadav, watch the rear,'* he ordered. *'We need to be ready for anything.'*

Nadav nodded, his voice steady. *'I've got it, Yossi. Keep moving.'*

Yossi knew the dangers - IEDs, traps, hidden enemies. They trained to detect and neutralise threats, working in near silence. Every sound was magnified, every breath seemed too loud. The tension was suffocating, but Yossi kept his focus, guiding his men through the darkness, trusting his instincts and their training.

By the third week, Yossi's unit was exhausted but sharper than ever. The training shifted to advanced technologies and full-scale simulations.

Yossi's platoon was introduced to augmented reality (AR) tools using the *Elbit Systems' X-Sight* and *IronVision*, which displayed vital battlefield information directly onto their visor and Matrice 300 drones, enhancing their tactical capabilities. Yossi adapted quickly to the new technology. *'Nadav, get the drone up,'* he instructed during one exercise. *'We need eyes on the rooftops.'*

Nadav nodded, launching the drone and guiding it expertly. They watched the live feed on their AR screens, coordinating their movements based on real-time intelligence. It was a new way of fighting, but Yossi knew they had to master it if they were to succeed in Rafah.

The final days brought the ultimate simulations - full-scale exercises replicating the assault on Rafah. Yossi and Nadav led their platoon through complex urban terrain, engaging in firefights, securing buildings, and rescuing hostages. Every decision was critical, every move had to be perfect.

After each simulation, they endured intense debriefings. The instructors did not hold back, pointing out every mistake, every hesitation. Yossi listened carefully, analysing his choices, understanding where he could improve. He knew his men depended on him, and he was determined not to let them down.

As the final week ended, Yossi stood beside Nadav, watching their men pack up. The training had been brutal, but they had come through stronger.

Nadav looked at Yossi, a rare smile on his face. *'You did well, Segen,'* he said, using Yossi's new rank with a touch of irony.

Yossi chuckled. *'Thanks, Samar. Couldn't have done it without you.'*

Nadav nodded. *'We've been through worse, right?'*

Yossi smiled, the weight of the last three weeks lifting slightly. *'Yeah,'* he agreed. *'But this... this was something else. We're ready, Nadav. I know we are.'*

Nadav clapped him on the shoulder. *'Ready or not, it's coming.'*

Yossi felt a surge of confidence. The men looked to him, and he knew they would follow him into whatever lay ahead. *'Yeah,'* he said, his voice steady. *'And we'll face it together, like always.'*

The training was over, but the real test was yet to come. Rafah awaited, and Yossi knew they would have to be better than they had ever been. But as he looked at his men, at Nadav, he felt a sense of calm. They were ready - together, they could face anything.

The sun dipped low over the Negev Desert, casting long shadows across the Baladia Urban Warfare Training Centre. The harsh light softened as it hit the assembled soldiers of the Parachute Brigade, who stood in neat lines, their faces marked by exhaustion but also determination. Yossi stood among them, his eyes fixed on Lieutenant Colonel Arad, their CO, who had just stepped onto the raised platform at the front. A hush fell over the group, every soldier knew this was the moment they had been preparing for.

Arad didn't need to speak loudly to command attention. His presence alone was enough to bring everyone to silence. Yossi felt the weight of anticipation settle in his chest, mirrored by the men around him, including Nadav, who stood at his side, his posture relaxed but his eyes sharp.

'Men,' Arad began, his voice firm but even, *'over the last three weeks, you have trained harder than ever before. You've faced challenges, pushed past your limits, and shown exactly why you were chosen for this mission.'*

Yossi felt a swell of pride in his chest, but he kept his expression steady, his eyes on Arad. He knew his men were looking to him for cues, and he wanted to set the tone - calm, focused, ready.

'You've learned to navigate every obstacle,' Arad continued, *'to fight in every environment, and to rely on each other with absolute trust. These are the skills you will soon put to the test. Very soon, you will be using everything you have learned here at Baladia to take the fight to Hamas.'*

A ripple of energy moved through the assembled soldiers. Yossi could feel the adrenaline kicking in, his senses sharpening as he listened. He glanced at Nadav, who gave him a quick nod, a shared acknowledgment of what was coming.

Arad's gaze swept over the crowd, his face serious but filled with quiet confidence. *"You are part of a Battle Group that will be on the front lines, and your mission will be critical to the success of our operation. This is not a small task - it will demand everything you have, every ounce of courage, skill, and determination."*

Yossi tightened his jaw, feeling the gravity of Arad's words. He knew the risks, the stakes, but he also knew his men were prepared. This was what they had trained for, what they had committed themselves to.

Arad paused for a moment, letting his words settle. *'I want to thank each of you for your efforts and dedication during this training. You have proven yourselves ready for the challenge ahead. The date of the attack will be announced very soon. Until then, I encourage you to rest, recharge, and contact your families. Speak to them, but remember - do not mention our intentions or what is to come. The success of our mission depends on our silence.'*

Yossi nodded to himself, understanding the importance of keeping quiet. He knew the men around him did too. They had all seen what happened when information leaked, how it could jeopardise everything. Still, he also knew how much it would mean to hear a familiar voice, even just for a few minutes.

Arad gave a final nod. *'Stay sharp, stay focused, and be ready. Dismissed.'*

As the soldiers began to disperse, Yossi stood for a moment, taking in the atmosphere around him. Some of the men were already heading to find a quiet spot, others moving toward the phones. He felt a hand on his shoulder and turned to see Nadav.

'What do you think, Yossi?' Nadav asked with a faint smile, though his eyes remained serious.

Yossi exhaled, a small smile playing at the corner of his mouth. *'Time to get some rest... maybe make a call home,'* he said, a hint of weariness in his voice.

Nadav nodded. *'Yeah, good idea. We've got to take whatever moments we can, right?'*

'*Exactly,*' Yossi replied. He looked around at his men, sensing their quiet resolve, their readiness. He felt a wave of calmness settle over him. '*Whatever comes next, we're ready for it.*'

Nadav nodded again, clapping Yossi on the shoulder. '*We've got this, Yossi. And when the time comes, we'll do what we have to do.*'

Yossi nodded back. '*We will,*' he agreed. '*We face it together, like always.*'

The training was over, but the real challenge was just beginning. As Yossi made his way to the phone to make his call, he felt a sense of calm resolve. The waiting was nearly over, and soon they would be taking the fight to the enemy, side by side, just as they always had.

Yossi made his way directly to the row of phones set up along the side of a large tent. The sun had dipped below the horizon, and the cool of the desert evening began to settle over the base, a welcome relief after the relentless heat of the day.

He stood in line, his thoughts racing, his heartbeat louder than usual. The anticipation of hearing Yael's voice was a strange mix of comfort and anxiety. He hadn't spoken to her in weeks, not since the training had begun, and he knew she would be worried. He reached the front of the line, picked up the receiver, and dialled her number from memory, his fingers moving quickly over the buttons.

The phone rang a few times before he heard her voice, soft but clear. '*Hello?*'

Yossi felt a surge of emotion. '*Yael, it's me,*' he said, trying to keep his voice steady.

There was a brief pause, then he heard her sigh, filled with both relief and worry. '*Yossi... finally. I've been waiting to hear from you,*' she replied, her voice trembling slightly. '*Are you okay? Where are you?*'

'*I'm okay,*' he assured her, leaning against the tent, his voice calm. '*We've been training hard. It's been... intense. But we're ready for whatever comes next.*'

Yael was quiet for a moment, and Yossi could almost picture her biting her lip, trying to hold back her emotions. '*I've been worried,*' she admitted. '*I know you can't tell me much, but... just hearing your voice, it helps.*'

Yossi nodded, even though she couldn't see him. *'I know, Yael. I'm sorry it's been so long. Things have been busy, but I wanted to call you, to hear your voice too.'*

There was a pause before she spoke again, her voice softer now. *'Yossi... just promise me you'll be careful, okay? Whatever happens, just come back to me.'*

Yossi closed his eyes, feeling the weight of her words. *'I promise,'* he said quietly. *'I'll do everything I can to come back to you. You know that.'*

Yael's voice softened further, barely a whisper. *'I love you, Yossi.'*

He felt a tightness in his chest, a longing he couldn't quite put into words. *'I love you too, Yael. More than anything. Just hold on for a little while longer. I'll be home soon.'*

They shared a few more words, quiet reassurances, before saying their goodbyes. Yossi hung up the phone, taking a deep breath, feeling a mix of resolve and sadness settle over him. He needed that call, needed to hear her voice, but it also reminded him of everything he had to fight for - everything waiting for him back home.

As Yossi stepped away, Nadav took his place at the phone, his expression unreadable. He dialled quickly, fingers moving over the numbers with a practised ease. The call connected after a moment, and he heard Leila's voice on the other end.

'Nadav?' she answered, sounding surprised, and he could hear the background noise of the hospital where she worked.

'Leila, it's me,' he replied, a small smile forming despite himself. *'I'm sorry it's been a while. Things have been... complicated.'*

Leila's voice softened immediately. *'Nadav... I was worried. You're okay?'*

Nadav leaned back against the tent pole, his smile fading slightly. *'Yeah, I'm okay. Tired, but okay. We've been training non-stop, getting ready for... whatever comes next.'*

Leila was quiet for a moment. *'I know you can't tell me much,'* she said finally, *'but just knowing you're safe, that's enough for now.'*

Nadav felt a surge of warmth at her words. *'I'm safe,'* he assured her, trying to keep his tone light. *'And I'm thinking of you, Leila. Every day.'*

He heard her sigh on the other end, a mix of relief and worry. *'I think of you too,'* she whispered. *'I just... I just want you to come back to me, in one piece. That's all I ask.'*

Nadav chuckled softly, though his heart ached. *'That's the plan,'* he replied. *'I'll do my best to make it happen.'*

They talked for a few more minutes, about small things, mundane things, avoiding the reality of what was to come. Finally, Leila's voice dropped to a whisper again. *'Just... take care of yourself, okay? Promise me that.'*

'I promise,' Nadav said, his voice firm. *'I'll come back to you, Leila. I swear it.'*

When they finally hung up, Nadav stood there for a moment, staring at the phone. He felt a heaviness in his chest but also a sense of calm. He had done what he could to reassure her, to let her know he was okay. Now, all he could do was keep his promise - to her, to Yossi, to himself.

He turned to find Yossi waiting for him, a knowing look on his face. *'Everything good?'* Yossi asked.

Nadav nodded, a small smile playing on his lips. *'Yeah, everything's good. As good as it can be.'*

Yossi clapped him on the shoulder. *'That's all we can ask for right now.'*

They walked back towards their unit, side by side, ready to face whatever came next. They had made their calls, said their goodbyes, and now it was time to focus on the mission ahead.

Chapter Fifty One

AHMED

The tunnels were filled with an uneasy quiet, the kind that settles before a storm. Ahmed pressed his back against the cool, damp earthen wall, listening intently to the faint sounds echoing through the underground network. Snatches of hurried conversation, the shuffle of feet, and the distant hum of drones patrolling above filtered down through the still air. The tension was suffocating, thick enough to choke on. Something was happening.

Khaled appeared beside him, his face drawn and his eyes sharp with urgency. *"Ahmed,"* he whispered, *"they're moving the civilians out of Rafah."*

Ahmed's pulse quickened, though his expression remained calm. He had suspected this would happen, but hearing it confirmed sent a wave of dread through him. *"How do you know?"* he asked, his voice low, almost lost in the distant rumble of machinery.

Khaled tapped the small radio clipped to his belt. *"IDF broadcasts are coming through every channel,"* he replied. *"They're telling people to evacuate. Leaflets, loudspeakers, even local stations - they're all saying the same thing."*

Ahmed's brow furrowed. His mind spun with possibilities. *"They're clearing the civilians out,"* he murmured, more to himself than to Khaled. *"They're preparing to move in. We need to be ready."*

Above ground, Rafah was gripped by panic and confusion. Israeli aircraft circled menacingly overhead, dropping thousands of leaflets that drifted down like a sinister snowfall. Each flier carried the same chilling message:

"To the residents of Rafah: The IDF will be conducting a military operation in this area soon. For your safety, evacuate to the designated safe zones in the southern Gaza Strip. Use the marked routes and avoid all military areas. Leave immediately to avoid being caught in the crossfire."

The streets below were a chaotic tangle of desperate humanity. Families, the elderly, and young children struggled through the congested alleyways, clutching whatever belongings they could carry. Some gripped the leaflets tightly, their eyes darting back and forth over the crude maps, frantically searching for the safest route. Others pushed through the crowd with a frantic energy, fear driving them onwards.

Everywhere, the shrill beeping of mobile phones announced the relentless stream of automated warnings: *"Evacuate immediately. Move to the designated safe zones. Do not remain in the area."* IDF vehicles patrolled slowly through the neighbourhoods, their loudspeakers blaring the same message in Arabic: *"For your safety, evacuate now. Move to the designated areas. Do not delay."*

Salma found herself swept along in the tide of people, her hand wrapped tightly around her younger brother's. He stared up at her, his eyes wide and frightened. Her mother, pale and drawn with exhaustion, struggled to keep pace, clutching a small bag of their remaining possessions.

"Stay close to me," Salma whispered urgently, glancing over her shoulder. *"Don't let go, no matter what happens."*

Her mother's voice was thin and strained. *"We must keep moving. We have to reach the safe zones."*

The leaflets fluttered around them, dancing in the gusts stirred up by the panicked movement of hundreds of feet. Salma's heart hammered in her chest as they wove through the narrow streets, trying to avoid the surging mass of bodies around them. Everywhere she looked, she saw fear etched into faces - mothers clutching babies to their chests, old men leaning heavily on walking sticks, children stumbling along with tear-streaked cheeks. The city was a madhouse, a hive of misery and confusion.

The distant thunder of explosions reverberated through the ground, each rumble feeding the rising sense of terror. Salma glanced upwards again, squinting at the black silhouettes of jets circling high above like steel birds of prey. The leaflets rustled as they settled onto the ground around her, covering the streets like a mournful shroud.

She tightened her grip on her brother's hand. *"Keep your head down and stay with me,"* she murmured. *"We'll be all right."*

But even as she said it, she wasn't sure she believed it.

As they pushed on, the IDF's announcements grew louder, more insistent. The throngs of people around them surged forward in a frantic wave, driven by an unspoken fear of being left behind. Salma could feel the desperation in every face, the silent urgency pressing against her like a physical force. Then, from a loudspeaker mounted on a passing vehicle, a new warning crackled to life:

"Evacuate now. The operation is imminent. This is your final warning."

Salma's heart leapt in her chest. *"We need to move faster,"* she whispered, glancing anxiously at her mother, who nodded weakly in response.

"Keep going," her mother panted, her voice tight with strain. *"We can't stop now."*

In the tunnels below, Ahmed listened intently to the muffled voices, engines, and distant announcements from above. His mind raced. The IDF was making its move. The evacuation was the final warning before the assault.

He turned to his men, who stood clustered around him, their faces tight with anxiety. *"They're clearing out the civilians,"* he said, his voice firm and commanding. *"That means the attack is coming. We need to secure these tunnels and keep the supply lines open."*

Hadi, ever quick to act, stepped forward. *"Shall we set more traps? Increase the patrols?"*

Ahmed nodded. *"Yes. Double the guards at every access point. Place tripwires and mines near the entrances. Make sure the routes to Rafah are secure. Keep the IDF guessing, don't let them figure out our movements."*

Khaled's eyes flashed with grim determination. *"If they come, they'll regret every inch they take."*

"Exactly," Ahmed agreed. *"We fight for every inch. These tunnels are our lifeline. We cannot afford to lose them."*

As his men dispersed to carry out his orders, Ahmed felt a cold resolve settle over him. Time was running out, and the battle was inevitable. They had to hold their ground.

But as his men disappeared into the dim tunnels, a small doubt crept into Ahmed's mind - a whisper that had been growing louder with each passing day. *Is this really what we've fought for all these years?* They were promised support from the Arab nations, told that they would drive the Jews into the sea. *And yet...*

Frustration flared. *Where are our leaders now, when we fight and die?* They sat in their palaces, far removed from the blood and ruin, delivering speeches while their fighters were buried in the dirt. *Victory was supposed to be certain. Allah was supposed to deliver us...*

Ahmed shook his head, pushing the thoughts aside. *I can't think like this. Not now. Not when so much depends on us holding this ground.* Yet the doubts lingered, a shadow at the edge of his mind.

The road ahead seemed endless, a treacherous maze of rubble and debris, clogged with bodies pushing and shoving to escape. Salma glanced around, trying to make sense of the chaos. There were too many people, too many frightened, desperate faces. The fear was palpable, like a suffocating blanket smothering them all.

Finally, they reached the southern edge of Rafah. The scene before them was one of utter bedlam. Cars and trucks, piled high with belongings, crept along at a snail's pace. Families perched precariously atop the swaying loads, clutching everything they owned - mattresses, blankets, cooking utensils - anything that could be salvaged. Children peered wide-eyed over the teetering stacks, their faces pale with exhaustion and fear.

Nearby, a line of makeshift tents stretched along the roadside, flimsy structures of canvas and tarpaulin that offered little protection from the harsh sun. The ground was churned to mud by the constant press of feet, and the acrid smell of sweat, fear, and unwashed bodies filled the air. Every few metres, people huddled together in small clusters, sharing whispered conversations or staring blankly at the endless stream of humanity moving past them.

Salma's brother whimpered softly, his small hand trembling in hers. *"I'm tired,"* he whispered, his voice barely audible above the din.

Salma glanced down, her heart breaking at the sight of his pinched, weary face. *"Just a little longer,"* she murmured, forcing a smile. *"We're almost there."*

Her mother staggered, her face white with fatigue. Salma caught her arm, steadying her. *"You're all right, Mama?"*

Her mother nodded shakily, her lips pressed into a thin line. *"I'm fine,"* she whispered, but Salma could see the strain in her eyes. The weight of the past weeks was etched deeply into her features - lines of worry and exhaustion that hadn't been there before.

Pushing on, they joined the column of vehicles inching its way along the cracked, dusty road. Every step was an ordeal, every metre a battle against the press of bodies around them. But slowly, painfully, they made their way south, towards the IDF-designated *"safe zone"* stretching from al-Mawasi to Khan Younis and Deir al-Balah. It was supposed to be a refuge, a place of relative safety, but Salma couldn't shake the uneasy feeling twisting in her gut.

The road stretched on and on, a winding snake of misery and desperation that seemed to have no end. All around her, the refugees moved in silence, their eyes fixed blankly ahead. The air was thick with dust and smoke, the sun beating down mercilessly from a sky bleached white by the heat.

Finally, after what felt like an eternity, the tents of the humanitarian zone came into view - a sprawling mass of white fabric pitched haphazardly across the barren landscape. The sight sent a fresh wave of weariness crashing over Salma, but she forced herself to keep moving. They had made it this far. They couldn't stop now.

They stumbled into the camp, their legs trembling with exhaustion. The relief workers barely glanced at them as they passed, their faces drawn with fatigue. Salma found a small patch of ground near the edge of the camp and helped her mother ease herself down. Her brother sank onto the ground beside her, curling up like a small, exhausted animal.

Salma looked around, her eyes scanning the endless rows of tents, the huddled families, the haunted, hollow-eyed faces staring blankly back at her. This was safety? This crowded, filthy, sun-baked strip of land? She swallowed hard, the reality of their situation settling over her like a suffocating weight.

But they had no choice. This was where they would stay - at least for now.

"We made it," she whispered softly, brushing her brother's hair back from his sweaty forehead. *"We're safe, little one. We're safe."*

By the first week of May, Rafah had become a ghost town. The once-bustling streets now stood silent and empty. Over a million people had evacuated in less than five days, leaving behind a desolate, abandoned city.

Buildings lay vacant, windows shattered, doors left swinging open. Leaflets, which had once fluttered through the air, now littered the ground, swept into corners and gutters. A strange, hollow quiet had descended over the city, broken only by the occasional echo of artillery fire.

Ahmed emerged cautiously from one of the tunnel exits, lifting the cover to peer above. The scene sent a chill through him - emptiness, abandonment, an eerie stillness. The evacuation had worked. Rafah had been emptied of its civilians, leaving only fighters like him and his men behind.

"It's like a ghost town out there," he murmured, almost reverently.

Khaled nodded grimly. *"That means they're ready. The airstrikes will begin soon."*

Ahmed glanced at Khaled, then over to Hadi, who stood by the edge of the tunnel, his weapon ready. *"We have to hold our positions. The IDF will strike hard, and when they do, we must be ready to move, to strike back."*

Hadi's jaw tightened as he nodded. *"We know what to do, Ahmed. We're prepared."*

That evening, as the sun dipped below the horizon, a low rumble began to grow. Ahmed felt it before he heard it - a deep vibration that seemed to resonate through the earth, growing steadily louder. He knew the sound. Jets were approaching. Death was coming.

Through the narrow gap in the tunnel cover, he watched the streaks of light from Israeli jets cutting through the darkening sky. The air was still, as if waiting for the inevitable.

Then, the first explosion hit.

The deafening roar shook the ground, sending dust and debris cascading from the ceiling. Ahmed ducked instinctively, pulling his scarf over his face as a cloud of dust billowed through the tunnel.

Where are our allies now? he thought bitterly. *Where are the armies we were promised?* But there was no answer, only the sound of the next explosion, louder and closer.

"Get back inside!" Ahmed shouted, motioning for his men to retreat deeper into the tunnel. *"They're starting their bombardment."*

Khaled and Hadi swiftly ushered the others back. The lights flickered overhead as the ground continued to shake with each impact.

For hours, the bombardment continued. Airstrikes came in relentless waves, each one more intense than the last. The distant whine of drones and the booming detonations of bombs filled the air.

Ahmed crouched in a small chamber deep within the tunnels, sweat dripping down his face. His radio crackled with fragmented reports from other units -

fighters calling out positions, confirming hits, trying to maintain communication amidst the chaos.

And where are our leaders? Safe in their homes, sending messages of courage from afar. Ahmed pushed down his rising anger.

"The southern sector is taking heavy fire," came a voice over the radio. *"They're targeting the entrances!"*

Ahmed grabbed the radio, pressing the button hard. *"This is Ahmed. Hold your positions. Reinforcements are on the way. Keep the supply lines secure at all costs."*

He turned to Khaled and Hadi. *"Take a team and reinforce the southern sector. We can't let them breach the tunnels."*

Khaled nodded, already moving. *"Understood, Ahmed. We'll hold them back."*

Hadi grabbed his weapon, giving Ahmed a confident nod before disappearing into the dark.

Ahmed knew this was only the beginning. The real battle had not yet started. The airstrikes were just the prelude.

"We've prepared for this," he muttered. *"We hold these tunnels, we keep the supplies moving, and we make them fight for every inch."*

His men moved with discipline, their faces set with determination. Ahmed knew they were ready. But as the airstrikes continued above, he also knew that the days ahead would test them to their limits.

The fight for Rafah had begun, and there was no turning back now.

Chapter Fifty Two

YOSSI

Yossi stood near the forward line with his unit, the desert air thick with tension. The sun was dipping below the horizon, casting a reddish hue over the landscape. The whole brigade was positioned close to the border, waiting for the signal to launch their assault on Rafah. It was the fifth of May, and Yossi could feel the anticipation crackling in the air like static electricity.

His eyes swept across the battlefield—a sea of military might. Merkava IV tanks gleamed under the fading sun, their colossal forms casting long shadows across the desert. Namer infantry fighting vehicles (IFVs) stood alongside them, their engines rumbling softly. Artillery pieces further back, fired intermittently, sending shockwaves through the ground. The constant booms were the prelude to the storm of battle that loomed ahead.

For days, Yossi had watched as Rafah endured relentless bombardment. Airstrikes lit up the night sky, flashes of light followed by dark columns of smoke rising from the city like blackened pillars. The artillery had pummelled the enemy's command centres, tunnel entrances, and positions in an unyielding rhythm. Yossi knew this was only the beginning.

The weight of the moment settled heavily upon him. Every soldier in his unit shared a quiet understanding: this would be a battle unlike any other. The narrow, twisting streets of Rafah, with their labyrinthine network of tunnels and makeshift defences, would test them to their limits.

To his left, Yossi watched the tank crews making their final checks. Soldiers scrambled over the hulls of the Merkava IVs, tightening bolts, testing the reactive armour, adjusting the sights with a precision born of muscle memory—years of training crystallised into these moments. Around the IFVs and armoured personnel carriers (APCs), his men drilled with machine-like efficiency, practising rapid dismounts and formations.

"*Faster, faster!*" Yossi barked. His voice cracked through the desert air like a whip. "*We need to be out and moving before they even know what hit them!*"

His men responded immediately, their movements quick and practised. Yossi watched them closely, his eyes sharp. Every second mattered. Every motion, every gesture needed to be seamless once they hit the city streets. The slightest hesitation could mean the difference between life and death.

Nadav approached, his arms crossed as he observed the men. "*They're moving well,*" he said, though his tone was reserved. "*But they're still not tight enough. The delay between exiting the vehicles and forming up is too long.*"

Yossi nodded without taking his eyes off his soldiers. "*They're close. But close isn't good enough. We drill until it's perfect.*"

Nadav's gaze flickered in agreement. "*Because once we're in, there'll be no margin for error.*"

Around them, the rest of the battle group was a flurry of activity. Combat Engineers prepped their hulking D9 bulldozers—massive machines, armoured and reinforced to clear debris, breach barriers, and destroy tunnel networks. Medics were setting up triage stations in preparation for the inevitable casualties, their movements swift but solemn. The hum of engines, the scent of diesel, and the sweat dripping from every brow—all combined to form a heady mix of preparation and impending destruction.

Yossi glanced at his men once more. They were as ready as they could be. Weapons were loaded, gunners poised behind heavy machine guns, every eye locked onto their next command. Yet, as prepared as they were, Yossi knew nothing could truly ready them for the fight ahead.

He cleared his throat, raising his voice. *"Alright, listen up! When we hit those streets, there's no room for hesitation. Disembark fast, form up faster, and move with purpose. Every second counts out there. They'll be waiting, and we need to stay one step ahead."*

His men nodded in unison, their faces grim and resolute. *"Yes, Segen!"* they shouted.

Yossi could see the nerves in some of them, the youngest ones, still green to combat. But there was determination in their eyes too, the look of men who understood what was at stake and were willing to face it.

"We'll run it again," Yossi ordered, his voice steady. *"This time, I want you out of those vehicles as if your lives depend on it… because they do."*

The drill repeated, faster, sharper. Soldiers leapt from APCs in practised motions, rifles raised, forming up with fluid precision. They were getting there. Yossi caught Nadav's eye, and Nadav gave a slight nod.

"We keep this up until it's second nature," Yossi murmured. *"No stopping until they can do it in their sleep."*

Nadav's reply was quiet but firm. *"We'll get there. We always do."*

The order finally came. The radio crackled with the command, a single word that sent a jolt of electricity through Yossi's veins. It was time.

Engines roared to life. The ground trembled as the armoured vehicles surged forward, and the air was filled with the guttural rumble of machinery moving into battle formation. Yossi's heart pounded as his APC lurched forward. His grip tightened on his rifle, feeling its familiar weight against his shoulder, the cold metal steadying him.

The convoy advanced towards Rafah, the landscape a blur of dust and smoke. The city loomed ahead, a maze of narrow streets and shattered buildings, the remnants of weeks of bombardment. Fires still burned in the distance, thick black smoke rising like funeral pyres.

THROUGH THEIR EYES

Yossi's eyes scanned the convoy through the narrow viewport of the APC as it rumbled towards Rafah. Dust swirled in the air, and the vibrations from the engine hummed through his body, but his mind was focused, alert. He knew Nadav's vehicle wasn't far behind, always keeping a tight formation.

Yossi keyed the radio, his voice cutting through the static. *"Nadav, how's it looking back there?"*

There was a brief crackle before Nadav's calm voice came through. *"All good, Yossi. We're right behind you. Once we hit the city, we'll move fast. No stopping."*

Yossi nodded, even though Nadav couldn't see him. *"Stay close. We need to stay tight once we disembark. No gaps in formation."*

"Got it. We'll stick tight," Nadav's reply was steady, the reassurance that Yossi needed as they approached the chaotic urban environment ahead.

The tight alleys of Rafah forced the vehicles into single file, their engines growling with effort as they pushed through rubble and debris. Yossi's muscles tensed as small arms fire erupted from the surrounding buildings, bullets pinging off the APC's armour with a metallic whine. His instincts kicked in.

"Here we go," Yossi muttered. *"Everyone, eyes open! Snipers could be anywhere!"*

His APC reached the edge of their first target zone, and Yossi gave the order. *"Disembark!"*

The door hissed open, and his men poured out, rifles at the ready, moving with speed and purpose. The heat of the street hit them like a wall, dust, smoke, and the stench of burning fuel thick in the air. Yossi dropped down, landing in a crouch, his senses on high alert. They were in enemy territory now.

"Cover me!" Yossi barked as he moved behind a low wall. The rattle of machine guns echoed around them, and the unmistakable crack of sniper fire cut through the chaos.

"Nadav, take your squad left!" Yossi shouted, gesturing towards a nearby building. *"We'll cover you. Secure that structure!"*

Nadav signalled his men, and they moved swiftly, darting from cover to cover. Yossi tracked their movements, heart in his throat. His eyes scanned the windows of the surrounding buildings, every flicker of movement a potential threat.

A burst of gunfire erupted, and one of Nadav's men went down hard. Yossi's pulse surged.

"Sniper!" Yossi yelled. *"Get down!"*

His men dove for cover, rifles raised. Yossi spotted a glint from a nearby window and squeezed off a burst of his own. The sniper's position went silent, but Yossi knew there were more. They were everywhere, hiding in the rubble, slipping in and out of the tunnel networks like ghosts.

The advance was slow and gruelling. Every step deeper into Rafah felt like stepping into a trap. The enemy fighters knew the terrain, using the warren of tunnels and buildings to strike and disappear like shadows. It was urban warfare at its most brutal, close-quarters combat in a city that had become a battlefield.

"Stay sharp!" Yossi's voice rang out. *"Every building, every corner could be a trap."*

Combat Engineers followed closely, using drones to scout ahead, their screens showing live feeds of rooftops and alleyways, searching for hidden enemy positions. Each step was calculated, each advance measured against the possibility of an ambush. The streets were a tangle of rubble and chaos, every intersection a potential deathtrap.

"Drones up!" Yossi commanded, watching as the small machines buzzed into the air, scanning for enemy movement.

The enemy fought with a mixture of desperation and cunning. They struck from tunnels, launched hit-and-run attacks, and vanished into the labyrinth beneath the city. Yossi's men were constantly on edge, their nerves fraying with each firefight, each near miss.

Tanks fired on fortified positions, shells tearing through the walls of buildings that refused to yield. The roar of explosions filled the air, followed by the unsettling quiet that came after—the calm before the next wave of gunfire.

Yossi's thoughts flickered briefly to the training they had endured, how they had drilled for this kind of warfare in the mock urban environments of the Tze'elim base. Every room they cleared, every alley they secured, was a reflection of those days, only now the stakes were higher. Mistakes cost lives.

"Nadav, flank left!" Yossi called over the radio. *"Push them out of that building."*

His men moved with determination, but Yossi could see the strain on their faces, feel the weight of the fight in their movements. The enemy was relentless, popping out from tunnels, firing, then disappearing underground before Yossi's men could retaliate.

"They're using the tunnels," Nadav's voice crackled through the radio. *"We've found three entrances so far, but there could be more."*

"Seal them," Yossi ordered. *"We can't leave any way for them to escape."*

The Engineers worked swiftly, setting charges at tunnel entrances, sealing off the underground routes that gave the enemy their greatest advantage. But for every tunnel they sealed, it felt like two more opened.

Yossi could feel the exhaustion creeping in. His body was drenched in sweat, his muscles sore from hours of combat. But there was no time to rest. The fight wasn't over. Not yet.

The deeper they moved into Rafah, the more hostile the environment became. The city, already reduced to rubble by the bombardment, felt like a maze of death. Every street corner, every shadowed window was a potential hiding spot for snipers or ambush teams. Yossi could feel the weight of the city bearing down on him, a suffocating tension that gnawed at his nerves.

His men moved with caution, their eyes scanning every building, every shattered window. The training had prepared them for this, but now that they were in the thick of it, Yossi could see how different the real fight was. The enemy wasn't a predictable target in a mock-up village... it was invisible, waiting, striking from nowhere.

They had cleared several streets when Yossi's radio crackled into life. *"Segen, we've found another tunnel entrance. Looks active... fighters are using it to move between buildings."*

It was one of the engineers, his voice tense but controlled.

"Seal it," Yossi responded, his voice firm. *"We can't let them keep moving beneath us. Set charges and block every route."*

The engineer confirmed, and Yossi shifted his focus back to the immediate threat. The street ahead was narrow, the buildings packed tightly together, their crumbling facades showing the scars of previous strikes. This part of Rafah was particularly treacherous; it felt like stepping into the heart of the enemy's stronghold.

"Nadav," Yossi called through the radio. *"I need your team to flank the right side. We'll take the left and push forward. Watch for crossfire... this street's too tight."*

"Copy that, Yossi," came the steady reply.

Yossi motioned to his men, leading them to the left side of the street. They moved in a line, using the rubble and broken walls as cover. The sound of distant gunfire echoed through the city, but here it was eerily quiet, a silence that only increased the tension.

As they approached the next building, Yossi held up his hand, signalling for his men to stop. Something wasn't right. The building looked intact, but there was a stillness that made Yossi's instincts scream.

"Hold position," he muttered into the radio. *"We'll clear this building. Too quiet for my liking."*

He motioned for two of his men to follow him. They approached the entrance cautiously, weapons raised, eyes scanning every possible angle. Yossi's heart raced as they neared the door, his grip tightening on his rifle.

Suddenly, a burst of gunfire erupted from the upper floor, shredding the doorway and forcing Yossi and his men to dive for cover. The air filled with the deafening roar of machine-gun fire, the bullets ricocheting off the rubble around them.

"Sniper! Upper floor!" Yossi shouted, his voice barely audible over the gunfire. *"Get down!"*

His men scrambled to take cover, their backs pressed against the walls. Yossi risked a glance upwards and spotted the muzzle flash from a broken window. They were pinned down.

"Nadav, we've got a sniper on the upper floor. We need support," Yossi radioed, his breath coming in short bursts. He could feel the adrenaline coursing through his veins, the familiar rush that came with the chaos of battle.

"On it, Yossi. Hold tight," Nadav's voice came back, calm despite the situation.

Moments later, the roar of a tank's cannon echoed through the streets, the shell smashing into the upper floor of the building. The explosion sent debris flying, and the gunfire ceased.

Yossi took a deep breath, signalling his men to move. *"Now! Get inside and clear the building!"*

They charged forward, storming the entrance with weapons raised. The interior was dim, filled with dust and the acrid smell of explosives. Yossi moved swiftly, his rifle sweeping the room. His men followed closely, clearing each corner with the precision they had drilled into their bones during the long days of training.

The building was empty, save for the sniper's shattered body lying in the rubble of the upper floor.

"Clear!" one of Yossi's men called out.

Yossi nodded, his eyes scanning the room for any signs of further threats. The silence was unnerving. He could hear his own breathing, heavy and laboured, mingling with the distant sounds of battle.

"Nadav," Yossi said into the radio, *"we're moving to the next street. Keep your men tight."*

The radio crackled with static before Nadav's response came through. *"Understood. We'll flank from the east and push them back."*

Yossi stepped outside, the air thick with the stench of smoke and dust. His men followed, their faces grim but determined. The sun was setting now, casting long shadows over the ruined city, making it harder to see, harder to anticipate where the next attack might come from.

The night was closing in, but the battle was far from over.

The fighting continued well into the night. Every metre of ground was hard-fought, the enemy using guerrilla tactics to slow their advance. Yossi's men were exhausted, their movements slower, but their resolve had not faltered. They knew that any hesitation, any lapse in concentration, could be fatal.

"Keep moving!" Yossi urged, his voice hoarse from shouting. *"We're close to securing this sector."*

The street ahead opened into a small square, littered with debris and the burnt-out remains of vehicles. Yossi knew this would be a choke point, an ideal location for an ambush. He immediately signalled for the drones to scout ahead, their buzzing filling the otherwise quiet night.

The live feed from the drones showed movement in the buildings surrounding the square. The enemy was entrenched, waiting for Yossi's men to advance into the kill zone. Yossi scanned the drone footage, his gut telling him the enemy was preparing to pin them down if they tried to move across the open ground.

He turned to his Forward Air Controller, Segen Tomer Avidan, standing just behind him with a headset on, eyes glued to his tablet, which was linked to the drones and targeting systems. Yossi tapped him on the shoulder.

"Tomer, we're not moving through that square until it's cleared. Mark those buildings and get fast air to hit them. I want those positions gone before we step foot out there."

Tomer nodded sharply, immediately tuning his radio to the air support frequency. *"Roger that, Yossi. I'll mark the targets and call in fast air."*

Tomer worked quickly, coordinating with the drone operator and marking the enemy positions on his tablet. *"This is Viper Four Actual, requesting immedi-*

ate air support at grid coordinates Alpha-Six-Three. Target buildings marked for strike, requesting fast movers. How copy?"

A moment later, the radio crackled with a response. *"Viper Four Actual, airstrike confirmed. Fast movers inbound, ETA two minutes. Hold your position."*

Tomer turned to Yossi, giving a thumbs-up. *"Airstrike inbound in two minutes, Segen. Targets locked."*

Yossi gave a curt nod, then relayed the information to his squad over the radio. *"Hold position. Fast air is inbound. We'll clear that square from the air before we move in."*

The minutes stretched out, the tension thick in the air. Yossi crouched behind the cover of a collapsed wall, his eyes flicking between Barak and the sky. His men stayed low, alert but still, waiting for the imminent airstrike that would soften up the enemy positions.

Then, they heard it—the distant roar of jets growing louder. The tension peaked as the aircraft screamed overhead, followed by the unmistakable whoosh of bombs being released.

Seconds later, the square lit up in a series of blinding explosions. The targeted buildings erupted as the ordnance found its mark, the thunderous roar shaking the ground beneath Yossi and his men. Flames and debris shot into the air, the shockwave slamming against the surrounding structures. Dust and smoke engulfed the area, blotting out the sky for a moment.

Tomer scanned the aftermath on his tablet, the drone feed now showing little more than rubble where the enemy had been entrenched.

"Direct hits, Yossi. Enemy positions are neutralised."

Yossi didn't waste a moment. He keyed his radio again, giving the next command. *"Tanks, move up. Clear any remaining positions."*

The Merkava IV tanks rumbled forward, their cannons aimed at what remained of the enemy fortifications. The deep thud of tank shells followed, further pulverising the area. Each shot tore through what was left of the enemy defences, leaving little to stand in their way.

When the dust began to settle, Yossi called for Nadav's squad. *"Nadav, take your men in now. We'll provide cover from the flanks. Sweep the buildings."*

Nadav's voice crackled back in affirmation. *"Roger, moving in."*

Yossi's heart raced as he watched Nadav's men dart from cover, advancing into the square in tactical formation, covering each other as they approached the shattered buildings. Yossi's men provided overwatch, eyes scanning for any hidden threats, but the airstrike and tank shells had done their job. What little remained of the enemy resistance was swept away as Nadav's men cleared the interior, moving swiftly and efficiently from room to room.

"Clear!" Nadav's voice called out over the radio.

Yossi gave the signal for his own squad to move in and secure the perimeter. His men advanced cautiously but steadily, securing the square as they cleared the last of the debris. Inside, they found the remnants of the enemy force,,, bodies and shattered equipment buried beneath the rubble.

Finally, after what felt like an eternity, the gunfire ceased. The square was theirs.

Yossi lowered his rifle, his chest heaving from the exertion. He scanned the battlefield, the flickering flames from destroyed vehicles casting an eerie glow over the carnage. His men stood around him, their faces drawn but triumphant.

"Sector secure," Yossi called into the radio. His voice was thick with exhaustion, but there was a note of satisfaction. They had done it. But as he looked around, he knew this was just the beginning.

The square was secured, but the victory felt hollow. The battle had been brutal, and Yossi could see the toll it was taking on his men. As the night deepened, the exhaustion was visible in every face, the weight of the fight etched into the lines of their expressions. Yossi wiped the sweat from his brow, leaning heavily against a crumbled wall. His body ached, and his mind buzzed with the aftermath of adrenaline, exhaustion, and worry.

His radio crackled to life, and Nadav's voice came through, tired but steady. *"Yossi, we've swept the area. No sign of more fighters for now. We'll set up a temporary perimeter and hold here until morning."*

"Understood," Yossi replied, glancing around at his men, slumped against walls, rifles resting in their laps, eyes scanning the darkness for any sign of movement. The lull in fighting was a welcome reprieve, but Yossi knew it was only temporary. The battle was far from over.

That night, they set up a temporary perimeter in the shell of a destroyed building. The men took shifts, some resting, others keeping watch. Yossi sat on the cold ground, his rifle across his lap, and for the first time in days, his thoughts drifted to Yael.

He wondered if she thought of him often, if she had any idea how close he'd come to not making it through another day. He pictured her face, the way she smiled when he returned home, but even the memory felt distant now, as though the war had built an invisible wall between them. *Would he be the same man when he returned? Would she even recognise who he had become?*

Nadav appeared beside him, his footsteps barely audible over the crackle of the small fire they had built. He lowered himself to the ground, stretching his legs out, the exhaustion clear in his posture.

"Thinking about home?" Nadav asked, his voice quieter than usual.

Yossi nodded, his thoughts still far away. *"Yeah. Just... thinking about how different everything feels now. I don't know if I'll be the same when all this is over."*

Nadav was silent for a moment, staring at the flickering flames. *"I get that. It's like... we're changing out here. I wonder how much we'll leave behind when this is all done. It's hard to know how to even talk about it with someone who hasn't been through it."*

Yossi glanced over at Nadav, the shared concern clear between them. They had both seen so much, endured so much, that it felt impossible to imagine going back to the normality of life before the war.

"I keep thinking about Yael," Yossi said quietly. *"Wondering if she'd even recognise me if she saw me now. I don't know if I'd recognise myself."*

Nadav nodded, his expression unreadable for a moment. *"I think about that too. How this is going to change everything. Leila... she probably still sees me the way I was when I left. But now? We're not the same anymore, are we?"*

The weight of Nadav's words settled heavily on Yossi. It wasn't just about surviving this battle. It was about what would be left of them when it was all over.

"We'll make it back," Nadav added, a touch of resolve creeping into his voice. *"We've come this far. We just have to keep going."*

Yossi nodded, but the weight of doubt lingered. He had to believe Nadav was right... he had to keep moving forward for the sake of his men, for himself, and for the life waiting for him outside this nightmare.

The deeper they went into Rafah, the more the strain began to show, not only on Yossi, but on his entire unit. Fatigue etched itself into their faces, their movements slower, their responses more cautious. Yossi could see the same exhaustion in his own reflection every time he caught a glimpse of himself in a broken window.

One night, after another brutal encounter, Nadav pulled Yossi aside, his voice laced with concern.

"You're running on fumes, Yossi," he said, keeping his tone level but firm. *"I've seen you pushing yourself harder than anyone, but you're close to burning out. We need you to keep your head straight."*

Yossi leaned against the wall, rubbing his eyes. *"I'm fine, Nadav. I can keep going."*

Nadav shook his head. *"You're not fine. We've been through a lot, and I get it. I feel it too. But the difference is, you're the one who everyone's looking to. If you start falling apart, the whole unit's going to feel it."*

Yossi's shoulders slumped, and for the first time, he didn't argue. The truth was, he felt like he was falling apart. The responsibility, the guilt, the constant loss—it was grinding him down, and he didn't know how to stop it.

Nadav's voice softened. *"We'll make it through this, Yossi. Just don't carry it all by yourself. Let the rest of us carry some of that weight. You don't have to do it alone."*

Yossi nodded, though the weight in his chest didn't lift. But he trusted Nadav. He had to.

By the sixth day, Yossi could barely tell if it was morning or night. His hands trembled from fatigue, and his mind was clouded by the endless hours of combat. Every decision weighed heavily on him, each one critical, each one potentially life or death. The fatigue ran deeper than just lack of sleep; it was the mental exhaustion of leadership—the constant pressure of keeping his men alive.

He fought to keep his focus, but the toll of the battle was becoming harder to ignore. Each moment was spent calculating the next move, the next order. The responsibility to lead, to be decisive, never let up. There was no room for doubt, no space for hesitation, and Yossi knew his men were watching him... depending on him. It was the unspoken burden that kept him upright when his body wanted to give in.

Nadav had been watching him closely for days, sensing the strain building behind Yossi's controlled exterior. That evening, as they paused to regroup in the ruins of a building, Nadav approached him quietly, his expression serious but gentle.

"Enough's enough, Yossi," Nadav said, his voice firm but not harsh. *"You've been pushing too hard for days, and it's showing. We can't afford to lose you, not now."*

Yossi straightened slightly, instinctively ready to deflect the concern. *"I'm fine,"* he muttered, the words hollow even as they left his mouth. He wasn't fine, but admitting it felt like weakness, and weakness wasn't something a commander could afford.

But Nadav wasn't having it. *"You're not fine,"* he said, taking a step closer. *"Look at yourself. You haven't slept properly in days. You're running on nothing but adrenaline, and that's going to run out. Soon."*

Yossi's jaw tightened, his eyes flicking over to his men, then back to Nadav. He could feel the exhaustion pulling at him, the fog in his mind making it harder to think clearly, but the idea of stepping back... of letting someone else take the weight, even for a moment, felt impossible. *"I can't,"* he whispered, his voice betraying the deep weariness he hadn't allowed himself to acknowledge. *"I don't know how to stop. If I stop..."*

Nadav's eyes softened, the edges of his voice turning from firmness to understanding. *"You don't have to stop, Yossi. Just... take a step back for a minute. Let us carry some of this. You've done enough. The men need you at your best, not on the edge of collapse."*

Yossi's shoulders slumped slightly, the tension he'd been carrying seeping out, though he still fought it. *"I just... I can't let them down,"* he said, his voice rough. *"Every decision... every time we move... it's on me. If I make a mistake..."*

Nadav placed a hand on Yossi's shoulder, his grip firm, grounding. *"And you haven't let them down,"* he said quietly. *"But you're not alone in this. You've got me, you've got the rest of the team. Trust us to carry the load for a bit. You've led us this far, we'll keep moving forward, but we need you in this for the long haul. Not burning out before it's over."*

For a long moment, Yossi didn't respond. His gaze drifted out over the ruins, his men resting where they could, some slumped against walls, others keeping watch, faces etched with exhaustion. He thought about every choice he had made, every order he had given. The responsibility had become so ingrained, it was hard to imagine letting it go even for a second.

But Nadav was right. The fatigue was dulling his edge. He was close to running on empty, and if he pushed any harder, he knew it would cost them all.

Yossi met Nadav's gaze, the tension in his body easing just slightly. For the first time in days, he allowed himself to breathe deeply, the weight shifting from his shoulders, if only for a moment. *"Maybe you're right,"* he admitted quietly. *"Maybe I don't have to carry all of it."*

Nadav gave a small, encouraging nod. *"You don't,"* he said. *"We're in this together. Take some rest. I'll keep an eye on things."*

That night, Yossi found a quiet corner in the rubble and allowed himself to sit, the weight of his rifle heavy in his lap. His body ached, his muscles stiff from the constant strain. The exhaustion was like a lead weight pressing down on his chest. He leaned back against the cold stone wall, closing his eyes, trying to shut out the sounds of the war outside, if only for a moment.

His sleep, when it came, was restless… haunted by the faces of his fallen men, the sounds of gunfire and explosions weaving through his dreams. He woke more than once, heart pounding, convinced he had heard something, only to see Nadav sitting nearby, keeping watch. Each time, Nadav would meet his eyes, giving a small nod, a silent reassurance that he had things under control. It wasn't much, but it was enough to let Yossi close his eyes again.

In the haze of his thoughts, Yossi found a small spark of resolve. He wasn't alone. He still had his men, and he still had Nadav, standing by him.

And tomorrow, they would fight again.

Chapter Fifty Three

AHMED

Ahmed crouched in the tunnels beneath Rafah, his body tense as the earth shuddered with each impact from above. For days now, the relentless pounding of artillery by day and airstrikes by night had turned the city into a hellscape. The violent rhythm of explosions never ceased a brutal reminder that they were being pummelled from all sides. Every blast seemed closer than the last, as though the land itself were breaking under the weight of the assault.

The air down here was thick... choked with dust and the acrid stench of explosives. The constant thudding of artillery reverberated through the tunnel walls, a low, bone-rattling rumble that made Ahmed's teeth vibrate. Each tremor sent tiny clouds of grit cascading from the ceilings, making the very earth feel alive, groaning under the bombardment. Every few minutes, another airstrike would hit, and the tunnels would tremble, as though wincing from the pain.

Ahmed closed his eyes for a moment, the darkness behind his eyelids a brief refuge. He tried to focus, to calm his breathing, but the chaos above made it impossible. The tunnels were meant to be their sanctuary, their stronghold against the Israeli bombardment. But today, it felt like a tomb waiting to be sealed.

Around him, the men were in constant motion... darting between sections of the tunnel, barking orders. Some scrambled to reinforce parts of the underground system where cracks had started to appear in the walls. Others sat huddled, staring at nothing, their faces pale and drawn. Sweat clung to their skin, mixing with the ever-present dust, giving them a ghostly appearance in the dim light. The atmosphere was thick with tension, the weight of dread palpable.

Ahmed's mind drifted, if only for a moment. How many times had they been through this? He had lived through countless bombardments, but each one felt worse than the last. Each time, the strikes came closer, more precise. He wondered how long they could hold out… how long the tunnels could hold before they all collapsed.

A sudden blast shook the ground violently, slamming Ahmed against the wall. His breath caught in his throat as the shockwave rolled through the tunnel. He coughed, spitting out dirt as his ears rang from the explosion. The lights flickered, throwing the tunnels into brief darkness before stabilising again. Shouts erupted from deeper within the tunnel as the ground shifted, groaning under the pressure. Dust filled the air, so thick that it was nearly impossible to see.

"*Get back! Move! Move!*" someone yelled, their voice barely audible over the sound of collapsing earth.

Ahmad pulled himself to his feet, wiping the grit from his eyes. His heart pounded in his chest, but he forced himself to stay calm, to keep moving. He glanced at the men around him… some were wide-eyed with panic, others frozen in place.

Bunker-busters, Ahmed muttered to himself, his voice hoarse. He had heard of these bombs… designed to dig deep into the ground before exploding, collapsing tunnels like the one they stood in now. His mouth was dry, the dust mixing with the metallic taste of fear.

Suddenly, there was a shout from further down the tunnel. Fighters were sprinting towards him, their faces streaked with dirt and panic.

"*It's collapsed*!" one of them gasped, breathless and wide-eyed. "*They hit one of the main tunnels. We've got men trapped!*"

Ahmed felt his blood run cold. He grabbed his rifle and sprinted towards the collapsed section, the ground unsteady beneath his feet. Dust choked the air, and the tunnel seemed narrower than ever. As he reached the site, he found a group of fighters already clawing at the rubble with their hands, desperate to free those buried beneath. Their hands were raw and bleeding, but they didn't stop.

"*Get the shovels!*" Ahmed shouted, his voice raw with urgency. "*We need to dig them out!*"

The men scrambled to find tools, their movements frantic and desperate. The tunnel echoed with the sound of shouts, coughing, and the occasional rumble from the artillery above. Ahmed knelt beside the rubble and began pulling at the dirt and debris with his bare hands, ignoring the sharp stings as his skin tore.

"*Keep digging!*" he urged, his breath coming in shallow, ragged gasps. Each second felt like an eternity as they fought against the earth itself, trying to free their comrades. The ground above could give way again at any moment, and they all knew it.

"*Ahmed!*" one of the fighters called out, pointing to a small gap in the rubble. "*I can hear someone!*"

Ahmed crawled closer, pressing his ear against the debris. Faint, muffled voices reached him from beneath the rubble. They were alive but trapped. His heart pounded as he shouted through the small opening.

"*Hold on! We're coming! We'll get you out!*"

The men dug with renewed energy, shovels and hands working in unison as the air grew heavier with dust. Ahmed's lungs burned with each breath, the thick air making it harder to think, harder to move. But he didn't stop. He couldn't. Time seemed to warp, each second dragging as they fought against the earth, the booms of distant strikes punctuating their efforts.

Finally, after what felt like hours, they managed to claw a small opening through the rubble. One by one, the trapped fighters were pulled free, their faces pale, their bodies caked in dirt and blood. Some coughed violently, gasping for air as they were dragged to safety.

"**We've got them**," one of the men panted, collapsing beside Ahmed, his chest heaving. "*They're out.*"

Ahmed nodded, his body too exhausted to respond properly. He stared at the collapsed section of the tunnel, his thoughts racing. This was only the beginning. The Israelis were getting closer, their strikes more precise, more devastating. The tunnels that had once been their sanctuary were now turning into death traps. How long before the entire network was destroyed? *How long before there was nowhere left to hide?*

Another distant explosion echoed through the tunnel, the ground trembling once more. Ahmed closed his eyes, trying to shut out the overwhelming fear gnawing at his gut.

"They'll be sending the ground troops soon," he muttered, more to himself than anyone else.

One of the older fighters, his face lined with dust and exhaustion, sat down beside him and nodded grimly. "*We'll be ready.*"

But Ahmed wasn't sure. They had trained for this, prepared for it... but no amount of preparation could steel them against the fear, the constant sound of collapsing tunnels, the sight of men buried alive. *How much longer could they hold out*?

As he sat there in the dim light of the tunnels, Ahmed felt the weight of the earth pressing down on him, the dust clogging his lungs, the air too thick to breathe. Rafah was being swallowed, bit by bit, and he wondered if they would be buried with it.

And the ground attack hadn't even begun yet.

The bombardment had stopped. For the first time in days, there was an eerie silence over Rafah. Ahmed stood in the tunnel, listening intently as the tremors that had shaken the earth for what seemed like an eternity faded into nothing. He glanced at the men around him—Khaled, Bilal, Hadi—and saw the same tension mirrored in their faces. Dust still hung thick in the air, clinging to their sweat-soaked skin. But now, everything felt too quiet.

"*They've stopped the strikes,*" Khaled murmured, his voice low. "*Why?*"

Ahmed didn't need to answer. They all knew. The silence was more terrifying than the noise. It meant only one thing.

"*They're coming,*" Ahmed said, his voice steady despite the dread tightening in his chest. "*Get ready.*"

Around him, the fighters began to move with purpose. Khaled barked orders, sending men to their positions, while Bilal and Hadi checked their rifles. Ahmad's mind raced, even as he fought to stay calm. He had lived through bombardments before—endured the constant strikes that turned Rafah into a smoking ruin... but this silence felt different. It was the prelude to something far worse.

"*Move quickly,*" Ahmad ordered, scanning the crumbling buildings around them. The dust hung in the air like a thick veil, and every shadow seemed to hide danger. "*We need to reposition before they're on top of us.*"

He turned to Khaled and Bilal, both standing nearby, their faces set with grim determination.

"*Khaled, take your team and set up an ambush near the square,*" Ahmed said, pointing toward the far side of the open area that would soon be crawling with Israeli troops. "Hit them hard when they enter. Bilal, you'll need a better vantage point. Find a new sniper position and cover Khaled from above."

Bilal nodded, already scanning the shattered skyline for the highest point, his sniper rifle slung over his shoulder. Khaled adjusted his gear and gave a quick nod before heading out, his team following closely behind, their movements swift and practised despite the tension in the air.

Ahmed's gaze shifted to Hadi, who had been silent, waiting for orders. "*Hadi,*" Ahmed said, lowering his voice, "*take your men into the tunnels. Try to come up behind them. We'll draw their attention from the square... hit them from the rear if you can.*"

Hadi's eyes met Ahmed's, a flicker of understanding passing between them. They both knew the risks. The tunnels were a lifeline, but they were also death traps. One wrong move, and they could be buried alive. But Ahmed had no choice.

"*I'll do what I can*," Hadi replied, his voice tight but resolute.

"*Be careful*," Ahmed added, placing a firm hand on Hadi's shoulder. "*If they've got engineers up there, the tunnels won't be safe for long.*"

Hadi gave a grim smile before turning to his men. "*Let's go. We need to move fast.*"

Ahmed watched as Hadi and his team disappeared into the tunnel entrance, the darkness swallowing them. He turned back to the street, his pulse quickening. The Israelis would be here soon, and they had to be ready.

The tunnel was a labyrinth of shadows, the air thick with the taste of earth and anxiety. Hadi led his men through the narrow, dim passage, their footsteps echoing faintly. Every step seemed heavier, the oppressive weight of the earth pressing down on them from above. Each distant explosion shook the ground beneath their feet, sending fine dust cascading from the ceiling.

"*Keep moving*!" Hadi called back to his men, his voice hoarse. He could feel the strain in his legs, exhaustion creeping in, but he pushed it aside. They were close to the western exit, their only chance to flank the Israelis and catch them off guard.

The faint light from the tunnel exit flickered ahead, a sliver of hope in the oppressive darkness. Hadi's heart pounded in his chest as he urged his men forward. "*Almost there*!" he shouted, glancing back at the weary faces behind him. They were close... just a few more steps.

And then, the world erupted.

The tunnel groaned as the ground above was torn apart by a blast. The Israeli engineers had blown the exit, and the shockwave hit them like a freight train. Hadi was thrown to the ground, the air crushed from his lungs as debris rained down. He gasped for breath, struggling to regain his senses. The tunnel was filled with dust, choking the air, turning every breath into a fight for survival.

He tried to stand, but his legs wouldn't move. His lower body was pinned beneath the collapsed earth. Panic surged through him, his chest tightening as he realised the gravity of his situation. Around him, his men were shouting, their voices muffled by the weight of the debris. Hadi clawed at the dirt, trying to free himself, but it was no use.

"*No... no, no, no!*" Hadi groaned, his fingers digging into the soil, his vision blurring. The dust filled his throat, making it impossible to call out for help. His men were trapped, just like him, buried under the earth they had once relied on.

"*Hadi!*" a voice called out, faint and desperate.

Hadi tried to respond, but the words wouldn't come. His vision dimmed, the dust swirling around him like a shroud. He could feel the weight of the tunnel pressing down on him, the last glimmer of light fading as more debris fell, sealing their fate.

The world went dark.

Ahmed could hear the distant booms of explosives and the relentless rattle of gunfire echoing through the ruins of Rafah. Every corner, every shadowed alleyway felt like a trap. His eyes darted between the crumbling buildings, tension gnawing at him. Khaled and his men were still securing their positions at the far end of the square, preparing for the ambush that would come later. Bilal had already repositioned, setting up in a tall building with a clear view of the streets below, ready to cover Khaled's team.

But there was something else. A growing unease twisted in Ahmad's gut.

Hadi and his team had gone silent.

Ahmed keyed his radio, static crackling in his ear. "*Hadi, do you copy?*"

Nothing.

His heart sank, the weight of dread settling over him like a thick fog. He tried again, his voice more urgent. "*Hadi, do you copy?*"

The radio remained silent.

Ahmed's grip tightened around his rifle as he glanced towards Bilal's position, the sniper perched high in the ruins, completely focused on the streets below.

Khaled's men continued preparing the ambush at the far side of the square, but Ahmed's mind was elsewhere. Hadi's silence gnawed at him. His friend, his brother-in-arms, was somewhere underground, perhaps trapped, perhaps worse.

Come on, Hadi, he muttered under his breath, his fists clenched. But there was no answer. Only silence.

From his vantage point, Bilal scanned the streets below, his finger hovering near the trigger. He had been in countless firefights before, but something about this felt different. The tension was suffocating, the silence between gunfire almost unbearable. Through the scope, he could see the Israeli soldiers moving cautiously through the rubble, advancing with precision.

And then he saw it... an opportunity. He lined up his shot, heart steady, breath controlled. With a sharp crack, the sniper rifle spat fire, and an Israeli soldier dropped to the ground.

"*Good shot*," Ahmed whispered to himself from his position, watching Bilal from a distance. But the momentary relief was short-lived.

Suddenly, the roar of a tank's cannon echoed through the narrow streets. Ahmad's eyes widened as the shell smashed into Bilal's building. The explosion sent debris flying, and the structure shuddered under the impact. Ahmad froze, his breath catching in his throat as he watched the building begin to crumble.

"*Bilal, get out*!" Ahmed shouted into the radio, panic lacing his voice.

There was no reply.

The building collapsed in on itself, a cloud of dust rising into the air as the walls came down, burying Bilal beneath the rubble. Ahmed stood, frozen in place, his mind reeling. Bilal was gone... just like Hadi. The weight of the losses pressed down on him, suffocating him as the city seemed to close in.

Bilal... Ahmad whispered, his voice barely audible, his heart heavy with grief.

For a brief moment, everything was still. Then the sounds of the battle returned—distant gunfire, the roar of engines, the ever-present hum of war.

But for Ahmed, the world had gone silent.

Ahmed crouched low, his eyes scanning the narrow streets as dusk fell over Rafah. The distant rumble of engines and sporadic bursts of gunfire echoed through the city, signalling that the Israeli forces were advancing slowly but relentlessly. The streets were in chaos, rubble from the shelling piled high, and the once-familiar corners of Rafah now held only danger. He wiped the sweat and dust from his face, heart pounding in his chest.

"*What's holding them up?*" Ahmad muttered to himself, glancing towards the square where Khaled and his men had taken position.

Khaled was stationed at the far end of the square, ready to spring an ambush on the approaching Israeli soldiers. Ahmad had counted on that ambush to at least slow their advance and give them a fighting chance, but something felt wrong. They hadn't moved for minutes, and there was an eerie stillness in the air. Then, from the distant side of the square, Khaled's voice crackled through the radio.

"*Ahmad, they're not advancing. They're holding back on the other side of the square.*" Khaled's voice was tense. "*Something's wrong. Why aren't they moving?*"

Ahmed's gut twisted. He felt the heavy weight of dread settle over him, but before he could respond, he heard it… a soft, buzzing sound overhead. His heart sank as the realisation hit him.

Drones… Ahmad whispered, his mouth going dry. The familiar, insidious sound of Israeli surveillance drones hovering above sent a wave of panic through him. "*Khaled, it's the drones. Get out of there. Now!*"

Ahmed's voice rose with urgency, but Khaled's reply was laced with fear. "We can't, Ahmed. They'll see us if we move…"

Before Khaled could finish, Ahmed heard the unmistakable roar of approaching jets. His breath caught in his throat, his pulse quickening in pure terror. He knew what was coming next.

"*Get out! Khaled, get out of the building! They're calling in an airstrike!*" Ahmed's voice cracked with desperation, but even as he shouted, he knew it was too late.

The roar of the jets grew louder, and then he heard the whoosh of missiles being released. Ahmed's eyes widened, his mouth opening to scream, but the words never came. The explosion ripped through the air before he could warn Khaled again.

The square lit up in a violent flash of light and sound. The ground shook violently as the building where Khaled and his men had been stationed was reduced to rubble in an instant. Ahmed stumbled back, the force of the blast reverberating through the streets. The shockwave hit him like a hammer, knocking the wind from his lungs as dust and debris clouded the air. For a few terrifying seconds, there was nothing but blinding dust and the deafening roar of destruction.

When the dust began to settle, the square was unrecognisable. Flames licked at the remnants of the building, sending thick black smoke spiralling into the sky. Ahmed stood frozen, his chest heaving as he stared at the destruction.

Khaled... The name formed on his lips, but he couldn't say it. He couldn't bring himself to accept what had just happened. His mind reeled as he realised the extent of the loss. Khaled, Bilal, Hadi—all gone.

Everything was gone.

Ahmed's knees buckled, and he sank to the ground, his hands gripping the dirt beneath him. He couldn't tear his eyes away from the flaming wreckage. The weight of everything crashed down on him... his friends, his family, his home in Jabalia and now here in Rafah. It had all been ripped away, and he was powerless to stop it.

The radio crackled faintly, but Ahmed didn't respond. He couldn't. His body trembled as he realised how empty the world felt now. The comrades who had stood by his side, the men he had fought with, laughed with, and bled with... they were all gone, consumed by the fire and rubble of this endless war. Rafah was falling apart brick by brick. And for the first time, it felt like there was nothing left worth fighting for.

His vision blurred with tears he couldn't suppress, his heart heavy with the weight of despair. The glow of the flames reflected in his dark, hollow eyes, and for a moment, he felt nothing but numbness. The world around him faded, the sounds of battle becoming distant echoes in his mind. He was alone, utterly and completely alone.

With trembling hands, Ahmed turned away from the burning square. He couldn't look at it any longer. The loss was too great, the pain too deep. Without a word, he rose to his feet, feeling the crushing weight of his defeat settling into his bones. He didn't care about the battle anymore, didn't care about the war. It was over for him. His spirit had been broken, shattered by the deaths of the men he had once called his brothers.

Slowly, Ahmed walked towards the tunnel entrance, his movements sluggish, as though every step took all the strength he had left. The flickering flames illuminated his path, casting long shadows on the crumbling walls around him.

As he descended into the dark, suffocating tunnel complex, the world above seemed to disappear. The noise, the gunfire, the explosions... all of it faded into the background, leaving only the oppressive silence of the underground.

Ahmed dropped the radio, his hands trembling, his mind reeling from the loss. Khaled, Bilal, Hadi—his closest friends, his brothers... were gone. The ambush had failed, the square obliterated by the airstrike, and the tunnels, their last hope, were collapsing. Every path he had taken, every decision he had made, seemed to lead only to this—trapped, entombed with the ghosts of his fallen comrades.

The tunnel was a mess of confusion and panic. Fighters stumbled through the dimly lit corridors, their faces pale and smeared with dust. Some barked frantic orders, while others tried in vain to shore up the collapsing walls. The dull, muffled thud of distant explosions above reverberated through the earth, sending tremors along the narrow passageways. Every few moments, another section of the tunnel would groan and shift, sending more dirt and debris raining down from the ceiling.

Ahmed could barely recognise the men around him. The weariness and terror etched into their faces made them look more like spectres than soldiers. The constant bombardment above had broken something in them... these men, once so full of resolve, now moved with the hollow-eyed resignation of the condemned.

There was no escape. The exits were sealed, the Israeli forces were tightening their grip, and their sanctuary beneath the city was crumbling.

Ahmed's breath was shallow, the dust clogging his lungs. He pushed forward, weaving through the chaos, trying to ignore the panic in the eyes of those he passed. His mind was spinning, the weight of it all pressing down on him, suffocating him. Everywhere he turned, there were reminders of how much he had lost. How much they had all lost.

"We're running out of time!" a voice cried out nearby. One of the younger fighters, his hands shaking as he tried to dig through the rubble blocking an exit. His face was smeared with dirt and streaked with tears. *"The whole tunnel's coming down!"*

Ahmed didn't respond. He couldn't. His throat tightened as he tried to suppress the growing panic. He forced himself to keep moving, the screams and shouts around him fading into a dull roar in the back of his mind. He needed to think, to focus, but every step felt heavier, as if the earth itself was pulling him down, dragging him deeper into despair.

Suddenly, a loud crack echoed through the tunnel, followed by the groan of shifting earth. The ceiling above him buckled, and Ahmed stumbled backwards as a section of the wall collapsed, sending a cloud of dust and rocks crashing down. A chorus of panicked shouts followed, and Ahmed's heart raced as he realised just how close he had come to being buried alive.

For a moment, he stood frozen, his legs trembling beneath him. The tunnel was caving in all around them, and there was nothing they could do. He glanced at the men around him, some scrambling to find new exits, others simply staring at the destruction, their eyes wide with fear.

And then, the faces returned.

Bilal, Khaled, Hadi... each of them staring at him through the dust and the chaos, their expressions frozen in that last moment before they were taken from him. Ahmed blinked, trying to shake the images from his mind, but they wouldn't leave. He had failed them. He had failed them all.

He stumbled forward again, his body moving on instinct as his mind struggled to keep up. The tunnel was quieter now, the sounds of men digging and shouting gradually fading into the background. Ahmed found himself alone in a narrow passage, his breath coming in short, ragged gasps. His hands shook, and for a moment, he thought he might collapse.

That night, as the tunnel grew quieter, Ahmed found himself alone with his thoughts. Sleep, when it came, was restless, haunted by the faces of Bilal, Khaled, Hadi… by the men who had followed him into this war, who had given everything for him, and who now lay dead, buried beneath the rubble.

And then there were the faces of the dead from the massacre on Route 232. Faces twisted in fear and pain, faces that had once been faceless enemies but now haunted him like spectres, tormenting him with the weight of their deaths.

The atrocities of October 7th replayed in his mind… the bloodshed, the chaos, the screams. He had justified it then, convinced himself that it was necessary, that it was the price of their struggle. But now, in the quiet darkness of the tunnel, the memories clung to him like shadows. He saw their faces… the men, the women and he couldn't shake the feeling that he had become something monstrous.

And then, there was Salma. Her words echoed in his mind, soft and pleading.

"Ahmed, I just want you to stay true to yourself."

He had brushed her off, ignored her warnings. But now, he couldn't escape the question that gnawed at him: *had he lost himself? Had he become the very thing they had once fought against?*

The next morning, the tunnel was eerily silent. The air was thick with dust, and the walls seemed to close in on him more than ever. Ahmed knew what he had to do. He couldn't stay down here any longer. There was no escape underground.

The sounds of battle grew louder, closer, like a drumbeat marching toward them. Ahmed knew the IDF soldiers were near; his time was running out. He felt a strange calm settle over him, a clarity that cut through the fear and fatigue. He moved deeper into the tunnels, choosing a path that led up toward the surface, toward an abandoned building close to the tunnel entrance.

Ahmed emerged into the dim, dust-choked light of a half-collapsed room. The ceiling was partially caved in, beams hanging precariously, and debris scattered across the floor. He felt the harsh grit of sand in his mouth, tasted the metallic bitterness of blood where he had bitten his lip.

He knew he needed to get back underground, to regroup, but his legs felt heavy, his body aching with exhaustion. His muscles burned, every movement a struggle. He could hear the distant sounds of IDF soldiers moving closer, their boots crunching on broken glass and rubble, their voices low but tense. Each step sent a tremor through the floor.

He started towards the tunnel entrance, his steps unsteady. His mind raced with thoughts of Khaled, Bilal, Hadi, Tariq... all the men he had led, all the men he had lost. Their faces flashed before his eyes, a parade of ghosts, and he felt the sting of guilt and failure press hard against his chest, a weight he could barely carry.

He was almost at the entrance when he heard a faint noise behind him... the creak of a floorboard, the subtle rustle of movement. Ahmed froze, his breath catching in his throat, the hairs on the back of his neck standing on end. Slowly, he turned, his heart pounding in his ears, and found himself face to face with an IDF soldier standing in the doorway.

For a moment, time seemed to stop. The soldier's eyes met Ahmed's, wide with surprise and recognition. Ahmed could see the tension in the man's stance, the rifle raised but hesitating, just like him.

Ahmed's breath came in shallow gasps, his chest tight. He knew there was nowhere to run, no more options. He closed his eyes slowly, waiting for the inevitable, a strange peace settling over him. He had fought long and hard. Now, he would face whatever came next, even if it was the end.

And then everything erupted.

The blast ripped through the building, the walls buckling as fire and force tore them apart. Ahmed was hurled forward, his body slamming against the ground. Agony exploded through his chest, the impact knocking the wind from his lungs. His vision swam, the world tilting as chunks of debris crashed around him. The air turned thick with ash and smoke, burning his throat and coating his tongue with grit.

He tried to push himself up, but his body refused, limbs heavy and unresponsive. The ringing in his ears drowned out every other sound. For a moment, all he could do was lie there, gasping, his mind struggling to piece together what had happened.

Through the swirling dust and pain, Ahmed spotted the soldier, just a few feet away, crumpled and unmoving. A trickle of blood ran down the man's temple, his chest rising and falling in shallow, strained breaths. They were both trapped, both shattered.

Their eyes met once more. And in that moment, Ahmed didn't see a threat.

Just a man.

Chapter Fifty Four

YOSSI

The sounds of battle outside were muffled as Yossi moved cautiously through the abandoned building. His heart raced in his chest, the tension coiling inside him like a spring ready to snap. The air was thick with dust, acrid with smoke, and every step he took was a reminder of the destruction surrounding him. The narrow streets of Rafah were a maze of collapsed buildings and debris, and the tunnels snaking beneath them made the entire landscape feel unpredictable... dangerous.

Every breath Yossi took was laced with the smell of smoke, oil, and the sharp metallic tang of blood, mingling with the ever-present stench of sweat clinging to his skin. The heat from the day still clung to the air, making the atmosphere oppressive, like the whole city was pressing down on him. He could taste the grit in his mouth, dry and bitter, and the taste of fear lingered, though he pushed it down.

Keep moving, he told himself, gripping his rifle tighter. *One step at a time. Don't think about what could happen. Focus.*

Yossi could feel the weight of the mission pressing on him. The airstrikes had softened the enemy positions, but now it was up to him and his men to clear the remaining fighters. His boots crunched on broken glass, the sound too loud in the eerie silence. Every noise, every shift of rubble underfoot, set his nerves on edge. The air felt heavy, thick with the tension of the unknown.

The quiet was too thick. *They're here*, he thought, his eyes darting between the crumbling walls, the shadows stretching out like fingers across the floor. Somewhere close, hiding, waiting.

He edged deeper into the building, senses heightened. He could hear his own breath, shallow and quick, the thudding of his heartbeat echoing in his ears. Sweat trickled down his back, mixing with the grime and dust clinging to his uniform. He was tired, more tired than he had been in days, but he couldn't afford to stop.

The building was deathly still, the only light coming from the dim, dusty rays filtering through shattered windows. Yossi's eyes strained in the half-light, scanning every corner, every shadow. His mind flashed to his men outside, to Nadav, and then… just for a moment… to Yael. The thought of her waiting for him tugged at the corners of his mind, but he forced it away.

Not now. Stay focused.

Suddenly, a faint creak broke the silence, the soft groan of a floorboard shifting. Yossi's body tensed instantly, adrenaline flooding his system. Instinctively, he raised his rifle, his pulse quickening. His breath caught as he saw the outline of a figure near the entrance to the tunnels.

A man.

For a moment, time seemed to stop. The fighter turned slowly, his face illuminated by a shaft of light spilling through the cracks in the wall. Yossi's heart skipped a beat. He could see the dirt and grime streaking the man's face, the bloodshot eyes, hollow from days of fighting. The man's clothes were torn, stained with sweat and dust, his body rigid with exhaustion. Yet there was something else in his gaze… something familiar.

Fear.

Not the wild, desperate fear of a trapped animal, but something quieter. Resigned.

Yossi froze, his finger hovering over the trigger. He should fire. He knew he should. *He's the enemy*, he reminded himself, but his body wouldn't respond. The man wasn't raising his rifle. He wasn't aiming. He was just standing there, staring at Yossi with an expression that was... human.

In that moment, Yossi felt the lines between soldier and enemy blur. The man's face looked so tired, so broken. Yossi's mind raced. *He's just like me*, he realised. Another soldier, another man fighting for his life. The wave of empathy crashed over him, catching him off guard. He hadn't expected this... hadn't expected to see his enemy as anything other than a faceless threat. But here he was, a man just like Yossi, trapped in the wreckage of a war neither of them had started.

The fighter's eyes softened. His chest rose and fell with laboured breaths, his hands trembling as they gripped his weapon. He didn't raise it. He didn't fire. He just... waited. Yossi could see the understanding in his gaze. The man had accepted what was about to happen.

Yossi's finger rested lightly on the trigger. *I should shoot him*, he told himself. *I have to. This is war.* But his hand wouldn't move. The moment stretched between them, heavy with unspoken understanding.

He's just like me.

The fighter slowly closed his eyes, waiting for the inevitable. Waiting for Yossi to pull the trigger.

And then everything exploded.

A deafening blast tore through the air. The ground shook violently as the walls around them collapsed under the force of the explosion. Yossi felt himself being thrown backward, his body slamming into the concrete floor. Pain exploded in his side, the breath knocked from his lungs. His vision blurred, the world spinning as debris rained down from the ceiling. Dust filled the air, choking him, the taste of earth and ash thick in his mouth.

He tried to move, but his limbs felt heavy, unresponsive. The ringing in his ears drowned out everything else. For a moment, all he could do was lie there, gasping for breath, disoriented, his mind struggling to catch up with what had just happened.

Through the haze of dust and pain, Yossi saw the fighter lying just a few feet away, crumpled against the wall, his body limp. Blood trickled from a cut on his forehead, his chest rising and falling in shallow, ragged breaths. They were both trapped, both injured. Yossi could feel the weight of the rubble pinning him down, the sharp pain in his side making it hard to breathe.

Their eyes met again. And this time, Yossi didn't see an enemy.

Just a mirror of himself.

There, in the dust-choked room, with the sounds of battle fading into the background, Yossi realised something. It didn't matter who had started this war, or who would claim victory. In the end, they were both caught in the same trap. Soldiers, fighting for causes larger than themselves, trapped in a war neither of them truly controlled.

The world outside continued to rage, but in that moment, Yossi felt only silence.

Nadav watched Yossi move toward the crumbling building. His movements were cautious but confident, just like always. Yossi had always been the steady one, the one who kept his cool when everything went to hell. Nadav trusted him with his life, and that trust had carried them through more than one close call.

But something about today felt different. The air was thick with the sounds of battle... the distant thud of explosions, the crack of gunfire echoing through the ravaged streets of Rafah. Nadav could feel the weight of the mission pressing down on him, heavier than usual. Yossi had been through worse, but still... a knot of worry tightened in Nadav's chest as he watched his friend disappear into the half-collapsed structure.

A distant explosion rocked the air, sending a plume of dust into the sky. Nadav's heart skipped a beat. He could feel the tension rising in his chest, a sense of dread creeping over him like a shadow.

Stay focused, he told himself. *Yossi knows what he's doing. He'll be fine.*

But then it happened.

The explosion.

A massive blast shook the ground, a deafening roar that sent shockwaves through the rubble-strewn street. Nadav's heart leapt into his throat. He saw the plume of dust and debris shoot out from the building Yossi had entered. His mind froze, and for a split second, everything went silent.

"*Yossi*!" The scream tore from his throat before he even realised what was happening. Panic twisted in his chest, tightening like a vice as he fumbled for his radio. His fingers shook, trembling as he pressed the button. "*Yossi, come in! Yossi, do you copy*?!"

Static.

"*Yossi*!" Nadav screamed again, his voice raw with fear. "*Answer me, damn it*!"

Still nothing.

The world shrank around him. The sound of battle faded into the background, leaving only the pounding of his heart, the blood rushing in his ears. All he could think about was Yossi... his best friend... trapped inside that building.

No. Not like this. Not him.

Without thinking, Nadav bolted toward the building, his legs moving on instinct. "*Follow me*!" he shouted at the platoon, already sprinting across the debris-strewn street. His heart pounded in his chest, his mind racing with panic. *I have to get to him. I have to get to Yossi.*

He burst into the building, the dust from the explosion still hanging in the air like a thick fog. His boots crunched on shattered glass and rubble as he scanned the room, his breath coming in short, ragged gasps.

And then he saw him.

Yossi lay crumpled on the floor, half-buried under a pile of debris. Blood and dust covered his uniform, and for a terrifying moment, Nadav thought... *No.* He couldn't finish the thought. He couldn't allow himself to go there.

"*Medic!*" Nadav screamed, dropping to his knees beside Yossi. "*Medic, now!*" His hands shook as he reached for Yossi, brushing the dust from his face, searching for any sign of life.

"*Yossi, can you hear me? Stay with me, Yossi.*" Nadav's voice cracked, the fear clawing at him. "*You're gonna be okay. You're gonna be fine.*"

But Yossi didn't respond. His breathing was shallow, his eyes closed, his body limp.

Nadav knelt beside Yossi, his heart hammering in his chest as he watched his best friend lie still, motionless. His breath came in short, frantic bursts, his mind racing to comprehend what had just happened. Yossi was never still. He was always the strong one, the one who held everyone together. Seeing him like this—vulnerable, unmoving—sent a wave of panic crashing over Nadav, threatening to drown him.

Come on, Yossi, Nadav whispered, his voice barely a breath, thick with fear. *Don't do this. Stay with me. You have to stay with me.* His hands were trembling as he touched Yossi's shoulder, hoping for a response, a flicker of life. But there was nothing.

The medic arrived, sliding to a stop beside them, his face pale but focused. "*Step back!*" he barked, quickly assessing Yossi's condition. Nadav watched helplessly as the medic worked, feeling utterly useless.

This can't be happening, Nadav thought, his heart sinking deeper into his chest with every passing second. *Not Yossi. Not him.*

His hands clenched into fists at his sides as the medic worked with quick precision, stabilising Yossi, checking for fractures, monitoring his vitals. Nadav could feel the sweat dripping down his back, his throat tight as he struggled to hold himself together.

Behind them, the platoon members secured the Hamas fighter, binding his hands behind his back, but Nadav barely noticed. His entire world had shrunk to the sight of Yossi's limp body, his shallow breathing barely noticeable beneath the dust and blood staining his uniform.

"*You need to move him now,*" the medic said urgently. "*We need to get him to an evac point before the swelling gets worse.*"

Nadav nodded numbly, his mind barely processing the words. He watched as they lifted Yossi onto a stretcher, securing him carefully. Everything moved in slow motion, the world around him a blur of noise and chaos. He couldn't breathe. The fear of losing Yossi was a knot in his chest, tightening with each heartbeat.

"*Move!*" the medic shouted, and the team carrying Yossi rushed toward the waiting vehicles. Nadav ran after them, his legs heavy, his mind a whirl of panic and guilt.

I should have gone in with him. I should have been there.

The thought hammered in his head, loud and accusing. *This is my fault. I let him go in alone.*

As they reached the evacuation point, Nadav's mind raced with what was about to come next. The triage unit, the medics, the hospital in Tel Aviv. He couldn't picture it—couldn't imagine Yossi lying in a hospital bed, hooked up to machines.

He has to wake up. He has to be okay. He has to come back.

As the helicopter lifted Yossi into the sky, Nadav watched it disappear into the distance, his heart aching with every second it carried his friend away. He felt rooted to the spot, paralysed with fear and uncertainty. The war outside raged on, but here, in this moment, all Nadav could feel was the emptiness left behind by Yossi's absence.

He sank down against a nearby wall, his head in his hands. His entire body felt heavy, weighed down by exhaustion and the suffocating fear that he might lose Yossi. The world around him faded into the background, and for the first time since this nightmare had begun, Nadav let himself break. His shoulders shook as he wept, the fear and frustration pouring out of him in waves.

The helicopter touched down with a jolt, its rotors whipping up a furious wind that sent dust swirling across the landing pad. Inside, the medics moved swiftly, their movements precise as they worked over Yossi's unconscious form. The interior of the helicopter was loud, filled with the constant thrum of the blades and the beeping of medical equipment monitoring his vitals.

Leila stood at the edge of the landing pad, her heart pounding in her chest. The second the helicopter came into view, her stomach had knotted, and now, as the medics unloaded Yossi's stretcher, she felt the world close in around her. She was a nurse, a professional, and she'd seen her share of injuries... but this was Yossi, her oldest friend. The sight of him, unconscious, pale, his body covered in debris and his clothes bloodied, made her legs weak.

"*Yossi...*" The whisper escaped her lips as the medics hurried him off the helicopter. One of the team briefly called out his injuries... multiple fractures, a suspected traumatic brain injury from the blast, though it looked like the worst of the explosion had missed him, shielded by a crumbling wall. He was alive, but the damage had been done. The concussion had rendered him unconscious, and the swelling in his brain was the immediate danger.

Leila barely registered the words. All she could focus on was Yossi's still form, the faint rise and fall of his chest beneath the medical equipment. Her mind kept repeating, *This is Yossi. He's strong, he'll make it.* But as she stared at the bruises on his face and the blood on his uniform, the reality of the situation hit her like a physical blow.

She felt a hand grip her shoulder and turned to see one of her colleagues, concern etched on their face. "*We've got this, Leila. Step back, we'll stabilise him first.*"

She shook her head, stepping closer, her voice trembling. "*I can help,*" she insisted. "*Please, I need to be there.*" Her hands clenched tightly around the edges of her nurse's uniform, the tension building in her chest. Memories of their childhood flashed through her mind... the three of them: her, Nadav, and Yossi, inseparable. And now here he was, battered and broken before her eyes.

The lead medic nodded, understanding her desperation. "*Okay, but stay focused, Leila. He's critical.*"

Leila swallowed hard, steeling herself as they wheeled Yossi into the emergency room. As she moved alongside the stretcher, she couldn't stop herself from looking at his face, bruised but familiar. Her pulse was racing, and the sterile smell of the hospital hit her all at once, mixing with the acrid scent of blood and antiseptic. She thought of Yael, of how she would break the news to her best friend, and of Nadav, who was probably still out there, devastated, thinking he might lose his best friend. The weight of it all pressed down on her, making her feel small, helpless, despite her years of experience.

Inside the trauma unit, the medical team swarmed around Yossi, calling out numbers, measurements, and urgent instructions. Leila forced herself to stay calm, to be the nurse he needed her to be, not just his friend. But inside, her heart was breaking.

"We need to control the swelling. Get him ready for a CT scan," one of the doctors ordered. *"Let's check for internal bleeding. We need those x-rays now."*

Leila was by Yossi's side, gripping his hand for a moment as they readied him. She leaned in close, her voice barely a whisper. *Hold on, Yossi. You can't leave us now. Yael's waiting, and Nadav... he needs you.*

The trauma room was a flurry of activity as the medical team worked around Yossi, stabilising him for the CT scan and addressing his injuries one by one. Leila forced herself to focus, compartmentalising her emotions as she assisted, her hands moving automatically through the familiar motions of medical care. But every glance at Yossi's face reminded her of the boy she had grown up with, the friend who had been by her side through thick and thin, now fighting for his life.

This is Yossi, she reminded herself over and over. *Strong. Resilient. He'll pull through.* But the reality of his injuries was undeniable, and the critical nature of the trauma shook her to the core.

The minutes passed in a blur of medical jargon, the beeping of machines, and the quiet hum of the hospital around them. The doctors and nurses worked with practised efficiency, stabilising Yossi, ensuring he was ready to be wheeled off to radiology. Leila stayed by his side as long as she could, her heart aching with every passing second.

Finally, the urgency began to settle as the medical team prepared to move him for scans. The room cleared a little, and for the first time since Yossi had arrived, there was a moment of stillness.

Leila stepped back, her hands shaking slightly. She ran a hand over her face, trying to keep herself together. Her chest felt tight, and she knew she needed to step outside for air. But something weighed heavier on her now... something unavoidable. Yael. Her best friend needed to know. She couldn't keep this from her, but the thought of making that call terrified her.

"He's going to the CT scan now," one of the nurses said softly, touching Leila's arm. *"We've got it under control."*

Leila nodded, her voice caught in her throat. *"I'll... I'll check in after the scan. I just need a minute."*

She left the trauma room, moving quickly down the hallway toward a quieter corner of the hospital. Her legs felt weak beneath her as she found an empty waiting area and sat down heavily. The weight of everything... Nadav, Yossi, the memories of their childhood, and the unbearable thought of telling Yael, pressed down on her. She took a deep, shaky breath, fumbling for her phone in her pocket.

Leila stared at the screen for a moment, her thumb hovering over Yael's name. *How do I tell her this?* she thought, her heart pounding. *How do I break the news that Yossi... that her husband... is fighting for his life?*

Finally, she pressed the call button. The phone rang once, twice, and then Yael's familiar voice came through the line. *"Leila? Is everything okay?"* Yael sounded a little out of breath, her tone tinged with worry.

Leila swallowed hard, her throat tight. *"Yael..."* she began, but her voice cracked. She took a breath, forcing herself to stay calm. *"It's Yossi. He's been hurt."*

There was a pause on the other end of the line. *"What do you mean? What happened?"* Yael's voice was rising with panic.

Leila blinked back the tears threatening to spill over. *"There was an explosion. He was caught in it. He's... he's unconscious right now, and they're running tests. He has some broken ribs, a fracture, and..."* She trailed off, struggling to say the words. *"They think he has a brain injury, but we don't know how bad yet."*

The silence on the other end of the line felt like a punch to the chest. Leila could almost hear Yael's breath catching, the fear taking hold. *"Is he... is he going to be okay?"* Yael whispered, her voice trembling.

"He's stable," Leila replied quickly, trying to offer some reassurance. *"The doctors are doing everything they can. He's strong, Yael. You know that. He's going to fight through this."*

There was another long pause. *"I need to come,"* Yael said finally, her voice thick with emotion. *"I need to be there with him."*

"Of course," Leila said softly, her heart breaking for her friend. *"Come as soon as you can. I'll be here, waiting for you."*

The call ended, and Leila sat there for a moment, staring at her phone, feeling the weight of the world pressing down on her shoulders. She had just delivered the worst news a wife could hear, and she hated every second of it.

She leaned forward, burying her face in her hands as the tears she had held back finally came. She let herself cry for a few moments, the grief and fear pouring out of her. But then she wiped her eyes, took a deep breath, and stood up. *Yossi needs me. And so does Yael.*

The moment Yael ended the call with Leila, her hands started trembling uncontrollably. *Yossi. Hurt. Unconscious.* The words rang in her head like a deafening alarm, her thoughts spinning in a whirlwind of panic and fear. Her body moved on autopilot, grabbing her bag, slipping on shoes, and rushing out of the door.

As she fumbled to start the car, her hands shook so violently that she had to pause and grip the steering wheel, taking several shaky breaths. Her mind kept replaying the fragmented words from Leila. *Explosion. Brain injury. Tests.* Every terrifying word made her stomach lurch. *Focus. Just get there.*

But then her heart clenched painfully. *Yossi's parents.* They needed to know. With a trembling hand, Yael pulled out her phone, hesitating for just a moment before dialling Yossi's mother.

The phone rang three times, and finally, Yossi's mother, Ruth, picked up. "*Yael, honey, what's wrong?*" Ruth's voice was soft but concerned, sensing the tension immediately.

Yael's voice cracked as she spoke. "*Ruth... it's Yossi. He's been hurt... There was an explosion during the fighting. He's in the hospital, unconscious. I'm on my way there now.*"

There was a long pause on the other end of the line. "*What? Hurt?*" Ruth's voice was shaky, struggling to understand. "*How bad is it?*"

Yael took a deep, steadying breath, trying to hold herself together. "*It's bad... but they're saying he's stable. He's unconscious, and they're running tests. He might have a brain injury, but Leila says they're hopeful. I don't know any more than that yet.*"

She could hear Ruth's sharp intake of breath, followed by the muffled sound of Yossi's father, David, in the background asking what was going on.

"*We'll meet you there. We're coming right now,*" Ruth said, her voice shaky but resolute. "*Yael... he's going to be okay. He has to be.*"

Yael nodded, even though Ruth couldn't see her. "*I'll see you there,*" she whispered, hanging up the phone.

The drive to the hospital was a blur of tears and prayers. Every traffic light felt like torture, every second lost an eternity. Her heart raced in her chest, beating in sync with the overwhelming fear in her mind. *What if he doesn't wake up? What if he's...?* She forced the thought away, shaking her head as if physically trying to rid herself of the possibility. *No, he's strong. He'll pull through. He always does.*

When Yael finally reached the hospital, she practically stumbled out of the car, not even caring if she parked it correctly. She rushed through the sliding doors, her breath coming in short, panicked gasps as she looked around for any sign of Leila or a doctor.

The cold, sterile air of the hospital hit her like a wave, and for a moment, she froze in place. Everything felt surreal, like a bad dream she couldn't wake up from.

Then, through the blur of panic, she spotted Leila standing near the entrance to the trauma wing.

"*Leila!*" Yael called out, her voice breaking as she ran to her friend.

Leila turned, her face etched with a mix of worry and exhaustion. The moment Yael reached her, Leila pulled her into a tight hug, holding her for a long moment as Yael's body shook with fear.

"*I'm so sorry, Yael,*" Leila whispered, her own voice strained with emotion. "*But he's stable. The doctors are running tests now. I was with him when he arrived. He's unconscious, but they're hopeful.*"

Yael nodded, tears streaming down her face as she clung to Leila. "*I need to see him,*" she whispered, her voice trembling. "*I need to see him.*"

"*You will,*" Leila reassured her, pulling back gently. "*The doctors will talk to us soon.*"

Just as she spoke, Yael saw Ruth and David rush through the doors, their faces pale and drawn. They hurried over, embracing Yael as the reality of the situation settled in.

"*Where is he? What do the doctors say?*" David asked, his voice thick with emotion.

Leila stepped forward, addressing them both. "*He's in the trauma unit right now. They're stabilising him, and they've already done a CT scan. They're checking for internal injuries and fractures. He's stable, but he hasn't woken up yet.*"

Ruth's face crumpled with worry as she clutched David's arm. "*Is it... is it serious? Will he...?*" Her voice broke, unable to finish the question.

Leila took a deep breath. "*He's suffered a moderate brain injury, and there's swelling. His ribs are broken, and his arm is fractured. But there's no sign of internal bleeding, and the doctors are optimistic. It's early, and we need to monitor him closely, but the signs are good. He's going to need surgery for the fractures, but... he's alive.*"

The relief was palpable, but it was tinged with the fear of the unknown. The words *brain injury* and *unconscious* hung in the air, reminding them all that Yossi wasn't out of the woods yet.

"*Can we see him?*" Yael asked, her voice barely a whisper.

Leila nodded. "*They're moving him to a room now. You can sit with him, but he's still unconscious.*"

The walk to Yossi's room felt like the longest of Yael's life. Her hands were clammy, her heart racing in her chest as they approached the door. When she stepped inside, her breath caught in her throat.

Yossi lay still in the hospital bed, hooked up to multiple monitors that beeped softly, tracking his vital signs. His face was pale, and his body was covered in bruises. His right arm was in a sling, and his chest was bandaged from the broken ribs. An oxygen mask covered his mouth, helping him breathe, and a machine by his bedside tracked the pressure in his brain, monitoring the swelling.

For a moment, Yael couldn't move. The sight of him like this... so vulnerable, so still... was almost too much to bear. She felt Ruth's hand on her shoulder, gently urging her forward.

She took a few hesitant steps until she was standing next to him. She reached out, her fingers trembling as she took his hand in hers. His skin was warm, but the feeling was distant, like she was holding onto someone who wasn't quite there.

"*Yossi,*" she whispered, her voice cracking. "*Please, wake up. I'm here. We're all here.*"

Tears blurred her vision as she stood there, holding his hand, willing him to open his eyes, to squeeze her fingers... anything to show that he was still with her.

Ruth and David stood quietly by the door, their faces etched with worry as they looked at their son, helpless to do anything but wait. Leila lingered nearby, ready to help but knowing this was a moment for the family.

The hours passed in a haze of worry and exhaustion. Doctors came in and out, checking Yossi's vitals, adjusting the machines, but there was no change. He remained unconscious, his body fighting to heal from the trauma.

Yael stayed by his side the whole time, barely moving, her eyes never leaving his face. Ruth and David sat quietly in the room, their hands clasped tightly together as they waited, each minute stretching into an eternity.

The days following Yossi's arrival were a blur of waiting, praying, and watching. Yael spent every moment at his bedside, speaking softly to him, telling him stories, hoping that somewhere in his unconscious mind, he could hear her voice. Ruth and David stayed as long as they could, returning home only to rest briefly before coming back to sit with their son.

Leila checked on them constantly, making sure they had everything they needed and providing updates from the doctors. She felt the weight of her role in their lives... Yossi's friend, Nadav's girlfriend, Yael's support and it drove her to work tirelessly, ensuring Yossi received the best care possible.

Yossi remained unconscious, his body healing slowly. The swelling in his brain began to subside, but the doctors were cautious, monitoring him closely for any signs of improvement. Yael refused to leave his side, her heart breaking a little more with every day that passed without him waking up.

But even in the darkness, there was hope. Yossi was stable, and though the road to recovery would be long, the doctors believed he would wake up soon. He had survived the explosion, and now it was a matter of time, patience, and love.

And Yael, Ruth, David, and Leila would be there, every step of the way.

Chapter Fifty Five

AHMED

The chaos of the battlefield had long faded into a dull, persistent memory. The moment Ahmed was captured replayed over and over in his mind... the explosion, the dust-filled air, the IDF storming the building. He had offered no resistance, feeling the weight of defeat long before they laid their hands on him. They had blindfolded him, bound his hands, and tossed him into the back of an armoured vehicle. But the real prison wasn't the vehicle, nor the shackles on his wrists. It was the memories... each one gnawing at him like a relentless wound that would never heal.

The cold of the steel cuffs bit into Ahmed's wrists, the bruises along his arms and ribs aching with every jolt of the vehicle. His body felt heavy... broken, but not in a way that the bruises and cuts could explain. It was as if the weight of all that had happened... the deaths, the failures, pressed down on him more than the shackles ever could.

As the vehicle rumbled forward, jostling him on the cold steel floor, Ahmed's thoughts drifted back to his earliest days. His father's face flickered before him... martyred in 2009, a shahid in the eyes of their people. He had grown up hearing stories of his father's bravery, of how he had fought the IDF until the bitter end. It was a legacy Ahmed had been proud of, one that had shaped every decision he made. His uncle Yusuf had ensured that Ahmed's childhood was steeped in the lore of the struggle, a path of vengeance that left little room for doubt or self-reflection.

But now, sitting here, bound and captured, the weight of that legacy felt like a lie. *Was it worth it?* The question dug into him like a splinter, sharp and persistent. He thought of Yusuf, of how his uncle had groomed him, filled his head with stories of glorious martyrdom, of their rightful land taken by force. Hatred had been his inheritance.

His mind wandered further back, to the days he had spent in the tunnels beneath Gaza. He, Tariq, Bilal, and Khaled had been practically inseparable since childhood. They were bound not just by the war that surrounded them, but by the dreams they had built together as boys. Those tunnels had been their playground, their training ground. Back then, they mimicked the fighters they idolised, unaware that one day, they would be drawn into the very conflict they pretended to fight.

He thought of Tariq... always the one with the plan. Ahmed could see his face, serious even in their boyhood, as they whispered about the future in the dimly lit tunnels. They had all looked up to him, following without question. And Bilal, the quiet thinker, the one who never rushed into anything without considering every angle. His advice had kept them alive more than once. Then there was Khaled, always laughing, always ready for a fight. His violent nature had been both a strength and a curse, but it was that fire that had made him their shield. And Hadi... the youngest, eager to prove himself, full of energy and dreams.

Later, Hadi joined them, younger but eager to prove himself. Ahmed had taken him under his wing, guiding him, just as Tariq had guided them. Together, they trained, fought, and planned for a victory they thought was certain.

But now, they were all gone.

Every last one of them... dead because of him, because of his orders.

His hands, bound in the cold steel cuffs, clenched involuntarily. The weight of their deaths was crushing. Tariq, Bilal, Khaled, Hadi. He had led them into the fire, promising that victory was just within reach. He had convinced them that if they sacrificed enough, fought hard enough, it would all be worth it.

Ahmed swallowed hard, his throat tight. What had he truly given them? Friends who had once laughed and dreamed with him were now cold corpses buried beneath the rubble. He had given them nothing but early graves.

They had dragged him from the armoured vehicle, pulling him through the cold, grey corridors of the facility until he found himself in a small, sterile room. The smell of antiseptic clung to the air, mixing with the faint scent of sweat and metal. They shoved him into a metal chair, his wrists still bound. The blindfold was ripped off, leaving him blinking under the harsh fluorescent lights.

Opposite him sat two interrogators, their faces unreadable, yet grim with purpose. They laid a folder on the table, the edges of surveillance images visible. Ahmed stared at the folder, his mind barely registering its contents. His wrists ached from the bindings, but the pain was nothing compared to the storm raging in his head.

"Let's begin again," one of the interrogators said, his voice steady but with the weariness of a man who had done this many times before. *"You were on Route 232 on the 7th of October, coordinating the attacks. We know your men led the assault on Kibbutz Be'eri, and you ordered the massacre at the Nova Festival."*

Ahmed remained silent. The truth of what he had done, the orders he had given, weighed heavy on his chest. He had led his men into those operations with a clear mind, believing that it was for the greater good. But now, with everything stripped away, what was left?

"We have footage," the interrogator continued, opening the folder. *"Your men's bodycams, Ahmed. Hamas was proud of what you did, weren't they?"*

They slid a tablet across the table. Ahmed's eyes were drawn to the screen, and there it was... the morning of the attacks. His voice rang out, steady, as he gave his commanders their instructions. He watched himself issue orders, cold and calculated. The footage shifted, showing the carnage on Route 232, the burning vehicles, the civilians trying to flee, the dead left in their wake.

His chest tightened. His hands, bound by the cold metal cuffs, trembled ever so slightly. He had seen this footage before... through the lens of pride, of righteous vengeance... but now... now it felt different. Now it felt wrong.

The screen flickered again, showing his men storming Kibbutz Be'eri. His orders, followed to the letter, without mercy, without hesitation.

"You led this massacre, Ahmed," the interrogator said softly. *"You coordinated everything. Route 232, the Nova Festival, Kibbutz Be'eri. You knew exactly what you were doing."*

Ahmed's throat felt like it was closing. There was no denying it. No escaping it.

"We also have questions about Salma," the interrogator's voice shifted, softer but no less heavy. *"We know she wanted peace, Ahmed. Did you ever stop to listen to her?"*

Salma. The image of her face flickered in his mind, clear amidst the haze of violence. Her soft voice, the way she had always urged him to look beyond the bloodshed. *There's another way, Ahmed. We don't have to destroy everything to survive.* She had believed in peace, in building something better. She had wanted him to believe too, but he had ignored her. He had turned away from her dream.

The interrogators pressed again, *"Is she alive?"*

Ahmed shook his head slowly. He didn't know.

"She wanted something different," he said finally, his voice raw. *"She always wanted peace… a better place to live."*

Days blurred into weeks, and Ahmed found himself alone in his cell, surrounded only by his thoughts and the unrelenting weight of his choices. The prison was high-security, reserved for men like him, men who had orchestrated the bloodshed of October 7th. The clang of metal doors, the heavy footsteps of guards, were the sounds that now defined his existence.

But the real prison wasn't the concrete walls or the iron bars… it was the memories.

He thought of his father, the man whose death had been glorified, turned into a beacon for their cause. His father had died fighting the IDF, a martyr in their people's eyes. But now, Ahmed wondered, had his father ever questioned the cycle of violence before it claimed him too?

His mind wandered back to his uncle Yusuf, the man who had filled the void left by his father's death. Yusuf had planted the seeds of hatred deep in Ahmed's soul, ensuring they would grow into something unshakeable. And then, later, there had been men like Abu Khaled, leaders who had promised victory through bloodshed, who had threatened those he loved if he did not obey.

But Salma. Her face lingered in his thoughts, clearer than ever. Her voice, the only one that had ever made him question this path.

Was she right all along? Could we have built something instead of destroying everything?

Now, it was too late. Salma was either dead or lost to him, just as his childhood friends were gone. Tariq, Bilal, Khaled, Hadi... brothers who had trusted him, followed him, and died because of him. Their blood was on his hands, and the streets they had fought for were now stained with their sacrifice.

Ahmed leaned back against the cold wall of his cell, closing his eyes. The sound of the prison doors echoed in the distance, the finality of his fate settling in. He would spend the rest of his days here, locked away, listening to the distant footsteps, the doors closing behind him. And for what? What had all the death and destruction truly achieved?

In the silence, the answer came to him, sharp and undeniable: *Nothing.*

Everything he had fought for, everything he had sacrificed, had been for nothing. He had destroyed the world he once knew, and in its place, he had built only ruins.

Chapter Fifty Six

YOSSI

The days following Yossi's injuries blurred into an endless stretch of time. Each one felt like a lifetime. Yael stayed by his side through it all, holding his hand, whispering words of encouragement, even when he couldn't respond. His parents, Ruth and David, came and went, their faces etched with the deep worry that never seemed to lift. Leila visited often, always with Nadav close behind, their shared concern for Yossi palpable. Though Leila took on the role of quiet supporter, Nadav's presence was steady... a rock that, though strong, seemed to strain under the weight of fear for his best friend.

Yossi's condition had improved, little by little. The swelling in his brain had finally subsided, and the doctors told the family that it was only a matter of time before he woke. The words, meant to comfort, hung in the air like fragile hope, ready to shatter at the slightest misstep.

Then, on one quiet morning, the stillness was broken. It was a small movement... so slight that Yael wasn't sure at first if she had imagined it. But then, it happened again. His fingers twitched in her hand. Her heart raced.

"*Yossi?*" she whispered, her voice trembling, thick with hope.

Slowly, his eyelids fluttered open. He took a deep, strained breath, his chest rising and falling as though his body was relearning the rhythm of life. His eyes blinked, unfocused, until they found her. Recognition sparked in their depths.

"*Yael...*" His voice was rough, weak, barely more than a croak, but it was him. It was Yossi.

Tears filled Yael's eyes, her heart swelling with relief so intense it nearly knocked the breath out of her. She squeezed his hand, her voice breaking.

"I'm here, Yossi. I'm here."

Yossi's brow furrowed as he struggled to piece together what had happened. "*What... what happened?*" His voice was little more than a whisper, each word a strain, but the confusion in his gaze was unmistakable.

"*You were hurt,*" Yael explained, brushing her fingers through his hair, her voice thick with emotion. "An explosion. You've been unconscious, but you're safe now. The doctors... they say you're going to be okay."

Yossi's gaze flickered with concern. He winced as he shifted slightly, the pain in his ribs sharp. "*Nadav... is he... did he make it?*"

Yael smiled through her tears, her heart aching at the concern etched on his face. "*He's fine. He's been here, worried sick about you.*"

Yossi exhaled a slow, relieved breath, his body sinking back into the bed. Nadav was alive. They had both made it.

A few weeks later, Nadav visited. His nerves were palpable as he entered the room, though he tried to hide them behind his usual grin. Walking in this time felt different. The knot in his stomach tightened as he approached Yossi's bed.

But the moment he saw Yossi sitting up, a grin spread across his face.

"*You stubborn idiot,*" Nadav said, shaking his head as he approached. "*You've got nine lives, don't you?*"

Yossi chuckled, though it quickly turned into a grimace as he clutched his ribs. "Not exactly by choice."

Leila, who had been standing quietly beside Nadav, smiled softly, though her eyes betrayed the depth of her emotion. *"You scared us, Yossi,"* she said, her voice gentle but filled with the weight of what they had been through. *"We thought we'd lost you this time."*

Yossi met her gaze, a lump forming in his throat. They had all grown up together. Leila, Nadav, Yael... they had been his family long before the war took over their lives. Looking at them now, he felt the weight of everything they had been through together.

"I'm still here," he said quietly, his words carrying more than just the relief of surviving the explosion. They were a promise... a reminder that they had all fought together, and they had all made it out.

Nadav, never one for emotional moments, brushed it off with a half-smile. *"You owe me a drink when this is over,"* he quipped, though his voice cracked slightly, betraying the emotion he was trying to hide.

Leila stood by, her heart swelling with relief. Seeing Yossi alive, talking, healing... it was like a piece of her was being mended too. She had been quiet throughout his recovery, offering her support through actions rather than words, but Yossi could feel her presence. As steady and reliable as she had always been.

Several weeks later, Yossi received unexpected news. Senior officers would be visiting him, and his parents, Yael, and several close friends were all expected to be there. Yossi had no idea what to make of it.

"I don't get it," Yossi muttered as Yael helped him adjust his blanket. *"Why the formalities?"*

"Just relax," Yael said with a soft smile. *"It's probably about your recovery. You know how they like to keep things formal."*

Still, the unease gnawed at Yossi. There was something more to this—he could feel it.

The morning of the visit, Leila arrived early to help Yael prepare Yossi. She brushed his hair, smoothed his clothes, treating him with the care of a patient she'd known her whole life. Yossi, impatient as always, grumbled.

"Leila, it's not like I'm meeting the President," he said, though his voice held a nervous edge.

Leila smirked, glancing at Yael. *"You might as well be."*

Soon after, Yossi was moved to a larger room. When he was wheeled in, his heart skipped a beat. He wasn't expecting this. His parents, Ruth and David, were there. So were Yael's parents, Nadav's parents, and Leila's family... everyone who had stood by him.

And then the doors opened. Lieutenant General Oren Tal, the highest-ranking officer in the Israel Defence Forces, entered, flanked by senior officers, including Lieutenant Colonel Arad.

Yossi's heart raced. *What was happening?*

The room grew quiet as Lieutenant General Tal approached Yossi's bed. The air was thick with anticipation, and Yossi could feel his pulse quicken. His parents, Ruth and David, sat nearby, their expressions unreadable. Yael stood at his side, her hand gripping his as though she could sense his rising nerves. Nadav, always his solid anchor, stood just behind them, Leila by his side, offering her quiet support.

Lieutenant General Tal's expression was solemn but filled with pride. *"Segen Rosenberg, Samar Levy, we have gathered extensive witness statements regarding your actions on October 7th,"* he began, his voice resonating through the room, commanding everyone's attention.

Yossi's heart skipped a beat. *This was about October 7th. What was he about to hear?*

The general's eyes swept across the room, landing briefly on Yossi's family before continuing. *"Many here may not fully know the details of what transpired that day. But today, we will share them."*

Yossi's parents exchanged nervous glances, their confusion evident. They had heard fragments about that day but never the full story.

Lieutenant General Tal took a deep breath and began recounting the events: the sudden attack at the Erez Crossing, the chaos that followed, and how Yossi and Nadav, without hesitation, diverted to help the civilians in Sderot who were under siege. His voice grew more serious as he described how they had coordinated the rescue efforts, facing overwhelming odds, engaging the enemy to protect innocent lives.

"They could have retreated. They could have waited for reinforcements. But they didn't," General Tal continued. *"Instead, these two men—despite being outnumbered—fought back, helping to evacuate over 150 civilians from Sderot and the surrounding area."*

Yossi's parents listened, their faces pale with shock. Ruth clutched David's hand, her eyes wide and tear-filled as the reality of her son's actions began to sink in.

"But that wasn't all," the general went on, his gaze now focused on Nadav. *"Samar Levy provided suppressive fire, allowing Segen Rosenberg to lead multiple groups of civilians to safety, while engaging directly with enemy fighters. They both risked their lives again and again, ensuring not just civilians but fellow soldiers made it out alive."*

Nadav stood rigid, his face betraying a mix of disbelief and humility. He hadn't expected this. He had come here to support Yossi, to be by his side... he hadn't anticipated recognition for himself.

"These men saved lives that day... countless lives," General Tal concluded. *"And they did so with bravery and selflessness that few can ever understand."*

The room was silent. Yossi's parents looked stunned, Ruth's hand covering her mouth in shock. Nadav's parents had tears in their eyes, overwhelmed by the weight of what they were hearing. Leila stood beside Nadav, gripping his hand so tightly her knuckles were white.

Yossi felt light-headed, his mind racing. He remembered fragments of the day... the chaos, the gunfire, the civilians' panicked faces. But hearing it laid out like this, hearing that they had saved over 150 people... it was too much to take in all at once.

Then, Lieutenant General Tal's voice softened. *"In recognition of your extraordinary actions on October 7th, it is my honour to award both of you the Medal of Valor, the highest honour the Israel Defence Forces can bestow."*

Yossi's breath caught in his throat. He hadn't expected this. He hadn't fought for medals or recognition; he had fought because it was the only choice he had. But now, seeing the gravity of what they had accomplished, hearing the stories of those they had saved, the weight of it all settled over him like a blanket.

The general pinned the medal onto Yossi's hospital gown with deliberate care. The metal felt cold against his chest, its significance far heavier than its physical weight. He glanced over at Nadav, who stood equally stunned, the same medal being pinned to his own chest. For once, Nadav was speechless.

The room erupted into applause. Yossi's heart pounded in his chest, a mixture of pride, disbelief, and deep humility washing over him. His parents, both teary-eyed, embraced him, and he could see the mixture of relief and pride in their expressions.

"You're a hero, Yossi," Ruth whispered, her voice thick with emotion. *"You and Nadav both."*

Yael stood beside him, her eyes filled with tears of pride. She leaned in close, her voice soft but steady. *"You did it, Yossi. You saved them."*

Yossi squeezed her hand, overwhelmed by the moment. His gaze shifted to Nadav, who stood in stunned silence beside Leila, his eyes wide with disbelief. Yossi could see the same turmoil in his friend's expression... the same shock at being honoured for something that had felt, in the moment, like simple survival.

Nadav's father stepped forward, his voice cracking with emotion. *"We couldn't be prouder of you, son."*

Nadav looked at his father, unable to speak, but the pride in his eyes was unmistakable. Leila wrapped her arms around him, her tears finally spilling over as she whispered, *"You're a hero, Nadav. You always have been."*

Yossi looked at the medal on his chest, his thoughts racing. He hadn't done this for glory. He had fought to protect the people he loved, to make sure they all made it through that dark day. And somehow, they had.

As the ceremony concluded, Yossi sat quietly in his hospital bed, surrounded by his family and friends. The applause had died down, and the room was filled with the quiet hum of conversation. But for Yossi, the weight of the medal on his chest was a constant reminder of everything that had happened... everything they had survived.

Nadav sat beside him, still shaking his head in disbelief. *"I can't believe this is real,"* he muttered. *"We were just... doing our jobs."*

Yossi smiled, though it didn't quite reach his eyes. *"It wasn't just a job, Nadav. We saved people. That matters."*

Nadav glanced down at the medal pinned to his chest and nodded slowly. *"Yeah. I guess it does."*

Leila leaned in, resting her hand on Nadav's arm. *"It does, Nadav. More than you know."*

Yael sat beside Yossi, her hand resting gently on his. *"You both did something incredible. Don't ever forget that."*

Yossi looked around the room, at the faces of the people he loved—the people he had fought for. And in that moment, he realised that the medals didn't matter nearly as much as the fact that they had all survived.

As the day wound down, and the visitors slowly trickled out of the room, Yossi was left alone with Yael, her hand still resting in his. The room was quiet, the noise of the hospital muted now that the crowd had gone.

"I never thought it would end like this," Yossi said softly, his eyes distant. *"A medal... after everything."*

Yael looked at him, her expression gentle. *"You deserve it, Yossi. You and Nadav. You both saved lives, and that's something that can't be ignored."*

Yossi sighed, leaning back into his pillow. *"I didn't do it for a medal."*

Yael smiled, brushing a strand of hair from his forehead. *"I know. That's what makes you a hero."*

For the first time in what felt like months, Yossi allowed himself to relax, to let the tension slip away. He had fought. He had survived. And now, as he looked at Yael, at the life they still had ahead of them, he felt something he hadn't felt in a long time.

Hope.

Billy MacLeod MBE

Author Biography

Billy MacLeod MBE

Billy MacLeod MBE is the Chief Operations Officer at **Veterans in Action (VIA)**, a charity dedicated to helping former soldiers rebuild their lives after the psychological impact of war. His unwavering commitment to supporting veterans suffering from PTSD and other war-related challenges has defined his career and inspired his debut novel, *Through Their Eyes: A Journey of Two Worlds*.

As a soldier, Billy experienced the stark realities of conflict firsthand. His journey didn't end when he left the military; it evolved into a mission to aid others in their recovery. Billy was recognised with an **MBE (Member of the Order of the British Empire)** for his outstanding service to veterans and his local community. His charity work, which includes pioneering adventure-based therapy for veterans, has supported over **1,700 veterans** and taken more than **500 on**

life-changing expeditions. These experiences have given Billy a unique insight into the human cost of conflict, which is woven deeply into his writing.

Billy's time in the British Army and his extensive work with **Veterans in Action** not only inform his understanding of war's lasting effects but also provide a foundation for his novel's exploration of the human spirit. *Through Their Eyes* tells the story of two boys—one Palestinian and one Israeli—caught on opposite sides of the Israeli-Palestinian conflict. It's a powerful tale of resilience, identity, and the hope for peace, all told through the lens of children navigating the scars of war.

What sets Billy apart as a storyteller is his **first-hand experience** of the conflict zones and regions depicted in his novel. He has personally travelled to some of the most affected areas in the Middle East, gathering stories from those directly impacted by the ongoing Israeli-Palestinian conflict. These visits gave him profound insights into the lives of people caught in the crossfire, which he has infused into the emotional complexity of his characters and the authenticity of their struggles.

Billy's charity's hands-on approach, alongside his time spent in these conflict regions, has helped him craft an empathetic and humanising portrayal of characters struggling with their identities amidst turmoil. His writing resonates with a profound understanding of trauma and healing, reflecting his passion for building bridges between divided communities.

Billy's work transcends borders and backgrounds, offering readers an honest and heartfelt exploration of war, survival, and the universal desire for peace. He continues to dedicate his life to highlighting the impact of conflict, especially on young people, while using his platform to inspire understanding, reconciliation, and hope.

Printed in Great Britain
by Amazon